THE LIFEHOUSE TRILOGY

Baen Books
by
Spider Robinson
❖❖❖

Callahan's Lady
Lady Slings the Booze
The Stardance Trilogy (with Jeanne Robinson)
The Lifehouse Trilogy
User Friendly
Telempath
Very Bad Deaths
Very Hard Choices (forthcoming)

THE LIFEHOUSE TRILOGY

BY
SPIDER ROBINSON

THE LIFEHOUSE TRILOGY

Mindkiller copyright © 1982, Time Pressure copyright © 1987, Lifehouse copyright © 1997; all by Spider Robinson

A Baen Book

Baen Publishing Enterprises
P.O. Box 1403
Riverdale, NY 10471
www.baen.com

ISBN 10: 1-4165-5511-0
ISBN 13: 978-1-4165-5511-7

Cover art by Stephen Hickman

First Baen printing, December 2007

Distributed by Simon & Schuster
1230 Avenue of the Americas
New York, NY 10020

Library of Congress Cataloging-in-Publication Data

Robinson, Spider.
  The lifehouse trilogy / by Spider Robinson.
     p. cm.
  ISBN 1-4165-5511-0
  1. Science fiction, American. I. Title.
  PS3568.O3156L54 2007
  813'.54--dc22

2007035652

Printed in the United States of America

10 9 8 7 6 5 4 3 2 1

❖CONTENTS❖

MINDKILLER

❖❖

**This book is dedicated to Psyche
and to Allison.**

❖ACKNOWLEDGMENTS❖

IN WRITING THIS NOVEL I have borrowed from the ideas, insights, and observations of many people. In no particular order, they are:

Dr. Jim Lynch, my oldest friend, who first put me onto brain reward; Larry Niven, whose novella "Death by Ecstasy" is probably the definitive story on the subject; Dr. Jerry Pournelle; Dr. Adam Reed of Rockefeller University; Bob Shaw; Aryeh Routtenberg, whose article in the November 1978 *Scientific American* was the final spark for the creation of this book; John D. MacDonald; Robert A. Heinlein; and of course Olds and Milner, who started the whole thing by poking electrodes into rat brains at McGill University in the 1950s. None of these gentlemen is to blame for what I have done with their ideas; as I write, only two are even aware that I have borrowed from them.

Research assistance was given me by Bob Atkinson, Bill Jones, John Bell, George Allanson, and Andrew Gilbert; Bob Atkinson typed more than half the manuscript while my arm was in a cast. Invaluable suggestions were made by my editor, Donald Hutter of Holt, Rinehart and Winston, and by my agent, Kirby McCauley. Jeanne, my other leg, read the whole thing in progress, called me back from the blind alleys, and helped me patch the leaks. Heartfelt thanks to them all. Oh, and thanks to the Gunner in Brattleboro for the Atcheson Assault Twelve and to the Sea Breeze Inn in St. Margaret's Bay for the hospitality.

Any resemblance between characters in this book and real people, living or dead, is unintentional. A character's opinions should *never* necessarily be taken to be those of the author, but I would like at this time to specifically repudiate any derogatory opinions about the city of Halifax expressed by characters hereinafter. It is the nicest city I have ever inhabited. But try persuading a New Yorker of that!

For those interested in influences, this book was written on a steady diet of Charlie Parker, Jon Hendricks, Frank Zappa, John Lennon, Tom Waits, and the Dixie Dregs.

—HALIFAX, 1981

✵1✵

2006

HALIFAX HARBOR at night is a beautiful sight, and June usually finds the MacDonald Bridge lined with lovers and other appreciators. But in Halifax even June can turn on one with icy claws.

A thermometer sheltered from the brisk wind would have shown a little below Centigrade zero. Norman Kent had the magnificent scenery all to himself.

He was aware of the view; it was before his face, and his eyes were not closed. He was aware of the cold too, because occasionally when he worked his face frozen tears would break and fall from his cheeks. Neither meant anything to him. He was even vaguely aware of the sound of steady traffic behind him, successive dopplers like the rhythmic moaning of some wounded giant. They meant nothing to him either. On careful reflection Norman could think of nothing that *did* mean anything to him, and so he put one leg over the outer rail.

A voice came out of the night. "Hey, Cap, *don't!*"

He froze for a long moment. Running footsteps approached from the Dartmouth end of the bridge. Norman turned and saw the man coming up fast in the wash of passing headlights, and that decided him. He got the other leg over and stood teetering on the narrow ledge, the wind full in his face. His hat blew off, and insanely he spun around after it and incredibly he caught it, and was caught himself at wrist and forearm by two very strong hands. They dragged him bodily back over the rail again, nearly breaking his arm, and deposited him hard on his back on the pedestrian walkway. His breath left him, and he lay there blinking up at bridge structure and midnight sky for perhaps half a minute.

5

He became aware that his unwanted rescuer was sitting beside him, back against the rail and to the wind, breathing heavily. Norman rolled his head, felt cold stone bite his cheek, saw a large man in a shabby coat, silhouetted against a pool of light. From the frosted breath he knew that the large man was shaking his head.

Norman lifted himself on his elbows and sat beside the other, lifting his collar against the cold. He fumbled out a pack of Players Light and lit one with a flameless lighter. He held it out to the man, who accepted it silently, and lit another for himself.

"My wife left me," Norman said. "Six years this August, and she left me. Six *years!* Said she married too soon, she had to 'find herself.' And the semester's almost over, I've bitched it all up, nothing at all lined up for the summer, and there's a really good chance I won't be hired back in September. Old MacLeod with his hoary hints about austerity and sacrifices and a department chairman's heavy responsibility, he wouldn't even come right out and tell me! *Find* herself, for Christ's stinking sake! Got herself a nineteen-year-old plumbing student, he's going to help her *find* herself." He broke off and smoked for a while. When he could speak again he said, "Perhaps I could have handled either one, but the two together is . . . it's only fair to tell you, I'm going to try again, and you can't stop me forever."

The other spoke for the first time. His voice was deep and gravelly and dispassionate. "Don't let me stop you."

Norman turned to stare. "Then why—?" He stopped then, for the knife picked up the oncoming headlights very well.

"I never meant to *stop* you, Cap," the large man said calmly. "Just, uh—heh, heh—hold you up a little."

He was not even troubling to keep the knife hidden from the traffic. Norman glanced briefly at the oncoming cars; as in a slapstick movie sequence he saw four drivers, one after the other, do the identical single-take and then return their eyes grimly to the road. He yanked his own eyes back to the knife. It was quite large and looked sharp. The large man held it as though he knew how, and all at once it came to Norman that he had cashed a check today, and had two hundred New dollars in twenties in his wallet.

He let go of his cigarette and the wind took it. He put his gloved left hand palm up on his lap. On it he placed his wallet, his cigarettes, a half-empty pack of joints, and the small lighter. As he peeled the watch from the inside of his wrist he noticed that both hands were shaking badly. Oh, yes, he told himself, that's right, it is very cold. He added the watch to the pile, worked the right glove off against his hip, and took his pocket change in that hand.

"On my lap, brother," the large man directed. "Then go. Back to town or over the side, it's all the same to me."

Norman sighed deeply, and flung everything high and to his right. Nearly all of it went over the rail and into the harbor; a few bills were blown into traffic and toward the other rail.

The large man sat motionless. His eyes did not follow the loot but remained fixed on Norman, who stared back.

At last the large man got to his feet. "Cap," he said, shaking his head again, "you got a lot of hard bark on you." The knife disappeared. "Sorry I bothered you." He turned and began walking back toward Dartmouth, hunching against the wind, still smoking Norman's cigarette.

"You gutless bastard," Norman whispered, and wondered who he was talking to.

Norman Kent was thirty years old. He was one hundred and sixty-five centimeters tall and weighed fifty-five kilograms—although, having been born in America in 1977, he habitually thought of himself as five-five and a hundred and twenty pounds. Despite his actual stature, people usually remembered him as being of average height: there was a solidity to his body and movements. It implied a strength and physical conditioning he had not actually possessed since leaving the United States Army six years before. His face was passable, with wide-set grey eyes, a perfect aquiline nose, and a chin that would have seemed strong if it had not been topped by a mouth a fraction too wide. Overdeveloped folds at each corner of the mouth made it seem, when at rest, to be a faint, smug smile.

One could have flattered him most by calling him elegant. He had shaved for his suicide. The suit was tasteful enough to befit an assistant professor of English—it was his best suit—and the topcoat was pure quality. At thirty his hairline had not yet receded visibly. He wore his hair moderately long; the wind had whipped it into a fantastic sculpture and kept revising the design. The only nonconformist indulgence he permitted himself was his necktie, which looked like a riot in a paint shop.

After a time he put his glove back on, got stiffly to his feet, and left the bridge at the Halifax end, stamping his feet to restore circulation. He had not known genuine physical fear in six years, and he had forgotten the exhilaration that comes with survival. It was a twenty-minute walk home, and he savored every step. The smell of the harbor, the seedy waterfront squalor of Hollis Street, the brave, forlorn hookers too frozen to display their wares, the fake stained glass in the front windows of Skipper's Lounge, the special and inimitable color of leaves backlit by a street light, the clacking sounds of traffic lights and the laboring power plant of Victoria General Hospital—all were brand new again, treasures to be appreciated for the first time. He walked happily, mindless as a child. When he reached his apartment tower on Wellington Street, he was whistling. On the way up in the elevator, he graduated to humming, and by the time he reached his floor he was singing the words too, whereupon he was amused to discover that the tune he had been humming so merrily was the old Tom Lehrer song, "Poisoning Pigeons in the Park."

Half the lights were out in the hall, as usual, including the one by his door, but he did not care. He felt preternaturally observant, as though all his organs of perception had been recently fine-tuned and the gain stepped up, and along with this came such a feeling of euphoria that when he reached his apartment door and perceived coming out from under it not the sounds of the tuner, which he had left on, but the soft light of the lamp, which he had not, the implications failed to disturb him in the slightest. Got to be junkies, he thought calmly, Lois is off on the Mountain for the weekend. Ho ho. Ought to go right back downshaft and wake up old Julius, have him phone this in. Yes indeed.

As recently as the night before, he would have done precisely that, while congratulating himself on being too much of an old soldier to walk unheeding into danger.

Still singing, he took his keys from his pocket, making a noisy production of it. He was heartened to notice that the security camera over his door was intact, as were the ones at either end of the hall—his antagonists must be idiots. The cameras did not depend on visible light. Let's see, he thought, the gun is in the bottom left-hand drawer of the desk: one long run and I'm there, claw it open from underneath, kick the legs out from under the bookcase to spoil their aim, and roll behind the corner sofa—it'll stop bullets. Then try to negotiate.

A part of his mind was startled to learn that a mild-mannered assistant professor could undertake anything like this so cheerily—it had been a long time—but he was in no wise afraid. It was not fear that made time slow so drastically for him now, but something more like joy. He shucked off topcoat, jacket, tie, and gloves. He unlocked the door, dropped into a sprinter's crouch so as to convey his head into the room at an unexpected height, and threw the door open— hard, but not so hard that it would rebound into him. He got a good start, clearing the frame just as the door got out of his way, staying low and gaining speed with every step, still singing lustily about poisoning pigeons in the park.

The room was poorly lit by the lamp, but he saw the desk at once, unrifled, drawers all closed, gun presumably undiscovered. Glance left: no hostiles visible. Glance right: one in deep shadow, very long hair, half hidden by the couch, possibly more in the hall or other room. He wanted to study the one he could see for at least another tenth of a second, because both hands were beginning to come up and he wanted to know what was in them, but his subconscious insisted on yanking his gaze back in front of him again. It was very nearly in time, but by the time he saw the *Village Voice* lying where he had left it on the floor, he was committed to stepping on it. His feet went out from under him and he went airborne. He lowered his head automatically, and even managed to get both hands up in front of him, with the net result that the top of his skull impacted with great force against both fists. He dropped heavily on his face on the carpet.

Remarkably, he was unstunned. He sprang to his knees at once and yanked the drawer open, expecting at any second to experience some kind of impact. The gun seemed to spring into his hand; he whirled on one knee and located the long-haired one, frozen in an attitude of shock. "Hold it right there," Norman rapped.

The other burst into sudden, uproarious, unmistakably feminine laughter.

Now he was stunned. He lowered the gun involuntarily, then simply let go. It landed unheeded and safely, the safety still locked. He fell off his heels and sat down hard on the carpet.

"Jesus Christ in rhinestones," he said hoarsely. "Maddy. What are *you* doing here?"

She could not stop laughing. "Don't . . . don't kill me, brother," she managed, and doubled over.

He found that he was giggling himself, and it felt very good, so he let it build into deep laughter until he too was doubled over. The aching of his hands and the throbbing of his head were hilarious. The shared laughter went on for a long time, and when it might have stopped she said, "Poisoning pigeons," and they were off again. It was one of the great laughs.

At last she came around from behind the couch and sat in front of him, taking both his hands. "Hello, old younger brother," she said in a Swiss French accent. "It is very good to see you again."

"It is *incredibly* good to see you," he responded enthusiastically, and hugged her close.

Madeleine Kent was four years older than her brother, and a good eight centimeters taller. The resemblance was fairly pronounced: she had his audiotape-colored hair, his perfect nose and perfect teeth, and on her the overwide mouth looked good. But a different character had built on those features; a polite stranger would have called her not elegant but bold. Or possibly daring . . . but not quite reckless, there was too much wry wisdom in the eyes for that. The facial difference between the siblings was subtle but unmistakable. Norman looked like a man who had been around; Madeleine looked like a woman who had been around and still was. Her voice was deeper than he remembered, a throaty contralto that was quite sexy. Her clothes were impeccable and expensive. Her arms were strong.

The hug stretched out, and then they both became self-conscious and disengaged. Madeleine smiled uneasily, then got to her feet and stepped back a few paces. She turned away and put both hands on a bookcase.

"I'm a little bit embarrassed at how good it is to see you," she said.

"You speak English like a Swiss," he said, getting up.

She started. "Do I? Why, I *do.*" She made an effort and dropped the accent. "Habit, I guess. An American is not a good thing to be in Switzerland these days."

"Why is it that I'm embarrassed too? At how good it is to see you."

She pulled a volume at random from the bookcase and appeared to examine it closely. "Why *I* am embarrassed is that you and I have never been the very best of friends."

"Maddy—"

"Let me say it, no? It's been ten years, I don't write many letters. I'll be honest, in that ten years I might have thought of you ten times. Well, give or take five."

He had to smile. "Much the same with me."

She turned to face him, and smiled when she saw his smile. But hers was tight, unconvincing. "Now here I am on your doorstep. *Past* your doorstep, there are four suitcases in your bedroom. I needed a place to be, and it came to me that you are the only close family I have left in all the world, and Norman, I need close family very badly right now. Can I stay here for a while?"

Norman was still smiling, but his eyes glistened in the lamplight. "Maddy, if you haven't written much in ten years, you haven't left any letters unanswered either. I have this crazy impulse to apologize because I didn't pop up and see you when I was in Africa. I will confess here and now that if you had called ahead first, I would have tried to put you off. But the moment I recognized you, it came to me that you are all the family I have left in the world. As you speak, I realize that I need close family very badly now too. Please stay."

Relief showed in her face, and they hugged again, without reservation this time.

"Have you eaten?" he asked, fetching his outer clothes from the hallway.

"No. I showed the security guard downstairs—Julius, is it?—my identification and got him to let me in, but I didn't feel right prowling around in your home while you—"

"Our home. Let's eat."

"Well—coffee? Black and sweet?"

"And toasted English, lots of jam, Irish in the coffee."

"*Merveilleux.* Go ahead, I'll join you in a minute."

She was true to her word; he had only just finished producing two cups of fresh coffee and toast, a sixty-second job, when she came into the kitchen, carrying a package of unmistakable shape: an old-fashioned vinyl audio-only analog record, primitive ancestor of a compact disk.

"A present for you," she said. "It was quite a job getting it past customs."

It was a copy of Lambert, Hendricks, and Ross's first Columbia recording, "The Hottest New Group in Jazz." Not the 1974 reissue, the original. It was older than he was, one of the first stereo jazz albums. The cardboard jacket was also original, in impeccable condition.

"Holy God," he breathed.

The inner sleeve was new, a paper-and-plastic disc preserver. He took it from the jacket and slid the record out with a practiced hand, touching it only at the rim and label. The disc was immaculate. It did not appear ever to have been played, it had that special sheen. He could not guess at its worth in dollars. Not many people bothered with the obsolete analog format for their music these days; simply as an artifact, the thing was priceless.

She saw his awe. "I chose wisely, then?"

"Dear God, Maddy, it's—" Words failed him. "Thank you. Thank you. God, if they'd caught you at customs, they'd have had your bloody *head.*"

"I remembered that you liked their music, and I didn't think you had this one in your collection. I was certain you didn't have it in vinyl."

"I've heard it through twice in my life. It's never been put onto CD. There might be half a dozen copies in North America, and none of them would be virgin. Maddy, where did you get it? *How* did you get it?"

"A present from—from a friend. Forget it. Where do I sleep tonight, the couch?" She picked up her coffee and looked for sugar.

He fetched it, and found that he was terrified of dropping his new treasure but could not bear to set it down anywhere in the kitchen. "Nonsense, I've got a bed set up in the den, I'll doss there and you take the queen-size." He went to the living room, stored the record safely by the antique turntable, looked at it and sighed, and returned to the kitchen. She had already demolished her English muffin and finished half her coffee. He thought: She was really hungry and she waited for me to get back home. Maybe this is going to work out okay.

"Listen," he said, "I don't know how to thank you."

She smiled. "I'm glad you're pleased."

Her smile seemed to fade a bit too quickly. "Hey, I'm sorry. You spoke of bed."

"Oh, I didn't mean right now, necessarily . . . unless *you*—"

"Wait a minute now, let me get the chronology straight. It's—" He tried to look at his watch, but it was not there.

"Ten o'clock," she supplied.

"Then it must be the middle of the morning by your internal clock. You must be dead on your feet . . . or have I got it backwards?"

"Here, it's simple. I left my apartment in Zurich at 4:30 P.M., flew straight to London, and caught an Air Canada flight to here. Total transit time, ten hours, eight of that in the air. I got here half an hour ago, at 9:30 Atlantic Standard Time. By my 'clock' it's 3:00 A.M."

"Then let's get you to bed—"

"Hold it. First of all, my customary bedtime is about 2:00 A.M."

"But jet lag—"

"—is not so bad traveling west as it is traveling east. I chased the sun all day, so for me it has only been a few hours since sunset. I'm not sleepy yet." She finished her coffee. "But that's not it. *You* don't look at all sleepy . . ."

He considered it. "No. Not at all."

". . . and somehow I get the impression that you have a good deal on your mind that you want very much to talk about."

He considered that. "Yes, I do. How did you know?"

She hesitated. "Well, partly from the fact that Lois isn't here and there's no trace of her in the apartment and you haven't said a word about her."

He winced. "Ah, yes," he said, in halfhearted imitation of W. C. Fields, but dropped it at once. "And there would, I suppose, be a general overall spoor of the bachelor male in his anguish about the place, wouldn't there? Laundry all about, bed unmade, ashtrays full—"

"—bottles empty," she agreed. "If you've been having any fun lately, it hasn't been here."

"It hasn't been anywhere. Till you showed up."

"Norman, if . . . look, if you need any money, just to tide you over, I can—"

"Money? What gave you the idea I needed money? That's the only problem I don't have."

"Well, you've no hat—your hair looks like something out of Dali. And I know you pawned your watch—I can see the little stickum patch where it used to be on your wrist."

He looked blank for a second, and then suddenly burst into laughter. "I will be go to hell!"

She looked politely puzzled.

"That's just too perfect." He gave himself to his laughter for a moment. "No, it's all right, I'll tell you. Look, let's go into the living room; this is going to take a while."

They took freshened cups of coffee relaced with Bushmill's. It was excellent coffee, and he was faintly miffed that she had not commented on it. Perhaps in the circles she'd been traveling in, first-rate coffee was taken for granted.

"Now, what's so funny?" she said when they were seated.

"The watch and the hat. The watch is at this moment lying on the bottom of Halifax Harbor, and the hat is almost certainly floating somewhere in the selfsame harbor. That's the funny part. If it wasn't for that hat, I'd undoubtedly be down there with the watch—do you know I simply never gave it a thought until you mentioned it?" He chuckled again.

"What do you mean?" she said, and being self-involved he missed the urgency in her tone.

"Well, it's kind of embarrassing. What I was doing—about the time you were talking Julius into letting you in here, I think—I was committing suicide."

He glanced down at his coffee, and so he failed to notice that at that last word she actually relaxed slightly.

"Seems silly now, but it made sense at the time. I wasn't toying with the idea, I was fucking well *doing* it—until I was stopped by a Bad Samaritan."

He narrated the story of his interrupted suicide, cheerily and in some detail.

"You see?" he finished. "If I hadn't tried to save that idiot hat, he'd never have gotten me, I'd have been over the side and gone. The damned thing was important enough to give up dying for, and from that instant until the time you mentioned it, I never gave it another thought. It must have blown off the bridge while I was being mugged!"

He began to laugh again, and to his utter astonishment the fourth "ha" came out *"oh!"* as did the fifth and sixth, each harsher and louder than the last, by which time he was jack-knifed so drastically that he fell forward between his own knees. She had begun to move on the second *"oh!"*; her knees hit the carpet at the same instant as his, and she caught him before he could land on his face. With unsuspected strength she heaved him up into a kneeling position and wrapped her arms around him. It broke the stuttering rhythm of his diaphragm, and like an engine catching he settled into great cyclic sobs that filled and emptied his chest.

They rocked together on their knees, clutching like a pair of drowners, and his sorrow was a long time draining. Well before awareness returned to him, his hips began to move against her in the unconscious instinct of one who has been too near death, but she did something neither verbal nor physical, that was neither acceptance nor rejection, and something in him understood and he stopped. It did not come to his conscious attention because he had none then; his memory banks were in playback mode. Firmly but not suddenly, she moved so that she was sitting on the rug and he was lying across her lap, and he flowed like quicksilver into the new embrace without knowing it. Something about the position changed his weeping, or perhaps it was sheer lack of air; the sobs came shorter and closer together, the pitch rose and fell wildly. He had been weeping as a man does; now he wept as a child. It might have been neither the position nor anoxia, just childhood imprinting of the smell of Big Sister, who has time for your smashed toe when Mother is at work and Dad is drinking. More than one species of pain left him in that weeping, more than one wound or one kind of wound closed over and began to scab. After a time his sobs trailed off into deep slow breathing, and she stroked his hair.

His first conscious thought was that something was hurting his cheek. It was one of the silver cashew-shaped buttons of her blouse, and when he moved he knew it had left an imprint that would last an hour or more. With that, reality came back in a rush, and he rolled away and sat up. Her arms, which had been so strong a moment ago, fell away at once when he moved, and she met a searching gaze squarely. He looked for scorn or amusement or pity, and found none of them. As an afterthought he looked within himself for scorn or shame or self-pity, and again came up empty.

"Lord have mercy," he said shakily. "I thought I got it all out in that laugh before." He grinned experimentally. "Thanks, sis."

She had found Kleenex. "Sure. Here."

Why do people always roll up their eyes when they wipe away tears? he wondered, and thought at once of the last time he had wondered that. "God, I missed you at the funeral, Mad."

She smiled briefly.

"I'm sorry, stupid thing to say, of course you couldn't come. I just meant—"

"It's all right, Norman. Really." She patted his hand. "I said good-bye to both of them in my heart before I left for Europe, and they to me."

"Yes." They both smiled now.

"Can you tell me about it now?" she asked.

"Why I was trying to do myself in tonight? I think so."

He sat on the couch again and lit a cigarette. Seeing this, she produced a pack of Gauloise from her vest and raised an inquiring eyebrow. This surprised and pleased him. To a smoker of North American cigarettes, Gauloise smell like a burning outhouse—a fact of which most Gauloise smokers are sublimely unaware. She had not smoked since she arrived, had not even asked until she was sure that he smoked himself.

He nodded permission at once, and she lit up gratefully. "*Now* we're even," he said, making them both grin.

"All right," he went on. "Lois. I suppose I should start from the beginning. I'm just not certain where that is."

"Then do it backwards. Where does she live now?"

Norman pointed toward the living room window. "About a thousand meters that way and eight floors down. A second-and-third-story duplex apartment across the street. They're away for the moment, at Lois's place in the Valley. She's living with a third-year plumbing student named, God help us all, Rock, and she's still working at the V.G. Hospital up the street from here. She's got a floor now, Neurosurgery."

"How long has she been gone?"

He smiled. "That's another of those difficult questions."

"When did she move out?" she amended patiently.

"Well, over a period of several months, but she took her TV six months ago. I've always sort of considered that conclusive. After that she came by about twice a week for a while, to pick up something or other or share some new insight, and since then she seems to find some reason to drop by on the average of every other week. Her appearances are always unannounced and usually inconvenient for me, and I always let her in. I would estimate that we fuck two visits out of three. She is always gone in the morning. It's a lot like having a leg rebroken every time it's begun to knit." His voice was calm, unemotional.

"What is this Rock like?"

"Aside from biographical trivia, location of aunts and so forth, all Lois has ever seen fit to tell me is that he is nineteen, that he lets her be herself, and that he is a better lover than me. From my own experience I can report only that he is very large and very fast and all over hair and has knuckles like pig iron."

"You fought with him?"

"Oh, yes. As you saw from my entrance tonight, I haven't lost that fine edge of physical conditioning I had in the army. The trained killing machine. I lost a tooth I was fond of, and a suit I wasn't. So I sucker-punched him. Lois gave me hell, and carried him offstage cooing sympathetically."

"Why did she leave you?"

He made no answer, did not move a muscle.

"Why did she say she was leaving?"

The answer was slow in coming. "As nearly as I can understand it, her gist was that in living with her for six years I have acquired some sense of who she is and what she's like. This, to her way of thinking, limits her. Makes it impossible for her to become something new."

"You disagree."

"Not at all. I see and concede the point. People tend to behave the way you expect them to, in direct ratio to your certainty and their own insecurity. It is why marriages often require extended solo vacations. I would happily have given her one if she'd asked for it. Instead she—"

"Perhaps she didn't want to ask."

"—had to go and—what?"

"Nothing."

"—to go and throw *every*thing away, smash the whole business. I came home one night at the usual time and found her in bed with another man. Absolutely the first I knew of any serious discontent, and my God, the blowup we had. You know, she had never once yelled at me before, never once lost her temper and told me to—I— she walked out and didn't come back for a week. I—this is only my perspective, my biased—I don't believe that I ever got a single opening, from that day on. She never gave me a chance. You should smoke the new ashless kind."

She carefully conveyed her hand to the ashtray beside her chair, flicked ash into it.

"I know," he went on, "to be surprised by the whole thing implies that I had blinders on for years. How well could I have known her, to be so stunned? Well, I've run that mental loop about six million times, and I can't buy it. Oh, to some extent, of course—you can't be fooled that well for that long without wanting to be fooled. But *God*, Maddy, I swear there were no clues to be seen, no hints to be picked up. She never paid me the compliment of telling me what she disliked about me and our life, never trusted me to help anything. *I could have tried.*" He stubbed out his cigarette angrily. "I would have."

She sat perfectly still. He lit another cigarette, drew on it harshly, and during this she was motionless and silent. Norman felt that his relationship with his sister had come to another crux. For all of his life Madeleine had been four years older, smarter, stronger, more knowledgeable, and by the time he was twenty and the age difference would have begun to mean less, she was gone to Europe. At the time of her departure they had been on friendly terms, but not friends. He had not seen her since, had seldom heard from or of her, had never had an occasion or an opportunity to put aside a lifetime of subconscious resentment. And from the moment of her reentry into his life he had behaved like an idiot, blundering into his own fists, waving a safetied gun like a spastic desperado, weeping in her lap. Norman perceived his resentment now, to which he had not given a conscious thought in years, tasted it afresh and in full. Against it he balanced the fact that she was an extremely well-mannered house guest who had brought him an extremely valuable guest's gift.

No. It was more than that. It was valuable *to him*. She had remembered his tastes in music, picked one that would have endured for the decade she had been gone.

He hadn't the remotest idea what her tastes in music were.

"That came out rather glibly, didn't it?" His decision process had lasted the span of a deep drag on his new cigarette.

"She's been gone for six months," she said at once. "The story gets polished with repetition."

He smiled. "Almost enough to be really convincing. Thanks, Maddy, but I'm a liar. The signs *were* there. Some of them were there the day I met her. I chose not to see them."

"And she chose to let you."

He nodded. "That's true." He got a thoughtful look, and she left him with it, finishing her coffee. Presently he said, "And ever since she left I've been behaving like a perfect jackass. It hasn't *seemed* like it. I haven't felt as though I've even had any choices—more as if I were on tracks. But what I've been doing is systematically harvesting every opportunity for pain that the situation affords. Because . . . because she enjoys it, and I—I seem to feel I *owe* it to her. I've known this all along. Why didn't I know I knew it?"

"You weren't ready yet."

"It has been harder saying this—to you—than it was weeping on your collar. Why is that, I wonder?"

She thought about it. "It is hard for a person, especially a man perhaps, to admit to being in pain. But I think for you it has always been even harder to admit stupidity. I think you got that from me."

At the last sentence he sat up straighter. He remembered for the first time that upon her arrival she had tacitly admitted to being in pain herself. "I could certainly have used you, these ten years past," he said suddenly. "You're a good sister, Madeleine. And after thirty years I think it is past time I became your friend. You've helped me to see clearer. Perhaps it's time I looked past my own nose. What brings you to Halifax?"

It was not quite a bodily flinch. Her face acquired the expression of one suppressing a sneeze. "Norman . . ." She paused. "Look, the bare outline is easy. I loved—I love—a man. I've given him half a year of my life. And then I found out . . . things that make me suspect he is not . . . not who I thought him to be, not what I thought him to be. I found out that I had been closing my eyes too, like you. I *think* I have. It's hard to be certain. But if I'm right, I've been giving my love to—to a—to someone unworthy." She hesitated. "But that's just the bare outline. And I'm afraid it's all I can tell you now, Norman." She held up a hand. "Wait. I'm not trying to cheat you, honestly I'm not. I'm not too proud to swap stupidity stories with you—and if what I fear is true, I've made you look like a genius. But I *mustn't* speak about it yet. Will you trust me, brother? For perhaps as long as a week or two?"

But maybe I can help! was what he started to say, but something in her face stopped him. "Are you sure that's what you want?"

"I'm sure."

"You know," he said cheerfully and at once, "ever since you got here I've been trying to put my finger on exactly what the hell the 'continental look' is. Because you've got it—I'd never have taken you for an American. It's more than just the accent. Something about the way you carry yourself."

It was her first smile of its kind, unplanned and soft at the edges; it destroyed temporarily the "look" to which he had just alluded. For the first time she reminded him powerfully of the Maddy he had known as a child. "A friend of mine said something very like that once," she murmured wistfully. "His theory was that Americans make a fetish of appearing strong, and Europeans just naturally are." Norman saw her pursue that line of thought and find something that made her hastily retrace her steps. "I'm not sure about Canadians."

"Oh, Canadians are insecure and don't care who knows about it," Norman said with a grin. "Look at Halifax, capital of this great province. No Sunday news programming, no Saturday postal service, and within fifteen minutes' drive you can find whole communities with outdoor plumbing, sound-only phones, and copper cables. There's no opera, next to no dance, a shocking amount of fake country music, and from one end of the city to the other there might be two hundred people who have ever heard of Miles Davis. You can draw a blank with Ray Charles.

"And do you know what? I love this town. I've been walking the streets unarmed for over five years, and tonight was only the second time I've been hit on—it *almost* made me homesick for New York, but not quite. Ordinary glass is good enough for windows here, and you can drink tap water with the right filter. Police service is still voluntary; you can enter a mall without having to go through a god damned metal detector. You never have to wait for computer time.

Even though a goodly amount of North America's heroin enters at this port, none of it stays—you could fit all the junkies in town into three or four squad cars. For a city it's pretty pleasant, in other words."

"Compared to Zurich, it sounds like paradise. I can live without opera."

"Well, at least we've got good music here—thanks to you. What say we heat up the old turntable, if the drive band hasn't rotted by now? I keep having this feeling that I should get that record copied before lightning strikes it."

"That sounds wonderful. They *are* the ones who wrote 'Shiny Stockings,' aren't they?"

"Jon Hendricks did, yes," he said, getting up and retrieving both their empties. "With a guy named . . ." He stopped. He stood as if listening for a moment, then cleared his throat and met her eyes. "Madeleine, I know I said this already, but it's awfully good to have you here."

"It's good to have here to be."

It was 4:00 A.M. for him, and 9:00 A.M. for her, when they finally broke it up and went to bed; fortunately it was Saturday. That set the pattern for the next week: every hour not occupied by mundane necessities they spent talking together. Some of the talk was catching up on the ten years they had spent apart, essentially a swapping of accumulated anecdotes. Another, perhaps larger part of the talk involved reliving their respective childhoods, each giving their own perspective on the formative years of the other, and comparing their memories of shared experiences. By the end of the week, Norman felt that he knew himself better than he ever had, and knew that Madeleine felt something similar. A kind of tension went out of both of them as they talked, to be replaced by something like peace.

This mutual spiritual progression was not accomplished smoothly in tandem, but more the way a tractor operator works his way out of deep mud, feeding power to alternate wheels in fits and starts. It was their firm connection that made any progress possible.

By the second week, conversation had achieved about all it could on its own. He began introducing her, carefully and thoughtfully, to certain of his friends, and was satisfied with the results. The end-of-term madness was beginning to snowball at the University, and he was startled to discover how little it troubled him. Dr. MacLeod, the department chairman, actually paid him a grudging compliment. Norman met an attractive and interesting woman, a single parent who had come to his office to discuss her son's prospects of passing his course, and saw small signs that his interest was returned. One night he dug out the half-forgotten, half-finished manuscript of The Book and read it through; he threw out half the chapters and made extensive notes for the replacement.

Madeleine fit right into the rhythms of his home life, enhancing it in many small ways and disrupting nothing he cared about. She had a fanatic neatness learned in a country where living space was at a premium, and an easy tolerance of his own looser standards. She was seriously impressed by parts of his music library, which flattered him, and one day she came home with an armful of CDs that startled him just as pleasurably. They swapped favorite books and videos, favorite recipes and jokes. She displayed no inclination to look for work, but she used her free time to do household maintenance chores he had been forced to neglect. And she did not appear to lack for money—indeed, he had to be quite firm before she would let him reimburse her for half of the groceries and staples she bought. She respected his privacy and welcomed his company, cleaned up her own messes and left his the hell alone.

The only thing that bothered him was concern for the private pain of which she still would not tell him, and which she could not altogether hide. She did not tantalize him with it; he acquired only by accident some idea of the depth and extent of her hurt, when he woke quite late one rainy night and heard her weeping in the next room. He nearly went to her then, but something told him that it was the wrong thing to do. He waited, listening. He heard her moan, in a voice softer than her sobs but still plainly audible: "Jacques, who are you? *What* are you?" Then her weeping became wordless again, and after a time it was over and they both slept. In the morning she was so relaxed and jolly that he wondered if he had been dreaming.

He noted certain subtle signs that she was becoming attracted to his good friend Charlie, who lived eight blocks away with three male roommates. Norman gave the chemistry careful thought, and decided that he approved. On the twenty-first day of her residence he saw to it that they were both invited to a party at Charlie's, and that night when it was time to go he announced that a whole day of processing final exams had tired him out, why didn't she go along without him? He was going to turn in at once and sleep the night away, would doubtless be sound asleep whenever she might return, early or late. He smiled to himself at how she tried to keep the pleasantness of her surprise from showing, bundled her out the door, and retired at once to his bed in the den, where he lay with the lights out. In point of fact he was wide awake, but he resolved to lie there in the dark till sleep did come. Charlie, he knew, was not a slow worker, and Madeleine seemed to have a European directness of her own.

Nonetheless, they had not showed up by the time he finally fell genuinely asleep at midnight.

In the morning he tiptoed about, trying to make breakfast as quietly as possible so as not to wake them . . . until he noticed that the bedroom door was open. He found that she had not come home the night before, and went off to work wondering what the hell Charlie had done with his three roommates and the party.

She was not home when he returned, which did not surprise him inordinately, but she had left no message in the phone, which did. He swallowed his prurient curiosity and a solitary dinner and put his attention on the work he had brought home for the weekend. To his credit, it was eleven-thirty before he broke down and phoned Charlie's place.

Charlie answered the phone. The screen showed him in bed with a pleasant-looking Oriental woman whom Norman vaguely recognized. Charlie was quite certain of his facts. Madeleine had arrived at the party, had not been overly depressed at finding Charlie already paired off with Mei-Ling, had stayed and drunk and smoked and laughed and danced with several men without settling on any of them. She had sung them all a devastating impromptu parody of the new Mindfuckers single. She had left the party, unquestionably alone, cheerful and not overly stoned, at about one in the morning.

In his guts, Norman *knew* before he had hung up the phone. But it was a full three days before he could get it through his head as well that Madeleine was never going to come back.

2

2011

I SMELLED HER before I saw her. Even so, the first sight was shocking.

She was sitting in a tan plastic-surfaced armchair, the kind where the front comes up as the back goes down. It was back as far as it would go. It was placed beside the large living room window, which was transparent. A plastic block table next to it held a clock, a dozen unopened packages of self-lighting Peter Jackson cigarettes, an empty ashtray, a full vial of cocaine, and a lamp with a bulb of at least a hundred and fifty watts. It illuminated her with brutal clarity.

She was naked. Her skin was the color of vanilla pudding. Her hair was in rats, her nails unpainted and untended, some overlong and some broken. There was dust on her. She sat in a ghastly sludge of feces and urine. Dried vomit was caked on her chin and between her breasts, and down her ribs to the chair.

These were only part of what I had smelled. The predominant odor was of fresh-baked bread. It is the smell of a person who is starving to death. The combined effluvia had prepared me to find a senior citizen, paralyzed by a stroke or some such crisis.

I judged her to be about twenty-five years old.

I moved to where she could see me, and she did not see me. That was probably just as well, because I had just seen the two most horrible things. The first was the smile. They say that when the bomb went off at Hiroshima, some people's shadows were baked onto walls by it. I think that smile got baked on the surface of my brain in much the same way. I don't want to talk about that smile.

The second horrible thing was the one that explained all the rest. From where I now stood, I could see a triple socket in the wall beneath the window. Into it were plugged the lamp, the clock, and her.

I knew about wireheading, of course—I had lost a couple of acquaintances and one friend to the juice. But I had never *seen* a wirehead. It is by definition a solitary vice, and all the public usually gets to see is a sheeted figure being carried out to the wagon.

The transformer lay on the floor beside the chair, where it had been dropped. The switch was on, and the timer had been jiggered so that instead of providing one five- or ten- or fifteen-second jolt per hour, it allowed continuous flow. That timer is required by law on all juice rigs sold, and you need special tools to defeat it. Say, a nail file. The input cord was long, and fell in crazy coils from the wall socket. The output cord disappeared beneath the chair, but I knew where it ended. It ended in the tangled snarl of her hair, at the crown of her head, in a miniplug. The plug was snapped into a jack surgically implanted in her skull, and from the jack tiny wires snaked their way through the wet jelly to the hypothalamus, to the specific place in the medial forebrain bundle where the major pleasure center of her brain was located. She had sat there in total transcendent ecstasy for at least five days.

I moved finally. I moved closer, which surprised me. She saw me now, and impossibly the smile became a bit wider. I was marvelous. I was captivating. I was her perfect lover. I could not look at the smile; a small plastic tube ran from one corner of the smile and my eyes followed it gratefully. It was held in place by small bits of surgi-cal tape at her jaw, neck, and shoulder, and from there it ran in a lazy curve to the big fifty-liter water-cooler bottle on the floor. She had plainly meant her suicide to last: she had arranged to die of hunger rather than thirst, which would have been quicker. She could take a drink when she happened to think of it; and if she forgot, well, what the hell.

My intention must have shown on my face, and I think she even understood it—the smile began to fade. That decided me. I moved before she could force her neglected body to react, whipped the plug out of the wall, and stepped back warily.

Her body did not go rigid as if galvanized. It had already been so for many days. What it did was the exact opposite, and the effect was just as striking. She seemed to shrink. Her eyes slammed shut. She slumped. Well, I thought, it'll be a long day and a night before *she* can move a voluntary muscle again, and then she hit me before I knew she had left the chair, breaking my nose with the heel of one fist and bouncing the other off the side of my head. We cannoned off each other and I managed to keep my feet; she whirled and grabbed the lamp. Its cord was stapled to the floor and would not yield, so she set her feet and yanked and it snapped off clean at the base. In near-total darkness she raised the lamp on high and came at me and I lunged inside the arc of her swing and punched her in the solar plexus. She said *guff!* and went down.

I staggered to a couch and sat down and felt my nose and fainted.

I don't think I was out very long. The blood tasted fresh. I woke with a sense of terrible urgency. It took me a while to work out why. When someone has been simultaneously starved and unceasingly stimulated for days on end, it is not the best idea in the world to depress their respiratory center. I lurched to my feet.

It was not completely dark, there was a moon somewhere out there. She lay on her back, arms at her sides, perfectly relaxed. Her ribs rose and fell in great slow swells. A pulse showed strongly at her throat. As I knelt beside her she began to snore, deeply and rhythmically.

I had time for second thoughts now. It seemed incredible that my impulsive action had not killed her. Perhaps that had been my subconscious intent. Five days of wire-heading alone should have killed her, never mind sudden cold turkey.

I probed in the tangle of hair, found the empty jack. The hair around it was dry. If she hadn't torn the skin in yanking herself loose, it was unlikely that she had sustained any more serious damage within. I continued probing, found no soft places on the skull. Her forehead felt cool and sticky to my hand. The fecal smell was overpowering the baking bread now.

There was no pain in my nose yet, but it felt immense and pulsing. I did not want to touch it, or to think about it. My shirt was soaked with blood; I wiped my face with it and tossed it into a corner. It took everything I had to lift her. She was unreasonably heavy, and I say that having carried drunks and corpses. There was a hall off the living room, and all halls lead to a bathroom. I headed that way in a clumsy staggering trot, and just as I reached the deeper darkness, with my pulse at its maximum, my nose woke up and began screaming.

I nearly dropped her then and clapped my hands to my face; the temptation was overwhelming. Instead I whimpered like a dog and kept going. Childhood feeling: runny nose you can't wipe. At each door I came to, I teetered on one leg and kicked it open, and the third one gave the right small-room, acoustic-tile echo. The light switch was where they almost always are; I rubbed it on with my shoulder and the room flooded with light.

Large aquamarine tub, styrofoam recliner pillow at the head end, nonslip bottom. Aquamarine sink with ornate handles, cluttered with toiletries and cigarette butts and broken shards of mirror from the medicine cabinet above. Aquamarine commode, lid up and seat down. Brown throw rug, expensive. Scale shoved back into a corner, covered with dust in which two footprints showed. I made a massive effort and managed to set her reasonably gently in the tub. I rinsed my face and hands of blood at the sink, ignoring the broken glass, and stuffed the bleeding nostril with toilet paper. I adjusted her head, fixed the chin strap. I held both feet away from the faucet until I had the water adjusted, and then left with one hand on my nose and the other beating against my hip, in search of her liquor.

There was plenty to choose from. I found some Metaxa in the kitchen. I took great care not to bring it near my nose, sneaking it up on my mouth from below. It tasted like burning lighter fluid, and made sweat spring out on my forehead. I found a roll of paper towels, and on my way back to the bathroom I used a great wad of them to swab most of the sludge off the chair and rug. There was a growing pool of water siphoning from the plastic tube, and I stopped that. When I got back to the bathroom the water was lapping over her bloated belly, and horrible tendrils were weaving up from beneath her. It took three rinses before I was satisfied with the body. I found a hose-and-spray under the sink that mated with the tub's faucet, and that made the hair easy.

I had to dry her there in the tub. There was only one towel left, none too clean. I found a first-aid spray that incorporated a good topical anesthetic, and put it on the sores on her back and butt. I had located her bedroom on the way to the Metaxa. Wet hair slapped my arm as I carried her there. She seemed even heavier, as though she had become waterlogged. I eased the door shut behind me and tried the light-switch trick again, and it wasn't there. I moved forward into a footlocker and lost her and went down amid multiple crashes, putting all my attention into guarding my nose. She made no sound at all, not even a grunt.

The light switch turned out to be a pull-chain over the bed. She was on her side, still breathing slow and deep. I wanted to punt her up onto the bed. My nose was a blossom of pain. I nearly couldn't lift her the third time. I was moaning with frustration by the time I had her on her left side on the king-size mattress. It was a big brass four-poster bed, and with satin sheets and pillowcases, all dirty. The blankets were shoved to the bottom. I checked her skull and pulse again, peeled up each eyelid, and found uniform pupils. Her forehead and cheek still felt cool, so I covered her. Then I kicked the footlocker clear into the corner, turned out the light, and left her snoring like a chain saw.

Her vital papers and documents were in her study, locked in a strongbox on the closet shelf. It was an expensive box, quite sturdy and proof against anything short of nuclear explosion. It had a combination lock with all of twenty-seven possible combinations. It was stuffed with papers. I laid her life out on her desk like a losing hand of solitaire, and studied it with a growing frustration.

Her name was Karen Scholz, but she used the name Karen Shaw, which I thought phony. She was twenty-two. Divorced her parents at fourteen, uncontested no-fault. Since then she had been, at various times, waitress, secretary to a lamp salesman, painter, free-lance typist, motorcycle mechanic, and unlicensed masseuse. The most recent paycheck stub was from the Hard Corps, a massage parlor with a cut-rate reputation. It was dated almost a year ago. Her bank balance combined with paraphernalia I had found in the closet to tell me that she was currently self-employed as a tootlegger, a cocaine dealer. The richness of the apartment and furnishings told me that she was a foolish one. Even if the narcs missed her, very shortly the IRS was going to come down on her like a ton of bricks. Perhaps subconsciously she had not expected to be around.

Nothing there; I kept digging. She had attended community college for one semester as an art major, and dropped out failing. She had defaulted on a lease three years ago. She had wrecked a car once, and been shafted by her insurance company. Trivia. Only one major trauma in recent years: a year and a half ago she had contracted out as host-mother to a couple named Lombard/Smyth. It was a pretty good fee—she had good hips and the right rare blood type—but six months into the pregnancy they had caught her using tobacco and canceled the contract. She fought, but they had photographs. And better lawyers, naturally. She had to repay the advance, and pay for the abortion, of course, and she got socked for court costs besides.

It didn't make sense. To show clean lungs at the physical, she had to have been off cigarettes for at least three to six months. Why backslide, with so much at stake? Like the minor traumas, it felt more like an effect than a cause. Self-destructive behavior. I kept looking.

Near the bottom I found something that looked promising. Both her parents had been killed in a car smash when she was eighteen. Their obituary was paperclipped to her father's will. That will was one of the most extraordinary documents I have ever read. I could understand an angry father cutting off his only child without a dime. But what he had done was worse. He had left all his money to the church, and to her "a hundred dollars, the going rate."

Damn it, that didn't work either. So-there suicides don't wait four years. And they don't use such a garish method either; it devalues the tragedy. I decided it had to be either a very big and dangerous coke deal gone bad, or a very reptilian lover. No, not a coke deal. They would never have left her in her own apartment to die the way she wanted to. It could not be murder: even the most unscrupulous wire surgeon needs an awake, consenting subject to place the wire correctly.

A lover, then. I was relieved, pleased with my sagacity, and irritated as hell. I didn't know why. I chalked it up to my nose. It felt as though a large shark with rubber teeth was rhythmically biting it as hard as he could. I shoveled the papers back into the box, locked and replaced it, and went to the bathroom.

Her medicine cabinet would have impressed a pharmacist. She had lots of allergies. It took me five minutes to find aspirin. I took four. I picked the largest shard of mirror out of the sink, propped it on the toilet tank, and sat down backward on the seat. My nose was visibly displaced to the right, and the swelling was just hitting its stride. I removed the toilet-tissue plug from my nostril, and it resumed bleeding. There was a box of Kleenex on the floor. I ripped it apart, took out all the tissues, and stuffed them into my mouth. Then I grabbed my nose with my right hand and tugged out to the left, simultaneously flushing the toilet with my left hand. The flushing coincided with the scream, and my front teeth met through the Kleenex. When I could see again, the nose looked straight and my breathing was unimpaired. When the bleeding stopped again I gingerly washed my face and hands and left. A moment later I returned; something had caught my eye. It was the glass and tooth-brush holder. There was only one toothbrush in it. I looked through the medicine chest again, and noticed this time that there was no shaving cream, no razor, no masculine toiletries of any kind. All the prescriptions were in her name.

I went thoughtfully to the kitchen, mixed myself a Preacher's Downfall by moonlight, and took it to her bedroom. The bedside clock said five. I lit a match, moved the footlocker in front of an arm-chair, sat down, and put my feet up. I sipped my drink and listened to her snore and watched her breathe in the feeble light of the clock. I decided to run through all the possibilities, and as I was formulat-ing the first one, daylight smacked me hard in the nose.

My hands went up reflexively and I poured my drink on my head and hurt my nose more. I wake up hard in the best of times. She was still snoring. I nearly threw the empty glass at her.

It was just past noon, now; light came strongly through the heavy curtains, illuminating so much mess and disorder that I could not decide whether she had trashed her bedroom herself or it had been tossed by a pro. I finally settled on the former: the armchair I'd slept on was intact. Or had the pro found what he wanted before he got that far?

I gave it up and went to make myself breakfast. The milk was bad, of course, but I found a tolerable egg and makings of an omelet. I don't care for black coffee, but Javanese brewed from frozen beans needs no augmentation. I drank three cups.

It took me an hour or two to clean up and air out the living room. The cord and transformer went down the oubliette, along with most of the perished items from the fridge. The dishes took three full cycles for each load, a couple of hours all told. I passed the time vacuuming and dusting and snooping, learning nothing more of significance.

The phone rang. She had no answering program in circuit, of course. I energized the screen. It was a young man in a business tunic, wearing the doggedly amiable look of the stranger who wants you to accept the call anyway. After some thought I did accept, audio-only, and let him speak first. He wanted to sell us a marvelous building lot in Forest Acres, South Dakota. I was making up a shopping list about fifteen minutes later when I heard her moan. I reached her bedroom door in seconds, waited in the doorway with both hands in sight, and said slowly and clearly, "My name is Joseph Templeton, Karen. I am a friend. You are all right now."

Her eyes were those of a small, tormented animal.

"Please don't try to get up. Your muscles won't work properly and you may hurt yourself."

No answer.

"Karen, are you hungry?"

"Your voice is ugly," she said despairingly, and her own voice was so hoarse I winced. "*My* voice is ugly," she added, and sobbed gently. "It's *all* ugly." She screwed her eyes shut.

She was clearly incapable of movement. I told her I would be right back, and went to the kitchen. I made up a tray of clear strong broth, unbuttered toast, tea with maltose, and saltine crackers. She was staring at the ceiling when I got back, and apparently it was vile. I put the tray down, lifted her, and made a backrest of pillows.

"I want a drink."

"After you eat," I said agreeably.

"Who're you?"

"Mother Templeton. Eat."

"The soup, maybe. Not the toast." She got about half of it down, did nibble at the toast, accepted some tea. I didn't want to overfill her. "My drink."

"Sure thing." I took the tray back to the kitchen, finished my shopping list, put away the last of the dishes, and put a frozen steak into the oven for my lunch. When I got back she was fast asleep.

Emaciation was near total; except for breasts and bloated belly, she was all bone and taut skin. Her pulse was steady. At her best she would not have been very attractive by conventional standards. Passable. Too much waist, not enough neck, upper legs a bit too thick for the rest of her. It's hard to evaluate a starved and unconscious face, but her jaw was a bit too square, her nose a trifle hooked, her blue eyes just the least little bit too far apart. Animated, the face might have been beautiful—any set of features can support beauty—but even a superb makeup job could not have made her pretty. There was an old bruise on her chin, another on her left hip. Her hair was sandy blonde, long and thin; it had dried in snarls that would take hours to comb out. Her breasts were magnificent, and that saddened me. In this world, a woman whose breasts are her best feature is in for a rough time.

I was putting together a picture of a life that would have depressed anyone with the sensitivity of a rhino. Back when I had first seen her, when her features were alive, she had looked sensitive. Or had that been a trick of the juice? Impossible to say now.

But damn it all to hell, I could find nothing to really explain the socket in her skull. You can hear worse life stories in any bar, on any street corner. Wireheads are usually addictive personalities, who decide at last to skip the small shit. There were no tracks on her anywhere, no nasal damage, no sign that she used any of the coke she sold. Her work history, pitiful and fragmented as it was, was too steady for any kind of serious jones; she had undeniably been hitting the sauce hard lately, but only lately. Tobacco seemed to be her only serious addiction.

That left the hypothetical bastard lover. I worried at that for a while to see if I could make it fit. To have done so much psychic damage, he would almost *have* to have lived with her . . . but where was his spoor?

At that point I went to the bathroom, and that settled it. When I lifted the seat to urinate, I found written on the underside with magic marker: "It's so nice to have a man around the house!" The handwriting was hers. She had lived alone.

I was relieved, because I hadn't relished thinking about my hypothetical monster or the necessity of tracking and killing him. But I was irritated as hell again.

I wanted to *understand*.

For something to do, I took my steak and a mug of coffee to the study and heated up her computer. I tried all the typical access codes, her birthdate and her name in numbers and such, but none of them would unlock it. Then on a hunch I tried the date of her parents' death, and that did it. I ordered the groceries she needed, instructed the lobby door to accept delivery, and tried everything I could think of to get a diary or a journal out of the damned thing, without success. So I punched up the public library and asked the catalog for *Britannica* on wire-heading. It referred me to brain-reward, autostimulus of. I skipped over the history, from discovery by Olds and others in 1956 to emergence as a social problem in the late twentieth century, when surgery got simple; declined the offered diagrams, graphs, and technical specs; finally found a brief section on motivations.

There was indeed one type of typical user I had overlooked. The terminally ill.

Could that really be it? At her age? I went to the bathroom and checked the prescriptions. Nothing for heavy pain, nothing indicating anything more serious than allergies. Back before telephones had cameras I might have conned something out of her personal physician, but it would have been a chancy thing even then. There was no way to test the hypothesis.

It was possible, even plausible—but it just wasn't *likely* enough to satisfy the thing inside me that demanded an explanation. I booted a game of four-wall squash, and made sure the computer would let me win. I was almost enjoying myself when she screamed.

It wasn't much of a scream; her throat was shot. But it fetched me at once. I saw the problem as I cleared the door. The topical anesthetic had worn off the large sores on her back and buttocks, and the pain had woken her. Now that I thought about it, it should have happened earlier; that spray was only supposed to be good for a few hours. I decided that her pleasure-pain system was weakened by overload.

The sores were bad; she would have scars. I resprayed them, and her moans stopped nearly at once. I could devise no means of securing her on her belly that would not be nightmare-inducing, and decided it was unnecessary. I thought she was out again, and started to leave. Her voice, muffled by pillows, stopped me in my tracks.

"I don't know you. Maybe you're not even real. I can tell you."

"Save your energy, Karen. You—"

"Shut up. You wanted the karma, you got it."

I shut up.

Her voice was flat, dead. "All my friends were dating at twelve. *He* made me wait until fourteen. Said I couldn't be trusted. Tommy came to take me to the dance, and he gave Tommy a hard time. I was so embarrassed. The dance was nice for a couple of hours. Then Tommy started chasing after Jo Tompkins. He just left me and went off with her. I went into the ladies' room and cried for a long time. A couple of girls got the story out of me, and one of them had a bottle of vodka in her purse. I never drank before. When I started tearing up cars in the parking lot, one of the girls got ahold of Tommy. She gave him shit and made him take me home. I don't remember it, I found out later."

Her throat gave out and I got water. She accepted it without meeting my eyes, turned her face away and continued.

"Tommy got me in the door somehow. I was out cold by then. He'd been fooling around with me a little in the car, I think. He must have been too scared to try and get me upstairs. He left me on the couch and my underpants on the rug and went home. The next thing I knew, I was on the floor and my face hurt. *He* was standing over me. Whore he said. I got up and tried to explain and he hit me a couple of times. I ran for the door but he hit me hard in the back. I went into the stairs and banged my head real hard."

Feeling began to come into her voice for the first time. The feeling was fear. I dared not move.

"When I woke up it was day. Mama must have bandaged my head and put me to bed. My head hurt a lot. When I came out of the bathroom I heard him call me. Him and Mama were in bed. He started in on me. Wouldn't let me talk, and he kept getting madder and madder. Finally I hollered back at him. He got up off the bed and started in hitting me again. My robe came off. He kept hitting me in the belly and tits, and his fists were like hammers. Slut, he kept saying. Whore. I thought he was going to kill me so I grabbed one arm and bit. He roared like a dragon and threw me across the room. Onto the bed. Mama jumped up. Then he pulled down his underpants and it was big and purple. I screamed and screamed and tore at his back and Mama just stood there. Her eyes were big and round, just like in cartoons. His breath stank and I screamed and screamed and—"

She broke off short and her shoulders knotted. When she continued, her voice was stone dead again. "I woke up in my own bed again. I took a real long shower and went downstairs. Mama was making pancakes. I sat down and she gave me one and I ate it, and then I threw it up right there on the table and ran out the door. She never said a word, never called me back. After school that day I found a Sanctuary and started the divorce proceedings. I never saw either of them again. I never told this to anybody before."

The pause was so long I thought she had fallen asleep. "Since that time I've tried it with men and women and boys and girls, in the dark and in the desert sun, with people I cared for and people I didn't give a damn about, and I have never understood the pleasure in it. The best it's ever been for me is not uncomfortable. God, how I've wondered . . . now I know." She was starting to drift. "Only thing my whole life turned out *better*'n cracked up to be." She snorted sleepily. "Even alone."

I sat there for a long time without moving. My legs trembled when I got up, and my hands trembled while I made supper.

That was the last time she was lucid for nearly forty-eight hours. I plied her with successively stronger soups every time she woke up, and once I got a couple of pieces of tea-soggy toast into her. Sometimes she called me by others' names, and sometimes she didn't know I was there, and everything she said was disjointed. I listened to her CDs, watched some of her video, charged some books and games to her computer account. I took a lot of her aspirin. And drank surprisingly little of her booze.

It was frustrating. I still couldn't make it all fit together. There was a large piece missing. The animal who sired and raised her had planted the charge, of course, and I perceived that it was big enough to blow her apart. But why had it taken eight years to go off? If his death four years ago had not triggered it, what had? I could not leave until I knew.

Midway through the second day her plumbing started working again; I had to change the sheets. The next morning a noise woke me and I found her on the bathroom floor on her knees in a pool of urine. I got her clean and back to bed, and just as I thought she was going to drift off she started yelling at me. "Lousy son of a bitch, it could have been over! I'll never have the guts again now! How could you do that, you *bastard,* it was so *nice!*" She turned violently away from me and curled up. I had to make a hard choice then, and I gambled on what I knew of loneliness and sat on the edge of the bed and stroked her hair as gently and impersonally as I knew how. It was a good guess. She began to cry, in great racking heaves first, then the steady wail of total heartbreak. I had been praying for this, and did not begrudge the strength it cost her.

By the time she fell off the edge into sleep, she had cried for so long that every muscle in my body ached from sitting still. She never felt me get up, stiff and clumsy as I was. There was something different about her sleeping face now. It was not slack but relaxed. I limped out, feeling as close to peace as I had since I arrived, and as I was passing the living room on the way to the liquor, I heard the phone.

As I had before, I looked over the caller. The picture was under-contrasted and snowy; it was a pay phone. He looked like an immigrant construction worker, massive and florid and neckless, almost brutish. And, at the moment, under great stress. He was crushing a hat in his hands, mortally embarrassed. I mentally shrugged and accepted.

"Sharon, don't hang up," he was saying. "I *gotta* find out what this is all about."

Nothing could have made me hang up.

"Sharon? Sharon, I know you're there. Jo Ann says you ain't there, she says she called you every day for almost a week and banged on your door a few times. But I know you're there, now anyway. I walked past your place an hour ago and I seen the bathroom light go on and off. Sharon, will you please tell me what the hell is going on? Are you listening to me? I know you're listening to me. Look, you gotta understand, I thought it was all set, see? I mean I thought it was *set*. Arranged. I put it to Jo Ann, cause she's my regular, and she says not *me*, lover, but I know a gal. Look, was she lying to me or what? She told me for another bill you play them kind of games, sometimes."

Regular two-hundred-dollar bank deposits plus a cardboard box full of scales, vials, razor, mirror, and milk powder makes her a coke dealer—right, Travis McGee? Don't be misled by the fact that the box was shoved in a corner, sealed with tape, and covered with dust. After all, the only other illicit profession that pays regular sums at regular intervals is hooker, and *two* bills is too much for square-jawed, hook-nosed, wide-eyed little Karen, breasts or no breasts.

For a garden-variety hooker . . .

"Dammit, she told me she *called* you and set it up, she give me your *apartment* number." He shook his head violently. "I can't make no sense out of this. Dammit, she *couldn't* be lying to me. It don't figure. You let me in, didn't even turn the camera on first, it was all arranged. Then you screamed and . . . I was real careful not to really hurt you, I know I was. Then I put on my pants and I'm putting the envelope on the dresser and you bust that chair on me and come at me with that knife and I hadda bust you one. It just don't make no sense, will you *goddammit say something to me?* I'm twisted up inside going on two weeks now. I can't even eat."

I went to shut off the phone, and my hand was shaking so bad I missed, spinning the volume knob to minimum. "Sharon you gotta believe me," he hollered from far far away, "I'm into rape fantasy, I'm not into rape!" and then I had found the right switch and he was gone.

I got up very slowly and toddled off to the liquor cabinet, and I stood in front of it taking pulls from different bottles at random until I could no longer see his face—his earnest, baffled, half-ashamed face.

Because his hair was thin sandy blond, and his jaw was a bit too square, and his nose was a trifle hooked, and his blue eyes were just the least little bit too far apart. They say everyone has a double somewhere. And Fate is such a witty little motherfucker, isn't he?

I don't remember how I got to bed.

I woke later that night with the feeling that I would have to bang my head on the floor a couple of times to get my heart started again. I was on my makeshift doss of pillows and blankets beside her bed, and when I finally peeled my eyes open she was sitting up in bed staring at me. She had fixed her hair somehow, and her nails were trimmed. We looked at each other for a long time. Her color was returning somewhat, and the edge was off her bones.

She sighed. "What did Jo Ann say when you told her?"

I said nothing.

"Come on, Jo Ann's got the only other key to this place, and she wouldn't give it to you if you weren't a friend. So what did she say?"

I got painfully up out of the tangle and walked to the window. A phallic church steeple rose above the low-rises a couple of blocks away.

"God is an iron," I said. "Did you know that?"

I turned to look at her and she was staring. She laughed experimentally, stopped when I failed to join in. "And I'm a pair of pants with a hole scorched through the ass?"

"If a person who indulges in gluttony is a glutton, and a person who commits a felony is a felon, then God is an iron. Or else He's the dumbest designer that ever lived."

Of a thousand possible snap reactions, she picked the most flattering and hence most irritating. She kept silent, kept looking at me, and thought about what I had said. At last she said, "I agree. What particular design screwup did you have in mind?"

"The one that nearly left you dead in a pile of your own shit," I said harshly. "Everybody talks about the new menace, wireheading, eighth most common cause of death in less than a decade. Wireheading's not new—it's just a technical refinement."

"I don't follow."

"Are you familiar with the old cliche, 'Everything in the world I like is either illegal, immoral, or fattening'?"

"Sure."

"Didn't that ever strike you as damned odd? What's the most nutritionally useless and physiologically dangerous 'food' substance in the world? White sugar. Glucose. And it seems to be beyond the power of the human nervous system to resist it. They put it in virtually all the processed food there is, which is next to all the food there is, because *nobody can resist it.* And so we poison ourselves and whipsaw our dispositions and rot our teeth. Maltose is just as sweet, but it's less popular, precisely because it doesn't kick your blood sugar in the ass and then depress it again. Isn't that odd? There is a primitive programming in our skulls that rewards us, literally overwhelmingly, every time we do something damned silly. Like smoke a poison, or eat or drink or snort or shoot a poison. Or *overeat good* foods. Or engage in complicated sexual behavior without procreative intent, which, if it were not for the pleasure, would be pointless and insane. And which, if pursued for the pleasure alone, quickly becomes pointless and insane anyway. A suicidal brain-reward system is built into us."

"But the reward system is for survival."

"So how the hell did ours get wired up so that survival-threatening behavior gets rewarded best of all? Even the pro-survival pleasure stimuli are wired so that a dangerous *overload* produces the maximum pleasure. On a purely biological level, man is programmed to strive hugely for more than he needs, more than he can profitably use. Add in intelligence and everything goes to hell. Man is capable of outgrowing any ecological niche you put him in—he survives at all because he is The Animal That Moves. Given half a chance he kills himself of surfeit."

My knees were trembling so badly I had to sit down. I felt feverish and somehow larger than myself, and I knew I was talking much too fast. She had nothing whatever to say—with voice, face, or body.

"It is illuminating," I went on, fingering my aching nose, "to note that the two ultimate refinements of hedonism are the pleasure of cruelty and the pleasure of the despoliation of innocence. Consider: no sane person in search of sheerly physical sexual pleasure would select an inexperienced partner. Everyone knows that mature, experienced lovers are more competent, confident, and skilled. Yet there is not a skin mag in the world that prints pictures of men or women over twenty if they can possibly help it. Don't tell me about recapturing lost youth: the root is that a fantasy object over twenty cannot plausibly possess innocence, can no longer be corrupted.

"Man has historically devoted *much* more subtle and ingenious thought to inflicting cruelty than to giving others pleasure—which, given his gregarious nature, would seem a much more survival-oriented behavior. Poll any hundred people at random and you'll find *at least* twenty or thirty who know all there is to know about psychological torture and psychic castration—and maybe two who know how to give a terrific back-rub. That business of your father leaving all his money to the church and leaving you 'a hundred dollars, the going rate'—that was *artistry*. I can't imagine a way to make you feel as good as that made you feel rotten. But for *him* it must have been pure pleasure."

"Maybe the Puritans were right," she said. "Maybe pleasure is the root of all evil. Oh, God! but life is bleak without it."

"One of my most precious possessions," I went on blindly, "is a button that my friend Slinky John used to hand-paint and sell below cost. He was the only practicing anarchist I ever met. The button reads: 'GO, LEMMINGS, GO!' A lemming surely feels intense pleasure as he gallops to the sea. His self-destruction is programmed by nature, a part of the very same life force that insisted on being conceived and born in the first place. If it feels good, do it." I laughed, and she flinched. "So it seems to me that God is either an iron, or a colossal jackass. I don't know whether to be admiring or contemptuous."

All at once I was out of words, and out of strength. I yanked my gaze away from hers and stared at my knees for a long time. I felt vaguely ashamed, as befits one who has thrown a tantrum in a sick-room.

After a time she said, "You talk good on your feet."

I kept looking at my knees. "I think I used to be an actor once."

"I would have gues—"

Hiatus.

I was standing by the door, facing out into the hall, and she was still speaking. "I said, will you tell me something?"

"If I can."

"What was the pleasure in putting me back together again?"

I flinched.

"Look at me. There. I've got a half-ass idea of what shape I was in when you met me, and I can guess what it's been like since. I don't know if I'd have done as much for Jo Ann, and she's my best friend. You don't look like a guy your favorite kick is sick fems, and you sure as *hell* don't look like you're so rich you got time on your hands. So what's been your pleasure, these last few days?"

"Trying to understand," I snapped. "I'm nosy."

"And do you understand?"

"Yeah. I put it together."

"So you'll be going now?"

"Not yet," I said automatically. "You're not—"

And caught myself.

"There's something else besides pleasure," she said. "Another system of reward, only I don't think it has much to do with the one I got wired up to my scalp here. Not brain-reward. Call it mind-reward.

Call it . . . joy. The thing like pleasure that you feel when you've done a good thing or passed up a real tempting chance to do a bad thing. Or when the unfolding of the universe just seems especially apt. It's nowhere near as flashy and intense as pleasure can be. Believe me! But it's got *some*thing going for it. Something that can make you do without pleasure, or even accept a lot of pain, to get it.

"That stuff you're talking about, that's there, that's true. But you said yourself, Man is the animal that outgrows and moves. Evolution works slow, is all." She pushed hair back from her face. "It took a couple of hundred million years to develop a thinking ape, and you want a smart one in a lousy few hundred thou? That lemming drive you're talking about is there—but there's another kind of drive, another kind of force that's working against it. Or else there wouldn't still be any people and there wouldn't be the words to have this conversation and—" She paused, looked down at herself. "And I wouldn't be here to say them."

"That was just random chance."

She snorted. "What isn't?"

"Well, that's *fine,*" I shouted. "That's *fine.* Since the world is saved and you've got everything under control I'll just be going along."

I've got a lot of voice when I yell. She ignored it utterly, continued speaking as if nothing had happened. "Now I can say that I have sampled the spectrum of the pleasure system at both ends—none and all there is—and I think the rest of my life I will dedicate myself to the middle of the road and see how that works out. Starting with the very weak tea and toast I'm going to ask you to bring me in another ten minutes or so. With maltose. But as for this other stuff, this joy thing, that I would like to begin learning about, as much as I can. I don't really know a God damned thing about it, but I understand it has something to do with sharing and caring and what did you say your name was?"

"It doesn't matter," I yelled.

"All right. What can *I* do for *you?*"

"Nothing!"

"What did you come here for?"

I was angry enough to be honest. "To burgle your fucking apartment!"

Her eyes opened wide, and then she slumped back against the

pillows and laughed until the tears came, and I tried and could not help myself and laughed too, and we shared laughter for a long time, as long as we had shared her tears the night before.

And then, straight-faced, she said, "Wait'll I'm on my feet; you're gonna need help with those stereo speakers. Butter on the toast."

⊰3⊱

2006

THE ROOM WAS RIPE with the pungencies of sex and sweat. Darkness was total, and now that their pulse and breathing had slowed, the stillness was complete. Norman tensed his stomach muscles briefly, felt the warm honeyed weight of Phyllis from his left shin to left shoulder, felt the barely perceptible movement with which she nestled a breast more comfortably into his armpit, tasted the sour sweetness of her breath. Idly he moved his left hand up and down the smooth length of her, reflected on how pleasant it was to caress a body whose dimensions were not precisely and thoroughly known, how very pleasant to encounter unfamiliar swellings and taperings, and in the encountering to trigger unpredictable responses and quickenings.

This caused him to wonder why, in all his five years of marriage to Lois, he had never been seriously tempted to be unfaithful. He had been experienced when he met her, aware of the sweetness of novelty, and during the course of their marriage perhaps a dozen women had inspired lust in him at one time or another. But he had allowed only a handful of those temptations to progress even as far as the fantasy stage—and in retrospect those were the only ones where actual fulfillment of the fantasy was out of the question. Ever since their estrangement he had sought no other partner until now. From the vantage point of satiation, he wondered why he had waited so long.

Well, he answered himself, if you consistently pass up a chance at something very pleasant, it must be because you're afraid of risking something else, something that's *better* than very pleasant. There must be something about long-term intimacy, about familiarity, that is sweeter than variety; something more to life than that spiciest of its spices.

He considered the lovemaking just now finished, and he thought, Well, that was definitely more . . . explosive than anything Lois and I have had in years. But he didn't know if he could say it was more satisfying. There had been clumsinesses, false starts, and missed signals. It is a tricky, finicky road to orgasm, different for everyone on Earth. If this woman and he remained lovers for any length of time, they would have to learn each other's ways—such a clumsy, self-conscious process.

And then Norman understood the sweetness of familiarity. Some say it breeds contempt, but he saw now that there was a tremendous security in having someone who knew you inside and out, who had found it worth the time and trouble to learn where your buttons were and when and how to push them, and whose own personal buttons you could find in the dark. It was worth some loss of mystery. In that moment he learned what it had been about his marriage that was so sweet that, over the past half-year, he had bartered away most of his self-respect for occasional morsels of counterfeit.

And with that learning he knew that the thing he still yearned for so badly—having someone so close to you that they become your other leg—was gone for good, and that counterfeit was all he would ever have of it again from Lois—that it was finally and forever over, irretrievably lost, and that he must find someone else and work five more years ever to have anything like it again. The last scrap of hope, nourished for so long, left him at last. His heart turned over inside him, and his eyes stung fiercely

Phyllis rolled away from him suddenly. It was a single quick movement, but it was made up of many subtle parts, the drag of breast across his chest, the pleasant pulling apart of fleshes cemented by dried sweat, tiny tugs of intertangled hairs separating, moist sounds from her loins. She left a hand palm up on his belly to maintain contact between them, and rummaged in the tangle of clothing beside the bed. She struggled up into a sitting position, replaced the hand with a leg across his leg, and used both hands to shatter the darkness with a struck match.

The effect was rather like that of a star shell going off over a deserted battlefield, for Norman's bedroom was a mess. But he saw only her, the sudden and terrible beauty of her nakedness. She was flat-chested compared to Lois, but he was not comparing her to Lois; Lois was gone from his mind, and his sorrow with her. This was Phyllis, and she was lovely. When her weight had come off him he had automatically taken a deeper breath; now he could not exhale it.

The sight lasted only long enough for her to light two Player's and pass one to him; then she whipped the match flame to death. But he took the opportunity to take several mental photographs, apply fixative, and store for easy access. In the sudden return of darkness, his breath left him whistling. He replaced it with tobacco smoke.

"That," she said softly, "was good enough to be illegal."

"Madam, your son just passed Victorian Poetry."

She chuckled. "You bastard. 'Passed'? That was B-plus at the very least."

"He'll graduate Mama Cum Loudly," he assured her, and she pinched him.

"Seriously, Norman . . ." She drew on her cigarette, and her face and one shoulder reappeared briefly and ectoplasmically. "I don't make a habit of bolstering my lovers' egos, but that was extraordinary."

"Wasn't my doing. Wasn't even our doing. We were both privileged to be present at an extraordinary event."

"Bullshit. It may have taken me till five-thirty in the morning to seduce you, but it was worth waiting for. You're a very good lover, don't you know that?"

A flip answer died on his tongue and left a strange taste. "No," he said finally, "I didn't."

"Well, then, let me tell you: in the last hour or so you fulfilled just about every fantasy I had left, and showed me at least one erogenous zone I didn't know I had. Listen, I'll be honest: I've had better. But I've never had a better first time, and I doubt I ever will."

He could think of nothing to say.

"Hey, look, I don't want to belabor this. I didn't mean to make you self-conscious. I just . . . I guess I just wanted to say thanks. It's . . . well, there's been a long line of guys who couldn't have cared less if I'd been *awake* or not."

It startled him. "Why the hell would anyone want to have fun alone? Given an alternative like you?"

"The ultimate test of cool. Maintain independence even in the ultimate sharing. You, now: you've got more guts than that. You've given me a piece of yourself, and for all you know I might rip you off."

"Phyllis," he said gently, butting out his smoke, "my checkbook and credit cards are on the bureau. Clean me out and we'll be about even. You've done me a world of good." He sat up, and she hugged him.

When they separated again, he realized that he could dimly see her outlines now; a warm glow was faintly visible at the edges of the window shade. "Jesus. It's come morning." All at once, and for the first time in many hours, he was immensely tired. He lay back down and closed his eyes.

"Norman?" she began, and from the tone in her voice he knew at least in general where she was going, and started to protest his fatigue, but she kept on talking, saying, "Do *you* have any unfulfilled fantasies?"

Fatigue gone. "Uh . . . sexual fantasies, you mean?"

"Chicken. Come on, be honest. Aren't there any secret wishes *I* can make come true for *you?*" Her hand found him, began working gently.

"Well . . ."

"Come on, you're stalling, trying to think of something else plausible to ask me for, in place of whatever you first thought of."

Even Lois had not pushed *all* his buttons. He made his decision. "How do you feel about being tied up?"

Even in the semidarkness he could tell she was frowning; her hand stopped.

"Further than you wanted to go?" he asked after a while.

"You know," she said slowly, "I'm not sure." She lit another cigarette, cupping it so that all the light was reflected down away from her face. "I had a friend, once. She and her husband were into master-slave stuff, I mean they were incredible. She wore a collar around her neck, had whip scars, and I swear to God she was as proud and happy as hell. I thought it was weird."

"Jesus," he said, "so do I."

"I used to ask her how she could stand to be degraded like that. She said it was like the ultimate proof of her love for him. I asked her if he ever proved *his* love, and she said it didn't work that way, that she gave him what he needed and he gave her what she needed."

"Christ on a skateboard. They still together?"

"Of course not. After a while she had no more to give him, so he dumped her. I haven't seen either of 'em in years."

"Uh . . . that's considerably stronger than what I had in mind. I don't think I'd go for bullwhips and pain and abuse."

It was light enough now to see her grin as her hand squeezed. "But hearing about it got you hard, didn't it?"

He could not deny it.

"I'll tell you something. I think she was off the wall, I mean industrial-strength crazy . . . but once in a long while I think about it and I get wet myself. Isn't that sick?"

"First tell me what 'sick' means when applied to a normal condition. *Nobody* leaves the TV for a snack during the rape scene. That does not necessarily mean that *anybody* wants a rape for Christmas." He took another cigarette himself, and she lit it for him with hers. "Look, my subconscious is as screwed up as anyone's. Just from the little I've told you about Lois and me, you must be able to see that there's probably a lot of hostility toward women buried in me right now, certainly toward one woman. But—well, I don't know if this will make any sense or not, but a fantasy is not necessarily a wish."

"All right, then," she said, and began gently stroking his penis. "Tell me about your *wishes.*" He could make out her features now, and she was looking him square in the eye. He could not look away. Involuntarily his back began to arch, his buttocks to clench.

"I would like to tie you down to this bed," he said thickly, "and tease, tantalize, and otherwise titillate your fair young body until you scream for mercy. The only kind of pain I have in mind—beyond the occasional pinch or scratch we've already tried—is the sweet agony of wanting to come so badly you can't see straight or remember your name."

Her busy hand paused, and she grinned suddenly. "That *does* sound more interesting than scrambled eggs and coffee. I just don't know if I understand the tying-up part."

He disposed of his cigarette and she followed suit. "Well, partly it's the symbolic trust, of course, which is fairly heady stuff. But most of it is a sheerly muscular thing. I mean, sex is a process of allowing tension to build to a peak and then release, right?"

"When you're doing it right."

"All right—but ordinarily there's a certain point beyond which your subconscious will not let you build that tension—because if you did, the sheer intensity of the climax would break your partner's back, or nose, or whatever. But when you're restrained, you can exert total effort safely. Every muscle in your body can turn into steel cable, and it's okay."

She was looking thoughtful. "You sound as if you've had it done to you."

"Once, a long time ago. A woman I lived with."

"You enjoyed it?"

"Very much."

"How come only that once, then?"

"She didn't want to talk about it afterward. I think she was deeply disturbed by how much she enjoyed it. Which was her privilege; I didn't push it."

"But you'd try it again?"

"Well, I have to admit that these days it's not what I'd call one of my premier urges. I guess I just feel like I've had my fill of being helpless, this last year. But if you wanted to, I guess I could get behind it."

"Another time, perhaps," she said softly, and lay down spread-eagled on her back. "Right now I'm yours on toast. Bring on your ropes."

He used neckties, and was careful about circulation.

"Norman," she said as he was securing the last knot, "can you see my handbag?"

"Sure, what do you need?"

"In the inside compartment there's a vibrator."

"Oh." He fetched it, stopped on the way back to the bed. "You know, this is a hell of a first date."

All the tension blew away in their shared laughter.

He opened the shade, and it was well and truly morning now, an impossibly rosy dawn from some Tourist Bureau postcard. He spared it only a glance, then brought his gaze back to her vulnerable nakedness.

"You know," she said, "there *is* something thrilling about being helpless . . . when your subconscious is convinced that there's nothing to be really afraid of."

"Thank you," he said. He tried the vibrator: it sounded like an alarm clock buzzer. He grinned at her. "Never tried one of these."

"The single mother's home companion. It'll be a learning experience for both of us."

"That it will."

After fifteen minutes she begged for a gag. "Honest to God, I've gotta scream so bad, I'll wake up the whole building." He insisted that they work out signals first by which she could communicate the concepts "stop doing that" and "I need a breather." Half an hour later he still had not allowed release to either of them. His penis was iron-hard and uncharacteristically standing completely upright against his belly, and she was in a state somewhere beyond babbling incoherency, when the doorbell rang.

He ignored it, of course. It penetrated his attention only just far enough to cause him to tuck the vibrator under a sheet, muffling it, and continue manually. Phyllis was beyond noticing anything external.

Of course the bell rang again; he was expecting that, and paid it no more mind than he had the first time. From somewhere Phyllis had found the strength to begin whimpering again.

But the third time it rang, long and hard, he began idly wondering who it could be that was *not* going to get access to Norman Kent's attention that morning. Certainly not Lois. From nine at night or two or three in the morning was her visiting range—one reason it had taken Phyllis so long to seduce him. Not Spandrell, he'd have given up after the second ring. Little George could scarcely be imagined ambulatory before noon, and the Bobcat was gone south for the summer. Some stranger? Norman's rhythm faltered slightly.

The fourth time it rang it didn't stop.

Anger welled in him, and his hands ceased work altogether. In ten or twenty seconds Phyllis's eyes had unrolled and she heard it too. By that time he had found his slippers. He was blazing mad, but he did *not* want the first thing she saw to be an angry face, so he made a terrific effort and produced a fair smile. "It's all right, darling," he said, caressing her cheek. "Some impertinent idiot. I'll blow him out into the hall and be back in thirty seconds."

She nodded and he rose and left the room. He stuck his head back in, said, "Now, don't go away," and closed the bedroom door carefully and firmly behind him. As it clicked shut, her leg spasmed; the vibrator dropped to the floor and lay buzzing.

Norman went to the door naked and fully hard, fervently hoping that whoever was on the other side would prove to be shockable. Already composing his opening blast, he slipped the locks and flung the door open, and his breath left him.

Lois took her finger off the bell. "Good morning," she said brightly.

"God damn it," he said, and lost his voice again.

she glanced at his erection and grinned. "Got you up, I see." She gripped it briefly, in a proprietary way, and stepped into the apartment, starched whites rustling. "You always did wake up hard."

Somewhere in his highly educated brain were the words he wanted now, needed now, but all that came to mind was "Get out of here. I don't want to see you now," and he could not say those words to Lois. Moreover, he knew she would not obey them.

"God, this place is a wreck. That's not like you, Norman."

"Lois—" His throat and mouth were too dry to produce speech; hastily he went to the fridge and threw orange juice past his teeth. "Lois, *listen to me—*"

"Jesus Christ, you must have been on some binge last night, you've slept right through your alarm. I hear it buzzing."

"NO!"

Too late, she was already halfway down the hall, he dropped the orange juice and *ran* flat out but she was already opening the bedroom door.

"Lois, God damn it—"

She screamed.

Through the door came the muffled sound of Phyllis screaming too, and with weirdness incredible the screams harmonized. As Norman crashed into his ex-wife he roared himself, a great bellow of unendurable frustration, and when they had landed in a mock-obscene tangle on the hallway floor and the last of his bellow had left him, in that moment of stillness before the world could come crashing down around all of them, the doorbell rang again.

Lois heaved him off her and headed for the door in a stumbling, scrabbling run, nurse's cap askew. For an insane moment he wondered why she should want so badly to answer the doorbell, why anyone would *ever* want to answer a doorbell. Such was not Lois's intention.

To her the door was not a gadget for letting people in; it was a gadget for letting them out. Norman heard a loud crash, Lois's war cry ascending the scale, sounds of violent body contact, an astonishing chorus of voices expressing shock and/or indignation, and Lois's footsteps rapidly receding in the direction of the elevator. By then he was on his hands and knees, shaking his head in a perfectly futile attempt to clear it.

"Time out," he said plaintively to the universe in general.

"It's okay," one of his unseen callers told the rest. "He says he'll be right out." Thus reassured, they began entering the apartment—perhaps a dozen of them, by the sound.

Norman had *started* this overtired. He yearned most to race to Phyllis, but he did not want to leave a large number of strangers alone in his apartment until he had at least examined them and learned their business. On the other hand, he was loath to greet them naked. In a few seconds they would have progressed far enough into the apartment to command a view of the hallway. *If only the God damned vibrator would stop buzzing . . .*

All human brains have a component that takes over problem-solving when the conscious mind is stunned. Often it does as well or better. Norman's had gotten him out of the jungle alive six years before, and it did its best now.

"Hang on, Phyllis," he said urgently, and got to the bathroom a split second before the first uninvited guest came even with the hallway. It should have been the work of a moment to deploy a towel, but incredibly he was still erect. Cold water, he thought wildly, and raced for the sink, but halfway there he decided that the noises coming from the living room sounded somehow technological in nature, and he recalled that there was a two-thousand-dollar sound-and-video system in the living room. He whimpered, spun on his heel, and left the bathroom, doing the best he could with the towel

There is no way to evaluate a dozen people quickly. They looked like a dozen people. The first thing that registered was the source of the technological sounds. Three network-quality video cameras on tripods, four camcorders, a still camera and assorted video gear. Every outlet in the room was in use, and two people were setting up high-intensity lights.

Norman stared at the people, and the people stared at him.

An extremely fat lady with a single eyebrow recovered first. "You *were* expecting us?"

"No."

"Oh, dear. I am Alexandra Saint Phillip."

He had never heard of her. It was obvious that he had never heard of her. She could *not* believe he had never heard of her.

"Alexandra Saint *Phillip*," she explained. "And this is Rene[aa Ge[aarin-LaJoie." She indicated a short dapper man with a monocle. "And Harry Doyle, of course, and Gloria Delemar, and—"

Norman had never heard of any of these people, and every second he left Phyllis alone lowered the already-low probability of his ever seeing her again. "What do you want?"

"The story, of course," Ge[aarin-LaJoie said impatiently. "Today, if possible. There's a fire over on Spring Garden Road we could be covering."

Is that so? Norman thought. "What story? *Hold it,*" he added as a bearded man began to walk down the hall in search of another outlet. The man paused expectantly.

"You *are* the young man whose sister has disappeared?" Saint Phillip asked in astonishment.

In the two and a half weeks since Maddy had failed to come home, there had literally not been a waking hour in which she was absent from his thoughts—until ten o'clock the previous night. Being reminded was like being slapped in the face with a two-by-four.

"Oh," he said weakly. "Oh, my." Pain twisted his face.

"This kitchen's all over orange juice," complained a dwarf with a fake Oxford accent and a Nagra stereo deck.

"He's the one, Alex," Ge[aarin-LaJoie said. "And we couldn't all have gotten the appointment wrong—so MacLeod must have failed to reach him." He turned to Norman. "Obviously our names ring no bell, Monsieur. Perhaps it is more helpful to say that I am ATV News, and Alex is CBC. These other people are the other major Halifax media. We have come at the behest of your department chairman to publicize the disappearance of Madeleine Kent."

"Wait here," Norman said suddenly. "Please, wait right here. I *must go*, I'll be back in a moment. Make coffee if—" The phone rang. The new picture phone in the bedroom. "Oh, slithering Jesus."

"I'll get it," the technician in the hallway said helpfully.

"NO!" Norman screamed, stopping him in his tracks. Alexandra Saint Phillip's single eyebrow became a circumflex, and Gérin-LaJoie's ears seemed to grow points. "Please wait here."

Norman hurried to the bedroom, losing his towel just as he got the door safely shut behind him. Phyllis was bright red; whether with fury or shame was unclear. He saw at once that it was MacLeod on the phone, in the process of recording a message.

"—concerned after our last conversation," the department chairman was saying, "and then your estranged wife came to see me. She told me a bit more about your situation, and—well, I called in a few favors. I hope you're there, Norman, they'll be arriving any minute now. Lois said she'd drop by and warn you on her way to work, but I wasn't—"

With what was intended as a reassuring smile at Phyllis, Norman spun the phone carefully away from her, adjusted the camera to show him only from the collarbone up, and activated his end. "Yes doctor they're here right now I have to go thank you *very* much," he said, and cut the connection.

He expected MacLeod's image to look startled as it faded out of existence. But: *that* startled? Instinctively, Norman glanced over his shoulder. There was the bureau mirror, perfectly angled to catch Phyllis's reflection.

He literally fell down laughing.

The horror fed the laughter in the vicious feedback loop of hysteria. He made a last massive effort and beat at his head with his fists, barely succeeded in disrupting the loop. Even before he had his breath back he was hunching across the floor toward her like a brokenbacked snake.

He said no word as he untied her bonds, partly from an awareness that it is impossible to apologize to a captive audience, and partly because he could not conceive of anything to say. She stared fixedly at the ceiling until he was done, then rolled convulsively from the bed.

Of course her legs would not support her. No more would her hands break her fall; she landed heavily on her face.

"Are you all right, Mr. Kent?" the technician called from the hallway.

Sure thing, Jimmy, Norman thought for the millionth time in his life, just changing into Superman. "*Yes,*" he roared. "Right out."

"That's what he said the last time," Norman heard the dwarf complain.

He managed to heave Phyllis up onto the bed. She bit him as he did so, and he let her. When she let go, he began dressing at once. "Phyllis, listen. Stay right there. Get dressed when you can, leave when they're gone. There's no second choice. There's a gun in my desk, I'd appreciate it if you could blow my fucking brains out before you go."

She had the gag down now. "Do it yourself, mother-fucker."

He shook his head. "If I had the guts I'd never have waited this long." He finished sealing his trousers and decided slippers eliminated the need for socks. "Phyllis, I *have* to talk to these people, now. That's CBC and ATV and both papers and most of the FMs out there, they want to know about *Maddy*. I might—it could—she could be—" His jaw worked. "Phyl, for the love of God wait until they're gone. If you go out there now with rope marks on your wrists they're going to think I killed Maddy and ate her. *I've got to get her picture on the air.*"

Without waiting for an answer he left the room, returned at once, shut off the vibrator, left again.

He held up his hands as he entered the living room, partly to head off conversation and partly to save his eyesight—his living room was now hellbright. "Hold it, ladies and gentlemen. I'm still not here yet, it just looks like it. Is coffee made?"

"Let's just get a reading on you, darling," the dwarf said.

"No," he said firmly. "I'm a different color when I've had my coffee."

"See here—"

"No, you see here. Every piece of equipment in this room has its own battery pack, and you're all draining my wall outlets. I'll accept that, because I want the opportunity to shout with your voice. But I will damned well have coffee first."

One of them had figured out the machine; ten cups of coffee were ready. Norman took his cup back into the glare of video lights.

"Now," he said, sitting in his desk chair, "explain something to me. Dr. MacLeod has a good deal of influence in this town—but this big a turnout is ridiculous. I ignore news myself, but you people are obviously the first string. Since when does the first string cover a simple missing-persons story?"

"Since Samantha Ann Bent was found dead in a stand of alders outside of Kentville," Gérin-LaJoie said, coming back with his coffee.

Norman's ears began to buzz. "I don't believe I—" The dwarf thrust a light meter in his face and clipped a mini-mike to his shirt.

"She disappeared from Halifax two days after your sister. She was . . . it was a sex crime. A very ghastly sex crime."

Coffee slopped on his legs. He set the cup down on the desk with exquisite care and lit a cigarette. "Where was she last seen?" he asked mildly.

"Kempt Road," Saint Phillip supplied. "Near the all-night donut place, at about four o'clock in the morning."

"What did she look like?"

"Mr. Kent, I don't know if you want to—"

"Before, dammit!"

"Oh. She was blonde, dyed blonde, and rather short. About seventeen or eighteen, but she looked younger, I should say. Perhaps fifty kilos. A rather bad complexion, and a sort of teenybopper figure, with—"

"They searched the area where her body was found?"

"For others, you mean? Yes, I imagine so. Probably still at it now."

"Any leads on the killer?"

"Nothing yet," from Gérin-LaJoie. "Except that he is very sick."

Norman let out a great slow breath, and worked his shoulders briefly. "All right. I think it's okay. I don't think the same man got Maddy."

Gérin-LaJoie murmured something into his deck. "Why not, Monsieur Kent?"

"Well, I'm not positive—but it doesn't feel right. My understanding is that sex killers pick a type and stick with it. Maddy was—is—thirty-four years old, brown hair exactly the same shade as mine, about three inches taller than I am, and a good sixty-five kilos. Her figure was excellent and her skin superb. When I last saw her she was not dressed remotely like the way seventeen-year-olds dress these days. She dressed sensibly, tastefully. Her clothes were European, with those loose lines, and that air of durability we stopped respecting over here a long time ago." He ran down awkwardly.

"Sex criminals don't always stay with a type," Gérin-LaJoie said. "Some like variety."

"The circumstances don't match. This Bent girl was way over at the North End at 4:00 A.M. Maddy was last seen downtown, on Argyle Street, planning to walk down one block to Barrington and catch a bus, at a little after midnight. The whole MO is different." He puffed on his cigarette and frowned. "Perhaps I shouldn't be telling you all this. If a tie-in gives it more news value—"

"Mr. Kent," Saint Phillip said, "when two women disappear off the streets of Halifax within forty-eight hours, it is news even if one is built like a hippo and the other a giraffe. It is not inconceivable that two killers independently—" She broke off. "I'm sorry, I—"

"No, you're right." Norman's face was stony. "None of this makes things look any brighter for Maddy. But at least I don't think it was your butcher-crazy that got her."

"Monsieur Kent," Gérin-LaJoie said, "forgive me please, I have not had a chance to familiarize myself with your case. Is there no chance that your sister could have . . . taken it into her head to—"

"I don't think so." Norman frowned. "Look, in your business you must hear a lot of people tell you, 'but she had no reason to.' Maddy not only had no reason to, she had reason *not* to. It's too long a story to explain, but—will you just accept it that Sergeant Amesby down at Missing Persons believes she was abducted? He's a rather skeptical man."

"Hell yes," the dwarf agreed. "If *Amesby* says she was snatched—"

"Hadn't she been in Switzerland for ten years?" asked Saint Phillip, who had plainly done her homework. "Couldn't she have—"

"Leaving everything she owned? It's been almost three weeks, and Interpol comes up empty," Norman said.

The bedroom door opened, and Phyllis entered the living room. She wore her own jeans and one of his shirts, with the sleeves buttoned. "Goodbye, Norman," she said icily, and exited. There was a brief pause.

"Look, are you ready to tape?" Norman asked.

"Yes."

He ran his hands through his hair. "Okay." He looked at the

largest of the videocameras, told himself it was an old and understanding friend who happened to have one round eye. "My deepest
sympathies go to the family of Samantha Ann Bent. I think I know
something of what they are feeling now. But I don't believe that the
beast who took their girl got my sister Madeleine. Their physical
types and the manner of their disappearances are too dissimilar. I'm
all the family Maddy has left and I don't know *what* has happened to
her." He took a folder from his top desk drawer, selected a large color
glossy. He held it up to the cameras, which all trucked in. "This is my
sister, Madeleine Kent. She is thirty-four. She was last seen on June
twelfth near Barrington and Argyle, wearing a tan calf-length skirt,
matching jacket and pale yellow blouse, carrying a yellow purse. She
had just returned from ten years in Switzerland, and she tended to
speak as though English were a learned language, although she was
losing the tendency. If you have any information which could help us
locate her, I beg you to contact Sergeant Amesby of the Halifax
police, or the RCMP. Complete anonymity can be guaranteed.

"My sister has been gone for eighteen days. I am worried sick. If
you know anything at all, if you saw anything unusual near Argyle or
Barrington streets on Friday, June twelfth, *please* . . . call Missing
Persons. I—" His voice broke. "I need your help. Thank you." He
sucked hard on his cigarette. "Okay?"

"In the can." "Got it." "Good take." At once all the video people
and half the others lit cigarettes.

"All right." He drained the coffee, set it on the desk, and took a
folio from the same drawer. Most of the journalists came closer,
gathered round the desk. "You newspaper people, here is a dossier
I've compiled on Madeleine. I gave a copy to Sergeant Amesby, but
he won't have let you see it. It contains everything I know or was able
to find out about Maddy, everything known about her last evening.
Statements from people who were at the party. A copy of the posters
I distributed to all the cab companies. Still shots of Maddy, ten years
out of date. She had a home videocassette in her belongings that
seems fairly recent. I've had some stills made up from that. You can
see that she hasn't changed a great deal in ten years."

"More worldly-wise," Saint Phillips said. "A faint flavor of cynical
amusement. Of self-assurance. She was a very beautiful woman, Mr.
Kent."

Norman clenched his teeth. "And still is, so far as I know."

"Oh, my God, I'm sorry. Of *course* she—"

"As for you print and radio people, perhaps it would save us all a good deal of time if I simply ran off several copies of this dossier for you to take with you. Then if you have any questions you can phone me; I have full-range audio."

"Can we borrow these photos, Mr. Kent?" one of the print journalists asked.

"I'll fax them to you, if you'll all be so kind as to give me your access." He started a notepad circulating. "If there are no more questions, I'll start these through the printer. Please feel free to start a fresh pot of coffee, and there are munchables in the first cabinet on the left."

He went down the hall to the library and started printing out copies. As he was collating the second set, he became aware that he was not alone.

"Mr. Kent?" Alexandra Saint Phillip said.

He did not turn.

"Mr. Kent, it is my business to listen to sad stories all day long. In my darker hours I think of myself as a sob-sucker. I know how to give sincere condolences to people I don't give a damn about. I . . . I just . . . I'm sorry, Mr. Kent. I'm sorry for your sister, who looks like she is a hell of a woman. But most of all I'm sorry for you. Whatever happened to her, at least she knows it."

He continued collating the printouts as they collected, perhaps a little more clumsily.

"I've been a journalist a long time, Mr. Kent. You start to get a feeling. I can't be sure, of course, but I don't think you are ever going to know any more than you do now. I don't think she'll ever be found."

Norman stopped shuffling paper. His shoulders knotted. "I don't think so either."

"You are either going to learn how to live with that, or you aren't. I read you as the kind of man who has what it takes to survive something like this. But—forgive me, aren't you in the midst of a divorce right now?"

"That was my ex who greeted you at the door."

"Yes. Look, I have no wish to pry. I'm not trying to get a juicier story, this is off the record. But I think if you own a gun you should throw it away. If you own a razor, buy an electric one instead. Perhaps I talk too much. I—if there's anything at all I can do—well, here."

He turned to see her offering a card. Past her he saw the dwarf looking through the open bedroom door. "Get the hell out of there," he barked.

"Certainly, old man. Thought it was the loo."

"Try the one I came out of wearing a towel," Norman suggested bitterly.

"Sorry."

Norman turned back to Saint Phillip. "Madam," he said slowly, "I don't know if I'm the kind of man who can take a lifetime of this. But I value your opinion. And your concern. Thank you very much."

She smiled, a very sad smile. "Take the card. It's the one with office *and* home numbers. I don't give it out often. My husband's name is Willoughby. Go on with your collating."

After they all left he noticed that the orange juice had been mopped from the kitchen floor, and knew that she had done it.

That evening he took another walk out onto the MacDonald Bridge. He watched the clouds slide past the moon for several hours, and once he sang a song, and at eleven-thirty he threw his gun over the side into the harbor.

❧4❧

2011

I WOKE the next morning with less headache than I deserved. The nose hurt worse. I was alone in the bedroom. I heard distant kitchen sounds, smelled something burnt. I found I was irritated. I had not cleared Karen for solo flight yet. That made me laugh sourly at myself, and any kind of laugh will do to get a morning started.

I found her sitting on a pillow in the dining area adjacent to the kitchen. She did not acknowledge my arrival. She was staring expressionlessly at what she had intended to be an omelet. It was the toast that had burned, and these days it's hard to burn toast.

Breakfast with a stranger is always awkward. You come upon each other before you have had time to buckle on your armor. And so the question becomes, how urgent is the need? Even if you made love the night before it doesn't necessarily help: you can get to know someone better than you wanted to over first breakfast. Neither of us was capable of making love, but I knew Karen fairly well, in terms of the pattern of her history. But the Karen I knew had died, had committed suicide. The new Karen I had created by aborting her suicide I did not know at all.

I found that I wanted to know her. As a man who has accidentally caused an avalanche cannot prevent himself from watching to learn the full extent of the damage, I needed to know, now that it was too late, what I had done by my meddling. I wanted to like her. That would make me a hero.

I took the omelet and toast from in front of her. She started indignantly, a good sign. I dumped the stuff down the oubliette and took new ingredients from the fridge. On a hunch I went back and

60

took a sip of her coffee. I pitched that too and got the beans from the freezer.

I mixed and sliced and grated, assembled and seasoned the resultants, and arrayed them in the cooker. I studied the controls. The combination she had programmed was straight out of the owner's manual, with one plain error. I had figured out the quirks of this particular model—extensive ones—the first day I had been in the apartment. She was a rotten cook. I set it correctly and initiated.

"I think I'm going to move out of this dump," she said.

I nodded. I did not ask where she would go. I prepared cups to receive coffee. Her sugar had been stored in a cabinet, so she didn't take any. Expensive cream was on her shopping list, so she used it.

"Hey, that smells *good.*"

I dealt out onion-and-cheddar omelets, bacon, crisped English muffins. I put two straws in a quart of orange juice and poured Javanese coffee. The shopping-list program had been her own. She was in the habit of ruining some very expensive food. Well, she earned her money. She started to dig in, pulled up short. "You think I'm ready for a meal this size?"

I had reoriented her stomach with tea, soup, and other soft foods. "If it looks good to you, you should certainly have at least a little of everything."

She fell to at once, but ate with some caution. She did not talk while she ate, which suited me. We paid respectful attention to the food. She made occasional small sounds of enjoyment. I found this remarkable. It did not seem that any of the jelly of her hypothalamus had been boiled away. Her pleasure center was functional. Remarkable.

While the food occupied her attention, I studied her. Her hair had been washed, dried, and brushed. She looked squeaky clean. She wore a glossy fluff-collar robe that covered her to the chin. She wore no makeup, no jewelry. Her hands were reasonably steady, her color okay.

After a while she caught me studying her. Without hesitation she began to study me right back. For a few seconds it got like two kids trying to outstare each other, but there is a limit to the amount of time two chewing people can do that and keep a straight face. We shared a small explosion of laughter, then smiled at each other for a few seconds more and went back to our food.

I had given her a portion a third the size of my own. Though she chewed much more slowly, she finished first. At once she reached for a nearby package of Peter Jackson. I did not react, kept eating. She looked down, saw her fingers taking a cigarette from the pack, and put it back. Though I still gave no sign of noticing, I chalked up a point for her.

When I was done, she took the cigarette back out and touched it alight on the side of the pack. "Gasper?" she asked, offering me the pack.

"Don't use it, thanks."

"Grass in the freezer."

"That either."

She was surprised. "You don't get high?"

" 'Reality is for those who don't have the strength of character to handle drugs,' " I quoted. "That's me."

She pursed her lips, nodded. "Uh-huh." She took a deep drag. "You're a good cook, Joe. Thanks. Very much."

"Yeah."

She held her cigarettes down between middle and ring fingers. It seems like one of those meaningless affectations, until you notice that with each puff, half of the face is hidden. The inverse is to hold the cigarette like a home-rolled joint between thumb and forefinger tips, minimizing facial coverage. Now that I saw her with her hair brushed, on a head held upright, I saw that the hair too was styled for maximum concealment, in long bangs and forward-sweeping wings. If she'd been a man she'd have worn a full beard.

"Joe what? I forget."

Embarrassing. So did I. "Nixon," I tried at random.

"Temple something. Templar . . . Templeton."

"Well, I knew it was a rat's name," I said. She didn't laugh, of course. She had been a small child when the pack brought Nixon down, and nobody reads *Charlotte's Web* anymore these days. But she could tell that I thought I'd said something witty, so she smiled. She had manners.

"You don't have to tell me the real one," she lied. "It doesn't matter."

Do you ever learn things from your mouth? I have a hundred glib evasions and outright lies on file for the question "What is your name?" To my astonishment I heard myself tell her the truth.

"There is no real one."

"Eh?"

"I don't exist."

She could tell I had stopped kidding, even if she still didn't understand. "You lost me. I'm dumb in the morning."

Nothing to do for it now. "I'm not on file. I'm not on tape. The government and I don't recognize each other. I'm a non-person. I have no Social Security number."

"No shit?" Though she had hidden it well, she had been just a trifle annoyed, thinking I was withholding my real name out of mistrust. Now she was realizing how much I did trust her. So was I. "God, that's fantastic. How did you do it?" She caught herself. "I'm sorry. That's not a proper question."

I was beginning to like her. "It's okay, Karen. I have told two people what I just told you. Both of them asked me how I pulled it off, I told them both the truth, and neither one believed me. Not at first, or ever. So I don't mind telling you."

"Okay. How'd you do it?"

"I haven't the faintest idea."

She thought about it. "Yeah. Yeah, that's kind of hard to get a handle on, all right." She puffed on her cigarette. "I take it there's about a two-hour rap that explains it."

"Yeah. It gets less probable with each sentence."

She nodded. "And you don't especially feel like going into it right now?"

Definitely beginning to like her. "Another time. Why'd you stop dealing coke?"

Her eyebrows rose a fraction of an inch. "Tossed the place, eh? I liked it too much. The toot and the loot. Contentment is not in my pattern, if you dig. I'm a Pisces. When the situation's been comfortable too long, I find some way to kick it apart. There are so many. In this case I got involved with my supplier, and when the relationship went sour, so did the career. Of course I couldn't have predicted this without going to the trouble of thinking about it for a second. I believe you, by the way."

"I know."

There went her no-hitter. I hate people who do that, look you in the eye and tell you matter-of-factly how screwed up they are. I have this conviction that screwed-up people are *supposed* to be embarrassed about it. It's as common a vice as smoking these days, and at least as much nuisance to those around you. It lowers the general morale.

On the other hand, I make a habit of bitterly criticizing every aspect of reality *except* myself—which is also bad for general morale.

"After a while I found myself owing considerable money to some very sandy people," she said. "Well, I'd always told myself I could hook if times got bad. I thought it out and made my move, and it didn't work out very well. I mean, I got paid all three times, but I could tell they weren't real happy. They weren't repeat business, they weren't word-of-mouth. A girl could starve that way.

"The fourth one set me straight. We talked afterwards, and he was nice. I told him just a little about me, just that my first time was a rape. 'That's it,' he says. 'You're not a bad little actress, but Señorita, no *way* will you ever convince anyone that you like it.' About a day and a half later it hit me that that wasn't a drawback, it was an advantage, and I changed my PR and tripled my price. I paid off my people in a week. So that's"—she grinned bitterly—"that's what a bimbo like me is doing in a class joint like this." She took a last puff, pinched the filter harder than necessary, and tossed the butt, before it had quite finished going out, in the general direction of the oubliette.

I sat perfectly still. I had scrubbed that floor on my hands and knees—but not by invitation. You don't *own* the place, I reminded myself, you're just robbing it.

But if I had not been irritated (I'm embarrassed to admit), if the effort of not wrinkling up my nose hadn't made it throb, I might have been humane enough to save the obvious next question for another day or two.

"What will you do now?"

She visibly flinched, and dropped her gaze. Of course I felt like a jerk at once. Of course that irritated me more. She rose suddenly from the table. I was between her and one exit, so she took the other. Into the living room.

When she stiffened, I opened my mouth, slapped myself in the forehead, and raced after her. I was days too late. There in the same

position between the lamp and the plastic table, from which I had
never thought to move it, was the God damned armchair. Framed
and lit like a tableau at Madame Tussaud's, lacking only a waxy
body . . .

A moist noise in her throat decided not to be a word after all. She
looked around, hesitated. She was *not* going to sit those bedsores on
the chair that had put them there. But if she sat on the couch she had
to *look* at the chair. I stepped past her, turned the chair so that it
faced away from the window, and tilted it back as far as it would go,
bringing up the footrest. With some throw pillows from the couch,
the result was a cushioned flat surface about thirty degrees from hor-
izontal, the high end facing the window.

"Come here," I said in what I hoped was a kindly but firm tone.
She did not move. "I'll clear the window. Lie on your belly and watch
the sun try to brighten the Hudson Sewer." She still didn't move.
"What do you do when you fall off a horse, Karen?"

She nodded, crossed the room, and stretched out without further
hesitation. I dialed the window transparent and fetched her cigarettes. She lit one gratefully. "Joe?"

"Yah."

"Would you rub some more of that anesthetic gunk on my ass?
And could I have some rum?"

"Just what your system needs. How about some aspirin? If I can
find any in that haystack."

She sighed. "Okay."

I fetched cream, aspirin, and water from the bathroom and pulled
a footstool near her chair. She lay with her face toward me while I
applied the cream, and though she sucked air a few times she didn't
cry out. One excellent test of trust is the ability to receive a butt-mas-
sage unselfconsciously, and she paid me that compliment. As I
worked up to the sores on her back I looked around the room. I had
given her story CDs a B-minus. A boxed set of historical romances
had cost her points. On the other hand, she kept a handful of real
books, good ones. Maybe the set was a gift. She had a fairly good
multipurpose music collection, deficient in classical but otherwise
sound; there were items I had already stolen. Her video library was
strictly tape-of-the-month club, but with the incongruous addition
of some classic early Emsh. An overall rating was hard to decide. A

C-plus would have been strictly fair, but a B-minus could have been justified to the . . .

Hiatus.

I was sitting on the couch with half a drink in my hand, and she was looking out the window, smoking a cigarette I didn't remember her lighting. The sun was high over the river now. It looked hot out there. I saw a gull make a dead-stick landing on a distant roof and lay where it hit. What boils up off the Hudson at mid-day would take pages just to catalog. How come pigeons have adapted to pollution and gulls haven't?

After a while she pinched out a cigarette, dropped it on the rug. She got up and put the robe back on. She walked over to the window and stood staring out over lower buildings, watching faraway boats trying to slice the water. "One thing for sure, I've gotta get out of this pit. I always wanted to live in a place like this. My old man's life savings couldn't have bought a month in a place like this. The week before last I found myself sitting in front of the video with the stereo playing and a story on the reader on my lap. I looked around and on the table next to me was a burning cigarette, a burning joint of Supremo, a couple lines of coke, and a drink with the ice all melted. Four kinds of munchies. It came to me that I was bored. I couldn't think of one thing on earth to do that I would enjoy." She turned around, leaned back against the window, and surveyed the room. "It's kind of like that now. I need to change the channel. This just isn't the kind of place where you figure out what to do with the rest of your life."

She was as close as she could come to asking. I was reluctant. "What about, uh, Jo Ann?"

"She lives with two other girls, it's like Times Square."

So think about it. Crazy little hooker with a socket in her scalp, miserable cook, slob, sexual cripple, two kinds of smoker.

Tough as a Harlem rat, in both mind and body. With pretty good manners. She had respected my privacy considerably more than I had respected hers. And she knew what you do when you fall off a horse. In many ways she was the ideal roommate for someone like me, at least for a while. Maybe my own life had gotten a little boring.

"You can crash at my place," I said. "I'll put up with tobacco, but no grass. I do all the cooking, you do all the dishes, I do all the rest of the housework. You can bring five percent of the contents of that medicine cabinet."

Relief was plain on her face. "I'm grateful, Joe. Really grateful. You're sure it's okay," she added, not quite making it a question. I answered it anyway.

"Sure."

"I won't be putting you out any?"

"Karen, why don't you just figure out what questions you want to ask me and ask me? I don't promise to answer any, but we'll save time that way."

She smiled. "Fair enough. You live alone?"

"Yeah."

"Involved with anybody?"

"No."

"Born New Yorker?"

"I don't think so."

She blinked, but let it pass. "Got any family?"

"I don't know."

"You don't *know?*"

"Next question."

"How come you burgle?"

"It's the only job my background has prepared me for. I'm trying to furnish a flat."

"How'd your nose get all broke up like that?"

"I don't know how I got the first break. You broke it the second time, when I unplugged you."

"Jesus wept and died. I'm *sorry,* Joe, I—how can you not know how you broke your nose?"

"I wish to God I knew."

"Jesus."

That ended the Twenty Questions for a while. She paced and thought about what I had said, absently lighting another smoke. I could see her working it out. Most of what I had told her made no sense. Lord, who knows better than I? But I had not been smiling when I had said it, so she believed me implicitly. Therefore there had to be a startling but logical explanation, and I must have reasons of my own for not wanting to go into it.

I wished that were so.

It was a little annoying, how implicitly she trusted me. Perhaps it is vaguely unflattering to be considered harmless. Or a little *too* flattering: more responsibility than I liked.

I was just as annoyed at how implicitly *I* seemed to trust *her*. I depend on my instincts—I have to in my position—but sometime soon I was going to have to sit down with them and ask them exactly why they had had me offer my two most dangerous secrets to her. I must stand to gain something from the ultimate risk—but what?

"Look," she said, still pacing, "maybe there's one thing more we should—" She saw my face and stopped. "No," she said thoughtfully. "No, I guess I don't have to discuss that with you. Okay, look. Can you wait another day or two? I know I promised to help you with these speakers, but honest to God I don't think I could make it to the corner right now. If I don't lay down soon, I'll—"

"Go to bed, Karen. I'll get the dishes. Maybe the day after tomorrow, maybe the day after that. My time is my own." Something made that last sentence taste bitter in my mouth.

"Thanks, Joe. Thanks a lot."

"Take two more aspirin."

After she left I got up from the couch and selected one of her CDs. I intended to steal it, or at least dub it onto my home system, but my subconscious felt like hearing it now: Waits's classic *Blue Valentine*. I adjusted the headphones and sat back.

His courageous version of "Somewhere" made me smile sadly as always. For all us losers and thieves and junkies and nighthawks there is a place, somewhere. But: *my* place? The next track also seemed apropos, "Christmas Card from a Hooker in Minneapolis," but only in that Karen could have written such a letter. It did not explain why I had answered as I had. I drifted through the next track, and then my ears woke me up again in the middle of the hypnotic blues "$29," and I had it. Waits's whiskey-and-Old-Gold rasp filled my head.

When the streets get hungry baby
You can almost hear 'em growl
Someone's settin' a place for you
When the dogs begin to howl
When the streets are dead
They creep up and take whatever's left on the bone

Suckers always make mistakes
Far away from home
Chicken in the pot
Whoever gets there first
Gonna get himself $29 and an alligator purse . . .

I had already taken all her cash myself, and planned to take other items. Still, there were other thieves on the street who would consider me shockingly wasteful. If I left her here to work out her destiny, I was morally certain that she would drift back to hooking within a week or two. The money is addictive. But she had been working as an independent for a surprisingly long time. Such luck could not last; luck had never lasted for Karen. One day soon she would come to the attention of an entrepreneur. When his training period was over, even a woman as tough and strong as she would be docile, obedient, and tremblingly eager to please. In this largest city in the land of the free, it happens every day.

I could not leave her to the slavers. I hated and feared slavery too much myself.

But it was more than that.

I had meddled. I had forcibly prevented her from ending her life when and as she wished. Stated that way, my action was morally repugnant to me; as a kid I had canvassed and petitioned vigorously for Right to Death, and cheered when it became law of the land. I had no defense now, no excuse: I had acted out of "instinctive" revulsion, which is never an excuse for overriding morality. She had been fleeing from a life that was misery occasionally leavened with horror. If I simply returned her to that life and washed my hands, I was a monster.

I hoped it would not take her too long to find some new kind of direction, some kind of plan or purpose. Because I was stuck with her until she did.

I found myself cursing her for having been so inconsiderate as to pick a slow, pleasant death, and laughed out loud at myself. And went to do the breakfast dishes.

It was actually three days before I clouted a delivery van over on Broadway, and drove us and the plunder I had selected to my place. What I didn't want she left behind. The rent would keep paying itself,

the lights would go on and off in random patterns simulating inhab-
itance, the rugs would clean themselves once a week, from now until
her lease ran out in another two years or her credit balance dropped
too low. That was the rent she paid to stay at my place: the maintenance of a legal address elsewhere on all the proper databases.

I had told her almost nothing about the place. So few people ever
see it that it's fun to savor the reactions.

She was neither impressed nor dismayed when we pulled up
behind the warehouse. It was a moonless night and there were no
lights, but a warehouse does not look impressive even in the daytime.
The daytime appearance of mine is, in fact, particularly weatherbeaten
and long-abandoned, even for the neighborhood.

It was probably just about what she had expected, and I would
guess she had lived in worse circumstances before. "Do we unload
now?" was all she said.

"Yeah."

We took the swag in the back way and by candlelight we stacked
it, for the moment, where burglar's plunder should be stored, in a
corner where casual random search of the warehouse would probably
not find it.

An office module formed a block in the center of the warehouse. I
led her toward it through the black maze by memory, having left the
candles where they would be useful. Most people being led through
total darkness are a pain in the ass, but she knew how to move in the
dark. As we rounded a stack of packing crates something subliminal
warned me. I tightened my grip on her hand and flung her bodily
into an aisle between two rows of boxes. That changed the position
of my head, so the sap came down on the point of my extended
shoulder. My right arm died. There is no good way to get a gun from
under your left armpit with your left hand. For me to have tried it
would have presented my one remaining elbow to that sap. I back-
pedaled, spun, and bugged out.

He followed. Not many could have followed me through my own
turf in the dark, but he was one of the few. I tried angling toward the
crowbar pile, but he guessed it and moved to cut me off. He pressed
me too closely to give me a chance to spill the gun and pick it up. I
took us to a cleared space large enough to allow room to work and
spun at bay, feeling pessimistic. He pulled up just out of reach and

puffed and chuckled. I kicked one shoe up into the air, sent the other in another direction, hoping to misdirect him. He flinched as the first one hit, but by the second he had figured it out. He chuckled some more.

"I couldn't get in your place . . . this time either, Sammy," he puffed. "But you'll take me in . . . won't you? You'll beg for the chance."

His sap arm would be behind him; no matter where or how I hit him, he'd have a terrific shot at my head. I should have saved one shoe to flip into his face. Dumb.

"Hey, thanks for throwing in the fem, Sam. She'll never find her way outta here in the dark. You saved me another twenty bucks."

I had to make my move soon, he was getting his breath back. Go for the gun? Try to yank my belt free left-handed? Charge and hope for a break? They all sucked.

"Hey, no hard feelings, huh?"

A shinbone was the least risk; I got ready to try a kick, rehearsing what I would do after he broke my leg. "No hard feelings, Wishbone."

If it is possible to grunt above high C, that is what he did then. He came at me in a shambling walk, hissing, and when he cannoned into me he embraced me. I was too startled to react. The hiss ended in the word "Shit," and then he slid slowly down me.

God damn it, was my whole house full of armed hostiles? I stepped out of his arms, bent and searched hastily for the sap without success.

"Twenty bucks, huh?" Karen said. "Mother fucker."

I got slowly to my feet. "What the hell did you do to him?"

"Put a fist through his goddam kidney. Son of a bitch. Help me find his crotch, I want to kick it."

"Take it easy. Your honor is satisfied."

"But—"

"He sapped me. It's *my* turn."

"Oh. Are you okay?"

"I'll be okay for another couple of minutes, until this arm comes back to life. Then I will be very disconsolate for a long time."

"How can I help?"

"Help me drag him over here."

We arranged him on a low flatbed handtruck. He was making mewing sounds. He wanted to scream, but he would give up the idea long before he had the breath. I was glad she had hit me only a glancing blow that first day; full strength and she might have killed me, and wouldn't that have made interesting copy for the *Daily News*?

"Who the hell is he?"

"Wishbone Jones. Small-time mugger and a little of this and that. Skinny as a stork and stronger than I am. Lives down by the wharf. Not bright, but a good fighter. We've tangled." By now I had my gun out. I gave it to her and sat down on the handtruck beside him. My arm and shoulder were just beginning to catch fire, but that was mitigated to some extent by the exhilaration of survival. "Hello, Wishbone."

"H—hi, Sam." He was getting back under control.

"Bad day at the track, Wishbone?"

"Nuh . . . no."

"Then it's got to be basketball or poker."

"Neither one. My ex from Columbus caught up with me."

"Yep. That's karma for you. Well, I believe we discussed this the last time?"

He grimaced. "Aw, *shit,* Sam. If I go to the hospital they give me the cure."

"We *did* discuss it."

He shook his head. "Ah, shit. Yeah." He gave me his arm.

"No hard feelings." He closed his eyes and I broke the arm across the edge of the handtruck as quickly and cleanly as I could. He screamed and fainted.

Karen had not uttered a sound when I had suddenly flung her into the darkness, but she yelped now.

I slumped, exhausted and unutterably depressed. I wanted to vomit, and I wanted to scream from the pain in my shoulder, and I wanted to cry. I stood up. "Let's go inside."

It took one metal key and a five-number combination to get us into the office module. The windows are not boarded, they're plated. The door is too heavy to batter and the roof is reinforced. Still, it is no more secure than the average New York apartment. A cleverer cracksman than Wishbone could have opened it in fifteen minutes with the right tools. There is no such thing as an unbeatable lock, just incompetent craftsmen.

"What about him?" she asked as we stepped in.

"Wishbone will find his way home. To the hospital if he's smart. But Wishbone's not smart. Damn his eyes." I sealed the door and turned on the light.

She was looking at me expressionlessly. She came suddenly close, took my face in her hands, and studied it. Nearly at once she nodded. "You hated it."

"God damn you, did you think I enjoyed it?" I yelled, flinging her hands away.

She shook her head. "No. Not for a second." She backed away one step. "But for just a minute there I was scared to death that you didn't give a damn, one way or the other."

I dropped my eyes. "Fair enough," I turned around and walked a few steps. "Simulating total ruthlessness is, I guess, the hardest thing I've ever had to do in my life. Sometimes it's necessary."

"Yeah, I know."

I whirled, ready to flare up at any sign of pity or sympathy, but there was neither. Only a total understanding of, and agreement with, what I had said.

"Come on," I said. "I'll show you around." My shoulder ached like hell, but as I said, I wanted to see her reaction.

The room we were in had not been substantially altered since the last time it was used as an office, perhaps fifteen or twenty years ago. The alterations I had made had not involved cleaning. There wasn't much to see that was worth looking at, unless she had a thing for busts of President Kennedy the Second. I led her into the back, throwing on lights as we went.

It was obvious that a bachelor burglar of no great fastidiousness lived here. Three inner offices were converted to living space, furnished with things too rickety, threadbare, or ugly to fence. Empties lay here and there, and all the wastebaskets were overflowing. The "kitchen" could produce anything from peanut butter on moldy white bread to a tolerable mulligan, and not much in between, if you didn't count the beer. The office with the toilet had perforce become the master bedroom. A truly astonishing calendar hung on the wall. The mattress lay on the floor, and the sheets had that lived-in look. A rancid glass of orange juice sat beside the bed, next to a sound-only phone and a disorderly pile of recent newspapers all opened to the society page.

She really did have manners. She kept a poker face, made no comment at anything she saw, just looked around at each room and nodded. Perhaps she had lived in worse. Finally my shoulder hurt too much. I decided I had milked it for all it was worth and took her back to the outer office.

She lit a Peter Jackson. "By the way, how many names have you got, Sam?"

"How many are there? Sit over on that desk, 'Sharon.' "

She complied.

"Now lift your feet off the floor, completely, and keep them there."

I waited until she had done so. Initiating dislock sequence while there is additional human-size mass anywhere in the room *except* on the four places where those desk legs meet the floor will cause the room to be blown out of the warehouse. When she was seated correctly I turned to the desk nearest me. I opened the middle drawer. Then I crossed the room and flipped the switch for the ventilation fan that no longer works. On, off, on. I went back to the desk and closed the drawer. What looked just like a battered old Royal manual typewriter sat on a rubber pad on the desk's typing shelf; I typed some words. Karen watched all this without expression, but I could tell that she was wondering if I had sustained any head injuries in the scuffle with Wishbone.

I walked over in front of the bust of Kennedy and smiled at it. Its right eye winked at me. A large section of floor hinged back and up like a snake sitting up, soundlessly. Carpeted stairs led down into a place of soft lights.

"Now I'll show you where I really live."

"You bastard," she said.

I bowed and gestured: after you.

"You bastard," she said again softly. "*This* you *did* enjoy."

I lost control and grinned hugely. "Bet your ass." I gestured again. "Come on. You can get down off there now. Or do you *want* to spend the night up here?"

She came off the desk with a you'll-get-yours grin, tugged her skirt around, and whacked dust from it. "The secret temple of Karnak. Do I have to take my shoes off?"

"Not even your dress." Perhaps an indelicate joke, but I had found that she *liked* being kidded about her occupation.

She grimaced. "That's another buck for ironing, chump." She came to the stairs and went down. I followed. I didn't crash into her on the bottom step because I was expecting her to stop dead. I waited while she stared, and when she finally stepped into the living room I moved past her.

She was still staring around her, with an astonishment that refused to fade. No matter where she looked, she could find nothing unremarkable. I drank her astonishment thirstily.

Perhaps I am excessively houseproud. But I have some reason to be. The location is a large part of its value, of course—but as a conventional apartment it was worth two and a half of hers, and she had not been living cheaply by any means. I seldom indulge my weakness; Karen was the fifth person to come down those stairs with me. Almost all of the others had lived with me *upstairs* for at least a week before I let them into my real house.

She would not say a word.

"This is the living room," I said, and she jumped. "If you'll step this way . . . ?" Oh, I was disgusting.

She remained resolutely silent during the rest of the tour, but it cost her. It took a good ten minutes; my house has a little more than twice the cubic of the office complex that sits on it.

As we walked I flipped switches and brought the house back up to active status, started the coffee program, and turned up the fans to accommodate her inevitable cigarettes.

The message light on the phone panel was not lit. Maybe one day I will come home and find it lit. When that happens I will drop to the floor and pray that the end is quick.

At last my shoulder made me cut it short. I led us back to the living room and dropped into the nearest Lounger, drawing its attention to my shoulder. "Excuse me," I said. "This won't wait any longer."

She nodded. The chair began doing indescribable things to my shoulder girdle, and I closed my eyes. When I could open them again, she was standing on the same spot in the same stance, looking at me with the same lack of expression. My chair cut back to subliminal purring. I tried the shoulder and winced, but decided against repeating the massage cycle.

"Joe," she said finally, "you are a *good* burglar."

"I'm a very good burglar."

"If that grin gets any bigger, you're gonna split your face clear back to your ears. Just before that happens, would it be all right if I were to ask some of the obvious questions?"

"I'll tell you anything I can."

"All right." She took out cigarettes and lit up. Then she put her fists on her hips. *"What the fuck is this place?"*

"Are you familiar with the expression, 'to go to the mattresses'?"

"Sure. Are you trying to tell me that all *this*"—she swept her hand around the room—"is some kind of gangster's command post?"

"No. But I am telling you that big multinationals sometimes have to go to the mattresses too."

Her eyes widened. "But—that's silly. Multinationals don't have shooting w—well, yes they do, but not in *New York.*"

"Not on page one, no. They tend to be much neater, much subtler."

She thought it through. "So it's a corporate command bunker. What corporation?"

"I don't know."

"It looks like it would make a great fortress. How come the original owners aren't here?"

"My guess is undeclared war, a sneak attack. The secret of this place would naturally be known only by a few—presumably 'one grenade got them all.' I estimate that it has been abandoned for almost fifteen years, since about '97. I found it about ten years back, and nobody's come around since, that I know of. Could happen any time, of course."

"So how the hell could you happen to 'stumble across' that song-and-dance routine you did upstairs to open the door?"

"I can't imagine."

She frowned. "Conversation with you certainly has a lot of punctuation. Forget I asked." She looked around again. "Who pays the utilities? Since you don't exist, I mean."

"Nobody."

"What do I look like, an idiot? That's a full-service phone over there, and two powered chairs, and your tape console computer alone must draw . . . not to mention that computer in the bedroom, and lights and climate and—don't tell me. There's an inconspicuous solar collector on top of the abandoned warehouse, no bigger than Washington Square."

I smiled. "I misspoke myself. I should have said 'everybody.' I get my power and phone from the same place you do—I just don't pay for it."

"But they've got hunter programs monitoring for unmetered drain—"

"Programs written and administered by corruptible, fallible human beings. Whoever built this place built it well. I never get a bill."

"I'll be damned." She stared at the phone. "But how can anybody call *you?* You can't have a number, the switching syst—"

"Nobody can call me. It's the perfect phone."

Her grin was sudden. "I'll be go to hell. So it is." She took off her rucksack and checked to make sure she had broken or crushed nothing when she fell. "Where should I stash my stuff?"

"I'll do it. Sit down."

I gestured toward the other Lounger. She put down the sack and went to it, stroked the headrest reverently. "For *years* I've wanted one of these. Never could afford it." She shook her head. "I guess crime pays."

"No, but the perks are terrific. Go on, try it."

She sat, made a small sound as she realized that it did not hurt her sores, then made another as the chair adjusted to her skeletal shape and body temperature. I set it for gentle massage and took her bag to the spare bedroom. When I got back I had her chair mix a Preacher's Downfall for me and a rum-and-rum for her. (I had satisfied myself by then that wireheading had cured her of compulsive overboozing. A marvelous therapeutic tool, save that its side effects included death.)

She did not see me at once; her eyes were rolled back into her head. But after a while her ears told her that ice cubes were clinking nearby, and she came slowly back to the external world. "Joe," she said, smiling happily, "you're a *good* burglar."

It was nice to see her sitting back in a chair, with a smile that I *liked* on her face.

We drank and talked for an hour or so. Then on impulse I put on some Brindle to see if she knew the difference between music you talk over and music you don't. Sure enough, three bars in she shut up and smiled and sat back to listen. When the CD was through she was ready to admire my bathroom, and then I showed her her bedroom. By then she was too tired to admire anything. I started to head for my own room, but she caught my arm.

"Joe . . ." She looked me in the eye. "Would you sleep with me tonight?"

I studied her face until I was sure the question was meant literally. "Sure."

"You're a *good* burglar," she murmured, peeling out of her tunic.

It did feel almighty good to have arms around me in bed. I fell asleep no more than five seconds after we had achieved a comfortable spoon. She beat me by several seconds. From that day on, if we slept at the same time it was together.

I introduced her to the bust of Kennedy, who filed her in his permanents. I showed her the defense systems and emergency exits. I showed her my meditation place down by the river, and how to get there and back safely. She started spending a lot of time alone there, even though she couldn't smoke while filtered and goggled. She did not discuss what she thought about there, and I did not ask. I could search her home, rifle her strongbox, and milk her computer—but some things are personal. Four days went by this way.

I was sitting in the Lounger having my neck rubbed and planning my next job when I heard the dislock sequence initiate. I glanced up, expecting Karen. But when the door cycled up it was the Fader who came down the stairs, with a tape in his hand.

Fader Takhalous is fiftyish and just as nondescript as a man can be. I have mistaken half a dozen strangers for him, and once failed to recognize him until he spoke to me. He could mug you in broad daylight and rent a room from you the next day. I held much the same relationship to him that Karen held to me, except four years further along. I only saw him two or three times a year, and was surprised to see him now; I hadn't been expecting him for another few months.

But the tape explained it. He nodded hello on his way to the stereo; I nodded back, but he didn't see it. He fed the tape to the heads and turned the treble back to flat. He sat in the other Lounger, leaving it turned off, and stared at the ceiling. I dialed the lights down and shut my own chair off. The music was almost unbearably good, a synthesizer piece that was alternately stark and lush, spare and majestic; that took chances and succeeded. It reminded me of early-period Rubbico & Spangler. The Fader smoked a joint while we listened, and for once I didn't mind the faint buzz that breathing his waste smoke brought; the music made it okay.

And about the time I could tell that the unknown composer was building to the finish, Karen did come home, the music masking the noise of her arrival. I had not thought this through. As she came down the stairs she took in the scene, threw me a hello smile, and headed for the kitchen, carrying groceries.

When she returned she sat on the couch without a word and listened, staring at the ceiling. The Fader raised an approving eyebrow, then returned his own attention to the music.

When it had ended we awarded it ten seconds of silence. Then the Fader rose from his chair. He bowed to Karen. "You listen well, Miss—"

"Karen Shaw. That was worth listening to."

"They call me the Fader. Which is what I'm about to do. A pleasure to meet you." She offered her hand and he kissed it. Then he turned to me. "Pop me that tape, son. I'll bring it back for duping another time. I just remembered I left the kettle on."

I got the tape and gave it to him. "What's your hurry?"

"A small matter of business." His eyes slid briefly to Karen.

"She's okay, Fader. She's a friend. She's *here,* right?"

He relaxed slightly. "I've got a mark up to Phase Two, and I just now thought of a way I could take him straight to Phase Four in one jump. If it works it cuts down the seed-money investment substantially—but it has to happen *now.* I'll let you know how it turns out."

I grinned. "Ah, the delicious urgency of the creative impulse. Good luck." He smiled and nodded at Karen again, and was gone.

"Nice old duck," she said when the door had closed behind him. "I get the funny feeling maybe I . . . frightened him away somehow. I'm sorry if I did, that music was *nice.*"

"You're the sorriest thing I've seen all day," I said. "What did you buy us for dinner, and why aren't you pouring it?"

"Whups." She left and came back with whiskey and cashews and raisins. "I'm cooking stew."

"The hell you say."

"God damn it, Joe. *I* know I'm no good with a microwave. My folks were too poor to have micro. But you've got that old-fashioned stove that still works in there, and a perfectly good pressure cooker, and that's what I learned at my mother's knee. So shut up and wait till you taste it before you—"

"All right, all right, I'll take a chance."

She found the Fader's joint on the rug, which thank heaven is burnproof, and looked up inquiringly. I nodded, and she toked it back to life. After two or three deep puffs, she set it down on what we still call an "ashtray'" even though it's been years since cigarettes or joints produced ashes, probably because "buttrest" seems indelicate. "Hey, Joe. Guess what? I think I figured out what I want to do when I grow up."

I sat up straighter and felt myself smiling. "Tell me about it." It was the best news I'd had in a long while. I hadn't been sure whether her meditation was helping or hurting her.

"You remember that conversation we had back at my place, back on Day One? About joy? As distinguished from pleasure?"

"Sure."

"So there's two kinds: the kind from doing a good thing, and the kind from passing up a real tempting chance to do a bad one. The second kind's easy. It is really tempting to go back to the life, the money's fabulous—and it's giving me great joy not to, because the life is a bad thing."

"You don't rationalize that it's therapeutic for the customers?"

"If acting out aggression drained it, there'd be fistfights *before* football games instead of after. I did my customers no favor, and I charged 'em plenty for it.

"But dumping that is only a kind of negative joy. I've been looking for a *good* thing to *do*. Something really worthwhile, something to benefit the world in a significant way, and commensurate with my talents and background."

"Uh-huh."

"Well, that's the hard part. I've never learned how to do anything really useful except fuck and fix motorcycles, and I can't go back to bikes because I can't stand working on the junk they make nowadays. Besides, the existence of motorcycles in good running order isn't all *that* great a boon to mankind. I figure I can do better than that."

"I'm sure of it," I agreed. "What have you selected?"

"Well, I got to thinking about this socket in my skull. I got to thinking about people who have 'em put there, and why. Self-destruction's too quick an answer. I've been over it in my head a lot, and I can't be certain, but I think if that option hadn't been there—if there hadn't been a friendly neighborhood wireshop all of six blocks away—if wireheading hadn't come along and presented itself, I do *not* think I would have just found some other way to suicide. Other than tobacco and a risky lifestyle, I mean.

"I mean, I don't think dying is what I wanted at all. I don't think hardly any of the people the juice has killed wanted to die, as such, exactly. I think we just . . . just wanted to *have it all,* just for once, just for a little while to have it all and not be hungry anymore. And if dying was the ticket price, well, okay."

I wasn't certain I agreed, but then I'd never asked a wirehead's opinion. Very few people ever get to. I remembered the great lengths she had gone to with the water bottle to prolong her own last ride as far as possible.

"So it seems to me, now, that the existence of that option is an evil thing. An attractive nuisance, like the swimming pools and old refrigerators little kids get into. It makes it so that people past a certain point of instability are unbearably tempted. Maybe I'm rationalizing, trying to shift some blame for what I did from myself."

She finished her drink and lit a Peter Jackson, masking the last fragrances of the Fader's joint. "So what I'd like to do is everything I can to remove that option."

I sat there trying not to frown. "How, exactly?"

"I haven't exactly got detailed plans yet—"

"Phone your congresscritter? Write a letter to *The Village Voice?* Shoot every wire-surgeon in town?"

"The shock docs don't matter one way or another. They'd just as soon be botching abortions and faking draft deferments. It's the corporations that make and market the hardware that are the real villains."

"Anybody can put together a juice rig."

"The wire and transformer, sure—but the droud itself, the microfilaments and the technology to place them properly, that's not workbench stuff. Without the corporations, wireheading just wouldn't happen."

"Do you have any *idea* how many corporations are involved?" I asked sarcastically. I had no firm idea myself.

"Three."

"Nonsense. There have to be at least—"

"Three. The shock doc I picked took it out in trade, and he felt talkative afterward. I didn't think I was listening at the time, but I was. There are over a dozen juice-rig models on the market, but they all get their basic modules from one of three corporations. There used to be five, but two of them went under. And the doc said he had his eyes and ears open, and he had a hunch that two of the three were really different arms of a single outfit that nobody knows."

"How could a juice-head company go broke?"

"How should I know? Sampling the merchandise, maybe. Anyway, all the basic patents are held by a Swiss outfit, so that makes a total of three targets and four avenues of approach."

"Infiltrate and destroy, huh?"

"Something like that. Free-lance industrial espionage."

"I repeat, what's your plan? See how many executives you can poison before they get you?"

"I thought of it," she admitted.

"Pointless and stupid. Honey, you start killing sharks, they just start showing up faster than you can kill them."

"Yeah, but that's not why I gave up the idea. I don't think I've got it in me to kill."

That impressed me. Most of the children of television are convinced that they have in them what it takes to murder in cold blood. The overwhelming majority of them are wrong. Surprisingly few have what it takes to murder in *hot* blood, or even self-defense. "Congratulations."

"But there are other ways. There's no such thing as an honest corporation. A hooker often learns things, without even trying, that the IRS would love to know. Or the Securities and Exchange Commission. Or the Justice Department, or—"

"Or *Newsday,* right. They pay the best, you might as well get a terrific coffin out of the deal. I'm certainly glad to hear that you have no death-wish."

"I'm not especially afraid of death. Not anymore. Someday, no matter what I do, random chance is going to strike me dead. I might as well be doing something worthwhile at the time. It should be a shame that I died."

"It sure will be. Karen, the kind of people you're talking about have all the access they could ever want, and more leverage than you can believe. There is no way you can sell that kind of information and not be traced. Hell, they'll be able to follow the path of the check."

"I won't sell the information, then. I'll give it away."

"Don't be silly. Who'd trust free information?"

"But I could—"

"Damn it to hell, listen to me. I was professionally trained to infiltrate and destroy once, by experts. I've been on the con for a long time now, and I have a unique advantage you don't share. I can't be traced. If my *life* depended on it, *I* wouldn't get within a hundred miles of a scam like this. With a crack team of about a dozen, and an unlimited bankroll, you could maybe put a big bruise on people like that and live to admire it. No way is *any*body going to bring them *down*. Let alone a single commando, let alone a crusading hooker with a hole in her head. Get serious, will you—"

"Shut the fuck up!"

I am not used to being outshouted. I hadn't even known I was shouting.

"Don't talk down to me! I don't care how old you are, don't talk down to me. I'm sick of that shit. I don't have to listen to that. I have been around, chump. I've been in on enough scams to know what I can do. I'm pretty smart and I'm pretty tough, and I don't scare worth a damn. God damn it, I've been hooking for almost a year in this town and *nobody owns me.* I'm a fucking independent, do you know that? Do you know what that means?"

Of course I did—but I had never thought it through, never considered the cleverness and strength it implied. She saw me working it out and grinned. "There's a sucker out on the street now with three new creases on his face. One that I put there, and two from worrying about where I might put the next one. Joe, *I know the way things are.* I know this job is too big for me, and I expect to enjoy it right up to the end, and I don't need any lectures. Oh, *Jesus,* the stew!"

She leaped up and galloped to the kitchen. I sat there with my empty glass, listened to the squeal and hiss and clatter of the silly obsolete pressure cooker, listened to oh-shit noises turn to dubious *mmms* and finally to mollified *nnns* and a last triumphant *ha.*

Once I blew a radiator hose on the highway. A Good Samaritan stopped to help me. He acted very knowledgeable about cars. While I was getting the spare hose out of the trunk, he helpfully topped off my transmission fluid for me. With the brake fluid I kept behind the right headlight. "Oh, it's all the same stuff," he assured me. "They just put in different dyes and charge you more money." It took me three days to get a tranny shop to flush and refill the system, and for those three days the transmission slipped so badly that I nearly went crazy. The engine would roar smoothly in response to the accelerator, while the car crept along in fits and starts as it slipped in and out of gear. It was a helpless, frustrated feeling. I had all the horsepower in the world, and it took me two city blocks to coax her up to thirty.

At the moment that was the inside of my head. High revs, but it wouldn't *go* anywhere. I attributed it to the pot smoke I had breathed. The thought train went like so:

(I'm much too agitated.) (Well, sure I am, my new friend is planning something dangerous and stupid.) (No, there's more to it than that.) (Something else?) (Yes.) (What else?) (. . . my new friend is planning something dangerous and stupid.) (No, there's more to it than that.) (What else?) (. . . my new friend is planning . . .)

Pull back on the accelerator and try again.

(Why must there be something else?) (Because I'm much too agitated.) (Why?) (Because my new . . .)

Same loop. Try again.

(Why do I feel my agitation is "too much"?) (Because if I were only concerned about my friend, I'd be trying to persuade her to drop her plans.) (And . . . ?) (And getting agitated is the wrong way to persuade her.) (Sure?) (Yes; it will only strengthen her resolve.) (Conclusion?) (I'm not really trying to talk her out of it.) (What *am* I doing, then?) (Getting very agitated.) *(Why?)* (My new friend is planning something . . .)

Christ.

The aroma of stew struck like a symphony, disrupting the inner loop. I heard silverware being assembled, bowls being ladled full. I saw the cigarette she had left burning give one last puff of smoke and expire. Stop the brain, put it away, maybe after dinner . . .

(What *should* I be doing?) (Talking her out of it.) (How?) (By going along with the gag.) (By—?) (Wait for her own doubts to emerge, wait for her to falter—and she will—and then nudge.) (Con my friend?) (That, or stubborn her up and send her out there alone. There's no third choice.) (I can't do that.) *(Why not?)* (It's dangerous.) (What do you mean, dangerous?) (It makes me very agitated.) (Why?) (My new friend is planning to . . .)

(I'm trying to talk *myself* out of it!)

She brought two bowls into the room, and the symphony of smells crescendoed. She put them on the coffee table, left, and reentered with a jug and two glasses. She poured for us. She left again for garlic-and-butter-toasted French bread, and then she sat opposite me. I started to dig in.

"Joe? It should cool a little first."

"Right."

"Look . . . I just did some thinking. I had no call to blow up at you that way, no right. It's just that you came on kind of . . . paternal, and you're about forty." That made me wince. In my head I'm twenty-eight. "About the same age as *he* was when . . . I'm sorry I yelled at you."

"I'm sorry I yelled too. I don't know why I did."

We ate the stew. It was superb, and I told her so.

"Joe?"

"Yeah."

"Look, you've done an awful lot for me. You saved my life, you put me—"

"Please."

"—back together again, let me say it, you gave me this place to come to and a warm bed every night, you never ask when I'm gonna get it together and *do* something, you give me all this and I give you bupkiss."

"My ass. I got all your cash and a terrific pair of speakers."

"You're a good man, Joe, and only a selfish bitch would ask you for anything more."

"The way you're about to?"

"The way I'm about to."

I tried to sigh, but a belch spoiled it. "Ask away, honey. Your stew has softened my heart."

"Your terminal has just about all the access there is. I want you to get me readings on all my targets."

The fear was back, a muffled yammering in a distant compartment of my skull.

"Just give me a deep reading of each one. That's all. I'm not asking you to come in on the scam. It's not personal with you, it's not your crusade. But you could save me weeks of legwork—maybe months."

"I'm sorry, Karen. I can't."

"Why not?"

(Why not?) "The kind of information you're talking about is ringed around with alarms, tricky ones. If I trip one, a tracer program could start hunting me back."

"So what? You don't exist, not in the Net."

"Exactly. How come you're still an independent? Forget about how tough and smart you are—what's the main reason?"

She frowned. "Well . . . my johns don't talk much. Not even to their best friends."

"Bullseye. How long do you think you'd last in this town if The Man heard about you and decided he could use you? A couple of gentlemen would call on you, and when they were done you'd be terribly, terribly anxious to do any little thing that might please them. Now suppose that you're a big-time corporate shark. The kind whose attention The Man himself tries not to attract. Somebody tries to crack your shields, and when you investigate you discover that the interloper has no legal existence. Could you not find uses for such a person? Important uses? Would it not be worth a *lot* of time and trouble to track him down and enslave him? Honey, I continue to exist as an independent for the same reason you do, or anybody else with something special to offer. The bastards haven't noticed me yet. Should I stick my nose in their window and start sniffing?"

We both listened to the argument as it came out of my mouth. It convinced her, and it should have convinced me. My subconscious had done a good job on it. It was a pretty good argument, with only a couple of holes in it, and it was indeed something to be afraid of.

But it wasn't what I feared. I could tell.

But she bought it. She didn't even bother poking at the holes in the logic to see what I had them stuffed with. If a good friend doesn't want to do you a favor, there's no point in arguing.

"I guess you're right. I hadn't thought it through." She sat crestfallen for a moment, then squared her shoulders. "Well, there are other keyboard men in town."

"Sure. Professionals with equipment almost as good as mine. Better connected, better protected. But Karen . . . listen, no matter how you go about this, it's suicide city, I'm telling you. Give it up."

"Two weeks ago I was willing to die just to find out what pleasure was like."

"If all you want is a socially useful kamikaze mission, just stop paying off your draft board. You'll be on the New York police force the next day, and stiff in the South Bronx before the year is out."

"And chase guys like you? And chippies like me? Don't be silly. Look, I've got to piss—you stay here till I get back. Surprise dessert in the kitchen." She leaped up and was gone.

I sat there trying to figure out what I was really afraid of.

It was astonishingly, frustratingly difficult. I knew that the answer was in my possession, that some part of my mind held the knowledge. I could even tell in what "direction" that part lay. But every time I steered that way and gave her the gas, the transmission slipped. It could run away faster than I could pursue. Stubbornly, hopelessly, I stalked it, knowing only that it tasted like nightmares.

Something yanked me out of my brown study; the outside world was demanding my attention. But why? Everything looked okay. I smelled nothing burning, all I heard was the distant sound of Karen urinating . . .

I played back the tape, and discovered that I had been hearing that sound for an impossibly long time.

I didn't even bother to run. She had found a small length of hose under the sink, and used adhesive tape to run a siphon from the toilet tank, to simulate the sound of urination. Then she had left, by the second of my two emergency exits. The one I had not told her about. On the face of the lid she had left a lipstick message: "Enjoy the speakers, Joe. I'm glad that fucker landlord didn't get them. Thanks for everything."

I nodded my head. "You're welcome," I said out loud. I went to the kitchen, made a pitcher of five-to-one martinis, frowned, dumped it in the sink, made a pitcher of six-to-one martinis, nodded and smiled, brought it into the living room, and hurled it carefully through the television screen. Then I rummaged in the ashtray for the Fader's roach, and got three good deep tokes out of it before I burned my lip. I had not smoked in many years; it smacked me hard.

"Lady," I said to her empty stew bowl, "if you can con me that well, maybe—just maybe—you've got a snowball's chance."

❖5❖

2006

NORMAN HALTED just outside the front door of his apartment building, let it close behind him, and sighed. Fall had always seemed to him a silly time to begin the new school year. Like hibernating bears, scholars sealed themselves away from the world just when it was at its most beautiful. A farmer would have been his most involved with the outdoors now, trying to outguess the frosts and prepare his home for winter. Norman could not even yield to the temptation to kick apart heaps of rainbow leaves in his path, for an assistant professor in public can no more take off his dignity than his trousers.

It was only a block to the campus, but Norman was running late. He sneered at his briefcase, turned right, and began the walk to work. As he passed the underground garage ramp it blatted at him and emitted a Toyota. Norman watched the car as he got out of its way, wondering for the thousandth time why anyone living in this city would want to own a car. Walking was much cheaper, much less trouble—and healthier too.

If you're such a health nut, he asked himself, why have you let yourself get so badly out of shape? In the six years since he had left the army, Norman's only sustained regular exercise had been this daily two blocks' walk to and from the university. He had long since given up even pretending that he was trying to control his tobacco habit, and he knew he weighed more than he should. He could remember what it had felt like in the army, to be in shape, and wondered why he had let such a good feeling go out of his life upon his discharge, without a backward glance. He had known an echo of that easy confidence, that readiness for anything, the night when Maddy arrived and he had thought her a prowler. But the absurd failure of his charge that night proved that it was only an echo, an adrenalin memory, that he no longer deserved that confidence. Norman resolved to begin a rigorous program of calisthenics that very night, and to sign up for swimming privileges at the university pool that very afternoon, whereupon he lit a cigarette.

This whole thought-train had occupied only the space of time necessary to glance at the puffing Toyota and then down into his jacket pocket for his cigarettes. His cupped hands came away from his face, and the one holding the match began to shake it out, and instead held the match upside down long enough to burn him. Lois stood before him on the pavement—tall, slim and beautiful—frosting at the mouth and shivering. She wore no coat. Her hair and makeup were impeccable, and her expression was somewhere between afraid and exhilarated.

"I'm late," he said at once, and then, "Ouch." He disposed of the match, making his hundredth mental note to switch to the new self-lighting cigarettes.

"I know. I nearly froze my face off waiting in my lobby for you to come by." She could not meet his eyes, though not for lack of trying.

"Lois, for God's sake, it's the first *day*. I've got—"

"I planned it this way. First I thought I'd have you over for coffee and spend about three hours leading you around to it, and then I decided that would be dishonest and you'd resent being manipulated, so I thought I'd just say it bang and let you have time to think about it before you say anything. That way you sort of don't just say something, like, spontaneously, and then feel like you have to live up to it or something."

This was a more or less familiar ritual with them. When she had, say, lent five hundred (Old) dollars they couldn't spare to a friend who couldn't possibly be imagined repaying them, she would begin the news like this. And he would think, What is the most horrible thing she could possibly say next? and then he would be relieved when it wasn't that. So he thought now of the most horrible thing she could possibly say next, and she said it.

"I want to come back to you."

He stared at her, waited for a punchline, for the alarm clock to go off, for a freak meteorite to come and drill him through the heart.

"I'm off today at three, I'll be home all night, call me when you're ready."

She was gone.

Since his path was no longer blocked, he resumed walking. At this particular time her proposition—no, damn it, her proposal—was simply and literally unthinkable. He placed it firmly out of his mind and walked on, thinking of pushups versus situps and wondering if the bookstore had gotten his texts in yet. When he had gone about twenty steps he paused, spun on his heels, and roared at absolute maximum volume, *"What about the plumber, then?"*

Across the street a second-floor landing window slid open on Lois's building. "He moved out a week ago," she called back, and closed the window.

A handful of students on either side of the street were motionless, staring at Norman with some apprehension. He glared back, and all but one resumed their own migrations. That one continued to stare, quite expressionlessly, past glasses that doubled the apparent size of his eyes.

"Moved out of his own apartment, by God," Norman muttered to himself. He puffed furiously on his cigarette. There had to be *some* way to make that insolent bookstore manager show a little respect. Norman couldn't complain to MacLeod . . . but perhaps he could mention it to someone who *would* tell MacLeod. Yes, that idea had promise . . .

He walked on.

His first sight of the campus delighted his sense of irony. The original layout designer had placed concrete walkways where he thought they would look nice. Generations of students had taken more convenient paths, destroying grass and creating muddy ruts. Generations of administrators had taken this as a personal affront, and had struck back with strict, unenforceable prohibitions. The current administration had faced reality: all the previous summer they had torn up and reseeded the walkways, poured new ones where the students' ruts were. Now Norman saw at once that the majority of the upper-class students were ignoring the new walkways and following the old paths they had always scorned, through the new grass. In one place a small circular flower plot stood precisely on a no longer-extant path: Norman watched a student walk directly to it, circle its perimeter carefully, and continue on the imaginary walkway.

Having just made himself a public spectacle before students who might well be his own, Norman walked where he was meant to walk. But he resented having to do so.

He picked up memos and schedule revisions at the department office, stored his hat and coat in his office, and went to deal with the bookstore. By a stroke of luck the assistant departmental chairman was present when Norman said in a slightly raised voice, "Another *month*? But these were ordered in March. Of last year." The assistant chairman glanced up, and Norman had the satisfaction of hearing the store manager hastily give an excuse that was not only patently false, but checkably false; a memo from the Chancellor would reach the manager within twenty-four hours, and Norman's students would have their textbooks before the close of the add-drop period. He reached his first class, Introduction to Joyce, in a cocky, go-to-hell state of mind, and when he looked about the room and saw at least a dozen versions of the same mask—eager interest mixed with respectful politeness—something clicked in his head and he made an impulsive decision. Norman had always been rather conservative for an English teacher, had never needed to be given MacLeod's Number Three Lecture on The Irresponsibility of the Maverick, had always respected even the forms and traditions which he personally found silly. Ever since the army he had been willing to pay lip service to any ritual-system that promised stability—or even only familiarity. But all at once he heard himself say to his students the very same words that had nearly ended his father's career twenty-five years before.

"Is there anyone here who does not want an A?"

Total silence.

"I say, is there anyone here who objects to being given an A in this course, for the semester, here and now?"

One hand rose near the back, a skeptical woman sensing some kind of trap. (Norman's father had drawn three of them.)

Norman nodded. "Okay. Come see me in my office sometime, we'll discuss it. The rest of you, you've all got an A in this course. You can go home now."

Pandemonium. Hands shot up all over, and no one moved from their seats. (Twenty-five years before, several students had whooped with glee and left the room by this point.) When the general outcry reached its first lull, Norman spoke up and overrode it.

"I am perfectly serious. Those of you who signed up for this course because you needed another three credits in English may now leave, satisfied. You have what you paid for, and are spared six months of diligent hypocrisy."

"And then when we take you up on it and leave, you fail us, right?" said the woman who had first raised her hand.

Norman frowned. "You have nearly managed to insult me, Ms. . . ."

"Porter."

"Ms. Porter. Let me assure you: I say what I mean, and vice versa. Those who choose to leave have my blessing, and my thanks. I will not even make a list of your names, since everyone except Ms. Porter is getting the same grade. I will not so much as look with private disapproval on those of you who choose to go. I fully understand that the existing system pressures you to matriculate at the expense of learning about anything you're interested in, and acquiring a necessary job credential seems to me as valid a reason as any for attending a university. God help us. If that is your purpose, accept it and be proud of it and do it efficiently. And don't clutter up my classroom. Because you see, I happen to be enormously interested in—and greatly confused by—the writing of James Joyce. Some of the things he wrote stir up my brains and haunt my off-hours, and other things he wrote mystify or bore me to tears. And I propose to spend a couple of hours a week for the next several months in the *exclusive* company of people who are also enormously interested in the writing of James Joyce. I believe this will increase my own knowledge and appreciation of Joyce, and I'm confident that it will increase yours."

A young man who wore the only necktie in the room besides Norman's spoke up in a nasal voice. "Will there be any tests?"

"Well, I should hope there will be at least one or two in every class-room period, but not the way you mean, no."

"Papers?" asked a short rat-faced woman.

"Anytime you feel you have the makings of a paper, cogent or otherwise, write it up and leave it in my office. The very best I will help you to have published, if you're interested. Those and the second best will be photocopied, distributed, and discussed. The bad ones will be discussed privately. They'll all get A's."

The necktied young man supplied Norman with the straight line he'd been hoping for. "But Dr. Kent, if we've all got A's . . . what's supposed to motivate us to work?"

Happily, Norman again quoted his late father. "Why, bless you, the intrinsic interest of the material itself."

Blank faces stared at him. He waited, and after a few moments a third of the class left the room. Ms. Porter was among them. Most of the remaining two-thirds looked mightily interested.

Be damned, Norman thought, history does repeat itself.

He repeated the procedure at Victorian Poetry, his only other class that day, with similar results.

At nine o'clock that night he stubbed out an expensive marijuana cigarette, set his phone for *record*, shook his head at it, and said, "Not a chance." He played it back, nodded, and punched Lois's number. When his board told him that she had answered, he fed the recording on a loop. His own screen stayed dark, and after a while she hung up. He put Lambert, Hendricks, and Ross on the stereo, lit another of the cigarettes, and after some while cried himself to sleep.

The next morning history continued to repeat itself. The summons was waiting on his desk, and the reaming was thorough. It did not help at all that MacLeod knew the story about Norman's father. MacLeod had made all the allowances he was going to make for Norman's personal misfortunes; for the rest of the semester, and perhaps the year, Norman was on sudden-death overtime. The next mistake would be his last. He was obliged to contact all the students who had left and advise them that he had been overruled. No part of that was fun.

Thoroughly sobered at last, lusting again for any kind of security, Norman became over the next three or four months a model teacher—that is, a tireless and blindingly efficient robot. He shouldered a tremendous course load including two freshman World Lit courses and a two-night-a-week seminar, and performed brilliantly in all of them. He completed and published an exemplary paper on Dwyer's 1978 "Ariana Olisvos" hoax, which was anthologized nearly at once.

He took over the campus literary magazine when old Boudreau died, restructured the staff to tremendous effect, and figured out a way to get the printing done at half cost. He kept his promise to himself: he spent every hour not used for work or sleep in hard exercise at either the gym or the pool. He gave up tobacco and cannabis and cut down on alcohol. Good physical condition came back hard at his age, after nearly seven years of neglect, but he pursued it hard. His students either loved or hated him; none was indifferent. MacLeod allowed himself to become friendly again.

To those around him Norman came to seem almost unnaturally alert and rational. In fact, he was in a kind of trance, the peace of the dervish.

At Christmastime came Minnie and the Bear.

Both sets of parents had guessed wrong. A man christened Chesley Withbert should not be very tall, very broad, immensely strong, and covered all over with curly black hair; it is unfair to those tempted to laugh. His inevitable nickname was first given to him at age eight. Similarly, a woman born Minnie Rodenta should not be five feet high and mouse-faced, but no nickname had been found for her yet that was not worse. To Norman they were beloved friends, not seen in three years and frequently missed. He was greatly cheered by their arrival in that loneliest of all seasons, which of course was why they had come.

Norman and the Bear had served together in Africa; each had saved the other's life once. Norman had been wounded and discharged first, but by the time he was out of the hospital the Bear was out of the army, and had moved to Nova Scotia. While Norman was sitting in New York, pondering what the hell to do with his life, he got a letter from the Bear, inviting him up to Halifax for a couple of weeks. Halifax is one of the few remaining North American cities from which one can reach raw nature in ten minutes' drive; by the middle of the second week Norman knew that he could never go back to New York. There was a regional shortage of trained English teachers, the only job for which his prewar degree had prepared him; he overcame his lack of experience with a brilliant interview and was hired. Presently the Bear and his new lover, Minnie, introduced him to a girl Minnie worked with at Victoria General Hospital. Named

Lois. Both couples spent a great deal of time together, swapped twice experimentally, and gave it up when it seemed to interfere with their friendship. They were married within three months of each other.

Then three years ago Minnie's work had taken her to Toronto. Bear had by then established himself as a copy-hack, and was earning a fair living knocking out tecs, sits and scifis for several software networks; he had no strong objection to moving. Since that time the two couples had communicated largely by birthday phone call, and in the last year even that had been interrupted by the collapse of Norman's and Lois's marriage. The reunion now was explosively enthusiastic on both sides.

"Jesus," the Bear rumbled as he released Norman from one of his classic hugs. "You're in great shape, man."

Norman's grin flickered momentarily. "Some ways, brother, some ways," he said, and then Minnie was taking her hug. Her first words were, "Sorry it took us so long, Norm. It's been crazy out."

"Nonsense. I'd've been too busy to be a proper host if you'd come sooner. God, it's good to see you two. I've been on eleventerhooks ever since you called." He took their suitcases, showed them where to put their coats and boots and where to find the liquor cabinet. As soon as they were all seated in the living room he raised his glass high. "To great friendship," he said, drained the glass, and flung it across the room. It smashed on the baseboard heater.

Minnie and the Bear broke up. They faced each other, said in unison, "We've missed him," and followed his example.

"Missed me again," he said exultantly, and then, "Oh, God, I've been hanging out with ordinary people for so long. Thank you two."

"There are crazies in Hogtown," Minnie said, "but few with your elegance." Norman rose from his chair, bowed, and produced more glasses, threading his way carefully through the scatter of glass on the carpet.

"This is fantastic," he said wonderingly. "You two have been here less than a minute, and it's as though you'd never left. All the time between has just disappeared." He giggled. "How thoughtful of it." Suddenly he looked away.

The Bear lay in magnificent repose in one of Norman's huge bean-bag chairs, looking rather like a beached whale covered with colorful tarpaulins and black seaweed. He made a joint appear, tapped it alight, and sucked hugely. "So? Which side brings the other up to date first?" He passed the joint.

Norman hesitated, decided training was shot to hell anyway, and took a toke. "Is yours cheerful?" he croaked, passing the joint to Minnie. With her nose wrinkled up she looked even more mouselike.

The Bear looked thoughtful. "Yeah, on the whole. A couple of real bright spots, and one genuine tall tale."

"Then we'll save it for catharsis, okay?"

The two nodded at once. "Lois?" Minnie asked economically.

"Yes and no," Norman said. "Not really; I think I've got that under control now. It's more Madeleine. And, I suppose, mostly it's me. It's been a hard-luck voyage, mates. I—you didn't get here any too soon."

"Damn straight," the Bear agreed. "I still see double yellow lines and headlights coming at me. So talk."

Norman brought them up to date, beginning with Lois's first request for a separation and including his botched suicide, Maddy's arrival and disappearance, and subsequent events. The Bear interrupted frequently with questions, Minnie more seldom.

"Argyle, Barrington area, huh? Pedestrians around there all night long on a Saturday."

"And a little bit of residential. Enough so that a scream could *not* go unheard."

The Bear nodded. "Two blocks over nobody'd pay any attention. But right there it'd cause phone calls. And you're sure she didn't know anyone in Halifax well enough to get into a car with them at 1:00 A.M.?"

"No one in North America. Except Charlie, who was occupied."

"And alibied by many witnesses," Bear clarified. "So, that leaves two possibilities."

"Psycho cabbie or rogue cop."

"Right. Nowhere except in the crap I write do you take an armed and able-bodied citizen off a public street with no fuss at all. Only a fool would try it. And from what you say, she could take care of herself. You checked out both angles?"

Norman produced a file folder from his desk, took two sheets of paper out, and gave one to each. "This is the poster I put up everywhere a cabbie might conceivably see one. It's got a good recent picture, her description and the circumstances of her disappearance, and my phone number. While I was putting them up I questioned all the dispatchers and half the drivers in town. I pieced together people's memories and accounted for every driver seen in that area during that time, with some computer assistance."

"That leaves a cop." The Bear frowned. "Hard to track."

"Sergeant Amesby at Missing Persons brought up that theory before I could think of a graceful way to phrase it. He's been running his own check with a lot better data, and he comes up empty too."

"Yeah, but is he really looking?"

"I've been living in Amesby's pocket for months. I know him. He looked."

"A cop with no partner can fake his whereabouts."

"Not so Amesby couldn't catch it. Believe me, Bear, he's good."

"Most fortunate. We'll dismiss the notion of a citizen in a cop suit."

"That he sewed himself, right." He passed them the rest of the folder's contents, mostly press clippings and blowup facials of Madeleine taken over a period of fifteen years. "The firm she worked for in Zurich supplied some company videotapes with footage of Maddy in them, and I had stills made."

"You got terrific coverage," Minnie observed.

"Saturation. A woman named Saint Phillip has been very helpful. No woman in the Maritimes has died mysteriously without a paragraph mentioning that police do *not* believe this case is connected with the disappearance of Madeleine Kent, followed by a three-paragraph synopsis. I've been on all three local stations and the CBC twice each. Lots of results, none worth talking about."

The Bear finished off the joint and lay back thoughtfully into the chair. "Well," he said, gazing at the ceiling, "when you have eliminated the impossible, whatever remains, however improbable, et cetera. So a total nut pulls up to the curb, shoots a total stranger in the head with a silenced gat—"

"In the *back* of the head. She went armed, and she was fast."

"Right. Yanks her into his car before anybody comes around the corner, and departs at a moderate speed, takes her out up into the maples. He's local, woods-wise enough to find a spot where no one will walk—which is *much* harder than a city killer could imagine—and he's immensely strong, because he can haul the corpse of a pretty big woman *to* that spot without aid. In the dark. Oh, goat berries, I don't believe it for a second." He grimaced ferociously.

"Wait a minute," Minnie objected. "Why does it have to be woods, just because there's so much of 'em around here? How about that business from your last, darling? The newly poured concrete?"

The Bear nodded. "And the psycho who happens to have unrestricted access. You will recall that I didn't put my own name on that one."

"But I mean what about some urban or suburban disposal site?"

The Bear looked pained. "Darling, this was *summer.*"

"Oh. That's right. Well, what about the harbor?"

"Darling, remember how many summer Friday nights we tried to find a spot along the water uncrowded enough to make love? Imagine trying to dump a corpse. You *might* pull it off—but would you bet on it?"

Norman suddenly smiled. "You know, except for Amesby, you two are the first people I've spoken to since Maddy left that don't use euphemisms. I can't tell you how grateful I am."

The Bear grinned back at him. "Damn straight. Not many people are understanding enough not to be understanding. You, for instance, are not one of those offensively oversolicitous hosts, who fusses about making sure one's glass is full and offering one coffee and such."

Norman shook his head sadly. "How can you live with such a snide bastard, Min?" He got up and headed for the coffee-maker.

"I beat him regularly."

"Damn straight," the Bear agreed. "I keep thinking: *this* time I'm gonna fill that straight."

"You fill practically anything, dear." They grinned lewdly at each other.

"I'm about ready to fill a strait*jacket* myself," Norman called from the kitchen. "You two still take cinnamon?"

"Yeah."

He came back with three coffees and cake on a tray. "So what all this comes d—what are you doing?"

The Bear was lighting another joint. "Dr. Withbert's famous bluesectomy procedure. First get nuked with good friends, then . . . haven't we done this before?"

Norman hesitated. It was a Friday night, but . . . "I've been keeping myself on a short leash the last few months. The accumulated stash—"

"Is what we came a thousand miles to drain," Minnie said firmly. "Listen to the doctor."

"Remember the Ukrainian proverb," the Bear boomed. " 'The church is near—but the roads are icy. The tavern is far—but I will walk carefully.' How long has it been since your last confession, my son?"

Norman remembered, and set down the coffee. "Gimme that joint."

"So what this all left me with," he went on a few puffs later, "was the natural logarithm of one."

"I still like the rogue-cop idea," Bear said, gulping coffee. "Who else could be confident of getting away with it?"

"Maybe," Minnie said, "but the trouble with any psycho theory, cop or civilian, is that psychos usually aren't one-shots. They keep on performing until they get caught. But you say there's been nothing with a similar MO—"

"Psychos make their own patterns, my love," the Bear said drily. "Maybe he takes six months to wind up to each one. Maybe he's wealthy and does this in a different city each week for sport."

"I don't buy either one," Minnie persisted.

"So what's left?"

"Well, if it's not a flat-out killcrazy, it's got to be someone she'd lower her guard for. Norm, how would she react if, say, a carful of *women* offered her a lift?"

"She's like me, she loves to walk. It was a beautiful night. She'd spent the last ten years in *Europe,* Minnie. I don't think she'd accept a ride from any stranger."

"Hey," the Bear said, sitting erect with some difficulty. "How about that? Somebody from Switzerland?" He frowned again. "He locates her at 1:00 A.M. on a Friday night without asking memorable questions of anyone she knew here. Bear, you *are* a jackass. Forgive me."

Norman squinted at the Bear. "That last joint get you high?"

His old friend recognized the beginning of a litany that had been written in the jungle years before, grinned, and gave the antiphon. "Nah. You?"

Norman frowned and stuck out his lower lip. "Nah."

The Bear shook his head sadly. "Cheap weed."

"Blackskin man give me bad deal."

"Burned again."

"Yeah, Sarge."

"Only one thing to do."

"Check."

The Bear produced the pack, and they choroused, *Smoke some more!*"

Minnie had endured all this with patience and, since she had not heard it in three years, some amusement. "Count me out, thanks. I'm not about to try and keep up with you two."

But by the time the third joint was half consumed, the smiles had faded and the topic remained. "I kind of liked the Switzerland angle myself. She was hanging around with some *very* comfortably fixed people, and she dropped a few teasers about an unhappy affair. But Amesby's got some friends at Interpol that he respects, and anybody Amesby respects I respect, and they come up empty. As near as we can learn, no one she dealt with in business had any motive to have her kidnapped or hit. It wasn't that kind of business. Electrical supply, micro-electronics widgetry and software, related items. They have an excellent reputation, as a stodgily honest old firm, just big enough to be unambitious. Harbin-Schellmann is the name, I think. They were sorry to see her go, but not that kind of sorry. Anyway, as you say, a Swiss hit squad passing through town would be bound to leave spoor. So that's out too." He took the last toke, held it awhile with his eyes closed. "So I consulted a couple of psychics."

The Bear opened his mouth and then closed it firmly. Minnie only nodded. "What'd you get?" she asked.

"The first one was recommended by the RCMP, they'd worked with him several times with pretty good results. He was about sixty and looked like a grocery store clerk, dressed like one, everything. He was very irritable, very disinclined to try and like you. That made me suspect he might be into something."

Minnie nodded. "Nurses have to learn that one. Patients are clients, problems you try hard to solve. You become their friend only if they've *got* to have one, and then you get chewed up some."

"I saw it happen with Lois. I think she got a shade *too* good at disassociating."

"We'll carve that one next,"Minnie said firmly. "Let's close up this one first. What did the psychic say?"

"How much did he ask?" the Bear wanted to know.

"He got every known salient fact out of me—he said straight out that as far as he was concerned his only talent was for having very reliable hunches, which required *all* available data at a minimum. He got things out of me about Maddy that I hadn't known I remembered. Then he . . . well, it sounds anticlimactic, but he just seemed to sit there and think about it awhile."

"While you were watching?" Bear asked.

"I saw him forget me. Except as part of the puzzle, I mean. After about ten extremely boring minutes he told me that Maddy was in a house, a private home, on the order of a hundred and fifty klicks from here. Direction uncertain. Two men were with her. He said he didn't feel any hostility or violence or aggression in them, but their relationship to Maddy was not clear. He said she came through as so passive that she might have been drugged or simply ill. She had not been physically harmed or mistreated, and she wasn't being interrogated. He said there was a large body of water right out in front of the house, but he couldn't tell whether it was the Bay of Fundy or the Atlantic or what. One other house in sight nearby, uninhabited. He told me that it was a very beautiful spot, woods all around the house and a brook nearby that was unsafe to drink. He said he had not felt any fear from Madeleine. He apologized for the fact that all this information was perfectly useless, and he charged me fifteen dollars for an hour of his time."

"Do you think he was into something?" the Bear asked, leaning forward intently.

Norman shook his head. "I don't know. I don't know, Bear. I was straining not to be skeptical, and I found I didn't have to strain so hard. I'll stipulate that he's sincere. But I just don't know. The damned evidence always turns out to be unobtainable, doesn't it? But I keep getting this funny feeling. Like the story makes so little sense that it makes sense." He giggled. "Does that make sense?"

"It butters no parsnips," the Bear said, sitting back. "What'd the second one say?"

"The second one was recommended by some friends of Lois's, which made it harder to be open-minded. But I was desperate. He religioned it up a good deal more. He said 'cosmic' and 'universal' a bit too often to suit me, but—"

"So did Gandhi,"Minnie interjected.

"Right. He shaved his head and wore fake Tibetan clothes from Eaton's and one gold earring and he had no last name, but I have no really valid reason to sneer at any of those things either. And even if I did, nothing says a jerk can't be psychic." Norman rubbed the bridge of his nose. "He was strange. Kind of . . . well, I started to say 'wild-eyed,' but that's not accurate. He looked . . . subtly *wrong* somehow, off-register in some indefinable way. You had the feeling that at any moment you would put your finger on it. It kept you just a little bit off balance, but he didn't seem to realize that or exploit it in any way.

"Anyway. His rap . . ." Norman consulted some notes from the folder. "He said she was in a motel, no idea where or how far away but definitely not in Halifax Metro. Two men were with her, and she loved them both very much. He thought they might be her brothers until I told him she had none but me. Anyway, she was not being held against her will, she very much wanted to be there and was having a wonderful time. She had not been in the motel for very long, she had been brought there recently from the country."

The Bear's eyes flashed and he shifted his weight in the beanbag chair.

"Right. Let's see, right at that point he reversed himself a little on location, said the motel was definitely somewhere in the Annapolis Valley. I asked him how he knew and he said he 'recognized the spiritual flavor of the region.' He said she had just come from somewhere up over the mountain, very close to the Bay. He repeated that she loved and trusted the two men very much."

"Did he mention if they were Swiss?"

"He said he couldn't feel them at all directly, only Maddy's perceptions of them. I told him a little about her background and asked if he could get their nationality, but all he could say was that she thought about them in English. *All* the rest of this, by the way, he gave me with no information whatsoever, using only a picture of her and a rosary of hers he had me fetch along."

"All he had to do was read a paper or watch the news," the Bear noted.

"I know, I know. He said he hadn't, but who knows? But honestly, it was hard to picture him reading the crime news. Anyway, he—"

"What's this about a rosary?" Minnie interrupted.

"He'd asked me over the phone if I had access to any small 'religious objects' belonging to the missing person. She had a rosary our mother gave her when she was a little girl, I'd run across it in her things. He said that would be fine, bring it along."

"Point for him," she muttered. "Go on."

Norman consulted his notes. "That's about it. Oh, wait, he said one man seemed to be the dominant one, smarter or stronger than the other. The other deferred to him. That was all he got, and for his fee he made me donate a hundred New dollars to the UN Disaster Fund. He wouldn't take a cent himself."

"A motel in the valley . . ." Minnie said thoughtfully.

"A week later," Norman continued, "the first man called me back. He said he'd seen the same house again, in a dream this time. He said it was empty now, but it was a very clear night and so now he could make out New Brunswick on the horizon, pick out the lights of a large city against the sky."

"Fundy shore," the Bear breathed. "Up over the mountain from the Annapolis Valley. It fits." He interlocked his big fingers and played tug-of-war with himself; his triceps bulged, then relaxed. "No help. Blue sky pieces."

"Eh?"

"You know him and puzzles," Minnie said. "The two stories don't contradict; they interlock pretty good, like jigsaw pieces. But they're blue sky pieces: no useful informational content."

"Except in context," the Bear agreed. "Which we don't have yet. I assume your Lieutenant Amesby checked with Valley RCMP?"

"Sergeant. Of course he did—I tell you, the man is good at what he does. Good enough that I can't understand what he's doing in the Halifax Police Department. In addition to that, I had copies of the poster put in every bank, credit union, post office, and Liquor Commission outlet from Digby to Wolfville. Result: the cube root of fuck-all."

"Plus the number of sentient beings in Parliament," the Bear agreed. He placed his knuckles together; this time it was his biceps that swelled alarmingly. "Well my son, this is some hard bananas you bring me, but fortunately you've come to the right man. A trivial problem, really, although I can see that some of its subtler aspects might well have eluded a mere trained professional such as Amesby—or a workaday genius like yourself, Norman—for several months. 'Watson, you know my methods?'"

Minnie nodded. "Certainly, Holmes." She turned to Norman. "He comes up with the cube root of fuck-all."

The Bear beamed. "Excellent, Watson. A very concise summary."

Norman felt all his breath leave him with a rush. "Bear, you don't know how much I hoped you'd come up with a decent hunch," he said bleakly. "I've gone over it and over it until my head spins, I wake up in the morning trying to *make* it make sense, and nothing. You two have got maverick and supple brains, and I was hoping you'd see something Amesby and I missed. Damn it, there *is* no probable answer. Least improbable would I guess be some variant of the random-psycho theory—and at this point I'm afraid I'd be grateful if I could just believe it and get started with the mourning. But it's so bloody *unlikely*." A brandy decanter stood nearby; he uncapped it and drank, passed the bottle.

The Bear looked greatly distressed now. "*Compadre,* I'm sorry to say I don't even have suggestions, and the day I can't give bad advice . . ." He smote both thighs with his fists, hard enough to make the beanbag chair start violently.

"I've got suggestions," Minnie said.

Both men looked at her.

"Two of them. First, can we all stop lying to each other?"

Norman and the Bear flinched guiltily.

"All three of us know better. When there is no logic, you go on feelings, and I think we all have the same hunch, am I right?"

The two men exchanged glances. "All right," they said together.

"Allow me," Norman said to his friend. "Okay, the only reasonable hunch is Switzerland. Someone from there, call him . . . well, for the sake of argument let's call him Jacques. Maddy mentioned that name once. If the psychics are even close to accurate, it *has* to be Jacques. Nobody else could have the resources. Even if the psychics are both frauds, it has more logic than the lone-psycho theory. Okay so far?" His friends nodded. "So the logical next step—"

"—is to go to Switzerland and nose around," Minnie finished. "And you're hesitating."

"I'm right on the fence," Norman agreed. "Have been for a couple of weeks. I was hoping you two would help me decide one way or the other—"

"—and instead, he who defecates in arboreal regions here tried to play dumb. And you let him," Minnie said. "And now he and I are being as neutral as we can manage. All right, you're doing great, keep going: Why are we being neutral?"

"Because I've got a job and responsibilities, and if you agree with me that Switzerland is the key, I'd dump the job in a minute and blow my career on a hunch. And you're friends, so you don't want—"

"Think again," the Bear said grimly.

Norman looked puzzled.

"Brother," the Bear went on, "if that's the only reason you can think of, I just got you down off that fence. On this side."

"I don't follow."

"Exactly. Look, postulate Jacques. For reasons unknown he reaches across an ocean, locates a particular person without the slightest difficulty, leaving no trail, and puts on her a snatch so perfect that a pro like Amesby doesn't smell him. Jacques tap-dances around everybody from Interpol on down and vanishes without a trace. Now tell me, and this will sting a little but hang on, it's the killer: *What has a guy like that got to fear from an English teacher?*"

Norman opened his mouth, closed it, and seemed to deflate. He looked down. "I can take care of myself."

"Norman, look at me. Listen to me. We were in cocky khaki together, and I'll certify that you were sudden death with both hands, okay? Just looking at you I can see that you're in real good shape, maybe *almost* as good as you were when you were a kid, even. Norman, our whole platoon couldn't have made Jacques uneasy. Not with full combat ordnance and the air support we never used to get. The *best* you can accomplish is quick suicide."

Norman's face was in his hands. "But Bear," he said hoarsely, *"she could still be alive."*

"Certainly. That's why suicide is the best you could accomplish. Look, if he's got her, best guess is she's involved in something he wants kept secret with a capital S. If she's still alive, it's because he doesn't absolutely need her to be dead. But if *you* come poking around . . ."

"But maybe I could—"

"FORGET IT, NORMAN!" the Bear thundered, and furniture danced.

"Your subconscious made the right decision," Minnie went on in what seemed a murmur by comparison, "even if it didn't keep you informed. There is nothing you can do that will help. We could all be wrong—it might be a nut that got your sister—and if so there's no point in blowing your job. If we're right you might endanger Maddy. If you ever get *proof* that she's dead, and that a Swiss did it, *then* maybe I'd say it's time to go lose your life in something too big for you. But not now—you don't dare."

Norman was silent.

The Bear shifted his weight uneasily. "My dear, a while back you said you had two suggestions. I've only heard one."

Minnie's face lost all expression. "There's only one thing you can do, Norman."

"Go on," he said.

"Kill her."

Norman jumped.

Her voice was mercilessly hard. "Sit back in a comfortable chair. Get thoroughly stoned. Pick a psycho killer from Central Casting and replay Madeleine's murder in your mind. In complete and vivid detail, 3-D stereo, a couple of instant replays. Feel the pain and the fear and the *unfairness* of it. Pick a possible method of corpse disposal and walk him through it—say, he walks her out onto the McDonald Bridge to where he has wire and weights waiting. Picture her drifting in the currents under the harbor, bloating and being chewed, and when the horror is more than you can bear, cut it off. Sharp. Get drunk. Have her declared dead, and have a symbolic funeral. Picture her *in* that empty coffin, throw flowers on it, and begin formal mourning. Say goodbye to her in your heart, Norman, and get on with your own life. Pray that they catch the poor crazy before he does it again, but *say goodbye to Maddy*.

"Otherwise you'll—" She caught herself. "You could crack."

Norman sat perfectly still, features expressionless. But his skin was pale and his palms were sweaty. There was a moment of silence.

"God, this is depressing," the Bear boomed finally. "What a party. Let's talk about something cheerful for a change. How'd your marriage come apart?"

Norman broke up, and his friends joined him. The laugh went on for some time, faltered, steadied, became one of the great laughs, one of those where every time it starts to pause for breath, someone gasps out another punchline and it's off again. A great laugh with the Bear participating took on epic proportions.

Whereafter in due course Norman documented the decline and fall of his marriage, Minnie described life in the Neuro Ward of a big-city hospital, and the Bear narrated an intricate and hilarious story of revenge on a critic, which had generated income as a side effect. Having compared the water lately gone under their respective bridges, they let their conversation become more general, and by the time the brandy was annihilated and they had switched to Irish coffee they had remembered and retold all the jokes, puns, and anecdotes they had been saving for each other, and were waxing philosophical. The Bear propounded his Leech Theory of Economic Dislocation: arguing that no organism can survive without some control of the size of its parasites, he called for the establishment of a legal Maximum Wage. Then Minnie tried to explain in layman's terms why the researchers attempting to crack the information-storage code of the human brain, who had been so confident fifteen years before, were now frankly stymied.

That triggered Norman to bring up the newest and most alarming campus problem: a few students were having a plug surgically inserted in the skull, which allowed direct stimulus of the hypothalamus. Wireheading baffled Norman to the soles of his feet, and he said so. Minnie spoke at length about medical and psychological aspects of the new phenomenon, and the Bear described it as the natural bastard child of the two cultural imperatives *be happy* and *be efficient,* with a postscript on why wireheading would *not* be made illegal as lysergic acid had been forty years before. That led them into recounting old drug experiences, which they gradually came to realize everyone present had already heard anyway, and by then the coffeepot was empty and the hour was late. Norman showed them the guest room, bathroom, and location of breakfast makings, hugs were again exchanged, and all three went to bed.

Norman hovered on the edge of sleep for what seemed a long time before he heard his door click open. He rolled over slowly, and found his arms full of Minnie.

"Where's Bear?" he asked sleepily.

"Too tired," she whispered. "Heavy driving plus heavy drinking zonks him out. Just as well, this bed's too small anyway."

"Heavy drinking zonks me out too."

Her lips touched him delicately at a place where neck joined shoulders, and simultaneously two of her fingernails found a certain precise spot with a facility that, all things considered, implied either terrific tactile memory or a high compliment. She pulled back and examined the results. "Wrong."

"Uh, I take a long time when I'm drunk."

"No, love. You *give* a long time when you're drunk. I remember. Now stop being so fucking polite and shut up."

"Make me," he punned, and she did.

❖6❖

2011

I SAT THERE for an indeterminate time after Karen had left, paralyzed by internal confusion: the slipping-transmission phenomenon
mentioned earlier, except that now there were *several* thought loops
cycling simultaneously. Intuitively I felt that something urgent needed
doing, but I could not for the life of me imagine what it might be.

No matter how many times I ran it through, I got the same answer:
I had discharged all my moral obligations to Karen Scholz. She and I
were square, all debts paid. I had meddled in her suicide, an immoral
act. In reparation I had done all I could to ease her transition back
into living. I had made her a present of my most essential secrets,
given her the power to tamper with my own obituary date if she so
chose. I had supported and maintained her at the absolute peak of
creature comfort while she took stock and decided what to do next.
When what she came up with was a more elaborate form of suicide,
I had done my best to talk her out of it. Perhaps I had been small in
refusing to get the computer readings she wanted, but the procedure
really was uniquely dangerous for me, and any of a dozen other
professionals in New York could oblige her with less risk.

She would have her crusade, and perhaps she would manage to die
with joy, and perhaps it *would* be better than dying with pleasure.

In my case, it was her choice and my responsibility was ended. It
saddened me that she intended to kamikaze, but I had no rights in
the matter. She had made it plain that she did not want my advice or
assistance. Case closed. Exit Karen, urinating.

Exit Karen.

Yes, that was the way of it; she would surely fall. As a fighter she was all heart and no style at all; they would crush her like a bug. More likely sooner than later. Doña Quixote on a spavined horse, armored in rust, fielding a balsa lance against a twenty-megawatt, high-torque Wind Energy Module, in defense of righteousness. In defense of the right of people not to be tempted to their deaths. She wanted to slay the Sirens, she who had heard their Song and lived.

She was welcome to try. If she saw herself as Doña Quixote, that was her business. I saw no percentage in playing Pancho Sanza. I am not capable of that kind of love. I think I was once, but something happened to me in a jungle. Enough brushes with death will permanently inhibit your urge to place your life on the line for *any* cause. When that final day came, when I heard the click-snap-*spung!* and saw the mine pop up to head height and ducked to try and take it on the helmet, I had a very clear idea of the sacrifice I had made for my country. When, much later, I discovered that I had survived the event, and the war, it left a lasting impression. As Monsieur Rick said, I stick my neck out for nobody. (And I *never* burgle veterans.)

Furthermore, I was not at all certain that I approved of her crusade. If I had been wrong to meddle in her suicide, what right had she to tamper with the suicides of the hundreds, perhaps thousands, who would plug themselves in over the next few years? People *wanted* juice rigs. It seemed to me a self-correcting problem: in a few generations all the people who could be tempted by pushbutton ecstasy would be bred out of the race.

People like Karen . . .

Who, let's face it, was a loser. The term *loser* does not necessarily denote incompetence, stupidity, or major personality defect. It says that you lose a lot. She had been, through no fault of hers that I could discern, consistently unlucky all her life long. That can break even the toughest fighting spirit.

Perhaps wireheading bred the race not just for competence and survival drive . . . but for luck?

If so, was I *that* strict a Malthusian? Misfortune was no stranger to me, and might remember me at any moment. Out there in the jungle I had smoked opium admixed with heroin, though I had known it was insane. What would I have done if someone had offered me a juice rig then? What would any of us in my unit have done?

This was stupid. Stipulating that the existence of the wirehead trade was undesirable, Karen's silly secret-agent stunt was the wrong way to go about abolishing it. Lone operators do not bring down big multinationals. At best she would bring about a restructuring of personnel, a redivision of the pie. I did not see *any* effective way to put the egg back into the shell. Certainly, prohibiting wireheading could accomplish nothing useful, and I couldn't design an effective way to regulate it.

Regardless of whether or not I could see any right answer, I knew Karen's way was a wrong answer. So I certainly did not want to chase after her to join her. There was no point in chasing after her to try and dissuade her; I'd had one fair try at that and failed. And there was no way in hell I was going to chase after her and forcibly restrain her. I had, in short, no visible motive to chase after her.

And I wanted to get up from my chair and track her. It scared me to death.

If we had even once made love, or even fucked, I could have attributed it to my glands. I had never so much as had an erection over her.

What in *Hell's* name was wrong with me?

After a time I got tired of running it through, and decided to snap out of it. Find something useful to do.

It was not hard. As soon as I let my eyes see what they were looking at, my search was ended. My television was a total loss. Its gaping glassfanged face had long since ceased to drool good gin on the carpet beneath. The air conditioning had left only a memory of a very bad smell.

I got up and dried the carpet, cleaned up the glass, and disconnected the tube from the system, not bothering to reset all the tripped circuit breakers. The way I had it wired, not only had I lost phone, commercial and cable TV programming, computer display and storyscreen, but I would not have stereo until I could scare up some more patchcords. The most efficient system design is not necessarily the best. All I had left was books and booze.

So the first thing to do . . . no, the first was to dispose of the dead telly. That took me fifteen minutes. The *second* was to steal another.

It was a good plan. It steadied my mind, for while I am working I do not chew over my problems. I give it my full attention, by long habit.

First I had my computer ask the power company computer for a list of customers whose power-consumption profile had been identical for more than five consecutive days, just as usual save that I had to work with printouts instead of display. When the list was filed down to a twenty-block radius from my home turf, it contained eighteen possibles. I had the computer dial all eighteen phone numbers and strike from the list those that had a record-a-message program active. Those absentee tenants probably planned to be home soon. The no-answers numbered seven. I asked the NYPD computer for information on defensive structures of those seven buildings, and selected the one that was hardest to crack. That tenant would have the most expensive TV. Standard procedure would then have been to tell that building's security cameras to recognize me as a bona fide tenant, and take it from there. But this particular building also employed live guards in the lobby. Still no problem: the pigeon had recorded a message-program in his own voice, it just wasn't in service. I hooked in the voder and had my computer use his phone and a fair imitation of his voice to call downstairs. It told the door guard to expect a TV repairman from TH Electronics. The guard welcomed it home, and it thanked him. It hung up and printed out a work order for me.

My computer has so many interesting capabilities that to use it for something as trivial as grand larceny is almost a crime. But to exploit anything like its full potential I would have to compromise an even greater asset: invisibility. I am the man no one is looking for, and I like that a lot.

I am deeply curious to know more about the extraordinary person who had that machine built and programmed. Almost I yearn to meet him or her. My recurring fear is that I shall: intuitively I know I would not survive the encounter.

But surely he or she must be long dead. That's what I tell myself when I wake up sweaty.

I wiped all records of my transactions at both ends, stood up, and got disguise number four from the closet. Faded green coveralls, a GI jungle cap, grimy work boots laced with speaker cable, a tool belt that would have made Batman laugh out loud, and a stained shoulder satchel bulging with assorted electronic testing gear. I checked the picture ID in the wallet that went with the outfit, and corrected my facial appearance to match. It is a part of my job I really enjoy: trying on new faces. None of them, even the one I start and end with, ever looks familiar. I can't imagine what would.

I spilled coffee on the work order, blotted it with a dirty cloth, wadded it up and stuffed it in my breast pocket, and left. I was back within two hours with the tube and a couple of interesting audiocassettes from the van I'd clouted. I wired the new glass teat into the system, ran a few tests, and made a few adjustments. I punched for news display and sat down in front of it. I had the chair make me a bourbon and distilled water. After two sips I killed the news readout and concentrated on the drink. I had nearly finished it before I allowed myself to ask me:

What is the *next* thing to do?

(Follow Karen, of course. Do what you said earlier: play along and wait for her own momentum to falter, then give her something to distract her attention. Once she gets the readings she wants from someone else, the immediate danger to you is past.)

Yeah, but getting those readings from *anybody* could make *her* hot. I could catch something meant for her.

(Yeah, you're really hooked on a safe, sedentary lifestyle. I can see that.)

All right, I find a moderate amount of risk stimulating . . .

(And you won't do something stimulating to save a friend's neck?)

But how do I know she'd let me—

(She's used to you meddling in her life. For some reason she doesn't mind.)

Yeah. Father figure.

(Okay, jerk. You adopted her. Be a responsible father. You're *in loco parentis,* just like—)

Hiatus.

I was sitting at the keyboard, fingers at rest on my lap. I didn't recall resolving the internal debate, but evidently my subconscious thought it was settled. I even had some idea what I intended to program. Instead I swore, spun the chair around, hugged myself, and folded over until I hit the floor. My mouth was wide open, my teeth clenched tight, my forehead knotted, and I snarled softly in the back of my throat. When I could, I pounded the rug with my fist and wept.

I *hate* them. Those sudden gaps in my life, those sudden jump-cuts like slipshod editing, like little bits of tape snipped out of my recording. It must be much like this to have epilepsy, except that I never seem to convulse, or hurt myself while I'm blacked out. Some sort of automatic pilot cuts in; other people rarely even notice. But I resent those missing bits of tape. One of them is six years long.

It all comes of being careless in jungles, I guess.

I was pretty used to it by now. I rarely threw that kind of frustration tantrum anymore, *never* when I was not alone. But I was about to involve myself in something that I could sense was much more dangerous than my average heist and it was maddening to be reminded that I did not have guaranteed access to my own brains.

But eventually I had cursed and cried out all the fury and frustration. I got up off the rug and sat back down at the keyboard. I had wasted enough time.

Karen's credit account showed no activity, either savings or charge, since she had left her apartment to move in with me. She had left my place with enough cash to rent a flop, but she had not yet paid a deposit to a keyboard man. I set up a monitor on her credit, so that when she did pay I would know who she hired. I knew, or knew of, perhaps half the boys in town, and I could locate the rest and pick up her trail. If she paid in advance, as she almost certainly would have to, there was an excellent chance I could "tap the line" and listen in on whatever her operator found out. That would be less dangerous than initiating the probe myself—although more dangerous than simply trying to trail her physically from the site. If her operator *did* trip a guard program, it might be sophisticated enough to notice me "listening on the extension." I wondered if it was worth the risk. If I knew what she knew, I could figure the first place she'd go and get there first, be waiting for her. It would be a good argument for taking me on as a partner.

I realized something and cursed. Karen didn't have to touch her credit. If no friend was willing to lend her a couple hundred, she would surely know how to locate at least a few of her regular customers. They would be happy to make any requested donation, and they would *prefer* to use cash. I wasn't thinking clearly.

Damn it, that left me flat. There was nothing she had to do that had to appear somewhere in the network. She could get her sightings, pick a target, and skip town without leaving a trace in the system. She couldn't get through a dragnet, but I am not a dragnet. I could not find Karen if she did not wish to be found, not quickly anyway.

Perhaps I would after all have to run the inquiry program she had asked me for.

That decision could be postponed. "If she did not wish to be found . . ." That was the key. I suddenly recalled the wording of the goodbye message she had scrawled on my toilet seat; she had *not* written, "Don't bother to try and come after me." Could I assume that she was trying to prevent me from trailing her?

I decided to see how the hand played out. I left my watchdog program monitoring her credit account, wired to light and sound alarms. Any withdrawal or deposit would bring me out of a sound sleep. If she wanted to be found, or didn't care one way or the other, she'd trip that alarm. If she was actively trying to shake me off, if she hadn't touched her credit or reentered her apartment within, say, twenty-four hours . . . well, then I could sit down and decide whether I wanted to catch up with her badly enough to stick my neck out. I told her apartment terminal to notify me if it was used.

I nodded and got up from my terminal, rotating my head to pop my neck. What's the *next* thing to do?

It was a tight contest between go *to sleep* and *get piefaced drunk*. I didn't feel remotely sleepy, and I didn't want to answer that alarm drunk or hung over. But finally I was forced to admit that I was so wound up I would probably be more effective hung over. And I might not have to answer any alarm . . .

Nor did I. The hangover was somewhere between average and classic. I could find no music that would soothe it. Finally I gave up and took aspirin. It muted the headache and increased the queasiness. I let the Lounger rub my neck for almost an hour, and as my strength came trickling back I used it to get agitated again. After a while I became aware that I had for the past ten minutes been composing variations on the expression "hair of the dog." Puppy fuzz. Cur fur. Pug rug. *Toupé du chien.* I said a powerful word out loud and went out for a walk. I knew I would not drink among strangers—and I wanted to go see some people, in the same way that other people infrequently feel like going to the zoo.

And on the streets I found signs and wonders, things strange and different. I saw a man with one leg walking a dog with three. I saw two women dancing together on the roof of a station wagon; oddly, neither one seemed to be enjoying it. I passed three young toughs in leather and mylar, cheeks tattooed and noses pierced, the oldest of them perhaps fourteen. (This is the first generation of "juvenile delinquents" whose resignation from society is irrevocable. They cannot change their minds when they get older. It will be interesting to see how that works out.) I saw a pimp feeding cocaine to his golden retriever. On a sloping street I saw a short squat ancient woman in a black print dress and babushka stop on the opposite sidewalk, sigh, squat a little more, and begin urinating copiously. A vast puddle gathered at her feet and rushed down the hill. I stood frozen, as though at some personal religious revelation, vouchsafed to me alone. It was not that everyone else on that street ignored the woman. They literally did not see her. People sidestepped the rushing river without noticing it. The hair stood up on the back of my neck and my head throbbed. The old woman urinated for a full minute; then the flood cased, she straightened, sighed again, and resumed walking uphill, leaving damp footprints of orthopedic shoes. A few minutes later I shook off my trance and resumed my own walk.

I passed a sidewalk cockfight; noticed that they were betting Old dollars. I passed an alley in which a young whore was on her knees before a cop, paying her weekly insurance premium. He was looking at his watch. I passed six pawnshops in a row, then a political party's precinct headquarters, then four pornshops in a row. I rounded a corner and nearly tripped over a wirehead sitting on the sidewalk in front of a hole-in-the-wall hardware store.

He was new to it: the hair had not yet grown in around his droud, and he had obviously just learned the one about wiring in a third battery to produce a threshold overdose. He grinned at me and I saw Karen in his face. I hurried past; almost immediately my stomach knotted and I had to sit down on a stoop with my face in my hands. Out of the corner of my eye I saw the hardware shop proprietor stick his head out of his shop, look around furtively. He bent over the wirehead and extracted his wallet. The boy blinked up at him, grinning, then suddenly understood and roared with laughter. "Right, man," he said, "square deal," and he laughed and laughed.

I found myself walking toward the proprietor with no idea why.

He flinched when he saw me, flinched again when he saw my face, then became aggressive. "This man owes me money—you just heard him say so. Mind your own—" He shifted gears, held out the wallet, and said "please," and then I jacked one up under his ribs, his gut should feel like mine.

As he went down and backwards the wallet flew into my hands. I took all the money that was in it and tore it into tiny shreds, tossed the shreds down a sewer. The wirehead laughed and laughed. I threw the wallet in his face and walked away. Behind me I could hear him, ripping up all his identification and photos and giggling.

I bought a Coke at a dog-stand. It tasted like burned sugar. I used it to wash down four drugstore aspirins and decided to go home and check my alarms. Automatically I took a different route toward home, and so passed something genuinely unique:

A wirehead shop with a large sign taped in its window saying "FREE SAMPLES."

I stopped in my tracks and stared at that sign.

Free samples? How in God's name could you give free samples of radical neurosurgery? *And what if it were true?*

I entered the shop.

The shock doc was old and thin and red-nosed. His clothes were baggy everywhere they weren't shiny. His hands shook at rest. They were almost the only sign of life; his face and eyes looked newly dead. A potential customer was gibbering and gesticulating at him like a speed freak, babbling something about installment plans, and he was not reacting in any way at all, not laughing or anything. Eventually the customer realized he was wasting his time and went for his gun. It was a sure sign that he was stone crazy—was he going to hold a gun on the doc through surgery?—and I started to backflip out the door. But the doc stood his ground; one of those shaking hands shot up and slapped the man, *crack, crack,* forehand and backhand. They stared at each other over the gun. The excited man was no longer excited, he was quite calm. He put his piece away, spun, and brushed past me on his way out. His expression made me think of Moses traveling away from the Promised Land. When I turned back to the doc he was giving me precisely the same dead stare he had given my predecessor.

Now I noticed that his other hand was in his pocket. It was not alone in there. He looked me over very carefully before he took it out, empty.

I was doing my best to look like a man at the very end of his rope; con man's chameleon reflex. The room helped. Surely to God his operating theater was bright and well lit, but this office-anteroom was dingy and dark and depressing as hell. Unnaturally depressing; I suspected subsonics at high gain. The predominant color was black, and it's not true that a black wall can't look dirty. Even the storefront window was blacked over; the only illumination came from a forty-watt bulb on the ceiling. There was no decor. Behind the doc an L-shaped affair that might have been either a counter or a desk grew out of the wall, a chair on either side. One had to pass the thing to get to the door that must lead to the operating theater. On the opposite side of the doorway from the desk was a tall steel cabinet with a good lock. A black box sat on top of the desk, and connected to it by telephone cord was what looked like an oversized black army helmet.

I shuffled my feet. "I, uh . . . good, uh . . ."

"You saw the new sign and you want to ask me some questions," he said. His voice was flat, sepulchral. "That sign is going to make me rich."

I have known cripples and cops and killers, people who *must* learn how to get numb and stay that way, and I have never met anyone remotely so inhuman as that man. It was impossible to picture him as a child.

"I, uh, always understood there was no way to . . ."

"Until this year that was correct," he agreed. "It still can't be done anywhere but here. Yet. The device that makes it possible is my own invention." He displayed no visible sign of pride. Or, for that matter, shame.

"How does it, uh . . . ?"

"It is based on inductance principles. I do not intend to discuss it further. My patent application went in this week; that sign has only been up for an hour."

"Well, but I mean, how would I . . ." I trailed off.

He stared at me for a long time, hands shaking. "Step over there against that wall. Behind the sonoscope."

Hesitantly, heavily, I obeyed. The sonoscope looked just like the one in every emergency room, rather like an old fluoroscope, except that the face of the display had a fine-mesh grid inscribed on it. I stood in the proper spot while he candled my head with ultrasonics. He grunted at his first look. "Trauma there. And there."

I nodded. "War wound."

"Hold your head still. I will have to offset the droud a bit—"

"Hey, listen," I interrupted, "I'm not sure I'm going to do this. I just—"

His shoulders slumped a little more. "Of course. The sample first. This way."

He led me to the desk counter, sat me down, and went around behind it. He made three adjustments to the black box, one to the inside of the "army helmet." He passed it to me. "Put this on. That way front."

I eyed it dubiously.

He did not sigh. "When I activate this unit, it will set up a localized inductance field in the area where I calculate your medial forebrain bundle to be. For a period of five seconds you will experience intense pleasure. The effect will be almost precisely half as strong as that produced by a conventional droud from standard house current."

"What if my medial thing isn't where everybody else's is?"

"That is unlikely. If so, the most probable result would be that you would feel nothing, and I would recalibrate and try again."

"What about *least* probable? Are there any potentially dangerous near-misses?"

"Not lethal ones, no. There is a chance, which I compute as less than five percent, that you might experience a feeling of either intense heat or intense cold. If so, tell me and I'll disconnect."

"This thing has been tested a lot?" I temporized. "I mean, you said your patent thing just went in this week."

"Exhaustively tested, by me, for a year at Bellevue."

I raised an eyebrow. "Volunteers?"

"Mental patients." No, in other words.

I kept on looking at the damned helmet.

What was I doing here? Research? Investigating the subject of Karen's crusade, so that I could understand it better, understand her better? What was to be gained here that was worth sticking my head into a giant homemade light socket?

Was it really that tempting? To know pure pleasure for once, for just this once, to let go all the way and find out what happens when you let go? If I did let go, could I find my way back?

"Doctor, do you consider conventional wireheading addictive?"

He didn't flinch. "Yes."

"Is *this* addictive?"

"No."

"Is it habituating?"

"It can't be. One free sample per customer. I am not a candy store."

I had a thought. "Can you cut it back to one-*quarter* droud strength?"

"Yes. That would still be your only sample."

Still I waited and debated. He was making no slightest effort to influence my decision either way, or to hurry it along. He was dead. I thought of Karen in the harsh light of her living room lamp, and of the young wirehead I had left shredding his identification. I thought of what Karen wanted to do. She wanted to commit financial and/or physical violence on the people who ran this industry. She wanted to abolish this practice. I intended to try and con her out of it. *I had to know what it was like.*

I put my hands on the helmet, and I closed my eyes and tried to imagine what ecstasy would feel like, and—

Hiatus.

I was halfway out of my chair, rising, spinning toward the door, all in slow motion. The helmet was in mid-bounce. Just before the shock doc's face slid out of my peripheral vision, I thought I saw the mildest, most feeble trace of relief flicker across it. I was conscious of every muscle-action of running toward the exit. Someone was screaming; I didn't know his name. My time sense was so stretched out that I was able to open the door at a dead run, leaning out to pull it towards me, yanking my torso back away from it as it opened, pivoting on the handle so that I flung myself into the street. I hit the pavement feet first, perfectly banked for my turn; after three skidding steps I had my stride back and within ten I was settled into it. Shortly I had to brake for a busy intersection. As I did, my time sense suddenly snapped back to normal. I sat down on the curb, rushing traffic a meter from my shoes, and bent over and puked and puked into the gutter. The nausea lasted, off and on, through four or five light-changes. When it passed I sat there for another couple, and then I heard cat feet approaching and looked up to see who was desperate enough to roll a drunk in broad daylight. So I happened to be looking in the direction of the wireshop, a full block behind me, when its front wall danced across the street, hotly pursued by brightness intolerable, and struck the vacant storefront opposite like some monstrous charge of Brobdingnagian buckshot.

I flung myself back and sideways, away from traffic and into blast shadow, and the sound reached me as my face hit the pavement. I stayed down until it seemed like everything that was in the air had landed, then rolled to my feet fast.

My would-be mugger was glancing back and forth from me to the smoking wreckage, clearly of two minds. I put my hand on my gun butt. "Not today," I said, and he licked his lips and sprinted for the shop. He had delayed too long; five or ten people were already gingerly entering the store, wrapping various things around their hands so they wouldn't burn their fingers. They were a gang; two of them stood guard.

I joined the rest of the crowd. We stayed a half-block away on either side and stared and cursed the looters for getting there first and swapped completely bogus eyewitness reports. I decided it probably had not been an accidental explosion. It had taken artistry and skill to place a charge that would utterly wreck the wireshop without bringing down the floors above or seriously damaging the adjoining buildings. God is an iron, but He is seldom that finicky in his irony. That left me in three simultaneous states of mind. I was impressed. I was scared. And, strongest of all—

I was enormously intrigued.

I made my way home quickly, and when I smiled at President Kennedy he winked his *left* eye. I had a guest. One that Kennedy had recognized and admitted, or he would have winked both eyes several times. I am allergic to surprises, and never more so than that afternoon. My first thought was that anyone smart enough to crack my house was smart enough to tell the President which eye to wink. I wondered why I had never thought of that. I pulled my gun and made sure the collar wasn't in the way of the knife and told myself that it was purest paranoia to think the wireshop bombing could have anything to do with me. The hypothesis yielded a bomber of infinite resources, great ingenuity, and complete incompetence. More likely my guest was the Fader, who was about due. Or Old Jake, come with his guitar to play me a new song . . .

And when the door raised itself, music did indeed come drifting up the stairs. But it wasn't Old Jake. It was the Yardbird, these fifty-six years dead.

Whoever was down there was a friend.

It was Karen who sat in my living room, crosslegged on her usual chair. Even if the music had masked the sounds of my arrival she could not have helped seeing me peripherally, but she gave no sign, kept staring at the place where the far wall met the ceiling. I sat down quietly in the other Lounger, dialing for tea.

She was listening to one of the last Dial sessions at WOR, in '47, when Bird finally got the band he wanted in New York. Miles and Max Roach and Duke Jordan. And all the smack he wanted. There's a Mingus piece, usually called "Gunslingin' Bird," whose full title is "If Charlie Parker Was a Gunslinger, There'd Be a Lot of Dead Copycats." As my tea arrived, the thought jumped into my head: if Charlie Parker had been a wirehead, all those copycats would have had to work for a living.

When the last note of "Bird of Paradise" cut off, and not a moment before, Karen turned the stereo not down, but off. I remembered that the Fader had liked her.

"Hi, Joe."

"Hello, Karen."

"Anticlimax. The runaway child comes back home."

"Why?"

She took her time answering. "I don't know if I can put it into words. You . . . you've done . . . a lot for me, and, that means that you must . . . care about me some and I'm gonna go do something that's gonna get sticky and you wanted to talk me out of it and I didn't give you a *chance*, I got defensive and took it personal and cut you right off." She paused for air. "I mean, I'm gonna do this anyway but I just thought you'd feel better if you did your best to talk me out of it first, you know, like you'd be easier in your mind. It was wrong of me to leave like that, it was . . . it was like . . ." She was slowing down again.

". . . like not caring about *you*."

I was looking at my hands. "And you're not afraid I'll try to prevent you?"

"No. You're not my father."

"Have you hired a reader yet?"

"Not yet. I've been thinking."

I looked up and met her gaze. I had decided on the way home. "Good. You don't need one anymore."

She twitched her shoulders violently. "I—you—but—" She stopped herself and closed her eyes. She drew in a big lungful of air, pursed her lips, and blew it sl-o-owly through her teeth, *ssshh-hooooooo*, did it again slower. Then she opened her eyes and said, "Thank you, Joe."

My hangover was gone.

"When do we start?" she asked after a moment.

"Have you eaten?"

"I brought cornbread, and some pretty good preserves, and some Java coffee."

"We start after brunch."

As we were setting the table she took me by the shoulders and looked at me for a long moment. Her expression was faintly quizzical. Suddenly she closed in and came up on tiptoe and was kissing me thoroughly, her fingers digging into the back of my head. I had salad bowls in either hand and could neither resist nor cooperate. She did not kiss me the way a whore kisses her biggest spender. She kissed me the way a wife kisses a husband who remembered their fifth anni—

Hiatus.

She was two meters away, leaning back against the wall with her hands outspread. Her eyes were round. Salad dressing stained her blouse and dripped from her cheek, and there was lettuce all to hell and gone between us. I looked up at the ceiling. "Dammit," I cried bitterly, *"that* one wasn't fair!"

"Joe, I'm sorry, I'm sorry, I didn't—"

"I wasn't talking to you!" I stopped myself. I tried her exhaling trick and it helped a lot. "Karen, *I'm sorry.* That had nothing to do with you, nothing at all. It was—"

"I know. Somebody in your past."

I shrugged. "It could be. I honestly don't know." I told her about my blackout condition. I had never told anyone before—but she and I were going to go to war together, and she had a right to know.

When I was done explaining, all she said was, "Let me see if there's a safe dosage," and then she came into my arms and hugged me and kissed me, the way a friend kisses a friend, and that was just fine.

And we ate, and that was just fine too, and then we adjourned to the living room. Where I pulled the keyboard out of the wall recess and heated it up. And the next two hours were interesting indeed.

There are many better keyboard men than me. I came quite late to hacking, and will never have the genius level of aptitude that some are born with. On my good days I consider myself a talented amateur. There are enormous holes in my knowledge of computers, and probably always will be. But blind chance gifted me with a computer the equal of any in North America, with programmed-in owner's manual, at a point in my life during which I had nothing better to do than study it. It is so supple and flexible a machine that I have never been tempted to anthropomorphize it. It can interface with almost any network while remaining effectively invisible. Its own capacity is four terabytes, four times ten to the twelfth bytes.

Karen watched for the first half hour, but after the first ten minutes she was just being polite. Finally I told her to go dig Bird on the head-phones, and she did. At that point I was only puzzled. Subsequently I did some things with that most versatile of computers that would have shocked the IRS, a few that would have fascinated the CIA, and even one or two that might have surprised the computer's original owner if he or she were still alive. I went from puzzled through intrigued to mystified, stayed there for about an hour, then moved on to baffled, proceeding almost at once to frustrated. Karen heard me swearing and came over to sit wordlessly beside me with her hand at the base of my neck. Within another fifteen minutes, frustrated modulated into vaguely alarmed, and stayed there.

Finally I ordered hard copy printout and cleared. "'You got it, buddy,'" I growled in my best Tom Waits imitation. "'The large print giveth, and the small print taketh away.'"

"What is it, Joe?"

"I'm damned if I know, and I'm sure I can't explain it very well. You haven't studied economics, let alone business economics.

It's—" I broke off, groping for an analogy within her experience. "Like a motorcycle. You can break down what a motorcycle does, chart the path and interaction of different forces and materials, follow the power flow. If you can visualize the motorcycle as a series of power relationships, you can locate its weak points—where it can be most disabled with least effort. That's what I've been trying to do with the wirehead industry. But I can't get a computer-model that *works*. If you built a motorcycle like this it would whistle 'Night In Tunisia,' make a pot of coffee, and explode. I can't make sense of the power flow . . . and it seems to have only the most peripheral relationship to the money flow . . . damn it, there's nothing the IRS could object to. Stupidity isn't illegal. But it just . . . *feels* wrong, feels like something is being juggled. But I can't understand how or why or by whom. That makes me highly nervous."

"So, since you can't diagram out this motorcycle, you can't find the weak points?"

"I can't be sure. We've got to get inside and nose around, learn things that aren't in *any* computer. Field work."

She nodded. "Fine. *Where?*"

"That's another problem. There are three major corporations, as your source told you—and by the way, if two of them *are* really the same outfit, I can't prove it. We might get useful information at any of three places."

"Where?"

"Germany, Switzerland, Nova Scotia."

"Which is better?"

"The biggest outfit is the West German one, in Hamburg. That'd be the hardest to crack. I don't speak German—"

"I do."

"Point. The smallest of the three, and that ain't small, is in Geneva. We can get by with English in Switzerland but I think there's the least information to be had there. The middle-size bear is in Halifax—"

". . . and the Canadian border is a joke. That settles that. My stuff's still where I left it? I'll pack."

"Yes, do that," I said, and set immediately to making my own preparations for departure. I wasn't sure why she was impatient to be going, but I knew why I was. I could not shake the nagging fear that I had tripped some subtle watchdog program without knowing it.

There are ways to avoid being backtracked, and I believed I knew the best ones.

But I wasn't positive.

We took four days getting to Halifax. We had to keep changing vehicles, and one does not want to enter a strange city exhausted from travel. Especially not if one wishes to vanish as quickly as possible into the shadows of that strange city. We found a cheap apartment house that still accepted cash in the old part of town, on a sorry, broken-down sin-strip called Gottingen Street. If you went up on the roof you could see the harbor and the bridge to Dartmouth. You could also leave the building in any of three directions without special equipment, which was what closed the deal. We took a year's lease on a two bedroom as Mr. and Mrs. Something-or-Other, and by the time I hitchhiked back from where I'd dumped our final car, Karen had us unpacked and food in the fridge, coffee made.

"Oh, Joe, this is exciting. This town is so strange; I think I'm going to like it. Let's go for a walk and plan our first move."

"Wait," I said. "I don't think we should do either one just yet. I haven't needed to bring this up until now, but . . . let me tell you what happened to me on my last walk in New York." I did not do that, but I did give a brief outline of the wireshop incident. Her eyes were wide when I was done. "Do you see what I mean? It has the same *wrong* feel as I got when I took the readouts. That zombie was no genius inventor. When I saw that homemade helmet of his, I couldn't believe someone else hadn't thought of it five years ago. Hell, they could have built one of those in the eighties. But he had the only one I ever heard of. And he got blown away, along with the Mark I, the week his patent application went in—" I broke off and frowned. "You *can't* burgle the Patent Office's computer files. But maybe I can find out whether anyone has made official inquiries through channels about that particular patent. That's public record."

Before I had left my home I'd had my computer select three different acceptable but unused phone numbers in Halifax, diddle the Atlantic Tel computer into believing they were high-credit subscribers in good standing, initiate conference calls from all three, and leave those circuits open, on standby. Why not? I wasn't paying for it. I dialed one of those numbers now, and when I was put through I got out the portable terminal I travel with and clipped its squeaker to the phone. I was interfaced with my home computer.

I asked it my questions, frowned, and rephrased my questions. This time I got an answer, and it couldn't have been on screen for more than three seconds before I was ordering the computer to break circuit, wasting that means of access. I was scared enough to wet my pants.

"There is no such application on file," I said in a shaky voice. "No patent remotely related to wireheading or inductance or anything to do with the goddam brain has been sought by anybody in the last year. Current to three o'clock this afternoon."

"So either that shock doc was stone crazy—"

"Or someone can subvert the U.S. Patent Office. And we know about it. God's teeth. The only people with interest enough and leverage enough are the big wirehead outfits—and why the hell would they take risks like that to suppress something that would probably triple their income or better?"

"Jesus."

"It's wrong, it feels wrong, it's all just . . . *off*. And I'm getting very nervous. Let's *not* go for that walk."

We watched TV instead, curled up in the master bedroom, until we fell asleep. I slept poorly. Bad dreams.

When a week had gone by without incident or alarm, I began to relax. Until that time we made believe that we had never heard of wireheading, and kept to ourselves. We talked a lot. The entertainment facilities of our room were a joke, and I was not going to call home again until and unless I had to. Part of our talk involved practical matters of planning, a good many hours inasmuch as we had almost nothing to go on. We were able to kill much time inventing new contingencies. But there was a limit to how far we could stretch that, and finally there was nothing left for us to talk about except the stories of our lives.

Karen started it. She talked about her childhood, starting with the happy parts because they came first chronologically. They didn't last long. Her father had been a monster in almost a biological sense. She told me a great deal about him over the course of perhaps a week, first in a two-hour monologue she ended by vomiting to exhaustion, and then in a series of long conversations that wandered everywhere but always led back sooner or later to that extraordinary man. I use that last word reluctantly, but I can find no legitimate excuse to disown him. I wish I could. His death should have been celebrated. Well, it had been—by Karen surely, and likely many others—but I mean nationally. Planetarily.

But although he had never been especially intelligent, Wolfgang Scholz had always had the animal cunning never to hurt anyone who could effectively complain about it.

About her mother, Ilse, Karen told me little, and most of that simply involved incidents at which the woman had been present. Apparently she was one of those cipherlike people that true sadists keep around. Having no personality to destroy, they cannot be used up.

The telling of her life was good for Karen. She had told most of these anecdotes to others over the years—but she had never told anyone *all* of them. In telling them all together, perhaps she was able to perceive some kind of gestalt pattern she had previously missed. Perhaps by replaying every minute of her life with her father she was better able to exorcise him, one step closer to being able to accept and forget him. Every time you play the record, the signal-to-noise ratio gets worse. Her consumption of alcohol dropped steadily to zero. She cut way back on tobacco. She actually began to display signs of neatness, become more careful in personal grooming.

And finally it was my turn.

And of course there was nowhere to start but at the beginning.

I remember, as an infant remembers womb dreams, the click and the sight of the mine coming up like a featureless jack-in-the-box and very bright light and then very dark dark. And then I was born.

When I realized that I was alive, my first thought was that VA hospitals were better than I'd heard. I was in a powered bed in what looked like the bedroom of a captain of industry, with no medical equipment in sight. My head did not hurt nearly as badly as I thought it should, and nothing else hurt at all. Well, I said to myself, you've managed to come up smelling like a rose again, Corporal—

And paused.

Because what I intended to end that sentence with was my name. And I did not know it anymore.

It was not really *that* much of a shock, then. In all the books and movies, amnesia is always temporary. But I yelled. A man came in the door with an icebag. A man so completely nondescript that I could not tell whether I knew him or not. I thought that was symptomatic too at the time, but of course it was the Fader. He sat down and put the ice on my head and told me that he had gotten the son of a bitch.

I'm not sure which questions I asked first, but within a couple of days I had as much information as the Fader could give me. By the end of a month I knew almost all I was ever going to know.

When the mine went off in the jungle I was, as best I can reconstruct it, twenty-four or thereabouts. When I woke up in that bed under the offices of that deserted warehouse, for what I believed was the first time, I was—again, best guess—about thirty.

Of what I did, where I was, during the intervening six years, I have no slightest recollection.

Of my life before the mine went off I have only random shards of memory, disordered, fragmentary, incomplete. I do not for instance know my name, nor have I been able to discover it.

It's like a million file cards scattered across a great field, more than half of them facedown. Random bits of information are clear and sharp, but there is no context. I remember a family, remember childhood incidents involving three vividly recalled people, but I do not know their names or what has become of them. I remember growing up in a small town; if I ever see it I'll know it, but I doubt I'll ever find it. I remember that we moved to New York in my early adolescence, but in the four years since the Fader put that icebag on my head I have walked through most of the five boroughs without finding that street. Ten years is a long time in New York. It may not exist anymore.

I remember enlisting and bits of Basic and there's a lot of chaotic, badly edited video footage of the horrors of war—in fact, the army days are probably the period I retain most of. But to my sour amusement I cannot recall my serial number.

What the Fader had to say was mighty interesting. We had met a couple of months before in a bar. I had busted a stein over the head of someone who was attempting to knife him. We had become friends, and a couple of weeks ago I had invited him home, and a week ago I had showed him my *real* home. The Fader stated that he was a composer—who, the times being what they were, dabbled in the small-time con (mostly variations on the classic Man in the Street) and an occasional mugging. He told me that I was a burglar, apparently for the sheer love of it since I obviously had, as he put it, adequate resources.

How had I found my home? How would he know? He had been too polite to ask, and I had not volunteered the information. Or, unfortunately, much else.

One guess suggests itself. One of the two emergency exits from the underground apartment is a long tunnel, which at its far end is camouflaged, quite realistically, as an abandoned sewage outfall, malodorous and unattractive to inspection. Could I have been so afraid of someone or something that I tried to hide in there, and found myself in Wonderland?

The Fader said that we had been coming back from a large "mutual adventure" when a hijacker tried to take its proceeds from us. The hijacker had laid a sock full of potting soil against my skull, and the Fader had killed him with his hands. Then he had dragged me the rest of the way home, and since he knew the dislock sequence but had not been filed in the perms yet, he had a hell of a time propping me up in front of Kennedy to get the door open. (I added the weight-activated explosives later.) He had been nursing me for the past few days, through delirium and nausea, had run several medical texts through the reader before he decided he could safely refrain from taking me to a hospital.

This last because I had told him my secret: that I did not exist, that I was an invisible man.

At some point during my missing six years, and after I had stumbled upon my home, I must have seen the possibilities of its computer, and decided to resign from the human race. I had done a hellishly efficient job. God is an iron.

In between talking with the Fader, I watched and read a lot of news—and I heard nothing that made that decision seem like a bad idea.

I could, to my only mild surprise, think of no better place for me in the world than the one I seemed to have made and lucked into. Every goal or dream I ever had that I can recall was destroyed in the jungle. I looked around me and found it good, or at least tolerable. And I could imagine no other occupation or lifestyle that was.

The Fader showed me what ropes he knew, helped me relearn what life was like in the underworld, steeled me to the rogue. He helped me comb through the ragbag of my mind for scattered bits of memory; helped me try, with the aid of the computer, to find out who I was; helped me get drunk enough on the night that I finally accepted, emotionally, that I might never know. He had done for me what I later did for Karen, and when he had finished it he politely made his excuses and left me alone, visiting frequently for a while and then tapering off. He even found me women, until it became clear that it was a waste of everyone's time. According to my memory shards I had nothing against sex—but now I found myself as asexual as Karen herself.

"Jesus," Karen said at this point in my narrative, speaking for the first time in hours. "How could I read it so wrong? You never wake up hard in the morning, you never get hard at all, and so I figure you must be gay. What a jerk."

I looked away. "To be totally accurate," I said tightly, "I'm a little bit more than asexual. Maybe antisexual is closer."

"How do you mean?"

"Arousal frightens me. Angers me. I can remember enjoying sex in the past, but now on the rare occasions that I become aroused, I—I usually have one of those blackouts."

Karen shook her head. "Different with me. I just don't get anything at all. Not since I was a kid."

Suddenly I was crying, explosively, convulsively, and she was holding me, holding my head against her breast and rocking me in her lap, and I was hanging on to her for dear life. "I thought *I* had it tough," I heard her whisper, and I wept and wept. It was the first time in a long while that I had wept for anything but rage, and it drained away an enormous amount of pain and fear and left me spent. Karen half-carried me to bed, and it was like leaning on a rock with a soft surface.

There was a new bond between us the next day, and so it was late that afternoon that Karen had her own blowout, that her own psychic kettle came to a boil. I think it was that night that she finally forgave

God for creating her father, and I ended up holding her until she fell asleep. A deep and profound sleep, complete exhaustion plus successful catharsis. She never felt me undress her, never noticed me leave the bed, never heard the TV I watched as I mixed myself a drink and finished it. I took another one to the corner chair with the directional reading light, and I sipped while rereading computer printouts for the thirtieth time, trying to make a sensible pattern out of them.

The drink was long gone when I heard the first sensual moan.

I looked up and dropped the printout. She had worked the sheet off in her sleep and lay writhing on the bed. She was obviously having a deeply erotic dream. I had never known this to happen to her before, had never expected it to. I felt a trace of the faint distaste that sexual arousal usually elicits in me and wanted to look away.

But Karen—scarred, frigid little Karen, my true friend Karen—was whimpering with lust. Perhaps for the first time in years.

Something had finally unlocked, some door in her mind was opening. If it could happen in sleep it could happen in waking life. My patient was at a crisis. But *was* it happening? She thrashed on the bed, clenching and unclenching her thighs, making small sounds as she searched for release. Her hands flexed and grasped at her sides; she had never learned to masturbate, could not work it into whatever fantasy was stimulating her.

Surely a lifetime of deprivation would provide enough back pressure to allow release without any physical stimulus. But what if it didn't? If this attempt at sexuality ended in frustration, would it be repeated? When would conditions ever be better? Or as good?

I got up and approached her. She did not seem to feel my weight come on the bed. I looked her over from head to toe, dispassionately, as an intellectual problem. I thought it out. The more input I gave her, the more she had to work into the script of her dream; eventually the effort might bring at least partial awareness and failure. Her arousal was coming in slow waves that built to a peak, ebbed, then caught again. When I sensed a peak coming I reached out carefully. With infinite gentleness I put the tip of an index finger just above the top of her vulva, so slowly that for her there was probably no defined border between not feeling it and feeling it. As the peak arrived I moved my finger delicately down the shaft of her clitoris toward the glans. She was breathing in gasps, whistling on the exhale. As I approached the nub I began using a little fingernail, and when I had reached it my thumb was beneath it, trapping it, and she groaned and went over the edge.

It was not the spectacular, backbreaking orgasm I had rather expected. It was a mild thing, a gentle upwelling. But it was definite and unmistakable, and it left her soft and buttery and totally unconscious, all angles rounded, all edges softened. It left me with tears on my face and awe in my heart and a hollow feeling that hurt as bad as anything I've ever known. My sleep that night was an endless round of nightmares, and when I woke the sheet was pasted to me.

Two nights later the sequence essentially repeated. Except that she woke up after orgasm, and figured out what had just happened. We hugged and cried then. I had no nightmares that night. The next day she taught herself to masturbate while I was out shopping. She reported her success proudly, and I smiled and congratulated her, and was jovial as hell all that day, but I believe she caught on because she never again mentioned it or did it in my presence.

But she stared spending a lot of time in the bathroom.

I was confused about my own feelings. For her I felt genuinely happy and gratified. And relieved: I never again remembered that there was still a droud in her skull, which she could still use.

For me I felt nothing.

Then came the day when our impatience overcame our paranoia and it was time to begin our campaign. Karen had more than one motive to return to her profession now. Oh, she had cautioned herself not to expect too much. Sex with a random stranger whose only known attribute is that he or she has to pay for it is not liable to be great. But whatever happened, she could definitely abandon her former specialty and switch to straight whoring. She now knew, at least, how to pretend enjoyment. And as it turned out she was third-time-lucky, came several times, and refunded his money. From then on she went about one for three, as near as I could tell.

My own cover identity was pimp, part-time second-story man, and occasional dope runner. If I was home when she brought a client home, I remained discreetly out of sight in the other bedroom, with my eyes on the TV and my ears cocked for trouble. I wasn't always there; I had fish of my own to fry and she could handle herself.

A good part of what I was doing was running down exactly how, after we had established our personae, we would begin expanding her client list to include the people we wanted to get to know better, without its being too obvious that we were moving in that direction. I had to tail a couple of them to the homes of the whores they did patronize, learn what kind of women they liked and what they liked to do with them. I was able to get some information from three women by pretending to be looking for recruits for my own stable. With one of them it was necessary to express horror and shame at my unprecedented attack of impotence, and be laughed scornfully out of her room. I tried a fourth woman, and her man put a notch in my ear and a trivial slice on the back of my arm before I could apologize sincerely enough to suit him.

It was going well. We were both acquiring authentic reputations in the Halifax underworld, and I was learning just what class of johns our targets represented, so that we could specialize in that type and acquire them in the natural course of events.

I had decided to actually move a little coke for the sake of my cover, and I returned from a negotiating session in a pool hall with a tentative commitment and a good deal of optimism. When I got home, two coats were on the living room couch and the door to the working bedroom was closed, so I took coffee into the other room and watched a TV special about a zero-gravity dancer, in orbit. Very interesting stuff, very beautiful. I wondered why no one had ever thought of it before. After a while I heard the phone start to ring, but Karen must have picked up the extension at once because it cut off before I could move. Shortly I heard her door open, then the apartment door, then a male voice in brief conversation with Karen's, then the door closing. I put my coffee down; Karen's customer had gone and I wanted to ask her some things.

Only the customer wasn't gone. She and Karen sat at the kitchen table, both dressed, portioning out the pizza I had just heard being delivered. I stopped and waited diplomatically for my cue.

Karen looked up and brightened. I could tell that this had been one of the good ones. "Hi, baby. I didn't know you were home. Want some pizza? This is my old man," she said, turning to the client, and then her smile vanished.

The woman was not a regular. She was about my age, blond and tall and slim, quite beautiful by conventional standards. In my first glimpse of her, bending over the pizza, I had noted in her face and carriage small trace indicators of self-indulgence and bitterness, but I had also sensed strength and courage and will. She wore a starched white uniform, quite unwrinkled and spotless except for where it had been stained when the pizza leaped from her fingers.

She was staring at me, mouth open, eyes bulging with shock, hands gripping her elbows so tightly that the knuckles were turning white. She was looking at me as if I were death, as if I were all horror and all evil, and I could not for the life of me imagine why.

"Lois," Karen cried, "what's *wrong?*"

Her mouth worked. She swallowed. "Norman," she rasped and swallowed again. "Oh, my sweet Jesus fucking Christ you *are* alive." She tilted her head as if she had heard something, and fainted dead away.

❖7❖

2007

THE LAST TWO FACTORS in the complex causal-event-tree that killed Norman Kent were Semester Break and an old address book.

Each factor by itself was necessary but not sufficient cause. Norman might have gotten through Semester Break if it had not been for the address book; the book would probably not have killed him at any other time of the year. But the two factors coincided, and Norman's death ceased to be a matter of statistical probability and became virtually inevitable.

He even knew this when it happened.

He had followed the advice given him by Minnie and the Bear, had done his level best to declare Maddy dead in his mind. He had gone so far as to initiate the lengthy process of having her declared legally dead, which he had been putting off. The horrible impersonality of the procedure helped make the idea of her death more real to him. In his academic world the tendency was to smother the unpleasant realities of life in empty form—in dozens of empty forms, to be filled out in quintuplicate. It seemed fitting and correct that the bureaucratic world should deal with that most unpleasant reality of life—death—in the same way: by chanting the dry cold facts over and over again, on paper. It made it official, made it real.

The lesson was clear: pain could be buried, with enough shoveling. Norman had allowed himself to relax for the duration of his friends' visit, because this let him appreciate them. But when they left he plunged gratefully into the work that had backed up in a week of relaxation, and was soon producing like five driven men again.

His students began to transcend themselves, reaching new plateaus of insight and understanding almost against their will. He published a new paper, in which he coined a new critical term of fourteen syllables that meant nothing whatsoever and was to remain in serious critical usage for half a century after his death. Under his direction the campus literary magazine not only doubled its circulation and quintupled its readership, but brought several of its contributors reprint fees, and one a book contract. Norman practiced, and even came to enjoy, the art of Lunching for Advancement, which he had formerly considered an unpleasant obligation. Three jealous colleagues tried but failed to knife Norman; one was ruined by boomerang effect. Eighteen students, singly and in groups, in series and in parallel, failed to seduce him. Three carefully selected faculty wives succeeded. MacLeod, who was married to one of them, began to publicly praise his own sagacity in giving Norman one more chance to Find Himself, and dropped hints about early Total Tenure. Even the Chancellor deigned to nod to Norman when they passed one day on the quadrangle, both scrupulously following the unnaturally natural pathways.

Respect of a similar yet different kind was given to Norman by other teachers and students who were in no way connected with the university. Monday night was Fitness Canada Night at the YMCA, the basic RCAF program with assorted frills: Norman was first made a class demonstrator and then offered a part-time job, which he declined. Tuesday night was Jazz Beginner class at DancExchange: he was by now in the first row. Wednesday night was T'ai Chi, that splendid blend of dance and unarmed combat. Thursdays had given Norman a problem for a while: no course for which he was eligible involving physical exertion was offered anywhere in the city on that night. He settled for a pistol marksmanship class given by the police department. Friday night was unarmed-combat class at the Forces post on South Street, where again he was made a demonstrator. He jogged to and from all these activities—he jogged everywhere he went off campus—and did some serious running on weekends down at Point Pleasant Park. Every night he slept like a dead man, a kind of rehearsal.

He gave up forever tobacco and alcohol and marijuana and reading for pleasure and sex for pleasure. They were all ways to relax, and he had no wish to relax. He canceled the cablefeed service that brought entertainment and news to his video console. He abandoned all social life save that which would enhance his professional position, and pursued that with energy and something that was frequently mistaken for gusto.

He attained, in short, as has been said, a drastic kind of dynamic stability, the peace of the dervish, and maintained it for some time. As the work pressure on campus swelled, growing inevitably into the tidal wave of Exam Week, he rode it like a master surfer, until at last, when he was humming along at absolute peak velocity and efficiency, the wave suddenly broke and deposited him, shipwrecked, on the shores of Semester Break.

All the work, all the students, most of the faculty, all *went away*. Norman was far too organized to need to plan his next semester, and there was no First Semester work left undone. There was nothing to fill his days.

His evening prospects were not much better. Three of his five evening classes were also suspended while the students were away; marksmanship and hand-to-hand would continue, but it was easy to see that he would come home from them insufficiently exhausted. As for what might be called his curricular extracurricular activities, only one of his three faculty wives had failed to leave town for the vacation— and by Murphy's Law she was the least tiring, most tiresome, and least available of the three. There was not much to fill Norman's nights.

For the first few nights he bounced around his apartment like a Ping-Pong ball in a blender, a workaholic evading savage withdrawal. He added final touches to already exemplary housekeeping, got his apartment looking like an advertisement, then frowned and rearranged virtually every piece of furniture in it, three times. He cooked himself elaborate meals that required hours of preparation and extensive cleanup—then hours later he would realize that he had forgotten to enjoy them. He designed a way to increase the efficiency of his apartment's layout by tearing out a single wall, and gave it up only when the building super proved to him that the wall was load-bearing—that every wall in the massive tower was load-bearing. In desperation he dug out his novel, but put it aside after an hour. Writing was hard work, but it was not the kind of work that kept him from being alone with his thoughts.

He cast his mind back to the days when he had had both time and inclination for a hobby. He had once been something of a low-key computer enthusiast, had in fact built his own Other Head (a machine so versatile that its brand name was fast becoming a generic term) from a kit. He spent two days familiarizing himself with the state of the art, then redesigned and rebuilt and overhauled his system, hardware and software. After a day of playing with it he was again restless and irritable. He found himself hurling a glass against a wall because the grapefruit juice in it had become lukewarm.

Inanimate objects and total strangers began to conspire to drive him mad. An essential component of his typewriter snapped under no provocation at all—the dingus that held the paper against the platen-roller (it irked him immensely that he could not recall the name of that dingus). Norman did most of his typing on his computer, of course, but the few uses he still had for the old Selectric—fill in the blank forms, and the like—were *just* important enough to make it a necessity. Typewriter repairmen overcharged mercilessly; they had to. Norman decided an epoxy repair might just hold up and reached for his epoxy. Used up in rebuilding his Other Head. He went out into the bitter cold and bought more. When he opened it at home, the resin was solid throughout its tube; he had been sold epoxy several years old. Swearing, he went out again—it was snowing fiercely now—to a different store and purchased a cyanoacrylate adhesive, the kind that bonds skin instantly. He found that the tiny tube was too frail to withstand the force required to break the seal inside its tip, even with a very sharp pin and much care; two of his fingers bonded together before he could react and instinctively he yanked them apart, tearing the skin. Adhesive dripped down the length of his hand, dropped on his expensive slacks. He wanted to clench his fist in rage and did not dare. He bellowed and ran to the bathroom, flushed his hand as clean as possible, and dressed the bleeding finger; when he returned to his office the tube was bonded to the desk. He pierced the side of it to get some fresh adhesive, and made his repair job. The stuff claimed to bond in "seconds," so he gave it an hour. The join failed instantly on the first test. With trembling hands, Norman removed the tube of adhesive from the desk, scarring the desk irreparably and getting adhesive on his shoes. He found himself in the living room, holding the massive IBM over his head, the power cord tangled on one arm, and realized that he was looking for the most satisfyng object through which to hurl the thing. He set it down with great gentleness on the rug, then stood erect and filled his lungs. People who live in apartment towers do not generally visualize God as their upstairs neighbor, but Norman looked upward now and screamed, *"What is it, then?"*

Silence came for answer.

"You've got my attention, damn your flabby heart! *Now what the fuck are you trying to tell me?* I'm *listening!"* He swayed on the balls of his feet, shoulders hunched, breathing heavily. His head ached, his fingers throbbed, his throat was torn by the violence and volume of his challenge. *"Well?"* he shrieked, damaging it further.

At this third provocation the woman living above Norman called out to her husband. That man's name was Howard, but there was a floor and a ceiling and a perfunctory attempt at insulation between the woman and Norman, so that the word he heard filtering down to him from on high was:

"—coward?"

His eyes bulged. The blood drained from his head.

"—coward, what's he doing?"

He bent and grabbed the IBM, heaved it up to chest height. But the cord had his ankle now, so he yanked his right foot out from under him; he lost the IBM and went down howling. He saw the great gray bulk coming down at his face, rolled convulsively out of the way, and smacked his skull solidly into a leg of the coffee table. It was excuse enough to lose consciousness.

His awakening was strange, only partial. He had no recollection of the incident, did not ask himself how he came to be lying on his living room floor with a sore head and assorted aches. He simply got up, moved the typewriter to where he kept the trash, and made coffee. Thoughts of any kind came slowly and far apart. One fragment of the metaprogramming part of his mind recognized that he was in shock, but did not care. Decisions were handled by something like a random-number generator somewhere in the murky cavern of his brain; Norman went along for the ride, his consciousness on hold, or perhaps "on standby" would be more accurate.

He found himself seated at his desk, rubbing a finger uselessly over the new scar as though it could be erased. His coffee was cold. He recalled that there was an immersion coil in one of the desk drawers and looked for it. He got sidetracked: the desk badly needed straightening out. Been meaning to get this organized, he thought, and began weeding out superfluous items.

One of the first was the address book.

It was quite out of date. Norman had built his Other Head on his honeymoon, with wedding money; both he and Lois had fed their address and phone files into it and dumped the original books and lists. This was an old one that had been overlooked. Norman was about to trash it—it was surely obsolete—and then he hesitated. Some part of his somnolent mind decided that he might just run across the name of some forgotten old friend or lover he could call or look up, as a means of harmlessly killing some time. There might be one or two other items worth adding to his computer files. He opened the book and began browsing.

The first twenty pages were just what he could have expected: a mildly bemusing, mildly depressing trip down memory lane. I wonder if she ever forgave me. Say, I remember that jerk. And Ed, so promising, yeah, dead in the Second Riot in Philly. Old Ginny, wow, what are the odds she's still single? On and on for twenty pages— right up through the J's. There was nothing worth salvaging.

Then he turned the page and saw Madeleine's old address and phone code in Switzerland.

The violence was all internal this time, too titanic to escape his skull in any form whatever. The full recollection of the evening past came crashing out of its cage, the surface of his soul fissured and split to reveal something disgusting, the last seven years of his life snapped suddenly into meaningful pattern, agonizing pattern, he understood at once that he *must* now undo every single day of that seven years and that their undoing would almost certainly bring his death to him within a period measured in days—and an unobservant person seated across the room would probably have failed to notice a thing. Norman did not so much as flinch. He sat quite still for perhaps ten seconds, forgetting to breathe. Then, very gently, he sighed.

"All right," he said, looking straight ahead at nothing. "I hear you."

Then, sitting bolt upright, the address book still perched on his lap, he fell asleep in the chair.

❖❖ ❖❖ ❖❖

Some hours later his eyes opened. It was just morning. He rotated his head on its socket three slow times, cracked his spine, put his hands on the desk, and stood carefully. The book fell unnoticed from his lap; he would never notice it again. He knew what he needed to do and what he needed to learn and much of how to do it. Most of all he knew how much it would cost him—and was only glad he had the price.

It was quite simple. Somewhere in the African bush he had decided to hell with self-worth, given it up as a lost cause, settled for mere pride. A villain or a coward may have pride. Academic life had gradually eroded most of that pride—not because he failed at it but because he succeeded at it, turning out generations of students whose imaginations had been stimulated precisely where the department chairman wanted them stimulated and nowhere else. He had sold everything for security, gelded himself for security. Small wonder his wife had left him for someone more dangerous. When he had failed to learn from that lesson, life had, with the infinite patience of the great teacher, spent more than a year kicking him repeatedly in the heart, brain, and balls. You didn't need to catch Norman Kent between the eyes with the million-pound shit-hammer more than forty or fifty times before he got the message:

Pride is not enough to get you through this world. You have to have self-worth too, or you won't be able to take the gaff.

Sam Spade had hit the nail squarely, more than half a century before. When a man's partner is killed, he's supposed to do something about it. Madeleine Kent had been, for a brief time but in full measure, Norman's partner, and someone had come and taken her away, and Norman was supposed to do something about it. Self-worth required it.

To die in pursuit of self-worth is much better than to live without it. So said all his life since the jungle days, now that he had the wit to read it. The supersaturated solution had at last crystallized, all at once. Norman caught himself humming as he headed for the door, and realized on some preconscious level that he was happy for the first time in a long while.

He walked south to Point Pleasant Park while he planned his campaign. The horrid cold sharpened his thought.

Known for certain: Madeleine was gone. Period.

High probabilities, in order: Maddy was dead. She had been killed by a man known to her and perhaps named Jacques, or by agents of that man. Jacques was very puissant and very clever, possessed of enormous resources.

Slightly lower probability: Jacques had been a colleague or business associate of Madeleine in Switzerland. Perhaps not—he could be a tennis pro she had met in a bar, or the man who came to fix the microwave. But would she then have felt it necessary to leave her job, leave the career she had built so painstakingly, leave her ten-year home in Switzerland, and come to Canada to avoid Jacques?

She had not left Switzerland because she *feared* Jacques, of that Norman was certain. She had not been even half expecting to be kidnapped or harmed. During her stay with Norman, Maddy had sometimes slipped and showed hurt; she had never shown fear.

Assuming all this, she must without realizing it have possessed information that Jacques considered damaging to him. No other motive made sense; a lover spurned does not take on Interpol and the RCMP. Norman yearned mightily to possess information that Jacques would consider damaging.

How do you approach an enemy ten times your size?

In disguise, smiling.

First step: locate Jacques. Without being caught at it. Norman did not intend to underestimate Jacques; he assumed that his Other Head and his credit account were bugged and monitored. He could not afford to access information about Maddy's firm from any terminal in Halifax Metro, for that matter, if he wanted to be *certain* of coming up on Jacques's blind side. There must be no evidential record even hinting at Norman's interest in Jacques. One day soon Jacques might have reason to wonder if someone was taking a bead on him, and if he could learn that someone in Metro had been asking questions about him at or shortly after the time that Norman Kent had dropped out of sight, he would add two and two. Norman needed information that had already been accessed, which left only one way to go, and so he gave ten dollars to the first wino he met at Point Pleasant Park.

He stood outside the phone booth, watching a filthy superfreighter belly up to the containerport across from the park, while the wino phoned up the city police and asked for Sergeant Amesby. Norman kept better track of missing-persons stories than most citizens, had discussed most of them at length with Amesby. Thus briefed, the wino was able to convince Amesby that he was in possession of important information regarding a recent case quite unconnected with Maddy's, and demanded a face-to-face meeting at a remote spot near St. Margaret's Bay, many kilometers to the west. He had corroborative data not known to the general public. Amesby went for it. The drunk hung up grinning, and Norman gave him the additional twenty he had promised for a successful job. With three of Norman's ten-dollar bills in his hand, the unshaven and tattered man asked Norman for a quarter. He used it to call a cab, to take him to the Liquor Commission store.

Norman walked to police headquarters. Amesby was gone when he arrived. Norman was known there, and had long ago made it a point to be liked there; they brought him to Amesby's office and let him wait.

Thank goodness for the cheapness of the voters! Amesby's files were actual files of paper, in big bulky drawers, rather than electrical patterns on tape or disc. Norman used gloves, and within half an hour he knew everything that Amesby knew about Maddy's situation in Switzerland, her acquaintances, and the firm she had worked for. He used Amesby's battered Selectric to note down a few addresses, phone numbers, and bits of information.

Amesby was efficient, and had paid attention when Norman told him about Maddy's single cryptic mention of the name Jacques. In the web of acquaintances that Amesby had had Interpol draw up for Madeleine, there were two men named Jacques, with dossiers for each.

The first and seemingly most obvious candidate was her immediate superior at Harbin-Schellman, Jacques DuBois. But Norman rejected him at once when he saw the photograph. Maddy could not have become emotionally involved with that face. The second was a man named Jacques LeBlanc. Norman could read nothing at all from his face; the man was nondescript. He was executive vice-president of Psytronics International, the much larger consortium that had absorbed Harbin-Schellman in the last year. He apparently had extensive contact with Maddy in the course of the takeover, would have been an ideal candidate for a lover, save that Interpol could not turn up even a rumor of a romance between the two. What made that lack of evidence significant was that LeBlanc was not married. If he and Maddy had become involved, there would have been no reason to conceal it. Unless . . . could he have been using Maddy for secret leverage in the takeover? No, she would not have played along; Maddy had old-fashioned ideas about loyalty.

All right. Jacques's last name was LeBlanc, until events proved otherwise.

Amesby's copier was down the hall, useless to Norman. He typed an abbreviated version of LeBlanc's dossier, removed all traces of his work, and left. On his way out he told the desk man it was nothing important, not to bother telling Amesby to phone him.

He stepped from the police station into the incredible wall of wind that howls past Citadel Hill in winter, and leaned into it. With the wind-chill factor, the sudden temperature differential was on the order of a hundred and ten Fahrenheit degrees; Norman ignored it and plodded on, making plans.

On his way home he got twenty dollars worth of change from a bank. He fed some into a sound-only pay phone in the quiet base-ment of a moribund restaurant and called Zurich, where it was now three o'clock in the afternoon.

It was necessary to locate Jacques; according to Interpol, he traveled a lot. It would be difficult enough for Norman to get to Switzerland untraceably—but it would be stupid to manage it and find that his quarry was in Tokyo or Brasilia. The dossier mentioned an interest that Jacques shared with Norman, and it gave Norman an idea. They both collected classic jazz. He summoned up the New York accent that he had by now almost succeeded in obliterating, and located in his wallet the number of the illegal New York tie-line that one of his faculty wives had told him about.

"DiscFinders, N'Yawk, callin' long distance for Mr. Jock Le Blank."

"One moment, please."

So Jacques was in Switzerland. That was all Norman wanted to know—but he was curious to hear his enemy's voice. He decided to try and sell Jacques a rare Betty Carter side.

But the next voice was female. "Monsieur LeBlanc's office, may I 'elp you?"

"Hullo, this is DiscFinders in N'Yawk, lemme speak to Masseur Le Blank, please."

"I yam sorree, Monsieur LeBlanc is out of the city at present."

Norman was glad he had waited. "When's he comin' back?"

Slight hesitation. "Not for some time. May I 'elp you?"

"Well, where is he?"

"I yam sorree, I cannot give out that—"

"Listen here, sister, what I got here is a mint copy of Betty Carter's birthday album, on her own label, there can't be another one mint inna world. Five thousand bucks expenses Mr. Le Blank fronted us to find it, another fifteen on delivery. I think he wants to hear this record, what do you think?"

"If you will send it 'ere, we—"

"Bullshit, lady, didn't you hear me? Fifteen grand, New dollars, the day Mr. Le Blank gets this record in his hand. You think I'm gonna ship it over there and let some clown in your mailroom leave it on the rad for a week before he forwards it fourth class? I send it direct to Le Blank by courier, *personally,* or I peddle it elsewhere."

"Monsieur, I yam afraid I must—"

"I am the best record finder in the world," Norman roared, desperate. "I don't need this bullshit. I know three other people, old customers, 'ud buy this fuckin' thing in a minute, I'll send Le Blank a registered letter tellin' him where his expense money went, how did you say you spell your last name?"

"Monsieur LeBlanc is vacationing in Nova Scotia, in a place called Phinney's Cove. The postmaster in the town of 'Ampton can direct your courier. 'Ave him say that Madame Girardaux approved it. You understand this information is to be absolutely confidential?"

"That's more like it. Pleasure doin' business wit' ya, Miss Jeerado." Dueling Accents. He hung up.

His first reaction was elation at his lucky break. Jacques was right here in the province, a scant hundred and fifty kilometers away. Norman owned a small cottage and a couple of acres not twenty klicks from Phinney's Cove—which community comprised perhaps fifteen homes along the Fundy Shore—and knew the area fairly well.

He had not been looking forward to stalking Jacques on the latter's home ground, in an unfamiliar country, and he was immensely cheered to find Jacques on something like his own turf.

Then he had second thoughts. The hair prickled on the back of his neck. Jacques had been standing unseen just behind his back for an indeterminate time; perhaps this was not wonderful news after all. Could Jacques be wondering if Maddy had passed on something incriminating to her brother before she'd been killed? If so, he must by now have concluded that Norman did not *know* he had anything incriminating . . . mustn't he? Or was he even now deciding to play it safe and have Norman killed too? Norman went from joy to fear like a speeding car thrown suddenly into reverse.

Then he had third thoughts. He remembered what the two psychics had told him about Maddy's surroundings after her disappearance. The descriptions given would fit Phinney's Cove—the city lights on the horizon would be St. John, New Brunswick, across the Bay of Fundy. *Perhaps Maddy was not dead!*

He forced himself to leave the restaurant at a slow walk. A block away, after satisfying himself that he was not being tailed, he did run the remaining three blocks to his home.

He had to take a small risk, then. He needed information he could only obtain from his own Other Head. But it was not the sort of information that Jacques would be likely to find significant, even if he learned of the accessing. From long years of living with Lois, Norman still had a line to the data banks of the hospital just up the street. To play it safe, he charged the tap to Lois's code; someone reviewing the record might reasonably suppose that she had made a routine retrieval while visiting her ex-husband.

The readout he got in response to his query elated him. A male Caucasian of Norman's approximate age and size had died within the confines of the hospital during the previous forty-eight hours. More important, the late Aloysius Butt had been a pauper with no known relatives, was awaiting burial by the province. Since the demographics of Halifax bulged markedly in Norman's age bracket, this could not be considered an incredible stroke of fortune, but Norman definitely took it for a good omen. Aloysius Butt was the one lucky break Norman required for the plan he was forming. Had Aloysius not had the grace to die so timely, Norman would have had to postpone his campaign until a suitable candidate presented himself, and Norman could not bear the thought of enforced inactivity at this point. He did not want too much time for reflection, for doubt and worry. Fortunately fate had given him the one factor that his wits could not provide, just when he needed it. It was railroading time!

Now for traveling cash. Back out to another pay phone.

"This is me, no need for names."

"Not if you say so," the other said agreeably. "To what do I—"

"I am prepared to sell you, under certain conditions, my entire collection. You know what they're worth, can you get that much cash by tonight?"

"What conditions?"

"You tell nobody where they came from. I don't mean just Revenue Canada Taxation or your mistress, I mean *nobody*. You get them in different jackets—same goods, in Angel sleeves, but the jackets'll be from junk, I keep the original jackets. And it has to go down tonight, at 3:00 A.M."

"Without the jackets, the resale value depreciates. There would have to be a small dis—"

"No it doesn't and no there won't. You have no intention of selling them. Book value, take it or leave it."

"I don't know if I can get that much cash by tonight. Can I give you a check for the last five thousand or so? You know I am good for it."

"My friend, this is a one-time-only offer, and nothing in it is negotiable. The Swede wouldn't treat these as well as you would, he wouldn't *appreciate* them—but I know he'll have the cash at home."

The barest hesitation. "Come up the back way and knock two paradiddles. Thank you for thinking of me."

Details filled the rest of the afternoon. Norman picked out two complete sets of clothing, put on the first and folded the second into a compact package. He carefully filled a backpack, his two prime considerations being that the backpack should sustain him for an indeterminate time on the road, and that no one subsequently searching his apartment should be able to deduce that such a backpack had been filled. He did not, for instance, pack his salt shaker, but poured half its contents into an old perfume vial of Lois's. Any essential of which he could not leave behind a convincing amount in its original container he abandoned, to be replaced out of his operating capital on the road. When he was done with his preparations he examined his entire apartment in detail—and shook his head. I am, he thought, an unreasonably neat man. The apartment was, as always, so neat and organized as to give the impression that its owner was away on vacation—which was exactly wrong. He un-neated it a little, gave it a spurious kind of lived-in look. He went so far as to cook himself a dinner—an undistinguished one, when what he wanted was a grand Last Feast, a farewell to his gourmet's kitchen—and leave the dishes in the sink.

He spent the next six hours in his armchair with headphones on, saying goodbye to his music. At midnight he shut off the system and transferred a carton full of extremely rare jazz records, many of them deathgifts from his mother, into the jackets of cheap ordinary records, and vice versa. He put the disguised rare records into another carton, then selected eight more mundane records from his shelves and put them, in their original jackets, into the carton full of rare records. In three unobserved trips, he brought both cartons, his backpack, and his spare set of clothing down to the lobby, stashing them in the dark community room.

One A.M. Lois should have just returned home from work by now.

He flinched at the cold as he left his building. He hurried across the street, noting that the window he wanted was lighted. He used a key he had possessed for some time, but never before used, to let himself into the ancient three-story apartment building. The hall heaters were not working, and more than half the lightbulbs were dead. There were no security cameras to record comings and goings. Norman climbed to the top floor, located a door. He had a key for this door too, but did not wish to use it; he knocked.

Lois answered the door. She started with surprise when she recognized him. "Why, Norman!" she said in a voice that seemed a bit too loud. "What brings you here?" She made no move to step aside and let him in.

"I've got to talk to you, Lois. Business, very urgent."

"Can't it wait until tomorrow? I just got in from work and—"

"Sorry. It can't wait."

She hesitated.

"Come on, it's cold out here. It won't take a second."

Still she hesitated.

"I always let *you* in."

She let him in. A woman, also in nurse's uniform, was seated in Lois's living room; as he saw her, her hands were just coming down from the top button of her smock. Pillows were spread on the floor before her, and he noted that the stockings below her uniform were distinctly non-regulation. He turned back to Lois and, now that the light was better, observed a lipstick smear on the side of her throat. So Lois was trying to change her luck, and was embarrassed about it. Wonderful! She would be flustered, anxious to get rid of him, and the presence of her lover would allow him to be as vague as possible.

"Leslie, this is Norman, my ex. Norman, this is Leslie; she and I have to prepare a report together by tomorrow. What can I do for you?"

"Those records you borrowed. King Pleasure, Ray Charles Trio, Lord Buckley, the Lennon outtakes. I need them all back, right away."

Lois bit her lip."Uh . . . I haven't had a chance to tape them yet."

"It's been over a year."

"Well . . . can I borrow them back and tape them later?"

Lie. "Sure."

If she had been alone she would have argued. "Well . . . wait here, I'll get them."

She left the room. Norman smiled sweetly at the other nurse, and sat down across from her. "Hello, Leslie. Or should I call you Lez?" He was ashamed at once of the cheap shot, but it could not be recalled.

Leslie started to speak, then changed her mind and stood. "Excuse me," she said coldly, the only words she had spoken since he arrived. She left, following Lois, and shortly he heard the buzz of low conversation in the adjoining room. Lois came back alone with eight records, each jacket sprayed with preservative plastic.

"Here. Take them and go."

Now for the dirtiest trick. Well, it couldn't be helped. "Lois—let me borrow your car for tonight."

"I need it tomorrow."

"No problem. I'll leave it under the building, keys in the usual spot. But I've got to do a lot of traveling tonight, and a taxi just won't make it."

She frowned.

"Lois, this cancels us, okay? I'll never ask you for another favor. *Please.*"

Again she hesitated. Then: "Norman . . . promise that it won't be the last favor you ever ask me, and you've got a deal."

That one hurt; it was an effort not to wince. "Okay," he lied at last.

She handed over her key ring, and unexpectedly she kissed him—a long, smoldering kiss that was painfully evocative. For the thousandth time in his life, Norman wished there were some truly effective way of erasing memories. The worst of it was having to cooperate in the kiss, to put a false promise into it. "I'll be here alone tomorrow night," Lois murmured as the kiss ended. "Come tell me about your night's travels." Norman was silent, regretting. She searched for words that would bind him to her, and what she came up with was, "I miss your prick." The regret faded; he promised and made for the door.

Still he paused on the threshold. "Lois . . . thanks."

"No problem, Norman, really."

"No, I mean . . . thanks for the good times, all right?"

He turned and fled down the hallway, annoyed with himself for yielding to melodrama. That had sounded too much like an exit line for a suicide.

In case she was watching, he took the car for a several-block drive before doubling back to their street, where he parked in front of his own building. Loading the car with records, backpack, and clothing took no appreciable time and, as far as he could tell, went unobserved. Once inside the car again, he switched jackets between the eight records Lois had returned and the eight mundanes he had fetched. The mundane records, now in jackets claiming that they were rares, he put in the trunk of the car.

Walter, the collector who *appreciated* jazz rarities, had been able to acquire the cash Norman demanded. As Norman had expected, Walter accepted the jacket swapping and other skullduggery as a scheme to defraud Revenue Canada, and was quite happy to collaborate, as Walter's own tax position was chronically less than optimal. He actually drooled as he rummaged through the carton, establishing the identity and condition of each disc. His pudgy hands trembled as he gave Norman the suitcase full of used bills in low denominations—but only because the hands yearned to return to the records. Norman did not bother to open the case and count the money. He forestalled the attempts at conversation that Walter was really too excited to make, and left as soon as he decently could.

It was approaching four in the morning when he reached the hospital. His effortless success there had very little to do with luck. He knew the hospital layout intimately, knew where to park and where the few graveyard-shift personnel could be expected to be cooping and where spare uniforms could be had. And of course he had Lois's key ring. The late Aloysius Butt never had a chance. His absence, in fact, went unnoticed for several days, and when discovered was attributed to the notoriously twisted sense of humor of interns, so obviously was it an inside job.

By the time the sun was rising, Norman had succeeded in hitching the first in a series of rides, and was well content. He wanted to go west, and so he had hitched his first ride east. His hair was parted on the opposite side, and his hairline had receded a full inch. He wore entirely bogus eyeglasses that Lois had once given him as a birthday joke to make him look more "professorial." Cheek inserts subtly changed the shape of his face. His dress did not match his station in life, but looked at home on him. He was unshaven, and could not possibly have been mistaken for a dapper academic. He had a suitcase full of untraceable cash.

Behind him in Halifax, the local newspaper, famed for many years as not only the worst daily newspaper in Canada, but very likely the worst newspaper possible, was preparing to misinform its readers on at least one count for which, for a change, it could not reasonably be blamed. A story and photos on pages one and three alleged that a local English professor named Norman Kent had crashed his wife's car into an oil-storage tank at the foot of the hill by the waterfront, totally destroying the tank, the car, himself, and an extremely valuable rare-record collection whose ruins were discovered in the wreckage.

Norman was ready to hunt him some Jacques.

❧8❧

2011

THE RE WAS ONE timeless frozen instant in which I could close my eyes and murmur, "Oh, *shit*." Then Karen and I were both in motion. We got the unconscious woman to a couch. We laid her out gently. Karen loosened her uniform collar. It has been my experience that fainters usually revive at this point, but she showed no signs of recovery at all. Her color remained pale. The pulse in her throat fluttered. Her breathing was shallow.

"Jesus, Joe," Karen said. "Jesus." Her eyes were wide.

There was too much in my head. I was dangerously close to fainting myself, and dared not. "You sure can pick 'em." I turned slowly round, looked at the room and everything in it. "Oh, my, yes."

"Joe, she's—"

"—big trouble, right. No telling how big." I went to the table and sat down. "Not until she wakes up—and before then we have to decide which way to jump."

"I—what do you mean?"

I wanted to bark, kept my voice low with an effort. "We are engaged in a criminal conspiracy to wreck a billion-dollar industry. We require darkness and quiet. This client of yours has taken me for someone she knew and believed dead—someone who obviously meant a great deal to her."

"Her ex-husband, Norman. She talked about him a lot."

"Oh, fine. So as soon as she wakes up she is going to turn on all the searchlights and sound all the alarms. 'Oh, you're not my dead husband, Norman? Who are you, then? Can you prove it? What a terrific coincidence this is—I must get to know you better, there

154

must be dozens of little nuances of irony here. I can't wait to tell all the girls down at the hospital.'" I frowned. "We need this like an extra bowel. You know what—"

"Joe!"

I trailed off.

"How do you know you're not Norman?"

My face must have turned bright red. I could feel my nostrils flare as I sucked in enough breath for a bellow. My teeth ached. It took all the strength I possessed to keep my vocal cords out of circuit while I exhaled. A shout might wake the sleeping nurse.

I gazed at her across the room.

Her uniform cap was askew. Her blonde hair was mussed. Now that she was unconscious, her face looked petulant. I scrutinized the face very carefully, and then the generous body. I was prepared to swear that I had never seen her before in my life.

Which meant nothing.

Or did it? It depended on which theory of amnesia you bought. Amnesia the way it is in the movies, or amnesia the way you think it really must be, or amnesia the way it really is.

Movie amnesia: if this blonde fem really was my wife once, I would unquestionably have remembered her at once, regaining my memory on the spot. Love is stronger than brain damage. Hate, too—since she was alleged to be an *ex*-wife.

Amnesia as one imagines it: no such pat, instant abreaction—but at least *some* few small bells should ring. A spouse becomes familiar on so many levels that you almost relate to them from your spinal column—the way a pianist will remember his way around his instrument, regardless of whether or not he can recall his name at the moment. This woman was a stranger. In odd hours I have tried to guess what kind of woman I would want, if I wanted women. As far as I could tell, this ex-wife was not even my type.

Amnesia as documented: in 1924, baker Benjamin Levy disappeared from his home in Brooklyn. Two years later a Catholic street sweeper named Frank Lloyd flatly refused to believe he had ever been a Jew, a baker, or named Levy—even when they proved it to him with fingerprints and handwriting analysis. He was quite suspicious, and only when other relatives were able to pick him out of a crowd did he decide there might be something to it. Reluctantly he moved back in with his wife and daughter in Brooklyn. He had to get to know them all over again, and to his dying day he claimed he had no recollection of his early life as Levy.

The mind is stranger than it can imagine.

I had myself back in control now. I looked up, saw Karen staring at me.

"What if I am?" I asked her calmly.

She started to explode.

I overrode her. "We are stalking some very dangerous game, and we are committed now. Maybe they know someone is angling for them, maybe they don't. We could be on borrowed time right now. Suppose this woman *does* hold the key to the missing half of my brain—is now the time to get into it? Either way it blows my cover, jerks me off the rails." I grimaced. "In fact, there's a mighty funny smell to the way she popped up just at this time in our lives. A nurse could be involved in wireheading . . ."

"But if she was sent here she wouldn't have fainted—and that faint is genuine."

"True . . ."

"You don't recognize her *at all?*"

I shook my head. "Proves nothing, though."

"Jesus Christ, Joe, aren't you curious?"

"Not half as much as I am scared. I want to defuse this one, fast. If there's anything to it, I can always come back to it when the job's done."

"You could die! You could die never knowing!"

"So what?" I snarled. "Maybe she was the whole world to me once—but right now she's a live grenade on my sofa. Let's try and get the pin back in." I got up from my chair. I took the headset off the phone and laid it down on the end table. I punched my New York number and put my portable terminal next to the headset. I told the computer to record audio from this location at maximum gain. I told it to transmit a constant dial tone to the phone's earpiece and filter it from both the recording and the extension phone in my bedroom here in Nova Scotia. I gave the computer a one-syllable audio-disconnect cue, which could wipe the whole circuit and all records save for the recording in its own impregnable memory. Then I switched off the terminal and put it away. The phone now looked and sounded as if it had been left off the hook for privacy, rather than for the opposite.

"I'm going into my room, so the shock of seeing me when she comes to doesn't start a loop. And so I can eavesdrop on the extension. When she comes around, convince her she made a mistake—and *pump* her for everything you can get on this Norman."

"She'll want to see you."

"And I won't want to upset her. But when she really insists, I'll have to come out and persuade her I'm not Norman. Which is why you have to get every drop of information you can *first*, so I can do a convincing job. Keep her talking."

"How do you keep someone talking?"

"Be fascinated. You can't fake it. Find her every vagrant thought interesting. Make small involuntary sounds of wonder and sympathy. Nod slightly from time to time. This fem could get us both killed, honey; be fascinated."

Karen took a deep breath. "I guess you're right. We play it your way." She shook her head slightly. "But I just don't know . . ."

"The most probable answer is coincidence. There's nothing unique about my face. Remember your last client in New York? Lots of people, not enough faces to go around."

The reminder jarred her. "Yeah. All right—split. I think she's coming around."

I slipped into my room and closed the door.

I knew the beginnings of the conversation would be rather predictable and of no value to me. I found the Irish and poured a stiff one, and drank it down before I did anything else. My pulse was racing. I hoped the whiskey and the adrenalin would meet in my bloodstream and strike a bargain. That damned nurse bothered me, scared me. And the reasons I had given Karen were not the whole of it. I did not know the whole of it myself. I was only intellectually sure that I wanted to.

The whiskey helped. I picked up the phone.

Karen:—him a *long* time, honey. I'm telling you, this is the first time he's been north of Boston in his life.

Nurse: (pause) Then—(pause) God, how weird. I'd have—no, of course he isn't. He didn't know me—and Norman never could act worth a damn.

K: (laughing) That describes Joe, too.

N: Listen, I'm sorry for the way I—

K: No, no, that's cool—

N: Some prize customer I turn out to—

K: Really, it's all right.

N: Look, can I give you a little extra for your—

K: It's real nice of you to offer, no, thanks.

N: But I feel as though I—

K: Look, if you want to do something for me, help me kill my curiosity. How come you flipped?

N: I told you, he looks just like—

K: —a dead man, right. You told me about him before, you even told me what he looked like when you buried him. If I buried a burned roast and a few years later I saw a guy that looked just like him, I'd think, 'Gee, he looks just like my ex.' But what you said was, 'Norman—you *are* alive.' Like the idea wasn't new to you.

N: (long pause) Karen, can I trust you?

K: Look at me. I've hurt a few people in my time. Now watch my lips. I. Have. Never. Hurt anyone who didn't hurt me first. And you ain't hurt me. You made me feel good. Real good.

N: Do you have any pot? (sounds of a joint being lit, then a longer pause) I don't remember how much I told you. Eight or nine months after he threw me out, his sister, Madeleine, came home from Switzerland.

K: When was this?

N: Just as the '06 school year was starting, it was. She'd been working in Switzerland for years. A very beautiful woman. (long toke) Then a few weeks later she just . . . disappeared. All her things left behind, she just didn't come home one night. It was all in the papers and such, Norman did an excellent job of beating the bushes, but no trace of her was ever found. He took it badly. I went to talk to him one day, let myself in, and he . . . had a woman tied down on his bed, all naked and . . . he . . he changed, you know? He turned cold to me, and he got strange.

K: You think he had something going with the sister?

N: Perhaps. I'm not sure. But her disappearance affected him deeply.

K: And then?

N: A few months later, during Semester Break, he knocked on my door, unannounced, at one o'clock in the morning. He woke me up. He wanted me to return some of his old jazz records.

K: What kind of records?

N: Oh, really old things. Charlie Parker, Jack Teagarden. Lester Young. Ray Charles Trio. Obscure people—King Pleasure, Lord Buckley, Jon Hendricks.

K: You gave them back?

N: There wasn't much else I could do. He wouldn't explain. Then he borrowed my car to transport them. The son of a bitch. A few hours later they called me up and told me he was dead. He and the car both burned to the frame. The ruins of the record collection were in the trunk.

K: They didn't burn?

N: Oh, there was plastic soup everywhere. But these were rare; Norman had sprayed the jackets with preservative, and it turned out to be fireproof. The jackets weren't entirely destroyed.

K: So why aren't you sure he's dead?

N: The last thing he ever said to me was, 'Thanks for all the good times,' and then he left. I thought it was a little odd at the time. Like an exit line in a movie. Norman Maine goes for a little swim. So when I heard he'd crashed I thought the bastard had decided to use my car to suicide in. I'll tell you the truth, my initial reaction, I wanted to kill him. He could just as easily have jumped off the roof of his building. That little Chrysler cost me six months of Neuro Ward.

K: What changed your mind?

N: Little things at first. That plastic soup in the trunk had scraps of charred labels floating in it—and I happened to notice that one of the labels was from a ghastly disco album one of his students had given him, worthless from any standpoint. That stuck in my mind. Later that day I let myself into his apartment, and I looked for the jacket to that record. It was gone. Then I noticed that there were too many empty spaces on the shelves. He'd had about twenty other rare records, in addition to the eight I returned—and there were many more than that missing. Maybe twice as many. And the *other* missing records were utterly ordinary, of no value.

K: So you figured he swapped jackets and tried a switched-package con? And maybe it blew up in his face?

N: Actually, I did think something of the sort. You're very quick. I almost went to the police, but . . . I decided not to.

K: Sure.

N: Then a day or two later I went back to work and the rumor was that some crazy intern had swiped a pauper's body from the morgue. Things like that go on all the time. One time . . . anyway, we all waited for a few days for the other shoe to drop—for the corpse to turn up nude in the ladies' room, or in Maternity, or fully clothed with a magazine on its lap in the lobby. Nothing happened. After a few days, just as everyone else was beginning to forget it, I happened to remember that the key ring I'd lent Norman that night had held *all* my keys.

K: Oh.

N: He knew that hospital as well as anyone. Better than some. Once, just after we were married, we . . . used to meet down in the morgue, in the small hours, and make love. Anyway. So I accessed the coroner's report on Norman, and tried to compare it to his X-rays and things.

K: Yeah?

N: I couldn't be sure. Not enough data. It might have been Norman that burned. It might have not been him. And I couldn't get more data without giving a reason. You can picture that: "You say you think your dead ex did *what*? He had a set of keys? You *gave* them to him?" Dentals would have sewn it up, but there were none on file for the burnt corpse and I didn't have access to Norman's.

K: Wow. What did you do?

N: I thought it over, and I went to see a policeman I knew. A Sergeant Amesby at Missing Persons. I met him when Madeleine vanished, a very good-looking man in an odd sort of way. He impressed me a good deal, and I trusted him. I brought my suspicions to him.

K: How'd it turn out?

N: He heard me out, and then he slapped his forehead and said something about a wild-goose chase. He called the front desk and asked if Norman had been in looking for him on the day he died, and they said yes. He pulled the file on Madeleine and nothing was missing.

He frowned and thought for a while. All of a sudden he jumped out of his chair and yelled and dove at the wastebasket. I thought he'd gone bug. He took a used-up IBM typewriter ribbon out of it and began unreeling the ribbon on the floor and squinting at it. After a while he growled and unreeled more slowly.

K: You mean—?

N: Norman had used Amesby's typewriter to copy off some information from Maddy's file. Information about a man she'd worked with named Jacques LeBlanc.

K: Worked with where? Here or in Switzerland?

N: Switzerland. Not in her firm, some related group. Uh, Psytronics International, I think. Did I say something wrong? No? Well, Norman decided, for some reason, apparently, that this LeBlanc character was involved in Madeleine's disappearance.

K: I don't get it. Norman thought this guy had his sister snatched. So he switched some records, snatched a stiff, and died?

N: This LeBlanc is apparently a very wealthy man. If Norman decided to go after him, he'd need a new identity, and untraceable cash. And some way to account for his own disappearance.

K: Jesus. That's brilliant. You're really smart.

N: Well, Sergeant Amesby did most of the deduction.

K: After you got him started. Your subconscious was smarter than his conscious. Well? What happened?

N: Well, Amesby cautioned me to keep quiet, of course, and said he'd check into it. A few days later he called up and said we were wrong. He'd checked dental records, and it was definitely Norman I had buried. He'd investigated LeBlanc, and positively cleared the man.

K: You didn't believe him.

N: (long pause) I didn't know. I still don't. He was very convincing. He offered to show me the dentals.

K: But you couldn't help wondering if maybe a phone call came down from on high: lay off the rich guy.

N: Exactly. You *are* quick.

K: (slyly) Not as quick as you were . . . an hour ago.

N: Oh! (pause) A tribute to your talent, darling. and your beauty.

K: Why, you sweet thing! (rustling sounds) Come here.

N: But—I—

K: Come on. A friendly freebee, okay? I've been on my own time for the last half hour. And you could use some cuddling.

N: I—

K: Couldn't you?

(sounds of embrace, wet slow kissing, whispering fabric)

N: Wait.

K: Uh? Are you kidding?

N: Wait. Before we . . . God, I'm inhibited. Verbally, I mean. Before you suck me off and make me crazy again, I want to see him. Meet your Joe, I mean. Then maybe I can get all this tangled old karma out of my mind. May I?

K: In the morning, maybe?

N: Please, darling. I'll be able to relax better. I'll make it worth your while. (gasp) Oh! Not with money, I mean—I mean—damn my primness! What I *mean* to say is, I believe I could make *you* crazy— once I get this out of my system.

(rustles)

K: (groaning) Oh, you naughty bitch. All right, you've convinced me. Just a second while I—(rustles, sigh) There. Don't take long on this, now, you've got me all hot.

N: I won't, darling—

K: Mmmm, yes.

N: Stop, now. Say—won't Joe object to a freebee, as you put it?

K: Naw. I told you, he's more of a friend than a pimp. In fact, *I* got *him* into the business. Joe's a sweetheart. HEY, JOE!

I answered her second call, "Just a sec," I yelled. I drank more whiskey from the bottle. I turned the TV on, yanked out the earplug so they could hear me turn the set off, and joined them.

The room smelled of pot and of girl. It made me edgy. "I'm terribly sorry I frightened you, Miss . . ."

"Mrs. Kent," she murmured automatically. "God, this is fantastic! Oh—forgive me. You didn't frighten me, Joe. I frightened myself. Excuse me, but would you mind stepping over here into the light?"

"Sure." I moved closer. She rose and approached me.

"Fantastic," she said again. "I can see the differences now, but—Joe, I mistook you for my ex-husband. He's been dead for almost five years now, and you look remarkably like him. The corpse I saw could have been anyone, it was that bad. I mean, it was just barely possible—"

I looked astonished. "No wonder you keeled over. Uh . . . how close is the resemblance? Now that you can see me better."

"Startlingly close. I can see now that you couldn't possibly be him, of course. For one thing, you're much more than five years older than he was when he died. But you could be his older brother. Could you bend your head down?"

I did so.

"Fantastic. You both have scars on your scalps. Yours are in different places, of course. His were from an old war wound."

"Mine are from a less official war."

"Could I ask you a terribly personal question?"

"You can try."

"Well . . . are you circumcised?"

An impulse uncommon to me made me answer truthfully. "Yes."

She nodded. "That settles *that* forever. Norman wasn't. And not for any reason can I imagine him disguising his penis with a knife. Not that it wasn't settled already, Joe . . . I just meant—"

"Look, Miz Kent—"

"Call me Lois, please."

I grinned. "Lois Kent? Like Mrs. Superman?"

She burst out laughing. "Now *that* settles it. Norman always said if he heard that joke one more time he was going to end up on Neuro with hysterical deafness. Thanks, Joe—you've put even my subconscious at rest."

We laughed with her. I made my excuses and left.

There was a chance that Karen might get something more from her. I went to the phone again.

Lois:—to bring this up without asking you about it first, but . . . is there some way I could persuade Joe to join us? It would be so much like a fantasy I've had.

Karen: (startled) Wow. Hey, I see what you mean. Sorry, honey— Joe doesn't go for girls.

L: Damn. What a shame. Uh . . . (long pause, rustle of clothing) Karen? Couldn't he be persuaded . . . well, to just watch? That'd be almost as—

K: Sorry, honey. I don't think so.

L: I just don't understand monosexuals. It just isn't *natural.*

K: Well, there you go. (pause) And there you go. And there . . .

I put the phone down. The room was very hot. I undressed and sat naked on my bed. Something was wrong with my stomach. I took a long gulp of whiskey and sat on the bed clutching my knees and shivered. The world closed in around me and shimmered. It was very much like a bad drug experience, too much strychnine in the acid, and that made it a little less scary. I found that if I concentrated, I could make the world shimmer at the same cyclic rate as my shivering. Somehow that helped.

After a few hundred years the door opened and Karen slipped in. She looked and smelled well used. "She's gone," she murmured, and found my whiskey. I began to calm down.

"I think I convinced her to keep her mouth shut, Joe—"

"Great. She won't tell more than fifteen other fems. I probably won't hear the story in a bar any sooner than the day after tomorrow."

She frowned but said nothing.

"I'm sorry, Karen. You done good. Weird little fem—maybe she will keep her mouth shut. It must be tough to be a gay nurse—or she wouldn't have had to come to you in the first place. Hell, she's probably wishing she'd kept her mouth shut herself, right now. You pumped her good, Karen."

"That's an awful pun, friend."

"Well . . ." I scratched my bare thighs.

"You want to talk about it now or later?"

I sighed. "Now. You caught the name of the outfit this LeBlanc character worked for?"

"Catch it? I thought I'd shit."

"Psytronics International. Our target. I wonder why there's no Jacques LeBlanc on our hit list?" I reached out, got the phone, and asked the computer. We watched the readout on the terminal together. "Retired, huh? Shortly after this Norman Kent business. Hey, look! Lives in Nova Scotia, by God. Where the hell is Phinney's Cove? Aha. Fundy Shore. Maybe a hundred miles from here. Hey!" Something struck me. "Remember that old army buddy I told you about that used to live in Nova Scotia? The Bear?"

"Sure. You tried to look him up when you got here."

"Yeah. No joy. Maybe he never came home from the jolly green jungle. But he used to live not far from where this LeBlanc is supposed to be." I scowled. "The more I pick at this, the more it bleeds. And the worse it smells."

"Joe? You *can't* be Norman, right? No bells ring at all? Different scars, no foreskin?"

"None of these things are conclusive. You disguise scalp scars with a skin graft that leaves new scars. Circumcision's a simple operation. There are just too fucking many coincidences. I look enough like Norman to fool his wife in fairly bright light. We both took head wounds in the war. We both like vintage jazz. We're both tricky— that switched-bodies scam was a beaut." I scowled again. I was uncomfortable; I slipped into tailor's seat. "And in the end, we may have both met our ends by trying to tackle Psytronics." I finished my drink. "I don't like this. If I am . . . if I used to be Norman Kent, then this Jacques has something that scares me to death. The world's first genuinely effective method of washing brains."

Karen was staring at the wall. "I can't think of anything that's more obscene."

"Neither can I. Until half an hour ago I would have said that was a meaningless word. But if what happened to me . . . was . . . was *done* to me, by a human being—"

She turned to me, and gasped. "Joe!"

I looked at her, followed her gaze.

I had a powerful erection.

I stared at it for a long time. It did not seem, did not feel, like a true part of me. Then as I watched, it started to. I was fascinated, repelled. It swayed rhythmically with my pulse, like an old tree in gale winds. I had the idiot impulse to throw my hands up and cry, Don't shoot.

Out of the corner of my eye I saw Karen's hand gingerly approaching, fingers forming the ancient shape—

"*Leave it!*"

She started at the volume and jerked her hand back.

We sat in silence for a while, watching the phenomenon together. Gradually, but steadily, it subsided. Each pulse raised it less than the last, until it was only the familiar flaccid appendage. After a while she rose and went to the door.

"Karen?" I called after her.

She turned.

"We're going to kill that motherfucker. You and I."

Slowly she nodded. "Yes. We are. Get some sleep."

She left, to sleep in her work-bed.

I found it surprisingly easy to take her advice.

❖9❖

2007

VIRTUALLY EVERY INCH of the Fundy Shore, Nova Scotia's northern coast, is stunningly beautiful at any time of day or year, under any weather conditions. But to sit on a sun-warmed rock at the high-tide line beside a brook that chuckles as it covers the last few meters to the Bay of Fundy, on the first really nice day in weeks—at sunset—is pure Beethoven. Norman had come down to the water's edge for a few minutes only, to pay his respects to the Bay before going about his business—more than an hour ago. The sun was almost down now, but he knew the light-show in the sky had a good half hour yet to run. And then the stars! And the moon! To one on the Fundy Shore, the world is mostly sky; no grander canvas exists anywhere on the planet's surface. Norman had been living without sky for too long, and could not tear himself away. Nova Scotia winter is savage and merciless, and every year the same thing happens: spring, heeding the frantic prayers of the cabinbound, comes forth to do battle with winter *much* too early—about the end of January or early February—and is utterly destroyed within a week or two. Thaw, as the period is called, is a pleasant time, but subsequent to it, winter returns with redoubled ferocity and remains until about mid-June, when it suddenly gives way to summer without transition. Norman could not be sure, but it felt as though this were one of the last days of Thaw. Good reason to get up and resume the hunt, before the hammer came down and made everything more complicated.

Yet he could not get up. Norman Kent had not felt good in quite some time, and right now he felt very good. He had self-worth. He felt fast and tricky and lucky and dangerous. He remembered flashes of a similar feeling from eight years ago, from his earliest days as a grunt in Africa. But this was different, was better. This time he understood what he was fighting for, knew his enemy to be genuinely evil, this time he was a volunteer! The old skills were coming back, he could feel it. All the mad activity of the last several months had formed a kind of Basic Training, leaning him down and toughening him up, and with the return of good physical condition came muscle-memories of deadly games once taught him by weary old professionals and by clever enemies. He expected to die on this venture—but he was certain that Jacques would predecease him. Norman was even fairly sure that he could manage to persuade Jacques to answer a number of questions before dying.

At last he had drunk his fill of the place. He rose as the sun's last gleam winked out, stretched carefully, and clambered up over vast white driftwood mounds to the marsh flats and the road beyond. He made his way with care, for he did not know this ground; although he was in a beautiful spot, he was not in Paradise.

Norman's own getaway cabin *was* in Paradise. Its postal address was Rural Route 2, Paradise, Nova Scotia—although in fact it was situated well up over the North Mountain from that sleepy and well named little Annapolis Valley community. The cabin could be reached by foot, four-wheel drive, or horseback. It was heated by wood, powered by Canadian Tire solar collector and wood-alcohol combustion, had neither telephone nor television. Norman never considered going anywhere near it. It is said around the Valley that if a man breaks wind on the North Mountain, noses will wrinkle on the South Mountain. Norman was entirely too well known around Paradise, and even if he had reached the cabin unobserved he could not have hidden his chimney smoke.

Phinney's Cove, his target area, lay about twenty kilometers west of his cabin, just inside the radius within which Norman could reasonably expect to meet someone he knew along the road, and thus come to the attention of the jungle drums. So instead of hitching the North Shore routes, Norman had followed the province's *southern* coast, then taken 8 North past Kejimkujik National Park and crossed the North Mountain at Annapolis Royal, some fifteen klicks *west* of Phinney's Cove—avoiding the region where he was known, and approaching Jacques from the opposite direction. He was now on a part of the shore called Delap's Cove.

But the fact that he was not known here did not mean that he did not know anyone here. Civilization on the North Mountain is spread thin, scattered so widely that anyone who has lived there for any length of time comes to know at least a few people who live many klicks from his home. Norman had once needed water found, and so he had come to know old Bert Manchette.

He crossed the Shore Road (only the Tourist Bureau called it "The Fundy Trail" anymore) and entered the woods. The ground rose steadily before him; he was now climbing the gentle slope of the Mountain's north face. Fifty yards in from the road, well out of sight of passing traffic (perhaps one car per hour), he found a distinctive stand of white birch. He stopped, took two balled-up green plastic garbage sacks from his backpack, and shook them out. He removed a few hundred dollars from his suitcase of cash, sealed the case with a combination lock, and double-bagged it tightly against moisture. Then he rammed it beneath a rotting deadfall and concealed it with dead leaves and bark. He had marked the spot where he had entered the woods; nonetheless, knowing from experience how hard it can be to locate a particular patch of forest again, he used the woodsman's knife that now hung at his hip to blaze a few of the surrounding birch—about a meter *above* eye level, where the scores might go unnoticed by another.

He continued on uphill. The sun was well and truly down now, and the moon not yet risen; yet the darkness was far from total. The sky was clear, the branches naked overhead, and a city dweller might be astonished by the amount of starlight to be found in a forest. And Norman could hardly have gotten lost. The directions to Bert's were simple: proceed uphill until you strike the old overgrown road, then follow it east until you reach the ruins of the mill. Straight uphill from there half a klick to Bert's Ridge, and hullo the house from just outside buckshot range.

The walk gave rise to thoughts about eternity and entropy. Once this whole forest had been settled and populated. The overgrown trail Norman walked had once been a busy road, bustling with carts and buggies and wagons and hitched oxen and running children. Then, more than seventy years ago, for reasons Norman still did not fully understand, the Mountain community had died back. The people had all . . . gone away. Houses fell in upon themselves. Cultivated fields vanished under the alders. Nature, which had been literally driven away with a pitchfork a century before, had returned as the Roman maxim prophesied.

The region was actually less spooky by night than by day. The bones did not show—the occasional glimpse of foundation and sills in the undergrowth, the odd bottle-and-can heap, every so often an orange axe head or fitting or fastening slowly oxidizing on the ground. All of these were invisible in the dark, and Norman was able to keep mortality from the surface of his thoughts for some time. The air was inexpressibly clear and good, the smell of woods had all the subtle nuances of flavor of a truly great dessert, the earth was springy beneath his feet. Rotted leaves and branches and occasional unmelted patches of snow crunched under his boots, and the quality of the sound told him the true size of the room within which he walked. He was aware of distant deer avoiding him, and caught a brief glimpse of a weasel silhouetted against the sky.

Then Norman heard the sound of the stream that meant he was approaching the ruined sawmill, and he was reminded of all the ghosts that lived along this road.

He forced the thought from his mind. He drank from the stream with cupped hands, and took time to enjoy the almost forgotten taste of unchlorinated water. Then he left the stream, which cut sharply east, and struck straight uphill—giving the sawmill a wide berth.

Norman had spent enough time in jungles and woods to know how to move without undue noise—quietly enough to sneak up on a city man, certainly—but he made no effort to use his skill as he neared the Ridge. There was no telling when old Bert might take a notion to go grocery shopping, and Norman was walking through Bert's pantry. He even went so far as to whistle, to remove the possibility of being mistaken for a moose. No moose had walked the North Mountain for twenty years or more—but there was no telling how good Bert's memory was these days. If he still lived, of which Norman was certain only intuitively, he was a hundred and four years old.

Norman had never, in the dozen or so times he had visited old Bert, met another guest on the Ridge, and he knew Bert seldom left it. Nonetheless the old man knew everything that happened on the North or South Mountains (he paid only slight attention to "doings" in the more civilized Valley—or indeed, anywhere else on the planet). Most every mountain dweller at least knew of him; he was a fixture, an area landmark. Most people believed him to be half crazy—but no one laughed at his dowsing rod. The cost of having a well drilled ran upwards of thirty dollars a meter these days, and a man fool enough to sink a well without consulting Bert might easily rack up three or four thirty-meter dry holes before getting lucky. Enough money can make even the most cynical superstitious.

Five years ago, Norman had heeded the earnest counsel of his friend Bear, and told the men to drill where Bert said to drill. He had seen the drill-boss's face change when he gave the order, and so he had been prepared when they struck sweet water at four and a half meters. The next day Norman had fetched a bottle of good Cointreau up to Bert's Ridge, and stayed long enough to annoy the hell out of Lois.

He smiled now as he replayed for perhaps the hundredth time the memory-tape of that first visit. He had come upon old Bert, ninety-nine years old then, chainsawing logs into stove-length behind his house—with bedroom slippers on his feet. Norman had been told, by several different locals, that Bert was "some strange," but this seemed to call for comment. "Hey, Bert," he had hollered over the yatter of the big old Stihl saw, "didn't you ever hear of steel-toe boots?"

Bert had let the saw finish its cut, then throttled back to idle, thumbing the oil feed to lube the chain. Idling, the ancient Stihl sounded like a motorcycle with no muffler, but Bert's voice had carried over it easily. "Yuh. Tried dem once." He smiled evilly. "Dull too many blades."

V-rrrooooooooom, back to cutting—and how the logs had danced!

The moon was coming up as Norman reached the Ridge. From here one could catch glimpses of the Bay through the spruce and pine. The sky was clear enough for him to make out the faint ribbon of light which was the province of New Brunswick on the horizon. The sight tempted him to stop and gawk, but he kept walking. He was pleased at how little winded he was by the climb just past, feeling his second wind strong in his chest, eager to be about his business. Bert would not mind being kept up late, but it would be impolite. Wind from the south, from the Valley—shit, that probably meant snow by morning. Oh, well.

He was still whistling softly when he first saw the lights of Bert's house. An instant later the whistle chopped off and he stopped in midstride. A woman crying out in pain . . .

He shrugged the backpack off his shoulders and held it by its straps in his left hand; his right pulled the knife he had bought on Route 8. He used all his woodcraft now, approached Bert's house rapidly but without ever exposing himself needlessly to fire from any direction. His awareness of the world expanded spherically. The cries came clearer as he neared the house. Sounds like upstairs. Sounds young. Sounds like someone's beating hell out of her. Sounds like . . .

All at once Norman grabbed a maple and stopped. His eyes widened. He dropped pack and knife, slapped both hands over his mouth, and quaked. He dropped to his knees, then fell over on his side.

The cries intensified, built to one wrenching terminal shriek. Norman curled up in a ball and bit the heel of one fist while the other pounded the outside of his thigh. Even so, he could not completely stifle the sounds he made—but he did a creditable job. No one more than three meters away could have heard him laughing.

The smothered laughter was some time in passing. When he had his breath back, Norman sat up against the maple and tried to light a cigarette, but the giggles kept returning and it took him three matches. He smoked it down, then leaned back against the tree with his hands laced behind his head, and waited.

Presently the door of Bert's house opened and alcohol light spilled out. A girl no older than fifteen emerged, wearing jeans and a garment more collar than coat. "Go on now," Bert's voice came after her. "Your mudder be mad if you late on a school night."

"Screw her," the girl said boldly.

"Not in twenty years, more's de pity."

She laughed, blew him a kiss, and left. Norman watched her disappear into the forest, shaking his head and grinning.

Bert was still alive, all right.

In 1755 the British kicked the French the hell out of Nova Scotia. The few Acadians who survived and stayed were herded together, on the French Shore, a godforsaken stretch of the Fundy coast between Yarmouth and Digby, some fifty to a hundred and fifty klicks west of Bert's Ridge. The region is one of the proudest and most fiercely self-sufficient in the world. Norman had only driven through the French

Shore—few Anglophones are at home there—and so Bert was the only Acadian he had ever met. Nothing could make the old man divulge the reason he had left the French Shore so long ago.

But once in a while Norman believed he could guess.

When he was sure the girl was beyond earshot, Norman stood and called out Bert's name, then approached the house slowly. Bert came to the door at once. Mountain folk do not greet each other with "Hello," or "Hi, how are you?" The preferred greeting is an insulting commentary on whatever the greetee happens to be doing.

"Don't you ever poke yourself, Bert?"

Bert showed no surprise at finding Norman at his door, betrayed his pleasure only by the faintest of smiles. "How you mean?"

"Getting the diapers back on 'em afterwards."

The smile widened. "By de Jesus, dat's true. Worth it, dough. Come on in and set."

Norman came in, took off his boots, and sat. There was a small but elegant tea ritual, involving both kinds of tea (Bert grew his own marijuana), and a sharing of the Cointreau that Norman had fetched in his pack. The next step then would have been a swapping of lies, regarding what had happened to each of them since their last meeting. But Bert broke tradition.

"You got troubles, man?"

Norman took a deep breath. "Yes, Bert. I do."

"Taught so, by Jesus."

Norman sipped Cointreau before speaking again. "No reason to burden you with them. But I need your help."

"Yah?"

"Phinney's Cove, Bert. Two men and a woman, a few months ago. She was probably quite ill. Uh . . . woods around the house—and a stream hard by, that isn't fit to drink. At least one of the men is there now: Jacques LeBlanc. *Pas Acadien.* A Swiss. The only way I have of locating them is to ask Wayne down to the Hampton post office— and I mustn't let him, or anyone, so much as know I'm in the area."

Bert nodded. "Shoor. You supposed to be dead."

Norman stared. Bert had no radio, no TV, and the only newspapers he ever saw were donated firestarter, months old. Norman's "death" had taken place less than twenty-four hours before. The old man was uncanny.

"If anyone can help me, you can, Bert."

"Shoor. De old DeMarco place. Just past Lester and Beth's, hard by de fisherman's markers, you know? One man dere now, maybe de woman too, I dunno. Big place, used to be painted red, dere's a wreck out back used to be a goat shed. You want to sneak up on dem, you go through Lester's woodlot to de bog, den go right downhill when you reach de bust-up tractor. Watch out for a 'lectric fence."

A wave of relief spread over Norman. "Bert, you're a godsend."

"Some say. What else?"

"I want your outlaw gun, the one that isn't registered. And all the dynamite you can spare. A meal—I've been on the road since sunup—and a place to crash, I guess." Bert nodded imperturbably at each request. "Down by the road, by the little stream, there's a stand of white birch with my mark about a meter above eye level. You remember my mark?"

"I know de birches."

"Right. There's a suitcase buried there, combination lock. You remember my birthday?"

"Shoor. First of January—you never had a birthday party in your life. Forget de year, dough."

"Seventy-seven. Dial the numbers and take whatever you think is fair for the gun and dynamite. Stash the rest, I may need it fast."

Bert nodded. "You look at the Bay before you come up?"

Norman's heart sank. "Oh, hell. Tell me." Bert could glance at the Bay and, from its color alone (he claimed), give you a weather forecast for the next week, more accurate than satellite tracking.

'In two hours hit begin to snow like a fucker. Snow mebbe two, tree days."

"Damn. Skip the crash, then, and I'll need that gun and at least a little dynamite right away."

"Eat first. Straighten you head."

"I can't, old friend. I have to scout *now*, before I'll leave tracks. I may be back around dawn, I may not."

Bert frowned but did not argue. He got up from his ancient rocker and left the house, returning with an ancient but impeccably maintained M-1 and a satchel. "Dynamite, detonators, fuses, ammo for de gun. We ever get time for a proper drunk, you and me?"

Norman hesitated, then answered honestly. "I don't think so, Bert. I don't expect to live through this."

Bert frowned again. "Like I taught. De lady, she be your sister, eh?"

"I think so. I hope so." He took the gun and satchel, got his pack, and headed for the door. "Thanks, Bert. Thanks more than I can say. I should have come here months ago."

"No," Bert said surprisingly. "No, you wasn't ready den. You ready now. You always was a good boy, Norman."

Norman found that his eyes stung. He reached the door and put his boots back on. "Hey, Bert," he said as he straightened. "I always heard that as a man gets older, his interest in the ladies kind of diminishes. They say sooner or later it goes away altogether. You think there's any truth in that?"

"Aw, shoor," Bert replied at once. "God's troot, by de Jesus." He relit his pipe full of homegrown. "You first notice it come on, oh . . ." He paused reflectively. ". . . oh, about ten minutes after dey lay you in de ground."

Norman laughed. "Thanks again, Bert." He shouldered his gear and left at once.

Bert called after him. "Hey, Norman—catch!" Norman saw something sail at him against the door light, stuck up his free hand, and caught it. It was a large hunk of ham. He smiled toward Bert's silhouette in the doorway, and chewed off a piece.

"Bon chance," the old man called. "Be careful, Norman."

Norman took the advice to heart. The gathering clouds overhead made him risk a hitch up to Phinney's Cove, but once in that region he stopped being in a hurry. He finished the ham, and drank from one of the many streams that seek the Bay. He took to the trees on foot, following Bert's directions, and moved as cautiously as he knew how. He spotted the electric fence in plenty of time, cleared it with practiced skill. Half a klick farther downhill he located, identified, and passed a sleeping guard. He was expecting an infrared scanner; he moved as a deer would move, walked where a deer would walk. He did it very well; he was actually in sight of the house before they bagged him.

Suddenly he was very very happy.

❖10❖

2011

PERHAPS A COCKROACH cleared its throat. I woke up on my feet, in streetfighter's crouch, hands and feet prepared to kill the first thing that moved. A few seconds passed. I tried to laugh at myself, but the sound frightened me even more. I made myself sit on the floor and breathe deeply and slowly. Soon I was calm enough to notice how much my neck hurt. I decided that was all the improvement I could stand and left the bedroom. The door to the medicine cabinet stood ajar. While I was urinating I caught sight of my face in the mirror. It didn't look any more familiar than ever. "Hi, Norman," I said to it. It said the same thing to me. Only one voice heard. Conclusion unmistakable. Shake it and flush, let's us both go have breakfast.

Karen was waiting for me. She had started the coffee. She knew better than to attempt breakfast herself. I mixed up things while the coffee finished dripping, drank some while I cooked. She had the table ready when the food was. We ate. She was halfway through her cigarette when she broke the silence.

"Okay, let's break it down. What do we know for sure, what do we guess, what do we propose?"

I nodded approvingly. "Good. Okay, known for sure . . ." I paused. "Not much."

"We know you look like a man named—"

"No, we don't."

"But—oh. I see."

"Right. Who vouches for Lois Kent? What evidence did she offer?"

"Um. None at all."

176

"So known for sure is: we are in Halifax, drawing a bead on Psytronics Int. A woman has alleged that I look a lot, but not completely, like her ex-husband. In support of this proposition she offers a detailed circumstantial account that she says convinces her that I am not this gent, but which makes *us* suspect that I might be. Her story is checkable on several major points, so before we go any further, let's check it out. The whole story could be some kind of ploy by PsyInt, to set us up for something."

"Okay."

I suppose I could have used my terminal. But I was feeling paranoid; we took a bus to the library.

The newspaper morgue backed Lois Kent on the disappearance of her ex-sister-in-law and the spectacular fiery death of her ex-husband. There was a picture of the deceased English teacher. He looked like me—but like me ten or fifteen years younger than I looked now, rather than three or four. The sister had indeed worked for a company in Switzerland, and shortly before she left it, it had been absorbed by the Swiss wireheading outfit that I suspected of being secretly allied to Psytronics International. There was an extraordinary amount of followup for a missing-persons case, even a beautiful female one. Norman Kent must have been industrious.

What tore it were the photos of Madeleine Kent.

I knew her. That is, I had known her. She was the grownup version of the sister I dimly remembered from my childhood but could not name.

"She's different," I told Karen. "She looks like she grew up into a nicer person than I remember. But most kids do. That's my big sister."

"Does the name Madeleine—or Maddy—ring a bell?"

"Not at all. But I do have a vague recollection that my sister went away somewhere when I was in college, and I guess it could have been Switzerland. Let's see . . . assuming Norman's birthday is mine . . . yep, dates match."

"Let's get out of here."

"In a minute."

I found a sound-only pay phone and called the city police. I asked the desk man for Missing Persons. Shortly a voice said, "Missing Persons, Amesby."

"Never mind, Officer—he just came in the door. Bobby, *where* have you been?" I hung up. Another detail of the nurse's story confirmed: there was a Missing Persons cop named Amesby.

"Now let's get out of here."

We walked to Citadel Hill. It is an amazing monument to the thought processes of generals. I'd read the brochure while dealing dope there. The Citadel—the first Citadel—was built by the British Army in 1749, to protect settlers from Indian attack. Nineteen days after its completion, a group of wood-cutters were attacked and killed by Indians under its guns. For some reason the settlers had refused to help in its construction. It was completely torn down and rebuilt three times in the next century, in response to the threats of the American Revolution, Napoleon, and the War of 1812, and each rebuilding was obsolete well before completion. There has never been a day on which it was not obsolete. No shot was ever fired in anger by or at any of the four Citadels. Haligonians are fiercely proud of this boondoggle, which cost hundreds of thousands of pounds. They say it was an important base for the subjugation of Quebec— but *was* Quebec subjugated? During World War I, it was a detention camp for radicals and other suspicious types. Leon Trotsky is said— falsely—to have done time there. It has been a tourist trap for over forty years. High-rises block its view of the harbor.

Perhaps I'm being harsh. Halifax is a splendid port, and no invader ever so much as tried to take it. Was that *because* of the Citadel? You tell me.

But you can still see water and sky from there. The entire Halifax Peninsula is laid out around you, the best view in town. The obsolete fort, crumbling in the sun, whispers of entropy and Herculean labor wasted. It is a good spot for thinking.

Karen and I used it so.

That early on a workday, it was almost deserted. We walked around to the southeast section, closed off for repairs, and found that completely deserted. There was heavy construction equipment here and there, but a strike had kept all the workers home. By our standards it was chilly for August, but not intolerably. The breeze was surprisingly light for such an exposed location. Nonetheless, I shivered as I thought.

After ten minutes I was done thinking.

A deep trench encircles the Citadel. It is perhaps twenty feet deep and thirty across. It prevents access except by the gate on the east or harbor side, and provides a breastwork around the fort, which, like everything else, was obsolete before completion. We were sitting a few yards from the trench. On the far side an iron staircase gave access from the floor of the trench to a sally port in the side of the Citadel proper. I nudged Karen, got up, and went to the trench. Fifteen feet below me, a construction flatbed of some kind stood abandoned. I lay down on my stomach and swung my legs over the stone lip of the trench.

"Joe, what—"

I shushed her. I lowered myself in stages until I was hanging from the edge by my hands. There were footholds in the stone block wall that any spider would have found more than adequate. I glanced down, kicked slightly away from the wall, and let go. I landed well, and waved her to join me, holding a finger to my lips for silence.

Shaking her head, she followed my example. She also landed well. We got down from the flatbed and sat cross-legged on the ground facing each other.

"This strikes me as a hard spot to mike from a distance," I said.

"Oh. Good thinking. And we can go up those stairs to the inside and out the main gate."

"So let's talk."

"Joe—me first, okay?"

"Go ahead."

"I think we should go back to New York, right away."

"Karen—"

"Let me finish! The evidence says that you already took on this Jacques LeBlanc once—and lost. Pretty decisively. I can find something else to do with my life."

"The man who took on LeBlanc five years ago is dead. I am not him. And I carry none of the excess baggage—broken marriage, kidnapped sister—that he had." I chucked her under the chin. "Plus, he didn't have *you*. Or anybody."

"Then you think we may have a chance?"

"Not for a second. We're dead; question of when."

She didn't flinch. "Not even if we cut and run?"

"Much too late. *Think* about it, baby. Visualize the enemy. If he can erase specific memories, no *wonder* the power flow in the wire-heading industry has no relation to the money flow! What the fuck would Jacques want with money? If he can scrub brains, suck memories, what is there that he cannot do? We are to him as bacilli to a whale."

"So maybe he'll overlook us."

"You're still not thinking. If I am—if I was once Norman Kent, *whose computer is that down in New York?*"

Now she flinched. "Oh, my sweet . . . and you recorded that whole scene with Lois . . ."

"Yeah. The really surprising thing is that we woke up this morning. And are breathing now. We're blown, baby."

"Maybe he's not monitoring—maybe we've got some time!"

"Unlikely. But it's hard to argue with the fact that we're alive. But we can't have *much* time."

"So what's our next move?"

"All-out attack. Crazed-wolverine style. Get out of here, clout a good car, run out to Phinney's Cove. Fake it from there. Maybe turn the car into a bomb and run it through his kitchen. Maybe stick up the nearest Mountie detachment for some automatic weapons. Christ, I wish I had an atom bomb. I wish I'd brought more ammo when I left the house this morning. I wish I hadn't paid the rent last week, I'm never going to see the place again. Well, let's—"

"Joe—something we ought to do first."

"Yeah?"

"Make a record of everything we know."

"What, for leverage on Jacques? To warn the world? Don't you und—"

"No, no, for *us.*"

"Huh?"

"Look, the evidence says, anyway suggests, that Jacques doesn't kill. Doesn't kill bodies, I mean. He doesn't need to; he's the mind-killer. Suppose he follows his pattern: wipes our brains and turns us loose. And then we find a record we left for ourselves . . . get it? He can't steal all our memories if we stash a few. Maybe two or three tries from now we kill him."

"No."

"But—"

"One: no time. It'd take too long to write out even the basics, we're not holding enough cash for a tapedeck, and there's no time to steal one. Two: where would we leave the record? Three: when the mindkiller gets us, he opens up our brains and finds out where we left the record. Let's get moving."

"You're right. Maybe we'll get one clear shot before we go down."

Someone yanked the sun across the sky.

Shadows leaped, and froze where they landed. The breeze changed direction and speed radically. The temperature dropped a couple of Celsius degrees in an instant. Internal changes were subtler but no less perceptible. My folded legs were suddenly stiffer. My mouth tasted slightly different. An exhalation was suddenly an inhalation. My breakfast was slightly farther along my gut.

The oddest part was the absence of terror. A parallel example *should* have been an earthquake. Humans require constant sensory reassurance of reality. When the solid earth dances and a thousand dogs howl, when the evidence of your senses is suddenly placed in doubt, you experience primeval terror. I received, in a single instant, a number of sensory reports that were simply impossible—and the terror did not come. I seemed to be too exhausted to be terrified, as though all my strength had fled from me in that same instant. Karen was gaping at me, clearly as stunned as I.

"What—" I croaked.

And then I got it. It was as well that I was too exhausted for terror, or my heart might have exploded then.

There is an old Zen conundrum: if a tree falls and no one is there to hear it, does it make a sound? Here is a related question: if a man's brain is awake, but his memories are not allowed to form, is he conscious? Does he, in fact, exist?

My (hiatus)es usually averaged five to ten seconds in duration, with fuzzy edges, like a sloppy job of record-muting. This one had lasted at least ten minutes, and it was a clean splice. This one had not been preprogrammed. This one had come from the source. Jacques, or an agent of his, had shut off our minds from a distance.

"Joe, God oh God Joe, God—"

She was staring at the ground between us.

A folded piece of eight-and-a-half-by-eleven paper lay there.

Excellent paper, a heavy linen parchment, cream-colored. The calligraphic type on it read:

I request the pleasure of your company this evening at my country retreat. Ask for the Old DeMarco Place. Dress informal; weapons optional. I promise to give you both at least temporary possession of any information you desire.

—J.

It was unsigned.

My hands went instinctively to my weapons. They were in place. I looked around, pulled the gun, confirmed that it was loaded and live, and put it away. We both got stiffly to our feet. I tucked the letter into my shirt pocket.

"Well," I said.

Karen could not speak. She trembled just perceptibly.

"Hoy," came a voice from above our heads.

I jumped a clear foot in the air, came down with one arm around Karen. I never even tried to go for the gun. Just for her. We gaped upward together.

A uniformed security guard stood at the edge above, looking down at us with detached interest. I was glad I hadn't tried for my gun. All the Citadel guards are experienced war veterans. He seemed vaguely relieved. He looked quite tidy and dapper, and when he spoke his accent said that he was British by birth, of cultured origins, and had a sense of humor about his job. His left sleeve was pinned up to the shoulder.

"You two seem on friendly enough terms."

Instinct came to my rescue. Agree with the nice policeman. "We are."

"What was all that screaming about a minute ago, then? Two screams, one from each of you. Sounded like black murder being done; I heard you both all the way over in the North Ravelin. You haven't murdered anyone, have you?"

Lie. "Yes."

He raised an eyebrow. "Really?"

"My father. Well, actually, my primal rage at my father. You're familiar with Janov's work?"

"Can't say I think much of it. Particularly in urban areas." He turned his gaze to Karen. "I suppose *your* father—"

"—makes his look like the Easter Bunny," Karen said. Her voice sounded okay. It held the ring of sincerity.

"I suppose you know you're not permitted to be down there, primal screaming or otherwise?"

"We're just leaving," Karen said.

"Splendid. I'll just meet you round at the Main Gate and see you both safely on your way home."

He didn't buy our story for a minute, but there was little he could do. He checked our ID. I always buy good ID. It's worth the extra money. He arched his brow at me a few times, admired Karen's ass, and let us go.

There seemed no reason to go back to the apartment. At a supermarket I bought ammo, food, and common household items with which I could make a cottage-industry bomb capable of converting a cottage into splinters. I got lucky, stole a four-wheel-drive with real muscle and a rifle behind the seat. Neither of us was hungry, but we ate anyway, and then hit the highway. It was sundown as we left the city behind.

About ten miles farther on, I pulled over at a place that was wall-to-wall forest. We walked a ways into the woods. We both sighted in the rifle and practiced with it a bit. Our unknown benefactor had bequeathed us two full boxes of slugs. The rifle was a thirty-oh-six with good action. It threw high and to the left. Karen, an indifferent pistol marksman, turned out to be damn good with a rifle. We got back in the truck and drove on.

Neither of us had had a thing to say since we had left the Citadel, barring short functional sentences. There seemed nothing to say. As we were passing Wolfville, after an hour of silence, I thought of something, and said it.

"I'm sorry I got you into this, baby."

Karen jumped. "Christ!"

"What?" The truck swerved.

"That's *spooky*, man. I was just opening my mouth to say those identical words to you."

"To *me?*" I growled. "What—"

"Yeah," she snapped back. "To you. I'm sorry I got you into this."

"I was into this before I ever laid eyes on—"

"Well, if I hadn't dragged you into this wirehead scam—"

"If I hadn't spoiled a perfectly good suicide—"

"*Dammit—*"

She stopped, and I stopped, and there was a pause, and then we both broke up. I laughed so hard I had to pull over and put it in park. We held each other awkwardly in the cramped cab and laughed on each other's shoulders.

After an immeasurable time I heard her voice in my ear. "Don't be sorry, Joe."

"You either. I might have lived out my life in New York, never knowing the Mindkiller *existed.* I might have died never knowing what my mother called me. Now at least I'm going to get some answers before I die." ("Again," I did not add.)

"I'm satisfied too. I told you once I want it should be a shame that I died. Well, if I go down before I get to shoot that mother-fucker in the belly, it'll be the dirtiest shame I ever heard of."

"That it will."

"What do you suppose his game is?"

"Power. What else? As long as he can snip sections out of memory-tape, and keep a monopoly on the secret, he's God. And it looks like he can keep a monopoly on the secret. It's that kind of secret. It has to have something to do with wireheading; remember the joint that blew up just before we left New York, and the inductance patent that wasn't in the files?"

"Sure. Inductance—that means wireheading at a distance, right? Jacques—or his agent—used some kind of wirehead field to keep us docile while he picked our brains and left us his invitation. That's why that guard heard us screaming on Citadel Hill. I bet I screamed first. And loudest." She sat up and lit a cigarette. "Do you know," she said, dragging deeply, "that there is a part of me that can't wait to get to Phinney's Cove and get another dose of the juice? Even if I don't get to keep the memory?"

I shuddered slightly. I wanted to say something to break the silence, but nothing came. I listened to the engine idling in the cool evening. I rolled down the window to let her smoke out, and heard some kind of mournful bird call. I wondered if that was an owl.

"Karen? I . . ." It wouldn't come out right. "I'm—I'm glad I've known you."

She didn't react at once. She took two more drags on her smoke, then stubbed it out and turned to face me. "I love you too, Joe."

We embraced again.

"Maybe," she said a while later, "he'll turn us loose together . . ."

"No!" I said sharply, and disengaged.

"Huh?"

"Don't think that way. Don't let there be any favor he can do for us, any boon he can grant, any hold over us. I love you and in a couple of hours we're going to die and that's the end of it."

She thought. "Yeah. You're right. God, I wish I could make it with you just once."

I kept my voice even. "Karen, I accept the compliment, and in theory I agree. But the thought makes me twitchy."

"That's cool," she said at once. "I . . . I think I kind of know exactly what you mean. I used to feel that way when I was with someone I loved."

"I think I could make *you* come."

"Yeah," she agreed. "But don't. Let's drive."

I put the van in gear.

We took the main highway all the way through the Annapolis Valley to Bridgetown, then drove up over an immense mountain. The road resembled telephone cord hanging from the ceiling, an endless upward zigzag. I was glad I'd stolen a good vehicle. Despite the extreme hairiness of the road, we were twice overtaken and passed on blind curves by farmers in battered pickups. Just after the second one yanked in front of us, a half-ton loaded to the gunwales with hardwood appeared round that blind curve, plunging downhill at terrifying speed. Its driver and the driver of the pickup waved to each other as they passed.

Eventually the road yanked around one last vicious bend and leveled out. It stayed level for a good two hundred yards, then began sloping down. About the time that the Bay of Fundy became visible below us in the moonlight, demanding our attention, the slope suddenly became drastic. I had my hands full there for a while. Then the road went into rollercoaster dips and rises for a bit before settling down to a last long downward plunge. There was a stop sign at the bottom of it. I never considered obeying it, but I was very disconcerted to learn that the road turned into gravel just past the stop sign. We damn near went into a ditch.

I got us heading west on the Fundy Trail. It was a lovely drive by moonlight and must have been stunning by day. I drank it in thirstily—and almost succumbed to the road's last crafty attempt to kill us, with a blind curve/vertical drop/vertical ascent/blind curve pattern that must have afforded the locals much amusement in the tourist season.

A brief flurry of relatively modern houses—say, thirty to fifty—called Hampton, then almost at once we were in farmer and fisherman country. Big spreads, houses well over a hundred years old and widely spaced. Some were kept up, many were hulks. Some had as many as a couple of dozen junked cars scattered around them. All the ones that looked inhabited had a woodpile and a garden. I saw outhouses. Barns. Fishing nets and traps. Great fields of hay and corn. I nearly hit a deer. The Bay was never more than two hundred yards to our right, sometimes as close as a hundred feet. There was no other traffic, and no one walking the road. Most of the inhabitable homes had few or no lights showing—folks went to bed early hereabouts. I began to wonder how we would find the "Old DeMarco Place."

Just then the headlights picked up a pedestrian, walking in our direction. I pulled up past him and waited.

In the moonlight he looked two hundred years old. He wore a disreputable woodsman's cap and carried some kind of odd stick in his hand. Stick and hand were equally gnarled.

"Excuse me, sir," I said, and he came to the window.

" 'Allo," he said. Up close his face had so many wrinkles as to preclude expression of any kind. He was two hundred and fifty if he was a day.

"We're looking for the old DeMarco Place."

"Oh, shoor," he said. His breath smelled of whiskey. "Hit be up the road some." He gestured with his stick, and I realized with faint amusement that it was a dowsing rod. "Mebbe two, tree k'lometer. You been dere before?"

"No. How'll I know it?"

"You got paper, I draw you a map."

"Are you going that far?" Karen asked.

"A little ways past."

"Can we give you a lift?"

"Shoor ting."

He was slow getting in on her side. In the sudden overhead light he looked two hundred and seventy-five. He studied Karen and me dispassionately, and showed us a smile comprising three teeth. We drove on.

"What're those?" Karen asked, pointing to what looked like three tall billboards, facing the Bay in a row, two to our left and one to our right. The two we could see had large, simple designs painted on them.

"Navigation markers for de fishermen. Line dem tree up, you know just where you are."

"What do they do when the fog rolls in?" I asked.

"Navigate by potato."

"Beg pardon?"

"You keep a bunch of potatoes on de bow. Every couple minutes, you t'row one over de bow. If you don't hear no splash—*turn.*"

Karen and I chuckled politely.

"Dere," he said after some time, pointing. A mailbox with no name marked the beginning of a rude mud-rutted path that disappeared into the woods on the left. "You follow dat up a k'lometer or so, you be dere. Tanks for de ride." He got out.

As he walked on up the road, I turned to Karen. "This is it."

She nodded.

I drove just far enough up that trail to be out of sight of the road. I turned the vehicle around to face the road. I shut it down and arranged the ignition wires so that it could be jump-started again in a hurry.

We sat a moment in silence. My window was down. I smelled fresh sweet country smells I was too ignorant to identify. I heard night creatures I could not name, small things. A car went by on the road. Tall grasses and trees whispered. I felt a sensation I remembered from Africa. An eerie, unreasoning certainty. Someone or something had a dead bead on my head. It might be a sniper with nightscope, or a heat-seeking laser, or a small dark man with a blowgun, or an ICBM silo a hundred miles away, but I was standing on the spot marked X.

Karen lit a smoke. "We're targets, aren't we?"

"We're naked. Scanned, X-rayed, doppler ultrasounded, and the contents of our pockets inventoried. You feel it too?"

"Yeah. Was it like this in the war?"

"No. This is worse."

"I thought it was. Let's not bother with weapons. They're cumbersome."

"He said they were optional."

We got out of the van, leaving the firearms in it. I got out both of my knives and the sap and tossed them onto the front seat. Karen added items, then came around to my side.

We looked uphill. The road curved up into forest. She took my hand and we walked. After a few thousand yards the woods gave way to an immense cleared field, perhaps twenty acres, most of it waist-high in hay. At the far edge, where the land turned back into forest and began climbing again, stood a house. It was a big three-story with four chimneys, two of them in use. There were lights on in the ground floor, and a spotlight illuminating a yard on the right. A jeep, a four-wheel like ours, and a Jensen Interceptor were parked in the light. There were two outbuildings. A barn the size of my New York warehouse home stood to the right of the house, and a smaller building lay to the right of that. No people or defensive structures were in evidence anywhere, not so much as a chain-link fence.

The moon was high above the mountain. It made the scene as pretty as a postcard, and would make us tabletop targets all the way to the house. The hay had been cut back on either side of the path.

"Nice spot," Karen said, and we kept walking.

After a while we became aware of how much sky there was here. I could not remember the last time my world had held so much sky. I looked up, and stopped walking, momentarily stunned. Karen kept on a few paces, then turned and followed my gaze. *"Oh."*

We watched them for a few minutes together—until the temptation to lie down on our backs and watch them forever became acute. Then I dropped my eyes, and saw Karen drop hers. We looked at each other, sharing the wonder.

"Been a long time," she said softly.

I nodded. "First time I ever shared it."

I put my arm around her and we continued on.

❖ ❖ ❖

The house looked well over a hundred years old and poorly kept up. It had no door facing the Bay, but several windows, one of them gigantic. We went around to the lighted side and found the door. It had a brass knocker. I used it. The door opened and the Fader smiled at me.

"Hi, Joe."

"Hello, Jacques. You remember my friend Karen."

"Enchanted, my dear. Please, both of you, come in and make your-selves comfortable."

❖11❖

2007

NORMAN KENT no longer wished he could die. He had stopped wishing that hours ago. What he wished now was that he could *have* died, many months previously.

Preferably at the moment when he had stood on the edge of the MacDonald Bridge, ready to jump. When his biggest problems had been a failed marriage and disgust for his chosen work. When his death would have meant no more than the end of his life.

That had been his last golden opportunity, and he had thrown it away for a hat. A half hour after that, Madeleine had come back, so briefly, into his life, and started him on the treadmill that led to this place and this time.

This time was late evening. This place was the most beautiful, luxurious, and comfortable cell imaginable.

The clock, for instance, which apprised him of the time, was a world standard chronograph of Swiss-Japanese manufacture, simple, elegant, and utterly accurate. The light by which he saw both clock and room was artfully muted and placed so as to complement the room. The furnishings—chairs, desk, shelves, tables, bar, tape system—were quite expensive and exquisitely tasteful. (The bar had not functioned since his arrival; he was on limited fluid intake.) The books lining the shelves were, in his professional judgment, impeccable. So were the audio- and videotapes. The bed in which he reclined was a rich man's powered bed, a distant and highly evolved descendant of the hospital bed. The large bay window to his left offered a stupendous view of the Bay of Fundy and a cloud-strewn sky, the faint glow of distant New Brunswick serving to hold them apart.

It was very nearly the ideal room. Only two things were immediately apparent as odd about it. First, that such a triumph of wealth and leisure should exist in the most rural part of a rural province, on the third floor of a one-hundred-and-fifty-year-old house that seemed, from the outside, quite ramshackle. Second, that a room so carefully appointed should lack any telephone equipment whatsoever.

That omission, and the fact that the bay window was shatterproof, and the fact that the door would not open at Norman's will, made it a cell.

It contained means of suicide in abundance. But Norman could not bring himself to use them. He knew that his end was coming soon enough, and he knew that it would be more painful, and more horrible, than anything he could devise himself. It was interesting to learn that he was more afraid of pain than of horror. It was the latest in a series of unendurably interesting learnings, and he knew it was not—quite—the last.

The door slid open.

He lay motionless, head still turned toward the window, but he stopped seeing the Bay.

"It has been twenty-four hours, Norman. I must ask for your answer."

Norman turned his head slowly. He marveled again at the absolute nondescriptness of Jacques LeBlanc. The man could have been a fisherman or a night watchman or a bank teller or a member of Parliament. An actor would have killed for his face; he could play any part simply by dressing for it and altering his accent. On any street in the world, from the Bowery to Beverly Hills, from the Reeperbahn to the River Ganges, he could pass unnoticed unless he chose to draw attention to himself. For some reason the eye wanted to subtract him.

"Why ask," Norman said, "when you can fucking well *take* it?"

Jacques's face remained impassive. "Because I prefer to ask."

Norman considered lying. The lie could not survive longer than ten minutes—but it might not need to. If he could convince Jacques, just long enough to lull the man into a moment's unwariness, he might get a single chance to . . .

But Jacques understood that, and the object in his hand said that even the attempt would be pointless.

Norman answered honestly. "I'm against you. With my whole heart. I think you're the greatest madman the world has ever seen, and if I could kill you now I would, whatever it cost me."

Jacques nodded gravely. "I expected as much. I hope you are wrong. Goodbye, Norman."

And he activated the thing in his hand, and Norman Kent became ecstatic.

When Jacques turned on his heel and left the room, the ecstasy went with him, and Norman Kent followed it. Doggedly. Mindlessly. Urgently. And, since his legs were adequate to the task of keeping up with ecstasy, happily.

Jacques led him downstairs, and through a living room that made Norman's cell look like servants' quarters. Jacques activated an instrument board against one wall. "Make sure the area is not under observation," he muttered to himself, summoning up reports from various security installations. Shortly he needed both hands. He put the device that was the source of Norman's ecstasy down on an end table, then met Norman's eyes. "If you touch this," he said, "it will stop working."

Norman more than half believed that Jacques was lying. But he did not dare take the chance. He waited patiently while Jacques monitored the electromagnetic spectrum for Heisenbergian observers who might seek to interact with him by the process of observation.

None was apparent. Jacques cleared the screen and retrieved his ecstasy generator. He put on a coat, and made Norman put on his own. He opened the front door onto a combination woodshed/vestibule, which only a very discerning eye would have realized was also a serviceable airlock. He led Norman into it and thence to the world outside.

It was very cold now. Norman laughed and wept with joy at the sight of snow falling from the sky. He watched individual snowflakes as he followed Jacques, for he did not need eyes to follow the ecstasy. Then he tripped over a chopping block and roared with laughter. The laughter changed in an instant to a bleat of terror as he felt happiness slipping away, and from then on he used his eyes to help him follow his perfect master.

They walked past the larger of the two outbuildings, which seemed to be a barn, to the second one, which Norman had taken for some kind of workshop. The rustic, poorly hung door, which fastened with a piece of wood spinning around a nail in the jamb, revealed behind it a more substantial door with a Yale lock. Jacques used a key in that lock, then knocked two bars of "Take Five" and said, "Open." The door gave way and both men stepped through it.

They left their coats and snowy boots in an anteroom that Norman did not bother to examine. It gave onto a room that strongly resembled an operating theater. There were six fully equipped tables, but no surgeon or support team visible.

Jacques set down the ecstasy generator. Norman stopped in his tracks. "Sit down, please," Jacques said, pointing to a table. Norman complied at once, anxious that no thought or deed of his should offend the lord, from whom all blessings flowed. Jacques touched an intercom. "Come," he said.

Two people entered the room, gowned, gloved, and masked in white. Norman became slightly uneasy, but relaxed when he saw that they were as loyal to the master as he.

"Prepare him," Jacques said, and left the room. An air conditioner clicked on as the door closed.

The two undressed Norman with efficient skill. He experienced orgasm as they removed his trousers and shorts. The only reaction they displayed was to clean him carefully with disinfectant-impregnated toweling. They helped him to lie down, and arranged his head on a complicated cradle. He felt supremely comfortable, and grateful that his ending place had been so thoughtfully prepared for him. They strapped him down at ankles, thighs, waist, wrists, biceps, and head. The head straps were complex and kept his skull immobile. The shorter of the two attendants carefully shaved Norman's head to the scalp, then painted that with disinfectant. When this was done, the taller one caused the table to "kneel" at one end, so that Norman's cranium was raised to working height and conveniently deployed. The shorter one rolled a large, ungainly machine from the wall to a place near the table, and began separating and arraying a series of leads from the machine for easy access. On Norman's other side, the tall one prepared instruments of neurosurgery.

Visualizing his death in nuts-and-bolts detail for the first time, Norman came again. A catheter accepted his ejaculate.

Jacques reentered the room. He too was surgically clothed now. Without a word he took up a tool and laid open Norman's scalp.

It felt wonderful. It felt exciting and holy. The sensations of craniotomy were nuggets of joy, and when the living brain had been laid bare and the first probes inserted, Norman was slightly disappointed to learn that there was no such extra surge of pleasure; for the brain cannot feel.

The mind, however, can, and there was indeed some small place deep within Norman's gibbering mind that was horrified by everything that was being done to him, something that strove to fight ecstasy.

But the thrill of horror outweighed the horror; that small portion of his mind was like a single ensign in a battleship full of mutineers, trapped in the paint locker.

Then the first probe reached his medial forebrain bundle, and it was as if all the ecstasy *clicked* into focus for the first time. This was perfection, this was Nirvana. He orgasmed a third time. As an ejaculation it was insignificant, but subjectively it was the fiery birth of the macrocosmic universe; his consciousness fled at lightspeed in all directions at once.

From now on, his body would have an instinctive, mindless revulsion for ecstasy.

It was several hours before Jacques required him to be conscious. Bliss gave way to pleasure, then to simple euphoria and a dreamy, slow awareness of his surroundings. What a *nice* dream that had been. And how nice to find Jacques here upon awakening. It was going to be a *fine* day.

"Hi, Jacques."

"Hello. Listen to me. I must engage your subconscious mind as well, so listen to me. If you evade my questions, if you stop listening to my voice, I will take the pleasure away. Ah, I see that you understand. Good. Listen to my voice. What is your name?"

The ensign in the paint locker knew what would happen, watched hopelessly as it happened. Your magic carpet will perform flawlessly as long as you do not think of a blue camel. Norman Kent's name leaped into his mind, in response to the question—and vanished.

It was not simply the name itself that vanished. With it went the associations and mnemonics keyed to it in his memory. Jokes from childhood about Superman, jokes from adolescence about the Norman Conquest, jokes from the jungle about the Norman DeInvasion. An old Simon Templar novel he had read many years ago, and remembered all his life because it featured a hero named Norman Kent, who laid down his life for his friends. Certain times when the speaking of his name had been a memorable event. The sight of his dogtags. The nameplate on the desk in his office at the University. His face in the mirror.

If you take a hologram of the word "love" and try to read a page of print through it, you will see only a blur. But if the word "love" is printed anywhere on that page, in any typeface, you will see a very bright light at that spot on the page. In much the same way, one of the finest computers in the world riffled through the "pages" of Norman Kent's memory, scanning holographs with a reference standard consisting of the sound of his name. Each one that responded strongly was taken from him.

All this took place at computer speed. Without perceptible hesitation the man on the table answered honestly and happily, a puppy fetching a stick. "I don't know."

"Very good. What is your wife's name?"

"I don't know."

"What were your parents' names?"

"I don't know."

"Your sister's name?"

" . . . "

"What is your occupation?"

" . . . I . . . "

"Where are we?"

" . . . "

"What is my name?"

"You are . . ."

"What did you do when you left the army?"

" . . . "

The questioning took several hours. It would be extremely difficult to pinpoint just where in there Norman Kent ceased to exist. But by the end of the interrogation he was unquestionably dead. As he had yearned to be since the long-gone jungle days. The prayer he had prayed so fervently then was retroactively answered at last: his memories now stopped there. The paint locker was empty.

He was happier than he had been in years.

He remained on that table, cocooned in ultimate peace, for an unmeasurable time, drifting in and out of sleep. Jacques visited him from time to time, always alone. As intelligence reports trickled in from Halifax and New York and Washington, Jacques would ask him additional questions, covering loopholes, sealing leaks. A microchip was wired into five of the ultrafine filaments that skewered his brain, and tucked up into a fissure in his skull. The whole assembly would escape detection by anything short of a *very* thorough CAT scan, and it would briefly scramble the recording circuits of his short-term and long-term memory systems if certain thoughts entered his mind. Any direct or associational clue that might help him deduce his former identity would trigger a (hiatus). Thoughtfully, Jacques had added a fail-safe: if someone else ever suggested to this man that he had once been called Norman Kent, the microchip would self-destruct, allowing him to consider the idea dispassionately without going into suspicious fits of paralysis.

The man on the table experienced all this through a haze of bliss. But his memory-recording circuitry was in "erase" mode; none of the experience was retained. His consciousness had a duration of perhaps four seconds total. He simply marinated in pleasure, for what seemed like forever. His body achieved orgasm every time it was capable. At the end of a week he developed a prepuce infection necessitating circumcision. He never knew it; it transpired in his sleep.

There came a time when he slept and did not wake. His dreams were confused and painful, but he could not wake. He dreamed of plugs being drawn from tight sockets in his head, phone-jack plugs and DIN plugs and little RCA phono plugs. He dreamed that a man without a face was stirring his brains with a spatula, as though they were scrambled eggs that must not stick to the pan. He dreamed that a woman with blonde hair was holding him by one hand over a harbor he could not recognize, from a bridge he could not name. He dreamed that a bear and a mouse were calling a name that he ought to recognize, but did not. He dreamed that he was in his mother's womb, and refused to leave. He dreamed that he was a burglar, that a dry voice on audiotape was acquainting him with details of a burglar's trade, and when he had mastered the lessons the voice began to teach him the rudiments of high-level computer programming.

None of these memories recorded in his conscious mind. They were groundwork only: they would give a false "echo" of familiarity when his conscious mind "relearned" them.

At some point in his sleep the ecstasy began to fade, so gradually that he never experienced a distinct "crash" state. Eventually it was completely gone. And completely forgotten.

He woke with a hell of a headache in a strange place—a very strange place.

"It's good to see your eyes open," said a man he did not know. "You've been out for a long time; for a while there I was sure you'd bought it. I got the son of a bitch, by the way."

He knew his response was silly even as he said it. "What son of a bitch? It was a mine, a Bouncing Betty."

Then his eyes took in the room around him and he knew that he was somehow no longer in Africa.

✠12✠

2011

JACQUES LED US through the woodshed into the house proper.

"Sit down," he said, smiling warmly. "Can I offer you refreshment?"

"Nothing for me," Karen said.

"Thank you. Coffee for me."

"I have some twelve-year-old Irish whiskey—"

"Perhaps another time?"

That made his smile sharpen at the corners. "Well phrased. Please—make yourselves comfortable. I'll be back in a moment."

I was bemused by my host. He was unquestionably the man I had known as Fader Takhalous in New York. But his whole manner was different. He no longer had a Bronx accent. His speech was accentless now, newscaster's English, but somehow he was unmistakably a European. The Fader had been a tired old cynic; this man was a vigorous fiftyish with sparkling eyes. He was, I could sense, smarter and faster than the man I had been subconsciously expecting to meet.

If he was leaving us alone in the room, there was no point in searching it. It was large enough to have two distinct groupings of furniture. The set to our left faced a splendid bay window, now opaqued. The second, to our right, faced a large stone fireplace in which a fire was crackling. To the left of the hearth was a powered chair, the equal of my own in New York; to the right was a small sofa facing the chair. Between them a much larger couch and a second powered chair faced the fireplace, but we never considered sitting there. To do so would present our backs to both the front door and the door by which Jacques had left the room. Karen took the sofa; I sat down in the chair and swiveled it to face the room. I noticed that she moved the sofa slightly before sitting on it. It was a good idea, but my chair was bolted down.

Jacques returned almost at once, with nothing in his hands but a remote terminal. A table followed him. At his direction it rolled itself up to the fireplace, between Karen and me, and knelt, like a New York bus, to coffee-table height.

"Slick," I said. "How does it corner?"

He was surprised for a second. He had forgotten that the table was worthy of comment. He grinned then. "Poorly. But the mileage is good."

The table contained coffee, cups, spoons, sugar, honey, and cream. The cream was at least twenty-percent butterfat. The honey was local. The sugar was unrefined. The cups were lightweight plastic, double-walled with vacuum between—they would keep coffee drinking temperature for half an hour. The coffeepot too was thermal. A trigger in its handle operated the pour spout; there was no way to make it disgorge all its contents at once. Into someone's face, say. The cups had half-lids, open just enough to admit a spoon. You could pour out their contents, but not fling them. Jacques poured all three cups, adulterated his own to taste, and sat in the powered chair.

I sipped my own coffee. As I had expected, it was fresh brewed Blue Mountain, with just a trace of an excellent cinnamon. I added cream and Jacques waited politely for us to comment on the coffee.

"Why are we here?" I asked.

"To judge me."

"To *judge*—"

"—*you?*" Karen finished.

"Yes."

"Guilty," she said at once. "Die."

Jacques smiled sadly. "I will require you to go through the formality of a trial first. An old American tradition: allowing the accused to speak his piece before you hang him."

"Do you seriously suggest," I asked, "that there can be any justification for the things you have done? That would persuade *us?*"

"It is precisely because I cannot answer that question that you are both still alive. Consider this question: How is the most powerful man in the world to know whether he is sane or not? For *certain?*"

It was a good question.

"Why would he care?" Karen asked.

That was another.

"That is a good question," Jacques said. "I will give you an honest answer, and if it sounds melodramatic, I am sorry." His voice changed. For the first time he sounded like the Fader I had known. "If I am mad, the human race has had it."

"I am afraid," I said slowly, "that I agree with you. But again, why should you care?"

He sighed. "All humans with enough imagination to understand that they will die have an intolerable problem. They must reconcile themselves to extinction, or else work at something larger than themselves, something that will survive them. Their children, most often. The identity relationship between parent and child is direct, demonstrable, basic. Some are imaginative enough to see that their children are as ephemeral as they themselves, as susceptible to chance destruction. So they transfer allegiance and identity to something more than human. To a nation, or a notion, or a religion, or a school of art."

I was almost beginning to enjoy this. This was the Fader I knew. We'd had a dozen of these raps together. It was from him that I had picked up the habit of arguing in precise, formal language, like a lecturing professor. I found that it clarified thought.

Or *had* I picked it up from him? Apparently I had once *been* a professor.

"A few," he went on, "a very few, are afflicted with the insight that all those things too are mortal. For these few there is no alternative but to love their entire *species* above all else, to love the idea of sentient life." He paused and drank coffee. "I am thus accursed. I have thought it through. I will sacrifice anything to preserve the human race. Your lives. My life. Those I love. Anything. Nothing else that I know, not planets or stars or the universe itself, has as good a chance of living forever. It's the only game in town."

I let a few seconds of silence go by. "The argument has been made before," I said. "The classic reply is, 'Who appointed *you* preserver of the human race?'"

He nodded. "I call it random chance. My lover says it was God. You might split the difference and say, 'Fate.'"

"You, in other words."

The one time I had ever beaten him at chess, I saw him smile just like that. "Yes. I chose not to duck."

"Standard answer. But if I understand you correctly, you doubt your fitness for the job?"

"That is correct."

"Now that is something new." I turned to Karen. "Which would you say is worse, honey? A confident megalomaniac, or an insecure one? Generally speaking, I mean?"

"Shut up, Joe. I'm starting to like his vibes. Listen, Jacques—I assume we're formally introduced, yes?—if I understand you, you're telling us that you did not seek the power you've got. It's kind of something that happened to you?"

He looked sad. "I'd like to say yes, but that's not strictly true. I . . . saw that the power would come into existence, would come to *someone*. Once I knew that, I was obligated. I fought the idea for almost a decade, hoping that someone else would emerge more worthy of the power. No one did, and my hand was forced. I live for the day I can put down the burden. But I took it voluntarily and wield it ruthlessly."

"You know," I said, "I'd like to believe that. I have always felt that the best candidate for a position of power should be the one who wants it least. But you have, however reluctantly, wielded that power for at least five years now—"

"More like ten."

"—and what little I personally know of the accomplishments of your administration smells rancid. You have made money from the deaths of thousands, perhaps hundreds of thousands, of wireheads. Like my friend Karen. You have learned how to make involuntary wireheads, and used that ability to make sure it stays exclusively yours. You blew up a shock doc and his shop in New York, suborned the Patent Office—"

"You scooped out Joe's brains, and put back the pieces that suited you," Karen cut in. "You kidnapped his sister—"

"What did happen to her, Jacques?"

Karen saw my face. "Easy, Joe."

"She is upstairs."

I blinked.

"She was not certain whether or not she wished to meet you. I don't believe she was certain that she even wished to monitor the video feed from this room. She was holding back tears when I left her." He saw my expression and made that pained smile again. "She is the lover I mentioned, who thinks that God did this to me."

I thought that over for a measureless time. "Why isn't her opinion of your sanity good enough for you?"

"She loves me. You two hate me."

"Huh." I burned my tongue, having forgotten about the thermal cup. "Tell me something. That shock doc in New York—that *was* your doing, yes?"

"The bombing on the lower West Side? Yes. Pure chance you were passing by. But it was *not* luck that you were not hurt. My agent had orders to wait until he was certain there was no one else in the blast zone."

That was true. "Okay. Now tell me: why a bombing? Wouldn't it have been simpler and less risky to mindwipe him?"

He was shocked. "I have had to make my own rules. One of the most important is this: I never mindwipe a man if I can accomplish my purpose by merely killing him."

I looked him square in the eye. "That is a very good answer."

He relaxed and smiled. "For a moment I thought you were serious. The thought that I might have so seriously misjudged you scared me badly."

"Yeah. You know all about me. I want to know about you."

He nodded. "And the most important things I say will be the ones I hadn't planned to say. Keep prodding."

"Why do you sell the wire?" Karen asked. She got out cigarettes and lighter, and he watched her hands carefully while replying.

"For cover, and for money."

"Cover?"

"It gave me a plausible and legitimate reason for research into brain-reward, which is the key to memory—and it gave me a plausible and legitimate reason for keeping the results of that research secret."

"With mindwipe, what do you need with money?" I asked.

"I have had mindwipe for a little over four years. It was very expensive. Projects now on the drawing boards will be so immensely expensive that I will need every little billion."

"All right. We now know at least a smattering of your means. Next topic: What are the ends that you contend justify those means?"

He nodded. "Now we are getting somewhere. Let me refill your cup. This will take some time." He busied himself with the pot. "I must start from the beginning."

I accepted more coffee, and Karen took a cup. Maximum alertness here.

"I was born into the midst of planetary war. Literally the midst, for Switzerland is bounded by France, Germany, Austria, and Italy. It was the eye of the storm, and by the time I was old enough to truly understand the danger, it was past. When I was six, my father attempted to explain to me something of the significance of the atom bomb, which had just annihilated Hiroshima and Nagasaki. He was a director of what was then Switzerland's fourth largest banking firm, located in Basel. I'm sure he made an effort to soften the horror of it, he was not trying to scare me. But when I understood that *one* bomb had destroyed a city the size of Zurich, I was appalled. I had been taken there twice, and believed it to be the largest city on earth. But my father told me that the bomb meant the end of war. He said now the whole world would have to be as smart as Switzerland, would have to learn to live together in peace, because the weapons were now so terrible that it was too dangerous to start a fight. 'What if they're not?' I asked. As smart as Switzerland." He paused a moment in thought. "Strange. One of the things I admire the most about my country is that nothing is done without consensus. To raise taxes requires a national referendum and a constitutional amendment. We did not enfranchise women until I was thirty-two years old and my mother, a neurosurgeon, was dead. A coalition of major parties has ruled for nearly half a century, talking every issue to death before anything is done. And now I, a Swiss, am acting as unilaterally as any tyrant in history. On a scale that Genghis Khan could not have dreamed of."

"God is an iron," I said.

"Eh? Oh, yes, I remember the conceit. A person who commits irony is an iron. God knows, cold and hot iron have figured prominently in His ironies. Yes, God is an iron. Switzerland produced me, And my Uncle Albert. Not really my uncle. A friend of my mother's, a chemist who worked in the big laboratory across town."

A jigsaw piece clicked into place. "Jesus. Basel. Sandoz Laboratories. Dr. Albert Hofmann."

"It was the day after my fourth birthday. Uncle Albert ingested what he thought was an infinitesimal amount of LSD-25, climbed onto his bicycle to pedal home, and took the world's first trip. The day was beautiful; I was playing outside with my new toys when he pedaled past. Even at four years old I was aware that something extraordinary was going on with him. He seemed to shine. He saw me and he smiled at me as he rode past. He did not wave or call out; he only looked at me, turning his head as he went by, and smiled. You can think of the contact-high phenomenon if it suits you. I say that for those few seconds time stopped and we were telepathic. I remember today the exhilaration . . ." He frowned down at his coffee and drank of it.

"My," Karen murmured.

"Never, even with my parents, had I felt so close to another human being, adult or child. There was a bond between us. Eighteen years later to the day, the day after my twenty-first birthday, he gave me my first dose of lysergic acid diethylamide under controlled conditions. It had been decided before my birth, possibly before my conception, that I was to be a doctor. It was Uncle Albert who suggested I go into neuroanatomy. At that time there were less than a dozen neuroanatomists on this planet, and they were some of the most eccentric men alive. I fit right in. I was something of an odd duck."

"I can imagine."

"By this time, you see, I was already deeply interested in the interface between the brain and the mind. Next to nothing was known about the brain, and I felt that better maps might be the key. It was a wide-open field, an exciting puzzle with the answers seemingly *just* out of reach, possible of attainment.

"The year I began my medical training, I read an article in *Scientific American* about the work of two men, James Olds and Peter Milner, at McGill University in Canada. They had discovered that if you placed an electrode in a certain part of the brain of a rat—"

"We know about Olds," Karen interrupted. Her voice was harsh.

"Of course you do. Forgive me. I worked with Olds, later, and with others who followed him. Lilly, Routtenberg, Collier, Penfield. After a time I worked only with myself. Routtenberg had put me onto the connection between the brain-reward system and memory formation, and I was absolutely fascinated by memory. I had decided that life is the business of making happy memories—and I was offended as a neurophysiologist to be completely ignorant of the process by which this most basic task was accomplished.

"But I had no intention of publishing my results in *Scientific American*. Or anywhere else. I had learned from John Lilly's experiences with the CIA involving brain-reward research, and Uncle Albert's experiences with the same group and others like it, that the kinds of answers I was looking for were dangerous answers."

"Tell me about your personal life during all of this," Karen said.

He sighed and sipped coffee. He got up and poked the fire with an andiron, then put on more wood. "While I was acquiring an M.D. and becoming a neuroanatomist, there was of course not much personal life to talk about. I received my doctorate at twenty-six. I had friends. I had lovers, but only the friends lasted. I don't think there was enough of me left from my work to satisfy a lover, to give to her. When I was thirty-two I met Elsa. She was as stable as I was wild. She calmed me, housebroke me. She was a cyberneticist; she could make a computer do anything, and she was deeply interested in holography. We learned from each other. We were married and had six wonderful years. Then—"

He finished his coffee and put the cup down with infinite care and attention. Then the words came out a little faster than before.

"Then a piece of equipment exploded in her laboratory. Below and to the side; a fragment evaded anything vital and entered the skull. The hippocampus and several associated structures in both temporal lobes were virtually destroyed. She lived. With anterograde amnesia."

He was silent for a few moments.

"The skills and knowledge she had acquired up until that time remained largely intact. She seemed able to register limited amounts of new information. But she could no longer retain it. Her short-term memory system and her long-term storage had been disconnected. She never again learned to recognize anyone she had not known before the accident, not even the specialists who worked with her daily. Each time she met them was the first time. Her memory had a span of perhaps ten minutes. She lived another five years, perpetually puzzled by the fact that the date always seemed to be later than it could possibly be. She never got more than ten minutes past 1978, and it seemed to confuse her a little, the way the world went on ahead without her. But she was fairly happy in general.

"I was familiar with the syndrome from correspondence with Milner. I lived with it with her until she died, working ferociously to understand her condition so that I could alleviate it. I failed. When she died I gave myself to my work entirely, as a kind of memorial. If that word is not too ironic.

"She had given me many tools, many leads. She had taught me more about computers than any university could have. She had taught me much about holography. By the time of her death, it was well established that memory storage takes place in a manner analogous to holography."

Karen frowned. "I don't think I follow."

He seemed to come back from a far place, to recall that he had listeners and a reason for speaking. "If you cut the corner off a hologram transparency, you do *not* take a corner off the image it yields. Both it *and* the cut-off corner will produce the complete, uncut image. The former will be very slightly fuzzier than before the mutilation; the latter will be quite fuzzy, but still complete. Similarly, you cannot remove a given memory by removing a specific portion of the brain. Each memory is stored *all over* the brain, in the form of a multiple redundant *pattern*. Each neuron thus represents many potential bits of information—and there are as many neurons in a brain as there are stars in the galaxy."

"So the question," I said, "is how are the memories encoded and how are they retrieved?"

"Precisely. Computer theory was essential. And my hunch was right: brain-reward was the key to the puzzle. The brain-reward aspect of memory formation was the only one I knew how to detect, and to measure and track accurately. The task was rather like a space explorer studying purely economic data for a planet, then trying to deduce or infer the body of its inhabitants' psychology. But I knew where I was going, I had known for years, and I was determined to be the first one there. By that time I had transferred my personal allegiance to the human race. The last few decades have not been such as to encourage ethical behavior by scientists, and a relatively large number of people were chasing the secrets I sought. A psychologist stood up at a Triple-A-S meeting in the mid-seventies and declared that the information-storage code of the human brain would be cracked within ten years. That frightened me. While pursuing my own researches, I did my best to cripple the work of others by feeding false data into the literature. Red herrings, blind alleys, false trails. I succeeded. By the late 1990s, I was the only one still digging at the spot marked X, unnoticed by the crowd over at the other end of the field. Simple surgery and brain/computer interface were the last tools I needed. By 2003 I had a rudimentary and cumbersome, but fairly effective, version of mindwipe. It was of some help to me in capturing the wirehead industry, and concealing the extent of my own involvement in it."

"*You* run the whole thing?" Karen exploded.

"I am and plan to remain the whole thing. I assure you that no one now living can prove that statement—although you, Joe, guessed or learned more than I would have thought possible. But the whole industry is and has been my personal monopoly."

"How *could* you—" she began, and ran out of words. She had begun to like him, and could not swallow the new information.

"Most of the basic patents are mine, under an assortment of names. If I did not do it, someone else would. Once it became possible, it became inevitable. I accepted the responsibility, destroyed all would-be competitors, and kept the industry just as small and stunted as possible. Do you remember anything of how *fast* marijuana and LSD spread in the sixties and seventies, when organized crime realized their economic potential? Has the growth of the wirehead industry been anything like that?"

No. It had not. It got a lot of talk in the media, but the numbers said it was nothing like the social problem alcohol or cocaine posed. That had always struck me as odd. People dumb enough to flirt with *heroin* would not touch the wire; it was strictly for born losers. Could that be because the wire was simply not being marketed aggressively?

"Those who seek pleasure at any cost are those to whom ethics matter least. I have been weeding the human race of its most selfish and self-indulgent."

"I'm selfish and self-indulgent," Karen said darkly.

He smiled. "Is that what brings you to Nova Scotia?"

She got her knee out of the way in time; the spilt coffee landed on the rug.

"Of *course* you were obsessed with ecstasy, having been denied it all your life. Once you tasted it in full, you established normal relations with it—one of your customers reports to me—and turned your attention to other things. To an ethical task."

She frowned, but said nothing.

"And you, Joe. I supplied you with the most comfortable and carefree existence that modern society affords, no taxes, no mortgage, no bills, and what did you do? You dumped it all for a crusade. Or did you ever seriously expect to survive this?"

"No," I said. "Not once, even from the beginning. But I had a responsibility to Karen."

"To Karen? Why?"

"I meddled in her life, spoiled a perfectly good and painless suicide. I had to accept the con—"

"Bullshit," Karen snapped.

"She is right, Joe. Paramedics spoil suicide every day, then punch out and go home. You *perceived* a responsibility. Because it suited you. Underneath it is something else. You saw the horror of Karen's experience. In your heart, you believe her cause is just. You believe, like her, that every man's death diminishes you. Don't you?"

I said nothing.

"I could be wrong, of course. It could simply be emotional involvement—"

My voice was bleak. "You, of all people, should know that I am unable to love."

This smile reached his eyes. "I don't know any such thing."

The sentence hit me like a surprise slap in the face that bewilders, hurts, and angers. "The hell you don't!" I shouted.

"Your sex drive is disconnected, yes. But these days sex and love don't even write to each other much. I think your love for Karen is very much like the love your sister has for me. And Karen's love for you is much like mine for Madeleine."

I tried to gain control of my emotions. "Perhaps I do agree with Karen about wireheading. In any case, I believe I'm ready now to render the judgment you asked for."

"Be patient. I've given you the background. I have yet to present my defense."

I had to admire his nerve.

"Proceed," Karen said after a while. She struck another cigarette.

"Thank you. As to wireheading, you must admit that the way I set up the industry, it is something that can only happen by choice. The subject has to assist in the placement of the wire. Inductance—wireheading without consent, from outside the skull—is a childishly simple refinement. I have made it my business to kill any entrepreneur who tries to introduce it.

"Should I manufacture automobiles instead, and kill more people than wireheading does *without* the element of choice?

"What you dislike about wireheading is not the wire itself. There were wirehead personalities *long* before the wire existed. What it is that horrifies you is what it displays: the component of human nature that *wants* the wire, that wants pushbutton pleasure badly enough to pay any price, that is so blind and afraid that it will suicide with a smile. You would like, rightly, to eliminate that part of human nature. I tell you that *you cannot do that by eliminating the wire.*

"My first mindwipe technique was a very clumsy and primitive thing. I could *not* erase a memory pattern, but I could, in a sense, erase its retrieval code. The memory remained in the skull, but the mind could not access it. I redoubled my efforts, because I wanted direct access to memory itself."

"True mindwipe," I said.

"If you will," he agreed. "But recall this: the same man, Heinrich Dreser, discovered both heroin and aspirin. Consider an analogy, shall we? You are an aborigine genius. Someone gives you a good reel-to-reel tape recorder. He explains electronic theory in some detail, and you are so bright you follow most of it. Then he rips out the heads and all their circuitry, destroys them, and departs—leaving behind tapes containing directions to a buried fortune. The tape transport still functions, but the heads are gone.

"Now suppose, against all odds, you somehow manage to make that tape recorder functional again. Perhaps it only takes you a few hundred years and requires a complete reorganization of your tribe. Forget all that. *Which will you succeed in reinventing first: the record head or the erase head?*"

Answering the question took a split second; it was seconds later before the implications registered. Then I was startled speechless.

"The erase head, of course," he said. "It is a much simpler device—a single blanket signal that disrupts any and all frequencies. It is an infinitely simpler task to destroy information than to encode it in the first place. Which is easier to do: create a book, or burn it?"

"My God," Karen cried. "You weren't after mindwipe. You wanted—"

"Mind*fill*," he said quietly, and the room seemed to rock around me as my beliefs began rearranging themselves.

"To continue the analogy," he went on, "I have recently learned how to build both record and playback heads. Neither process will ever be as elegant and simple as the erasure process." Suddenly there was a weapon in his hand, so suddenly that neither Karen nor I jumped. It looked like a water pistol. "With this I could remove twenty-four hours from your mind, and put your memory on hold. You experienced a taste of the latter this afternoon. To dub off a copy of those twenty-four hours' worth of memories would require much more equipment, power, and time. To play my memories into your skull would take nearly twice as much of all three. *But I could do both of those things.*

"Understand me: to copy your memories from last night to *this* moment, I would have to wait several hours, until the information has had time to soak into long-term storage. And any information that your mind's metaprogrammer elected not to store would be lost."

"Then you haven't got a handle on short-term memory?" I said, watching the water pistol.

"I know only how to erase it. Record and playback heads for it will take about three or four years to develop . . . if all goes well."

"And then you'll have true telepathy," Karen breathed.

"That is correct. And I have devoted my life to ensuring that no individual, group, or government will gain exclusive control of these developments. At present, I have a monopoly. I live for the day when I can responsibly abdicate. My secrets must belong to all mankind—or to no one."

He fell silent then. He put the weapon away. I didn't even see where. He let us have about five minutes of silence, to think it through.

The first, and least important, implication was that the deadly threat of mindwipe could be at least partially mitigated. By the record head. If there is a memory you especially want to ensure against theft, make a recording of it and put it in a safe place. If someone wants to steal your memory of this moment, right now, you have several hours to try and escape him—though that may be difficult if he has a water pistol that destroys your short-term memory as it forms, holds you mindless and happy.

But the second implication! The playback head . . .

Suppose you could give a Hindu peasant the memories of, say, a scientific farmer? Not an *account* of those memories, translated into words and retranslated into print and retranslated into Hindi—but an actual, experiential memory. What soil *looks* like and *smells* like when it is most fruitful. The sound of a correctly tuned engine. The difference between hand-tight and wrench-tight. The smell of disease. Principles of health care. They say experience is not just the best, but the *only* teacher. What if it were willing to travel?

Suppose you could give a student the memories of a professor. Log tables. Tensor calculus. Conversational Russian. The extraordinary thing about Kemal Ataturk. Pages of Shakespeare. The Periodic Table.

Suppose you could give a child the memories of an adult—of several adults.

Suppose you could give an adult the memories of a child, fresh and vivid.

Suppose you could show a Ku Klux Klanner what it is really like to be black.

Suppose you could give a blind man memories of sight. Give music to the deaf. Give entrechats to a paraplegic. Orgasms to the impotent.

Suppose the desire to know everything about your lover could be satisfied.

Suppose your need to share your own life completely with your lover could be satisfied.

Suppose a historian had access to the memories of Alger Hiss, or Richard Nixon.

Suppose politicians were required to submit to periodic memory audit.

Suppose accountants were.

Suppose you were.

Suppose a doctor could determine incontrovertibly, in a matter of hours, your innocence of a crime.

Or your guilt.

Suppose all these things became the exclusive monopoly of anyone. Like Jacques's monopoly on wireheading . . .

I opened my mouth to ask Jacques a question. I don't remember what it would have been. A board lit up on the wall across the room, over his terminal, and he gave it instant, total attention. Almost at once he relaxed slightly, but got up from the chair nonetheless and walked to the board.

"No reason to be alarmed," he said. He punched a few buttons, studied a readout, and nodded. "Perfectly all right. For a moment I thought we had uninvited guests, but it is only an animal. No sentience-signature in the brain waves." He frowned. "Big animal, though. I thought—" Suddenly his voice was urgent. "*Fast* animal!" He punched more buttons in a great hurry, and fire erupted in the night outside through the big bay window. Laser come a-hunting. He half turned toward the window and it exploded into the room in a spray of glass, letting in fire and smoke and sudden thunder. A man came headfirst through the hole it left, rolled when he hit the floor, and came up on his feet. His gun covered all three of us, settled on Jacques.

Karen and I sat very still, sudden breeze fanning our hair.

✠13✠

2011

HIS EYES WERE BROWN. Black pants, turtleneck, and boots. Nightsight goggles pushed up onto his forehead. An odd headgear covered everything but his eyes. He seemed to have taken five yards of heavy-duty metal foil, painted it black, crumpled it until it was all over wrinkles, and then molded it around his head like a ski mask, in multiple layers. It distorted the shape and contours of his head. All at once I understood it. Jacques broke the silence. "My guards?"

"I got them both."

Jacques looked very sad. I liked his sadness. "Why are you here?"

His voice from under the foil was vaguely familiar. "I'm here to kill you, LeBlanc. And steal your magic."

"What do you know of my magic?"

"I know everything about you. For instance, you have a weapon. Give it to me very carefully. Very slowly."

Jacques complied.

"I've been tracking you for five years. And you know nothing about me."

"On the contrary, Sergeant Amesby. I know you to be one of the finest policemen in the world."

Amesby. The cop who had handled Maddy's case. My mind went into passing gear.

Being recognized rocked him a little; he tried not to show it. "I've put five years in on you, all by myself, without letting anyone else know what I was doing, because I had some kind of notion of how important you'd turn out to be. But I've left records where they'll be found in the event of my untimely death, so you daren't kill me even

213

if you could. And you can't brainwipe me as long as I'm wearing this helmet. And it isn't coming off until one of us is dead. I know all about you, LeBlanc."

"Who am I, then?"

"You are the first genuine ruler of the world. And I'm your successor."

Jacques burst out laughing. "*You* will replace *me?*"

"Why not? As of tonight, *everything you know belongs to me.*"

Jacques's laughter chopped off short.

"Why did you happen to pick tonight?" he said at last.

"Kent, here."

I blinked. Me, he meant.

"He's how I got into this—him and his sister—and he's the only part of it I never understood. What the *hell* he does for you that was worth all the trouble you took, I can't for the life of me figure out, and that makes me uneasy. I did a lot of sniffing around in this neighborhood, times you were off in Switzerland and Washington and places. Mapping your security perimeters, testing the helmet, asking questions of the locals. There's an old fart west of here used to know Kent. He was the last person to see Kent before he disappeared. He called me tonight, said he saw Kent and a woman come here, and he said Kent acted like he didn't know him anymore. That puzzled me. I remembered a phone call I got this morning, a voice that sounded familiar but I couldn't place it. It just didn't add up. I had Kent figured for dead. I've been thinking about making my move for a couple of months now. I decided if I did it tonight I might get the only answers I haven't got yet."

He turned to Karen and me.

The gun was a Yamaha Disruptor, with solenoid trigger and twenty-five-round capacity. A sneezing cat makes more noise. A slingshot has more recoil. The M-40 I used in the jungle has about the same stopping power. Two guards lay dead outside, presumably good guards. He had dodged a tracking laser. I feared him.

While he was looking at us, Jacques was situated at the extreme limit of his peripheral vision. Jacques shifted his stance very slightly—experimentally? hard to say—and Amesby, without moving his eyes a millimeter, produced a second Disruptor from a back-pocket holster and drew a dead bead on Jacques's nose.

Oh, my mind scrabbled around in my skull like a trapped rat.

Jacques had been right. This hick cop was *good,* was seriously dangerous. And he wanted answers I did not have and he was going to kill me if he didn't get them. Probably even if he did. I sensed that Jacques was worried, though he hid it well, and that realization nearly panicked me. If *he* had no ace up his sleeve, no rabbit in the hat—

Oh, God. He did have a rabbit—he was worried that the rabbit might be foolhardy enough to take on the fox. Maddy. Something about a video feed from this room . . .

"All right, Norman, talk to me. How do you figure in this business? Just where the hell do you fit?"

Now, there was a question—and the clock running out. I yearned for the comfort and security of a burglar's life.

I could see Jacques looking at me, wondering how I would play it. This was the first moment that day that I had not been under threat of instant death from Jacques, and we both knew that. If I could convince Amesby of that, maybe we could deal. I might convince him, too; I was sure he had scouted our four-wheel and seen the weapons we'd abandoned.

I think what decided me was the grief that had splashed across Jacques's features when he heard that his two guards were dead. I knew that he was one of the best actors alive—but the sadness had been too spontaneous to be faked. He cared when his employees died.

I took my face out of neutral. I gave Amesby mild, sour amusement. A very small smile, a slight shake of the head, a suggestion of a sigh. Then I turned away from him, powering the chair around thirty degrees to face Jacques. Because of Amesby's solenoid trigger, I wanted to do it very slowly. So I mashed the button down and whipped the chair around just as fast as it could go. Both my hands remained in sight; Amesby flinched but held fire.

"Sometimes being half smart is worse than being stupid." I smiled wickedly at Jacques. "Who'd know better than you, eh?"

Without waiting for his reaction, I whipped the chair back to face Amesby again. His flinch was not visible this time, but I knew that was twice he had decided not to kill me. A habit to encourage. He was now conditioned to permit sudden movements in front of his eyes.

I said, "I own you or I kill you, sonny, there's no third way. Make up your mind."

"*You* own—?"

I sighed. "*Look at me,* jerk."

He frowned and looked closer. The timing was important. In the split second *before* he got it I said, very softly, "Am I Norman Kent?"

"Jesus." He stared. "By Jesus, you're not! But who—"

I kept my eyes on his, held out my left hand toward Karen. "Cigarette, please," I murmured. And bless her, she was with me, she said "Yes, sir" quite smartly, struck a cigarette, and placed it between my spread fingers as smoothly as if she were accustomed to it. It is much easier to put across aristocratic superiority if you have a cigarette to work with. It is not necessary to smoke it.

As this business ended, Amesby got his first question formulated in words and drew breath to ask it. "Shut up," I said, with absolutely no whip-of-command in my voice. He obeyed. "You don't know *what's* going on, do you? You actually thought Le Blank here was the top man. You really thought I was Kent." I shook my head. "I don't know that you're bright enough to be worth keeping. How long did you say you'd been working on this? Five *years?*"

He was good. He was very good. His mind must have been racing at a thousand miles an hour, but his face gave away nothing at all. I glanced at the knuckles of his gun hand and saw that he was wondering, But why can't I just pull this trigger?

There were two places my sister could be. She could be upstairs with the video switched off, crying at the thought of her crippled baby brother down in the parlor. If so, she was safe. If not, she was standing about fifteen feet away, trying frantically to think of something. Only one door led from this room into the rest of the house. It lay well within Amesby's field of vision. I had been observant when Jacques had come through it with his coffee cart. It opened on a long hallway, not much wider than the doorway. The doorknob was on the right. From Madeleine's perspective it would be on the left, and the door would open toward her. She was right-handed. She could pull the door open with her left hand, wait for it to get out of her way, and fire backhand. Or she could pull the door with her right hand and try a left-handed shot. Neither was very good, against a man with one gun on her lover and another on her brother. Could I sucker his gaze away from the door? No, his instincts were too good, it would be pushing him too hard.

I knew she was there. I could feel her there. I could hear her pleading with me to come up with something. I was running out of seconds.

"*I'm* a layer or two from the top, sonny, and Le Blank here jumps when I say frog. If he's all you've come up with after five years, I don't think the firm will be interested in your services." I raised my voice. "Madeleine, dear, come in here, will you?"

Everyone turned to the door, and it opened, not too fast and not too slow, and Madeleine Kent walked into the room with both hands prominently empty. Her bearing was regal. Her eyes swept the room, dismissed everything but me. I did not recognize her.

"Yes, sir?"

"Radio the ship. Tell them there will be three bodies to be picked up for disposal. Oh, and tomorrow evening I want you to order a new bay window from Halifax, and arrange for something local until it arrives." I dropped my cigarette on Jacques's expensive rug and trod it out. "I think that's all."

"Very good, sir." She turned to go.

"Hold it right there," Amesby snapped, his voice cracking on the last word. One of his guns tracked her, trembling just perceptibly.

She came to a gradual stop, turned slowly, and stared at him as though he were something distasteful written on a wall. His gun did not even rate a glance. "Are you speaking to me?"

I had run this bluff just about as far as I could. I had him off balance, paranoid. I had kept him on the trembling verge of pressing that trigger for so long that his finger had to be tired. One disadvantage of a solenoid trigger. I had managed to introduce a fourth person into the room without provoking shots. Now he had four threats to cover with two guns. It takes an extraordinary mind to handle more than three of anything without time-sharing.

But he had an extraordinary mind. And in my scale of evaluations, the most expendable person in the room was me. I wanted insurance.

"What I'm doing, lady," he said, his voice dismayingly strong, "is promising to shoot you in the belly if you take a step or move some way I don't like."

"Do you know why you're still alive, Amesby?" I asked. "It's a matter of probabilities. I settled it to my satisfaction in Africa, a long time ago. Even if you put a nice heavy high-velocity load right on the money, just punch a couple of vertebrae right out and bounce the skull off the ceiling, there'll still be about a ten-to-fifteen-percent chance that the corpse's trigger finger will clench. Spasmodic nerve action, like a headless chicken. Ten to fifteen percent. I'll take those odds if I have to, if you even *look* like actually pressing a trigger. But frankly, I would rather negotiate."

He grinned. "Who's going to shoot me? Her?"

"Did you happen to catch Le Blank's face when you told him 'both' his guards were dead? How it took him a second to get a sad face on? You clown, *you missed the point man.*"

He did *not* turn to, or even glance toward, the shattered bay window to his right. I had never expected him to. Whether he bought the bluff or not, there was no point in turning to see. But he bought it, I could see him buy it in his heart. I had softened him up enough, hit him from enough different directions in a short enough time frame to give him the feeling that he had stumbled into a threshing machine. Now he had five things to keep track of.

"So I've got a ten-to-fifteen-percent chance of negotiating a mutually satisfactory settlement," he said at last. "Until we do, the first one of you that moves is catfood."

In that moment I respected him enormously. I was glad, because I knew he was going to kill me.

"The rest of you *sit still,*" I ordered. "I refuse to be killed by a headless clown, if it can be avoided." I hoped they would keep backing my play and follow orders. "All right, Amesby, what have you got to trade with?"

"I told you: I left evidence behind, in enough different places that even you can't find them all. Kill me and you're blown."

I smiled politely. "I don't think I'll lose much sleep over the Halifax Police Department—once you're retired from it."

"Yeah? How about Interpol and the—" He shut up and looked properly disgusted at himself for giving away information. "Believe me, you'll never find all the stashes I left. You'll blow LeBlanc, and that's got to be at least a large part of your organization."

I frowned and tried to look like I was not worried. Casually, I put my right foot up on the chair and rested an elbow on my knee. Now

I had one foot under me. At last I nodded. The good executive makes decisions without wasting time.

"All right. We'll make a place in the firm for you. You can be one of the lesser gods—but you'll wear a belly bomb just like the rest of us and you'll take orders." I raised my voice two notches. "If he puts up his guns, let him live."

He took a full ten seconds making up his mind. Then, slowly and deliberately, he pointed both guns at the ceiling and waited to see if he was going to be shot by my imaginary assassin.

Pointing at the ceiling wasn't good enough. He was too far away. I glanced toward the window, widened my eyes, and roared, "Dammit, *no!*"

I had to assume that this time he would go for it. As he began to pivot, I rocked forward and launched myself. I expected him to check in midstream and kill me, but I thought I could immobilize one or both of the guns long enough for Karen or one of the others to find a weapon and use it. I was so full of adrenalin the seconds were passing by like clouds.

There is a bit of movie film I will carry around in my skull forever. It is a silent movie, no soundtrack at all. I am partway to Amesby, in midair and in ultraslow motion, arms coming up. One of the Yamahas is arcing around toward me, almost there, while the rest of him continues to spin toward the window. Suddenly a hole appears in the neck of his helmet, under his Adam's Apple, the size of a Mason jar lid. I continue to drift toward him a few more inches, and see two vertebrae leave the back of his neck, one atop the other in stately procession, attended by gobbets of meat and larynx. A moment later his body begins to travel backward and his head starts to come forward. The body wins the uneven argument, but as it drifts back out of my way I see his nose hit his chest. The coffeepot, thrown by Karen, passes through the space his head used to occupy, trailing drops of the world's best coffee. I note with approval that his hands have reflexively *opened;* both guns are airborne. The sound of the shot arrives. I am still a few feet from the point at which we would have met if he had kept the appointment, beginning to think about my landing, when Madeleine slams into his shins from the side. Her intent is to knock his feet out from under him, but the slug that killed him has already made a pretty good start on that. One of his feet swings high and wide, impacts solidly on my left temple. There is a sudden jump-cut and I am on the floor on my belly, all the wind knocked out of me.

God, what a team! I though as reality returned to real-time. We *all* got him! But where did Jacques have that holdout hidden? I got one elbow under me, craned my head around, and took inventory. Amesby down. Madeleine getting up. Karen bending to retrieve one of Amesby's guns. Jacques right where I had left him, his mouth a comical O, his hands empty at his sides. His gun had fallen to the floor, then. No, it hadn't. But there wasn't anywhere *on* him to conceal a gun capable of blowing a spinal column in two.

The voice came from the window. "Corporal, that was the *busiest* fucking sixty seconds in the history of the world."

I recognized the voice and I recognized the words. Subjectively, I had last heard both five years ago, in a damp trench full of fresh corpses on the Tamburure Plains.

"Bear!"

I rolled and looked and indeed it was him, face darkened with mud. He stood just outside the ruined window with weapon still extended. It was an Atcheson Assault Twelve—a twelve-gauge shot-gun with a twenty-round drum and automatic or semiautomatic fire. He was ten years older than I remembered him. "Sergeant Bear, if you please." His eyes went to Jacques. "I assume Joe passes the exam?"

Jacques blinked, drew a deep breath, and nodded. "I would say so, yes."

He lowered the Atcheson then, and stepped gingerly in the window.

"Joe," Karen called. "You know this guy?"

"Bear Withbert. He saved my ass in Africa once. I told you about him." I smelled eucalyptus just seeing him. You crush the leaves and rub them on your hide for insect protection in the jungle. "If he's with Jacques, I am."

"Honest to Christ, Corporal, you damn near gave me fits for a while there. First you blow Madeleine's cover, and then you like to blow my own. And you know perfectly well there ain't more than a five-percent chance of a spinal shot going wrong. I couldn't figure out *how* the hell you wanted me to play it. How did you know I was out there?"

I got to my feet and worked my shoulders. For the first time in a very long while, I felt very good. "I didn't. I was just trying to divide up his attention too many ways."

He stared. "You were bluffing?" He turned to Jacques again. "Sign this one up, boss." He safetied the shotgun and set it down against the wall. He walked across the room, pulling out a handkerchief. He picked up Amesby's vertebrae in it. He rolled it up and tucked it into Amesby's pants pocket. He lifted Amesby's shoulders; the head dangled by the sterno-mastoid muscles. The metal foil made a crinkling sound. The features were deformed by hydrostatic pressure, eyes burst. "I'm afraid this rug is shot." He stripped off his black rainproof poncho and used it to wrap the upper portion of the body. He picked it up in his big arms and headed for the outside door. Madeleine held it open for him, then got the outer door. She closed and sealed both behind him.

"Madeleine," Jacques said, with just the right amount of irony, "please radio the ship and tell them there'll be three for disposal. And would you order a new window tomorrow?"

Karen glared at me.

"I was bluffing, I tell you," I said weakly. "It just seemed the logical way to handle the ones you use up."

"Jacques, stop teasing him," Madeleine said. "He was brilliant. I almost believed him myself." She came close to me, stopped, and looked me over carefully. She nodded slightly to herself. There were pain and guilt in her eyes, but there was courage there too. The pain was not crippling, the guilt not shameful. She was sorry, but unrepentant. "Thank you for saving Jacques. For saving everything. You did a good thing, Joe."

It was odd. With that last sentence she reminded me for the first time of the childhood sister I recalled; she had said that to me a hundred times while I was growing up. But she said "Joe," not "Norman." With that one sentence it was as though she were offering to transfer her sisterhood from Norman Kent to Joe, uh, Templeton. She saw that register on me, and waited for my response. I noticed that she had stopped breathing. Jacques too was watching me intently.

"My pleasure, sis."

She exhaled and her whole face lit up. Jacques relaxed. Karen got up and put an arm around me and kissed me on the cheek. I put an arm around her too. "So we're bright enough to be offered jobs, eh? Both of us?"

"I knew I wanted you both before I invited you here. The question was, did you want me? Yes, you're both in, and you won't be 'like gods,' but you won't wear belly bombs either. You probably will die unpleasantly, like Reese and Cutter outside, but you'll do it voluntarily."

"I knew that," I said. "I had to make the pitch plausible to Amesby's kind of man. Tell me something: how come I pass now? Why did I fail four and a half years ago?"

"I offered you the choice then. Join my conspiracy or be mind-wiped. You chose the latter. I've never been sure why."

It was hard to get a handle on. "Can mindwipe change personality that much?"

"Personality is built with memories."

"Joe, let me try," Madeleine said. "When I got to Nova Scotia from Switzerland, you were in *rotten* shape. The war had shattered you, busted your philosophy of life apart. You made a superficial adjustment, and in a few years it started to go sour. It all came apart on you. Your work, your marriage, your self-respect. You were suicidal when I arrived. I was confused myself. We leaned on each other. We became close. And so you were set up for the coup de grace.

"I had left Switzerland because I discovered, accidentally, that the man I had come to love was someone I did not know at all. I knew almost nothing—hints, little things that didn't add up—just enough to know that Jacques was something more than what he claimed to be. I presumed this to be sinister. International espionage, drugs, I suspected one of those. I left him without telling him I was leaving. I came to Canada, where I thought he could not find me, to think things through. And I smuggled a present for you through customs. A phonograph record. Lambert, Hendricks, and Ross, mint condition. It got past customs, but an agent of Jacques scanned my luggage more thoroughly and reported the package to him. He had to assume it was a laser disc full of damaging computer data that I was planning to use against him."

"It hurt to think that," Jacques said. "I had her watched very carefully for a few weeks. She did nothing alarming, but finally I decided

I could not afford to leave the situation unresolved. I ordered her kidnapped and taken into the country. I planned to come at once and interrogate her, but I was delayed."

"An assassination attempt," Maddy said drily. "He was a week recovering in hospital. Then he came here and told me who and what he was, and . . . well, we've been together ever since.

"But by that time it was too late to undo my 'kidnapping.' There was no explanation I could give you or the police, and besides, I could be of more use by remaining underground. I *had* to leave you in the dark; you were in no shape to handle anything like this.

"So you had the last pillar knocked out from under you. After a while, all that sustained you was fury at whoever had taken me from you. You kept digging until you found Jacques, and you came after him with a gun. Much like Amesby did tonight. Except that you were out for vengeance rather than gain."

"You weren't as good as Amesby then, Joe," Jacques said. "You never got close. I must say you did a much better job of stalking me the second time."

"I had more information this time. So you bagged me."

"By then," Maddy continued, "you had too much invested in hating Jacques. You couldn't shift gears. You didn't want to. You knew mindwipe was a kind of death, and you'd been wanting to die for some time."

"Jacques, why didn't you just kill me? I would have."

"I begged him not to," Maddy said, her voice firm and strong. "I argued that if you were taken back to the war years, and allowed to start all over again, you might just take a different path from there."

I grimaced. "So I spent four years doing nothing whatsoever and then became a crusader."

"Not so," Maddy insisted. "You spent four years coming to terms with the war."

"War can be exhilarating, exciting," Jacques said. "That is its dirty secret. A life-threatening situation is stimulating. If you know that, it is because you are the one that survived. So, if you are an introspective, sensitive man, you may mistakenly decide that it is killing that excites you—when in fact the exciting part is almost-being-killed. To encourage you to stay underground, I gave you enough illicit computer power to plunder banks at will—yet you chose to become a burglar. To put yourself on the line, to give your victims, and the police, a fair crack at you. You used the computer only to give you an edge. In that four years you had some very narrow squeaks, and you acquired some interesting scars, and you never killed anyone. Look at you: that little dance you just did with Amesby got you high, didn't it? The crucial element that was missing in the war, and that has been present in your life since I set you down in New York, is ethical confidence. You *believe* in the causes you fight for now. Or else you don't fight. I know I can trust your commitment, because you fought for me."

"How did the Bear come to work for you?"

Madeleine answered. "He and his wife, Minnie, moved to Toronto shortly after you moved up here. They came back to visit you before you dropped out of sight. You told them the whole story, and so when you did disappear, Bear and Minnie decided that Jacques had had you killed. It bothered them both—they both loved Norman Kent—but there was nothing they could do. They couldn't go off commandoing like you, they had responsibilities. Minnie was tied to her job, and Bear was inhibited by Minnie's being pregnant. Then, four months later, she was killed in an auto accident. When he was over his grief, Bear decided it would be good therapy to go look up Jacques. He went through much the same thing you have today—without the floor show. He's been with us ever since."

There was no way to take this all in; I filed it for later. Bear married, and widowered. I wondered if I had liked this Minnie, if Norman would have mourned her. "Everything has ripples, doesn't it?" I had a sudden alarming thought. "Hey! How badly is Amesby's planted evidence going to mess us up?"

Jacques smiled. "Not too badly, I think. You pumped him well; I believe he left leads only with the RCMP and Interpol, and we have both of them under control. It may even be possible to recover the evidence before his death is known."

"So where do we go from here?"

His smile widened. "Lots of places, Joe. Lots of places. I intend to loose mindfill on the world, for good or ill, in a little more than three years. We will be busy."

I was shocked. "Three years?"

"That soon?" Karen gasped.

"I'd like it to be longer. But I can't keep the lid on forever, even with mindwipe to help. The leaks keep getting harder to patch, and the assassins keep getting better. As it is, I don't know if I'll live to see even the first-order results of what I have done."

"But how can you get the world ready for a trauma like that in three years?" Karen shook her head. "Sounds to me like World War Three and a new Stone Age. You read the papers. The world ain't *ready.*"

Jacques nodded in agreement. "It will be necessary," he said in a perfectly normal, conversational tone of voice, "to conquer North and South America, Europe, Pan Africa, the Mideast, Greater India, Russia, China, Asia, Japan, Australia and Antarctica, without letting anyone know we've done it."

"Oh," she said weakly. "Well, as long as you've got it worked out, okay."

"Jacques," Madeleine said reprovingly, "you are an awful tease. Karen, honey, come here." She led Karen to the couch and sat them both down. "Who is the most powerful man in the United States?"

She gestured with her head toward Jacques. "Besides him?"

Madeleine smiled. "Yes, hon. Besides him."

"The President."

Madeleine kept smiling while she shook her head. "No. It's the man who pulls the President's strings, dear. For decades now, it has been impossible for a man suited to that power to be elected. Stevenson was the last to try. The rest of them accepted the inevitable and worked through electable figureheads. There hasn't been a president since Johnson who wasn't a ventriloquist's dummy. Some of them never knew it. The present incumbent, as a matter of fact, has no idea that he is owned and operated by a mathematician from Butler, Missouri. They've never been introduced. But *we* know—so we needn't waste time and energy trying to get past the Secret Service."

"I'm beginning to see how I can be of help to you," Karen said.

"You're very quick."

They smiled at each other. They were going to be friends.

I had reached that state of mind in which nothing can surprise. If Amesby had walked back into the room, on fire, I'd have offered him coffee. "So we conquer the world . . ."

"A necessary first step," Jacques agreed. "Then it gets harder." He laughed suddenly. "Listen to me, eh, Madeleine? All my life I have thought of myself as a rational anarchist. Albert Einstein said once, 'God punished me for my contempt for authority by making me an authority.' "

"Darling," my sister said, "lay out the Grand Plan later. Right now Joe has a choice to make."

He blinked. "Yes, my dear. Quite right."

Choice to make? Sure, anything, go on, ask me anything.

"Joe, would you like your memories back?"

I stopped moving. I stopped breathing. I stopped seeing. I stopping thinking. I kept hearing.

"You received the most primitive form of mindwipe. I spoke of it before. The memories themselves were not actually erased. They . . . they were hidden from your mind's metaprogrammer. The access codes were removed from the files. And placed, as carefully as the state of the art allowed, in *my* files. I can put them back now if you want."

He waited in vain for a response. He went on, his voice strained, "Some damage will always remain. If I restore your access to those memories, they will . . ." He reached for words. "Joe, one day soon I will play into your head a tape of my memories of the last thirty years. It will take a few hours. When I'm done, you will have access to everything I've done and seen and thought. You will be able to recall it all, experience it through the eyes of the viewpoint character. But you will not confuse those memories with your own experiences. The *identity* factor will be attenuated. The memories will have a kind of 'third person' feel—the experiences of someone not-you. Ego knows its own work.

"Memory is a living process—continually shuffling and rearranging itself. By fencing off some of your memories for so many years, I weakened them, blurred them slightly. The gestalt they were part of no longer—quite—exists. Those years I stole from you will, at best, always seem like something that happened to someone else. But they are not necessarily completely lost to you."

He stopped talking again for a time. Then: "It is the only restitution I can offer for what I have done to you. If you refuse, I will understand."

Then he shut up completely.

I sat down on something. Hot wetness occurred in my mouth. Coffee the way I like it. I swallowed. My vision cleared and I saw Karen staring into my eyes from a foot away. "Thanks," I said, and took the cup from her.

She turned to Jacques, her expression angry. "Will it make him whole again? Or mess him up more?"

Madeleine answered. "Karen, listen to me. I have in my skull the memories of more than a hundred people, in whole or in part. Jacques has nearly three times that many. Between us we know more about human psychology than anyone now alive. This will make him whole if anything can. It will be up to him. It always is."

I put down the cup. I got up and went to Madeleine. She was standing near the fire. It was only coals now, but still quite warm. I put my hands on her shoulders.

"Were there any good times in there at all, Maddy?"

I recognized her now. The expression on her face I had seen often in childhood. When I broke my tooth. When I failed Social Studies. When I got mugged. When my first love left me.

"Yes, little brother. A few, at least, that I know of; I've never audited your tapes. Not many, I won't lie to you. Those were not your best years, Norm—Joe. A man sets a mine that very nearly kills you, to further a cause that he believes in, and your mind can find no good excuse to hate him and your heart can't help it. That's hard to integrate. It got worse from there, steadily. But yes, there were good times. Just not enough. We got to know each other, at least, at last, and I loved you."

"Did I love you?"

"You needed me"

I turned to Jacques. "Do it. Tonight. Now."

They took me to a white sterile place like a cross between an operating theater and the bridge of the Space Commando's starship. They laid me down on a very comfortable table. They spoke soothingly to me. They placed under my head and neck what felt like a leather pillow. It was comfortable. They folded parts of it over across my forehead and secured them. My heart was racing.

Karen's face appeared over mine. Her voice was the only one that didn't seem to be coming from underwater.

"Joe? Remember how I'd forgotten most of that stuff about my father? And then after I told you about it, I could handle it? You're a brave son of a bitch, Joe, and someday I want to swap memories with you, if you're willing."

My mouth was very dry. "I love you too."

She kissed me, and her face withdrew. A tear landed on my chin. I tried to wipe it, but my arms seemed to be restrained.

"*Now*, Jacques!" Like two decks of cards being shuffled together.

First, large cuts, thick stacks.

I fought in the jungle burgled apartments taught English befriended pimps and thieves bungled a marriage found Karen in the living room found Maddy in the living room hunted the man behind her death hunted the man behind her death tracked him to Nova Scotia to Phinney's Cove died killed.

Then individual cards.

The hoarse panting breath of the mugger beside him on the MacDonald Bridge. The terrible smile on Karen's face as I cleared the doorway. Weeping in Maddy's arms, the top of his head bruised and sore. The smell of Karen's cigarettes. Naked at the door and Lois grinning at him from the hallway. The sound Karen made when she came the first time. Minnie in his arms, calling his name. "—coward, what's he doing?" The nurse calling me "Norman" and fainting. The Bay of Fundy as the sun goes down, magnificent and indifferent and I know I'm going to die soon. She's sorry she got me into this, and the sky is so full of stars! That luxurious cell, Jacques will be here soon for my decision. The flat, anechoic sound of the shot that killed Amesby. My God, what if Maddy's never *coming* back? The bitch broke my nose. God damn it, Sarge, the poor bastard's dead *we've got to bug out now!* He has to be the spitting image of her old man, oh, Christ. It's not really you I'm screwing, Mrs. MacLeod, it's your husband. The shock doc has the emptiest eyes I've ever seen. I'm gonna find that son of a bitch and kill him twice. This one's my size, no relatives, he'll do just fine. It's *his computer*, Karen, we're blown. We can really change the world. I love you too, Karen. Heinrich Dreser gave us both heroin and aspirin. God is an iron.

❖ ❖ ❖

This is my memory record of how I came to join the conspiracy. Since it is the third record you have audited, you will probably understand why I have ordered it as I have. I want you to see the two paths I took, and the choices they led to. It will shed some light on why, of two very similar people, one will opt to join our conspiracy and one will not. Later records will be even more instructive in this regard.

One of the very best things about pooling memories is that it allows us to learn from each other's mistakes. And from our own.

If we have not already met, I love you for the choice you have made. We will prevail!

Tomorrow's record will be that of my wife, Karen.

TIME PRESSURE

**For all my North Mountain friends, hippies,
locals and visitors,
and for Raoul Vezina and Steve Thomas**

✦PROLOGUE✦

I guarantee that every word of this story is a lie.

✤ONE✤

IT WAS A DARK and stormy night . . .

Your suspension of disbelief has probably just bust a leaf-spring: how can you believe in a story that begins that way? I know it's one of the hoariest clichés in pulp fiction; my writer friend Snaker uses the expression satirically often enough. "It was a dark and stormy night—when suddenly the shot rang out. . . ." But I don't especially want you to believe this story—I just want you to listen to it—and even if I were concerned with convincing you there wouldn't be anything I could do about it, the story begins where it begins and that's all there is to it.

And "dark" is *not* redundant. Most nights along the shore of the Bay of Fundy are not particularly dark, as nights go. There's a *lot* of sky on the Fundy Shore, as transparent as a politician's promise, and that makes for a lot of starlight even on Moonless evenings. When the Moon's up it turns the forest into a fairyland—and even when the big clouds roll in off the water and darken the sky, there is usually the glow of Saint John, New Brunswick on the horizon, tinting the underside of clouds sixty kilometers away across the Bay, mitigating the darkness. (In those days, just after Canada went totally metric, I would have thought "forty miles" instead of sixty klicks. Habits *can* be changed.)

The day had been chilly for late April and the wind had been steady from the south, so I was not at all surprised when the snowstorm began just after sundown. (Maybe you live somewhere that doesn't have snow in April; if so, I hope you appreciate it.) It was not a full-scale mankiller blizzard, the sort where you have to crack the attic window for breathing air and dig tunnels to the woodshed and the outhouse: a bit too late in the year for that.

Nonetheless it was indisputably a dark and stormy night in 1973— when suddenly the snot ran out. . . .

Nothing less could have made me suit up and go outside on such a night. Even a chimney fire might not have done it. There is a rope strung from my back porch to my outhouse during the winter, because when the big gusts sail in off that tabletop icewater and flay the North Mountain with snow and stinging hail, a man can become hopelessly lost on his way to the shitter and freeze to death within bowshot of his house. This storm was not of that caliber, but neither was it a Christmas-cardy sort of snowing, with little white petals drifting gently and photogenically down through the stillness. Windows rattled or hummed, their inner and outer coverings of plastic insulation shuddered and crackled, the outer doors strained and snarled at their fastenings, wind whistled through weatherstripping in a dozen places, shingles complained and threatened to leave, banshees took up residence in both my stovepipes (the two stoves, inflamed, raved and roared back at them), and beneath all the local noise could be heard the omnipresent sound of the wind trying to flog the forest to death and the Bay trying to smash the stone shore to flinders. They've both been at it for centuries, and one day they'll win.

My kitchen is one of the tightest rooms in Heartbreak Hotel; on both north and south it is buffered by large insulated areas of putatively dead air (the seldom-used, sealed-up porch on the Bay side and the back hall on the south). Nevertheless the kerosene lamp on the table flickered erratically enough to make shadows leap around the room like Baryshnikov on speed. From where I sat, rocking by the kitchen stove and sipping coffee, I could see that I had left about a dozen logs of maple and birch piled up on the sawhorse outside. I was not even remotely inclined to go back out there and get them under cover.

Dinner was over, the dishes washed, the kitchen stove's watertank refilled and warming, both stoves fed and cooking nicely, chores done. I cast about for some stormy night's entertainment, but the long hard winter just ending had sharply depleted the supply. I had drunk the last of my wine and homebrew a few weeks back, had smoked up most of the previous year's dope crop, read all the books in the house and all those to be borrowed on the Mountain, played every record and reel of tape I owned more than often enough to be sick of them, and the weather was ruining reception of CBC Radio (the only tolerable station of the three available, and incidentally one of the finest on Earth). So I decided to put in some time on the dulcimer I was building, and that meant that I needed Mucus the Moose, and when I couldn't find him after a Class One Search of the house I played back memory tape and realized, with a sinking feeling, that I was going to have to go outside after all.

I might not have done it for a friend—but if Mucus was out there, I had no choice.

Mucus the Moose is one of my most cherished possessions, one of my only mementoes of a very dear dead friend. He (the moose, not the friend) is about fifteen centimeters tall, and bears a striking physical resemblance to that noblest of all meece, Bullwinkle—save that Mucus is as potbellied as the Ashley stove in my living room. He is a pale translucent brown from the tips of his rack down to wherever the Plimsoll line happens to be, and pale translucent green thereafter. Picture Bullwinkle gone to fat and extremely seasick. His full name and station—Mucus Moose, the Mucilage Machine—are spelled out in raised letters on his round little tummy.

If you squeeze him gently right there, green glue comes out of his nostrils. . . .

If you don't understand why I love him so dearly, just let it go. Chalk it up to eccentricity or cabin fever—congenital insanity, I won't argue—but he was irreplaceable and special to me, and he was nowhere to be found. On rewind-search of my head I found that the last place I remembered putting him was in my jacket pocket, in order to fasten down the Styrofoam padding on Number Two hole in the outhouse, and he was not in the said pocket, and the last time that jacket pocket had been far enough from vertical for Mucus to fall out had been—

—that afternoon, by the sap pot, *halfway up the frigging Mountain,* more than a mile up into the woods. . . .

I have a special personal mantra for moments like that, but I believe that even in these enlightened times it is unprintable. I chanted it aloud as I filled both stoves with wood, pulled on a second shirt and pair of pants, added a sweater, zipped up the Snowmobile boots, put on the scarf and jacket and gloves and cap and stomped into the back hall like a space-suited astronaut entering the airlock, or a hardhat diver going into the decompression chamber.

The analogies are rather apt. When I popped the hook-and-eye and shouldered the kitchen door open (its spring hinge complaining bitterly enough to be heard over the general din), I entered a room whose ambient temperature was perhaps fifteen Celsius degrees colder than that of the kitchen—and the back hall was at least that much warmer than the world outside. I sealed the kitchen door behind me with the turnbuckle, zipped my jacket all the way up to my nose, took the heavy-duty flashlight from its perch near the chainsaw, and thumbed open the latch of the outside door.

It promptly flew open, hit me sharply in the face and across the shin, and knocked the flashlight spinning. I turned away from the incoming blast of wind-driven snow, in time to see the flashlight knock over the can of chainsaw gas/oil mixture, which spilled all over the split firewood. Not the big wood intended for the living room Ashley, the small stuff for the kitchen stove. I sleep above that kitchen stove at nights, and I was going to be smelling burning oil in my sleep for the next week or so.

I started my mantra over again from the beginning, more rhythmically and at twice the volume, retrieved the flashlight, and stomped out into the dark and stormy night, to rescue fifty cents worth of flexible plastic and a quarter-liter of green glue. Love is strange.

I had been mistaken about those banshees. They hadn't been inside my stovepipes, only hollering down them. They were out here, much too big to fit down a chimney and loud enough to fill the world, manifesting as ghostly curtains of snow that were torn apart by the wind as fast as they formed. I hooked the door shut before me, made a perfectly futile attempt to zip my jacket up higher—all the way up is as high as a zipper goes—and pushed away from the Hotel to meet them.

The woodshed grunted a dire warning as I passed. I ignored it; it had been threatening to fall over ever since I had known it, back in the days when it had been a goatshed. As I went by the outhouse I half turned to see if the new plastic window I'd stapled up last week had torn itself to pieces yet, and as I saw that it had, a shingle left the tiny roof with the sound of a busted E-string and came spinning at my eyes like a ninja deathstar. I'm pretty quick, but the distance was short and the closing velocity high; I took most of it on my hat but a corner of it put a small slice on my forehead. I was almost glad then for the cold. It numbed my forehead, the bleeding stopped fairly quickly for a forehead wound, and what there was swiftly froze and could be easily brushed off.

When I was clear of the house and outbuildings the wind steadied and gathered strength. It snowed horizontally. The wind had boxed the compass; wind and I were traveling in the same direction and, thanks to the sail-area of my back, at roughly the same speed. For seconds at a time the snow seemed to hang almost motionless in the air around me, like a cloud of white fireflies who had all decided to come jogging with me. It was weirdly beautiful. Magic. As the land sloped uphill, the snow appeared to settle in ultraslow motion, disappearing as it hit the ground.

Once I was up into the trees the wind slacked off considerably, confounded by the narrow and twisting path. The snow resumed normal behavior and I dropped back from a trot to a walk. As I came to the garden it weirded up again. Big sheets of air spilled over the tall trees into the cleared quarter-acre bowl and then smashed themselves to pieces against the trees on the far side. It looked like the kind of snowstorm they get inside those plastic paperweights when you shake them, skirling in all directions at once.

I realized that despite having fixed it in my mind no more than three hours ago, I had forgotten to bring the chamber pot with me from the house. I certainly wasn't going back for it, not into the teeth of that wind. Instead, it shouldn't be a total loss, I worked off one glove, got my fly undone and pissed along as much of the west perimeter as I could manage, that being the direction from which the deer most often approached.

Animals don't grok fences as territory markers because they cannot conceive of anyone *making* a fence. Fences occur; you bypass them. But borders of urine are made, by living creatures, and their message is ancient and universally understood. A big carnivore claims this manor. (The Sunrise Hill commune had tried everything else in the book, fences and limestone borders and pie-pan rattles and broken-mirror windchimes, and still lost a high percentage of their garden to critters. Vegetarian pee doesn't work.)

Past the garden the path began to slope upward steeply, and footing became important. It would be much worse in a few weeks, when the path turned into a trail of mud, oozing down the Mountain in ultraslow motion, but it was not an easy walk now. This far back up into the woods, the path was in shadow for most of the day, and long slicks of winter snow and ice remained unmelted here and there; on the other hand, there had been more than enough thawing to leave a lot of rocks yearning to change their position under my feet. My Snowmobile boots gave good traction and ankle support—and were as heavy as a couple of kilos of coffee strapped to my feet. The ground crunched beneath them, and I sympathized. I had to keep working my nose to break up the ice that formed in it, and my beard began to stiffen up from the exhalations trapped by my scarf. Mucus, I thought, I hope you appreciate the trouble I go through for you.

I thought of Frank then for a while, and a strange admixture of joy and sadness followed me up the trail. Frank was the piano-player/artist who had given me Mucus, back in Freshman year. Fragile little guy with black curls flying in all directions and a tongue of Sheffield steel. His hero was Richard Manuel of The Band. (Mine was Davy Graham then.) He only smiled in the presence of friends, and his smile always began and ended with just the lips. The corners of his mouth would curl all the way up into his cheeks as far as they could, the lips would peel back for a brief flash of good white teeth, then seal again.

The way our college worked it, there was a no-classes Study Week before the barrage of Finals Week. Frank and I were both in serious academic jeopardy, make-or-break time. We stayed awake together for the entire two weeks, studying. No high I've had before or since comes close to the heady combination of total fatigue and mortal terror. At one point in there, I've forgotten which night, we despaired completely and went off-campus to get drunk. We could not seem to manage it no matter how much alcohol we drank. After five or six hours we gave up and went back to studying. Over the next few days we transcended ourselves, reached an exhilarated plane on which we seemed to comprehend not only the individual subjects, but all of them together in synthesis. As Lord Buckley would say, we dug infinity.

By the vagaries of mass scheduling we both had all our exams on Thursday and Friday, three a day. We felt this was good luck. Maximum time to study, then one brutal final effort and it was all over. One or two exams a day would have been like Chinese water torture.

As the sun came up on Thursday morning I was a broken man, utterly whipped. Frank flailed at me with his hands, and then with that deadly tongue—Frank only used that on assholes, the kind of people who mocked you for wearing long hair—without reaching me. He and the rest of the world could go take Sociology exams: I was going to die, here, now. He left the room. In a few moments I heard him come back in. I kept my eyes shut, determined to ignore whatever he said, but he didn't say anything at all, so with an immense irritated effort I forced them open and he was holding out Mucus Moose the Mucilage Machine.

He knew I coveted the Moose. It was one of his most cherished belongings.

"I want you to have him, Sam," he said. "I've got a feeling if anything can hold you together now, it's Mucus."

I exploded laughing. That set him off, and we roared until the tears came. We were in that kind of shape. The laugh was like those pads they clap to the chests of fading cardiac patients; it shocked me reluctantly back to life.

"You son of a bitch," I said finally, wiping tears away. "Thanks." Then: "What about you?"

"What about me?"

"What's going to hold *you* together, if I take Mucus?"

His cheeks appled up, his lips peeled apart slowly, and the teeth flashed. "I'm feeling lucky. Come on, asshole."

I passed everything, in most cases by the skin of my teeth, but overall well enough to stagger through another semester of academic probation. Frank passed everything but not by enough and failed out.

If you want to really get to know someone, spend two weeks awake with them. I only saw him twice after that—he made the fatal mistake of trying to ignore an inconvenient asthma attack—but I will never forget him.

And I was not going to leave Mucus on a snowy mountainside with his only bodily fluid turned to green fudge in his belly.

As the trail made the sharp turn to the left, I saw a weasel a few meters off into the woods. He looked at me as though he had a low opinion of my intelligence. "You're out here too, jerk," I muttered into my scarf, and he vanished.

There was something electric in the air. It took me awhile to realize that this was more than a metaphor. I became aware of an ozone-y smell, like—but subtly different from—the smell of a NiCad battery charger when you crack the lid. You know the smell you get when you turn on an old tube amplifier that's been unused long enough to collect dust? If you'd sprinkled just a pinch of cinnamon and fine-ground basil on top first, it might smell like the air smelled that night, alive and tangy and sharp-edged. I knew the stimulant effect of ozone, had experienced it numerous times; this was different. Better. I knew a little about magic, more than I had before I'd moved to the North Mountain. Nova Scotia has many kinds of magic, but this was a different kind, one I didn't know.

I stopped minding the cold and the snow and the wind and the steepness of the trail. No, I kept minding them, but I became reconciled to them. Shortly a unicorn was going to step out from behind a stand of birch. Or perhaps a tornado was going to take me to Oz. Something wonderful was about to happen.

A part of my mind stood back and skeptically observed this, tried to analyze it, noted that the sensation increased as I progressed upslope (ozone was lighter than air, wasn't it?), wondered darkly if this was what it smelled like before lightning struck someplace, tried to remember what I'd read on the subject. Avoid tall trees. Avoid standing in water. Trees loomed all around me, of course, and my boots had been breaking through skins of ice into slushwater for the last half klick. (But that was silly, paranoid, you didn't get lightning with snow.) That part of my mind which thought of itself as rational urged me to turn around and go back downhill to a place of warmth and comfort, and to hell with the silly glue-dispenser and the funny smell and the electric night.

But that part of my mind had ruled me all my life. I had come here to Nova Scotia specifically to get in touch with the other part of my mind, the part that perceived and believed in magic, that tasted the crisp cold night and thrilled with anticipation, for something unknown, or perhaps forgotten. It had been a long cold winter, and a little shot of magic sounded good to me.

Besides, I was almost there. I kept on slogging uphill, breathing big deep lungfulls of sparkling air through the scarf, and in only a few hundred meters more I had reached my destination, the Place of Big Maples and the clearing where I boil sap.

That very afternoon I had hiked up here and done a boiling, one of the last of the season. Maple syrup takes a lot of hours, but it is extremely pleasant work. Starting in early Spring, you hammer little aluminum sap-taps into any maple thicker than your thigh for an acre on either side of the trail, and hang little plastic sap-trap pails from them. You take a chainsaw to about a Jesus-load and a half of alders (I'll define that measurement later) and stack them to dry in the resulting clearing. The trail is generously stocked with enough boulders to create a fireplace of any size desired. Every few days you hike up to the maple grove, collect the contents of the pails in big white plastic buckets, and dump the buckets into the big castiron sap pot. You build a fire of alder slash, pick a comfortable spot, and spend the next several hours with nothing to do but keep the fire going. . . .

You can read if you want, if the weather permits—it's hard turning pages with gloves on—and toward the end of sap season you sometimes can even bring a guitar up the Mountain with you, and sing to the forest while you watch the pot. Or you can just watch the world. From that high up the slope of the Mountain, at that time of year, you can see the Bay off through the trees, impersonal and majestic. I'm a city kid; I can sit and look at the woods around me for four or five hours and still be seeing things when it's time to go.

Sap takes a *lot* of boiling, and then some more. Raw maple sap has the look and consistency of weak sugar water, with just a hint of that maple taste. That afternoon had been a good run: I had collected enough to fill the pot, maybe fifty liters or so—then kept the fire roaring for hours, and eventually took a little more than three liters down the Mountain with me in a Mason jar. (Even that wasn't really proper maple syrup—when I had enough Mason jars I would boil them down further [and more gently] on the kitchen stove—but it was going to taste a hell of a lot better on my pancakes than the "maple" flavored fluid you buy in stores.)

At one point I had scrounged around and picked some wintergreen, dipped up some of the boiling sap in my ladle and brewed some fresh wintergreen tea with natural maple sugar flavoring, no artificial colour, no preservatives, and sipped it while I fed the fire. Nothing I could possibly have lugged uphill in a Thermos would have tasted half so good. I had not felt lonely, but only alone. It had been a good afternoon.

I remembered it now and felt even better than I had then—good in the same way, and good in a different and indefinable and complimentary way at the same time. This afternoon the world had felt *right*. Tonight felt *right, and about to get even better*—even the savage weather was an irrelevancy, without significance.

So of course luck was with me; Mucus was just where I'd hoped to find him, half-buried in the heap of dead leaves beside the stone fireplace, where I had for a time today lain back and stared through the treetops at the sky. I didn't even have to do any digging: the flashlight picked him out almost at once. He was facing me. His features were obscured by snow, but I knew that his expression would be sleepy-lidded contentment, the Buddha after a heavy meal.

"Hey, pal," I said softly, puffing just a little, "I'm sorry."

He said nothing.

"Hey, look, I came back for you." I worked my nose to crack the ice in my nostrils. "At this point, the only thing that can hold me together is Mucus." I giggled, and my lower eyelids began to burn. If I felt so goddam good, why did I suddenly want to burst out crying?

Did I want to burst out crying?

I wanted to do something—wanted it badly. But I didn't know what.

I picked up the silly little moose, wiped him clean of snow, probed at the hard little green ball in his guts, and poked at *his* nostrils to clear them. "Forgive me?"

But there was only the sound of wind sawing at the trees.

No. There was more.

A faint, distant sound. Omnidirectional, approaching slowly from all sides at once, and from overhead, *and* from beneath my feet, like a contracting globe with me at the center. No, slightly off-center. A high, soft, sighing, with an odd metallic edge, like some sort of electronically processed sound.

Trees began to stir and creak around me. *The wind,* I thought, and realized that the wind was gone. The snow was gone. The air was perfectly still.

When I first moved to Nova Scotia they told me, "If you don't like the weather, sit down and have a beer. Likely the weather you was lookin' for'll be along 'fore you finish." No climatic contortion no matter how unreasonable can surprise me anymore. This was the first snowstorm I'd ever known to have an eye, like a hurricane; fine.

But what was disturbing the trees?

They were *trembling.* I could see it with the flashlight. They vibrated like plucked strings, and part of the sound I was hearing was the chord they made. Occasionally one would emit a sharp cracking sound as rhythmic accompaniment to the chorus.

Well, of course they're making cracking sounds, said the rational part of my mind, *it's a good ten degrees warmer now—ten degrees warmer?*

A thrill of terror ran up my spine, I'd always thought that was just an expression but it wasn't, but was it terror or exhilaration, the cinnamony smell was very strong now and the trees were humming like the Sunrise Hill Gang chanting Om, a vast, world-sized sphere of sound contracted from all sides at once with increasing speed and power and yes I *was* a little off-center, it was going to converge right over *there—*

Crack!

A globe of soft blue light did actually appear in the epicenter, like a giant robin's egg, about fifty meters east of me and two or three meters off the ground. A yellow birch which had stood in that spot for at least thirty years despite anything wind or water could do obligingly disintegrated to make room for the globe. I mean no stump or flinders: the whole tree turned in an instant into an equivalent mass of sawdust and collapsed.

The humming sound reached a crescendo, a crazy chord full of anguish and hope.

The globe of light was a softly glowing blue, actinic white around the edges, and otherwise featureless. It threw out about as much light as a sixty-watt bulb. The sawdust that fell on it vanished, and the instant the last grain had vanished, the globe disappeared.

Silence. Total, utter stillness, such as is never heard in a forest in any weather. Complete starless Stygian darkness. It might have taken me a full second to bring the flashlight to bear.

Where the globe had been, suspended in the air in a half-crouch, was a naked bald woman, hugging herself.

She did not respond to the light. She moved, slightly, aimlessly, like someone floating in a transparent fluid, her eyes empty, her features slack. Suddenly she fell out of the light, dropped the meter and a half to the forest floor and landed limply on the heap of fresh sawdust. She made a small sound as she hit, a little animal grunt of dismay that chopped off.

I stood absolutely still for ten long seconds. The moment she hit the earth, the stillness ended and all the natural sounds of the night returned, the wind and the snow and the trees sighing at the memory of the effort they had just made and a distant owl and the sound of the Bay lapping at the shore.

I held the flashlight on her inert form.

A short dark slender bald woman. No, hairless from head to toe. Not entirely naked after all: she wore a gold headband, thin and intricately worked, that rode so high on her skull I wondered why it didn't fall off. Eurasian-looking features, but her hips were Caucasian-wide and she was dark enough to be a quadroon. Smiling joyously at the Moonless sky. Sprawled on her back. Magnificent tits. Aimlessly rolling eyes, and the blank look of a congenital idiot. Arms outflung in instinctive attempt to break her fall, but relaxed now. Long, slender hands.

Well, I had wanted an evening's entertainment . . .

❖TWO❖

I GUESS THIS is as good a place as any for your suspension of disbelief to snap through like an overstressed guitar string. I don't blame you a bit, and it only gets worse from here. Con-men work by getting you to swallow the hook a little at a time; first you are led to believe a small improbability, then there are a series of increasingly improbable complications, until finally you believe something so preposterous that afterward you cannot fathom your own foolishness. My writer friend Snaker says the only difference between a writer and a con-man is the writer has better hours, works at home, and can use his real name if it suits him.

So I guess I'm not a very good con-man. Without the assistance of Gertrude the Guitar, anyway. I'm giving you a pretty improbable thing to swallow right at the start. It's okay with me if you don't believe it, all right?

But let me try to explain to you why *I* believed it.

Despite the fact that I was then a

1) long-haired
2) bearded
3) American-born
4) guitar player and folksinger
5) college dropout
6) sometime user of powerful psychedelics and
7) bonafide non-card-carrying member of the completely unorganized network of mostly ex-American hippies and back-to-the-landers scattered up and down the Annapolis Valley—despite the fact that I could have called myself a spiritual seeker

without breaking up—nonetheless and notwithstanding I did *not* believe in astrology or auras or the Maharishi or Mahara Ji or Buddha or Jesus or Mohammed or Jahweh or Allah or Wa-Kon-Ton-Ka or vegetarianism or the Bermuda Triangle or flying saucers or the power of sunrise to end all wars if we would all only take enough drugs to stay up all night together, or even (they having broken up in a welter of lawsuits years earlier) the Beatles. I *did* believe in mathematics and the force of gravity and the laws of conservation of matter and energy and Murphy's Law.

I was pretty lonely, is what I guess I'm trying to tell you: the hippies frowned on me because I didn't abandon the rational part of my mind, while the straights disowned me because I didn't abandon the irrational part. I maintained, for instance, an open if rather disinterested mind on reincarnation and ESP and the sanity of Dr. Timothy Leary, and I was tentatively willing to give the Tarot the benefit of the doubt on the word of a science fiction writer I admired named Samuel Delany.

That's part of what I'm trying to convey. I had read science fiction since I'd been old enough to read, attracted by that sense of wonder they talk about—and read enough of it to have my sense of wonder gently abraded away over the years. People who read a lot of sf are the *least* gullible, most skeptical people on earth. A longtime reader of sf will examine the flying saucer very carefully and knowledgeably for concealed wires, hidden seams, gimmicks with mirrors: he's seen them all before. Spotting a fake is child's play for him. (A tough house for a musician is a roomful of other musicians.)

On the other hand, he'll recognize a *real* flying saucer, and he'll waste very little time on astonishment. Rearranging his entire personal universe in the light of startlingly new data is what he does for fun. One of sf's basic axioms, first propounded by Arthur Clarke, is that "any sufficiently advanced technology is indistinguishable from magic." Confronted with a nominally supernatural occurrence, a normal person will first freeze in shock, then back away in fear. An sf reader will pause cautiously, then move closer. The normal person will hastily review a checklist of escape-hatches—"I am drunk"; "I am dreaming"; "I have been drugged"; and so forth—hoping to find one which applies. The sf reader will check the same list—hoping to come up empty. But meanwhile he'll already have begun analyzing this new puzzle-piece which the game of life has offered him. What is it good for? What are its limitations? Where does it pinch? The thing he will be most afraid of is appearing stupid in retrospect.

So I must strain your credulity even further. I don't know what you would have done if a naked woman had materialized in front of you on a wooded hillside at night—and neither do you; you can only guess. But what *I* did was to grin hugely, take ten steps forward, and kneel beside her. I had spent my life training for this moment—for a moment like this—without ever truly expecting it to come.

If it helps any, I *did* drop Mucus on the way, and forgot his existence until the next day.

My first thought was, *those are absolutely* perfect *tits.*
My second was, *that's odd. . . .*
The nipples on those perfect teats were erect and rigid. Nothing odd there: it was freezing out, she was naked. But the rest of her body was not behaving correspondingly. The skin was not turning blue. No sign of goosebumps. A slight shiver, but it came and went. Teeth slightly apart in an idiot's smile, no sign of chattering.

It wasn't the cold stiffening her nipples. It was excitement.

What sort of excitement do you feel while you're unconscious? I wondered.

It seemed to be equal parts of triumph, fear, and sexual arousal. A sort of *by God, I made it! Or have I?* excitement, like someone disembarking from her first roller coaster ride—and finding herself in Coney Island, one of Brooklyn's gamier neighborhoods.

My eyes and nose found other evidences of the sexual component of her excitement—

—I looked away, obscurely embarrassed, and glanced back up to the other end. Her face was vacant, but that did not seem to be its natural condition. A lifetime of intelligence had written on that face before some sort of trauma had stunned it goofy. I guessed her age at forty.

So one way to approach it is to go through a long logic-chain. This woman had materialized amid thunderclaps and bright lights. Could she be an extraterrestrial? If so, either human stock was ubiquitous through the Galaxy, or there was something to the idea of parallel evolution, or she was in fact a three-legged thing with green tentacles (or some such) sending me a telepathic projection of a fellow human to soothe my nerves.

I don't know what strains your credulity. The idea of other planets full of human beings, while admittedly possible, strained mine. How did they get there? And why didn't their evolution and ours diverge over the several million years since *we* took root *here*?

Parallel evolution—the idea that the human shape is an inevitable one for evolution to select—had always seemed to me a silly notion, designed to simplify science fiction stories. Certainly, the human morphology is a good one for a tool-user, but there are others as good or better. (Whose idea was it to put all the eyes on one side of the head? And who thought two hands were enough?)

And I had difficulty believing in aliens who'd studied us closely enough to notice the behavior of nipples, but not closely enough to know that normal skin turns blue in temperatures well below zero. If what I saw was a telepathic illusion, how come it was semicomatose? To lull me into a false sense of . . . no, the thought was too silly to finish.

And if she *was* an alien, what had happened to her flying saucer, or rather flying robin's egg? Could she be smart enough to cross countless light-years, and clever enough to escape the attention of NORAD, and dumb enough to crash land in front of a witness?

No, she was not an E.T. (As no one but an sf reader would have phrased it in 1973.) But she was certainly not from *my* world. I knew much more than the average citizen about the current state of terrestrial technology, and no culture on earth could have staged the entrance I had just seen.

Hallucination was a hypothesis I never considered. At that time of my life, at age twenty-eight, I had experienced the effects of alcohol, pot, hash, opium, LSD, STP, MDA, DMT, mescaline (organic and synthetic), psilocybin (ditto), peyote, amanita muscaria, a few licks of crystal meth, and medically administered morphine. I knew a hallucination when I saw one.

So that left . . .

I did not go through this logic-chain, not consciously. I just knew that I was looking at a time traveler. Which both mildly annoyed and greatly tickled me, because I had not until then really believed in time travel. There are certain conventions of sf that are, in light of what we think we know about physics, preposterous . . . but which sf readers are willing to provisionally accept. Faster-than-light travel is, so far as anyone knows, flat-out impossible—but skeptical sf readers will accept it, grudgingly, because it's damned difficult to write a story set anywhere but in this Solar System without it.

Time travel too is considered flat-out impossible (or was at that time; physics has gone through some interesting changes lately) but tolerated for its story value. It's a delightful intellectual conceit, which gives rise to dozens of lovely paradoxes. The best of them were discovered and used by Robert Heinlein: the man who met himself coming and going, the man who was both of his own parents, and so forth.

That was, of course, why I did not truly believe in time travel, for any longer than it took to finish a Keith Laumer novel: its very existence implied paradoxes that no sane universe could tolerate. A culture smart enough to develop time travel would hopefully be wise enough not to *use* it. The risk of altering the past, changing history and thereby overstressing the fabric of reality, would be too great. What motive could induce intelligent people to take such a hideous gamble?

The clincher, of course, was the question, *where were they?* If (I had always reasoned with myself) time travel were ever going to be invented, in some hypothetical future, and used to go back in time . . . then where were the time travelers? Even if they maintained very tight security, you would expect there to be at least as many Silly Season reports of encounters with time travelers as there were of encounters with flying saucers (in which I emphatically did not believe)—and there weren't.

Since I had long ago relegated time travel to the category of fantasy, it was slightly irritating to be confronted with a time traveler. . . .

But I'd have bet cash. I could see no other possibility that met the facts. I was, further, convinced that she was one of the earliest time travelers (from the historically earliest point-of-origin, I mean), if not the very first.

She certainly seemed to have screwed up her landing—

I worked off one mitten and the glove beneath, quickly placed the back of my hand against her cheek. Its temperature was *neither* stone cold, nor the raging fever-heat mine would have had if I had been naked. Her skin temperature was . . . skin temperature. The same as my hand was in the instant that I slipped off my glove, but hers remained constant. Curiouser and curiouser. It occurred to me sadly that in her time Nova Scotia might be as overpopulated as Miami, its irresistible beauty no longer protected by its shield of horrid weather.

I hastily began to cover up my hand again. The instant my skin broke contact with hers, she made the first sound she had made since she had crashed to the forest floor. In combination with the happy-baby smile on her face, it was a shocking sound; the sound an infant makes when it is still terrified or starving, but too tired to cry any more. A high-pitched drawn out *nnnnnnnnn* sound, infinitely weary and utterly forlorn, punctuated with little hiccup-like inhalations. For the first time I began to consider the possibility that she was seriously hurt rather than stunned. Perhaps some unexpected side effect of materializing in my tree had boiled her brains in their bone pot. Perhaps she had simply gone mad. Perhaps some important internal organ had failed to complete the trip with her and she was dying.

Or perhaps her body's dazzling climate-control system took so much power under these overloaded conditions that there was none to spare for trivia like reason and speech. For all I knew, she had been expecting to materialize in Lesotho or Rio de Janeiro. (She could have been a Hawaiian who only moments before had dropped money into a wishing well and prayed to be somewhere cooler.) In any case, it was time for me to stop observing and marveling and do something resourceful.

Total elapsed time since her appearance, perhaps half a minute. Trip time to house (carrying load, downhill, on ice and loose rock, in the dark, during a snowstorm which was already back up to its original, pre-miracle fury), at least half a century.

⊹THREE⊹

DO YOU MIND if I don't describe that trip back home? If you really want to know what it felt like, perhaps therapy could help you.

No, wait, some parts were worth remembering. A fireman's carry doesn't work when you're dressed for Nova Scotia outdoors, she kept slipping off my shoulder, so I carried her most of the way in my arms, the way you carry a bride over the threshold. I could feel the warmth of her groin against my right arm through four layers of thick clothing, and in looking down to pick my footing I spent a lot of time watching those splendid breasts jiggle. Snowflakes seemed to melt and then evaporate instantly as they struck her, soft white kisses that left no mark. Her horrid moaning had stopped. In repose her features were beautiful. Perhaps there was a little of that ozone effect left in the air. By the time I emerged from the trees and sighted my home, windows glowing invitingly, twin streamers of smoke being torn from the chimneys, I suppose that I was feeling about as good as possible for a man in extreme physical distress. Better than you might suspect . . .

I don't remember covering the last hundred meters. I don't know how I got the outer and inner doors open and sealed again without dropping her. Instinctively I headed for the living room, the warmest room on the ground floor since it held the big Ashley fire-box. I vaguely recall a dopey confusion once I got there. I wanted her on the couch, but I wanted her closer to the fire than that. So It was necessary to move the couch. Hmmm, I was going to have to put her down first. Where? Say, how about on the couch? Minimize the number of trips I'd have to make back and forth. Brilliant. Very important to conserve energy. Set her down carefully. Oof. Oh well.

Circle couch, tacking like a sailboat, wedge self between it and wall. Final convulsive effort: heave! Good. Circle couch again. More difficult against the wind. Oh shit, we're going to capsize, try not to hit the Ashley—

Someone whacked me across both kneecaps with padded hammers, and then someone else with a naked sledge stove in the side of my head.

Two large beasts were fighting nearby. The nearer roared and growled deep in his throat, like King Kong in his wrath, or a dragon who has been told that this is the no-smoking section. The other had a high eldritch scream that rose and fell wildly, a banshee or a berserk unicorn. It sounded like they were tearing each other to pieces, destroying the entire soundstage in their fury.

Damn, it was hot here on Kong Island. Funny smell, like toasting mildew. Swimming in perspiration. Jungle so close it fit you like—

—a coat. A big heavy furry wet overcoat, and soggy hat and scarf and gloves and many sweat-saturated layers of undergarments. The shrieking unicorn was the storm outside, and mighty Kong was my Ashley stove . . . about a meter away! I rolled away quickly, and cracked my head on the couch. But for the cushioning of hat and hair, I'd have knocked myself out again.

If things would only slow down *for a minute, maybe I could get something done! Menstruating Christ, me head's broke. . . .*

I made it to my hands and knees. The dark naked woman on the couch caught my attention. So it was *that* kind of party, eh? Then I remembered. *Oh, hell yeah, that's just the dying time traveler I found up on the Mountain. Is she done yet?*

No, she was still working at it. Taking her time, too. She was asleep or unconscious, breathing in deep slow draughts. They called my attention to the fact that her nipples had finally detumesced. Fair enough. If I couldn't stand up, why should they? I began the long but familiar crawl to the kitchen, shedding wet clothes like a snake as I went until I got down to my Stanfields.

Fortunately there was always coffee on my kitchen stove, and I had overproof Navy grog in my pantry, and whipped cream from Mona's cow Daisy in my fridge; halfway though the second mug of Sassenach Coffee I had managed to become a shadow of my former self. I set the mug on the stove to keep warm and put my attention on first aid for my houseguest.

And screeched to a mental halt. What sort of first aid is indicated for someone who doesn't mind subzero temperature? What is the quick-cure for Time Traveler's Syndrome, for *mal de temps?*

It occurred to me to wonder if I had harmed her by bringing her into a warm environment. It didn't seem likely, but nothing about her seemed likely. I had only had a glimpse of her before crawling from the room. I forced myself up onto my weary feet and headed for the living room, cursing as my socks soaked up some of the ice water I had tracked indoors.

Her metabolism seemed to mind warmth no more than it had subarctic cold. Her pulse seemed unusually fast and unusually strong—for a human being. The skin of her wrist was soft and warm and smooth. So was her forehead. Somehow I was not surprised that it was not feverish.

The back of my hand brushed that silly golden crown perched high on her bald head—and failed to dislodge it, which did surprise me. I nudged it, found it firmly affixed. I investigated. There were three little protuberances around its circumference, barely big enough to grasp, one at each temple and one around behind. I tugged the one at her right temple experimentally and it slid outward about ten centimeters on a slender shaft. There was an increasing resistance, like spring-tension, but at its full extension it locked into place. So did the other. I cradled her head with one palm and pulled out the third, and the crown fell off onto the couch. I examined the frontal two holes, the skin around them horny as callus, and confirmed that the three locking pins had been socketed directly into her skull.

There was no apparent change in her condition. She did not seem to need the crown to survive—at least, not in this friendly environment.

It seemed to be pure gold. It weighed enough, for all its slenderness. Examined closely, it seemed to be made up of thousands of infinitely thin threads of gold, interwoven in strange complicated ways that made me think of photos I'd seen of the IC chips they were just beginning to put in pocket calculators in those days. It didn't *feel* like it was carrying any current, or hum or blink or act electronically alive in any way I recognized. (Then again, neither did a chip.) There were no visible control surfaces or connections beyond the three locking pins—which did seem conductive.

Who knew what the thing was? Perhaps it was her time machine. Perhaps it made people obey you. Or not see you. From my point of view, there was nothing to be gained, and much to be risked, by replacing it. When she regained consciousness, she could tell me what it was. Or babble in some strange tongue, in which case I might decide to gamble on the crown being a translating device. For now, it was a distraction. I hid it in the kitchen, wishing I knew whether I was being crafty or stupid.

When I got back to the living room, she had rolled over in her sleep to toast the other side. It was the first completely human thing she had done, and for the first time I felt genuine empathy with her. With it came a rush of guilt at playing Mickey Mouse games, stealing gold from an unconscious woman—

In the harsh light of the bare bulb overhead, she looked somewhat less dark than she had outside, but not much. She definitely did not have the hyperextended back and high rump of a black woman, nor the slender hips and flat fanny of an Asian. She was muscled like an athlete, and much too thin for my taste—about what the rest of North America would have considered stunningly beautiful. Her face was turned toward me, and I studied it.

Outside in the dark in a snowstorm, I had guessed her age at forty. With better light and less distraction, I decided I could not guess her age. She might have been fourteen. The hasty impression I had gotten of intelligence and character was still there, but it did not express itself in the usual way, in number and placement of wrinkles. I could not pin down where it did reside.

Thai eyes, Japanese cheeks, Italian nose, Portuguese mouth. Skin medium dark, somehow more like a Mayan or a lightskinned Negro than a heavily tanned Caucasian, though I can't explain the difference. The net effect was stunning. One thing either marred or enhanced it, I could not decide. She was *totally* hairless—she had no eyebrows, and no eyelashes. Striking feature, in a face that didn't need it.

I didn't know what to do for her. Would a couple of blankets take some strain off her odd metabolism—or put more on? I felt her forehead and cheek. Just as they had been out in the snowstorm, they

were skin temperature. She did not react to my touch. I thumbed
back one eyelid, did a slight double-take. The pupil beneath that
Asian eyelid was a blue so startlingly vivid and pure that it would
have been improbable on any face. Paul Newman's eyes weren't that
blue. I actually checked the other pupil to make sure it matched.

I decided, on no basis at all, that she was asleep rather than unconscious. I could think of nothing better for whatever it was that ailed
her. I lit the kerosene lamp and dimmed the overhead electric light
all the way down to darkness. I went back to the kitchen, picking up
my discarded outdoor clothes as I went. I hung most of them by the
kitchen stove to dry, put the mittens, gloves and outer pair of socks
in the warming oven over the stove, put the boots on top of the
warming oven. I finished the British coffee I had left on the stovetop.
I went to a shelf by the back door, found a spare pair of socks among
the mittens and scarves, swapped them for the wet pair I had on and
put on my house-slippers. My Stanfields were still damp with sweat,
so I got a fresh set of uppers and lowers from the shelf. I emptied the
kettle into a basin, added the last ladle of cold water from the bucket
behind the stove (the line to the sink pump would not unfreeze for
weeks yet), and took a hasty sponge bath at the sink, then toweled off
and changed into the clean Stanfields. The stove's firebox was almost
down to coals—bad habit to get into; I hoped time travelers weren't
going to be showing up every night—so I threw in a few sticks of softwood and a chunk of white birch from the woodbox behind the
stove. I made a fast trip out to the drafty back hall for more wood,
wedged the Ashley as full as possible, adjusted the thermostat and
damper, closed her up and hung up the poker. The plastic was peeling up at one of the living room windows, farting icy drafts, so I got
out the staple gun and fixed that. (I was not worried about waking
her. People who need to sleep bad enough cannot be wakened.
People who *can* be wakened can answer questions. Besides, it is
impossible to load an Ashley quietly. In any case, she did not wake.)
I went back to the kitchen, checked that the fire was rebuilding well,
added a stick of maple.

The petty chores of living in the country are so neverending that if
they don't send you gibbering back to the city they become a kind of
hypnotic, a rhythmic ritual, encouraging you to adopt a meditative
state of mind. I found that I was priming up the Kemac, the oil-fired

burner which took over for woodfire while I slept, and that told me that I had decided what I wanted to do. So I went back to the living room.

I had two choices: carry her upstairs to the bedroom above the Kemac—the only room that would stay "warm" all night long without help—or keep feeding the Ashley at intervals of no more than three or four hours. No choice at all; I could never have gotten her to the bedroom (Heartbreak Hotel grew room by room over a hundred and twenty years, at the whims of very eccentric people; it's not an easy house to get around in). I readjusted the damper on the Ashley, got blankets from the spare bedroom, put one over her, curled up in The Chair, and watched her sleep until I was asleep too. Roughly every three hours I rebuilt the fire. I don't remember doing so even once, but we were alive in the morning—in the country you develop *habits* rather quickly.

My dreams were bad, though. My father kept trying to tell me that something or someplace was mined, and a baby kept crying without making any sound, and I couldn't seem to find my body anywhere. . . .

⋇FOUR⋇

I WOKE AS soon as the room began to lighten up. Dawn, through two panes of warped glass and three layers of thick plastic, gives a room a surreal misty glow, like a photograph in *Penthouse*. She certainly looked right for the part.

Externally, at least. *Penthouse* models are always either looking you square in the eye while doing something unspeakably naughty, or else looking away in a scornful indifference which you both know is faked. My time traveling nude was out cold. (Not literally cold; I checked. Even though the room and I were.) She didn't budge as I got up and exercised out the kinks, the floorboards cracking like .22 fire, and she didn't budge as I pried up the heavy stove lid and stirred up the coals, enough for a restart thank God, and she didn't budge as I split some sticks down to starting size with the hatchet, even though as usual I got the blade stuck in a chunk of birch and had to hammer it free—she didn't even budge when a flying chip struck her blanket-covered hip. I checked her over very carefully for any sign that this might be other than healthful sleep. Pupils normal. Pulse very strong but not enough to alarm. Breathing free and rhythmic as hell. I visualized myself calling old Doc Hatherly, explaining how I had come into custody of this unconscious naked bald woman. ("Well you see, Doc, I had gone out into a blizzard at night to get Mucus the Moose, when suddenly there was a ball of fire, and this time traveler—what? Why yes, I do have long hair and a beard, what has that—eh? No, I've never taken any of that . . . anyway, not since the Solstice Dance at Louis's barn—Doc? *Doc?*)

The hell with it. She would wake up when she was ready. Or perhaps she would suddenly and quietly die, from causes I would never understand. Grim logic gleaned from a thousand sf stories suggested that this was perhaps one of the best things that could happen to a time traveler. Up behind the house were about ninety-five acres of woods; I knew places where the ground might be thawed enough to dig, with some effort, near the spot where she had appeared. Meanwhile, I wanted coffee and a piss, in that order.

But of course I had to have them the other way around. Peeing was simply a matter of reaching the chamberpot. For coffee, I had to:

—fill the kitchen firebox with wood, shut off the Kemac when the wood had caught, adjust dampers—

—put back on all of last night's stove-dried clothing, including outdoor gear, all of it smelling of ancient and tedious sin—

—carry two big white plastic buckets and the splitting axe down to the stream, a trifling two or three hundred meters without the slightest cover from the wind whipping in off the Bay—

—hack through the ice with the axe, *without* cutting off my feet—

—dig up two fullish buckets and seal them with lids that fit so snug they must be hammered, *without* wetting my gloves or other garments—

—carry both full buckets (heavy) and axe (awkward) back to the house—

—refill the kettle and assemble the Melitta rig—

—wait five or ten minutes for the kettle to boil—

—and start the coffee dripping. All of this in the zombie trance of Before Coffee. I seldom had the strength to imagine, much less undertake, a second trip, even though two buckets of water is (at best) precisely enough to carry you through to bedtime. Today I made the second trip. I had company. By the time I was back with the extra two buckets, water was ready to be poured over the coffee. (Every country home has at least a dozen spare white plastic buckets around. They coalesce out of air, like my guest. When they're old enough, they transmute themselves into Mason jars full of unidentifiable grains and beans.)

I toasted a slab of bread on the stove and reheated some of yesterday's porridge while the coffee was dripping. It is important to be done with breakfast by the time you have finished your coffee. Another of those habits I mentioned, which come from living in the cold winter woods. Twenty seconds after I finished the coffee, I was sprinting for the outhouse. Maybe it was as much as two and a half minutes before I was back indoors again, considerably lighter and much refreshed, ready to lick my weight in, say, baby rabbits.

I had fetched along four fresh eggs from the chicken coop; like the extra water, that turned out to be a happy thought. (Thirteen chickens, four eggs: a good day. I'm told they developed a strain of chicken that would reliably lay an egg a day. One unfortunate side effect; it was *too dumb to eat.*)

The weather had, with characteristic perversity, turned rather pleasant. Snow gone. Temperature creeping up to within hailing distance of Centigrade zero (well *above* zero in the scale I had grown up with). Wind moderate, and from the north—snow wind came from the south. Sky clear except for some scudding ribbons of cloud hastening over from New Brunswick. Sunrise beautiful as always, lacking the stunning colours of the pollution-refracted sunrises of my New York youth, but with a clarity and crispness that more than compensated. I was whistling *Good Day Sunshine* as I came in with the eggs.

I checked my guest. Other than shifted position (a good sign, I felt), there was no change. My kitchen was sunny and undrafty. I sat with my chair tipped back and my boots up on the stove and thought.

If she woke, we *were* going to talk—even if it took time for us to agree on language. If we did talk there was, it seemed to me, great risk of altering the past, thereby stressing the fabric of reality, perhaps destroying it altogether. I examined my curiosity, and found that it *didn't care* if it killed the cat—or even all cats. As I said, the logical thing to do was cut her throat. Of course I had no such intention. Perhaps it's a character defect: I don't have whatever it takes to murder a pretty naked woman on the basis of logical deductions concerning something which logic said couldn't be happening in the first place.

But suppose she had no such deficiency of character? Risky interaction between us could be avoided equally as well by *my* death. This intuition had caused me to hide her golden headband—but that might not be sufficient precaution. She looked well muscled; even asleep she looked like she had a lot of quick. I don't know even Twentieth Century karate.

I wanted leverage.

So I called Sunrise Hill.

"Hi, Malachi—is the Snaker up?"

"Ha, ha. Now I've got one for you."

"Would you wake him, man? It's kind of important."

"There's enough suffering in the cosmos, Sam—"

"Please, Malachi."

"I'll get Ruby to wake him up. Hang on."

Long pause. One advantage of commune life: there's always someone else to start the morning fires. One of the disadvantages of a spiritual commune: no coffee.

"Hazzit. Whiss?"

"Good morning, Snaker. Wake up, man, all the way up."

"S'na fucking wibbis?"

"Really, man, I got news—"

"Garf norble."

"What I tell you is true, brother. There's a time traveler in my living room."

"*—from what year?—*"

"I don't know. Unconscious since arrival."

"And you're sure it's a—" He lowered his voice drastically. "—what you said?"

"That, or an alien who arrives in a ball of fire in the woods, doesn't mind being naked in the snow, and has fabulous tits."

"Sam, you haven't by any chance—"

"Not since the dance at Louis's barn. I'm straight, Snaker."

"I've already left, but don't pour the coffee till you hear me coming over the horizon. Shit, wait—*who else knows?*"

"You, me, and God, if He's monitoring this sector at the moment."
"If He is, He's holding His breath. Damn, why does everything always have to happen in the middle of the night?"

"Snake—don't even tell Ruby, okay? Uh—" I cast about for a cover story that would account for what he'd said so far. "What you tell people there is, I've got a possible Beatles bootleg, reputed to date from 1962, and I've asked you to come over and help me decide if it's legit. Get it?"

Even half-awake, the Snaker has a quick uptake. "It's the drumming that'll tell the tale. If it's Ringo, it can't be '62."

"Good man, Snake."

"Look, it's hard to run full tilt like this and talk on the phone. See you sooner." He hung up.

The only other habitual science fiction reader on the Mountain. I had known he would come through.

I used the morning chores to calm myself down. Bank fires, replenish woodbox, feed chickens, stare at Bay. The last-named seldom fails to repair a fractured mood; I went back indoors feeling pretty good. Started to resume work on my half-finished dulcimer, and realized I had left Mucus up on the mountainside the night before. No time to get him now. I went back outside and looked at the Bay some more.

While I was wishing for the thousandth time that I shared old Bert Manchette's ability to forecast the weather by the color of the water in the Bay, I heard the thunder of an armored column approaching. It was Blue Meanie, The Surprise Hill Gang's ancient pickup truck, with the Snaker at the wheel. There was a mechanical roar of outrage as the Meanie went through the Haskell Hollow, a few klicks away, and minutes later the wretched thing came into view around the bend, bellowing in agony and trailing dark smoke like a squid under attack. When he shut it off at the foot of my driveway it seemed to slump.

The Snaker was well over six feet and thin as a farmer's hope. Which made him especially cold-sensitive, which made him wear so many layers of clothes he looked like a normal person. Nobody knew Yassir Arafat back then, so Snaker had the ugliest beard I'd ever seen. His brown hair was narrow gauge, neither straight nor curly, and extremely long even for a North Mountain Hippie. He was that indeterminate age that all of us were, somewhere between eighteen and thirty-five. God had seen fit to give him guitarist's fingers, without a guitarist's talent, and it drove him crazy. He had a good baritone, was named after Snaker Dave Ray, the baritone in the old Koerner-Ray-Glover ensemble. He'd sold a couple of stories to magazines in the States. I taught him licks. He lent me books. We were friends.

This morning he was as excited as I've ever seen him before noon. He leaped from the truck before it had stopped coughing, ran up to me.

"Fabulous tits, huh?"

"Well," I said in a softer voice than his, "you're awake enough to have your priorities straight."

"As good as Ruby's? Never mind, you can't compare tits. Let's see her—"

He started to move past me to the rear of the house. (Nobody keeps a door open to the wind on the Bay side of his house.) I grabbed him by the shoulder, sharply. "Hold it a second. Stand right there and don't move." I went to the living room window, got up on tiptoe and squinted in through the layers of plastic. She was still where I had left her, apparently still asleep.

The Snaker was trying to look over my shoulder. "I'll be—"

"*Shh!*" I led him back away from the window.

"Come on, man, let's go inside for a better look—"

"No."

"Why the fuck not?"

"Stand there and shut up and I'll tell you why not."

He nodded. I went inside, made two cups of coffee, put a small knock of grog in my own, stuck the golden crown dingus under my coat and went back outside. He was peering in the window again. "Dammit, come here."

I made him drink the coffee all the way down. "Tell me all," he said when he had swallowed the last gulp, "omitting no detail however slight." So I did. It took less time than I had expected.

"It comes clear," he said finally. "Your behavior begins to make sense."

"Right. When she wakes up and realizes her cover's blown, maybe she just pulls my brains out through my eyesockets to cover her tracks. It would be nice to have an ally she's never seen and can't locate, who is prepared to blow the secret skyhigh if I don't report in on time."

"Aren't you overlooking something? What if she's a telepath? Then after she does you she comes and pulls out *my* brains."

I shook my head. "If she is, we're screwed no matter what we do. Besides, I don't believe in telepathy. What I'm going to do is give you this headband gizmo to hold hostage. You take it down the line somewhere and wait 'til you hear my shotgun go off once. It could take hours, but stay alert. If the crown turns out to be some essential part of her life support or something, I want to be able to get you back here with it in a hurry. But *don't* tell me where you're going, and *don't* come back if I fire *both* barrels."

"What a nasty suspicious mind you have, my son."

"Thank you."

"Look, why didn't you just tell me all this when I first got here?"

"You couldn't have followed the logic-chain before coffee."

"Oh. True. Okay, slip me the headband. And Sam—good luck."

"Thanks, mate."

"And call me back as soon as you're sure it's safe. I'm dying to find out if you're right."

"I know what you mean." I grinned. "It's like getting a tax refund from God. I've always wanted to meet a time traveler."

"Knowing one exists would be a tax refund from God. Meeting one would be gravy. Delicious gravy, but just gravy."

"I don't follow."

"Sam, Sam! If a time traveler exists—*then the human race isn't going to annihilate itself in the near future.* Not completely, anyway."

"Huh! You're right, by Jesus."

"Of course I am. I've had coffee."

He took the golden headband, studied it and put it away. He got back into the truck, did something that made it scream. "Have a care, son," he called over the clashing of gears. "Never trust a naked time traveler." And he was gone in a spray of gravel.

❖FIVE❖

FOR LUNCH I fried up two of the morning's eggs with some of the last earthly remains of Tricky and Dicky, the pigs I had slaughtered the previous October. I half expected the smell to wake her, but no dice. I ate in the living room, watching her. I caught myself becoming irritated at her. I hate houseguests who sleep late; I yearn so badly to sleep late myself, and a country householder *can't*. Even a time traveler ought to have enough manners to grab forty winks *before* coming to work, I heard myself think, and that sounded so stupid I grinned at myself. I dislike grinning at myself, so I started getting irritated again—

There's one thing even better than contemplation of the Bay of Fundy for calming me down, so I got out Gertrude and a handful of Ernie Ball fingerpicks. As usual, the song chose itself without conscious thought on my part; as usual I couldn't have improved on it with a week's thought. Beloved Hoagy (still alive then) and Johnny Mercer: "Lazy Bones."

I try to do that song as close as possible to the definitive version Amos Garrett laid down on Geoff and Maria Muldaur's *Sweet Potatoes* album. I'm not fit to change Garrett's strings, I'm just barely good enough to get by professionally, but the tune is so sweet it almost plays itself. That afternoon it seemed to come out especially well. I watched her splendid chest rise and fall, and told her softly that sleeping in the sun was no way to get her day's work done. (What *was* her day's work? And what day, in what year?) For the first time in a while I attempted an instrumental chorus before the second bridge, and to my immense satisfaction it came off just fine.

266

I grinned and finished the song, warned her that if she slept away the day, she was never going to make a dime. (Where would she have *put* a dime?) I even managed to stumble through the Beiderbecke riff (from a tune charmingly entitled "I'm Coming, Virginia") that Garrett quotes to close the song, and let the final G chord ring in the room while I admired myself.

In the last line of that song the narrator offers to wager that his listener has not heard a thing he's said, and I believed as I sang it that such a bet would be a boat-race—had she not slept through the repeated filling of a toploader stove?—so when she opened her striking blue eyes and said, "That's not true," I started so sharply my thumbpick flew off.

I left it on the floor. I had already mentally prepared some sort of welcoming speech, designed to show in as few words as possible that I was clever enough to know what she was and ethical enough to pose no danger—but it flew right out of my head. I put Gertrude carefully back in her case, to give myself time to think. "I stand corrected," is what I finally said.

She sat up, and I thought of a Persian cat I had once loved named Rainy Midnight. "That was very beautiful." Her voice was a smoky alto. It came out so flat and expressionless that it put me in mind of Mister Spock. I found it oddly attractive.

I thanked her with only a shadow of my usual wince. It *hadn't* been too bad. Her next line was very interesting.

"Do you know what I am?"

I liked that question. In the rush of the moment, I had forgotten my earlier fear that she might be a telepath, it had not been in my conscious mind. I remembered it when she asked the question—and so her question was probably genuine. Unless, of course, she could somehow read thoughts below the conscious level, or was very clever. . . .

My voice came out steady. "I know that you are a very beautiful bald lady who blew up one of my best birch trees. I believe that you are a time traveler. If so, I will do my best not to screw things up for you."

"You're very quick," she said calmly. "You understand the dangers, then?"

This was great. "I doubt it. But my guesses scare me pretty good. Changing history and so forth. What year are you from?"

"That I will not tell you."

"Okay. Why are you here?"

She hesitated slightly; I thought she was going to refuse to answer that question too. "Think of me as—" She looked quizzical, then tried comically to look up at her own forehead, where her crown-thing should have been. "Can I have my ROM? I keep some specialized vocabulary in there." She touched her bald skull. "And I'll need it to start growing hair."

I blinked. ROM meant Read-Only-Memory. The damned thing *was* an overgrown IC chip! Stored computer data! "Direct brain-computer interface—"

She smiled. It was a nice smile, but somehow it looked like something she had just learned to do. "You read science fiction!"

I had to smile myself. "They still have it in your time, eh?" I'd always been a little afraid they'd run out of crazy ideas one day.

"You'd love it." She frowned slightly. "If you could understand it."

"I'm sorry about your ROM. It's not here now. I can get it in ten minutes' time."

She nodded. "For all you knew it was a weapon. I understand. All right, what is the current term for people who study people of the past?"

"There are several kinds. Historians study events in the relatively recent past, and try to interpret them. Archaeologists dug up evidence of the distant past, and anthropologists use the evidence, and observation of surviving primitive cultures, to make guesses about human social and cultural development throughout history. Then writers relate all that to the present."

"Think of me as a combination of all of those. The human race has come so far, its past has begun to seem unreal to it. I'm here to learn."

"How can I help you?"

"By keeping my secret, and by introducing me plausibly to your community. I promise that I will not harm anyone in any way."

"You aren't afraid of accidentally changing the past? Your past?"

"Not unless my secret becomes general knowledge."

"One other person knows. He'll keep his mouth shut," I added hastily, seeing her dismay. "He's smart enough to understand why. He's actually sold some science fiction to a magazine."

She looked dubious. "He might think it's good story material."

"Maybe—as fiction. Who'd believe a guy who's written science fiction? I'm not sure I'd believe this myself—if I hadn't seen you appear in blue fire."

"I'm sorry about your tree."

"That's okay. I'm surprised materializing where another mass already existed didn't kill you—or worse."

"So am I." I held a blink, and then stared. "That was a very bad mistake—somehow that clearing is closer to the path than the records indicate."

"Maybe I see your problem, if your fix was based on the path. The land slopes to the west just there. I wouldn't be surprised if over the next fifty years or so that section of trail just naturally migrates a few meters downhill."

"That could account for it." She shivered. "Perhaps I should not have come. That was a very dangerous error." She paused, acquired a strange expression. "I ask your pardon for having endangered you by my recklessness." She seemed to wait warily for my answer.

"Hell, that's okay. How were you to know?"

She relaxed. "Precisely my error. Thank you for pardoning it. How long was I unconscious?"

I calculated. "Maybe fourteen hours. You don't snore."

"I don't know the term."

Oh. "You sleep beautifully. And soundly."

"Thank you. I haven't had much practice."

Oh. "That must be nice."

"I have nothing to compare it to, but I suppose it is. Do you want me to put on clothes?"

"If you wish. There is a nudity taboo in this place and time, but I heed it only when others do or the weather insists. If I'd known when you were going to wake up, I'd have stripped myself to put you at ease: it's warm enough right here by the fire."

"Does it not cause you tension to be in the presence of a naked woman?" There was something odd about her voice. The subtext *don't you find me attractive?* was in there—but I sensed she had no ego involvement in the answer, was simply curious. That implied to me a cultural advantage at least as startling as time travel.

"Yes it does! And the day I stop enjoying such tension will be the day they plant me. Don't dress on my account."

"Thank you."

"But if any neighbors drop by, you'd better scamper upstairs. Oh, the nudity wouldn't cause too much talk, indoors, but women bald to the eyelashes are fairly scarce on the Mountain these days. Mind your head if you do; the wall sort of leans out at you at the top of the stairs. I think the upstairs was built by a dwarf who leaned to the left at a forty-five degree angle. You'll find clothes in the bedroom to the right. Some may fit you—and of course a robe fits any size."

"Thank you."

"Are you hungry?"

"Thank you." They were the most emotionally charged words she had spoken so far. "Yes. But . . . but first, can you get my ROM back? I'm uncomfortable without it: a lot of what I know about this here/now is in it."

"I can start getting it back at once; it'll arrive after breakfast. Can you walk?"

She could walk. We went to the kitchen. I warned her to expect a loud noise, stepped outside and let off a round of birdshot. Then I whipped up a scratch brunch. She said she could eat anything I could. The coffee and porridge were hot; eggs, bacon, orange juice and toast took perhaps ten minutes. I had to show her how to use a knife and fork. That was excellent bacon, I'd fed Tricky and Dicky real well; the toast was fresh whole wheat, with fresh-churned butter from Mona Bent's cow; my coffee is famous throughout the North Mountain; the eggs were so fresh the shells still had crumbs of chickenshit clinging to them. She demolished everything, slowly. Oddly, she ate it all impassively, displaying neither relish nor distaste. She used no salt, no pepper, no tamari, no cream, no sugar. Toward the end she did think to say, "This is delicious," but I noticed she said it while she was eating a burnt piece of crust. I wondered how I would have behaved if suddenly dropped into, say, a medieval banquet. I also wondered how—and what—they ate where she came from.

I had made enough for Snaker; I expected him to arrive before the food was ready to eat, and I knew he had not broken his fast. But he didn't get there until we were done eating—and she had not left anything unconsumed. "Goddamn transmission," he muttered as he came through the door, and then stopped short. He stared at her for a long moment, then became extremely polite. "Beautiful lady, good morning to you," he said, in a much deeper voice than usual, bowing deeply. Basic North Mountain Hippie bow, palms together before chest, not the punch-yourself-in-the-belly kind. She watched it, paused for an instant and then imitated it superbly, sitting down. It looked a lot better on her than it had on him. Snaker turned to me. "Oh sweet Double-Hipness," he said, quoting Lord Buckley, "straighten me . . . 'cause I'm *ready*."

"Groovy," I agreed. "Snaker O'Malley, I would like you—"

—and I skidded to a halt, feeling like a jerk, and waited—

—and waited—

—growing more embarrassed by the second. I *hate* that, starting to introduce two people whose names you should know and realizing too late that you're shy one name, and it seems to happen to me about every other time I have to make introductions. Okay, I hadn't thought to ask her name, which probably wasn't very polite—but I'd been *busy*, and anyway I hadn't *needed* a name for her, there was only the one of her—and dammit, she had demonstrated repeatedly that she was clever and quick, she had learned how to bow and extrapolated it to a sitting position at a single glance, why the hell wasn't she letting me off the hook?

After five seconds, beginning to blush and just hating it, I had to say, "I'm sorry; I didn't ask your name."

She should then have understood why I was blushing, realized she'd been leaving me hanging, and been a little embarrassed herself. When I'm in a strange place with strange customs and realize that I've embarrassed my host, *I* become embarrassed. What she said, in that cool Lady Spock voice, was, "That's all right." And then she stopped talking.

Snaker's bushy eyebrows lifted, and he gave me a glance which seemed to say, *and we thought she might be a telepath.*

So I played straightman. "What is your name?"

"Rachel."

"Snaker, this is Rachel; Rachel, Snaker; consider yourselves married in the eyes of God." It's a gag line I probably use too often, but the reaction this time was novel. She got up, went to the Snaker, wrapped him up in those big muscular arms and purely kissed the hell out of him.

I expected him to hesitate momentarily, then talk himself into it and cooperate. I guess he trusted my friendship; he skipped the preamble. Enthusiasm was displayed by both halves of the kiss. Gusto. *Joie de vivre.* For something to do I rolled a joint. When it ended, the Snaker had the grace to shoot me a quick apologetic glance before saying, "Rachel, your husband will be one *hell* of a lucky gent—but I'm afraid my pal was joking. I am already engaged to be married, and . . ." He glanced down at what was flattening the fur on his coat. ". . . and much as I might regret it, I don't regret it. If you follow me. But thank you from the bottom of my—thank you very much."

"You're welcome, Snaker. Thank you."

"Welcome to our little corner of space-time. I hope you'll like it here."

"Thank you again. I hope so too."

Dammit, I'd done all the work, and he was getting all the good lines.

She turned to me. "I don't know your name."

"Sam. Sam Meade."

"Sam, in several of the things you said earlier I found ambiguity which I took to be whimsy. May I ask you to refrain from that? I understand that you mean to put me at ease, but it will confuse rather than amuse me."

Jesus.

"In particular, reversed or multiple meanings will badly disorient me—"

Snaker and I exchanged a glance. Half the fun of being his friend is that we can both volley puns back and forth all night, an exercise which both sharpens, and displays, the wits.

Suddenly I remembered the time I had unthinkingly dropped a pun in conversation with old Lester Sabean, my nearest neighbor (perhaps a mile to the west). " 'Scuse me, Sam," he'd said mildly, chewing on his ratty pipe. "Was that one o' them plays on words there?" When I allowed that it had been, he looked me in the eye and arranged his leathery wrinkles into a forgiving smile. "Might just as well save them around me, I guess," he said. I've never punned in Lester's presence since. Flashing on that now, I lost a little of my irritation with Rachel. That kiss had been my own dumb fault—

—except that she kept on *chattering.* And she was starting to gesture, to take little steps, to glance around at things. Until now she had projected the kind of Buddhist serenity that every freak on the North Mountain was trying for. All of a sudden she was hyper, giving off sparks, spilling energy like city people when they first get here. "—inherent in the nature of humor, even though one would think the matrix itself was intrinsically—"

Well, I knew how to deal with that. I lit the joint.

She trailed off and stared at it. "This," I said from the back of my throat, holding the smoke in, "is marijuana, or reefer. Its active ingredient is delta-niner tetrahydrocannabinol. It is made of dried flowers. I grew it myself, and it will not do you any harm."

She looked dubious. "Thank you, Sam. I know that I ought to partake of all your native refreshments—"

I exhaled. "It is nonnarcotic, nonaddictive, habituating with prolonged use. It contains much more tar than processed tobacco. It is just barely illegal. It cures nausea, cramps, anxiety and sobriety. You are under no slightest obligation to accept it, and if the waste smoke bothers you we'll open the stove door and let the draft take it."

"—Thank you Sam I would prefer that please you see I am responsible to many people and drugs which cure anxiety dull alertness and that's—"

"They don't have coffee when you come from, do they?" Snaker asked.

"Beg pardon?"

Oh, hell. Of course. The half a pot she'd accepted from me had probably been the first coffee she'd ever had. I wasn't so sure I would like the future if it didn't have coffee in it. . . .

"I'm not trying to change your mind," he said. He came over by the stove and took the joint, had a toke. "But you've already ingested a mild psychedelic, and this might help counteract it. The hot black drink in your cup over here contains a stimulant called caffeine. It's legal and very common, but quite strong and fiendishly addictive. It makes you hyper, speedy—do you know those words?"

She looked dismayed. "I think I understand them."

"If you're not used to it, especially, it can make you paranoid. Anxious and uneasy. It revs you up too fast. This—" He took another hit. "—cools you out." He was trying to avoid speaking Hippie, but of course it's difficult to discuss subjective biochemical states in any other language.

"That sounds like what I am experiencing. Dammit, it's *hard* to stay stable in this environment. Cold I was prepared to deal with, but for vegetable poisons I expected more warning. And it seems so *sensible* to be this afraid. You're right, I must correct it. But I would rather do it myself, thank you." She looked at him and waited expectantly.

Snaker and I exchanged the joint and a glance.

"I'll need my ROM," she told him.

He sprayed smoke, thunderstruck. "They have Krishna in the future?"

Now she was baffled.

I lost my own toke laughing. "Spelled R-O-M, Snake."

"Read-Only-Memory-oh. *Oh.* I see." His eyes widened. "Wow." He frowned suddenly, glanced at me. "Yes, Sam?"

"Go ahead, man." I sucked more smoke in, feeling the buzz come on. I grow good reefer if I say so myself.

He shucked his coat, produced the crown/headband from a capacious inside pocket. He held it in his hands and gazed at it a minute. "Fucking fantastic. Smaller than that Altair is supposed to be, no moving parts, direct brain interface, no visible power source—how many bytes?"

"Beg pardon?"

"How much data can it hold?"

"I can't say until I access it. May I, please?" She looked like a cat that's heard the can opener working, as though she were fighting the impulse to take the crown by force.

"I'm very sorry," he said, and handed it to her at once.

"Thank you, Snaker O'Malley!"

I watched the way she put it on. The rear locking pin snapped in first, then she pulled out the other two, settled the golden ellipse down over her forehead, moved it slightly to seat the pins and let them slide home. Almost at once her face began to visibly change, in a way I found oddly difficult to grasp.

❖SIX❖

I HAD ANOTHER toke, and passed the bone to Snaker, and the light had changed and it was cooler in the room, even by the stove. "Well," I said, "as you can see, reefer not only makes you babble aimlessly, you get irresponsible: I've let my fires run down. You were wise to refuse it." I began to get up.

Snaker was already on his feet. "Sit, man. I'll get the wood, I did most of the talking." He refilled the kitchen firebox with small sticks, went out back for big wood for the Ashley.

"What were we talking about, again?"

"Whether or not I can stay here," she said seriously.

"Oh, *hell* yeah, sure you can," I said. "You don't even have to fuck me. That was a joke," I added hastily.

"I don't think so," she said. She was much more calm and serene again, now that she had her headband on.

I frowned. "Can I be completely honest with you?"

"I don't know." From another woman it might have been sarcasm, or irony. She meant that she didn't know.

"Well, I'll try, and I do better with honesty when I say it fast so pay attention: unlike Snaker I am not engaged to anybody and I would love to have sex with you at least once in the near future and maybe more but I am not in the market for any kind of romantic or even long-term sexual relationship but I *am* tremendously excited at the prospect of talking with a time traveler but you don't seem to want to *tell* me anything which is frustrating and furthermore I have some reservations about you as a roommate which are not particularly your fault but I'm a very ornery guy to live with, you have to be pretty tantric around me and unfortunately because of your cultural displacement and so forth you're not exactly the most tantric person in the world, but you wouldn't be in the way of anything and there's been a lot of cabin fever going around this winter, so for a while, hell, for as long as you want, you can stay, yeah, sure."

"Tantric? Which aspect of the Vedas—oh, you mean the sexual yogas?"

"Sorry. Hippie slang. Means, like . . ." I foundered. "Uh, intuitive. Sensitive. A tantric person can walk in and out of your bedroom without waking you up, can coexist with an angry drunk, becomes seamless with his own environment. Easy to get along with. Aware of the fine nuances of others' feelings. Perceptive of small clues. Also called telepathic." Her face changed subtly. "No offense, your manners are excellent, but you lack too much cultural context to notice subtleties the way an ideal roommate ought to. For all I know, I've got more in common with a Micmac. But I like you, and even though I'm kind of a hermit I'm willing to endure the aggravation of having you around for a while in exchange for the pleasure of your company. Besides, I don't know where the hell else you'd go."

"You're right. Your help will enormously simplify my work. Thank you for your hospitality, Sam." Her eyes were dreamy, slightly bloodshot.

"Tell me something: what the hell did you *expect* to happen?"

"How do you mean?"

"You materialize naked in the night on a cold hillside. Then what was the plan? What if I hadn't come along? How were you going to line up a place to live, a plausible identity, a set of long johns for that matter?"

"I intended to improvise."

I whistled. "You've got plenty of balls."

She blinked. "Just the one I came in."

"Sorry again. A sexist slang expression, meaning, 'you have audacity.' "

The word "sexist" puzzled her too, but she let it pass. "More like necessity. I had to come through naked if I was to come at all."

That was odd. If all she could bring back was herself, not even clothes, not even *hair*, how come the headband dingus had come along? Did that imply that it was—

—I forgot the matter. She was still talking: "That limited my options. I hoped to conceal myself in the woods and reconnoiter until I could plausibly construct an identity."

"Like I said, you've got balls. Courage."

Snaker came in with an armload, shedding bark and snow and breathing steam. I'd heard him filling up the woodbox out in the back hall while I talked with Rachel. "There's oil spilled over your kitchen wood stash out here, so I swapped it for fresh. Did you know the west roof of your woodshed's gone?" he asked cheerfully.

I rolled my eyes. "Jesus T. Murphy and His traveling flea circus. I think I'll just go back to sleep and try this day over again tomorrow." Rachel giggled—which I thought was rather out of character for her. I'd thought I was supposed to avoid whimsy.

"Bullshit," Snaker said. "We've got to build Rachel a cover story. Relax—I threw a tarp over the wood on that side. Besides, the wind hardly ever comes west this time of year. Except when it does. Make more coffee and let's get to work."

"Are you in a hurry, Snaker?" she asked drowsily.

"Eh? No. I live in a commune, none of us is ever in a hurry. Why?"

"I'd like your help in building a good persona, but first Sam and I want to have sex."

There was a silence.

"Have I been untantric again? You *did* say the near future, Sam?"

"I'll just leave you two alone and go feed the other stove for a while," Snaker said carefully.

"If you wish," she said, just as carefully. Her almond eyes were wide.

Snaker hesitated. "You don't mind if I stay?"

"Not if you want to. Three is good. Odd numbers are always good."

He smiled apologetically. "My Ruby and I are monogamous. I won't risk our relationship for anything, even for the thrill of making it with a beautiful time traveler. She's too important to me." He swallowed. "But our agreement is, we're allowed to look." He met my eyes. "You mind?"

I thought about it. "I don't believe I do." My penis certainly didn't seem to mind. "But I'm damned if I'm going to do it here. The floor's cold, and someone might drop in."

So we all adjourned to the upstairs bedroom. Snaker forgot to feed the living room fire, carried the armload of wood upstairs because he forgot he had it in his arms, and had to go back down again.

He hurried back up.

❖SEVEN❖

RACHEL HAD NO comment on my bedroom. Joel, who owned Heartbreak Hotel and let me live there, had insulated the puptent-shaped bedroom in typical North Mountain Hippie fashion: refrigerator-carton cardboard spread flat and nailed to the studs, with crumpled newspaper stuffed down behind. (You could have placed it on the standard insulation-efficiency scale, but you'd have needed three decimal places.) Then he had covered the facing surface of the cardboard with about fifty large Beardsley and Bosch prints. I have to admit I didn't spend much time up there in daylight. Also, the room's ceiling was the house's rooftree; the walls sloped sharply and a person my height could only stand erect within a four-foot-wide corridor. (Snaker couldn't manage it at all.)

But she did not seem to notice the prints, and we were not vertical for long. At some indeterminate point on the way upstairs, she had stopped being merely nude and become naked. Snaker came in and sat down as I was slipping my undershirt off; I tipped an imaginary hat, he smiled, and I turned back to Rachel. . . .

Of all that I've had to explain and describe so far, this is one of the hardest parts.

I don't suppose it's ever easy to "explain and describe" making love. Even on a purely surface, physical level, an encyclopedia could be written on what transpired during the least memorable encounter I've ever had in my life—much less this one. I remember every detail of what transpired that afternoon—and most of the parts that can be forced into words are the least important ones.

279

To begin with, my consciousness was fractured, asymmetrically. The largest portion was on Rachel-and-Me, which of course translates as Mostly Me. A smaller, equally self-conscious portion was on Snaker-and-Me, and that portion tried to make itself as inconspicuous as possible. Another portion was devoted to Rachel-and-Snaker, and still another to Rachel-and-Snaker-and-Me (in constantly shifting order of priority), on the thing we were building in my bedroom, and how it was changing all three of us individually.

Each of these self-nuggets was further fractured. The portion concentrating on Rachel-and-Me, for example, could not decide whether to focus on our minds or our bodies or our souls. Part of me was learning about Rachel as a person from the way she made love, and telling her of myself; part was concerned with the simple but awkward mechanics of coupling; part was distracted by the weirdly beautiful symmetry of lust spanning time itself, by the notion that the Oldest Mystery stretched both backward and forward through the centuries; yet another part of me was wondering what her people used for contraception and whether she was now using it, wondering how I would feel if she were not.

And if this was fiction—the kind the author wants you to believe—I would tell you that all these parts were drowned out by the sheerly overwhelming physical sensations of what we were doing together, that the future folk had made unimaginable advances in Sexual Voodoo, perfected unnameable new skills and indescribable new delights, and that Rachel was one of their Olympic champions.

She was okay.

For a First Time, on a purely physical level, a little better than okay. None of the usual awkwardness. Well, some at first, all on my part, but I got over it fast; it takes two (or more) to sustain awkwardness. She knew all the things an educated woman of my time would know, and did them about as well. She didn't do anything to me that startled me (though she most pleasantly surprised me a few times). She was quite direct about asking for what she wanted, using gestures or words, and didn't ask for anything I didn't know how to do. (I believe I may have surprised her once or twice myself.) She neither hid nor inflated her enjoyment. She was perhaps less vocal than women of my time tended to be, a little less inhibited than the women I had been sleeping with lately (that is, completely uninhibited), certainly much less self-conscious than any woman I had ever known. She came quickly, but didn't make a big squealing deal of her orgasms.

And yet, while she was not self-conscious, she was to some extent self-involved, removed. My ego might have liked it better if she *had* made a bigger deal of her orgasms. If I had expected some kind of magical union, some rapture of telepathic transport, I was disappointed.

I had; I was.

I had been prepared for, had been half-expecting, to "lose my ego," as we were so fond of saying on the Mountain in those days, to mingle identities with her in some way, to be taken out of myself. We've spent a million years trying to learn to leave the prison of our skull through lovemaking, with the same perpetually promising results, and I had hoped that the people of the future had made some dramatic breakthrough in that direction, and that I was equipped to learn it.

No such luck. As intimately as we joined, part of us was separate, just like always. She missed subtle clues. Some of the clues *she* gave must have been too subtle for me to follow. Twice my penis slipped out of her vagina because she zigged when I zagged. I could not leave my skull, my body, my identity—partly because I could tell that she was still in hers. I could feel it in a barely perceptible tension of her skin, and see it in her eyes. I could almost see her straining against the insides of those eyes, trying to break out. They reminded me of the eyes of a wolf I had seen once, born free but long in captivity. Resignation.

In some odd way lovemaking defined the barrier between us, and so made us further apart than we had been when we started.

And at the same time I learned a great many things about her in a short period. Some were of small consequence, like the highest note that her alto voice could reach. Others were of more importance, things that would have taken much longer to learn or intuit without the lovemaking, things that she might not have known herself.

Such as the fact that underneath a very professionally manufactured calm, she was terrified, scared right down to her bones. Scared of what, I could not say, but she *needed* sex, to calm her nerves. And it wasn't helping as much as she'd hoped it would.

This was not a simple linear learning; I was simply going in too many directions at once. The age-old question I Wonder What This Is Like For Her was complicated by I Wonder What This Is Like For Him. Since he was male, I could empathize more directly with Snaker. (But Rachel was *closer*.) And since he was a friend of mine, I couldn't help wondering What This Would Be Like For Ruby when she heard about it, and What *That* Would Be Like For Him. And for me; Ruby was my friend, too. Making all thought difficult were the four restrained but quite emphatic orgasms Rachel had while I was on my way to my first, each seeming strangely to ease her fear and compound her sadness. . . .

What with six things and another, it seemed to go on for countless hours and be over before it had begun. Compared to hers, my own completion was thunderous and abrupt. The "afterglow" period of delicious brainlessness was measurable in microseconds, and then, wham, I was back inside my skull, brain buzzing, chewing on *well, that wasn't as good as I hoped nor as bad as I feared* and *Jeez I've got my back to Snaker and my legs spread, will he think I?* and *all that perfect skin-temperature control and she* still *sweats like crazy when it's time to be slippery* and *I wonder what in hell she's so scared of?* and *God it's good to get laid again* and so forth.

A long exhalation came from Snaker. I twisted round to see him. He was smiling hugely, a skinny stoned Buddha. He was also sweating a lot. Wood chips on his flannel shirt. Visible bulge below. Dilated pupils. Little orange bunnies woven into his outer pair of socks. Happy maniac.

"That was beautiful," he said simply.

I reached down and pulled the blankets back up over me again; even the warmth of energetic sex was only briefly equal to the cold of my bedroom in late Winter. Rachel, of course, did not need the protection and stayed uncovered; as I watched, the perspiration on her skin seemed to evaporate, or perhaps be reabsorbed.

I read about a character in a book once who could make knives appear as if by magic at need, from no apparent source; they just seemed to materialize in his hand. The Snaker does that trick with joints. They appear, lit, in his hand as he passes them to you. I accepted it from him and toked, being careful not to drip ashes on Rachel, then offered it to her. She passed. As she did I realized I didn't want another toke myself.

"May I ask you about your feelings, Snaker?" she asked.

He glanced quickly down and to his right, then back again at once. I'd been his friend long enough to know that little eye gesture was what he did when he wanted to reconsider, perhaps edit, the first answer that popped into his mind. But his smile never flickered. "Sure."

"Why did you not masturbate?"

Down and to the right; back up. "I'm not sure." Pause. "I want to be straight with you because I know you're an anthropologist and you learn a lot about a culture from its sex mores, but I'm really not sure myself, Rachel. I mean, I've been trying to understand *my own* sex mores for almost a quarter of a century, and I'm still confused."

"Would Ruby have considered it an act of infidelity if you had pleasured yourself while you watched us?"

Down and to the right; back up. "Again, I'm not sure. I *think* perhaps not. Maybe when I tell her about this she'll say I should have gone ahead. But I hadn't thought it through beforehand . . . and I can't rely on any judgment I make while I have a hard-on."

"Would *you* have considered it an act of infidelity?"

"Again, I'm not sure. But I think so. Especially since we haven't defined our agreement in this area yet. Uh . . . frankly, I don't think either of us ever expected the situation to come up."

"People of your time never witness the lovemaking of others?"

"Frequently, but almost always second-hand. On film, not in person."

Briefly it occurred to me to be jealous. I mean, if any woman of my own time, lying in my arms in afterglow, had initiated a complex discussion with a third party, I'd have read it a certain way. But I couldn't manage to be jealous. It just felt natural. She and Snaker hadn't touched, so they had to use words, was all.

She pressed the point. "But you said you had a mutual agreement that it was okay to look."

He looked sheepish. "That was sort of a sophistry. What we meant by that was, if you see a sexy stranger go by, a temptation, it's okay to look and be aroused by it—as long as you bring the arousal home to your partner. And as long as you don't play with it, start flirting and talk yourself into a place where you might get tempted beyond your ability to control. I construed the word 'look' to cover this situation, a slippery extension—so I guess that's why I construed 'don't play with it' to mean literally don't play with it." He looked even more sheepish. "There's a chance Ruby might be angry or hurt when I tell her about this, and I guess I wanted to be able to cop a plea if I had to."

"Cop a plea?"

"Sorry. Wanted something to say in mitigation of my offense if necessary. And it might be necessary. I think if Ruby'd been here, we might well have masturbated each other while we watched you. But she isn't. I guess I've got it worked out in my head that if you don't come, you're not being unfaithful. If Ruby's as smart as I think she is, she'll accept the big charge of sexual energy that I'm going to be bringing home as a delightful gift from the gods, and we'll put it to good use together. For which I thank you. Both of you."

I smiled what was probably a pretty fatuous smile and nodded. "Our pleasure."

"You are welcome, Snaker," Rachel said. "And thank you for answering my questions. For trusting me."

"Don't thank me. I don't trust people by conscious choice. It happens, or it doesn't. Do people usually make love in public when you come from, Rachel?"

She started to answer, and then her face smoothed over.

"If I'm crowding some taboo—," Snaker began.

"No, no. It's just that your question doesn't quite translate into meaningful terms. If I take it literally, I cannot answer it, and I'd rather not get into a discussion of why not. But if I analogize its concepts, extrapolate, and translate back into your terms, the answer is, yes, we do."

"*Everyone* does?"

"Everyone," she assured me, patting my ass.

It had been a very long time since anyone patted my ass. I liked it. "Without self-consciousness?"

She looked momentarily puzzled, then smiled. "I've warned you about those multiple-meanings, Sam. The way you mean that term, yes, without self-consciousness. Without shame or fear or guilt or anxiety."

"*When does the next bus leave?*" Maybe I was half kidding. Maybe a quarter.

She smiled again. It was a perfectly ordinary smile, physically identical to the previous one, nothing measurable changed in the placement of lips or eyes or anything I could see, your basic garden variety smile. Somehow it hauled more freight than a smile can carry unassisted. I read in it fear and regret and determination, read them so clearly that I still believed in them when they were totally absent from her voice as she said:

"Never."

Snaker looks down and to the right; I hold a blink for a few extra beats. I held a blink for a few extra beats, and said, "There's no way you can take anybody back with you?"

"Analogizing to make the question meaningful again, no, I cannot. I cannot 'go back' myself in the sense you mean."

This time I held my eyelids shut for a period measurable in seconds. When I opened them again, she still had that smile. "You're telling me that you're stuck here. That you can't go back to when you came from."

"Yes."

"Jesus," the Snaker said.

I was thunderstruck. Energy fought for expression; I wanted to jump up and pace the room. Some instinct made me hug her instead. Some impulse made me gesture to Snaker before her arms locked tight around me. He was there at once, swarmed into our embrace without disturbing it, and we hugged us.

She had come God knew how many hundreds of years—on a one-way ticket. My opinion of her courage—already high—rose astronomically. And at the same time a little paranoia-voice made a soft *hmm* sound. This woman was in greater psychic stress than I had imagined, was doubtless in need of a great deal of emotional support, represented therefore a potential burden. . . .

Every year you live you learn a little more about yourself. It had been quite a few years since I had learned much of anything I liked.

"Rachel?" Snaker murmured in my ear, in a voice that said I've Just Had A Dreadful Thought.

"Yes, Snaker?"

"In your world—I mean, your time, when/where you came from—"

"My ficton," she said.

"What?"

"Ficton. It is the word for what you mean. I'm surprised—" She interrupted herself with a bark of laughter, and all three of us backed off a few inches.

"What's funny?" I asked.

She hesitated, then smiled. "I was about to say that I was surprised you didn't know the word, since it will be coined less than a decade from now." She gave that single small shout of laughter again, and Snaker and I both chuckled too. Let's face it: time travel makes funny problems. I remembered back to high school Latin when I had thought *I* had had *my* tenses mixed up, and laughed even harder.

A three-way laughing hug is a very nice thing to have had in your life.

But when our giggles subsided, Snaker still had his I've Had A Dreadful voice. "In your ficton, Rachel—"

See now, there again. Just the *damndest* thing. I was looking right at her from point-blank range, and not a muscle twitched in her head, and one minute it was just a smile, and the next it was that other thing that looked like one and was full of pain.

"—do people die?"

Snaker looks down and to the right; I hold a blink; Rachel does nothing at all. She did that for a few seconds. I think I stopped breathing.

"Analogously speaking, of course," Snaker added.

Suddenly, shockingly, moisture appeared in those striking eyes, welled over and spilled down her placid expression. She did not cry; she simply leaked saline water down her face.

"No," she said. "They do not."

"I didn't think they did," Snaker said softly. "But you'll die, now that you've come here, won't you?"

Her voice was nearly inaudible. "Yes, Snaker."

I held that blink a *long* time. When I finally opened my eyes, my pupils had contracted and the dim light that came through double-paned glass and three layers of plastic insulation seemed too bright.

"Rachel," I said very quietly, "let me get this straight. You were an immortal, and you gave it up? For the glorious privilege of inhabiting, for a short while, this wonderful 'ficton' of ours?"

"Yes, Sam."

Loud: "*Why?*"

"Because it needed doing. Because someone had to, and I wanted to the most."

"But—but—" I couldn't make it make sense. "*Why* did it need doing?"

"It became necessary to study this ficton—"

"Wh—"

"—for good and sufficient reasons I will not explain. You lack certain concepts; you lack even the words to form them."

"But for Christ's sake, Rachel—" I was aware that I was becoming furiously angry. I couldn't help it. "What the hell good is your research if you can't bring the data *back*?"

"I can't bring it back—but I can *send* it back."

"You can?" How? With that headband dingus?

"Certainly I can. You can send data to the future the same way, if you want. Give it to me, and I'll bury it in the same place I'm going to bury mine. When the time comes, it will be retrieved."

"Oh." Okay, so it did make sense. It was still stupid. This beautiful warm kind funny strange lady had condemned herself to death, for what seemed to be insufficient reason. Never mind that I and everyone I had ever known or heard of lived under the identical sentence of death. We hadn't chosen it!

"Do you have any idea how long you could live, here and now?" Snaker asked.

"With luck and care, about as long as you, I think. There is no way to be sure."

I rolled over on my back and closed my eyes. "Jesus Christ. That's the stupidest—literally the stupidest thing I've ever heard in my life!"

"Sam—," Snaker began.

"No, I mean it, Snaker. I'll concede that anthropology is not worthless, although eighty-five percent of it bores me to my boots and no two anthropologists can agree with each other on the other fifteen. I can imagine, if I strain, someone who would want to be an anthropologist badly enough to kill for it. But have you ever heard of anybody who wanted to be an anthropologist so badly they'd *die* for it? Especially an immortal, who needn't die for *anything*? Who could have saved a great deal of effort and energy by simply consenting to live forever? It's fucking nuts is what it is, Rachel!"

My voice was loud and full of anger, but as I turned from Snaker to Rachel on the last sentence all the steam went out of me. She was scared stiff, trying not to flinch away from me. I had two realizations concurrently. The first was that if I were sojourning in the distant past, chatting with a Neanderthal, and he suddenly began to get loud and angry, I'd be scared silly. The second realization was that, in such a situation, I would certainly have fetched along a weapon for such contingencies, and would be fingering it nervously.

Maybe Rachel was as unarmed as she seemed to me. (Would the Neanderthal have recognized a pistol as a threat?) In the absence of data, it seemed like a good idea, as well as simple politeness to a guest who had just fucked me sweetly, to calm down.

Well, I don't know about you, but I had never had much luck in getting anger to go away once established, just because the rational part of me thought it ought to. Trying usually just made me madder.

And Rachel found the handle. "Why are you angry, Sam?"

Good question: the first step in dealing with anger is to peel away the artichoke layers of rationalization and get to its true root. But it was just such a perfectly North Mountain Hippie thing to say that it made me laugh.

The first answers to her question that occurred to me I rejected as bullshit. Finally I said, "Rachel, every single thing that human beings do, from making love to looking for cancer-cures, comes from the striving for immortality, the wish to live forever. You had immortality, and threw it away, for what seem to me trivial reasons. That makes all the rest of us look like fools." I snorted and reached down to get the shirt I'd left on the floor. "Everybody wants to be rich and be loved and to live forever. I've been rich and it wasn't all that great. I've been loved and it wasn't all that great. If living forever isn't worth it, what the hell is the point of life anyway? If you people in the future don't know, who does? I mean hell, you've got unbelievable metabolic control, you wear a computer on your head, somehow I just expected you future folk to be *smart*. And then you come up with a one-way time machine!" I looked down, realized I had put my shirt on without putting on my undershirt first. I took a deep breath and started over, beginning to shiver slightly.

"Current theory in my ficton says that two-way time travel is not possible. The device we used can recycle existing reality, 'reverse the sign' of its entropic direction—but it cannot explore reality which doesn't exist yet, cannot *create* a future for an entire universe. Too many random elements. At any given moment, any number of futures *may* happen . . . but only one past *has*. If you use the device to send a copy of itself back in time, it arrives with the same limitation."

"But *what was your hurry?* You were fucking immortal! If it'd been me, I'd have talked myself into sitting tight for a while. Maybe in only another five hundred years or so somebody'd come up with a better theory of time travel and build a two-way machine, and *then* I'd make the trip."

"Even for an immortal, Sam, the past keeps *receding*. It took an immense amount of power and scarce resources to send me back this far. Five hundred years later the trip might not be possible at all."

"But why was the game worth the candle? Oh, I understand the value of historical research, but—"

"Every ficton needs to learn from its past. This place-and-time happens to be an especially interesting one. Here, and now, on this Mountain, for a brief period, First and Second and Third Wave technology all coexist side by side."

"I don't follow."

That strange bark of laughter again. "Sorry. Again I've used terminology which hasn't quite been invented yet. First Wave technology was the club and the plow, the Agricultural Revolution, things people could make with their hands. The Second Wave you now call the Industrial Revolution, things made in factories. The Third Wave has just begun—"

"The Silicon Revolution!" Snaker said excitedly. "The information economy, solid-state technology—"

"Yes. The coexistence of all three waves is of fascinating historical significance."

I picked up my jeans. "But I don't understand why you had to come study it *in corpus*. Why weren't the usual historical channels—" I looked down and realized that I was putting on my pants before my Stanfields. My second stupid move in less than a minute, and one that was literally freezing my ass, before witnesses; my irritation started to boil over, and I drew in breath for a shouted "DAMMIT!"—

—and before I could release it, a realization came to me, and I understood one of the roots of my anger, and I let that breath go, very slowly and quietly, with a little whistling sound. I shut my eyes for a moment. "Never mind," I said. I took the jeans off, yanked on my Stanfields and both sets of socks. "I think I just figured it out." I stood up and pulled on my jeans. Now that I was nearly dressed, I felt much colder than I had naked. More clothes wouldn't help. The numbing, spreading chill was coming from *inside*. . . .

"What is it, man?" Snaker asked. "What's the matter?"

I looked at Rachel. She said nothing, poker faced as always. "You're as smart as I am, brother. Figure it out. This ought to be the *best* documented age in human history to date. We've got record-keeping even the Romans wouldn't believe. Print. Computer files. Microfilm. Photocopies. Words. Pictures. *Moving* pictures. Sound. Documentaries, surveys, polls, studies, satellite reconnaissance, censi or whatever the plural of 'census' is, newspapers, magazines, film, videotapes, novels, archives, the Library of goddam Congress—this is the best-documented age in the fucking history of the world so far, Snake, and we're living in what has to be its best-documented culture; now you tell me: *why wouldn't Rachel's people have access to all that stuff?* Why would they have to send a kamikaze back to study the place?"

The Snaker's eyes were very wide. He looked at Rachel, and she looked impassively back at him. "Full-scale global thermonuclear war would do it," he said thoughtfully. "Most of our records are stored in perishable form. If civilization fell, they'd rot with the rest of it. Survivors'd be too busy to preserve them. It might be a long time before record-keeping progressed as far as the papyrus scroll again. Trivial details, like who started the war and why, might well be . . . lost to history—" He broke off and turned to me. He touched the breast pocket which held his makings. "Sam?"

I nodded. Ordinarily I didn't allow tobacco smoking in my house. This was a special occasion. Snaker nodded back and began to roll a cigarette with frowning concentration. I watched him in silence while I finished dressing. Usually he rolled his cigarettes sloppily, like joints, but this time he put a lot of attention into pulling and smoothing at the tobacco, trying to produce a perfect cylinder. Soon he had something that looked like a ready-made. He couldn't get it to stay lit. Rolling tobacco is finer and moister than the stuff they put in ready-mades; packed to the same consistency it won't draw right. Snaker knew that, of course.

I realized that what he was doing was putting on his jeans before he put on his Stanfields. Dithering. In his place I'd have been immensely irritated when I saw what I'd done. He just blinked at the useless cigarette, put it out and began to roll another. In the "night-table" crate on my side of the bed was a pack of Exports my friend Joanie had left behind—Joanie'd just as soon not fuck if she couldn't have a cigarette after—and I tossed it to him. "Fill your boots."

Through all this Rachel sat voiceless and expressionless and splendidly nude, that thin golden band around her head like a slipped halo. I looked at her. As long as I was rummaging in the crate anyway, I got the box of kleenex and tossed it to her.

"What is this for?"

They probably didn't get head-colds when she came from. "Wiping yourself." She still looked puzzled. "Drying your vagina; we just fucked, remember? And you're sitting on my pillow at the moment."

"Oh. It's not necessary, Sam."

I took a closer look, and she was right. Well, if her metabolism could disperse a whole body-surface worth of perspiration in a matter of seconds, five or ten *ccs* of sperm and seminal fluid probably didn't strain it any. Perhaps they *had* improved sex in the future. It sure simplified contraception.

"Rachel?" Snaker asked, puffing on his smoke. "Is Sam right?"

Her answer was slow in coming. "I . . . can neither confirm nor deny his theory."

"I know I'm right," I said bleakly. I met her eyes. "The human race has been tap dancing on the high wire over Armageddon for thirty years now, and the human race just ain't that graceful. What I want to know is: when? *How soon?*"

"Sam, I cannot—I must not—either confirm or deny what you suggest."

"*Dammit!*" I lowered my voice. "Don't you think we have a right to know?"

"No. You have already accepted the concept that there are certain things about the future I dare not tell you, for fear of causing changes in the past. Can you not see that this is one of those things? If I give you foreknowledge of the future, I risk altering history. If I alter history, even a little, all the civilizations that ever were, all of reality from the Big Bang up to my own ficton, could vanish into nothingness. Nuclear holocaust would be a trivial event by comparison.

"And even if I were *sure* that that would not happen, I would not tell you, whether you were right or wrong. I *like* you, Sam. Have you never skipped ahead to the ending of a book—and then wished you had not, because it spoiled your enjoyment of the story to know how it was going to come out?"

"Rachel's right, Sam," Snaker said. "Suzuki Roshi said you should live each day as if you're going to live forever, *and* as though your boat is about to sink. Knowing the future would make that impossible. If Rachel knew the hour and minute of my own death, I think I might kill her to keep her from telling me. I don't much want to know the hour and minute of my culture's death, either. Come to think of it, I wouldn't want to *know* the reverse, either, that we're safe from nuclear catastrophe and there's really nothing to worry about.

"Which could be true. You make a good case for your theory, Sam, but you don't convince me. There could be other reasons why Rachel's here."

I snorted. "Name two."

"There could be other reasons," he insisted.

"Name one."

"Maybe she needs to study something that can't be squeezed into historical accounts, something we don't think to keep records of. If you're trying to build a global weather model and you need data on day by day weather changes in the Middle Ages, you'll have to go back and get it, because the monks didn't think that information was worth hand-illuminating.

"Or maybe Rachel's people lost the fine distinction between fact and fiction, between history and legend—do you think you know what the Old West was *really* like? You've had a liberal education, you probably know more about the history of Rome than the average Roman citizen did—do you think you have an accurate gestalt of life in the Roman Empire? Are there records of the secret corruption that went on under Caesar's table, the true facts behind the public pronouncements? History is always written by the winning side, Sam, you know that: suppose you wanted to learn something that only the losers could have taught you?"

Rachel was still expressionless, taking in everything, putting out nothing whatsoever. I'd never seen such opacity; I made a mental note not to teach her poker.

"Fine, man," I said. "You believe what you want to believe. I know what logic tells me."

Snaker frowned slightly. "Sam . . . can you give me a reason why your theory is *logically* preferable to mine?"

I said nothing.

"I think *you're* the one who's believing what he wants to believe."

"All right, let's drop it, okay, Snake? You live as if you're going to live forever, and I'll live as if the boat is going to sink in the next ten minutes, and maybe between us we'll make up a sane human being. Meanwhile, we've got other fish to fry."

He accepted the impasse at once. "Right. Rachel needs a cover story."

"And clothes. And a wig."

Snake looked at me as if I had grown an extra nose.

"Snake, you and I like looking at her naked. So would any sensible human being. But in this weather it's bound to cause talk, no? Outdoors at least."

"Agreed. But I don't see the problem. You must have a change of clothes to your name."

He was right. She wasn't that much shorter than me, and on the North Mountain a lady in men's clothes a few sizes too large would draw no comment. Underwear other than Stanfields was optional for either sex in our social set. I had a spare pea coat that was too small for me. Enough socks and she'd fit into my boots. I went to the west end of the room, where a series of mismatched cardboard cartons and a length of rope constituted my closet, and began selecting items for her. "Right. Okay, the other two problems go together: any wig we can buy anywhere closer than Halifax will be a rug, so her cover story has to explain why even a cheap wig is better than—what are you gaping at?" I seemed to have grown a third nose. "Testing. Earth to Snaker. What'd I say?"

His voice was strange. "You pride yourself on being a pretty observant cat, don't you, Sam?"

Baffled, I turned to Rachel. She was poker-faced, of course. "Do you know what this burned-out hippie is talk—," I began, and stopped. I held a blink, and then bent down and picked up the clothes I had dropped.

Some changes happen too slowly to perceive. They say there used to be Micmacs on the Mountain who could walk right up to you in broad daylight without being seen, because they could move so preternaturally slowly and smoothly that they failed to trip your motion-detector alarms. All of a sudden they were in front of you. It's possible to gain on a white-noise signal so slowly from zero that people in the room are actually raising their voices to be heard before they consciously notice the sound.

Rachel had hair.

❖EIGHT❖

NOT MUCH HAIR, yet. About two weeks' growth of beard worth, from what I dimly remembered of shaving, and all of that on her scalp. I like to think that even in my distracted condition I would have noticed groin-bristles. It looked like it would grow up to be red and curly—which didn't match her complexion. That was okay. Bad taste in hair colour was easier to explain than baldness.

I felt doubly stupid. First, for missing it at such close quarters (now that I thought back, I *could* recall stubble against my cheek; somehow the sensation had gotten tangled up with thoughts of—I dropped that line of thought hastily.) Second, for being startled when I did twig. First you cure baldness. Then you build time machines.

"Sorry, Snake. I don't know what's wrong with me today."

"I'd say the problem is in your software," he said helpfully.

I ran a hand over the territory that my hairline had surrendered over the last few years (with far too little resistance, I thought), and sighed. "Rachel, if you can teach that trick, you'll be able to buy Canada out of petty cash within a few years."

"I'm sorry, Sam. I can't. It's a stored ROM routine—and you don't have the I/O ports."

I nodded. "I figured."

"How long should I let it get, Sam? I have seen no women of this ficton. Like that?" She pointed to a nearby Beardsley of a woman whose hair would have sufficed to secure a Christmas tree to a VW bug. Snaker and I both cracked up involuntarily, and she caught on at once. "As long as yours, then?"

Mary Travers of Peter, Paul and Mary used to perform with hair shorter than mine was then. Snaker's was longer than mine. "Sure, that'd be fine. Scale your eyebrows and lashes to mine, too. How long will that take you?"

She consulted the inside of her head, or maybe that headband computer. "Another hour, if I hurry."

I poked my tongue out through my lips, bit down on it, and nodded. "I see. I guess that'll be satisfactory." Irony, like puns, was lost on her. "If anybody asks why you never take your headband off, just say it's a yoga." Snaker grinned.

"All right. What does that mean?"

"It means, there is no rational reason why."

Snaker grinned again. "About that cover story," he said.

I shrugged. "Well, given a normal head of hair, the problem becomes trivial, doesn't it? All we have to account for is nosiness and a very slight accent."

"The story must explain my unfamiliarity with local customs," Rachel added.

Snaker and I both shook our heads. "People on the North Mountain are used to newcomers being unsophisticated," I said, "not knowing how to feed a fire or feed chickens or plant a garden or do anything useful. City people are expected to be ignorant. Their faux pas are politely ignored. Anything weird you do, folks'll just chalk it up to you being from civilization."

"Then we must explain why I am ignorant of the ways of the city."

"Naw. Nobody'll ask you about them. A city background is treated like a mildly embarrassing disease; folks just pretend not to notice until it's clear that you've been cured. If anybody does ask you about life where you come from, just say, 'I came here to forget about the city,' and they'll nod and mark you down as a sensible young lady. But nobody'll be really interested."

"I think you're a writer, Rachel," Snaker said. "You're doing a book on the Back-to-the-Land movement, or alternative lifestyles, or the rural experience or some such. It's innocuous enough; it'll get you into people's living rooms and get them to open up to you."

"Open up? Hell, she'll be a celebrity, Snake. Remember how popular you were until folks got it straight that you weren't going to write up their memoirs for them? If it's oral history you want, Rachel, people around here'll talk your ears off, hippies and locals alike."

"Where's she from, Sam?" Snaker asked. "She's dark enough to be African or Far Eastern, but that accent feels more like European to me."

"I'd buy Polynesian raised and educated in Europe. Say, Switzerland. Do you know anything about contemporary Switzerland, Rachel?"

She blinked. "I have some data in ROM. Enough, I think, to deal with surface-level inquiries."

"You won't have to pass a quiz. And nobody on this Mountain knows diddly about Polynesia. Come to think, *I* don't. So you were adopted by a Swiss couple who took you home with them to live. You were going to grad school at S.U.N.Y. Stony Brook, studying . . . let me see, what discipline do we *not* have any refugees from around here? Studying sociology, and you dropped out to travel and write a book."

"Why the Stony Brook part?" Snaker asked.

"Well, college student explains the excellent English, the hand-me-down wardrobe, and general weirdness—and Stony Brook is good because I went there, and nobody else on this Mountain has ever been near it. Somebody back there who used to know me told Rachel that there were still a few hippies around up here in Nova Scotia; that's why she came here to research her book. The point is, Rachel, that your cover story doesn't *have* to have a great deal of definition. The vaguer you are, the more you'll ring true. *Lots* of people around here are vague about their backgrounds, for one reason or another. Far more important than where you're from is what you're like."

As I was speaking, I got one last item from a "closet" carton and noticed my old portable cassette recorder at the bottom of the box. A piece of cheese, with one of those built-in cardioid mikes, but it was adequate for spoken-word, ideal for oral history. I wondered if Rachel could use it. Come to think of it, how *did* she plan to preserve her data? What media would survive centuries of burial? Written notes on acid-free paper in sealed atmosphere? Shorthand acid-etched on steel plates? Supershielded computer tapes? Or could she simply store information in her—

—I tabled the matter. She was speaking:

"What exactly do you mean, Sam?" Rachel asked.

"Nothing that need worry you. Whether you're comfortable to be around—and you are. Whether you pull your share of the load—and I'm sure you will. Whether your word is good—and I'm certain yours is."

"Thank you, Sam," she said soberly. "Your trust warms me as much as your lovemaking." She actually blushed. "A great deal."

"Here," I said gruffly, and gave her the clothes. "Try these on for fit and then we'll go downstairs. The decor up here is deafening."

"For you too?" she asked. Her relief and surprise were evident, but I'm damned if I know where. She still had the vocal and facial expressiveness of a female Vulcan.

"Hell, yes. I don't own the place; I just live here while the owner's away. The only way I'd feel okay about revising his decor would be if I were to materially improve the house in the process—say, by properly insulating this upstairs and finishing the walls. So far, I haven't minded the decor quite that much."

She began to dress. It is always a fascinating process to watch. With her, it was riveting. I was a little surprised at how little trouble she had with twentieth-century fastenings like zippers and buttons. She picked things up quickly; she was alert all the time.

"When does the owner return?"

"For longer than a few weeks? Never. Only he hasn't figured that out yet." She raised one eyebrow, so precisely like Star Trek's Mister Spock that I had to suppress a giggle, and I saw Snaker doing the same thing. "Joel's an American hippie with rich parents. He fell in love with this place hitchhiking through, and Dad cabled him the money to buy it. He plans to move up here and 'fix it up' in a couple of years, and he lets me stay here to keep a fire in the place. What he hasn't thought through is that he has at least two drug busts on his record, plus political busts, plus time on the U.S. welfare rolls. He'll never get Landed status. The buyer actually warned him, but Joel's an optimist—"

I'd told this story to several people, I was telling it on automatic pilot—and then all of a sudden I heard the words coming out of my mouth, and froze. Snaker got it too, and looked skyward and frowned at the same time.

"What is 'Landed Status'?" Rachel asked innocently.

"Thundering *shit!*" I said, smacking myself in the forehead with my palm. "*Papers!*"

"That does complicate things," Snaker agreed mournfully. "What'll we tell Whynot and Boucher?"

"What is wrong?" she asked.

"Rachel, there are three kinds of people living in Canada. Citizens, Landed Immigrants, and Visitors on temporary visas. The last two kinds need paper ID. Other than for academic purposes or special circumstances, a visitor can stay a maximum of three months, usually much less—and how much is entirely at the whim of the officer on duty at the border crossing you use. A Landed Immigrant, like Snaker and me, can live here indefinitely without relinquishing his original citizenship, and can do everything a citizen can do except vote. It's hard to get that status, gets harder every year, and because a lot of people want to live here on the Mountain without that much formality, the Department of Manpower and Immigration sends a couple of runners through here regular, looking for people who've overstayed their visa. When they find 'em, they very politely and firmly deport 'em. Considering the line of work they're in, Boucher and Whynot are nice guys, but they're very good at what they do. And we can't get you a visa or Landed status, and we can't pass you off as a citizen."

"Shit, Sam, with her color and accent she hasn't got a chance," Snaker said.

She was fully dressed now. I'd been preoccupied enough to miss some of the best parts. Damn. "Couldn't I simply avoid them?" she asked. "There are acres of forest outside. I could avoid even infrared detection methods—"

"Rachel, weird as it may sound, the country is the last place to hide effectively. It is said that if a man farts on the North Mountain, noses wrinkle across the Valley on the South Mountain. You savvy the expression, 'jungle drums'?" She nodded. "Snaker's right: with your beauty, let alone your exotic colouring, you'll be known up and down the whole damn Valley in a week. And once they know you exist, Boucher and Whynot'll find you if they have to get out blood-hounds."

"I can beat bloodhounds too—"

"It's the wrong way to go, Rachel. You can't do your work as a fugitive. That puts us under severe time pressure. We've got to have some kind of paperwork for you by the time the Bobbsey Twins make their next circuit through the area. When was their last pass, Snake?"

"Around Thaw, if I remember right." Thaw, a brief, inexplicable week of good weather, came each year around the end of January, first week of February. "Not much action for them this time of year, but I'd look to see them again in a month or two, when things start warming up again some. Around Solstice. On the other hand, they love surprises; they could pop in later this afternoon."

"What do we *do,* Snake?" Getting somebody Landed in those days was easy, old hat: simply arrange a bogus marriage to a citizen or Landed Immigrant. It didn't even have to be a good fake; like I said, Whynot and Boucher were easygoing guys. But then citizenship papers for some country of *origin* were essential.

"We're going to need fake papers," he said. "Tricky. I'm not entirely sure how to go about it. I've got a friend in Ottawa I could call—but one thing's for sure: if we can do it at all, it'll be fucking A expensive."

I frowned and nodded. That was certainly a serious problem, all right—

"That's not a serious problem," Rachel said.

We stared at her.

"It was foreseen that it might be useful for me to have local money. My ROM includes certain useful data. Given investment capital and lead time, I can generate whatever funds we need."

We said nothing, continued to stare.

She looked mildly embarrassed. "I'm sorry, Sam. Of course you assumed I was destitute. I will pay for the food I eat. Do you want me to pay rent?"

"No, no! I'm not paying Joel a dime, why should you? I'm just kicking myself for being stupid, that's all. Naturally you'd have provided for a simple thing like unlimited funding. Silly of me."

"You're sure you don't want some money? Really, Sam, it'll be no extra trouble for me—"

This conversation was turning surreal. "Rachel, I have enough money to feed my bad habits; more than that is a nuisance. Thanks anyway. But even with plenty of cash, getting you forged papers isn't going to be easy."

Snaker nodded, frowning. "One of the few really backward things about Canada: its civil servants are astonishingly hard to bribe. It can be done, but you need luck and the same kind of tact it takes to negotiate with a Black Panther for his sister's maidenhead. And you said you need lead time to get a bankroll, and the Immigration boys are due in a month or two—I say we've got a time pressure problem."

To my surprise, Rachel refused to be dismayed. "Don't worry, my First Friends. From what you say, this can be dealt with. I am confident that it will not be a problem."

I didn't entirely share her confidence, but I didn't see any point in depressing her by debating the matter, and I was distracted by her honorific. " 'First Friends.' I like that."

"Me too," Snaker said.

"You *are* my First Friends," she said. "Every other friend I have, I will not meet for years to come."

"Far out," Snaker said. "I'm proud to be a First Friend of yours."

I mimed clicking my heels and bowed. "And I'm honored to be First Lover. Shall we get out of this pyramid burial chamber?"

We went downstairs. Snaker and I gave Rachel her first lesson in North Mountain survival—the care and feeding of woodstoves. That killed half an hour, even though I'm quite sure she had grasped the essentials within the first few minutes. Anybody who lives with a woodstove can, and will, talk your ear off on the subject, and no two of them completely agree on technique. She listened with polite attention, and probably immense patience. Then she reached out and shut the damper on the Ashley, which I had failed to close after shutting up the stove again, and correctly adjusted the mechanical thermostat, and Snaker and I shut up.

"Can we go outside, please, Sam?" she asked.

"Oh, hell, of course. I should have expected claustrophobia from someone who's comfortable naked in a blizzard."

"It's not claustrophobia as I understand that term," she said. "It's just that I've been in your ficton for nearly a day, and all I've seen are a few seconds of nighttime forest and the inside of your home."

"I understand perfectly. But let's get you dressed for outdoors, just in case anybody happens to drive by." Spare pea coat, scarf, hat and mittens were no problem, but I had to duck back upstairs for enough socks to make my spare boots stay on her.

She watched carefully the whole airlock-like procedure of exiting through the back woodshed. Open hook-and-eye, shoulder inner door open against spring tension, step into shed, let door close, seal with wooden turnbuckle, stand clear of outer door, spin its turnbuckle open, let wind blow door open, step outside, yank door shut and secure with hook-and-eye latch.

"Sam," she said, "your home cannot be locked while you are away."

"Of course not," I said absently. "Suppose somebody came by while I was out. How would they get inside?" I was distracted, and dismayed, by the sight of my woodshed. Snaker had told me, but I had forgotten.

"It's only the one side," he said sympathetically.

Sure enough, the near side of the roof was intact. But even from here I could see that the far side was completely gone, torn free and blown clear. Four cords of drying firewood, representing endless hours of labor, were open to the next snow or rain that came along. "Snake," I said sadly, "tell me it didn't land where I think it did."

"Well, actually," he said brightly, "you got away lucky there. It only demolished the half of the shitter that you weren't using."

"God's teeth." At some point in its twisted history, Heartbreak Hotel had been what it still looked vaguely like, a little red schoolhouse, and so it had a divided four-holer outhouse, two for the boys, two for the girls. (My custom was to use one side at a time and seal up the other, rotating yearly; it kept down the aroma, and provided splendid fertilizer for the garden and the dope patch.) Snaker was right, I'd had a lucky break. Exposed firewood had to be dealt with soon, but a sheltered place to shit is a *necessity*. (Especially when company comes to stay; it's easier to share a toothbrush than a thundermug.) But I didn't *feel* lucky.

My pal sought to distract me. "I see it was a Gable roof."

I regarded him suspiciously. "I sense danger. What prompts this observation, Mr. Bones?"

He shrugged. "Gone with the wind."

I fell down laughing. so did he. We needed a good laugh. "Only to windward," I managed. "Looks fine over here on the Vivien Leigh side," and we were off again.

I realized that we must have left Rachel far behind, and looked around to apologize—and found that she had left us far behind. She was nowhere in sight; her footprints led around the house. Snaker and I sobered quickly and followed her tracks, worried about God knows what.

We found her at once—

—transfixed, banjaxed, struck dumb and frozen in her tracks—

—by the sight of the Bay of Fundy. . . .

Perhaps I felt more true *kinship* with Rachel in that moment than I had while we were making love. Until now she had been always a little off-beat, a little alien, a stranger in a strange land. But this we shared. For the first time I felt that I truly empathized with her, understood what she was feeling. I remembered my own first sight of the Bay, coming from a city background—and how much more over-populated must her world be than mine?

The first thing that had surprised me about nature, when first I made its acquaintance, was how *big* it was. I learned this first with my eyes, and then, almost at once, with my ears, and finally with the surface of my skin. In the city, where I grew up, my visual and auditory autopilots had a scan range of a couple of hundred meters at most. Visual stimuli farther away than that tended to be filtered out, unless they met certain alarm parameters. Similarly, my ears were usually presented with such a plethora of nearby stimuli that a gunshot over on the next block might have gone unheard.

Then I came to Parsons' Cove, and stood on the shore of the Bay of Fundy. Suddenly half of my universe was sky, more sky than I had known existed. In one direction an infinite series of trees climbed the gentle slope of the North Mountain; in the other, my eye had to leap fifty kilometers to the far shore of New Brunswick. If I stood still and listened, I could clearly hear living things kilometers away. My world expanded to encompass a larger hemisphere—all of it beautiful.

It blindsided me. I have not recovered yet. Perhaps I never will.

Snaker and I looked at each other and shared a wordless communication and smiled. The best part of that first glorious and terrifying moment when you fall in love with the Fundy Shore is that it will never really wear off. Even constant exposure doesn't build much tolerance. Remarkably sane people live along that Shore. It's really hard to generate an anger or fear or other craziness that will survive an hour of looking at the Bay, at all that immense sky and majestic water—and *sunset* on the Bay has been known to alleviate clinical psychosis.

Suddenly I was startled to realize how soon sunset was going to be.

"Jesus, Snaker, look at the sun!" I whispered, trying not to distract Rachel.

"Well, I'll be prepped for surgery. Where the hell did the time go?" he answered as quietly.

I replayed the day in my mind, oddly disturbed. The three of us had adjourned to my bedroom just after noon; I'd noted the time. Flatter myself and assume the sex had lasted half an hour; add an hour for chatter, half an hour for Snaker and me to argue about stove lore. It should be two o'clock—three at the outside. But the sun said it was five or later.

To city folk, this may seem trivial. But if you've ever lived without electricity, you know how you get pretty good at keeping track of how much working light is left, just like you get good at keeping track of which stoves were fed how long ago. A malfunction in one of those internal clocks can be serious business. (It's ironic to recall that when I first came to the Mountain, I thought country folk were *less* time-bound than city folk because they seldom checked a wristwatch or clock before doing something.)

"I always said you grow terrific reefer," Snaker murmured.

"I guess so! The whole day's shot to shit, and we're late starting supper."

"Fuck supper, and fuck the day. Let's bring Rachel over to the Hill and introduce her around; there'll be plenty of food there."

"Vegetarian food. Thanks."

"Ruby's making chili today."

"Oh. That's different. Still, man, isn't that rushing things? Is she ready to take on your whole crazy crew? I think we ought to fill her in a bit, give her a few books to read—"

Rachel turned and interrupted us. "I'm eager to meet Snaker's family. Can you leave now?"

I blinked. "Sure. Let me get my guitar."

❖NINE❖

BLUE MEANIE HAULED the three of us east from Parsons' Cove, lurching like a drunk, engine coughing up blood and transmission shrieking, as though the aged truck knew that ahead, on the unpaved Wellington Road, axle-shattering potholes lay in wait for it, grinning.

The journey itself might have been adventure enough for anyone used to methods of travel more civilized than, say, buckboard—but Rachel had no time to appreciate it (or, more likely, be terrified by it), because Snaker and I talked nonstop the whole trip, trying to prepare her for the Sunrise Hill Gang. It would have been difficult enough to "explain" the Sunrise crowd to a normal human being of my own place and time—but Rachel didn't even know what a hippie was, let alone a die-hard hippie. She seemed barely familiar with the Viet Nam war. We needed every minute of the ten-minute drive to brief her.

"How many are in your family?" Rachel asked.

Snaker frowned and caressed the steering wheel with his thumbs. "I knew this wasn't going to be easy. Uh, at the moment there are six or seven of us around, what you might call the hard core—as soon as winter comes down, a lot of folks find pressing spiritual or other reasons to be somewhere warmer. But as to how many of us there are altogether . . . well, I'm not sure anyone's ever counted, and I'm not sure an accurate count is possible."

Rachel said nothing.

"Last summer we had as many as thirty, and I guess it averages about fifteen or so. If it helps any, there are a dozen or so names on the land deed. But half of *those* folks have gone, with no plans to come back."

"They decided to go for an actual deed, eh?" I said.

"When they saw the size of the stack of paperwork for a land trust, yeah," Snaker said.

Rachel looked politely puzzled.

"You see," Snaker tried to explain, "some of the Gang don't hold with the concept of owning land—"

Now Rachel looked baffled. Well, it baffled me too.

"—but they finally got it through their heads that if they don't own the land, somebody else will."

She dropped the matter. "Tell me about the six or seven now present."

Snaker looked relieved to be back on solid ground. "Well, there's Ruby, of course—you might want to grab a handhold here—"

All at once he *wasn't* on solid ground. We had come to the Haskell Hollow. It is an amusing little road configuration. Around a blind left curve, without any warning, the road suddenly drops almost vertically for five hundred meters, yanks sharp right, rises almost vertically for another five hundred meters, and swings hard right again. Snaker took it at his usual eighty kph.

"—and you'll really like her; she's a painter and fucking good; she has brown hair and unbelievable eyes; she thinks she's too fat but she's full of shit—"

The proper way to run the Hollow was to start accelerating *hard* about two thirds of the way down the cliff. The man who lived at the bottom made a fair dollar renting out his tractor to tourists and other virgins who chickened out and, in the hairpin turn at the bottom, lost the momentum necessary to make the upgrade. Of course, the transit was trickier on poorly ploughed snow. Blue Meanie roared in berserker fury and went for it. Rachel could have been forgiven for dampening her (my) pants at any time during the episode—but she took her cue from Snaker and me, grabbed handholds but stayed calm.

"—and she's the best cook in the place, by a damnsight. Then there's Malachi: he and Ruby used to be together once; now he lives with Sally from the Valley—"

He yanked the wheel round with both hands (the Meanie predated power steering) and popped the clutch about fifty meters from the bottom. We skidded into proper orientation for the upcoming turn-and-climb, and he had correctly solved the equation of friction and time and distance: the wheels grabbed, hard, just as we were reaching the nadir. (Snaker maintained that since that was the place where

motorists tended to throw up, it should be called the Ralph Nadir.)
Every component of the truck capable of making noise did so to the
best of its ability; Snaker raised his voice.

"—he's big and black-haired and half-bald; carpenter and electrician;
weird as a fish's underwear—he'll be the one with the eyes—"

The rear end threatened to go. Literally standing up on the throttle
now, Snaker slammed his ass down on the seat and back up again,
and Blue Meanie shrieked and settled down to the climb.

"—Sally's got long straight yellow hair, gray eyes; moves kinda
slow and doesn't say much but she's in there; then there's Tommy,
Malachi's older sister; doesn't look a bit like him, curly red hair, wiry
and fiery, tiny woman but tougher'n pumpleather; she's far out.
Lucas, he's sort of the resident spiritual masochist, salivates at the
mention of the word 'discipline'; but he's one of the *decentest* people
I ever met, brown hair and reddish beard; real handsome."

We'd begun the climb at perhaps 120 kph. We covered the last
fifty meters to the summit at a speed that the speedometer claimed
was zero, slowing even further for the curve. Then we were back on
level road, entering the fishing village of Smithton.

"Then of course there's the Nazz. One of the craziest and most
delightful cats I ever met in my life, a man who has clearly taken too
much acid and is the better for it; a stone madman; you never know
what he'll do next except that he'll be smiling while he does it and
you'll be smiling when he's done. Curly black hair and beard, both
completely out of control. He's named after an old Lord Buckley rap
about Jesus—the *Nazz*-arene, dig it?—and it suits him."

That is how long it took us to completely traverse Smithton. At the
posted speed limit of 30 kph. Then Snaker accelerated sharply and
took the right onto the Mountain Road in a spray of gravel. The slope
is nowhere near as sharp as the back leg of the Haskell Hollow, but it
goes on forever, and in snow season better vehicles than the Meanie
have had to give up halfway, slide back down backwards and take a
second run at it. Snaker went for it.

"Rachel," I asked, "is any of this getting through?"

"Some. Most of it, I think."

"I'm surprised. He's been speaking Hippie."

"Somehow when Snaker uses idiom or colloquialism, I take his
meaning more often than not."

"Far out," he said apologetically. "Sorry Rachel, I wasn't thinking." He grinned. "When I first moved in with Ruby, my first day at the Hill, Malachi dropped by in the afternoon just after we'd finished making love, to talk something over with her. Damned if I know what it was. A few minutes before I'd been certain that Ruby and I were, like, totally telepathic for life—and then she and Malachi started talking, and I did not understand a single thing they said. They were using what sounded like English words, but I couldn't even grasp the general shape of the conversation, much less follow it. And remember, I was already fluent in Hippie . . . city Hippie, anyway. Uh, I'll ask people to try and stick to Standard English—shit—" He had lost the battle to keep the Meanie out of first gear.

"No, Snaker. Immersion is the best way to master a dialect. If I need an explanation, I'll ask for one."

"Don't be afraid to ask for one with others around," I said. "As an exchange student, you won't be expected to speak Hippie."

She nodded. "Can you give me a primer?"

So we did our best to outfit her with basic vocabulary. Dig, into, trip, groove, cool, out of sight, righteous, stoned, spaced out, holding a stash, copping, manifesting, agreement, yoga, freak out, and of course, the ubiquitous far out (an acceptable comment in any situation whatsoever). Since all of these terms had multiple (often contradictory) meanings, depending on context, tone of voice, and the daily Dow-Jones average, I could not be certain we were accomplishing anything, but she kept nodding. Blue Meanie kept swapping uphill momentum for engine noise, which didn't make it any easier.

Two thirds of the way up the north slope of the Mountain, we came to the Wellington Road. Snaker took the turn from half-plowed uphill pavement to level but unplowed dirt road with gusto, throwing Rachel hard against me. As Blue Meanie began to roar in triumph and gather speed, he coaxed the wretched thing into second gear and accelerated sharply; the wheels bit just in time to keep us out of the substantial drainage ditch on my side of the road. "As for the physical plant," he said mildly in the sudden comparative quiet, "we've got three and a half houses on either end of a big parcel of land, about a hundred acres altogether." He took it up to 70 klicks (about 45 mph) and held it there. He raised his voice again. "We'll come to the Holler first, stop and see if anybody wants a ride to dinner. Then we'll go on to Sunrise Hill, to the Big House, and you can meet Ruby."

"I look forward to meeting her," Rachel called back.

The engine noise was less now, but the unpaved road was a washboard rollercoaster and the truck a giant maraca. The net effect was noisier than the desperate uphill run had been, except for the relatively calm intervals when we were on an ice-slick and flying free. Every so often a pothole the size of a desk tried to shatter the driveshaft and axles, or failing that, our spines. "Sorry if this makes you nervous, Rachel," Snaker said, "but you can't drive this road slow in winter, or you get stuck."

"That would be bad," she agreed, straight-faced. "Is there anything else I should know, to be a proper guest? Local customs or manners?"

I was impressed by her control and courage. This kind of transportation had to be a nightmare for her, and all her attention seemed to be on the coming social challenge.

Snaker looked at me. "Sam, what do you think the Gang would consider excessively weird behavior in a guest?"

I thought about some of the people I'd seen come and go at the Hill. "Gunfire. Personal violence. Arson."

"There you go. Rachel, we're all pretty weird ourselves, by contemporary standards. It's made us kind of tolerant."

"Of outsiders," I added.

He nodded reluctantly. "Yeah. Among ourselves we sometimes get kind of conservative. But visitors are welcome to do pretty much as they please. As long as they respect our right to be weird, we'll respect theirs."

I couldn't let that pass. "Aw, come on, Snake. Tolerate, yes, but respect?"

Snaker started to answer, then closed his mouth. Rachel looked back and forth at the two of us, settled on me.

So I said, "The Sunrise Hill Gang have this thing about honesty and truth, Rachel. As defined by them. To be fair, they don't lay it on strangers too much—but what it comes down to is, the longer you hang around them, the friendlier you get with them, the more they feel they have the right to . . . well, to get into your thing." I paused. How to explain that concept? To anyone, much less a time traveler? "To ask you extremely personal questions, and criticize your answers. To question your behaviour and beliefs. Sometimes they can get pretty aggressive about it." I looked over at Snaker again, met his eyes. "I'll concede that their intentions are good—but I find them hard to take sometimes. Malachi in particular has a gift for figuring out just what topics of conversation will make you most uncomfortable, and then dwelling on them, in the friendliest, most infuriating manner imaginable. He so obviously genuinely sincerely wants to help you—whether you want help or not—that you can't even manage to dislike him for it. And that makes me want to punch him. Especially when the rest of the group gets the scent of blood and joins in."

I glanced at Snaker to see if he wanted to rebut. He frowned. "I've seen him straighten a lot of people, Sam. I'm not saying I find him easy to take, myself. There's a lot of stash between us because of Ruby. But I have to admit he's good with hangups. He's got the instinct of a good shrink. Uh, sorry, Rachel, a good psychiatrist. You savvy 'psychiatrist'?"

"Oh, yes."

"But he doesn't have the *training* of a good psychiatrist," I insisted, "or any kind of license to lead group-therapy practice on non-volunteers. Why I'm bringing this up, Rachel, is to warn you to be careful around Malachi. You've got a lot to hide, and evasive answers make his ears grow points. The man has industrial-strength intuition."

Snaker frowned even deeper. "I can't disagree. Malachi demands a pretty high truth level around him. If he gives you trouble, Rachel, I'll handle him."

"Does it bother *you* to conceal truth from your family, Snaker?" she asked.

"No," he answered at once. "I place high value on truth myself—but there are higher goods that can take precedence sometimes. That's where I part company with most of the rest of the Gang."

"What takes precedence over the truth?" she asked.

"Duty, sometimes. And compassion always wins if there's a tie. Also preservation of self or loved ones, I guess. I'd lie to save Ruby if I had to."

She touched his near arm. "Does it bother you to lie to Ruby?"

He began to answer, then exhaled through his nose and started again. "Yes. But I can handle it. I really do understand the stakes, Rachel: the continued existence of reality. Like I said, I'd lie to save Ruby—even lie to Ruby herself."

It was beginning to dawn on me that I had screwed up. "I'm sorry, Snake."

"For what, man?"

"I've put you in a difficult position by sharing Rachel's secret with you. And it turns out it wasn't even necessary."

"So how could you know that? You were protecting yourself the best way you knew against a reasonable presumption of danger. I'd have done the same in your shoes. Besides, can you imagine how stupid I'd feel if there was a time traveler on the Mountain and *I didn't know it?* Don't answer, I know that doesn't make sense." He grinned. "But I'm glad you told me."

What could I do but grin back?

"Yonder comes the Holler," he told Rachel, downshifting.

I glanced at her, realized how beautiful she was . . . and a sudden thought occurred to me. "Whistling Jesus—I nearly forgot. Rachel: stop growing your hair!" I don't know if she'd forgotten; she just nodded. Her hair, an uncombed sprawl of chestnut curls, was now short for a Hippie, but long for a straight person; it covered all of her golden headband except the span across her forehead. Brows and lashes were appropriate.

The road ahead sloped down gradually, ran over a culvert, and swung left to disappear behind the trees. Just past the culvert and before the curve, Snaker snapped the wheel to the left and locked the brakes. The Meanie spun off the road to the left, rotating as it went, and came to rest, nose out, precisely in the truck-sized carpark that had been shoveled out for it, its rear wheels nestled right up against the log barrier. He put the engine out of its misery and we got out. I watched, and Rachel's legs were steady. Perhaps her time had even more hair-raising modes of transit. But I felt she had simply decided to trust Snaker before getting into the truck, and then thought no more about it.

"It's very peaceful here," she said, looking around her. There was nothing much to see except a mailbox with no name on it and a lot of snowcapped maple and birch trees and a rough path winding away downhill among them.

"It's very peaceful anywhere that truck is not running," I said.

She shook her head. "I mean more than ambient soundlevel," she said. "It is *peaceful* here."

Snaker smiled broadly. "I know what you mean," he said. "It got to me too, my first time here. Tranquility. Wait'll you see the Tree House."

And at that there was a loud explosion as Blue Meanie's left front tire blew up, followed by a diminishing cascade of metallic groans as the noble old truck went down on one knee.

No, Rachel's bravery was neither ignorance nor faith in Snaker. He and I both jumped a foot in the air, and he certainly went white as a ghost and I probably did likewise as the implications sank in . . . and then we saw each other's expressions, and fell down laughing in the snow. But I was watching her when the tire let go, and here is what I saw. The instant the report sounded behind her she was in motion— but almost as the motion registered on my eyes it changed. One microsecond, she was crouching and spinning with unbelievable speed; the next, she had aborted the crouch and was simply turning toward the sound at normal human speed. The change came, I was sure, before she had turned far enough to have the truck in her visual field. She had to have deduced what the bang must be, and then come down off Red Alert, in a shaved instant. In her place, I'd probably have panicked; it seemed to me that someone who had grown up expecting to live centuries barring accidents would be *very* afraid of sudden loud noises.

But I didn't think much about this at the time. I was busy rolling in the snow and howling with laughter. It did not occur to me to wonder *how* she had deduced the source of the noise.

" 'Tranquility,' " Snaker whooped. "Oh, my stars!"

" 'Such peace,' " I agreed, flinging handfuls of snow in his direction.

An inquiring hoot came distantly up through the woods. Still giggling, Snaker and I helped each other to our feet and brushed snow from ourselves, and Snaker hooted back reassuringly.

The North Mountain Hoot is a rising falsetto *"Wuh!"* that carries a kilometer or two in the woods, and you can pack a surprising amount of information into its intonation and pitch. The hail meant "Hello," and "Are you all right?" and "Do you need help?", and Snaker's answer meant "Everything's cool," and "I'll be right there," and "I'm bringing company."

He went to Rachel and took her hands. "So long as you're with Snaker O'Malley," he said in a fake Irish brogue, "no harm can come to you."

"But it'll sure God bark outside your door a bit," I said, still grinning. "Well, what do you say, Snake? Fix the tire now, or come back with help?"

He looked sheepish. "Well, see, it doesn't even matter that we don't have a jack—"

"God's teeth." I could guess what was coming.

"—on account of we don't have a spare either."

"Shitfire." I thought it over. "Rachel, our options have narrowed. We either walk a few miles in the snow tonight, or we crash here. Pardon me: 'crash' meaning 'sleep' in Hippie, not the literal meaning. Do you have a preference?"

"Not yet."

"Let me know if you decide you need to split."

An odd thing happened. This was not the first time I had absently used a Hippie term she could not be expected to know—but it was the first time she seemed to get angry about it. Her eyes flashed. Then, in an instant, she cut loose of it. " 'Split' means 'to leave'?"

"Sorry. Yeah. If you want to split, slip me a wink when no one's looking and I'll extricate us. You savvy 'wink'?"

She winked. I fought the impulse to grin. Can you imagine Mister Spock tipping you a wink? "Good."

We set off downhill along the twisting path. It was not shoveled, of course, but there were enough prior footprints to let us negotiate it with minimal difficulty. Before long we came to the Gingerbread House. I was not surprised that it wrung an actual smile out of Rachel.

Picture the Gingerbread House that Hansel and Gretel found. Now alter it slightly to reflect the fact that it is constructed—brilliantly if eccentrically—out of the remnants of a hundred-year-old chicken coop plus whatever came to hand. Malachi ceremonially destroyed his T-square and plumb bob before beginning construction. There isn't a right angle in the structure. Every single board had to be measured and handcut. There are nutball cupolas and diamond-shaped windows and a round door. No two shingles are the same size and shape. The first time I saw the G.H. I thought of Bilbo Baggins.

But no one was inside at the moment, so we kept following the path downhill and took the first left. Now the path was *really* down-hill. Rachel, in unfamiliar boots, kept her footing expertly despite the large roots that lurked beneath the snow. It didn't seem likely that the skills of woodcraft could still exist in her ficton; I decided that she was just naturally graceful.

We came to the bottom, to the stream. It's not a big stream. At full run, as now, you could have crossed it in three long strides and got wet to the knees; in summer it sometimes disappeared for days at a time, leaving small dwindling pools full of frantic fish. But it had pervasive magic about it. Its murmuring chuckle permeated everything, pleasing the ear in some subconscious way, conveying a kind of low-level ozone high.

A footbridge spanned the stream and the path continued downstream to our right. But we stopped on the nearside and faced left, to give Rachel—and ourselves—a chance to dig the waterfall. Snaker lit a pre-rolled cigarette, and smoked it like it was a sacrament, blowing smoke to the four winds Indian-style.

It was not a Niagara-type straight-drop waterfall, but a gradual cascade. A stepped escarpment of shattered rock turned the stream into a hundred little waterfalls by which it dropped maybe twenty meters in the space of five. White water for three mice in a boat. At the bottom it regrouped and rushed off downstream to the sea. It wasn't really much noisier than the rest of the stream, just more treble-y. It was prettier than hell, primevally delightful.

Like the Fundy Shore, that waterfall was the kind of place that could ground you spiritually, lend perspective, bring your rushing thoughts to a temporary halt and allow you to take stock. I breathed deeply through my nose, absently walking in place to keep my feet warm, and reflected that my friend the science-fiction-writing hippie and I were bringing a time traveler to Sunrise Hill for dinner. The three of us were sitting on what might very well be the deadliest secret that had ever existed, and we were about to introduce her, after fifteen minutes' briefing, to the *nosiest* customers to be found anywhere in the Annapolis Valley. I had not thought this through.

It would be irony even beneath God's usual standards if it turned out that all of reality, every last human hope and aspiration, were to be destroyed by the passion of a bunch of die-hard hippies for truth.

Fuck it. *If that is the final punchline,* I told myself, *then let's get to it.* "Let's go. It's getting late."

Snaker looked around and nodded. Back up in the real world the sun had not quite set, but down here in the Holler it was already getting dark. "Right on," he agreed.

And we tried to explain to Rachel what "right on" meant as we walked downstream to the Tree House.

✣TEN✣

I DESPAIR OF describing the Tree House. You have nothing to compare it to. The Gingerbread House was an eccentric enough structure, but the Tree House made it look like a Levitt tract home.

It was never designed; it simply occurred. Over a period of three years or so, five or ten talented and twisted minds had, with no plan and little consultation, simply done whatever stoned them, as materials or tools or willing labor became available, or as their individual spirits moved them. If a contribution by one of them foiled another's plan, he looked upon it as a *bonsai* challenge and rethought his concept. Three of these minds belonged to expert carpenters, one of them world class. Another co-creator couldn't have driven a nail if it had automatic transmission. The taste of all of them differed widely but not sharply. As near as I can see, the only thing they all had in common was that each carefully considered the effect his efforts would have on the tree.

A man Snaker's height could have just managed to walk underneath the house upright with a top hat on his head, though there were substantial areas where he could have safely used a trampoline. (Of *course* the main floor was not level. What fun would that have been to build?) Above the more-or-less first floor the house bisected. Two asymmetrical structures wound up into different parts of the mighty rock maple tree: a substantial section of two additional stories, and a slimmer but taller one that had a tiny fourth-floor meditation chamber. One could travel between the two third-floors by stepping up onto a window ledge and swinging across on a rope. There were

315

strategically placed hand and footholds on the intervening tree trunk in case of screwups, and the drop to the roof below was not severe.

The tree itself was magnificent. It continued on up another fifteen or twenty meters above the highest point of the House, its two mighty arms in the attitude of a man caught yawning. There was not another tree that size in the Holler, and I'll never understand why the loggers passed it over decades ago. Just possibly they had a sense of poetry in them somewhere.

A tree has always seemed to me a sensible place to keep a house. You don't think so? Consider: in the winter you have plenty of sunshine, in summer plenty of shade. You have partial protection from rain and snow. There is never any standing water in the basement. When it's summer and the windows are open, birds wander in and out, cleaning the kitchen floor. In winter, it takes one holy *hell* of a snowdrift to block your door. And you can haul up the gangplank if you want . . .

I watched Rachel as we approached the Tree House. It's always interesting to catch people's first reactions to it. She had not commented on the Gingerbread House; perhaps "odd" and "quaint" and "funky" were not concepts that traveled well across the centuries. But I was willing to bet that any denizen of any human culture would find the Tree House striking.

I was not disappointed. Her jaw did not actually drop, of course. She stopped walking and her nostrils flared. She raised first her right eyebrow, then her left, and stared at the place for a long twenty seconds. Snaker and I left her alone with it. Finally she smiled. It was the broadest, happiest smile I had seen yet on her face.

She turned to us, her eyes shining. "Thank you, my First Friends. This is a good place."

We smiled at her, and then at each other, and then at her again. Snaker took a last puff on his smoke and put it out. We moved on.

When we were close, Tommy's voice rose faintly above the rushing streamsound. She was singing that John Prine song about blowing up your TV. As we passed between pilings and under the House, it emitted a man. Well, part of one. The cellar door dropped open suddenly and I was looking right into the merry eyes of the Nazz, no less unmistakable for being upside down, from a distance of perhaps twenty centimeters. He was grinning hugely. (In future, unless I say otherwise, assume Nazz is *always* grinning hugely.)

"Visual interface," he told me joyously.

I couldn't argue.

"Excuse me," he said. One arm emerged from the house, carrying a long peavey. He reached down with it and opened the hatch of the root cellar by our feet. Then most of his torso emerged from the House; he made a long stretch and came up with a bag of turnips on the end of the peavey. He removed half a dozen or so, tossing them back over his head, up and into the house. "Gotta soak overnight." He dropped the sack back down into the root cellar, tipped the lid shut, sealed the anticritter latch, and hauled himself partway back up so that he was at eye level with me again. "Pictorial, really. Evolved versus learned, right? Self-evident. Groks itself! Completely new operating system." The house reabsorbed him, with a sound exactly like the one Farfel the dog used to make at the end of the word "cha-a-w—clate" in the Nestlé's commercials.

Snaker and I looked at Rachel. She looked at us. We resumed walking. The Nazz reappeared briefly behind us, said, "Hello, pretty lady," and was gone again before we could turn.

There are several ways into the Tree House, but we took the elevator. It's a simple open-air affair. You haul yourself up on a good block-and-tackle. We got on, I put my hands to the rope, and feeling faintly silly as always, joined Snaker in the ritual shout that politeness demanded.

"Umgawa!"

And we hauled away, as the shout echoed through the Holler.

Okay, it's dopey. When in Rome, you shoot off Roman candles. To an inhabitant of the Tree House, that shout means, "A fellow hippie is here." Rachel made no comment.

We stepped off onto the porch, whacked snow from our pants, scraped and kicked it from our boots, untied our laces and entered through the keyhole-shaped door. Snaker and I each took an arm-load of wood in with us from the stack on the porch, and Rachel followed our example. Just inside the door we stepped out of our boots. There was welcome warmth, good smells of maple syrup and woodsmoke and reefer, the sound of crackling fires.

From the cheaply carpeted living room I could see Tommy working in the kitchen. She was cleaning the sap taps. There are eight set into the living wood of the kitchen wall, hoses running in parallel to a boiling pot on the stove. At the end of a day's run it's a good idea to wash out the hoses.

She turned and saw us through the kitchen doorway. "Howdy," she called. "Far out—good to see you, Sam. Be right there."

We added our firewood to the box by the living room stove, standing a few of the more snow-soaked sticks on end on the front of the battered old Franklin to dry. Rachel examined the room. It was furnished in Rural Hippie. Kerosene lamps. Candles. Psychedelic posters. Several mandalas. Macramé. Plants. An enormous and functional brass narghile with four mouthpieces. Cushions. Cabledrum tables. A superb old rocking chair painted paisley. Zen epigrams printed on the walls here and there. An arresting painting of Ruby's, a portrait of Malachi. A wrinkled print of Stephen Gaskin leading Monday Night Class at the Family Dog. A hand-sewn sampler depicting a field of daisies and bluebells surmounted by the legend: flowers eat shit. Along one wall a shelf was lined with paperbacks that all concerned cosmic consciousness and how to achieve or sustain it.

Tommy came in, wiping her hands on her shirt. "Hi," she said to Snaker and me, and then a separate, friendly "Hi," to Rachel. "What's happening, guys?" she went on. "Was that one of them damn hunters again? We thought maybe y'all got shot for a moose."

(The Sunrise Hill Gang don't seem to have the custom of introductions. A newcomer is welcome to introduce herself, or not, as suits her. If she chooses to wait a bit, perhaps pick a name that's not being used already, that's her business.)

"Naw," Snaker said. "It was Blue Meanie throwing a shoe."

"Far out," she said, grimacing sympathetically. "Looks like it was a good landing; you walked away. Is it in the ditch?"

"Happened just as we were slamming the doors, thank you Buddha."

"Wow. That's *far out.*" Her eyes sparkled. "What a trip."

"Tire's a total, no spare, so I guess we hike to dinner."

She shrugged, a gesture that thrust her chin out and flounced her red curls. "Far out. I don't know if I'm into dinner—"

"Ruby's making chili."

"Hey, Nazz! Quit doodlin' and get your coat. Ruby's making chili tonight!"

The Nazz's bushy head appeared around the kitchen doorway. "Out of state," he called. "Just a third." When Nazz uses clichés they come out all wrong. He doesn't do it to be cute, it's just a mental short circuit.

Tommy was already half-dressed for outdoors. "Did you bring your guitar, Sam?"

"Left her in the truck."

"I'll help you carry it if Snaker'll take my flute. You look real cute with your hair short like that, hon—I think I might try that myself."

When two women meet, they size each other up. It's not necessarily a competitive thing. They just take each other's measure. Men do it too, but they do it differently, and I'm not sure how it's different. Women seem to take a little longer. They don't rely as much on sight, but I don't know what they use in its place.

"It will look very good on you," Rachel said, and I knew they were going to be friends.

Which was nice, because Tommy weirded out a lot of women, particularly ones as emphatically feminine as Rachel. Even with her long and curly red hair, Tommy could easily have passed for a teenaged boy; her flat-chested hipless body, her manner and many of her mannerisms were masculine. She blended right in with a construction crew. She was by no means a lesbian. She was the only true neuter human I've ever known. She had absolutely no sex drive whatsoever, and by that point in her life, her mid-thirties, she had long since given up pretending—or minding. She told me about it the night I made my pass. No physiological dysfunction, no horrid childhood trauma—she simply wasn't interested. She was quite capable of orgasm—an experience she likened to a sneeze, both in intensity and desirability. She was baffled and amused by the importance everyone placed on it, convinced that it was enormously overpriced at best.

This placed a certain basic gulf between her and many other women—not to mention many men. City-folk in particular, sex-charged to the point of frenzy by media hype, frequently resented her. But Rachel seemed to take to her instantly, and Tommy, once she was sure it was genuine, responded.

(I was slowly getting it through my head that Rachel was not what I thought of as "city-people," that in spite of the logic of a million science fiction stories, the future was not necessarily going to urbanize to the point of inhumanity. Whatever it was like when she came from, they were still flexible and tolerant—which city folk, in my experience, were not. Including myself when I first came up here.)

The Nazz came bustling into the room, beaming and brandishing computer paper. Lord Buckley once said of his namesake, the carpenter-kitty from Bethlehem:

Nazz had them pretty eyes. He wanted everybody to see out his eyes so they could see how pretty it was.

and it suited this Nazz as well. He sweetened the climate where he was at. He waved two sheets of computer paper at us. "It just now came to me," he said. "Check 'em out." He handed me one. "Find a letter that was sent to Hewlett-Packard on February 18."

I looked at the sheet. It was a printed list of about fifty computer files, displaying title, type of file, date of creation, last modification and size in bytes, arranged alphabetically by title. I ran my eye down the list: there were ten files with "Hewlett-Packard" or "HP" in their title, six of those were letters, the second from the bottom was dated "18 Feb."

"Right here," I said, pointing.

"Four point nine seconds," Nazz announced happily, looking up from a stopwatch. "Gravy. Here. Find it again." He handed me the second sheet.

I blinked at it. It was hand-drawn. The same approximate number of files were represented—by arrays of little pictures in groups, with meticulously printed labels beneath each. Little three-ring binders indicated reports; little tear-sheets were article extracts; the little envelopes were obviously letters. My eye went to them at once. Beneath the pictures were names; "HP 18F" leaped up at me. "There," I said.

"One point eight. Sixty-three percent faster. Far fuckin' up."

"Visual interface," Snaker said wonderingly. "Pictorial, really."

"Hard on," Nazz agreed. "See, the ability of the brain to interpret *text* is learned behavior, no older than the pyramids. But the brain has been interpreting *pictures* from *in front*. Much older circuitry, much faster traffic-flow, much more information-density. It's why movies kill books. Your face and breasts are extremely beautiful."

This last, obviously, was to Rachel. She was not at all taken aback. "Your hands and mind are extremely beautiful," she said.

They smiled at each other. Two more friends.

"Let's go eat," I said. I was starving.

"Remind me to call Palo Alto when we get to the Hill." Nazz said. "Couple of guys I want to mention this to. Less intimidating than a bunch of text in the damn ugly computer font; it's *friendlier*. Need a whole new language, though, and one of those new eight-bit chips—"

"Christ, i'nt he something?" Tommy said admiringly. "Gets such a kick out of little pictures."

"They're going to change the world," he assured her.

"For sure. So is Ruby's chili. Come on!"

We filled up the Franklin while Nazz found his poncho, and all left together.

The sun was below the trees on our left, throwing long shadows across the Wellington Road to the trees on the other side. We walked in the ruts that trucks and cars had made in the snow. Usually there were just the two, right down the center of the road, but infrequently there was a place where two vehicles had met and managed to pass each other.

The trip from the Holler to Sunrise Hill can be done in five minutes, if you don't mind falling on your face on arrival. It took us nearer twenty. It was beginning to get cold out, making the footing slippery. Gertrude the Guitar slowed me down. And the Nazz lit a joint, an enormous spliff which he said he had been saving for a special occasion. He always says that. Always means it, too. To pass a doobie on slippery surface, you have to stop, so everyone else has to stop to wait for you, and eventually it seems sensible to just form a circle. So we did. Rachel joined it, but politely refused the joint. "Perhaps later," she murmured, and the Nazz beamed at her. The rest of us shared it in silence.

The forest on either side of me began to sparkle. The random dance of shadows on branches suddenly became a pattern, that teetered on the edge of recognition. I was suddenly aware of my position, clinging to the face of a vast spinning planet, whirling through the universe. I heard the stream behind me, every leaf that fluttered for a hundred meters in any direction, the sounds of birds and a deer to the north. My friends became Robin Hood's Merry Men. And I was very hungry.

"Good shit, brother," I said to Nazz. My voice came from a hundred miles away through a filter that removed all the treble.

He beamed. "Xerox PARC."

Snaker broke up. "*Xerox Park?* Like, where people go to reproduce?"

We all cracked up. "No, man," Nazz said, "Xerox pee eh are *see*. On the Coast, man, Palo Alto. Dude that gave me this weed works there. Synchronicity, man—he'll freak when I tell him about my flash. All I need now is a way to *point* to stuff on the screen . . . maybe that weird rat thing Doug came up with . . . only make it a *one*-eyed rat—"

None of us had the slightest idea what he was talking about. But you don't have to understand joy to share it. We congratulated him, and finished the joint, and resumed walking.

The Wellington Road was a fairy wonderland, a winter carnival. Magic was surely in the air. And soon enough, we came upon some.

Mona and Truman's place came up on the right. Mona and Truman Bent were locals in their mid-forties, products of a century of inbreeding and poverty, and some of the nicest people I knew. (If you are going to giggle about the name Bent, would you please do so now and get it over with? It is an extremely common and highly respected name in Nova Scotia, as are Butt and Rafuse and Whynot.) Their home was a small showpiece of rural industry, ingenuity and courage, inside and out. It sat close to the road, with a little bit of a lawn and a swing-set out front. A driveway led past it to the big tired-looking barn in back. Truman's immense one-ton truck was pulled halfway into the barn so he could work on the engine out of the weather. As with many properties on the North Mountain, the area around the barn was littered with almost a dozen wrecked vehicles and their guts—but the garden beyond the barn and the area around the house itself were neat as a pin. Mona is a fuss-budget, and tough as cast iron.

And a sweetheart. When we were close enough to recognize what was lying in the center of her driveway, right by the road, we stopped in our tracks.

"Oh *wow,* man," Tommy said.

"Is that far out or what?" Snaker agreed.

Nazz shivered with glee. "Rat own, Mona!"

The Bents kept a pair of old tires on either side of the driveway, with flowerboxes set into the hubs. In summer they brightened the driveway considerable. In winter they were usually buried under snow. Mona had evidently had Truman dig one up, remove the empty flowerbox, and leave the tire in the middle of the drive.

"I don't understand," Rachel said.

"They heard our tire blow," I explained. "That one's for us."

"How do you know?"

I shook my head. "I just do. Come on, I'll show you."

Sure enough, there was a note stuffed into the hub:

This ai'nt much but it wil get you to the gas station I guess

"See, there she is in the window," Tommy said. We all waved our thanks to Mona. She gave a single wave back. Snaker pantomimed that we would pick the tire up on our way back from dinner, and she waved again, then closed her curtains.

"Wow," Snaker said. "We gotta do something nice for those people."

"Right field," Nazz agreed. "Let's get the whole family thinking on it."

We trudged on. "Mona and Truman are amazing people," I told Rachel. "They can't have kids, so they foster parent. Constantly. There's always five or six kids around the place. She's strict as hell with them, and they always worship her. She'll take retarded kids, kids that are dying, kids that are crippled, whatever the agency sends. There are a couple of social workers that would die for her."

"And as you can see," Snaker called back over his shoulder, "she's adopted the whole goddamn Sunrise Hill Gang."

"I look forward to meeting her," Rachel said.

"She's a trip," Nazz called. "You'll love her."

"I already do," Rachel said, so softly that only I heard.

It was only another half a klick before the forest on the left side of the road ended and we were come to Sunrise Hill.

We all came to a halt again, because the sun was just setting over the Bay. Rachel took my hand and Snaker's.

After a time we roused ourselves, trudged past an acre of snow-covered garden, and came to Sunrise itself, also called The Big House.

It was a simple wood-frame two story perhaps fifty years old, a much more conventional structure than either the Gingerbread or Tree Houses, and larger than both of them put together. Unlike them it stood right by the roadside, in the middle of five or six more or less cleared acres. The only external signs of hippie esthetic were the small sprouting-greenhouse built onto the house in front and a solar shower in back. Fifty meters back from the house, and about the same distance apart, stood a small cedar-shake toolshed and a smaller outhouse. Between them was an ancient Massey-Ferguson tractor covered by an orange tarp, and next to that an even more ancient one-lung make-and-break engine under a black tarp.

We entered through the usual woodshed airlock, which also contained a wheezing old freezer and huge sacks of grains and beans. Inside, the Big House looked much more like a hippie dwelling. The downstairs was a single enormous room, with a giant front-loader woodstove at either end. The bare wood floor was completely covered with a once brightly colored painting, now faded, involving rainbows, dragons, and an immense myopic eyeball that stared biliously at the ceiling. The parts that Ruby had done looked great. On the left, a J-shaped counter and a small cookstove defined the kitchen. On the immediate right, a stupendous table which had begun life as the west wall of a boatshed defined the dining room and conference area. On its surface was painted a large vivid sunrise. Assorted wretched chairs lined one side of it; on the other was a single homemade bench three meters long. Beyond that an open staircase took two zigs and a zag to reach the upstairs. Past the stair-case was open area. Beanbag chairs, ratty cushions, cable-drum tables, shelves of hippie books, milk crates full of this and that, drying herbs hanging in bundles from the overhead rafters, a bunch of Ruby's canvases arrayed by the east window, a small shrine to the Buddha in the far right corner.

The kitchen window was the only one on the north or Bay side. It let in enough of the glory of sunset to make the enameled sunrise on the table even more vibrant, but it was getting time to fire up the kerosene lamps. Both fires were roaring away, with a lot of birch in the mix, and the whole building was suffused with the overwhelming fragrance of simmering chili.

Ruby turned as we entered, left off pumping water and made a beeline for Snaker, drying her hands on her apron as she came. I liked to watch those two meet. Their joining was like slapping together two chunks of uranium: the energy levels of both went through the ceiling. I envied them.

When they were done hugging and kissing and making small sounds of contentment, Ruby backed away. She looked Rachel up and down, smiled and opened her arms again. Rachel took the cue. "Hi, I'm Ruby," Ruby said over Rachel's shoulder. "Hi, I'm Rachel," Rachel said over hers. They disengaged in stages, first pulling back to hold each other by the upper arms, then backing away further until their hands joined, then separating altogether, a spontaneous and oddly graceful movement.

"Welcome to Sunrise Hill," Ruby added. "That's a beautiful head-band." Rachel thanked her gravely. "Hi, guys," she said to the rest of us. "You're just in time; dinner's nearly ready. Somebody set the table, a dishtowel for everybody, somebody else pump water and get the cider, somebody give a hoot out back for the others. Rachel, you sit, you're a guest. Sam, I could dig some music; would you mind pickin' a little?"

"Not if the Snaker can join me."

"Well," she said, glancing at him, "I had some other uses in mind for his hands. But that's a choice I'll never confront him with. Go ahead, babe. Oh, yeah, *was* it the Beatles?"

Snaker pulled a blank. So did I. And it was up to Rachel to save the situation. "I think we are agreed it is not. The drumming is too good to be either Pete Best or Ringo, and the accents are wrong. But it's an excellent fake."

Ruby nodded, said, "Too bad," and went back to the kitchen area. Snaker and I exchanged a glance and mimed sighs; we had forgotten the excuse we'd originally used to get Snaker over to my place. "Well," I said, unpacking my guitar, "there's the old philosophical question as to why a near-perfect forgery isn't as good as the real thing."

And we jawed about that while Snaker and I got tuned together and warmed up with instrumental blues in E. Ruby scatted along with us. As Tommy came in with her younger brother Malachi and Sally and Lucas, we were just starting that Jonathan Edwards song about laying around the shanty and getting a good buzz on, and everybody joined in on that one. When it was done, the table was set, Ruby was in the final stages of her magic-making, and there was barely time for a verse of Leon Russell's "Soul Food" before supper was on the table. As the lid came off and the smell reached us, Snaker and I stopped in the middle of a bar and put away our axes.

There were four loaves of fresh bread, two whole wheat and two rye, baked Tassajara-style. There were about fifteen litres of cider in one of the ubiquitous white buckets, with a dipper. There was an equal amount of well water in another bucket. There was a bowl big enough to be the hubcap off a 747, overflowing with lettuce-based salad; another full of carrot flake and raisin salad. Four homemade dressings. There were great bulk-purchase slabs of margarine (the Sunrise Gang were strict vegetarians). There were tamari and brewer's yeast and tofu and peanuts and sprouts and tahini and a little bit of soybean curry from the day before. To accommodate all this there were plates and bowls and mugs and silverware (no items matching). And in the center of the table, in a pot large enough to boil a missionary, were about thirty litres of Ruby's Chili.

When we dug in, the table was groaning and we each had a dish-towel of our own. A while later the dishtowels were all saturated with sweat and we were doing the groaning. And grinning.

"Is there a recipe written down for this, hon?" Snaker asked his lady, gulping cider.

"Sure," she said.

"Better destroy it. It's evidence of premeditation." She threw a piece of bread at him.

Between the happy cries of the scorched and the clatter of utensils and the roar of eight conversations going on at once and the growling hiss of the stoves and the thunderous volley of farts that attends any gathering of vegetarians, we made the rafters of the old house ring. Nonetheless most of my sense-memories of the occasion are oral. Ruby made *good* chili, so good I actually didn't miss the meat. I never did get to observe Rachel meeting Malachi, Lucas or Sally; it must have occurred at some point when my eyes were watering and the wax was running out of my ears. (I did notice that while Rachel shoveled in chili as rapidly as the rest of us, she didn't begin screwing up her face in Good Chili Spasm until all of us had been doing so for a while, and didn't begin to sweat until a few minutes after that. By the end of the meal she had it down.)

We drank the cider and water buckets dry, and another bucket and a half of water. We ate everything on the table, save for perhaps five litres of chili, which tomorrow would be folded into chapatis for lunch. And then the conversations all trailed off into heartfelt compliments to Ruby, and there was a moment or two of silent respectful appreciation, a contemplation of contentment and a sharing of that awareness. Shadows danced by kerosene lamplight, the simmering of dishwater on the stove became the loudest sound in the house . . .

Lucas broke the silence, with a diaphragm-deep "AAA-OOOOOOOOOOOOOOOMM—" Malachi and Snaker picked it up at once, an octave higher, Malachi on the tonic, Snaker on the dominant. The rest joined in raggedly in whatever octave was easiest for them, and the sound swelled and rose and steadied as we all sat up straighter and got our breathing behind it.

Have you ever done an Om with a large group of people? Large enough that the drone chant takes on a life of its own, and doesn't ever seem to change as individual chanters drop out to inhale? If you have not, put this book down and go find ten or fifteen people who aren't too hip to learn something, and give it a try. So many things happen on so many levels that I'm not sure I can explain it to you.

On a musical level alone, the experience is edifying. The harmonics are fantastic, and they actually get a little *better* if one or two folks can't carry a tune so good and the note "hunts" a little.

On a physiological level, there is a surprisingly strong tranquilizing effect. The AAAAAOOOOOOOOOOOOOOOOOOOOOOOOOMM-MM syllable is the oldest breath-regulating chant on the planet, basic and irreducible and autohypnotic.

On an emotional level, it's together-bringing and happy-making. It's proverbially impossible to get any three people to agree on what time it is; to get ten or fifteen together on even something as simple as a single pure sound is exhilarating. If you Om with people you don't know, you'll be friends when you're done. If you do it with friends . . .

On a spiritual level—well, if you're alive in the Eighties you probably don't believe there is such a thing, so I won't discuss it. Just try an "Om" sometime before you die. Come to it as cynically as you like.

Sunrise Oms were just a trifle frustrating for me, though, at that point in history. When the group had first spontaneously formed, a few years before, the Oms were the best I've ever been in, before or since. Partly because we had more participants, nearly thirty that summer, but mostly because the Oms were freeform improv, an unrestricted outpouring of the heart. Those who were not musicians—the majority, of course—held onto the tonic or dominant to keep us all centered, and those with musical talent jammed around the basic drone, sometimes adding harmonies to make chords, then spontaneously mutating them in weird shifting ways; sometimes throwing in deliberate and subtle dissonances, then resolving them creatively; sometimes doing raga scales, or Ray Charles gospel riffs, or whatever came out of our heads and hearts and mutual interaction. The results were always interesting and frequently breathtaking.

But of late the Sunrise Gang had, typically, gotten a little too spiritually conservative (read: "tight-assed") and had decided that having people chant all over the place offered too much encourage-ment to Ego (a word which had for them roughly the same emotional connotation that "Commie" held for their parents). Surely Ego was out of place in a spiritual event. So the current Agreement was to limit the Om to the tonic and dominant notes. That was more democratic. More pure. More basic and simple.

Also more boring—and as a guest, I was of course required by politeness to conform, and listen to my own solos only in my head. It itched me a little—and I knew it itched Snaker too, because we'd discussed it. Still, any Om is better than no Om, and I was simply too well-fed to sustain irritation. So I settled into contemplation of the sound we were making—

—and Rachel began to improvise—

—brilliantly, from the very first riff, I hadn't been fully aware until then that she was participating in the Om but Jesus you couldn't miss her warm-honey alto when she started to blow, it was something like the sudden appearance of a darting trout in a pellucid pool, and a shared thought-chain flashed around the table in an instant, *what the—? Oh, it's cool, she's a stranger, doesn't know any better; Jesus, listen to her* do *it,* as she wove a strange liquid melody line around her drone, and after a very slight staggered hesitation the Om steadied and came back in strong behind her.

Well. The ice having been broken by the guest, I wrestled with the part of me that Malachi insisted was my ego . . . and went into the tank. When my current breath ended, I sucked in a joyous deep new one, paused an instant, and took off after her. Her eyes met mine, and we both thought of our lovemaking that afternoon, and wrapped our voices around each other. We did a modal thing, started it simple, cluttered it a bit, brought it home again—measuring each other, feeling each other out, alto and my baritone seeking harmony—

—and I caught Snaker's eye and lifted my brows, and he took a deep breath and jumped in an octave above me, duplicating my line to show that he understood what was happening—

—Ruby hesitated a few seconds and then began to parallel Rachel's line—

—and we all looked to Rachel, and at her signal we banked sharply and cut in the afterburners, riding that magic carpet of drone like the Blue Angels, heading for the clouds in perfect wordless communication—

—and a long happy indescribable time later it was over, the statement was made, it hung in the air and in our minds' ear like a skywritten mandala, hung and spread and drifted and dissipated as the last breath of the last voice—Tommy's—ran out.

We all smiled in silence together for a long time, too happy to speak. It was clear to us that God had been here and gone, but that was okay: He'd be falling by again sometime.

"Wow, that was far out," Malachi said at last, and from the tone of his voice I knew we were in for a session. Well, Rachel had to meet him sometime or other.

"It sure was," Ruby said, ignoring the subtext of his tone with the long practice of an ex-lover. She was smiling dreamily at Snaker.

He was going to be very glad he had been a good boy at my place earlier.

"Right *up,*" Nazz agreed, also oblivious.

Malachi pounced. "It's far out how something can happen spontaneously like that and it's a stone, that one time, because it's like perfect for the moment, you know?" Malachi had the mad burning eyes of a born saint or poet or revolutionary, though he was none of these, deep-set eyes smoldering under shelves of forehead like banked coals at the back of deep caves. He could disappear into the woodwork when he wanted, but when he put on his guru voice, he drew attention effortlessly. "Rachel didn't know our custom about not hamming up the Oms but that's *far out,* because she brought good vibes to the party and that's what counts. Even if we wouldn't want to Om that way all the time."

"I'd like to Om like that all the time," Snaker said with just a little edge.

"I think we have Agreement on that," Malachi said softly.

To my surprise, Lucas spoke up. "Maybe we should examine the Agreement." He was staring at Rachel.

Malachi rolled with it. "Far out, maybe we should."

Lucas was wearing weights strapped to his wrists and ankles, for three reasons. Because it was good physical exercise, because it was good spiritual discipline, and because it hurt. Any of the three would have sufficed. "I could dig some more Oms like that. Once in a while, anyway." He looked away from Rachel suddenly. "I think I'd give my right arm if I could make my voice do that stuff."

"Uh huh. Isn't that kind of why we made the Agreement?" Malachi asked, and one or two people began to nod.

"What exactly do you mean by 'agreement'?" Rachel asked.

Malachi turned those eyes on her. When she didn't flinch, he seemed to smile slightly. "See, we're a spiritual community, so we have to make some basic Agreements to live together, and then stick to them. Like, it's our agreement to be strict vegetarian, and you can rap for days about whether that's far out or misguided—and we have, still do—but meanwhile it's our agreement to do that thing, so we do. And if that's a drag for some of us—" Snaker squirmed. "—well, hopefully the spiritual solidarity from the Agreement is worth the drag. The way you were Oming—please don't think I'm laying blame, it was beautiful and you didn't know—but we used to Om that way here, and we found that it was easy for it to turn into a kind of exclusive thing, almost an elitist trip. Like it divided us up into the talented and the drones, if you dig. It brought us apart instead of together, and we wanted an Om that was more symbolic that we were all doing the same thing here, so we made that Agreement. You see?"

I'd been subconsciously expecting something like this for hours. I'd always found Malachi infuriatingly difficult to argue with—as they say around the Mountain, he's slick as a cup of custard—and I just knew that Rachel was a match for him, that she was going to lay him out, stop his clock with some splendid zen epigram. And she sideswiped me.

"I think that is a wise decision for you," she said. "I will make that Agreement with you all."

Snaker's jaw dropped too. Ruby gave Rachel a Closer Look. Malachi blinked.

Irritated at how often and easily Malachi could make me irritated, I spoke up. "Look, I have no Agreements at all with you guys except the ones that come under being a good neighbor, but I'll tell you this: while that Om was happening I was part of God and totally stoned—"

"Me, too," Snaker said.

"—and that seems like a silly thing for a spiritual community to turn away from."

"That's the trip, Sam," Malachi said with exasperating compassion. "*You* were totally stoned. Not everybody was. We want to *all* be part of God."

I could see myself responding, *but we* were *all stoned,* and then going around the table, *you were stoned, weren't you?* only by that time half of them would be wondering if they *had* in fact been stoned, Malachi had that effect on them, and I had climbed these stairs before. So had Snaker; he shot me a look that said, *thanks for trying, brother.*

"Far out," I conceded reluctantly.

"Clean-up crew," Ruby said loudly and clearly.

People began scraping plates, and stacking them. I caught Rachel's eye and stood up. She took her cue and followed me to the sink. She was supposed to be from the city, so it was okay for me to lecture her on the art of dishwashing without running water. I don't think she'd ever washed a dish under any circumstances, but she was a very quick study. At one point she should have burned her wrist on the hot water kettle, but the skin declined to burn. Malachi was nearby, scraping leftovers into the compost bucket, but he didn't seem to notice. She and I traded off washing and drying while others cleared and washed the table and put away the dried dishes and stoked the fires and adjusted the lamps, and Ruby watched in regal contentment. (One of the commune's more sensible rules is that whoever cooks dinner gets to fuck off the rest of the night.) (Except that Ruby wasn't fucking off; she was, ninety-five percent certainty, thinking about her next painting.)

Though she was concentrating on the dishes, Rachel managed to take in the whole scene. One of her rare smiles lit her face. "This is beautiful," she murmured to me.

I looked around to see what she meant. I got it at once. Many people working in concert, with no wasted words, moving at high speed but never bumping into each other, a marvelous improvised choreography. Calmness in activity, a perfect Zen dance. It was what attracted me to Sunrise Hill, this quality; if the place had been like that all the time, perhaps I'd have moved in. My irritation with Malachi leaked from me, and I began to enjoy myself again almost as much as I had during the Om. And then a strange and terrible thing happened—

❖ELEVEN❖

I WAS WASHING Rachel was drying. I had pointed out to her where a particular bowl belonged, and turned away, then realized I'd misinformed her; I turned back to give a correction. Tommy was at the counter next to Rachel, whacking a stainless steel bowl against the underside of the cupboard to dislodge some sticky food into the compost bucket beneath it. Rachel was looking toward her, away from me. On top of that rickety cupboard were many large mason jars containing grains and beans. Tommy's energetic whanging of the heavy bowl was causing one of the big jars to dance forward on its ledge. I saw it—and saw that Rachel saw it too. I remembered her phenomenal reaction time when the tire had blown, knew she would react faster than I could—which was good because I was off-balance, leaning the wrong way.

And she did. It was over in an instant, but I saw what she did with terrible clarity, as if in slow motion. Her eyes widened slightly as she measured trajectory, realized the falling weight was going to catch Tommy leaning forward and slam her face down against the counter. Rachel's lips tightened as she computed the mass of the load: about three kilos of mung beans and a half-kilo of glass. She clearly understood that the impact could very well be fatal. Her mouth opened and her face began to contort for a shout and her whole body gathered itself to spring—

—and she relaxed. Her features smoothed over and her mouth closed.

She did not know that I could see. I wasted nearly a whole second gaping in disbelief, did not get off my own shout until the jar had actually overbalanced beyond recovery.

"Tommy, *duck!*"

The woman had a lot of quick; she nearly managed it. She did manage to duck her head enough so that the jar struck her a glancing blow at a favorable angle: her forehead *just* missed the counter. The jar did not, and broken glass and mung beans flew from hell to breakfast. Tommy straightened at once. In a loud, clear voice she said, "For my next magical trick—" Then her knees let go and she started to go down.

Rachel caught her under the arms.

It was twice as horrible because I understood it at once. I don't think there was an instant in which I blamed Rachel. In the moment that she did what she did—nothing—I realized exactly why she was doing it. I saw clearly that she hated doing it, and felt she had no choice; most horrible of all, I agreed with her. And all this transpired in the space of a second, yet it wrenched all the events of the last twenty-four hours out of my memory banks, and jammed them back into my head at a slightly different angle.

By traveling through time, Rachel had accepted the terrible risk of altering the past. But as an ethical time traveler, she must have a horror of altering the past *too much*. Reality was stretching to accommodate her existence in my timeline. If she overstressed it, it might tear.

But how much was *too much?* A good rule of thumb might be to avoid major changes . . . such as altering the birth or death dates of any person. If someone would have died without your presence in that ficton, then die she must—

—but Rachel *cared* for Tommy, I knew that despite her poker face. They had made eye-contact, they'd touched, they'd joined hands in the Om, it had been clear that they were friends-in-the-making.

—but she'd done it. Done what she had to do, which was (as far as she knew) to watch her new friend Tommy get her brains broken by a jug of mung beans. I totally understood the moral imperative behind this before I even got my own warning shout halfway up my throat . . . but I felt different about Rachel because she had been capable of it. Not blaming, certainly, I told myself. Just different.

It changes your perception of a house-guest, bed-partner, someone you've begun to think of as a friend, to learn that under no circumstances would they do anything to prevent your scheduled death—even at no cost to themselves. Even if you understand and approve the logic, it changes things.

I did not know just how, though, because the entire incident struck much too close to something I never ever even thought about, some*one* I never ever thought about, and the inner conflict was so painful that I needed the thirty seconds of total confusion which followed Tommy's narrow escape to recover my own equilibrium unnoticed. I wished desperately that I could take Snaker outside or upstairs, alone somewhere, and talk to him, tell him what had happened and ask him how I felt about it. Or Snaker and Ruby would be even better, this tasted like the kind of hurt she was good at mending . . . except that Snaker and I had promised not to tell her Rachel's secret.

I had felt uniquely blessed to be the man on the scene when the time traveler came—now I was realizing that history is made by the unlucky.

Before I was ready for it, Tommy was thanking me. I heard myself answer automatically. "Hell, Tommy, anybody would have done the same." And heard internal echoes: *anybody who* could *would have done the same,* and: *who are you to criticize, pal?*

Those echoes must have shown on my face; I saw Tommy frown. Alarm bells went off; the Sunrise Gang all had incredibly sensitive detectors for guilt, conflict and deception. They all firmly believed that when a hassle or a hangup was observed, the thing to do was haul it out on the table and get it straight before anything else was done. Neither politeness nor tact nor respect for personal privacy was allowed to stand in the way. The only things that made this practice forgivable were the remarkable compassion they displayed in rummaging around inside your psyche, the absolute tolerance they had for any honestly held opinion however startling, and their damnably impressive success rate. A person suffering from internal conflict tended to shrink from them the way a man with a stiff neck will avoid the company of a chiropractor. If he learns of your affliction, he will insist on hurting you—and most annoying, when he is done, you will feel better. You will thank him.

By approaching it as a spiritual conditioning exercise, I had learned to appreciate the custom—and as it made me stronger, I had come to enjoy it.

But I had a secret now. Truth was a contraindicated medicine. I didn't have the right to take it, for it might kill my friends. Everyone's friends.

Which awareness I kept from my face as I set about lying to my friend Tommy. "Whew," I said, shaking my head briefly but violently. "That shook me up. I saw you dead for a second there."

At once she was understanding. "Wow, yeah. Pretty heavy. Your death thing again."

"Yeah. 'Scuse me—I've got to go visit the shitter."

My "death thing" was an old, counterfeit hangup which had long since been taken as far as it would go. If Tommy insisted, I was willing to haul it out again, as a diversion. But she grinned and cut loose. "You've got to get more beans in your diet, Sam. Here, take a lantern."

I avoided Rachel's eyes on the way out. Maybe she avoided mine.

The Sunrise shitter was more than fifty meters down a sloping, well-trodden path from the Big House, both to keep it downhill of the well, and to make it as handy to the fields as to the house. Instead of following the path to it, I veered left as I exited the house and took an equally well-trod path through the snow to The Chapel. The Chapel is nothing but a ledge, where the land drops abruptly away perhaps fifteen or twenty meters. It is a chapel because from there you have an unobstructed view of the Bay in the distance. It is the origin of the name Sunrise Hill, and it is a good place to be at sunrise.

It was a good place to be at night, too. Saint John glowed on the horizon. The Moon was up. The sky was spattered with stars, vast and glorious. What wind there was came from the north, from the Bay into my face: no snow tomorrow.

The assumption Rachel was working under was very close to the hippie-borrowed concept of karma. Karma is subtly different from predestination—it says that you make your own predestination—but it has that same unpleasant taste of inexorability, implacable fate. You will pay for every sin, sooner or later; you will have to earn every lucky break; each new disaster is only what you deserve. Combined with the doctrine of reincarnation, it *becomes* predestination, for the bad choices you make in this life are a result of bad karma earned in an earlier life. It's sort of the spiritual equivalent of There Ain't No Such Thing As A Free Lunch, eternity as a zero-sum game.

But what does it do to your karma to watch a friend die?

That was a question to which I badly wanted an answer myself . . . so badly that I could not remember why . . .

If it had been a movie scenario, and the same choice set up, the screenwriter would have *had* to have Rachel opt to save Tommy, and to hell with the fate of all reality, or else the audience would have hated the picture. The choice she made was artistically unsatisfying. Unpalatable. Did that make it wrong? Her logic was remorseless. There's a classic story called "The Cold Equations" . . .

I was out there for a long time.

When I heard approaching footcrunch I guessed Rachel. But it was Snaker who came to me out there in The Chapel, and silently stood and shared it with me for a few minutes.

"What a night," he said at last.

Whatever he meant, I agreed with it.

"I got Ruby aside and talked with her privately."

"You didn't—"

"Naw. She wouldn't *want* me to have told her about Rachel's secret if I did. If I had. If you follow. But I had to tell her about watching you guys ball."

"Oh. Yeah. Uh . . . how did it go?"

"Amazingly well. I found an extraordinary woman, Sam. Get this: *she didn't interrupt.* She let me tell her how it was, and she didn't say a word until I was done. Then she ran it through intellectually and decided she had no reason to be jealous, looked me in the eye and decided *emotionally* she had no need to be jealous, and cut loose of jealousy: I could see it happen. She asked me what it'd been like, and I told her. Her pupils dilated. Finally, she validated my judgment, that what I'd done, and not done, was within the spirit of our Agreement, and she said she admired Rachel's courage. I think we're going to fuck our brains out later tonight."

"You lucked out, brother."

"Seem-so. But that was just for openers. Once we'd dispensed with the trivial distraction *I'd* brought up, Ruby dropped her own bomb."

I closed my eyes briefly. "Yeah?"

"The test results came back from Halifax. She's pregnant."

"No *shit?* Wow, that's *great!* Congratulations, man, that's the best news I've heard all winter. It couldn't have happened to two nicer people, really."

I was saying all the right things, and I did feel joy for my friend. But I was sort of sorry he had told me *then.* A large part of me was numb. Too much had happened to me in the last while, and I had no room left in my brain. Snaker and Ruby were pregnant; neat. Love was great. For those who could believe in it. Or were capable of it.

"It's a real stoner," he agreed happily. "Anyway, the long and short of it is, I am virtually *certain* we are going to spend tonight fucking our brains out. Which leads gracefully to why I am suddenly in a hurry to put Mona's old tire on the Meanie and get you two back to Heartbreak Hotel. You grok?"

"Oh." I thought about it. "Listen, Snake: a long walk rolling a tire through the snow, changing it, a half-hour round trip on bad roads in the dark with an undependable vehicle, and all the while your woman is cooling off back at home . . . fuggit. We can crash here."

"Uh—" Snaker began, and hesitated.

"Really, man, I'd just as soon let my stoves go out; I've been meaning to shovel out the ashes and—"

"Think it through, man. If you crash here, where do you crash?"

"Ah." Either in the same upstairs with Snaker and Ruby, or on bedrolls on the floor immediately underneath their room. The huge vent in their floor, designed to let warm air come up, would easily pass sound. In either direction. Lucas slept in the Big House, but he didn't count; his room was the only airtight, relatively soundproof one in the structure; he liked it that way because it was colder. The point was that if we stayed, Snaker and Ruby would have no privacy to celebrate their happy news.

"I think Ruby finds the *idea* of someone watching while she's making love stimulating. But I'm sure she's not ready to deal with the actuality just now. Some shit like that went down around the time she and Malachi were breaking up, before I got here. I gather it was pretty intense for her." I could well imagine. Malachi had put her and Sally through a horrid long time when he could not decide which he wanted to live with, and so lived with both to see if that would shed any light on the matter. It eventually did, but with the light came much waste heat, and Ruby was badly burned. Snaker had come to the Mountain just as I was nerving myself up to move her into my place, on an emergency first-aid basis.

"Snake, I'll try to say this just right. I like you and Ruby. I would be honored to be present sometime while you two made love, as observer or . . . whatever. But you don't owe me anything, okay? You two have something special and private to celebrate. Just because I showed you mine doesn't mean you have to show me hers."

"Or my own. I hear you, Sam. Thanks. For myself, I'd be happy to reciprocate if Ruby were willing. Maybe it'll happen some day. Meanwhile, I know I'll be thinking of you and Rachel at several points this evening."

" 'If it's a good lick, use it,' as Buckley used to say."

"Pun intended, of course."

We went back indoors, collected Rachel, said our goodbyes and set off on the journey back home. As the three of us walked along the Wellington Road, he told Rachel his and Ruby's happy news. She congratulated him gravely, breaking out one of her rare smiles for the occasion. I searched her features in vain for any sign of the kind of inner turmoil that was chewing me up. But how much could be accurately read from that stone face by moonlight?

I wondered why I had passed up the opportunity to discuss my own emotional turmoil with Snaker. He had missed Rachel's failure to prevent Tommy's accident, and I couldn't bring it up then, with Rachel walking along beside us. Slowly I realized I was never going to bring it up. Maybe it was like the secret he hadn't told Ruby: he wouldn't have wanted me to have told him, if I had. Still, I thought briefly, I ought to warn him, not to think of Rachel as someone he could depend on to get him out of a bad fix. But I did not.

In retrospect, I think I did not bring my problem to Snaker for the same reason I did not bring it before the whole rest of the Sunrise Hill Gang. Like them, he would have solved it—that is, have seen to the heart of it, forced *me* to solve it. And I was not willing to give it up, would have died to keep it . . .

The tire-change went smoothly. There was some idle chatter on the drive home, praise for Ruby's chili, anecdotes about some of the people Rachel had met and some of the more spectacularly tangled chains of relationships. She asked good questions. She had seen some of Ruby's paintings, and praised them intelligently. When we got to Heartbreak Hotel, Rachel asked Snaker if he would come in for a while. He grinned and gunned the engine. "Darlin'," he said, "it's too complicated to explain, but if I get *right* back home tonight, I'll wake a happy man, and if I'm two minutes late I'll have to cut my throat. It's a pleasure to know you, and I'll see you sometime again." I got out of the cab—

—and she leaned over and kissed him for a full minute, while I stood there as discreetly as I could—

—and she sprang from the cab and slammed the door, and "There goes my margin," Snaker said dizzily and was gone in a shower of slush and gravel. Blue Meanie dwindled in the dark, roaring at both ends, like a flatulent lion.

The Ashley was still going; I packed it full and damped it down for the night. The kitchen fire was dead; I lit the Kemac oil-jet in the back of the firebox, filled the firebox with softwood for a quick blast of heat to warm the bedroom above, and refilled the hot-water well. At my direction, Rachel replenished both stacks of wood from the shed. I came upon her in the living room, looking over the books and records. I wondered if any of the names could mean anything to her. I offered to show her how to use the stereo, and she politely declined. (I suppose if you dropped me back into Edison's home, even politeness and great respect could not make me sit through more than one or two of those damned scratchy cylinders.) I said that I was very tired.

She nodded. "Do you want me to sleep with you?"

I remembered she had once implied that she did not make a habit of sleeping. Or did she mean—?

I did not know what she meant, what she wanted. So I had to fall back on what *I* wanted. What I wanted was for her to decide. "Suit yourself," I said, and gave her a hug.

She pulled back far enough to look at me. "Sam? You have brought me much joy today. I have many new friends, I have learned so much."

"My pleasure."

She kissed me, more thoroughly than she had Snaker since we were not squeezed into a truck seat, and then let me go. I went upstairs and the last thing I remember is walking through the bedroom doorway. My mind must have fallen asleep before my body did.

TWELVE

SYMMETRICALLY ENOUGH, MY body woke up before my mind.

Have you ever awakened to find that you are making love? And have been for some indeterminate time, under the impression that you were dreaming? An indescribable, blessed experience.

My mind's awakening was a slow, sequential process, a series of cumulative steps. I am fucking. I live. No enemies near. I am a mammal. I'm home. This is nice. I'm a male human being. My head hurts. I don't care. This is good fucking I'm getting. Oh, I remember who I am—

—like that. If one must wake up, that is the way to do it. It was a sweet slow lazy time, a healing and a nourishing. I became aware of Rachel's existence almost in the instant I became aware of my own, and the distance that had been between us when I fell asleep was melted before I was awake enough to recall it.

And when I did recall it, she knew it, by the minute hesitation in my rhythm, and murmured in my ear, "Please forgive me, Sam."

I chuckled. "I forgave you in my sleep. My subconscious sentries passed you through sometime in the night, so you must belong here. Forgive me for sitting in judgment on you?"

Okay, it was a silly question. Her answer was nonverbal but quite emphatic. So I asked a few nonverbal questions, and the dialogue became spirited.

At some point in there we began singing together, literally singing in great rhythmic cadences, in weird harmonies that diverged and converged again—like the lovemaking itself, it had been going on for some time before I noticed it. Briefly she quoted a riff she had sung in last night's Om, and mockingly I answered it with the featureless drone Malachi preferred, and she pinched me. And then we let our voices go free as our bodies, and raised up both in song, and it was good, oh good. . . .

Did she really say, in the warm afterflow, "I knew you would understand"? Or did I imagine it?

Over breakfast she raised the subject of our Agreement, and we killed several hours refining it. She planned to spend her days traveling around the Mountain, interviewing people for her imaginary book, storing data and impressions in her headband in some fashion I didn't understand. In the mornings and evenings she was willing to lend a hand with chores. She did not know how to cook but was willing to learn, and would take a crack at anything else. She would follow my customs while under my roof. I would not ask her anything about her ficton or near-future events in my own—more accurately, I could ask, but I agreed in advance not to so much as frown if I got a circumscribed answer or none at all. She stated that within a few weeks she would supply me with ten thousand bona fide Canadian dollars, with which I agreed to try and arrange legal residence in Nova Scotia for her. I did not ask where her money was coming from. She offered to pay cash rent in addition to labour, but I refused it. As I was searching for a tantric way to raise the remaining aspects of our Agreement, she charged right in.

"These are all what you call 'material-plane' matters, Sam. Now we must make our emotional, spiritual and sexual Agreements."

I blinked, then grinned. "I've spent my life yearning for a woman who didn't bullshit around. The reality is a little unnerving. Okay, I'll take a hack at it. Would you know what I meant if I said, 'I love you'? I'm *not* saying it—I'm asking how good a language course you got before you left home."

She looked wary. "Good enough to treat that phrase like an armed bomb. According to my dictionary, it has dozens of mutually exclusive meanings, and guessing the one or ones intended is terribly important."

"That's one reason why I never use the word."

"It can mean, 'I will meet your price for sex,' or 'I am fond of you,' or 'Your happiness is essential to my own,' or 'I claim ownership of you,' or 'I feel that I am or could be your other half.' Are any of these close, Sam?"

I blinked. "Uh—yes to one and two. Emphatic no to three, four and five. I'll have sex with you whenever we both want to. I don't mind if you have sex with others as long as you keep the noise down when I'm trying to sleep. I may have sex with others myself from time to time, although I don't expect it to cause any great traffic problem. I care about you a lot. I don't think *anybody's* happiness is essential to my own. I don't keep slaves. I don't think half of me is missing. I will be your friend. I'll keep your secrets. I'll teach you anything you need to know about this ficton. I'll keep you from harm if I can, and I know and understand and accept that you can't make the same promises. And I'll help you with your work, even if that means leaving you alone with it and dying of curiosity. Your turn."

She didn't answer right away. Maybe she was thinking over everything I'd said. Maybe she was just looking at me. Whichever, it was nice. Usually I can take it or leave it alone. Being looked at, I mean. When Rachel looked at you she left eyetracks on you. "Part of my mission is to study sexual mores and customs at this pivotal juncture in history. I am surprised and pleased by your non-exclusivity clause."

"Careful! I'm unconventional for this ficton. So, at least in theory, are some of the other Hippies—but almost none of the Locals. As a rule of thumb, I'd suggest you use great discretion in offering sex to any man without both long hair and a beard, or any woman wearing a brassiere. Oh, there are a few sexually conservative Hippies—the Sunrise Gang in particular are strong on monogamy these days, and the Ashram crew down in the Valley are into celibacy—but they're all used to people who feel different, they won't be offended if you ask."

"Thank you, Sam. As for the rest of what you say, I echo most of it and agree to all of it. I care about you a great deal too. I will be the best friend I can be to you. I thank you for your generosity to an uninvited guest. Will you want me to sleep with you?"

"Huh? Oh—" I don't know about you, but when I'm talking with someone, half the time I'm not really listening, I'm thinking of what to say next or where I'd rather be or something. I was getting it through my head that you couldn't do that with Rachel. "Pardon me, the question has never come up before. At least not in this sense. Let's see. It certainly isn't reasonable to expect you to waste a third of your day lying still." Suddenly I felt almost guilty that I would be leaving her to her own devices for such long intervals. "Uh . . . times we make love at night, would you stay with me until I'm asleep, try to leave without waking me? And perhaps curl up with me from time to time when you weren't doing anything else anyway?"

"With great pleasure. And the house will be warmer at night if there is someone to keep the fires fed."

I smiled. "I think we have Agreement."

She smiled. "Shall we seal the bargain?"

I frowned. "The chickens are hungry."

She kept smiling, rose from her chair and stood before me. "Then we must hurry."

"Yes, we must."

That night she called me from Sunrise Hill, to say that she would not be home, as she was going to be having sex with Snaker and Ruby. I wished her joy, and banked my fires and went to bed.

And woke, by God, the same way I had the day before. . . .

I am fucking. I live. No enemies near. I am a mammal. I'm home, on my back. This is nice. I'm a male human being. My head hurts. I don't care. This is good fucking I'm getting. Oh, I remember who I am—

Jesus Christ, I'm fucking *Ruby!*

—she's even better than I thought she'd be—

Jesus Christ, Snaker's lying right beside me!

—Rachel rides him, as Ruby rides me—

Jesus Christ, this is dangerous!

—not necessarily—

Jesus Christ—

I was wide awake. At least three friendships and a marriage were at stake, and the point of no return was near, if not here and gone— quick, Sam, run it through!

An even number, that was good. Genders balanced, that was good. All friends, all reasonably sane, stable types, all grownups, all discreet, all clean. Neither female at risk: one protected, one pregnant. I cared about all three people. . . .

In the soft glow of dawn through layers of plastic, my eyes traveled up Ruby's splendid nude body, and she was wearing the smile of the canary who has swallowed the cat. "Good morning, Sam," she said, moving lazily up and down on me. "I've fantasized about this."

"Uh, me too. Good morning. Morning, Snake, Rachel."

"—mornin', brother—"

"—good morning, Sam—"

"And congratulations, Ruby—Snaker told me the happy news the other night."

She smiled even wider. "Thanks, Sam." We stared together at her naked belly, thinking of the life that lurked inside. Spontaneously we began to rock together.

I giggled suddenly. "Now do you see why folks around here don't lock their doors, Rachel?"

Rachel smiled. She reached over and stroked Ruby's shoulder, undid a snarl in her hair. Ruby turned to her and kissed her. They put an arm around each other. We all synchronized rhythm while they held the kiss. I watched them forever, hypnotized and profoundly aroused. *Why* are there so few Lesbians? I'll never understand it.

The obvious corollary probably struck me at the same instant that it did Snaker.

We must have looked comical. I turned my head quickly—to find his face a few inches away from mine. His mouth was open too. Both our mouths were open. Almost touching. Our shoulders *were* touching, our arms. Our hands.

His hand touched my belly, moved to the place where his lady and I were joined. I gasped. I reached blindly, touched his chest. It felt strange, weird, hairy and flat, warm, alive, interesting. My fingers came to a nipple, like a miniature of a woman's nipple. I experimented; he sipped air. A working miniature.

We both glanced up briefly to see Ruby and Rachel caressing as they rode us, and then our eyes met again and we kissed.

I had had two other sexual experiences with males, years before, brief, furtive, unsatisfactory. I had never kissed a man. It was even weirder than I had thought it must be, rough and prickly and *peculiar*. We did not kiss with our tongues—I had morning breath, he was a smoker—but we did not kiss tentatively or fraternally, and when I decided that it did not hurt, was not intrinsically disgusting, did not seem to leave a stain, and actually kind of felt nice, not only did the skies not fall, but I found myself even harder in Ruby's pelvic clutch. Or was she clutching me tighter? Someone's fingers were in my hair. We all seemed to be heading into the home stretch. Ruby and Rachel were humming, harmonizing; suddenly Snaker and I were too, humming into each other's mouths; we were making a drone, then a harmony; with the women we made a chord of transition that rose and fell as we rose and fell, that sought resolution as we did, that rose, rose, swelled until it was no longer song but shout; Snaker and I broke our kiss and pulled our women down to us and roared against their throats as the world blew up—

"Thank you, darling," Ruby said next to my ear awhile later.

"Whuffo?" Snaker asked. (How did he know—how did *I* know—that he was the darling addressed?)

"For holding off on your cigarette. I appreciate."

"Huh! Never thought of it, love."

The two most awkward moments at an orgy are just before undressing and just after the orgasms. "Uh . . . good morning to you guys, too," I said.

Ruby kissed me. "Sam, how come you and I never got around to this before?"

I thought about it. "Silly reasons at first, and for a while. And then Snaker came and you guys got engaged and decided to be monogamous."

She nodded. "We still are. It's just . . . well, Snaker says there is very little difference between you and him."

"Under the circumstances, I will not contest the slander at this time," I said. "Uh . . . how shall I put this? . . . to what do I owe this pleasure?"

Ruby grinned. "What the hell are we doing here, you mean? Good question." She reached across me and poked her husband in the ribs. "How *did* this happen, honey?"

On the far side of him, Rachel raised up on one elbow. Snaker is right: you can't compare tits. "It was the effortless unfolding of the universe," she murmured.

"It was like hell effortless," Snaker said, breathing like a smoker. "But they're right, Sam: it wasn't so much planned as discovered.

Ruby and I got to talking about me watching you and Rachel ball, and talking about it got us horny, and then we got to talking about that with Rachel, and we learned that Rachel enjoyed watching too, and then we learned that Ruby thought she'd like being watched, and shortly after that we learned Ruby liked *watching* too, and so when the three of us had been researching the whole phenomenon long enough that I couldn't seem to get another hard-on, Ruby pointed out that you had constituted an entire third of the original Broadway cast and might have interesting data to share—"

"You're telling me that you three screwed all night long and then, in the cold rosy dawn, came over here to get laid?"

"That's about the size of it," Snaker agreed.

"Perhaps there is a God. Uh, can I cook you folks breakfast?"

Ruby chuckled, a purring sound. "Rachel and I brought plenty to eat. And I don't know about her, but mine's getting cold while you guys are talking."

I began to roll up onto one elbow, with a view toward walking a few fingers down her belly toward the area under discussion—but she pushed me back down flat on the bed, flung a leg over me and quickly sat astride my chest. I got the palms of my hands on her buttocks and coaxed her forward. "Magnificent," I said with great sincerity as the sweet knurled pinkness came into view.

Ruby had terrific lips, and this pair were the best. If the genetic cards had been cut the other way and she'd been born male, she'd have been hung like a horse. If—as I did then—you were to reach around her thighs and take each of those lips between thumb and forefinger and tug them gently up and out, opening the orchid, you would understand—as I did then—what that symbol truly is which we call a heart, although a heart looks nothing like that; understand what it is we admire in the butterfly. Like butterfly wings I tugged them down toward me, pursed my own mouth and blew a stream of cool air up and down the channel they formed, heard Ruby's hiss of pleasure. I heard Rachel murmur something too soft to hear, and Snaker agree. The bouquet was rare, the sauce piquant, the meaty petals delicious, separately and together: I feasted. Ruby's fingers explored my hair, met behind my head and guided me. . . .

When I felt a mouth on me, on my belly and then on my penis, I wondered vaguely whose it was. But my vision was blocked in that direction, and it didn't seem important. There were *two* mouths on me, kissing each other around me, for several minutes before I noticed. Ruby's clitoris, proportioned to match those labia, was like a miniature penis under my tongue. I experimented; she gulped air. A working miniature. Her thighs clamped my ears, I tasted a trace of my own semen, a gentle finger opened me and I was neither male nor female nor gay nor straight nor even bi but only human—

Breakfast for four is four times easier than breakfast for one. Four pairs of hands—One of the few things I've ever really envied the Sunrise Gang, one of the few good points of communal living to my way of thinking, is the division of labor, and the ability to renegotiate that division. If you'll go chop us some water, and he'll take care of the chores and critters, and she'll get the house warm, I will happily rustle up the eggs and flapjacks and crack open the last jar of peach preserves, and breakfast will be a thing of joy instead of the first false step in an infinite cycle of frustrations alternating with disappoint-ments. Perhaps tomorrow I'll be the one who least minds suiting up and going outside to get the water, and you'll be in the mood to turn out some johnny-cake or porridge while others feed the stoves and chickens.

In the country, it is so much easier to live with almost anybody than it is to live alone, that a person who does live alone must be very fussy, or very timid, or very undesirable, or just plain stupid. I won-dered, that morning, which applied to me. Had I not lived alone too long?

Wood heat, for instance, is remorseless and implacable, worse than bondage to cocaine or tobacco or even one's own belly and bowels. Every forty-five minutes you must throw a stick of wood on one fire or the other. Think about it. Every forty-five minutes. You must. You can stretch it to an hour, to an hour and a half or more, but you will do so as seldom as possible, because when you do, you catch cold, and sniffle a lot.

So the presence of even one housemate means that you can with some confidence undertake an activity, or a thought train, of as long as an hour's duration, *without* having to literally pay through the nose. Luxury! *Three* companions is wealth.

Never mind three talented sex partners—

❖   ❖   ❖

"Why don't you two move in here?" I asked as we sat down to breakfast.

Snaker opened and closed his mouth, Ruby did the same, he looked at her to see why she wasn't answering, she did the same, he made an "after you" gesture just as she did the same, and the three of us broke into giggles. Rachel watched all this with grave interest.

"Because we're committed to Sunrise," Ruby said finally. Snaker said nothing.

"Yeah, but you'd have more *fun* here."

"There's more to life than having fun."

"Is there? What?"

"See what I mean, Sam? You're never serious."

"I've never been more serious. If there is a higher purpose in life than enjoying myself, it has yet to be demonstrated to me."

"Sam, please. We've had this rap. You want to live alone, fine. Snaker and I want to learn how to live with others, without ego or competition or hierarchy. We're trying to find out if people *have* to always be strangers, or if it's just easier. We're trying to get telepathic, to find out if brotherhood is more than just a word. It's important to us."

"And how are you doing?"

"Huh?"

"I say that what happened upstairs awhile ago was the most telepathic, sharing, ego-transcending thing that ever happened to me. How about you? Has anything that telepathic happened at Sunrise lately?"

That generated enough silence for me to get half my breakfast down.

"That last Om," Snaker said finally.

"And look how it turned out," I said, and ate the other half of my breakfast.

"Sam," Ruby said after a while, "why don't *you* move in with *us?*"

The notion startled me; I laughed in self-defense. "I'd sooner have an orchidectomy. Groups aren't my thing."

Snaker spoke up. "I wish you would, Sam. The community could use you. *I* could use you. It'd be nice not being the House Materialist for a change, you know? It'd be comforting to have one other person around who believed in rationality and logic and arithmetic and capitalism and that shit."

I had a sudden flash of insight. "No, it wouldn't."

"Why not?"

"Don't you see, Snake? They tolerate you *because* you're the House Materialist, the sole voice of and for reason. If there were two of you, they'd have to throw you out." I had another flash. "Sooner or later they will anyway."

"You're wrong!" Ruby said.

"Maybe so," I said obligingly. Why make Ruby feel bad when it cost nothing to lie?

But Snaker said nothing. So did Rachel.

As I was thinking about getting up and leaving the shitter, to try again another time, Snaker came in and took the adjacent hole. I grunted a greeting, and he mumbled a reply. Snaker and I had shared an outhouse before, shared a chamber pot—hell, we'd shat in the woods together and wiped our asses with leaves. This time we were uncomfortable. For a while the only sound was Styrofoam creaking under our butts as we shifted our weight.

"Good time, wasn't it?" he asked at last.

"It sure was. It sure was. Uh . . . I'd just as soon not repeat it real soon, if you know what I mean."

Relief was evident in his voice. "I know what you mean. As a regular thing, it'd . . ." He trailed off.

"Yeah." I wondered what he meant, what I meant. "That's one reason why I'll never move into Sunrise with you guys."

He looked surprised. "You mean, you think if we were around each other all the time . . . hell, Sam, that's just backwards. What happened last night would never have happened at all at Sunrise. The community is monogamous, you know that."

"Now that Malachi's satisfied with his partner, yeah. But you don't understand what I mean. I'm not talking about sex, I'm talking about intimacy."

"How do you mean?" he asked.

"Look, you and I had our conversation about bisexuality a year and more ago."

"Yeah. We both felt that if their heads weren't all full of mahooha, everybody'd be bisexual—which is why aggressive cultures make it their business to fill everybody's heads with mahooha."

"And you told me about your couple of experiences—"

"—and you told me about yours, and we agreed that intellectually it all made sense, but emotionally, having been raised in this culture, the best it'd ever been for either of us was Not Totally Awful. That we were both . . . how did you put it?"

" 'Bisexual in theory, monosexual in practice.' "

Snaker suddenly grinned. "Jesus Christ, I was hinting like crazy, wasn't I?" He glanced down and to the right, then back up. *"Flirting* is the fucking word for it, I was flirting." Down and to the right, back up, still grinning. "Wasn't I? And you, bless your heart, you played dumb."

"Yeah, man, I was scared. I hadn't had a friend as good as you in a long while. I didn't want to fuck it up. Besides, by then it was shaping up to be you-and-Ruby, and I didn't want to complicate her life either. Or mine, for that matter—but Ruby'd definitely had all the heartache she needed just then."

"Huh! You know, maybe that's why I was flirting with you. I was sensing how heavy it was going to get with Rube—and the part of me that liked being a swinging bachelor started looking around for an escape hatch. What do you know about that?" He had the wild frown of a man for whom many things have suddenly fallen into place.

"Right there," I said, "is why I'll never join your group."

"Huh?"

"It took you a year to be ready to have that insight. But you wouldn't have been allowed to *take* that long if the Gang had known about it. The Sunrise Gang believe in flushing every hang-up a person has out of its hiding place and stomping it to death, right now, right away, no excuses or delays, and that is *not only* intolerable, but wrong." He looked like he wanted to argue, but he said nothing. "Everybody there insists on messing in your thing, getting into your private hang-ups, knowing all your secrets—" A few things fell into place in my own head. "You remember back when Rachel first arrived, before she woke up? How scared I was of her at first?"

"That business with the shotgun signals and all? Yeah, I guess I thought you were being a little paranoid—"

"And you an sf reader. What I was afraid of—so afraid I damned near cut her throat instead of calling you—was that Rachel might be a telepath. *That's* why I wouldn't join Sunrise Hill in a hundred years.

You people are deliberately trying to become telepathic: you say so out loud. To the extent that you succeed you are terrifying and dangerous to me. To the extent that you try you seem insane. Snake, *human beings aren't supposed to be telepathic.* There are reasons why our minds are sealed in bone boxes. Look at Malachi. He *is* telepathic, a little bit—and what does he do with it? Snoops and probes and pries and chivvies and powertrips people, finds your weak-spots and lets you know he knows them, finds your blind-spots and stores the knowledge . . . Ask anybody, who's the leader of Sunrise Hill? Oh, we don't have a leader. But when was the last time the big bald son of a bitch lost an argument he really wanted to win? And *he* isn't even really telepathic—that's just hippie jargon for what he is, which is observant and empathic and clever and insightful and glib. The only reason he's tolerable is that there is no evil in him. And he can be fooled by someone as clever as himself.

"But a *real* telepath? Someone who knew your innermost thoughts and feelings and dreams and secrets? If I thought there was one near me, I'd try my best to kill him—and maybe the worst part is that I'd never succeed."

Snaker was frowning. He was busy. "Kill him why?" he grunted between waves.

"Two reasons, either one sufficient. First, plain old intelligent paranoia. A telepath *owns* you. You live at his sufferance. If he chooses to kill you, you can't stop him: he will *always* be one move ahead of you. Unforgivable. Intolerable. Even if his intentions are utterly benign . . . they could change. Get outside his effective range *fast,* whatever it is, and lob grenades at him. It's your only sensible option. Nobody should be able to see through the bone box. It's too much power for any human to have.

"And the second reason has to do with, like, intimacy, dignity, privacy, the right to be free from unreasonable search and seizure inside your own head. A telepath would be the ultimate Peeping Tom. The ultravoyeur. The eavesdropper and the diary-reader and the unethical hypnotherapist rolled into one and cubed. Invasion of privacy on that big a scale calls for the death penalty; I think so, anyway. I don't know about you, but I have secrets in *my* head that *I'd* kill to protect. Even from you, old buddy. Not even things that could be used against me, necessarily. Just private. Personal."

Snaker was looking thoughtful.

"It keeps coming back to what I was talking about before. Intimacy. When I moved up here from the States I hadn't been intimate with anyone or anything in . . . anyway a long time. Typical uptight city kid.

"Then I come up here. Wham! One by one my walls started tumbling, boundaries crumbling. People up here share a chamber pot and don't think anything of it. Men don't turn their backs to the road when they feel like taking a piss, ladies squat with you standing right there. A new kind of intimacy. Nobody locks their doors, or cars, or bedroom doors: another kind of nakedness. People swim and bathe literally naked together, for that matter, and work too, sometimes, I've seen the Sunrise women topless in the garden on a hot day just like the men. The hippies and the locals each have their own jungledrum networks, so interwoven they might as well be left and right hemispheres of the same brain, so efficient that as we sit here there are people down on the South Mountain, back up in the piney woods, who are already working out what they're going to say to the Chinee Book Writer Lady when she gets around to interviewing *them*. To live here in the Annapolis Valley is to be naked to everyone else in it.

"So I have—dubiously, reluctantly, suspiciously—taken off several layers of armor that I carried around with me for years. And on the whole it has been good for me. It's pretty safe around here without armor.

"But enough is enough. I have reached my limit. What happened between us last night is the most intimate I ever want to get with anyone, and I don't want to do *that* very often."

I reached up and touched Snaker's face, touched his left cheek above the beardline with three fingers of my right hand. He backed away. "You see? You flinch. So do I. Whether it's instinct or learned behavior, what's the difference? Even friends or lovers need at least a little bit of distance. There's a use for layers of formality, restraint, inhibition, that *prevent* telepathic exchange, that bottle up the moment-by-moment unpleasantnesses and uglinesses of consciousness and give us time to edit ourselves into tolerability." I stood up and adjusted my clothing, ladled a couple of scoops of stove ashes and lime into the hole, and handed the ladle to Snaker.

"I need you for a friend, Sam," he said, finishing his own ablutions.

"And I need you for a friend. If we lived together maybe we'd become more than that, and I don't know that I need that. If *you* do, you have Ruby for it. Everything doesn't always progress naturally toward blissful unity. Snake. Your problem is, you want to marry *everybody*. If you could get all your best friends and loved ones and soul mates in one room, and give us some new drug that made us all be telepathic together . . . we'd probably go for each others' throats."

Snaker was frowning and nodding, zipping up his overalls. "If my thought-dreams could be seen . . . Yeah, I read that Poul Anderson story, too, man. '. . . *Get out! I hate your bloody guts!*' said the only two telepaths in the world to each other. Is it really that disgusting inside a human head?"

"Isn't it?"

He hung the ladle, put the wooden lid down over number two hole and straightened up. I popped the hook-and-eye, the door flew open, and we stepped out into the cold wind. By tacit mutual agreement we walked past the house and halfway down the driveway to where we had a good view of the Bay and the sky. We shared it in silence for a few minutes. He had some ready-mades, Players, and smoked one. Being around smokers bothers me. It seems to comfort them so, the times it isn't just a reflex. I resent a crutch that I can't use, to the extent that it works. It's only fair that it should kill them.

"Yeah, I guess it is," he said softly at last.

He fieldstripped the butt and pocketed the filter. I watched the sun dance on the water.

"There's a hole in your logic, Sam. I can smell it." He sighed. "But I can't find it."

"You're a romantic, man. You want life to be perfectible. It ain't."

"What's the harm in trying? You know that old chestnut about the two frogs that fell into the bucket of cream."

"The Persistent Frog survived only because it was cream in that bucket. A bucket of shit, for instance, gets *softer* when you churn it. And the smell becomes more offensive. The thing about blind optimism, man, it's *blind.*"

"Your pessimism is just as blind, brother."

"Granted. But I know which way to bet. It'd be nice if the human race could *all* get telepathic and all love one another one day—but it ain't gonna happen. If, God forbid, some dedicated researcher does stumble across true telepathy, the race will be extinct in a generation. The handful who survive the Total War won't dare get close enough to anyone else to reproduce."

"Jesus!" He took out another ready-made. Eight matches later it was lit. "That's a hell of a story idea, you know. Creepy, but interesting."

"It's yours. If you sell it, buy me a flat of beer."

He looked thoughtful—then frowned. "No. It'd be a good story: I mean, it'd sell. But it's not the kind of story I want to write. Listen, Ruby and I have to get back—there's a meeting today, to start planning the garden."

I grinned. "Not a moment too soon."

Does it seem odd that the Sunrise Gang were planning their garden in late March, when nothing goes in the ground in Nova Scotia before the first of June? Then I haven't conveyed the Spirit of Sunrise: hot air. The Gang were perfectly capable of spending several weeks debating Whether It Was Far Out To Wear *Imitation* Leather Since That *Too* Bought Into The Karma Of Slaughtering Animals. Something as genuinely involving as The Next Year's Food—not to mention Three Months Of Backbreaking Labor—could easily take them over two months of constant discussion to thrash out. If D-Day had been as overplanned as a Sunrise Hill garden . . . it would probably have turned out just as chaotically, I suppose.

One thing I must admit: they seemed to have learned the secret of arguing without fighting, or wrangling without getting angry. In cabin-fever season, that is one *hell* of an impressive achievement, when you think about it.

"Yeah, we're thinking about adding a third acre. Soybeans."

"You're crazy. Soybeans won't grow here."

"Well . . . Nazz and Lucas have a theory. And we won't really be self-sufficient until we grow our own soybeans."

"It's your back, pal. Good luck. Listen, you mind if Rachel and I bum a ride a ways? I want to introduce her to Mona and Truman. She's been bugging me about it since Mona laid that tire on you the other day."

"Sure. She can sit . . . huh! I started to say, Rachel could be the one who gets to sit in the back, since she doesn't mind cold. But we'd never explain that to Ruby."

"We'll both ride in back, let you two lovebirds have the cab to yourselves."

"Begin redrawing the lines, Sam? Start puttin' the fences back up?"

"Isn't it time?"

Sigh. "Yeah. Yeah, it is."

He started to head back indoors. I stopped him, turned him, hesitated a split second and hugged him, hesitated an intact second and kissed him. He hugged me back and kissed me back without any hesitation.

It really is hard to manage two beards. Do you suppose that's why they invented shaving?

"It was fun," Snaker said finally, breaking the hug. "Ten years from now we'll do it again."

"Talk about extended foreplay. It's a deal. Uh . . . for what it's worth, you give good head."

"Yeah," he agreed. "Yeah, I do. I always thought I would, if it was somebody I cared about. So do you." He grinned. "But Ruby's better."

"You're a lucky man, Snaker."

"I know. I know."

❖**THIRTEEN**❖

LET ME TELL you about the last time I mistook Rachel for a city person.

Living in Nova Scotia had encouraged me to divide the human race into city people and country people, and since Rachel came from the future, and it was axiomatic to me that future meant huge population, higher and higher tech, progressive hyperurbanization, I thought of her as a city person. I assumed, for instance, her ignorance of wood-stoves and outhouses and gardening, woodcraft and carpentry and such things. In my own time, they seemed already nearly obsolete.

I *think* I was often right. But not always. It turned out, for instance, that she knew more about gardening than I'll ever know.

But the day I took her to meet the Bents, I finally shook the City Mouse stereotype out of my subconscious.

On the way over, huddled under a blanket in Blue Meanie's truckbed with her, I tried to brief her about Mona and Truman Bent. I've learned to see, a little bit, since I got here, and I can now see that Mona is very beautiful. But when I first arrived, a city person, my notion of beauty was not mature enough to stretch to encompass Mona's missing teeth, or her fireplug figure. Similarly, it took me some time to realize that her strident voice could seem mellifluous to some ears. It took me longest of all to understand why the herd of ragamuffin kids she tyrannized so ruthlessly loved her so unreservedly. To be sure, she handed out hugs and kisses and treats liberally to those who earned them, and her weirdly beautiful smiles were not too expensive for a child to earn. But she also enforced a stern and unyielding discipline by lashing them with her harsh voice, once in a while by cracking them across the mouth with a horny hand—and once I saw her kick a little mongoloid boy square in the ass.

It was that particular episode that triggered understanding at last, brought me to realize that orphaned inbred diseased retarded rejected foster children who had been shuffled around for months and years by bad luck and bureaucracy before landing at the Bents' might require a special kind of loving, and that unsophisticated uneducated Mona might just know more about it than I did. Seeing her kick that kid had reminded me of something.

When I was a teenager I did a couple of weekends of volunteer work. They sent three of us to an orphanage in Far Rockaway; we were supposed to take groups of orphans on outings, to see the Hayden Planetarium and the Statue of Liberty and so forth. Boys, aged seven to twelve, from the mean streets—the toughest little sons of bitches I've ever met in my life. Orphaned by murder or overdose or suicide or the electric chair or Castro's revolution, they were the kind of inner-city gutter rats you patted down for shanks before leaving the grounds. We were dumbass future-liberals from Long Island. The first day, a nine-year-old with his leg in a cast to the hip, a kid with the kind of sweet, almost effeminate features that make grand-mothers swoon, asked my friend Petey for a cigarette. Petey told him he was too young to smoke. The adorable little kid hauled off and broke Petey's shin with his cast. The other kids fell down laughing.

While the staff liaison was taking Petey off to the Infirmary, my only remaining partner Mike approached the kid with the cast. The boy put a hand into his pocket and left it there. Mike smiled at him, held up his hands in a conciliatory gesture, and with no windup at all kicked the kid in the balls so hard his cast banged back down on the floor. Mike took the kid's knife, turned to me and smiled and said, "The first step in training a mule is to get the mule's attention," and we had an uneventful visit to the Empire State Building that day. . . .

So when, years later, I saw Mona kick slack-jawed, almond-eyed Joey because he had deliberately hurt a smaller child, I swallowed my liberal instincts and watched to see how Joey took it. Like that sweet-faced thug with the cast, he acted not with anger or fear, but with something like respect, something oddly like satisfaction, relief, as though the essential order and correctness of the universe had been reaffirmed.

I tried to tell Rachel all of this and more, on her way to meet Mona and Truman for the first time, to prepare her, because I was thinking of Rachel as a city person and city people sometimes disapproved of Mona on first meeting. (It was usually three or four visits before people got enough sense of Truman to know whether they liked him or not.)

Rachel cut me off. "Sam, I must not allow your opinions to color my observations. I know you mean well, but please, let me form my own impressions." Exasperated, I agreed, and spent the rest of the trip worrying.

And of course, within ten seconds of the introduction, Mona and Rachel had established a rapport deeper and wider than I had managed in three years.

It wasn't anything they said. If I quoted you their dialogue it would bore you to tears. What happened was simply this: that in the moment their eyes met for the first time they knew each other. Recognition signals were exchanged, mutual respect was acknowledged, in some way I could dimly perceive but not even dimly understand. They forgot to pretend I was there.

I went out back and tried talking with Truman, which of course didn't work. Truman was a very pleasant man. He looked like Raymond Massey with three teeth missing. He never had any more or less than two days' growth of beard, and the beard was white even though his hair was brown. Truman didn't talk much. He hadn't learned how until he was fifteen. Mona had just plain bullied him into it. He never would learn to read, he simply wasn't equipped, but she wouldn't stop trying to teach him until one of them died. He was probably the *nicest,* most loving man I knew. Certainly the strongest: I once saw him carry a rock the size of a beer-fridge ten meters, his boots sinking ankle-deep in unturned soil. Like the kids, he worshipped Mona.

I found him splitting firewood. I got his spare axe and joined him, spent twenty minutes in "conversation" with him across the chopping block. As always I wondered if he appreciated the courtesy or dreaded the ordeal. Most of his vocabulary was "Guess so," and "I don't s'pose, naw."

If you are City-Folk, you may have the idea that Truman was stupid.

Once I came upon him in the midst of a disassembled combine. It is so complicated a machine I despair of describing it; its very complexity stuns the eye. He was *wearing* it, slick with grease and sweat. It looked as though some hideous insect lifeform had him half swallowed. "Figure you can get that thing back together again, Truman?" I asked.

He blinked at me and thought about it. "A man made it," he said, and went back to work. And had it running before nightfall.

You may suffer from the delusion that you know what intelligence is. I don't. Illiterate Truman owned his own home, owned (and maintained) the one-ton truck with which he earned enough to feed and clothe and warm a whole brood of raggedy kids, owned a great deal of land and other shrewd investments. I had a liberal arts education, sophisticated musical skills and a glib tongue—and I owned a guitar and some books and records. Talking with him always made *me* feel like a moron.

In the background I could hear Mona and Rachel talking a mile a minute, two kindred souls.

I left after half an hour and they never noticed. Rachel was standing behind Mona, kneading her shoulders; they were deep in conversation, thick as thieves. I wandered up the road to Sunrise and ate soyburger and got into the argument about their garden, a waste of time if there ever was one.

In the end, my stock with Mona went up because I was the one who had introduced her to Rachel.

"Sam," Rachel said to me after we got home that night, "you are exasperated about something. What is it?"

I'd been thinking about that very thing. "I think I'm jealous."

She looked surprised. For her. "Really?"

"Yeah. Of you and Mona. You and Sunrise Hill, for that matter."

Now she looked surprised even for a human being. "I don't understand, Sam."

"I'm not sure I do either. I'm working this out as I speak." We were in the living room, sharing the warmth of the fire before I went upstairs to sleep. It really was turning out to be nice, having someone to keep the fire going all night long, sometimes, waking up to a warm house. Well, a less cold one. "It's just that . . . that . . . dammit, I'm a science fiction reader, all my *life* I've been training to meet a time-traveler, here you are, I meet you . . . and people who've never read *anything* seem to know you better than I do, in ways that I can see, but will never understand. It just isn't right. If anyone on this goddam *Mountain* ought to know you, ought to have rapport with you, it's me. Snaker's the only other sf fan for a hundred miles, except maybe Nazz. And there is something between you and Mona for Chrissake Bent that is deeper and stronger than anything I've managed to build with her in three years' acquaintance. Sometimes I think you have more in common with the superstitious anti-tech clowns at Sunrise Hill than you do with me. You spend as much time over there as you do here, and whenever they start running down science and reason and I argue with them, like tonight when you came in on the Garden Meeting, *goddammit, you won't fucking back me up!*" I was pacing around the living room now, gesturing with the cast-iron poker. "I thought we'd have something special in common and we don't really seem to; you and Mona shouldn't have *anything* in common, but you do anyway. And I don't even understand what it is. Why did you hit it off so quickly with her?"

Sprawled gracefully in my recliner chair, Rachel watched me pace and gesticulate with grave interest. "What I love in Mona is her need to love."

"What do you mean?"

"We talked about you a lot, Sam. She thinks you badly need someone to love. Do you think she is right?"

The question came from left field; I answered automatically and honestly. "I have never been in love. I have successfully faked it eight times since I was sixteen years old—half those times in order to secure a steady sex partner, and the other half because I felt a need to convince myself that I was capable of loving. I gave up doing it for either reason. Not soon enough. Not when I realized how much pain I was causing to innocent ladies; considerably after that. Considerably. To my certain knowledge, I have not loved anyone since my mother. I have been sexually fixated for brief periods. I've been jealous of a mate, like, stingy with a possession. But I've never felt that thunderbolt they talk of, that dizzy compulsion to be with someone else constantly and make them happy and tear down all the walls between us. There has never been anyone in my life that I would die for.

"If love is what Robert Heinlein said, the condition in which the welfare and happiness of another are essential to your own, then I have never loved. The welfare and happiness of another have often been relevant to my own . . . but never really essential. I'm still undecided whether I'm a monster, or everyone else is kidding themselves."

(Jesus, the last time I had spoken thoughts like this aloud to anyone had been . . . Finals Week, to Frank. Which reminded me of something, but I couldn't pin it down.)

I opened up the Ashley and made elaborate unnecessary adjustments to the logs inside, banging and clanking and swearing under my breath as much as possible. Rachel watched in silence until I had closed it up and reset the damper. The only place I had ever seen faces *that* expressionless, not even a wrinkle to show that an expression had ever been there, was in a—

"Sam? When was the last time you pretended to be in love?"

I waited, honestly curious to know whether or not I would tell her; heard my voice decide: "No. That I won't talk about."

"That bad?"

"Look." My face was warm. "Look. You have things you won't talk about, right? Questions *I* have that aren't just idle curiosity or being polite, questions that really matter to me that you won't answer, right? Well, this is one of those for me."

"I'm not being polite, Sam—"

"—damn right you're not—"

"—or idly curious. Are the cases parallel? Do you say that reality itself might crumble if you answered my question?"

"No. I mean I don't want to talk about it, and I won't."

Very softly she said, "You'll have to talk about Barbara *some* day to *someone*—"

"How do you know her name?" I roared, the hair standing up on the back of my neck.

"Because what your conscious mind refuses to touch, your unconscious cannot leave alone. You cry out her name at night sometimes. Sometimes you talk to her."

I did like hell talk in my sleep! And if I did, it wouldn't be to Barbara. I started to say so—

—and paused. How did I know? How long had it been since anyone but Rachel had stayed the night? Could she possibly be right?

But Barbara was dead. Asleep or awake, I didn't believe in ghosts, and calling out someone's name in my sleep was just too corny. I could not believe it of myself.

But how else would Rachel have known her name?

I thought of a way, and it wasn't just the back of my neck now, my whole scalp was crawling. Either I wasn't nearly as tightly wrapped as I thought—

—or Rachel was a telepath after all. . . .

"What did I say to her in my sleep?"

"I can't say. You mumble. Uh, you apologize to her a lot."

"What for?"

"I don't know."

I searched and searched that unreadable face of hers. How much did I trust Rachel, after all? I had never caught her in a lie.

It came to me that if she *were* a telepath, I never would . . .

—which suggested the thought that if she *were* a telepath, I was thinking thoughts that could get me killed. . . .

—which suggested that since I was still breathing, she was not a telepath . . .

—or she was a very clever one.

My head began to hurt. I looked away from her almond eyes and opened the Ashley's damper a quarter turn to inspire the fire. "Let's change the subject."

"All right. Why did you come to Nova Scotia?"

The damper spun in three complete circles, sending smoke puffing out from under the lid of the stove, and the heavy iron poker dropped to the floor with a crash. I used the time it took me to pick it up to think hard.

Suppose that Rachel *was* a telepath. Surely, then, she knew that the moment I became convinced of that, there would be a death struggle between us. Was she now trying to provoke it?

Suppose she was *not* a telepath. How, then, in the *hell* did she know that "Who is Barbara?" and "Why did you come to Nova Scotia?" were the same question? I refused to believe that I could have talked enough in my sleep for that.

Or could it be total coincidence, one of those improbable synchronistic ironies that happen to everyone at times? At various times I had heard her ask the same question of Ruby, Tommy, Nazz,

Malachi and others. It was a logical question for a cultural anthropologist to ask an immigrant; only a matter of time until she'd gotten around to me.

It was just the timing that was so hard to swallow. It could easily be read as a refusal to change the subject. Malachi did that sometimes; he would "drop a subject" by approaching it from another direction. It was just the sort of thing Malachi would be doing now if he had a hint that I had a hangup called Barbara, if he ever suspected that my avowed reason for being here was a lie.

So there were only two ways to go. Make a break for the shotgun that hung over the back door, two rooms distant—and if I were right, die on the way. Or assume that Rachel was *not* privy to my secret thoughts, that her question was innocent, and give my avowed reason for being here.

It wasn't much of a choice.

"It wasn't much of a choice. I could go to a hot place where everyone shot at me, or a federal prison, or a cold place where everyone was friendly and decent. The day my draft board classified me 1-A, I crossed the border." I sat sideways on the couch facing her, head cradled on my forearm.

"You did not support the Viet Nam war."

"I never addressed the question. If people wanted to do that, they were welcome to. I just figured that if there was no person I loved enough to die for, then I certainly wasn't going to risk it for an abstraction. My father being a military man of rank, it became necessary to go somewhere far away. Here I am."

"You are a pacifist?"

"No, no, no. I am a *coward.* Cowards can't be pacifists. Pacifism involves a moral commitment, a willingness to die rather than use force. I'm not certain any such people exist. I am certain I'm not one of them."

"You could kill in self-defense?"

"And for no other reason I can think of."

"Would you kill for Snaker?"

I hesitated. "Maybe. If it was the only way to save his life, yeah, maybe. Ruby too, I guess. Hard to imagine."

"Would you die for them?"

"No, I'd like to think I would, but I wouldn't. Friends are nice, but

I can live without them. I can't live without me." I changed position, lay with my feet toward Rachel, looking up at the ceiling beams.

"Do you think Snaker would die for you?"

That one took me by surprise. I had to think a minute. "Yeah," I said finally. "As his lights went out he'd be regretting it, calling himself a jerk—but if he didn't have too much time to think about it, he probably would. There's a lot of people and things he'd probably die for. Snaker can love, or can kid himself that he does, which comes down to the same thing."

"Do you wish that you could?"

"Look what it gets him and Ruby. He loves her, and she loves him and the commune. One day soon she's going to have to choose between them—and he's scared to death."

"But you envy him."

"Sometimes. I used to more than I do these days. I'm pretty used to who I am by now. Simple intelligent self-interest seems to be enough to make me a decent neighbour. That'll do.

"But you, Rachel, what you've done I will never understand. Coming all this way, exiling yourself to a drastically shortened lifetime among strangers in a primitive time—to go through so much in pursuit of abstract knowledge—what drives you? I just don't get it. Is it love, duty, fear, need, what? Is this a sacred kamikaze mission for you, or is it your punishment for horrid crimes? Or is it just that immortals stop fearing death?"

"Some of all of those," she said. "It's like your Barbara. I won't talk about it."

Which left me no comeback. The subject was dropped.

It kept going like that, as Rachel worked her way across the North Mountain, "interviewing people for her book": the people I had expected her to have the most trouble relating to were usually the ones with whom she established immediate empathy and mutual respect. Locals, as we hippies called native Nova Scotians, did not, as a rule, "take to" strangers quickly. Oh, they'd be friendly, more than polite— but they held back something, they didn't really fully accept you into the community until you'd survived your third winter without quitting and moving south, been around a few years and shown some stuff, demonstrated that your word was good and your skull occupied.

But Rachel was the rare newcomer who was taken nearly at once to the collective bosom of the locals. She shared something with them that my hippie friends and I did not, and I could not for the life of me pin down just what it was. The phenomenon was not always as strong and noticeable as it had been with Mona Bent, but it was pretty nearly universal. It was as though they looked deeply *once* into her eyes and saw all they needed to see; within minutes they would be allowing her to rub their necks, and chattering happily about The Old Days. And telling her the real inside story, too, as near as I could tell.

There were exceptions, like old Wendell Rafuse, of course.

How can I explain Wendell? East of Heartbreak Hotel lies the home of Phylippa Brown, whose husband inconsiderately died a decade ago and left her with two girls, Pris and Cam, and damn little else. When Phyl's oil furnace died a couple of winters ago, the next morning two true cords of cut split stacked firewood had magically appeared by her front door, *without waking her or the girls*. That same winter, Wendell Rafuse's furnace failed too, and he was a frail sixty-two—but Wendell was known to have cheated his brother out of a valuable piece of land, by misusing a power of attorney while the brother was in hospital. No wood appeared outside Wendell's door. He could afford a new furnace . . . but he burned up a lot of furniture in the three days it took to get it delivered and installed.

People like Wendell tended to decline to be interviewed by some kind of Chinese nigger woman who paid no fee.

But even some of that type accepted Rachel, perhaps because her cover identity offered the hope of seeing themselves in print some day, perhaps simply because they were lonely.

Most of the local people let her into their homes, gave her tea and cakes, answered her questions, talked about their lives, many of them accepted her offer of a massage—a great many as the word began to spread about how good she was at it. She did not ever repeat anything she had been told in confidence, however juicy; somehow the word spread about that too. Blakey Sabean said of her once approvingly that, "She don't smile just to dry her teeth."

It surprised me how quickly and easily the local folk, both Mountain and Valley (and good books have been written on the subtle but important differences between the two kinds of people) took Rachel into their homes and their hearts. What surprised me even more was how easily the hippies took her into their beds.

Not the fact itself. Rachel was an attractive female, with dark exotic good looks, and early Summer was the traditional time for the hippie folk to play Musical Beds if they were going to. What surprised me almost to the point of awe was how gracefully and painlessly she managed it.

Her experience with Snaker and Ruby and me seemed to be typical. She had the mystic ability to enter a home, have sex with everyone in it, open them to new ways of loving, and then exit painlessly, leaving behind relationships *stronger* than before.

We had had sexual superstars pass through in previous years, attempting to seduce anything that wore clothes and often succeeding. But usually when such carnal comets blazed over the Mountain, they burned what they touched. This one left no trail of wreckage, no clap, no crabs, no regrets. Most extraordinary. This was the woman I had thought untantric.

Part of it must have been her very straightforwardness. Anyone could see that there was no evil in Rachel, no guile. When she gave of herself it was not to rack up a score, not for reasons of power or manipulativeness or bargaining or mischief, but just for the joy of it. She was a noncombatant in the battle of the sexes, and she was *temporary,* as perhaps a more textured personality could not have been.

Here is the closest I can come to explaining it:

One winter I was on a Greyhound bus, returning to college after Christmas vacation. A blizzard descended; the bus driver was forced to leave the Thruway. We were stranded for a week, totally snowed in, miles from civilization, nearly five dozen of us in a single large room.

A bar. All expenses paid by Greyhound. . . .

All the passengers were students, returning to assorted midstate colleges and universities. The male-female ratio approached parity. We had four guitars, a sax, a flute, and eight people who could play the house piano. We had unlimited food and booze, and adequate drugs. I guess you could call what developed an orgy. It was a vacation from reality. All the rules were suspended. You could create a new self, without necessarily having to live up to it. Everyone slept with everyone, without jealousy or pain. There were *no* fights, not so much as an argument. Amazing music was played. When the big plows finally came by we all found our clothes and boarded the bus and went back to our lives, and I do not believe any of us so much as wrote to one another. We had not exchanged names let alone addresses.

Can you imagine that head-space, the dreamy accepting state of mind in which you have the vague conviction that *this doesn't count*, that you are comped and covered and exempt and it's safe to go on instinct?

Rachel was that condition on two legs. And they spread easily.

But not wantonly. Her judgment was fine. She did not, for instance, make a pass at Tommy, nor at the monks-in-training down at the Ashram, nor at any of the handful of other voluntary celibates among the hippies. She side-stepped around Malachi and Sally when they were having struggle in their relationship, presumably out of a sense that it would be a destabilizing intrusion—and yet she made it with Zack and Jill while they were squabbling, and they came out of it stronger. She got it on with bachelors of both sexes, and with couples married and unmarried, and with the three-marriage over on the South Mountain and the six-marriage over in Mount Hanley and the two gay men who lived together but weren't lovers down in Port Lorne (when she left they were lovers). She did it with George and Annie from Outram a week before Annie gave birth—and was there for the birth, cut the cord I'm told. Maybe they had planned to name the kid Rachel anyway.

Whether she had sex with any of the locals, I could not say for sure. Their grapevine worked differently from ours; they were more reticent about such things. But I'm inclined to think that she did not . . . or that she did so rarely and quite selectively. Most of the locals lived by a different moral code, which precluded "fooling around." Extreme sexual openness tended to open hippie doors, but it would have closed most local ones. There were, of course, exceptions and borderline cases, especially among some of the younger locals. All I can say for certain is that the scandal I constantly half expected never materialized. No one shot or cut anyone—or even punched anyone—over Rachel.

If none of this is ringing true for you, if your stereotype of country folk is that they are conservative, intolerant, stiffnecked and deeply suspicious of anyone or anything strange . . . well, you haven't been to the North Mountain, that's all.

Rachel was extremely good at drawing them out, scribbling copious notes in an impressive impenetrable shorthand which she admitted privately was fake. Folks didn't all bond with her as solidly as Mona had, there was something special about that relationship. But they all brought out their best china for her, if that conveys anything to you. I went along with her on her first half-dozen calls, realized by the third that I was superfluous, realized by the sixth that I was a hindrance and stopped coming along. She was launched.

She used Heartbreak Hotel as a home base. Two or three days a week she would be there to help me with whatever work I was doing. Two or three nights a week she was there for me to have sex with, and held me until I fell asleep. In between she popped in for unexpected and always pleasant intervals, then disappeared again. She would tell me where she was going if I asked. Other than that I kept in contact with her mostly by grapevine. Fairly close contact, that is to say. I always had the sense that I was her Special Friend. But I never had encouragement or opportunity to be more than that, to come to depend on her in any sense.

A few months went by.

Those months were the ones that connect Winter to Summer in Nova Scotia. (We don't get Spring.) That made them the most achingly beautiful time of the year—in a province which is never less than stunning—and the second busiest. (The busiest time is when Winter is coming on fast and you still don't have your firewood cut or your house banked.)

With the approach of Summer, people who've spent months marking time, caning chairs, battling cabin fever, all suddenly step outdoors, blink at the absence of snow, tear off their Stanfields and become whirlwinds of activity as they realize that they will have a maximum of four months' grace to lay up enough nuts to last through the *next* Winter. To compensate them for this, the world turns warm and fecund and friendly; almost overnight the North Mountain turns into the Big Rock Candy Mountain, and people's faces start to hurt from smiling so much.

Fair-weather friends began to drift back to Sunrise Hill from all around the planet to help get the crops into the ground, repair the ravages of the winter past and initiate new construction. That year's crop of Hippie transients began passing through, backpacked and headbanded and Earthshoed and fluted. Summer-resident property owners made their annual appearance from Halifax or the States, to take their Mountain homesteads down off the blocks and jumpstart them again. The stinking goddamned snowmobiles were silenced, and the equally grating but somehow more tolerable sounds of chainsaws and rototillers and tractors were heard in the land. Deer and rabbits and weasels and crows were somehow synthesized out of the defrosting bedrock of the Mountain and began to scamper around the landscape, which turned several hundred colors, nearly all of them called "green" in our poor grunting language. The Bay suddenly filled with vessels of every kind and type, small fishing and lobstering boats close-in (one popular model looked very much like a phonebooth in a bathtub), and big tankers and freighters farther out. Those people who earned their living by milking tourists began sacrificing to the gods in hopes of a good harvest, and calculating how badly they dared burn Americans on the exchange rate. Farmers and seeds began making intricate conditional promises to one another, both sides with fingers crossed behind their backs. A busy, happy time, full of square-dances and house-raisings, shared work and shared pleasure, new lovers and old friends, fresh food and fresh dope, fresh faces and fresh hope.

Some of this I shared with Rachel—but as the weeks went by and Winter wore itself out, she spent less and less time at Heartbreak Hotel, and more and more time at her work, talking to the people of Annapolis Valley, resident and transient, hippie and local, asking them about their lives and the way they lived them, about the choices they had made and the choices they wished they had, what it was like here when they were children and how it had changed, the things they were most proud of and the things they regretted. And massaging them as they talked.

On the morning of the day before the big Summer Solstice Celebration, I saw her for the first time in over a week. She'd gone to the South Mountain for a while, an area so upcountry and backwoods that it makes the North Mountain seem like suburbia. (I met someone there once who claimed she had never in her life actually seen an electric light up close. I believed her.) We had breakfast together.

I remember the last time I saw Rachel in this life. I stood on the hard rock shore of the Bay of Fundy at low tide, spray at my back, rich shore smell in my nostrils, watching her walk toward me from my doorstep a hundred meters away, watching her cross the road, clamber down the four-meter hill, stride across fifty meters of scrubby marshland, pick her way with easy grace through the treacherous jumble of bleached driftwood that lines the shore, navigate the ankle-breaking rock of the shore itself without hesitation or awkwardness, walk right into my arms and into a kiss without ever having removed her eyes from mine from the moment she'd left the Hotel. "I have to go now, Sam," she said. "I promised Ted and Jayne and David I'd help them get the rest of their garden in the ground before it's too late."

"Sure, hon," I said. "Give them my best."

"I will. I'll come back tomorrow and help you carry things over to Louis's barn for the Solstice Feast."

"Thanks, Rachel. That'd be a help."

She let go of me, turned and retraced her steps to the road. The process was as beautiful to watch from behind as it had been from in front. "Sweet night," I called after her, and she nodded without turning. She turned right when she reached the road and started walking toward Parsons' Cove, in no hurry at all. When she was out of sight around the bend I turned back to the sea and returned to my thoughts.

And that was the day I had the thought that killed me.

❖FOURTEEN❖

THE SUMMER SOLSTICE part was sort of Woodstock Nation's Last Gasp, the sort of jamboree that, cynical travelers assured us, could no longer occur within the borders of the United States of America. There was nothing particularly structured, certainly nothing remotely commercial or professional about it. No organizers, no steering committee, no Board of Directors. No tickets; no steenkin bodges. It just seemed to happen every year: the annual Gathering of the Nova Scotia Hippies.

Primarily, of course, it was a gathering of Annapolis Valley Hippies, for that was where the province's hippie-density was highest. But New Age people came from as far away as Yarmouth, over a hundred kilometers west; from Barrington Passage, a hundred and fifty klicks south; from Amherst, nearly three hundred klicks' drive away up around the Minas Basin; and from Glace Bay four hundred and fifty klicks to the east, out where Cape Breton Island thrusts its jaw truculently out into the cold North Atlantic. For that matter, random travelers came from all over the planet—but the above parameters roughly defined the boundaries of the Hippie Grapevine, and incorporated most of the people who could expect to be recognized, by reputation if nothing else, when they arrived.

I remember an early Solstice with no more than fifty or sixty folks, held in a half-acre field out behind the Big House at Sunrise Hill. The year before this, there'd been well over five hundred, overflowing even Louis Amys' stupendous dairy barn, the pride of six counties. (Unlike Max Yasgur—and possibly because North Mountain Hippies as a group still felt collective guilt over that poor Woodstock farmer—Louis swore he'd never had such a good time in his life; he had not so much agreed, as demanded, to host it again this year, and in all future years. No one had any objection. A merry soul, Louis.)

What happened at a Solstice Festival (or Celebration, or Feast, or Party, or Thing—it's indicative that the name was not fixed) was simply that several hundred Aquarian flower children got together and ate immense quantities of each others' organically grown holistically prepared food, and drank immense quantities of each others' organic cider and beer and wine, and smoked immense quantities of each others' organic dope, and talked and sang and talked and danced and talked and laughed and talked and cried and talked and gave each other things. Two things perennially baffled the locals, who observed from a polite distance: that we did not break anything, and that there were never any fights.

Within those general parameters, it was different each year, and always a good time. There was a swimmin' hole just within walking distance, and Louis had hay fields enough to accommodate a hundred couples making love under the stars, or fucking as the case might be, and the acoustics in the barn's top floor were so splendid that even unrehearsed amateurs sounded good. I was particularly looking forward to one of the few things that could have been called a tradition in such a deliberately spontaneous event: to a five-hundred-throat Om. Without Sunrise restraints . . . yum!

I was also looking forward to The Jam, of course. To be sure, there would be at least forty musicians who would drive me out of my mind—nice people, doubtless from good families, who through no fault of their own had trouble with Bob Dylan and Leonard Cohen songs. Or who insisted on playing nothing else *but* Dylan and Cohen songs. But I could also expect anywhere from five to twenty real musicians, singly and in bunches.

Hey, listen, I don't care where you are, the woods of Nova Scotia, New York, L.A., Minneapolis even—you get a chance to play with twenty real musicians in a year, you're rich.

So the day before this Grand Pantechnicon I was sitting in my kitchen, dawdling over the remains of lunch. I was so eager for an excuse not to go back out into the sunshine and split more wood that I decided, quite unnecessarily, to Make Some Plans for the affair. If I had only properly grasped the Hippie ethos of "just let it unfold, man," it could have saved my life.

There would be at least two fiddles, a banjo or so, a few harmonicas, congas and bongos and a handful of people who could tease music out of Louis's beat-up upright piano. I knew for sure of a bass, a clarinet and—most delicious prospect of all—"Fast" Layne Francis from Halifax, the best sax player I ever heard. There was no telling what else would show; I wouldn't have been surprised by an alp horn or a solar-powered Moog.

But one thing was sure. There would be a surfeit of guitars.

I intended to play mine nevertheless. It was my main instrument, the one I was most at home on, the one I could jam best with. But it occurred to me that it would be nice to be able to switch off, from time to time, to some less clichéd, more exotic instruments. Add a little texture to the sound. Challenge myself. Impress folks with my eclecticism.

Flies buzzed around my kitchen, looking for the egress. I got up and scraped the leftovers into the compost bucket. Thank God the water line had finally unfrozen and the pump was working again. It made cleanup so much less painful. Not to mention morning coffee.

Let's see, I thought, I could bring along the autoharp, and the mandolin . . . say, I could finish up that dulcimer, there was just enough time left before the feast for the glue to—

Jesus Christ on a Snowmobile.

Mucus the Moose.

Abandoned—worse, *forgotten*—on a frozen hillside. For weeks. Weeks of the usual crazy climate extremes, at that. Temperature change might have already cracked the noble moose. He might be spilling his guts right now—

Pausing only to grab a shirt, I took off up the hill. I was heartsick at my stupidity. How could I have forgotten Mucus? For so long?

It was like tugging at the one thread that's sticking out of your sock. More questions kept getting teased out as I hiked up the trail.

How can something be important enough to you to bring you out into a blizzard . . . and so insignificant that you forget it for weeks? Leaving it lying forgotten in the Place of—

—*Maples*—

Jesus in gym shoes! I had completely forgotten the fucking maples!

The season had been almost over, that night when Rachel had arrived. But only almost. Damn it, I knew what I was going to find when I got up there. Plastic buckets brimful of rain and spoiled sap, dead insects of all kinds floating on top. Reproachful maple trees, their blood wasted, spilling on the ground.

Oh, the trees wouldn't really care; nature has no objection to waste, and trees don't much mind anything. But I would. A waste is a terrible thing to mind.

The trail leveled out at the garden and I paused to catch my breath. How in the hell could I have spaced out on my maple trees? Why, I had been right up here in the garden dozens of times, rototilling and seeding and weeding and deer-proofing; the Place of Maples was the next place-of-consequence uphill from here. You'd think it would have popped into my head before now.

Hypothesis: the psychological impact of Rachel's explosive appearance, that night, had been sufficient to drive anything associated with it out of my awareness and keep it out. The hypothesis covered both the maples and Mucus the Moose.

But it didn't *feel* right. I replayed my memories of that night. It was unquestionably the most memorable night of my life so far. I had to admit on reflection that I had not replayed that memory tape very often, not as often as I had replayed other memorable events in the past. But I couldn't find anything exactly *traumatic* in the memory, nothing I shuddered to recall. Oh, the trek back down to the Palace carrying Rachel had been pretty grim: not the sort of memory one kept handy for repeat playing. But it wasn't the sort of thing you walled away from awareness either. I had enough of those to know the difference.

Alternate hypothesis: years of occasional drug abuse were finally taking their toll on my brain; I had simply spaced out on moose and pancake-paint. A familiar hypothesis for many Sixties Survivors. It accounts for absolutely any weirdness in your life, and can neither be proved nor disproved.

But you never play with it for very long. No point. Assuming it leaves you with nothing to do. Except maybe regret.

Maybe you're a city person, and think that this was like forgetting to water the houseplants; no big deal. City people can afford to space out on things. The technical term for a country person who is absent-minded and lives alone is "corpse." If I could space out on my maples, I could space out on my fires.

Okay, the first step to solving any problem was defining the problem and its extent. Were there any other inconsistencies in my behaviour that might shed light on this pair of lapses?

How the hell would I know? How would I go about testing for them? How do you debug your head?

Forgetting Mucus, now that was irresponsible. But forgetting the maple sap, that was *dumb*. All that flapjack juice gone to waste—not to mention how hard it was going to be to extract taps that had been so long in the living wood.

What did the two screw-ups have in common?

Only location—and Rachel.

My stomach started to tighten up. I left the garden, turned left and headed up the trail.

How was it that I had taken so long to remember my unfinished dulcimer? I'd been looking forward to finishing it, that night I had gone out into the blizzard . . . and then I hadn't given it another thought until the Solstice Jam wedged it into my head again. Or had I? I couldn't be sure.

It was much cooler up here in the trees than it had been down by the chopping block; I was glad I had fetched the shirt. Cold sweat glued it to me. If you are like most people, the scariest, most starkly horrifying thing you can imagine is probably some exotic kind of harm to your body. My ultimate nightmare is damage to the integrity of my mind. As Buckley said, "The frame doesn't matter, if the *brain* is bent." I stopped suddenly and urinated to one side of the trail, copiously and with great force. My hands shook as I rezipped my jeans. I noticed that I was breathing high in my chest; tried to force it lower, breathe deeper; failed.

I remembered the mood of inexplicable optimism that had accompanied me up this trail the last time. This was the backwards of it. I knew perfectly well that I was going to my doom. I know now why I kept going—but I didn't, then, and it was killing me. Feeling foolish, I picked up two stones, one softball-size, one tennis ball. I knew they would not help me. I needed garlic. A cross. Wolfbane. Automatic weapons and a ninja sidekick. But I did not throw the stones away.

Why, I asked myself, didn't you think all this through when you were within arm's reach of a perfectly good shotgun?

I think, I answered, because someone has been stirring my brains. Someone I trusted . . .

The sense of foreboding increased as I climbed. Twice I stopped to try and control my breath and pulse. Each time nervous energy forced me on again before I could. I was going to see something I didn't like. Might as well get it over with.

But still I stopped when the Place of Maples was just around the last bend ahead. It wasn't too late to reconsider. I wasn't committed yet. I could turn around and go home. If Mucus had survived this long, he'd live through Summer. Perhaps the deer had drunk the sap. . . .

I actually turned and took two steps downhill. But it didn't help any; nothing eased. Sometimes the only way to avoid pain is to get past it. I spun on my heel and continued uphill.

There was a tool on my belt that I used half a dozen times a day, that hung there so permanently I was not truly aware of it anymore; just about every adult male on the Mountain wore one at his hip. Five inches of Sheffield steel with a handle on one end, it was technically known as a "knife," and it dawned on me at this last possible instant that the tool could be adapted for use as a weapon. Why, between it and my two rocks, I was a walking arsenal. . . .

Please, I said to whoever it is I'm talking to when I say things like that, let there be nothing to see around that bend. Let me find only Mucus the Moose and plastic pails of sour sap and a squashed look-ing place where a birch tree used to stand until it was pulverized by a blue Egg.

I rounded the last bend.

Things certainly had changed. It took a few seconds to sort things out.

The first thing that impressed itself on my attention, of course, was the new Egg.

Double bubble, toil and trouble . . .

Just like the one that Rachel had arrived in, huge and blue, except that it wasn't glowing and emitting loud noise and threatening to disintegrate—fair enough; it wasn't trying to digest the total energy of the total conversion of the total mass of a large tree—and it was translucent, almost transparent. It didn't have a beautiful naked woman inside it. Rather a disappointment all told. What it did have inside it was a bunch of things I did not recognize even vaguely but which I took to be machines or tools of some kind, though I could not have said why. I cannot describe them even roughly, nor name the material of which they were fashioned, nor the method of their fashioning; they certainly weren't machined or cast or carved. They filled the person-sized Egg over two thirds full. I disliked them on sight, whatever they were.

The shape of the landscape around the Egg was wrong. How?

There were trees missing. A dozen or more. But they had not been completely pulverized like the one Rachel had destroyed. I could see stumps and trimmings, and shortly I spotted where the trunks had been stacked, a ways off in the woods. With them was a damned big old-fashioned bow saw. Like a tall capital D, the straight line being the sawblade—the kind of saw that takes either a man on both ends or a hero on one. Someone had deliberately, and at great expense of effort, cleared the area.

Why use such a backbreaking tool? Oh, of course. A chainsaw or an axe might have been heard, downhill, by the chump whose land this nominally was. I might have come to investigate.

So what if I had? It was becoming increasingly apparent that Rachel had the ability to erase specific memories at will, without leaving a detectable gap. To do so could not be more difficult than felling several mature trees with a two-man handsaw, could it? So why not borrow my Stihl chainsaw, mow down as many trees as needed in a matter of minutes, and edit the memory from my personal tape?

For that matter, why had the saw blade not rusted out here?

What else was wrong with this picture?

No sap pails hanging forgotten from taps, after all. Pails and taps collected and stacked over by the fireplace. Big boiling bucket lidded. Probably full of salvaged sap, waiting to be reduced.

Huh. Shape of land wrong over there. A pile of turned earth. Jesus, a large excavation! A fucking hole in the ground. Easily distinguished from my ass, in this light.

Steady, boy, don't get giddy. Get a grip on—

What the fuck is that?

I dropped flat to the ground and covered my head with my arms. I waited. Wind ruffled my hair. In the distance a crow did a Joan Rivers impression. A blackfly tried to bite my ear. I thought about what I thought I had seen, and lifted my head and peeked. It still looked a lot like a weapon—but a dopey one, so it probably wasn't.

What it looked like was a mortar, or a starter's cannon, as modified by the prop department of a typical sci fi movie. It was not pointing at me or even especially near the trail, and it had not, as I'd hallucinated, swiveled instantly to track me, and now that I calmed down enough to look I saw that it *could not,* that its odd armature did not allow it enough traverse.

A satellite-tracking antenna—

I got up, feeling stupid. Crows laughed at me. I looked at the transparent blue spheroid full of high-tech artifacts, and down at the rocks in my hands, and suddenly I was angry. I tossed the rocks blindly back over my shoulders, hard; one hit a tree with a gratifying home-run *thunk* and the other started a small avalanche in a pile of alder slash. I walked slowly toward the blue Egg, feeling the anger build. If I couldn't find an access hatch or a zipper or a seam, I'd chew my way into the damned thing. . . .

It was my own damned fault, I knew. I had done exactly what all my favorite science fiction writers preached against. I had made unwarranted assumptions.

Because Rachel had arrived naked, and said that she must come naked or not at all through the membrane of time, I had assumed that whatever method of time travel her people had developed would work only on organic matter, would only transmit a living thing or something which, like the crown, was part of a living thing's bioelectrical field—

—whereas it was just as reasonable to suppose that the system could handle either organic or inorganic matter equally well, *as long as they weren't both in the same load.*

There was no telling whether this Egg was the second, or the twenty-second, no way to be sure just how advanced and dug-in the alien invasion of my ficton presently was, how big a beachhead my colossal stupidity had let them establish. Was Rachel still the only time traveler around these parts?

Or had I met dozens of her friends and colleagues . . . *and forgotten?*

Angry makes you bigger, and heartsick makes you smaller, and both at once was as bad as I'd ever felt. Yet I knew it would be even worse if they went away and left me with scared shitless. I wanted to kill a lion with my teeth, and then beat myself to death with the bones.

The Egg had no hatch or seam I could discern. Up close, the things inside were still just . . . things inside, quite unidentifiable. Parts seemed fixed, others seemed to *wave* in a way that made me wonder if the Egg could be full of some viscous liquid. I touched its surface with both my hands. Though the day was quite warm, the big spheroid was distinctly, strikingly cold to the touch. Yet there was no condensation, no exhaust heat.

I was beyond surprise or curiosity. I was going to bust this fucking egg open. Should have held onto the rocks; maybe my knife would—

I started to remove my hands from the surface of the Egg, felt something happen, clutched instinctively . . . and found that I was holding a gold headband. It had apparently been synthesized by the chilly surface of the Egg and gently pressed into my hands. It was warm.

I whistled an intricate little scrap of melody from Chick Corea's *My Spanish Heart,* and examined the thing carefully.

It was not exactly like Rachel's headband. It lacked the three retractable locking-pins that anchored hers into her skull, although there were knurled discontinuities like knotholes in their places. It was thinner in two dimensions, and the microengraving on it was an order of magnitude less complex. The gold seemed less pure. It looked like the Taiwanese knockoff copy.

I decided that nothing could possibly hurt me more than I hurt already, and that nothing could happen to me that I didn't deserve, and that I didn't even care if I was wrong. Strike three. I put the headband on my head and was Ruby—

—am Ruby fucking Sam feeling the unfamiliar dick up inside me and liking it (always thought I would) but feeling the touch of Snaker's nearby eyes more vividly than the touch of Sam's hands here on my tits (fingertips on right tit heavily callused) seeing Snaker's unseen staring face more clearly than Sam's wide-eyed here before me (Sam's mouth

is beautiful) hearing the catch in Snaker's breathing beside me more clearly than Sam's happy growl (God, Sam's a good fuck) what joy to help my lover make love to his friend, I hope this isn't a big mistake but I'll worry about it later, unnnnh-yes, like that, like that, like that, I like that, just like that, **YEAH-YEAH-YEAH-YEAH-YEAH!**—

I ripped the headband from my head; clumps of hair came away with it. I was on my side, in fetal position. My whole body trembled, my calves threatened to cramp, my vagina pulsed rhythmically, my teeth were novocaine-numb—

Oh . . . my . . . *God* . . .

I looked down at the gold oval in my hands. I wanted to throw it as far from me as I could. Farther than I could. I wanted it in the heart of the sun, or passing the orbit of Neptune at System escape velocity—

Did anyone ever leave the theater during the rape scene? Did anyone ever voluntarily stop fucking in the middle of an orgasm? Even if they wanted to?

I watched my hands come close, put the headband back on—

No sense trying to reproduce more of it. I reentered Ruby's head at the exact instant I had left it, between the fifth and sixth *yeahs* of her orgasm. It was like teleporting into the heart of an explosion. I hung on for dear life, trying to keep from being destroyed utterly by the primal fire of Shiva, and all the while the little sliver of myself that is never asleep or drunk or stoned or unconscious was taking notes.

—*Tiresias was right. It is better for them*—

—*Bizarre: you can't "come in in the middle"—there is no middle. In the instant of jacking in, anywhere in the sequence, you know who you are and where you are and what's going on—just the way the originator of those memories did, at the time. What-Has-Gone-Before is implicit in the Now*—

—*This is not right; I shouldn't be here in my friend's head, certainly not during such a private*—

—*Damn, she's right: I am a pretty good fuck. Wow, I can feel me coming; I always wondered if they could*—

—*oh, really?*

(This last because Ruby had just thought, *but my Snaker's better . . .*)

—*So many layers to this; I expected maybe a top layer of consciousness and then a layer of subconscious murmuring. But this is like a dozen-layer cake with consciousness icing, like a crowd gathered round a computer programmer all shouting instructions at once—*

—God damn, it goes on so long for them! So long, and all over . . .

—I've Got To Stop This—

She is hyperaware of Snaker and she isn't a bit jealous, his ecstasy is prolonging her orgasm, how can that be? It's like he's here in her head; he isn't really, but there's a little mental model of him that's very close to the real thing, and there's a third eye she never takes off of it. She constantly checks it (I Really Ought To Stop This Now) against the real Snaker and uses prediction errors as feedback to refine the model; one day she'll have a little Snaker in her head indistinguishable from the real one. Is that telepathy?—

—No! This is telepathy. What she is doing with Snaker is an inadequate substitute for telepathy, is what people do because they cannot be telepathic. In solitary confinement, you make up stories about those whose shouts and moans come distantly from neighboring cells. . . .

Jesus Christ, isn't she ever going to stop coming?—

—!I AM GOING TO STOP THIS RIGHT NOW!—

I was still lying on my side. There was dirt in my beard, and pine needles. An ant was portaging a piece of maple leaf a few millimeters from my eyes, in the pale shadow of the big Egg. The gold crown was clenched in my left fist. It was quite warm.

I was in shock. The little monitor sliver of me that took notes decided maybe humor would help.

Cushlamachree. Congratulations, Meade. You may just be the first living man in the history of the world to actually fuck himself.

I began to laugh, and in moments was laughing so hard I genuinely thought I might choke.

But you sure as hell aren't going to be the last—

No, humor wasn't all that helpful. The laughter trailed off. I got wearily to my feet. I realized that I now badly needed to kill at least two people and maybe dozens . . . and that an invulnerable invincible enemy was, exactly as surely as Hell, going to prevent me. I began to cry, like an infant, in frustration and outrage. With bleak logic I computed that the very best I could hope for was to be permitted to kill *one* of my targets.

Myself.

Might as well find out. The suspense was killing me. I put the gold headband down most carefully on the forest floor, and dried my sweaty palms on my pants, and took my woods knife from its sheath, and the Nazz took it away from me.

I screamed.

"I'm sorry, Sam," he said. "I thought I could stop you in time."

There was a terrific bruise coming up in the middle of his forehead, a small cut in the center of it trickling blood; soon there would be a whacking great lump. I remembered tossing a rock over my shoulder and hearing it strike a tree. *Now* it came to me that there had been no tree close behind me at that time. Tunnel vision.

Okay, open it out. How many are we? ("You don't want to count the elevator boy?") Just the two of us. Okay, iris back in on Nazz. He's different. How? Start thinking, Sam!

A forehead wound was a major alteration in a man as hairy as Nazz, his forehead being the majority of his visible face, and for once, he wasn't grinning. But there was something else. Something subtler, but more profound. This was Nazz, all right—but Nazz was a different man now. How, and how did I know?

Jesus—his eyes! *His eyes!*

For as long as I had known him, for as long as any of us had known him, Nazz had been mad. His behavior was manic and his thoughts were like tumbling kittens: one minute he'd come up with some genuine insight, like that visual-interface notion for computers, and the next minute he'd be apologizing to a chair for farting on it. But mostly it was the eyes that were the tip-off. No one meeting him ever had to wait the five seconds it would take for him to say something totally off the wall to realize that they were dealing with an acid casualty. Equally important, a benign one. Just one look at those sparkling gray eyes and you knew two things: this man was stone crazy, and he was perfectly harmless.

Neither was true anymore. Somehow, *the Nazz had gone sane.* And in so doing had reverted to what he had been before he went insane. Maybe I shouldn't have been surprised by what that was.

He was a soldier.

A good one. I recognized it in the eyes first. The alert, balanced

stance, the absence of his usual goofy grin, and the way he had effortlessly taken my knife away before I even knew he was there, all were
only confirmation. I knew the look; my father was an admiral. Nazz
was wearing his Army camouflage jacket—hell, *all* Hippies wore
those, but now it wasn't a costume anymore, now I could see that he
had *not* bought it at an Army-Navy store to make mockery of it, now
it was his uniform again. He wore a web belt that held a GI canteen,
ammo pouches, a coil of rope, a commando knife, and a woods knife
like mine. Every few seconds he glanced quickly from side to side,
like a cop, or a fugitive.

A lot of guys who came back from the Viet Namese jungle—the
ones who survived—got heavily into acid. And some of them moved
north, to a country where nobody called them "babykillers . . ."

When two men meet they often—I'm tempted to say, nearly
always—make an instant assessment. Even if they don't expect the
question to arise in a million years, they can't help quietly wondering: if it came to it, could I take him? (Interesting that the same word,
"take," means to beat a man or fuck a woman or steal property . . .)
Their two opinions as to the answer will subtly affect all their future
dealings.

Nazz was one of the few men concerning whom it had never
occurred to me to ask that question before. I did now—

I was candy.

"Holy shit," I greeted him.

"Yeah," he agreed, "I guess that's what it is."

I was full of many things, especially questions. Too many to sort. I
let them pick their own order. "That head hurt much?"

"Yah. I never saw you move that fast before, Sam,"

"Something about an alien invasion that pumps you up, I guess."

He let that pass. "How'd you know I was behind you?"

"Then you aren't reading my mind now?"

He shook his head. "It doesn't work that way." He grimaced.
"Unless you were reading mine. I'd swear I never made a sound."

"You didn't. I just figured rocks weren't going to help me any, so
I just threw 'em away."

He couldn't completely suppress a flash of Nazz-like smile. "No
shit?" He shook his head. "That's a relief. Between you dropping flat

all of a sudden, and then getting up and surprising me again, I thought maybe I'd lost it."

"Junglecraft? No, you haven't. How'd she get to you, Nazz?"

"Get to *me?* I got to her."

"Why?"

"Well, once I figured out what Rachel was—"

"How?"

"It was self-evident, Sam. All you had to do was look at her to know she was a stranger in a strange land, and that exchange student story of yours didn't make it. So I looked closer—and it was pretty easy to see that the body she was wearing wasn't the one she was born in."

I hadn't guessed that. "How do you figure?" Jesus, even his diction had changed.

"Sam, Sam. Not a wrinkle on her from head to foot, not smile-lines or frown-lines or stretch-marks or scars of vaccinations or *anything*. Nobody is that featureless except babies. Well, that made it obvious. Where do they grow brand-new, adult bodies, and change them like clothes? The future. How could people that smart miss such a glaring giveaway? Because they're telepaths—*they don't use facial expressions.*"

Hell. I should have figured that out. I even had clues Nazz hadn't had. If Rachel could take a golden crown through time with her, why not head- or body-hair? Because she hadn't grown any yet . . .

A trained jungle-fighter with a mind like this was about unbeatable.

No. Very difficult to beat. Rachel was unbeatable. I had managed to surprise Nazz. I was convinced that Rachel would have known I was going to throw those rocks before I did.

Well, maybe I could find some way to surprise him again. There's no telling what dumb luck can do for you.

I nodded. "Smart, man. Mind if I sit down?"

He sat, without using his hands. I joined him more slowly and stiffly. Jesus, he was in shape.

It seemed appropriate to quote Dick Buckley. "Straighten me, Nazz . . . 'cause I'm ready."

"What do you want to know, Sam?"

Which questions to ask first. "Who is Rachel, and what is she doing here?"

" 'They,' "

"Huh?"

"You mean, 'who *are* Rachel, and what are *they* doing here?"

"Repeat: you faded."

"Rachel is four people. You didn't know?"

"Can they all carry a tune?"

"Beg pardon?"

"Sorry, I'm getting giddy. I was just thinking how nice it would be to sing Mamas and Papas songs by myself. Or Buffalo Bills stuff. You were saying, Rachel is four people—"

"Yah. Uh, technically they're personality-fragments, I guess you'd say. Abridged clones, not originals."

I let that go by. "Who's the leader?" Of the club that's made for you and me—

"Jacques. The others call him Fader. It's like an inside joke. What he really is, is—" He broke off, hesitated for several seconds. "I guess you'd have to say he's . . . the Saviour. The Founder. The one who brought the New Age. The Deathkiller."

Oh really?

"His born name is Jacques LeBlanc. A Swiss neuroanatomist—his original incarnation was, I mean. He started *everything.* A couple of klicks from here, as a matter of fact, a decade from now."

"Run that by me again."

"He's going to be a neighbor of yours. The first Jacques LeBlanc, the forerunner of the one that's one-fourth of Rachel, is going to move into the old DeMarco Place, just up the road from here, in a few years. That's where it's going to happen, Sam—isn't that far out? Right here in Nova Scotia, your neighbour-to-be is going to have the conceptual breakthroughs that let him discover mindwipe, and then mindwrite, and finally true telepathy. That's why Rachel picked this area for an LZ: this is where the conquest of the world will begin. Amazing, huh?"

And I'd helped.

"Gee, Nazz, that's just keen. Who are the other three Rachels?"

"The other three parts of her, you mean. Well, there's Madeleine, the Co-Founder, she's Jacques' lady—"

"There had to be a woman in there somewhere—or a gay man."

"Because of how good she is in bed, you mean? Not really. Original gender-of-birth hasn't got much to do with it. Then there's Joe—he's sort of Maddy's brother, but not quite—and Joe's lady Karen. If any one of them is responsible for Rachel being such a good lay, it's Karen. She used to be a high-ticket hooker."

"Joe is Madeleine's brother, but not quite." If I kept on playing straight man, sooner or later this had to start making sense.

Or maybe not.

"Well, actually it's *Norman* who was Maddy's brother—but then he thought Jacques had killed Maddy, so he took off after Jacques and tried to kill him. Jacques had to screw up his head so drastically that there *wasn't* a Norman anymore, and the personality in that skull became Joe. By the time they got that all straightened out, and he got his memories back, he was happier being Joe than he ever had been being Norman, so he stayed Joe."

"Jacques hadn't killed his sister after all?"

"No. Just kidnapped her. It might have been smart to kill her, she was on the verge of blowing the whistle on the whole conspiracy. But he loved her. So he took a big chance. He made her his first confidante, his partner, the first person to be invited into the conspiracy. Uh, 'first' sequentially, of course, not chronologically."

"Of course. Who is the first, chronologically? You?"

"Why, I really don't know for sure, Sam. For all I know, my namesake from Bethlehem could have been in it."

I was absorbing about one word in ten of his. Mostly I just wanted to keep him talking while I tried to think of some foolproof way to kill him without weapons, skills, or the advantage of surprise. Or failing that, a way to suicide—since he apparently wasn't going to let me.

"I mean, they must be into the Bible," he went on. "That's where Rachel got her name from. '. . . Rachel, who mourned for her lost children, and would not be comforted, for they were no more.' Typical Joe sense of humor. *This* Rachel hurts for her lost *ancestors*, not her children. Does a lot more about it than mourns, too."

This was getting us nowhere. "What are you doing here, Nazz?"

"The Egg here—" He reached out and touched it gently, caressingly, "—arrived a week ago. Ever since, I've been trying to get it safely into the ground, and guarding it in the meantime."

"Guarding it? Here? Against what, the deer?"

"You know how it is with woods trails. Deerjackers, hikers, lovers, berry-pickers, kids playing, horse people out riding, you never know who's gonna come by when. They all tend to follow existing trails. But mostly I've been keeping watch for you, Sam."

"For me?"

"Rachel told me to expect you. Uh . . . this is the second time you've been up here in the last few days."

Aw, *shit*. Really?

I had no recollection of having been here since the night Rachel arrived.

"How did Rachel know I'd be coming?"

"That moose gadget of yours. You thought of coming back up here for it last week, for the dozenth time—and Rachel stopped you, took the memory of that thought out of your head. But she knew it'd recur, and she had pressing business elsewhere. She couldn't erase the moose altogether, the memory was rooted pretty deep and there would've been holes big enough for you to notice. Besides, your most recent memories of it were integral to your memory of Rachel's own arrival here. She didn't want to leave any suspicious holes in that sequence.

"But she knew that the Solstice Thing coming up would keep putting the moose back in your mind. So she told me to keep an eye and ear out for you."

"Wouldn't it have been simpler to ferry Mucus down to the house and plant a false memory that I'd retrieved him myself?"

He shook his head. "Doesn't work that way. I don't think anyone could put a convincing false memory into a man's head except himself. The mind knows its own handwriting."

So I had to be allowed to keep climbing up the damned Mountain, loop and replay—like Sisyphus. Like a robot with a faulty action program. Like a bird blindly banging its head against the window, trying to escape . . .

My voice sounded odd to me. "What happened the last time I got this far, Nazz? We fought, didn't we?"

"Yes, Sam."

"And I lost, and you cut out some of my memory. Jesus, you did a good job. There isn't the slightest sense of déjà vu."

"Not me, Sam. I'm not even really a novice at this stuff. Hell, I'm just barely a postulant. All I could do was put you on hold and call in Rachel—she did the surgery."

" 'Put me on hold'?"

"Yeah, it's not hard. The crown generates a phased induction field that hyperstimulates your septum. Your pleasure center, just over your hypothalamus. You sort of supersaturate with pleasure, and your mind goes away. Like, samadhi. Nirvana."

"Mother of God." I was trembling. No, shivering. " 'Death by Ecstasy'—"

He nodded. "That Niven story, yeah, it's a lot like that."

"Oh Christ." That story had figured prominently in some of my worst nightmares. A man's brain is wired up to a wall socket. Enslaved by ecstasy, he starves to death with a broad grin—because the cord isn't long enough to reach the kitchen without pulling out the plug. . . .

"It could be worse, Sam."

It echoed through the forest, stilled wildlife. "HOW?"

He waited until the echoes had faded. Then he said softly, "You could get the identical effect by supersaturating the pain center."

I sat and thought for a while. He seemed willing to let me. Nothing productive came to me. Just bitterness and regret and fury and profound terror.

"I'm really surprised that *you* joined the Pod People, Nazz. I'd have sworn that you'd be the last person on Earth vulnerable to a mental assault. Why haven't you tried to convert *me?*"

"I gave it my best shot last time. Didn't work."

I held up the golden crown I still had in my hand. "Not after what this thing showed me. Is this what you're going to . . . 'put me on hold' with?"

"Not that one, no. The Egg made it for *you,* for one thing, it wouldn't interface with my mind properly. Calibrated all wrong. And that'll be a Read-Only crown you've got there, a passive playback-module. It hasn't got tasp circuits. But the Egg knows I'm authorized for a Command Crown—"

He was wearing an ordinary cloth headband; he took it off and set it down on the ground, shaking his head to tousle his hair. He turned away from me, reached both hands palm first toward the Egg, closed his eyes momentarily—

I jammed my crown down over his hairy head.

It was worth a try—hell, I had no other move—and the results were gratifying. He screamed.

Maybe it was that my crown was "calibrated wrong" to "interface with his mind properly." Maybe it was being unexpectedly dropped into the midst of a woman's orgasm. Perhaps he misinterpreted that first surging rush, thought I had somehow acquired a Command Crown by mistake, and panicked.

Most likely it was a combination of all of those. For whatever reasons, there were two or three entire seconds there during which he was no longer a highly skilled killer commando who could wipe up the forest with me without working up a sweat, but a grinning, gaping space-case rather like the Nazz I had always known and liked—

—and before those two or three seconds had elapsed, I hit him with the heel of my fist, like pounding on a table, impacting solidly below his ear, whanging his head off the Egg so hard that the thing rang like a gong.

✦FIFTEEN✦

WHETHER THAT BLOW knocked him unconscious or merely stunned him I could not say for sure. I sprang to my feet and kicked him twice in the head. The second kick caught him on the jaw shelf and snapped his head around, and the crown flew from his head as he went down. By then he was definitely unconscious. I stood over him breathing in great gulps and trying to decide whether or not to kill him. There was some urgency in the question. If I did not do so now, while I was pumped up, I never would.

In those days I believed in the insanity defense. I did not believe that a man should be killed for something that was "not his fault." It was "not fair." Laugh if you will; I was young. The Nazz I knew would not have been held responsible for anything by any reasonable person. This new, sane Nazz was an enigma with an unknown half-life. Perhaps one day with luck this man could be made insane again. I decided I did not have the right to kill him. Then and only then did I let myself consider how inconvenient it was going to be keeping him alive.

First things first. I removed his web belt of tools. The braided rope belt under it that he used to hold up his pants turned out to be long enough to secure both wrists and both ankles behind him in a classic hogtie. His own bandanna headband, which he had taken off in favor of the golden one, made a serviceable gag. I checked him carefully for holdout weapons without finding any. Once he was secured I looked around carefully.

The excavation in which he planned to bury the Egg was only partly a dug hole. The Mountain is a glacier's footprint: there's so much bedrock to it that there might not have been soil deep enough to cover the Egg anywhere within a couple of klicks. So he'd dug what he could, and was now apparently in the process of *dissolving* an adequate hole in the bedrock with some kind of chemical reaction I didn't understand. There were reagents of harmless-looking clear liquids, carefully kept far apart from each other, and lab gloves, and goggles. At the bottom of the trench, a circular film of cloudy liquid was *seething*. There was a faint odor that reminded me of an over-heated engine. I guesstimated that in another couple of days he'd be able to get the bubble down in there and kick dirt over it.

Why use such a clumsy, dangerous and slow method when dyna-mite was so cheap? Because I would have heard the blast and come to investigate. If I "forgot," other neighbors would have heard, and would ask about it the next time they saw me.

I returned to Nazz. My impression was correct: he had not had time to retrieve his "command crown" from the bubble before I put his lights out. So I could not simply . . . "put him on hold," even if his crown would accept my orders and I could learn to use it. Part of me thought that a damn shame. Briefly I thought of trying to press his unconscious hands against the bubble, see if I could fool it. But I didn't think I could. And what if I succeeded—and won the ability to make Nazz a zombie?

Most of me, I think, was awash with gratitude at being spared the moral choice. I would much rather have killed my friend than done *that* to him.

I began to regret that I had not killed him. I couldn't leave him here overnight—he could catch pneumonia. But it was a long way back downhill to the Palace. He weighed more than Rachel had. All that hair. It's very hard to carry a hogtied man without dislocating both his shoulders. I dared not even leave him alone long enough to go borrow a wheelbarrow or a horse. Even trussed up, there might be some way he could use the Egg to free himself, or worse, call Rachel.

In the end I got a bunch of fresh alder boughs from the recent clearing activities, and built a makeshift travois. Probably a Micmac could have done a much better job. I laid Nazz on it on his left side, head end uphill. It was not necessary to lash him aboard.

And I towed the son of a bitch down the Mountain.

❖ ❖ ❖

To my mild astonishment it worked just fine. I only got stuck five or ten times. The grooves that travois handle put in my shoulders didn't quite break the skin or my collarbone. My cursing would probably not have killed anything outside a thirty-meter radius. Three fourths of the way down the trail, Nazz came to. He grunted behind his gag. I didn't feel like talking to him. I tried turning him over on his right side and maybe that solved his problem; in any case he stopped grunting. Lot of rocks in that trail; couldn't have been a comfortable ride.

After only a thousand years of pain the trail leveled off at the garden. I didn't hesitate. Couldn't afford to lose the momentum. Smashed the gate flat and went right up the middle, destroying seedlings of squash and corn and radishes and carrots, dill and chives and broccoli. What survived was mostly onions and peppers and tomatoes and basil. Italian food all next winter, if I lived that long. Flattened the gate at the other end, bringing down that whole end of the fence, and was heading downhill again.

When I got to the chicken coop I stopped, and thought. I rolled Nazz off the travois and into the coop. It was very difficult to get him through the low doorway without untying him, but I managed. He would not freeze at night here. Chickens are actually dumb enough to mistake a hogtied man for another chicken. They would snuggle up to him. And the henhouse was far enough from the house and road that he could yell all he wanted. (He would rub off that makeshift gag shortly after I left him alone—a good thing, too, as an effectively gagged man can die of the sniffles.)

Of course, Foghorn Leghorn my rooster was going to hate it. And Nazz wasn't going to enjoy the smell much. GIs have a proverbial hatred of chicken shit.

When he understood I meant to leave him there he began to grunt furiously and emphatically, and thrashed around as much as was possible to him. I couldn't blame him. His arms and legs must already have been cramping severely. Twenty-four hours in that position and he'd need expert physiotherapy, maybe surgery. Tough shit.

I knelt by the doorway and waited in silence until he stopped grunting.

"If I get Rachel, I'll come back for you. If she gets me, she'll come looking for you."

He grunted *uh huh*.

"If we take each other out, I guess you're fucked."

He grunted *uh huh* again. His unblinking eyes met mine, trying hard to speak volumes. They were, as Lord Buckley has noted, pretty eyes.

I looked away and prayed the oldest prayer in human history—*make it didn't happen*—and got to my feet. "So long, brother."

He grunted *Sam, wait!* and I left him.

As the house came into view I suddenly swore and punched myself viciously on the thigh. I had forgotten the God damned moose *again*.

It was good to see my little home. By now I knew it might be my last day there. I was *busy*—but I kept sneaking glances around me as I worked, cherishing what I was about to lose.

The golden crown that had broken my heart and blown Nazz's mind hung from my belt. The first thing I did was put it on the chopping block and whack it a few times with the splitting maul; that deformed it some but not enough to suit me, so I took it to my shop and clamped it in the vise and worked it over with heavy-duty pliers and a rat-tail file and the head-demagnetizer from my reel-to-reel; then I cut it into small pieces with boltcutters and softened each piece with a blowtorch and hammered them flat with a mallet and went outside and threw each piece in a different direction as far as I could. Then I gathered up all the tools I'd used and threw them away too. I started up the Kemac jet, boiled water, scrubbed my hands. As an afterthought I got a facecloth and scrubbed my forehead where the gold headband had rested.

Then I made a pot of coffee.

Halfway through the pot, I heard the Blue Meanie approaching from the east. The pitch of its scream did not change; it was just passing through, on the way west somewhere. I sprang to the window. Snaker was driving, alone. I ran outside and flagged him down.

"Hey, bro," he called when the engine finally quit. "Just heading for Annapolis, guess what? There's gonna be some honest-to-God MDA at the party!" He wore only jeans, a denim vest and boots. I've seen pictures of concentration camp survivors with more meat on them. His hair was tied back in a ponytail.

I was experiencing inner turmoil. Flagging down Snaker had been instinctive. Now I faced a difficult choice. I planned to fight Rachel, and more than half expected to lose. Did I get my best friend involved, and probably get him killed too? Or leave him in an ignorance that would, whenever Rachel took the notion, be too blissful by half?

He misinterpreted my expression. "Haven't you done MDA before? You'll really like it, honest: all the good features of acid, psilocybin and organic mesc, with none of the dis—wow, man, you look like hell."

It occurred to me that I had already *made* this choice—back when Rachel first arrived. The only difference was, now I *knew* the danger was real. "Come on inside."

"Are you all right?"

"Come on inside."

I could feel him studying me as we walked up the driveway and around behind the house. He was silent while I got him coffee. The interval was not enough for me to find the words I needed, so we just looked at each other for a few moments.

"What do you need?" he said at last.

"Shithouse luck."

He nodded slightly. "That can come to any man."

My hands hurt. I looked down. They both clutched my cup, and they were shaking so badly that hot coffee was slopping on them. I tried to set the cup down and bounced it on the table three times. At once Snaker's hand shot out, came down over the top of the cup, forced it firmly down onto the table and held it there until I could let go. It must have scalded the hell out of his palm.

Something broke in me and I was weeping without sound, panting like a dog or a woman in LaMaze labor.

God bless him, Snaker did not flinch or look embarrassed. He looked at me, now that I think of it, exactly as though I were *talking to him*, as if he were listening attentively to me and thinking about what I was saying. Or as though so many people had burst into tears in conversation with him that he had learned to understand weeping as well as words.

Maybe he had. When I finally ran down and got my breath control back, he said softly, "That's hard."

I blew my nose and wiped my face. "You don't know the half of it."

"Talk to me."

"Snake . . . you know how I feel about Rachel?"

"Sure. Same way I do."

"Pretty much, yeah." Deep breath. "I have to kill her, Snake."

His face turned to stone.

"And I am not at all sure I'm up to it. I nearly got greased once already today—by the Nazz, if you can believe that. Did you know he did time in Nam? And she's much more dangerous. We blew it, Snake, you and me, that first day. *She is a telepath.*"

Very slowly and deliberately, as if handling a delicate explosive, he removed his makings and a Riz-La machine from the pocket of his denim vest, and rolled a cigarette with the same care. "Tell me all, omitting no detail, however slight."

So I did.

It took us halfway into the next pot of coffee. Or in his terms, eight cigarettes.

"—so as near as I can see it, it comes down to a classic science fiction question: *how do you kill a telepath?* Ought to be right up your alley, Snake."

"There are two ways I know, actually. I started a story about it once. You have to assume that there's some limit on the telepath's range—"

"I'm still alive. I still have my memories—I think. In any case, I have memories damaging to her. And she could have gotten here from Parsons' cove by now. If I had to guess, I'd say her maximum range is on the order of, oh, say earshot."

"Check. So—carefully remaining out of range, you give one of the telepath's socks to an attack-trained Doberman and say 'Kill.' Plan B: you build a killer robot and give it the same instruction. A nonsentient animal or a sentient machine, either will turn the trick."

"Terrific. I doubt there's an attack dog anywhere in the Valley. And the only guy around here who could probably build a robot is up the hill a ways, wondering how hungry you have to be to eat a raw egg with its mother watching. Have you any *practical* thoughts?"

"Abort the mission."

"Snaker, come on! We haven't got time to fuck around—"

"I'm serious."

"I haven't got a chance, you mean? Dammit, don't you think I know that? *I'm asking you to help me pick the best way to die trying.*"

"Sam, Sam, why does it have to be life and death?"

I stared at him.

"Really, man. You have no coherent idea of what the hell Rachel is up to. The one thing you know for sure is that *she* won't kill *you,* for fear of destroying the future she comes from—"

"Wrong! Rachel would *prefer* not to kill my *body.* My mind is fair game. I am my memories, Snake. My 'self' *is* those memories. They are me. Rachel is the Mindkiller. I have to bring her down."

"But what exactly has she *done* to your memories?"

Why was he being so obtuse? "That's the fucking point: *I don't know!* How can I know what things I don't remember? How do I know what transpired while I was 'on hold,' smiling beatifically, my naked brain open to thief or voyeur? I have been raped so intimately that I will never *know* just how badly unless and until my rapist chooses to tell me. Intolerable. Unforgivable. You disagree?"

"No. I share your horror of mind-tampering. As I sit here I keep probing my own head for memory gaps, badly glued seams, the way you poke at a toothache with your tongue. It's a creepy feeling, knowing she's been in my head, your head, Ruby's head. I'm angry at her for it. I want to know what made her do it. I give her enough credit to believe she thought she had a good—"

"Of *course* she thinks she has a good reason. I am not remotely interested in what it is! There *is no good reason* for what she did to you and me and Ruby. She dies. End of story. If I thought I could safely immobilize her, I might ask her what her motives were before I killed her—and then again I might not."

He was shaking his head. "You're not *indifferent* to her motives. You actively refuse to learn them. I can only think of one reason why: you're afraid you might agree with them if you knew them."

"You're wrong, Snake. I really don't care one way or the other."

"Bullshit. It would be tactically sound to know! It would aid you in attacking her. And you're too smart not to realize that. Yet you have left your only source of military intelligence, the man who could tell all and is eager for the chance—our pal Nazz—lying in a chicken-coop."

"I think I understand her motives."

"Then you're way ahead of me."

"Think about a telepathic society, Snaker. Everybody knows everything about everybody. There's no more voyeurism. No more mystery. No such thing as a candid camera, an unposed picture, an unexamined life. Everyone's always 'on-camera,' wearing their 'company face,' even fantasies are constructed in the awareness that they will be public property. In effect, everyone is naked, and if you've ever spent any time in a nudist camp you know how bland and *boring* that becomes. A whole planet becomes jaded.

"So a market develops for memory-tapes with a 'candid camera' feel, the experiences of people who *didn't know anyone was looking*. There's only one place to get them, though. From the past, from people who lived in the day before all this brain-robbing technology was developed. From people so primitive they don't even have copy-protection on their brains. We're like the native women in *National Geographic,* too dumb and ignorant to know better than to go around naked. No wonder Rachel's been in and out of every hippie bed in Nova Scotia, and for all I know half the local beds too: better value for the entertainment dollar."

He swung around in his chair, used the wrought-iron lifter to remove the front access plate from the stovetop, dropped a cigarette butt into the firebox, and replaced the plate with more crash-bang than was necessary. "Stipulate that such memory dubs would be desirable, even marketable. Would they be worth exiling yourself to a strange and primitive world, for life? Would they be worth giving up immortality? For the golden privilege of burying them in the woods, for your contemporaries to dig up and enjoy after you're dust?" At the mention of mortality, he began to roll another cigarette.

"On what authority do we know that Rachel has given up immortality to come here?"

He winced. "Touché. For all we can prove, she has two-way time travel."

"No, that story I believe. If it were that easy to slide back home, she wouldn't be reduced to using local talent like Nazz. Snaker, all of this is totally irrelevant. I told you already: her motives don't matter. Whatever they are, she's ashamed to tell her best friends, but even that is unimportant. A dozen times since I found out what a

Command Crown was I have wished that I had one available to me . . . God help me. There is no material problem one of those could not solve. Rachel has brought absolute power into my world. I don't care whether she can be trusted with it. It shouldn't exist."

"But what can you do about it?"

"Snaker, I'm surprised at you. For a writer you aren't very inventive. I've thought of three ways to kill a telepath, in less than an hour." I got up and poured the last of the coffee. "Point of order. We keep calling Rachel a 'telepath.' Is that strictly accurate? She can dub my memory-record, stipulated. Apparently she has to switch off my consciousness to do so. Can she *perceive* memories *as they are forming?* Can she really 'read my mind,' or does she have to *stop* my mind, take a wax impression of it, and read *that?*"

"What the hell's the difference?"

"Earth to Snaker: if she isn't a true telepath, in the sf sense, if she's just a memory-thief who can 'put me on hold' when she wants to, I can walk up to her, smiling pleasantly, and cut her throat."

"Huh. I wouldn't try it. She may not have any facial expressions of her own—but she has gotten very very good at reading other peoples' in the last two months. I'm beginning to understand why. But I see another implication. You audited a dub of an experience with four people present—but you didn't play it through to the end. It might have been recorded later, at a time when she and Ruby were alone. It would be useful to know *how many* minds she can bliss-out at a time."

I saluted him. "You anticipate me. Method number one for killing a telepath: go uphill, palm that Egg about fifty times, bring fifty crowns to the Solstice Thing tomorrow and pass them out. You wouldn't even have to say a word. Rachel could never run far enough fast enough. But you've put your finger on the flaw: suppose she can handle fifty at once? Nobody at that party is going to be surprised if they wake up the next day with memory gaps. A lot of them are counting on it."

"So what's method number two?"

"Number two I wouldn't use myself, but it's a beaut. Pick a chump. Boobytrap him without his knowledge. Send him to see the telepath. Apologize profusely to the corpse."

"Nasty."

"I'm pinning my hopes on method number three. Boobytrap someplace you know the telepath is going to be. Retire well out of her range and stay there until you hear a loud noise."

He said nothing, played with his cigarette. I turned away and busied myself with washing the coffee pot. Wisely does Niven say the secret of good coffee is fanatic cleanliness.

"She'll be here tomorrow before the Solstice, to help me ferry stuff to the dance. I was thinking of going up the road and borrowing some dynamite from Lester anyway. Make me some scrambled Egg. I could borrow enough for two jobs." I thought a moment. "Actually, what I'd like to do is kick that damned blue bubble all the way downhill, roll it right inside here and do both jobs with the same blast. But it'd hang up somewhere on the way downtrail, sure as hell—or worse, start sending out SOS signals. Pity."

He didn't answer right away. I turned around and caught him staring out the window, looking off uphill toward the Place of Maples.

"I know what you're thinking," I said. "Knock it the fuck off."

He whirled to face me. "Eh?"

"Don't try to look innocent. You're thinking about how much you want to wander up that Mountain and put that sonofabitching crown on your stupid fucking head and find out what it's really like for Ruby when she comes. You transparent asshole, you're salivating thinking about it." I went to him, grabbed his vest with both fists, yanked his face to a position an inch from mine, spoke loudly and firmly. "By your love for your lady, I charge you to forget it. For the honour of your immortal soul, give it up. Love does not give you the right to do that. You don't have the right to that information. No one does. I shouldn't have that information. The second most horrid moment in my whole life was when I knew that I could not help myself, that I was going to put that crown back on again." I shook him gently. "You and Ruby have something special going. *Don't fuck it up.*"

He did not try to pull away or avoid my gaze. "I'll try, Sam."

"You'd better, you—oh, mother of Christ! Look at that—"

Peripheral vision had alerted me. Through my back window I could see Rachel approaching my back door from the direction of the chickencoop, Nazz walking stiffly and awkwardly behind her.

❖❖ ❖❖ ❖❖

I sprang for the woodbox behind the stove, snatched up the big double-bit axe. "Battle stations! Grab down that shotgun, Snake, it's full of double-ought; dammit, is there no fucking peace anywhere in the jurisdiction of Jesus? She must have come right up over the Mountain through forest, for God's sake! duck around the corner into the next room, man; I'll draw her attention, you pop out and try to skrag her—"

I stopped talking then. Snaker had the shotgun.

Pointed at my belly—

"No, she didn't," he said quietly. "Come through forest. She was lying flat in the truckbed. You didn't look close enough."

He hadn't been thinking of Ruby's memory-dub when I caught him looking out the window. He'd been wondering what the hell was keeping Rachel and Nazz.

"Sam," he said, "cut loose. Give it up, man, and Rachel'll *tell* you why she's doing all this."

"Sure," I snarled, "and any parts that don't make sense, I forget, right?"

"Sam, my brother—"

"When Rachel's head comes through that door, *my brother,* I am going to try to bisect it with this here axe. You do what you have to do." I shouldered the axe.

He cried out: "Sam, *please*—"

The door squeaked open. Rachel entered. The axe left my shoulders, began to swing. "Ah, *shit,*" Snaker said, and shot me in the chest with both barrels.

❖SIXTEEN❖

DO YOU HATE cliché as much as I do? Then perhaps you can imagine how exasperating it was for me to have, as the load of buckshot was traversing the distance from gun to my torso, my whole life pass before my eyes.

In detail, just like everybody said, the works, *z-z-z-ip!* The duration and rate of speed of the experience cannot be described in any meaningful way. I can say only that it seemed to go by very quickly, like speeded up Mack Sennett footage, yet not so quickly that I lost a single nuance of emotion or irony. Objectively, of course, it had to be over in considerably less than a second of real-time.

I did sort of appreciate the second look, although it went by too fast to enjoy. But it was a cliché I had never for a moment believed in—like time travel—and I was vastly irritated by its turning out to be true. For Chrissake, thought the part of me that watched the show, next I'll find myself floating over my own corpse—

I caught up to where I had come in.

WHACK!

There was no pain; the buckshot killed me, and then I was floating in the air, a few feet above my corpse. I looked like hell. Snaker was having weeping hysterics. Nazz kept saying oh wow man. Rachel was expressionless, saying something preposterous to Snaker. I tried to speak to Snaker myself, but it didn't work. I didn't seem to have vocal cords with me.

Oh, for God's *sake,* I thought. Now I rise up through the ceiling,

403

right? And after a while I'll find myself floating down a tunnel toward a green light?

I began to rise slowly, passed through the ceiling as though it were made of cobwebs, things began to spin and twist sideways and down, I was rocketing through the air just above the forest like a low-flying missile or a hedge-hopping pilot, my God, I was heading for the Place of Maples, the bubble came up fast and WHACK there was a sense of impact, a wrenching, a stutter in time, then a terrible rising acceleration like the ending of *2001: A Space Odyssey* like the ending of "A Day in the Life" like both of those there was a crescendo, a peaking, a cataclysmic explosion, then a long slow diminuendo, a gradual return to awareness of my surroundings—

—and there I was in a damned tunnel, big as the Grand Canyon, drifting with infinite slowness toward a green light at the far end of it. . . .

It was visually staggering, exhilarating in the way that *vastness* always exhilarates. It was also infuriating. I had long since settled to my satisfaction that all those Near Death Experiences, the Out-Of-Body reports by those who had briefly been clinically dead, were merely fading consciousness's last hallucination, the Final Dream, the hindbrain's last attempt to replay the birth trauma and have it come out all right. I was disgusted to find out that my own subconscious mind didn't seem to have a better imagination than anybody else's.

I thought of a Harlan Ellison collection I had liked once. DEATH-BIRD STORIES. Death was giving me the bird, all right.

Can you hear me, Death? This is *boring*. I'm Death-bored. Show a little originality, for God's sake. Is He around, by the way?

I say I was infuriated, exhilarated, disgusted, staggered, but all these sensations were only pale shadows of themselves, memories of emotions. I no longer had a limbic system to produce emotions; I continued to "feel" them from force of habit. Already a great sense of detachment was beginning to come upon me. I was no longer worried that my world was being invaded by brain-raping, zombie-making puppet mistresses. It wasn't my problem anymore. In time, I could tell, the echoes of all passion would fade. I mourned them, while I still could.

All my trials, Lord, soon be over . . .
Fat chance.

I had a lot of time to think, drifting lazily down that most Freudian
of tunnels. And a lot to work out.

I *seemed* to have a body. It was there if I looked for it; if I concentrated I could make myself turn slowly end over end by flapping my
arms. But I could also pass my hands through my trunk if I tried, and
when I clapped them together there was no sound. . . .

I was afraid. I could not have said of what. I certainly did not fear
the pains of Hell, nor for that matter anticipate anything like Heaven.
The Christian Heaven had always struck me as remarkably like an
early Christian martyr's last fantasy of turning the tables on his
Roman torturers. I go to a place where *I* shall be one of the elect and
wear white robes and live in a great white city with big gates and do
no work while listening to the screams of sinners being burned for
my amusement.

(I know that harps and haloes are no longer the official position of
any modern Christian church, at least not if you work your way up
to the top rank of intellectual theologians. But just try and pin one of
them down on just exactly what Heaven *is* like. These people claimed
that they had once hung out with God; they'd seen him nailed up,
watched him die, three days later the cat showed up for lunch so they
knew he was God—or if he wasn't, anyway he'd *been there,* he knew
all the answers to all the great mysteries—and they'd had him around
for thirty days, and nobody thought to ask him *what was it like being
dead?,* or if they did the answer wasn't worth writing down. How
does a story like that last two millennia?)

Indeed, the only reason I was not intellectually offended to the
point of stupefaction by the whole concept of an afterlife was a
conversation I'd had with my father once when I was seventeen.

My father was emphatically not a superstitious man. Unusual, perhaps, for an admiral. He held to his marriage contract and allowed
my mother to raise me as a Catholic, but he always tried to see to it
that Reason got its innings, too. At seventeen I told him that I had
decided I was an atheist, like him. He told me to sit down.

Three times in his life, he said, he had lain near death, in deep
coma. Each time he heard a voice in his head, a deep, warm,

compassionate voice as he described it. Each time it asked him, "Are you ready now?"

Each time, he told me, he had thought about it, and concluded that he was *not* ready yet. The first time there was too much of the world he had not yet seen, and there were men under his command. The second time there was my mother. The third time I was still too young to do without a father. There may have been other factors he did not name.

Each time, he said, the voice accepted his decision. And each time he awoke, and a doctor said, "Jesus, you know, for a minute there we thought we were going to lose you."

"An atheist," he told me, "would say I had three dreams. And might be perfectly correct. I have no way to refute the theory. If that voice was a god, it was no god I've ever heard of—because it evinced no desire whatever to be worshipped. But son, I am no longer an atheist. I am an agnostic. By all means hate dogma—but I advise you not to be dogmatic about it."

Two years after that they diagnosed his cancer—lung cancer, which usually takes so many merciless months of agony before it kills—and in less than a month he was gone. He was retired from active duty. I was grown. Perhaps he calculated that Mother would have a better chance of surviving and remarrying if she did not have to watch him die by slow degrees; in any case, she did both.

So I was able to tolerate the concept of an afterlife—here it was, big as life. I just didn't have the slightest idea what it would be like, nor any guesses.

Nor any way to guess. Insufficient data. With cold rigour I admitted to myself the possibility that in a little while I would come to a vast pair of Hollywood gates and have to account for myself to an old gentleman named Pete, who fronted for a particularly vicious and infantile paranoid-schizophrenic. (I hoped not. The one thing all Christian theologians seemed to agree on was that, *whatever* Heaven was like, there was no sinning there. It would make for a long eternity.)

Phooey. It was equally likely that the Buddha waited at the end of the tunnel to show me the Eightfold Path. It was, in fact, precisely as likely that at the end of the tunnel I would find a stupendous, universe-spanning Porky Pig, and he would say "Th-th-th-th-that's all, folks!", and I would cease to be. Until you know what the postulates are, all hypotheses are equally unlikely.

But my father had persuaded me to hedge my bets. Just in case I *was* going to have to account for myself to Someone or Something. . . .

Sitting in judgment upon oneself may be a uniquely human pastime; some feel we invented deities at least in part to take the job off our shoulders. (Whereas we always seem to have enough spare time to sit in judgment on others.) Lacking that assistance, I felt that I had, in my life, done a little more self-judgment than most, if less than some. I had tried, at least, to judge myself by my own rules—and accepted the responsibility of constantly judging those rules themselves in the light of experience, and changing them if it seemed necessary.

But I had never before had so much uninterrupted time in which to consider these questions, or so little emotional attachment to their answers. I had never managed to sustain, for more than the duration of an acid trip, the detached point of reference from which such judgments must be undertaken. And I had certainly never before had such a spectacular and useful visual aid as having my entire life pass before my eyes in a single gestalt, in such detail that I could, for instance, see at once both what my childhood had really been like, and the edited version of it I had allowed myself to carry into adulthood. The lies I had sold myself over my lifetime were made manifest to me, my very best rationalizations crumbled like ice sculpture in boiling water; I looked squarely at my life now past, and judged it. Coldly, dispassionately. Honestly, by my own lights, as they were written in my heart of hearts.

And if, as some maintain, a life must be judged on a pass-fail basis, then I failed.

I had loved no one; few had loved me. I had pissed away my talent. I had, in general and with rare exceptions, hated my neighbor. I had left the music business when the folk music market collapsed—not because I didn't like other kinds of music; I did—but because folk music was the only kind you could play alone. I had never truly learned to stand other people. They seemed to break down into two groups. The overwhelming majority were determinedly stupid, vulgar, cruel, tasteless, superstitious, dull, insensitive and invincibly ignorant. And then there were the neurotic artists and intellectuals. I was just plain too smart and sensitive for anybody, when I came down to it.

So I had fled my world for the woods of the north country, and there, out of two billion people I had managed to find a bare handful I could tolerate at arm's length. And I had let them down, failed to protect them from a menace I should have been best equipped to stop, had bungled things so badly that my best friend had killed me and the rest were being mind-raped.

If Philip José Farmer was right, and I "owed for the flesh," then I was going to duck out without paying. I had taken nothing with me from life. In no sense and at no time and no place in my life had I ever pulled my weight.

As that judgment coalesced in my mind, I learned that not all emotions require flesh to support them, for I was suffused with an overwhelming sense of—not shame, not guilt, I was beyond them now, but sorrow. Sorrow insupportable, grief implacable. I had failed, and it was too late to do anything about it. I had wasted my birthright, and now it was gone.

No wonder I had feared a telepath. This much honesty, back when I was still alive, would have killed me.

All intervals of time were now measureless; I lacked even heartbeats as a referent. After a measureless interval, I had marinated in my failure for as long as I could bear. I turned my attention to the immense tunnel in which I drifted.

It seemed, to whatever I was using for senses (probably the same memories I was using for emotions), to be composed of dark billowing smoke shot through with highlights of purple and silver. I thought of a thundercloud somehow constrained into a cylinder. I was equidistant from all sides. My body-image was wearing off; I could see through my hands. The cool green light in the distance was getting closer, but since I did not know its true size I could not tell how quickly. I could not even be sure if it was the end of the tunnel, or a light source suspended in the center.

It is said that the pessimist sees mostly the overwhelming darkness of the tunnel, and the optimist sees mostly the tiny point of light that promises the end of it . . . whereas the realist understands that the light is probably an oncoming train.

All three are shortsighted. The *real* realist knows the ultimate truth: that if you dodge the train, and reach the end of the tunnel . . . beyond it lies another tunnel.

I reviewed what I had read of Near Death Experiences. If this one continued to follow the basic *National Enquirer* script, shortly I would closely approach the green light, and there be met by my dead loved ones.

The problem with that was that I didn't *have* any loved ones. Dead or otherwise.

(Did dead friends and intimate acquaintances count? And if so, what would we have to say to each other, in these circumstances?)

Oh, it was possible I had loved my parents in childhood, though I doubted it strongly. I was sure that from the time I had the intellectual capacity to understand what the word 'love' meant, I no longer felt that for them if I ever had. As far as I knew I had *always* been selfish; my parents' welfare and happiness had meant nothing to me except insofar as, and precisely to the extent that, they affected my own. I'd had no siblings to practice loving on. My mother's love for me had generally struck me as a cloying annoyance whose sole virtue was that it could sometimes be exploited to advantage. As for my father, once my storms of adolescence were past I had come gradually to respect and admire him—but I had never loved him. Whether he had loved me or not, I honestly did not know.

I had to admit, though, that he was the most likely candidate to greet me if anyone would. Of all those I cared about who had died before me, he was the one who (I thought) most visited my dreams and most evaded my waking thoughts. I wondered if dead admirals wore their uniforms. Would he steam up to me in a floating aircraft carrier—or, more likely, his first command, the USS *Smartt?* Or would he manifest as I best remembered him, sitting bolt upright at his desk, chainsmoking Pall Malls and coughing like a snowmobile and doing incomprehensible things with paper that changed the lives of people halfway around the globe?

Let's get this show on the road, I thought, and as though in response, my universe began to change.

I'm not sure how to describe it. I'm certain I won't convey it. It was as though my senses of light, hearing, taste, smell and touch all coalesced into a single sense, with the special virtues of each and the limits of none. It seemed to me then that there had really only been one sense all along—the sense of touch—and that all the other senses had only been other ways of touching. This too was a new way of touching, as wide-ranging as sight and as intimate as taste. Nothing could block this vision, nor distort this hearing. It was similar to the LSD experience in several ways, not least of which is that I cannot describe it to you and you will not know what I mean until you have been there. As with acid, most of the metaphors that spring to mind are visual. The scales have fallen from my eyes. I once was blind and now I see. I can see clearly now. Oh, *there's* the forest—

With this new sense, I probed ahead of me, as one reaches out an exploratory hand in a dark cave. And found that I was come nigh the end of the tunnel. The "green light" was "blinding," but between it and me I dimly made out a number of . . . *somethings,* hovering on the edge of tangibility. One of them came to me, and without body or limbs or features somehow became an entity, a self, a person. Recognition was a massive jolt, even in that detached frame of mind. I should have expected to meet her. I had not. I was wrong about my father being the one who most visited my dreams. He was only the one who most visited the dreams I remembered on waking.

"Hello, Pooh Bear."

"Barbara!"

I tried frantically to back-pedal somehow, to flap my arms and escape, kick my legs and swim away back upstream like a salmon. I no longer had even phantom arms and legs, and the force that drew me was as inexorable as gravity.

We were touching.

So there was retribution in the afterlife after all. . . .

The others could "hear" us, but for a time they left us alone. I knew them not. Music was playing somewhere, and I paid no attention.

There was no hurry here. I tasted her, and all the memories flooded back with aching clarity, their emotional colorations faded almost to invisibility but none the less powerful for that. A black and white two dimensional photograph of Rodin's *The Lovers* can yet stir heart and loins.

She was no longer the Barbara I had known, of course, except in

the sense that the flower is still the seed, but her aspect was familiar.
I understood that she had put on that aspect to welcome me, as one
might nostalgically put on an old garment to greet an old love—and
that she had had to rummage a while in a musty trunk to find it.

To convey what happened then I must pretend that we used
words.

"Hello, Barbara."

"Hello, Sam."

"I'm sorry."

"For what?"

"I'm sorry that I didn't love you."

Her response will not really go into words. She was like one who
tries not to laugh at a child, but cannot help smiling, because his
fear is imaginary. None the less real for that, nor less painful—but
imaginary and thus comical too. "But you *did*."

I could make no response. Many times I had fantasized this
conversation, in the days before the wound had finally scabbed
over . . . but this statement I had never imagined Barbara making.
Could a ghost be mistaken?

"Truly you did."

"I never."

"You taught me to stand up straight. To be strong. To accept no
authority above my own reason. You stood up for me, even when it
cost."

"I cheated on you. And let you find out."

"You knew we were not meant to be permanent life-partners. I
didn't. You knew how badly you would hurt me if I stayed with you,
and tried to deal me the lesser hurt—at greater cost to yourself."

"Bullshit. I wanted to get laid and I just didn't care if it hurt you."

"Then why let me find out?"

I made no reply. Pressure of some kind built. Finally:

"Barbara, you *know* I did not love you. Or were you too busy there
at the end?"

"What do you mean, Sam?"

"Barbara . . . I killed you. And our child."

"You did not."

It boiled out of me so fast she recoiled, it spewed out like projectile
vomit or a burst boil or a slashed artery: "I let you both die! I saw the

truck coming, and there was time for me to run and slam into you and knock you out of its path, just like in the movies, plenty of time. *And I didn't.* It's what a man would have done. What even a worm would have done . . . for a woman he loved. There was time. I was not willing to die in your place. I stood there and watched the truck crush you. Your belly burst and our baby came out. He lay there in your giblets and kicked a little and died while I watched and tried to think what to do. Just as you had a moment before. I already thought I was a monster, I guessed when my grandparents died and I didn't give a damn, and I felt it again and stronger when Frank died and the first thought in my head was 'Thank God it was him and not me,' but that day as I watched you both die I knew for certain that I was not capable of love, and that *I must never again pretend to myself or anyone else that I was!*"

She waited until I had regained control. Then:

"First things first. Only one person died in that accident."

"I saw him, I tell you—"

"You saw 'it.' You *know* better, Sam. You've always understood the anthropomorphic fallacy. *I was less than four months gone.* What came out of my belly looked like a little tiny person . . . and was not, any more than a four-celled blastula is a person, or an ovum, or a fingernail clipping. It did not have *any* neural cells. No brain, no spinal column, nothing that could be called a central nervous system. Not an axon or a dendrite or a ganglion. Nothing that could support sensation, self, let alone self-awareness. It could have *become* a person in time, if chance had so ruled—but it did not, *or it would be here now.*"

I knew somehow that she was correct, and a part of my pain began slowly to recede. I clutched after it. "It was alive, and it was *going* to be our baby, and I let it die. I let you die."

"You had a split second in which to make a complex decision. You have just tasted your life as a single piece, grokked its fullness. Don't you see that if you and I had let pregnancy force a bad decision on us and talked ourselves into staying together, our marriage and our life would have been a misshapen, stunted thing, crippling both of us, *and* the child caught between us?"

"What has that got to do with it? It was my duty to save you. The crunch came and my true colors showed. I'd told myself I loved you, I had myself half convinced. But when the nitty gritty comes, when the chips are down, you can't lie anymore. Bullshit walks. And I stood still, and watched you die."

She did something that was even more like touching than what we had been doing, that was a caress and a hug and an embrace and a massage and a kiss, a thing that was infinitely soothing and comforting. Lacking a bloodstream to keep reinforcing it, my pain began to lessen, like a fist relaxing. I was baffled by her forgiveness.

"Sam," she said when I had relaxed enough, "I'd like you to think about two things. First, think about how much you've suffered, over all the years between, for what you think you did to someone you did not love.

"Second, replay that accident just one more time. I heard the air horn the same moment you did. I had precisely as long to jump out of the way as you had to knock me out of the way. And better motivation. *And I didn't move a muscle either.*"

And then she was gone and the next greeter came forward.

"Hello, Dad."

"Hello, son. It's good to see you."

"Guess you didn't hallucinate that voice after all, did you?"

"No."

"What's the procedure now?"

"The usual procedure is being modified."

"Really? How?"

"Barbara greeted you first because we all agreed that it was necessary for you to make your peace with her before anything else. You and I have our fish to fry, too, but it is not necessary that we do it now.

"There are things we will talk about, things unsaid between us, things I never gave you and things you never forgave me. There will be a time when I will make my apology to you, for letting my selfish motivations call you up out of nothingness to be born and suffer and die, and demanding that you be grateful. That time is not now. There are others here who would talk to you, and what they have to say is not urgent either. There is no time here, and so there is no hurry.

"Nonetheless, we are—all of us—under enormous time pressure."

"I don't understand."

"Son, you are a clever, self-serving son of a bitch. You managed to maneuver yourself into a position where you could die honorably and painlessly, commit suicide without getting busted for it. You had been wanting to for a long time, ever since Barbara died. It is not going to work."

"Huh?"

"You are going to have to go back."

"*What?*"

"But first you need a history lesson. You have to understand What Has Gone Before . . . and What Will Have Gone After."

What I got from him then was just what he said it would be. A lesson, a long monologue, which I did not interrupt even once, so I am going to abandon the quotation marks and dialogue format. (I *know* you're not supposed to drop a long lecture in near the end of your story. It's like that dark and stormy night business; this is the way it happened and there's nothing I can do about it.)

Mankind (my father told me) studied the brain for centuries, seeking the key to the mind/body problem. It began to achieve glimmerings of real understanding in the Nineteen-Forties and Fifties, as sophisticated brain surgery became technologically possible and ethically permissible. Newer and better approaches were found; newer and better tools made; newer and better models were built and studied and correlated: the brain is like a switchboard, the brain is like a computer, the brain is like a hologram, the brain is an incredibly complex ongoing chemical reaction, the brain is a reptile brain draped with a mammal brain with humanity a mere cherry on top. By the Sixties, it was obvious that many of the brain's deepest secrets were close to being solved. By the mid-Seventies, a few years after Snaker killed me, a respected scientist was willing to predict before the American Association for the Advancement of Science that the "information storage code" of the human brain could be cracked within a decade or two, that neuropsychology was on the verge of grasping how the brain wrote and stored memories, that science stood at the doorstep of Self.

In the audience, a lonely widower named Jacques LeBlanc

frowned. He was one of the half dozen neuroanatomists on Earth, and easily the best. He completely agreed with the prediction, and it terrified him. Alone in the room, he grasped the awful power implicit in understanding the brain, and he knew how power tends to be used. He had been alive when the atom bombs went off; a protégé of Dr. Albert Hoffman, he had seen LSD used by the CIA for mind-control experiments.

He saw that if you understood how memories were written and stored, why, then you could make direct copies of a memory, rich and vivid and multilayered copies, and give them to others, and that would be a wonderful thing. If the trick could eventually be extended to *short-term* memory, you would have something approaching telepathy, and if you could actually extend it to consciousness itself—

He saw just as clearly that those refinements might never come to pass.

All information is a code, and entropy says that it will always be easier to destroy information than to encode it in the first place. A library that took thousands of years to produce can be destroyed in an hour. A lifetime's memories can be ended by a stroke in an instant. A tape-recorder's "erase" head is a *much* simpler and cheaper device than its "record" and "playback" heads. First they invent a weapon; then they look for ways to use it as a tool.

So the first result of understanding memory would be mindwipe. LeBlanc knew that if that power were loosed on the world unchecked, then what may as well be called The Forces of Evil might win for centuries to come. Tyranny never had a greater ally than the ability to make your slave forget he opposes you. The other side of the coin—the aspect of memory that permits it to be *shared*—would be studied haltingly if at all, implemented slowly if ever. A preacher named Gaskin once said, "Between ego and entropy, there is no need for a Devil."

LeBlanc looked around him at his world, seeking some institution or individual who could be trusted with such power. He saw no one whom he trusted more than himself. He was one of those rare people who are not capable of evading responsibility once perceived. With trepidation, with great humility, he set about conquering the world.

He used his superior knowledge and prominence in his field to misdirect and confound all others, using disinformation, falsifying data, throwing out red herrings and sending trustful friends and colleagues down blind alleys. Meanwhile, he raced ahead alone down the true paths, learning in secret and keeping his knowledge to himself.

By 2001 he had a crude, cumbersome form of mindwipe. The conquest of the world began to pick up speed.

In the next decade surgery—including brain surgery—suddenly got drastically simpler, and computer power got drastically cheaper. By 2007 LeBlanc had married his second wife Madeleine, and thanks to insights she provided he made the breakthrough that brought him true mindwipe. He could now walk up to any person and, without surgery or drugs, using only an induction gun and a microcomputer the size of a wallet, turn off their mind and take from it what he wished. He could open the vault of long-term memory storage, rifle any memory more than a few hours old, Xerox it or erase it forever as suited him. He strongly preferred to kill his enemies, given a choice, but did not allow his scruples to keep him from raping minds by the dozens when he deemed it necessary. He did his level best to minimize the necessity.

From that point on, he effectively owned Terra. He moved through human society at will, yet apart from it, unseen, or at least unremembered, by all save those he chose. He had access to *anything* under the control of any human being. He built his conspiracy slowly, carefully, putting full trust in no one except Madeleine. She had come underground with him—and that was nearly his undoing, for when she vanished, her brother Norman Kent thought that LeBlanc had killed her. It became necessary for LeBlanc to do mindsurgery on Norman, creating a new, amnesiac personality named Joe. Four years later, Joe and a friend named Karen Shaw put enough of the pieces together to come after LeBlanc a second time.

LeBlanc told them everything. He showed Joe and Karen his own secret inner heart and asked them to judge him. They joined his conspiracy, and that very night killed a policeman to protect it.

Two years later, twelve years after he had achieved the first clumsy form of mindwipe, in the lucky year of A.D. 2013, Jacques LeBlanc, neuroanatomist and amateur tyrant, and Joe No Last Name, gifted programmer and professional burglar, together developed mindwrite, co-wrote the computer language called Mindtalk, and perfected the brain-computer interface. They had true telepathy.

They no longer lived alone in the dark in meat-wrapped bone boxes. They no longer needed meat or bone to exist, could survive if need be the destruction of the brains from which they had sprung, could grow if need be new brains with bone and meat to haul them around, could if they chose replicate themselves perfectly and indefinitely. Barring catastrophe, they could live forever; no enemy could threaten them. At long last, human beings had taken a significant step toward immortality. Four of them finally held that previously abstract and hypothetical commodity, absolute power—more of it than had ever existed to be grasped before now.

They spent another eleven years manufacturing terminals—golden headbands—in large numbers, and warehousing them all over the planet without drawing attention, and assembling an army that did not know it existed. And the moment that task was completed, with a sigh of relief that came to be audible all over the globe, the secret masters of the world abdicated.

For this was their secret, self-evident strength: those whose power is genuinely absolute are incorruptible.

There came a morning in 2024 when every news medium on the planet that had any connection to the world computer network (virtually all media), print, audio, video, electronic, all opened with the same lead, though not a reporter alive could remember having written it and no editor had approved it for publication.

THOU ART GOD, said the headlines and broadcasters and datafeeds, in a hundred languages and dialects, to people who built spaceships and to people who herded goats, to saints and sinners, generals and monks, geniuses and fools, pros and cons, graybeards and children.

As God does not appear to exist, they said, it became necessary to invent Him/Her. This is now being done. The Kingdom is at hand, and you are welcome to join. Any living human whatsoever may become a neuron in The Mind, and all are equal therein. Go to the nearest telephone company business office or switching facility. There will be a lot of golden crowns. Put one on. You need never fear anyone or anything again. No money down. Satisfaction guaranteed.

Act anytime you like; this offer will last. *But remember: a smarter God is up to* you.

And then viewers were returned to normal news programming.

Within minutes, curious people were logging on to the new system, and The Mind began to grow.

The CIA and KGB, the Joint Chiefs and the Politburo and their counterparts all around the Earth, the guardians of national security and the balance of terror and business as usual and the unnatural order of things, all went individually and then collectively berserk, for the end of status is the end of status quo. But as fast as their servants developed leads, they seemed to forget them. . . .

For so audacious a mind, Jacques LeBlanc was curiously conservative in his projection of the demand: in that first run he provided only three hundred million of the golden crowns. That is to say, he assumed that no more than one percent of humanity would take his offer within the first week.

Fortunately three hundred million minds in communion and concert can work just about any miracle they choose. What had taken Jacques, Maddy, Karen and Joe eleven years was duplicated in a week, and again in a day.

And *everything* changed.

To join The Mind you did not have to lose your ego, your identity or free will. You could leave The Mind and restore the walls around your own personal mind as easily as switching off a phone—that being in fact how it was done—and for as long as you chose. There were no constraints whatsoever on freedom except consensus; no one neuron of God's Brain had or could have any more, or less, power than any other. Conformity was finally no longer necessary, for there was no static "state" to be threatened by its lack. The codified and calcified rituals that form a state are what humans must do because they do not have telepathy. The Mind was not static; it flowed. The ancient stubborn human conviction was right; in most disagreements, one side is rightest—and now both could know which, neither could refuse to admit it. Nothing could supersede the truth, not who you were or who you knew, for everyone knew everyone and everyone knew the truth. Consensus decisions were self-enforcing. All came to learn what computer hackers had always intuited and prayed for: that in a shareware economy, with free flow of information, there can be no hierarchy, and all users are equal.

Not everyone joined The Mind, of course. It is possible to adapt so well to pain and fear that you cannot shift gears and adapt to their lack. Black Americans, knowing more about these things than most, had a colloquial expression for this common response to unremitting pain: *It got good to him,* they said. Those people who had made cruelty or malice or indifference into an essential integral part of their self-identity, a sadly large portion of humanity, found that they were forced to reinvent themselves, or leave The Mind. Cruelty is love twisted by pain, malice is love twisted by fear, and indifference is love twisted by loneliness, and there was no pain or fear or loneliness in The Mind.

Others were so incurably afflicted with intolerant religious doctrines of one sort or another that they could not accept the damnable heresy of human beings daring to make their own God, could not bear to live in any Heaven where they were not a privileged elite by virtue of birth.

Within a single generation, all gnosis was ended; every religion that did not have tolerance built right into the very marrow of its bones (most of them) had vanished—at long last!—from the face of the globe, and those who had been afflicted by them were forgiven by their surviving victims. Something like a new religion came into existence almost at once, quite superior to simple "secular humanism" (a fascist code-word for "intellectual liberty").

(The new religion was simple. Clearly the universe is mindless. Equally clearly it was written by a mind. A program of such immense size and self-consistency cannot form by random chance; the idea is ludicrous. The new religion sought The User, the intelligence that had written the program, for no other reason than that it was the most exciting game possible. Some individual minds felt that by the act of collapsing into The Mind, the human race had debugged itself and would thus soon attract the pleased attention of The User ["soon" defined by whatever he/she/it used for "realtime"]; others argued that The Mind was as yet no more than an integrated application, an automatic routine beneath notice, and would have to *deduce* The User from contemplation of the Operating System.)

Many tore crowns from their foreheads in rage or shame, and swore to fight The Mind and all it represented. Of course they never had a chance: by definition they were unable to cooperate enough, even with each other, to seriously threaten minds in perfect harmony. Evil, however clever, is always stupid: Fear and age distort judgement.

They were not punished for trying. In time, they forgot what they had been angry about, forgot that they had been angry, were allowed to live out their lives and (since they insisted on it) die in the fullness of their years without remembering their bitter defeat. Rugged individualists who could not live without their loneliness became nothing when their bodies died, and there is nothing lonelier than that, so perhaps they too had their Heaven. Within a few generations, physical assault on the Mind had ceased. Individual, solitary humans would continue to exist for at least another century, in uneasy truce with The Mind . . . but most of them found it necessary to band together (insofar as their natures allowed) in Australia—because their gene-pool was so terribly small. The Mind freely gave them that glorious continent, the only gift they would accept. The Mind came to regard old-style humans much as they had once regarded their own elderly: with the deference and respect due those who are blind, deaf, querulous and on their way to extinction.

But an astonishing number of even humanity's most bitter pessimists chose, freely, to reinvent themselves rather than leave The Mind once they had tasted of it. *Most* human bitterness had derived from lack of The Mind. All evil derives from fear.

And the majority of human beings had always, in their heart of hearts, at least *wanted* to love all mankind—if only there had been some sane, practical way to do so. The problem with living in total perpetual honesty and openness had always been making sure that no one *else* lied either. People had tended to be untrustworthy because they lacked trust, to be selfish because they needed to be, paranoid because it worked—but for a million years they had never lost the sneaking awareness that *it ought to be otherwise,* had never ceased dreaming of a society in which it *was* otherwise. People had feared that others might see their secret thoughts—because each and every one was convinced that *his* or *her* secret thoughts and sins were fouler and more shameful than anyone else's (a delusion that could not survive an instant in The Mind)—and yet had never given up the search for a lover or confessor to whom they could unburden themselves. They had always yearned to be telepathic, and yet had suppressed most tendencies toward planetary awareness that they did develop—because the first thing any telepath notices is that most of his brothers are starving to death *and there is nothing he can do about it.*

But once that last clause no longer obtained, once world hunger and the arms race and death and pain themselves were seen to be soluble problems, humanity leaped to embrace telepathy with such ardor that it was as though Jacques LeBlanc's golden crown had been a seed crystal dropped into the heart of a great supersaturated solution, which collapsed at once into a structure, a pattern, of awesome complexity and beauty.

In the instant that Loneliness and the Fear of Death were ended, Evil died for good and for all. Mankind—at *last*—stopped hurting itself and began healing itself, physically, mentally and spiritually.

At the point when there were approximately a billion minds in The Mind, there was a quantum change. A switch was thrown and a new kind of awareness came into existence. The pattern became a living, functioning, growing thing, learned how to teach itself, approached at long, long last both intelligence and wisdom.

On an evolutionary scale the change was instantaneous. At the computer rates of thoughtspeed now available to its members, it seemed subjectively to last for hundreds of millennia. In old-style, Homo sapiens terms, the metamorphosis was essentially complete in something under three months from a standing start.

By half a century or so later, The Mind was something utterly unknowable to any old-style human, indescribable in any preexisting language. But it can perhaps be imagined that it was both intelligent and wise. Some of its members had lived thousands of subjective lifetimes of uninterrupted thought, without ever losing a friend or a colleague to death. It can be understood that The Mind spread to fill its solar system, and began to contemplate how best to reach the stars. And it can be reported that it had discovered—and discarded as much too dangerous to have any practical purpose—a way to bend space in such a way as to travel backward (only) through time.

Then one day one of the neurons in The Mind had an astonishing idea—

⊰SEVENTEEN⊱

IT WAS ALMOST irrelevant that this particular neuron had once been known as Karen Shaw. Having been one of the original Four earned her respect—but not "status" or "authority," since these things no longer existed, and certainly not "worship," for worship is a kind of fear.

It was the idea itself that was so irresistibly appealing. It was suffused with the same sort of dazzling audacity that had led Jacques LeBlanc to conquer the world in order to save it, the same kind of arrogance it took to wipe minds and subvert wills in order to make a world in which no mind would be wiped or will subverted ever again.

We have (Karen argued) overcome Death but not yet conquered it. We've managed to plug the massive information leak it comprised. Half of the human minds that ever thought are thinking now, and their thoughts are no longer wasted—

—only half.

Perhaps (she proposed) humanity was now grown mighty enough, not only to beat Death, but to rob it. To wrest *back* from it the half of the human race it had stolen before we learned how to circumvent it. To recover the trillions of man-hours of human experience that had been stored as painfully-collected memories, and then ruined.

Perhaps (she urged) we could go back and rescue our dead.

It was odd and ironic that this idea should have been conceived by Karen Shaw, for she had less reason than most to love her dead parents. (Her father had been a sadistic child-molester, her mother a cipher.) Equally ironic that the first to agree with it was Joe, who had no parents . . . but less odd, for he and Karen were married, both old-style and in the fashion of The Mind. Together they communicated her thought to Madeleine Kent—who saw at once that it was just what her own husband needed.

Though basically at peace with himself, Jacques LeBlanc was still plagued with a lingering echo of something like guilt, a persistent regret for some of the things he had been forced to do in pursuit of his dream, pain which even the vindication of his judgment could not entirely ease. Chief among these was that he had—in order to preserve his secrets, until it was time for all secrets to be ended—been forced to kill quite a few men and women. Not all of them had been evil people.

He seized gladly on the idea that perhaps he could undo this harm. Perhaps the man who had once been called the Mindkiller could become Deathkiller.

And so The Four, reassembled once more, studied Karen's idea, refined it to a plan, polished it, and presented it to the rest of The Mind. . . .

The debate was titanic. Never in the history of The Mind had consensus been so hard to achieve.

The risk was horrible. Careless time travel could change history, shatter reality, destroy The Mind itself and the universe in which it inhered, waste everything that had been gained so far and all possibility of future gain.

(On the other hand, a race which had feared nothing for countless subjective lifetimes was not utterly opposed to some risk in a good cause. It did not seem reasonable that the dissolution of the universe could *hurt,* exactly, and who would be left to mourn?)

The sheer physical task was daunting: to place, somewhere in the spinal fluid of every human being that had ever lived, a tiny and fantastically complex descendant of a microchip which would copy every memory that brain formed, and every link of its DNA code—and when triggered by death trauma, would transmit that copy to the nearest buried "bubble" for storage and future recovery—all this without ever getting caught at it by touchy ancestors.

(On the other hand, this was a manageable problem for several billion supergeniuses who could subtract memories at need and had an entire solar system to plunder for parts.)

The cost was also daunting. Any individual mind that volunteered to go back in time would go *one-way,* to a ficton which did not contain The Mind. After a lifetime of solitary confinement in the equivalent of a deaf, dumb, blind and numb hulk, such a one would *die*—not permanently, to be sure, but it would *hurt.* Should its true intentions be suspected, and it be surrounded by more minds than it could control alone, it might very well be burned at the stake. . . .

The potential benefit was irresistible. To undo two million years of tragedy, the aching psychic weight of grief and mourning represented by billions of deaths! The Mind would almost precisely double in size, both in numbers of "neurons" and in man-years of human experience. *The Family would be together again!*

The debate surged through The Mind from one end to the other, provoking more vigorous disagreement than that entity had hereto-fore known. In objective terms, it must have taken over an hour.

It was decided to perform a careful experiment.

The Four made copies of themselves. Heavily edited copies, extremely abridged copies, versions of themselves so close to the solitary old-style humans they had once been that they believed the copies could live among such without going insane. They grew a body out of germ plasm which, by now, was thoroughly racially mixed, and poured themselves into it, and called themself Rachel. They picked a target ficton close to the historical moment of The Mind's birth, but enough short of it that there would be time for a proper forty-year test of the plan.

And then they hurled themselves through time and into my birch tree.

Because of that single unfortunate error (my father explained to me now), the secret was compromised from the start. By the time Rachel had recovered from the near-fatal trauma of blowing up that tree, got her crown back, and was once again physically capable of controlling my mind, I had shared what I knew with Snaker—and he and I had lived through too much subjective time. To edit our memories now would leave gaps too large to remain unnoticed for long—and by horrid mischance we were both science fiction readers, perfectly capable of deducing what had been done to us.

A practical solution would have been to kill us both. The part of

Rachel that had once been Jacques LeBlanc had had a bellyful of that particular practical solution.

Instead she opened Snaker and me up and examined us—and decided to invite Snaker into the conspiracy, and keep me in the dark. Between them they did their best to cure me of the spiritual illness that made me dangerous, the sickness that feared its cure . . . and when that failed, they committed themselves to keeping me in ignorance of Rachel's true mission.

They had very nearly pulled it off. They were foiled by the preposterous chance involvement of a plastic moose, and by the unexpected savagery with which I defended my poisoned mindset.

And so I had brought the universe to the brink of disaster, by making a change in history too great for it to heal itself around. By changing the date of my death.

Imagine an immense computer program composed of billions of files, quadrillions of megabytes of data, an immense and intricate array of ones and zeroes, of *yes*es and *no*s. A cosmic ray strikes one bit of data, alters it. Does the program crash? Of course not. A program that vast has mighty debugging routines written into it, or it could never have reached that size in the first place. As the altered bit causes tiny errors to accumulate, they are spotted, collated, analyzed, and the bit is "repaired," restored to its correct state. If it cannot be, through media failure, a good debugger will rewrite the program around the damaged sector.

But if a whole file, millions of bits of related data scattered through many discontiguous sectors, suddenly seizes up and dissipates prematurely—before the results of its operations are made available to the other subroutines that depend on it—if the discontinuity is too large to work around—

—then cascading errors ripple outward like shock waves and the system crashes. And all the information—in this case, *all information*—vanishes, lost forever.

It was explained to me that my premature death—first cause, Rachel choosing to use a time machine to monkey with history; final cause, Snaker choosing to pull two triggers—was just such a potentially catastrophic disruption.

It was further, and most humiliatingly, made clear to me that this was not because of any profoundly significant effect or affect upon the universe as a result of my premature absence. By the time of my death I was an ingrown toenail of a man, halfway to hermitage, interacting with my world as little as possible and doing my very best to influence no one's life. Between Death and the remaining life I had planned for myself there was very little difference. There were no children who would now be unborn, no albums that would go unrecorded.

What made my death significant to anyone but myself—what made my own personal folly the rock upon which the universe itself might be broken—was that in my blindness and fear I had forced Snaker to kill me.

For he *did* interact with the world. He was a writer, an artist, and it was written in his karma that he would one day be a fairly influential one. But some public explanation had to be found for my death, and policemen always bet the odds. History would now record that Snaker O'Malley had been convicted of murdering me because I had slept with his wife Ruby. Killing me would abort some of his greatest works, and distort all the others beyond recognition, with far-reaching effects on people neither of us would ever meet. Similarly, Ruby's paintings could never now be what they would have been, and she was fated to be a greater artist than her husband, though less commercially successful in her lifetime. And Nazz would, in his grief and guilt, fail to pass on to friends an off-the-wall, blue-sky insight that would have so profound an effect on computers in the Eighties as to forestall nuclear war in the Nineties. . . .

So disastrous was the projected outcome that there was only one solution. I must climb back on the Great Wheel of Karma, return to my own time and undo the damage I had caused.

My father finished speaking. It was time for me to make my reply.

"Dad," I said, "are you telling me you want me to go back to that miserable planet and live out another thirty-odd years of being a hermit and not accomplishing anything and not having children and knowing just when and how I'm going to die (it will be quite painful, I grok, not like the last time) and generally being a waste of space? You're saying that I can alter the basic shape a *little*—perhaps experiment with loving my friends just a little more—but not much, not enough to risk screwing up the shape of the miserable life I had planned out for myself?"

"Son," he said, "I'm saying that I hope it's what *you* want. As a voice said to me, once: *are you ready yet?*"

I thought about it.

I could choose as selfishly as I liked. No sanctions could be applied if I chose not to do this thing. No retribution would come to me—not even disapproval, for there would be no one left to disapprove of anything. Not even regret; no self to do the regretting. If I refused to abet this unimaginable Mind, then it and the universe in which it inhered would cease to exist, fade away like the Boojum. I would have what it seemed I had always wanted—death, nonexistence, the peace that passeth all understanding—as well as my ultimate revenge on a world that had failed to love me enough to soothe my fear.

As I pondered my answer, I contemplated the shimmering green light. Now that I knew it was The Mind, I found that I yearned toward it inexpressibly. Absently, I recognized one of the shadowy forms that floated between me and the light. I knew him by his flickering grin, and knew that I should have been expecting him.

"It serves me right, I guess," I told my father. "All things considered, I think I got off lucky, if you want to know the truth. Moses spent longer than that in the wilderness, just outside the city limits of Promised Land. I can do thirty years of solitary confinement standing on my head."

Can there be many feelings as good as your father's warm approval? "Thank you, son. You make me proud."

Something came out of the green light and approached me. A body. Not a person, like Barbara and Dad and the others, but a physical human body. I recognized it as it came near, even bald.

It was me.

"Sam," my father said, "don't forget to tell Rachel she must take tissue samples from your old ruined body and bury them in her Egg, so that this one can have been cloned without causality paradox."

"Yes, Dad."

"Sam?"

"Yes, Dad?"

"If you ever decide to share any of this with your mother . . . give her my love."

"I will, Pop."

Something else came out of the light. A Time-Egg, bisected open like a clam to receive me . . .

Experimentally I tried on the body. It was familiar, like getting back on your first bicycle. Everything seemed to work right—

With mild dismay I realized that I could not get back out of it again. I was committed. Dad and Barbara and the others, the time-less tunnel and the green light itself began to fade from my ken as I lost the senses with which I had perceived them.

Damn, I thought, it would have been good to talk with Frank again. I'd really missed him. I realized too late that the music which had been playing unheeded somewhere in the distant background of my thoughts had been his attempt to soothe me with wry humour: Dylan's "I Shall be Released."

Ah well. He would still be there when I returned. And perhaps by then I would have learned more about how to love him back.

The Egg closed around me and sealed. It filled with air, and my new body took its first breath.

Without tears—

I thought I heard my father say, "We'll all be waiting for you—"

And then he was gone and there was a me and a not-me, an up and a down, a sky and an earth, both tinted blue.

I could see the Place of Maples all around me. My Egg was two meters to the west of the one Nazz had been trying to get buried. I touched the inner surface. The Egg opened, and sunlight and colours seared my brand new eyes. I stepped out onto the forest floor, onto the planet Earth, into my life—which was already in progress.

I breathed clean country air, smelled the good smells of the woods, felt the cool breeze on my naked body and the pleasant discomfort of twigs and leaves and pine needles under my bare feet. The day was beautiful.

I checked the sun, decided that I probably could spare the time . . . and after a brief search, found Mucus the Moose. Rachel, or possibly Nazz, had stood him up in a shady spot where he had a good view of everything. We said hello, and I gave him Frank's regards.

When I was halfway down the hill I heard the shotgun go off, and began to hurry. . . .

❧EIGHTEEN❧

IT WAS A bright and balmy night.

The huge loft writhed with hundreds of hippies, colorfully costumed and exuberantly high. The air was saturated with sounds and smells and smoke. Sounds of greetings and laughter and music and gossip. Smells of beer and food and the sweat of happy horny hairy people, and, under all, the smells of the cows who customarily lived downstairs (boarded elsewhere for the night). Smoke of grass and hash and tobacco and kerosene. The great hardwood floor shuddered under dancing feet; the ceiling trembled with the roar of chattering throats; the walls quivered from the energy and merriment contained within them.

On a couple of hay bales, at the east end of the second story of Louis Amys' fabulous barn, I sat and played my new dulcimer with a dozen other musicians—three guitars I knew and two I was glad to meet, Skipper Beckwith's standup bass, Norman's flute, Layne on sax, Bill on electric piano, Eric with his bongos, Jarvis making a fiddle talk in three languages, and a lady I didn't know with a handmade lute; all of us jamming around a figure in 4/4 that was alternately folk, country, R&B and three different flavors of jazz—and told myself that if this was, as all reports indicated, the Sunset of the Age of Aquarius, it was in many ways as sweet or sweeter than the Dawning. The music was better, the drugs were better, the people just as goodhearted but less naive—even the damned war seemed to be nearing some kind of an end.

It was looking like a promising year. LBJ had died in January, his hair grown as long as any hippie's (little did we suspect he would be the last competent president in that century); that same day the U.S. Supreme Court had guaranteed a woman's right to an abortion in the first trimester; five days later the United States had abolished the draft. The Watergate pack were savaging Nixon like sharks in a feeding frenzy; a month before a black man had been elected mayor of Los Angeles; Brezhnev had that very day signed an agreement not to provoke a nuclear war; the first Skylab crew had splashed down that morning; and next month they were expecting over half a million people at a rock festival in Watkins Glen, New York. (They got 'em, too.) Telesat Canada had launched the Anik 2 satellite in April; the Montréal Canadiens had whipped the Chicago Blackhawks in six to take the Stanley Cup in May; the Canadian government was in the process of withdrawing its cease-fire observers from Viet Nam.

The ending of the U.S. draft alone would have been sufficient cause for joy in a community of mostly ex-American residents of Canada, and since that had occurred in January this was our first chance to celebrate as a tribe. Between that and Nixon's public humiliation and the splendidness of the weather, it seemed that this was fated to be the most festive Solstice Gathering ever held on the Mountain.

But the joy ran deeper than that. There was more to it than that.

I could see most of the Sunrise Gang from where I sat. Malachi, Tommy, Lucas and two of the summer crew, Roger and Elaine, all were doing an indescribable dance that Sally had made up and taught them, and several dozen others were trying to imitate it with only modest success. You had to have lived with your partners for a year or so; it was that kind of dance. But even those who couldn't quite get it right were having fun.

"Fast" Layne finished a solo, and somebody else yelled, "Let's go home," and we all jumped in on the final chorus, licks flying like fireworks, harmonies meshing like the gears in the wheel that winds the world. We finished with a barroom walkout, held it, held it, held it, grinning like thieves—then let it resolve, and beat that final chord to death with a stick.

The room exploded with applause, and we musicians smiled at each other without words or need for any, and people came and gave us homebrewed beer and apple cider pressed that day and joints and pipes of freshly cured homegrown reefer and handshakes and hugs and offers of sex and invitations to come play in their neck of the woods anytime, by Jesus.

George and Bert began to play the Beatles' "Come Together"; half of the room began to sing along. There was no place for a dulcimer, and the vocal was out of my key; I cased my instrument and decided to circulate a little. I greeted and was greeted by twenty people on the way across the room, three on the ladder, half a dozen at the foot of it and perhaps a dozen more on my way past the dairy stalls to the outdoors. As I passed out through the huge double doors I met my host, Louis, a broad-shouldered heavyset man with a pirate's grin, a philosopher's soul and the constitution of an ox, and congratulated him on throwing the best party since Christ was a cowboy, an assessment with which he heartily agreed. Louis was going to be a rare and special spice in The Mind one day.

I was a few yards into the shadows, finishing a piss, when I spotted Snaker and Ruby over by Louis's house, sitting on a huge chopping block and nuzzling each other. I ambled over and joined them. "Hi, you two. Sorry: you three. How are you?"

Snaker looked up and smiled. "Growing. Changing. All three of us."

"Well, there's only one way to avoid change."

Ruby shook her head. "Even that doesn't work. We know that now. When you die, you just end up in The Mind—and start going through the biggest changes of all."

I shook my own head. "You're right, but that's not what I meant."

"Oh." Now Snaker shook *his* head, violently, but she ignored him. "All right, how *do* you avoid change?"

"Never break a dollar."

She turned to Snaker. "In the future, my darling, I will place greater reliance on your judgment."

He nodded. "It's in the eyes. When his eyes get big and round and innocent like that, you know he's going to lay one of those."

"I'll remember."

He squinted up at me. Ruby had taken his glasses off. "Jesus, Sam, you look exhausted."

"With my factory-new, wrinkle-free face, how can you tell? People have been telling me all night how *young* I look."

"The way your shoulders slump. How do you feel?"

"Shot," I said, and then seeing his face, "Hey, I'm sorry, brother. Bad joke."

He looked down and to the right, back up, turned red—and shrugged. "It's okay, man. You're entitled. I never thought I could shoot at a guy and still be his friend—nevermind I *hit* the son of a bitch. I grant you the right to break my balls for life. It was just that I thought you were about to ruin *everything*—"

"I was."

"Rachel had already infected about five hundred people with her little microbugs, more than enough to see that The Mind would carry on the task—but you were talking about not just killing Rachel but *blowing up the Egg.* Wasting all the data. The experiment wouldn't have been repeated if it failed, you know? The Mind would have assumed that history had rejected the attempt to mess with it."

I put my hand on his shoulder and met his eyes squarely. What passed between us was not a true telepathic exchange, perhaps, but when it was over we both knew that we forgave each other. "This is not something I say a lot, but . . . thank you for killing me, my friend."

That took the sober look off his face. "My pleasure," he said, and giggled. "Any time." Ruby smiled approval at me. "Maybe you can do the same for me someday—" We were all laughing now. "—one good turn—" "He's bleeding terrible," Ruby cried, quoting a Carry On movie we all knew, and Snaker and I chorused the antiphon: "Never mind his qualifications, is he all right?" and before long we had laughed ourselves into anoxia.

"Ah God, Sammy," she said after a while, wiping tears, "it must have been so *weird* to bury yourself."

Sprawled on the ground, I giggled again. "I won't say it wasn't. But how many men get to attend their own funeral? Without getting soaked by a mortician for an arm and a leg?"

"Still," she said. "I'd be all sentimental about my first body."

Snaker snorted laughter. "Sentimental? You know what this fucking ghoul did? He robbed his own body!"

Ruby looked at me.

"Well, shit, I was naked. And they were my best Frye boots, I wasn't going to *bury* the—"

I'm not sure just what it was she threw at me; it was dark.

After a while they got up hand in hand. With his other hand Snaker did his magic trick, took a toke, gave one to Ruby, and passed it to me. "Here you go, Sam. Ruby and I are going to go over by Louis's lower forty and engage in a small religious ritual together."

"Really? Which god?"

"Pan," Ruby said demurely.

I accepted the joint. "Pot and Pan, a good combination. Joy, you two. Don't drown the baby."

When they left I took over their seat and contemplated the great barn full of party, blazing against the night, radiating happy sounds and good vibes. People passing in and out of the big doors seemed to move in groups of at least two. I saw no other singletons. Vehicles came and went. Mosquitoes sang, stoned to the eyebrows. The sound of Layne's sax drifted across the clear Summer night. Maybe a distant train whistle in the night is as poignant as a distant sax, and then again maybe it isn't. Ah, there was a singleton—

She looked around, saw me, and came to me. "There you are, Sam. Your hair and beard look good."

I'd been growing them all night. "Thanks, Rachel. What's happening?"

A smile was getting to look more and more natural on her face these days. She didn't have smile wrinkles yet, but maybe she was developing creases. "I'm having a wonderful time. I have met so many people, Sam! I understand people better when I see them in a large group, interacting in harmony."

I sighed. "You must really miss The Mind."

Her smile wavered slightly, then firmed. "I left behind most of my memories of it. Had to. I remember enough to know that it will be very good to rejoin it. Worth dying for. Yes, I miss it."

"So do I."

I relit the roach of Snaker's joint. Now that she no longer had to keep track of a complex lie around me, she could afford to toke with me, and did so.

After a little silence I said, "Rachel?"

"Yes?"

"It seems like I've got decades more of this shit to live through. It's going to be real hard, trying to live it just exactly as if I were the same jackass I was the day before yesterday."

"It doesn't have to be 'just exactly,' Sam. History can heal itself around small things, or else I could not be here. You must not—since you did not/have not/will not—marry or have children, and you must not die until your fate kills you. And it would be a good idea not to become famous if you can help it. But I don't think even natural law can command a man to be a fool." She took my hand.

"Huh." I pondered that for a while.

"Sam?"

"Uh?"

"I've been invited to so many communities around the province tonight that you will not be seeing a lot of me in the next year."

"Well, sure. That was the plan. The Task—"

"There's a ride leaving for Cape Breton next week."

"Oh. That soon, eh?"

"I can put it off if you need me. You've been through a lot."

"And you help. But a week should be plenty. Thank you for asking."

"I'm grateful to you, Sam. For everything."

"Well, I hate to think of some guy dying in Cape Breton next week and missing the boat because you were hung up on the North Mountain holding my hand."

She shook her head. "I'm just the first boat to hit the beach. The next wave will start a million years ago, and flood the ecosphere with indetectable little backup bugs that home on human neural tissue. We're not going to miss *anyone* if we can help it, Sam!"

"I believe you."

I tilted back my head and looked at the stars. "Rachel . . . do you suppose there are *other* Minds out there?"

"I think there must be. I wonder sometimes: if we could find them, and learn to bond with them as we have with ourselves—if a billion Minds become neurons in a Super-Mind—would we become The User? Would we go *all* the way back and begin and end everything with a Bang?"

"Wow." I watched the stars and thought about that one. A shooting star fell; I made a wish.

"Sam?"

"Yes?"

"Would you like to walk out under the stars with me now and make love?"

"Very much. But there's something else I have to do first before it gets too late. Come with?"

"Of course."

❖ ❖ ❖

When we got upstairs the crowd was still doing a mass sing-along, songs to which everybody knew the words, and most of the musicians had drifted away to readjust their bloodsugar. The Sunrise Gang were still where I'd left them. I brought Rachel over to the hay bale I'd been sitting on earlier, sat on an adjacent one facing her. The group singers were into the final mantra section of "Hey, Jude," and Rachel and I scatted with it until it was dissolved by common consent.

And then I began to Om.

She joined me with her strong smoky alto at once, and others nearby picked it up immediately. The Sunrise Gang came in with the particularly pure tone I had expected of them, and were reinforced by dozens of others. The note hunted, then steadied, tonic and dominant, a drone that grew and swelled and filled the barn, filled my head, filled the world—

—and Malachi caught my eye, and winked, and began to scat around the drone—

I laughed right in the middle of my chant, for sheer joy; it gave the sound a transient vibrato. And then I jumped in after him.

What we all built together then was—briefly, too briefly—something very like my mental picture of The Mind.

Remarkably so, when you consider that at that point in time, probably not more than twenty or thirty people in the room were actually members of Rachel's conspiracy. . . .

Does that seem like a lot? All I can say is, why not? Membership doesn't require a special, extraordinary, highly educated mind. A mind as simple and unsophisticated as Mona Bent's can encompass our conspiracy and accept telepathy. The mind need not be brilliant or well stocked with information to be one of us, to respond to our call: it need only not be suffused with self-hatred. And our membership committee is a telepath.

I know: hippies can't keep secrets, especially juicy ones.

Well, suppose each of us *had* spilled the beans to some one close friend, and in the end, half the hippies at the Solstice Party had learned the secret? Suppose further they even believed it. What would be the effect?

They would all begin to live their lives as though conscience meant something, as though karma was real, as though there is a god. Well, *most of them were trying to learn to do that anyway*, even though they knew better. Now they would know better than to know better, is all. They'd tend to leave the woods, over time, scatter over the planet and live as righteously as possible, find or invent all kinds of right livelihood. They'd stop banding together in self-defense, and spread out and go where they were needed, disappear into the mix.

Do you understand now why I'm telling this story to you, and why I don't care much one way or the other whether you believe it? If you choose to do so, all that you can do about it is to stop being so afraid of death, personal and planetary, and to start living as though you are one day going to have to account for your actions to everyone you've ever loved. How can that hurt?

It's now the Nineteen-Nineties, and pessimism and despair are in fashion. There are almost no hippies left on the Mountain. Fundamentalists rage through the world like hungry beasts. Belief in apocalypse is everywhere, and a numb dumb fatalistic yearning to *get it over with*. Wonderful excuses to abandon responsibility. Every day our news media bring us a billion cries of pain, and there is nothing we can do about any of them—as individuals. Small wonder we feel the growing urge to put ourselves out of our misery.

Hang on. Just for a couple of decades, that's all I ask. The cavalry is coming. It is a pitcher of cream you're drowning in: keep churning. If you don't, you're going to feel really stupid one day soon. Keep living as though it mattered—because it *does*.

If you've ever really wondered where all the Hippies went, and not merely used the question as a way of denying that they ever existed— well, I will tell you where *some* of them went: they diffused throughout the planet like invading viruses. They went underground in plain sight, simply by changing their appearance, and they put their attention on lowering their race's psychic immune system, dismantling its defenses of intolerance of anything new or different, and thus making it ready for the ultimate transplant, preparing it like an ovum for invasion.

And they all lived happily ever after.

⊹EPILOGUE⊹

I guarantee that every word of this story is the truth.

LIFEHOUSE

❖❖

For the two Evelyns
. . . may we meet again in The Mind . . .

We come spinning out of nothingness,
Scattering stars like dust.

Look at these worlds spinning out of nothingness:
This is within your power.

Out beyond ideas of right-doing and wrong-doing,
There is a field.
I'll meet you there . . .

—Rumi,
a thousand years ago in Lebanon

If the Eternal Return is not allowed by modern
physics,
and if the Heat Death can also be avoided,
then eternal progress is possible.

—Prof. Frank Tipler,
PHYSICS OF IMMORTALITY, 1993

❖PROLOGUE❖

THE TAR BABY'S ALARM caught them making love, or the whole emergency might never have happened.

It might seem odd that they let something as frivolous as sex distract them even momentarily from their responsibilities. They were as dedicated, motivated and committed to their work as any guardians in history, as responsible as it was possible to be. And they had, after all, been married to each other for over nine centuries at that point.

But then, theirs was—even for their kind—one of the Great Marriages. They had mutually agreed on their five hundredth anniversary that in their opinion, things were just getting really good, and as their millennial approached, both still felt the same. And perhaps even we mortals can dimly understand that any hobby which endures over such a span of time must have within it certain elements of obsession. They had long since taken into their lovemaking, as into their marriage itself, the spirit of the Biblical injunction, "Whatsoever thy hand findeth to do, do it with all thy might," and they were good at finding things to do.

The precise timing of the alarm, moreover, was more than diabolical: it was Murphian. For several hours they had been constructing a complex and beautiful choreography of ecstasy together, a four-dimensional structure of pleasure and joy extending through space and time. A DNA double-helix would actually be a fairly accurate three-dimensional model of it. It was itself part of a larger, more complicated structure that had been under creation for nearly a week, a sort of interwoven pattern of patterns of pleasure and joy, of which this particular movement was meant to be the capstone. The tocsin sounded in both their skulls *just* as, in the words of Jake Thackray, "They were getting to a very important bit . . ." and for two whole seconds, both honestly mistook it for a hyperbole of their imaginations. By the time they understood it was real, a necessity at once emotional, biological and artistic urged them to ignore it—just for a moment.

This, in their defense, they did not do. Their responsibility was too much a part of who they were. Orgasm may be the source of all meaning—but it needs a universe in which to mean. The instant they realized the alarm was not a shared hallucination they stopped doing what they were doing (or more precisely, stopped paying attention to the fact that they were doing it), queried the Tar Baby, downloaded a detailed report of the situation, and studied it, fully prepared to leap out of bed and hit the ground running if the emergency seemed to warrant it.

It did not. Indeed, it seemed to be practically over. Only one sophont appeared to be involved—and not a sophisticated one. It carried only a single (pathetic) weapon, and no data transmission gear of any kind. The Tar Baby reported no difficulty at all in investing it, and was even now reprogramming it. There was another higher lifeform of some kind present, about fifty meters away from the Egg, but it did not display sentience signatures and thus could not be a significant threat. To top it all off, the whole nonevent was taking place less than two thousand meters away, a distance they could cover in seconds.

Yes, doctrine did mandate a suspenders-and-belt physical visit to the site to obtain eyeball confirmation of all data. But doctrine did not (quite) say that it absolutely had to be done *this instant* . . . not unless there were complicating factors present. They both double-checked, and there were not. They very nearly triple-checked. They concluded, first separately and then in rapport, that a delay of as much as fifteen minutes in the on-site follow-up inspection could not reasonably pose a serious or even a significant risk. They ran their logic past the Tar Baby, which concurred. It agreed to notify them at once if the situation were to degenerate, and to preserve all data.

This whole process had taken perhaps three seconds, a total of five seconds since the alarm had gone off. The weeklong work of art was still salvageable. Sighing happily, they returned to their erotic choreography, and in under ten minutes brought it to a conclusion satisfactory in every sense of the word, the brief hiatus actually improving it trivially, both as sensation and as art. They spent an additional five minutes on breath recovery and afterglow, and were *just* about to get up, less than fifteen minutes after the Tar Baby's first call—when suddenly it called again.

And this time it *shrieked.*

They came that close to being vigilant enough. Less than fifteen minutes late on a pointless backup. Less than one minute *too* late.

Unfortunately, they were not playing horseshoes.

And so the whole universe very nearly ceased to ever have existed. . . .

❖CHAPTER 1❖
A Walk in the Park

JUNE BELLAMY was walking in the woods, listening to FM on dedicated headphones and thinking deep thoughts about mortality and love—or perhaps about love and mortality—the first time she came close to annihilating upwards of twenty billion people.

It was definitely the mook's fault, not June's—the whole thing. That is quite clear. All she wanted to do, at the start, was to grieve, and she had gone out of her way to do so privately. Nonetheless she was—thanks to the mook, and the headphones—the one who ended up personally endangering some twenty billion lives. Repeatedly. Whereas he was out of the story almost at once, never had more than a moment's worry over it, and would not even remember that for nearly a century.

It is almost enough to make one suspect God of a sense of irony.

It was a splendid Fall afternoon in Vancouver. June was thirty-three years old and in excellent health. The woods she walked through were part of the former University Endowment Lands now called Pacific Spirit Regional Park, adjoining the sprawling campus of the University of British Columbia: about the only land on the Vancouver peninsula that had never been settled by white people or developed, and at least in theory never would be. The trail she had chosen had good drainage; despite the fact that it had rained for twelve of the past fourteen days—excessive even for Vancouver— leaves that had been lying in sunshine today *crunched* under her walking shoes. There was just enough crispness in the air to encourage activity, and the trapped ozone of several thunderstorms to add alertness. Traffic and houses and bustling human activity were no more than a kilometer or so away in any direction—but no trace of them reached here, into the forest sanctum. There were surely other hikers in the woods—but not many, and few June was likely to meet. It was a wonderful place in which to be conflicted.

The only death she knew to be on her personal horizon was the impending death of her mother, in San Francisco, of colon cancer. She thought it more than enough reason to be conflicted.

She had just that day returned from what she knew would be her last visit with her mother. She had known since the first phone call from her father, the previous week, that Laura Bellamy had at best a matter of days left. The cancer had come out of nowhere and gutted her without warning or mercy: by the time she was symptomatic she was, as June's father put it on the phone, a dead woman walking.

And by the time June had arrived at her hospital bedside she was clearly done walking. She had looked shrunken and—the pun made June tremble the instant it occurred to her, because she could never ever share it with anyone—and *cured,* like leather: she had looked like someone who *ought* to have that many wires and tubes coming out of her. She was fifty-four, and looked ninety. June knew exactly the phrase her lover/partner Paul would have used to describe his almost-mother-in-law's condition if he'd been there: "circling the drain." She'd looked like a crude, ill-thought-out parody of Laura Bellamy, one that was not intended to be sustained for long.

But she had also looked—this was the part June could not get out of her mind, as she walked through the forest—fearless. June's mother had, to the best of her recollection, always had the usual human allotment of fears, doubts, and uncertainties. Now she had none. It was clear in her sunken, shining eyes. June had wanted mightily to ask her about that, to discuss it with her. But it had proven almost completely impossible.

That had been the very worst part of the whole depressing experience. Everyone in the room, including the Alzheimer's patient in the next bed, had known perfectly well that Laura Bellamy was terminal. But June's father, Frank, suffered from—clutched like a drowner—the illusion that his wife did not suspect anything of the sort. The notion that even a doctor who was trying to could have concealed such news from Laura Bellamy was ridiculous, but Frank was in deep denial—and, as always, needed his wife's help with it. He needed to believe he was protecting her from *something*, even if it was only knowledge of her doom. He had met June in the hospital lobby and explained solemnly that they must be very very careful not to let Laura suspect the Awful Truth. By the time June had realized he was serious, it was too late to protest; they were on their way in the door of her mother's room.

Where she found, to her horror, that Laura Bellamy would rather have died than admit in her husband's presence that she knew she was dying. Unlike most men of his generation, Frank Bellamy had not often needed his wife to simulate ignorance or stupidity; she was willing to indulge him, this once.

And therefore June, who had abandoned her partner in the middle of an important project and traveled thirteen hundred kilometers for the specific purpose of having her Last Conversation with her mother, who had rehearsed it in her mind for several tight-lipped dry-eyed days because she knew this was her one and only window, had been unable to have it . . . had been forced to smile and chatter cheery inanities about how everything was back home in Canada these days and even help, herself, to shore up the grotesque illusion that her mother was soon going to recover and resume her interrupted life.

Horror.

They'd held a wordless conversation with their eyes, of course, while the rest of their faces spoke hollow lines for Frank's benefit. But eye contact lacks bandwidth; the communication had been ambiguous, fragmentary, profoundly unsatisfactory for June.

Once—once—she had succeeded in inventing an errand that would require her father to leave the room for five minutes. And then she had gone and dithered away three of them, finishing up the useless surface conversational thread they'd been chewing when he left, too nervous to begin. Finally she'd said, "Mom—we *have* to talk."

"Yes, dear," her mother had said at once. "But if we take it out of the box now, there's no way we can have it all tucked back in again in two minutes . . . and that's when he'll be back."

She'd made the words come out calmly. "There probably isn't

going to be another chance. I've gotta get back to Canada, and I can't risk coming back."

"Yes, there will."

"Phone? He can't stay here twenty-four hours a day—"

Her mother had smiled at that. They had never had the clichéd mother-daughter phone relationship; Laura Bellamy felt that talking on the telephone was unsatisfactory, and that talking long-distance was like hemorrhaging: something to be done in brief bursts if absolutely necessary. "They won't let you have a cell phone around all this medical gear, and I'm afraid I'm just too lazy to hobble down the hall these days. Don't worry, dear: we'll talk."

"*When?* How?" Her voice had risen in pitch, and she was furious with herself for losing control. She was *not* here to add her own emotional burdens to her mother's obviously overfull agenda.

But her mother's serenity had only increased. "Do you know, I don't have the faintest idea? And I don't know how I know. But I'm quite certain—so don't worry, June. All the things we need to say to each other will be said . . . in time."

June's eyes had narrowed suspiciously. "What, are you going religious on me, Ma? Now?"

Laura had smiled. "I don't think so. I'm still just as fundamentally ignorant as I ever was, about all the important things. I have no Answers; I've had no revelations. But somehow . . ." Her face had changed subtly, in a way June could not classify. "Somehow, I'm not . . . not quite as *clueless* as I was. Just . . . just trust me. All right? We *will* get it all said, one day—and we'll probably find out that we already knew most of it. And meanwhile, it's all going to be alright."

And with theatrical timing, her father had reentered the room just then.

The next hour or so of their discourse had been transmitted by eye contact, with its terrible signal-to-noise ratio (was that a punctuation mark? or just a blink?), and hampered by the need to keep a plausible surface conversation going with an inarticulate man. Shortly June had found herself unable to decide whom she resented more: her father, who had the nerve to find his beloved wife's brutal dying too much to bear, or her mother, who, faced with a choice between her daughter's needs and her husband's, had the nerve to make the only choice she possibly could. And of course, awareness of her own irrational selfish resentment had made June despise herself, so she had resented them both for that, too.

And then, as visiting hours were drawing to a close, her mother had said, "You know, I read a book once, I forget who wrote it, but he said the most beautiful thing. He said—let me see if I can get this right—he said, 'There is really only one sense. It is the sense of touch. All of the other senses are merely other ways of touching.' "

And she had held out her hand—her shrunken, IV-trailing hand—and of course June had taken it, and—

—and something had happened. Even now, walking through the woods of Pacific Spirit Park back home in British Columbia with Coltrane whispering in her ears, June was not sure just what. But information exchange had taken place. Data of some kind had come surging up her arm from her mother's feeble grip, and data of some other and different kind had flowed in the other direction.

It had *not* been the "getting it all said" that her mother had spoken of earlier. The questions June had walked into that hospital room with were still unanswered; the words she had gone there to say were yet unspoken. But *some* kind of profound communication had taken place, something just as far *beyond* talking as talking was beyond eye contact. (And something, therefore, just as unsatisfying as eye contact had been—if for different reasons.) June did not have a mystical bone in her body . . . but she was quite certain that her mother had taken something from her in that brief physical contact, and imparted something important to her in return. Something almost tangible, in the form of an energy almost palpable. Some kind of change had occurred in June. She just wished she knew what, so she could explain it to Paul when she finally saw him again.

She was still trying to analyze it, as she wandered heedless through the woods, jazz saxophone playing softly in her FM headphones. *How,* she thought, *am I different?*

I am different in some way that I cannot define. Changed. I sense that the change is, or probably will be, temporary. Nonetheless it is important. And it reminds *me of something . . .*

The memory surfaced. It had taken awhile because it was a memory not of a real event but of an imagined one.

This is what I used to imagine it was like to have a magic spell put on you!

When she was a little girl, a voracious consumer of Tolkien and his disciples, she had often acted out fantasy scenarios of her own devising in her solitary play hours. This was what it had felt like just after the wizard had placed his enchantment upon her, and just before it was fully activated by the inevitable appearance of the handsome warrior. It had something to do with the inevitability of that appearance, and the certainty that they would recognize each other at once. It was, now that she thought of it, probably one of her earliest gropings, in imagination, toward the concept of empowerment.

Well, she already had a handsome warrior in inventory, thank you very much. She *had* recognized her Tall Paul on sight . . . and had basically won him in combat and directed that he be scrubbed and brought to her tent. Even better, he had a tent of his own now. She was as empowered in that area as she felt any need to be.

But she did, now that she thought of it, feel more than usually empowered today, in a strange sort of way. Usually when she was in raw nature like this, she felt like a stranger, who must be careful not to offend through thoughtlessness; like a visitor to the zoo, whose gawking curiosity is a kind of impertinence; like a tourist. Today she felt, for once, at home here in the woods. And the woods seemed to agree.

She saw more wildlife than usual, for instance. Several squirrels. A raccoon. Something she took to be a weasel, that browsed her with his eyes, like a penny-pinching shopper, and decided she was too expensive. Birds—June *never* saw birds in the woods, even when she was right underneath the chirping things and the branches were bare, but so far she had seen at least half a dozen, without even thinking about it. All of these wild things noticed her in return, and were wary of her—but none of them seemed to feel any need to flee. Perhaps they were all under the influence of the magic spell.

Between her light head and her heavy heart, she felt no alarm at all when she became aware of the man ahead of her on the trail, even though he was clearly a sleazebag.

She reached up to switch off her radio headphones, succeeded only in turning the volume all the way off, and settled for that.

She did not even momentarily wish she had her handsome warrior with her for backup. She was armed and competent—and more than that: somehow she knew that on this day of days, she could face down a mugger with impunity, calm a psycho with her gaze, unman any rapist. Death—not the concept but the grim reality, up close and personal, ravaging one of her loved ones—had in some odd way given her power, and she could sense it. She mistook an electric tingling in her earlobes for a symptom of it. She studied the sleaze-bag carefully, but her pulse remained steady.

Caucasian male, about her age. He looked like when he was five Santa had asked him what he wanted to be when he grew up, and he'd chirped, "A perpetrator." In the distant neighborhood where her lover had grown up, in a country adjoining America called The Bronx, he would have been termed a mook. He could not possibly have passed within a thousand meters of a cop in thick fog without instant radar lock taking place. At the moment, even in the middle of nowhere and believing himself unobserved, he was managing to skulk, mope, loiter, creep and look furtive, all at the same time—a virtuoso performance. He reminded her of a man she knew called Hopeless Harry.

He was well over two meters tall, and seemed to mass well under fifty kilos. He wore clothes meant for other people, who unless they were color-blind were not missing them, and a jailhouse haircut. On his back was a large designer backpack. Its designers had intended it to say *behold me: I am rich, stylish and fit* but on him it had the look of a false mustache, making him look, impossibly, even more suspicious.

June had been moving quietly, one with the forest, even before she saw him; now she became a Shao-Lin monk walking the rice paper, leaving no trace. Her first instinct had been to change course and avoid him . . . but that backpack intrigued her. An instinct only slightly younger on the evolutionary scale told her it contained treasure. June Bellamy liked treasure. And she was in the mood for a distraction from her thoughts.

She left the path and shadowed him for a little less than a hundred meters, paralleling the meandering trail. He was the kind of mook who could have been tailed through the French Quarter during Mardi Gras; for someone with a magic spell on her in a forest this damp he was candy. Twice, he spun craftily on his heel in the hope of surprising someone following him; both times his gaze passed right over her without stopping. *Call me Chingachcook,* she thought smugly.

He kept staring from side to side as he walked, looking for something. Occasionally he would leave the path, pick a spot at apparent random, paw at the earth briefly with his sneakered foot (it was probably the name that had first attracted him to sneakers), and then move on.

Finally his eye was caught by a large, freshly toppled tree about twenty meters from the trail. The bank on which it stood had been undercut by centuries of Vancouver rain, and the days of sustained downpour just ended had finished the job. The huge elm had fallen to a 45-degree angle before being caught like a drunk by its neighbors; roots clawed at the sky like tentacles frozen in spasm, bearded with brown glistening tendrils that made her think of shit tinsel. He looked around one last time, failed again to see her fifty meters away, and unslung his stylish backpack.

She began to understand when he removed a collapsible entrenching tool and assembled it. The earth the tree had lately protected was freshly turned, easy to dig. There was indeed treasure in that bag, and Captain Kidd there proposed to bury it. June smiled.

And almost instantly felt a stab of sadness. A week ago, such a gift from God would have been a blessing and a pure joy. Now it was a consolation prize. A prize booby.

Still, she was forced to admit to some interest in just *how much* consolation; she took a position of vantage and dropped into a squat as the mook began digging.

The longer he dug, the better she felt. The deeper he wanted his plunder buried, the more likely it was to console her. But when he began approaching a depth and dimensions which would have served for the grave of a child, nearly waist-deep in the hole he was making, she entertained a brief Pythonesque fantasy in which, having buried his treasure, he would protect its secret by shooting the guy who'd dug the hole. That way she wouldn't have to wait for him to pass out of earshot to uncover the swag, and there'd be that nice handy entrenching tool.

Come to think of it, digging up a grave wasn't something she was really in the mood for, just now—even one with treasure in it. She'd settle for marking the spot, and coming back with Paul sometime. Let him do the grunt work; that was what handsome warriors were for. Well, one of the things.

The mook's shovel, which had been saying *chuff—shrrrp* . . . *chuff—shrrrp* . . . *chuff—shrrrp* with decreasing rhythm like an asthmatic slowly recovering from an attack, suddenly said *chuff—shrrrp* . . . *clack!*

Not *clank!* as if it had hit a rock. Not *chup!* as if it had hit a root. *Clack!* As if it had struck . . . she didn't know, plastic or plexiglass or formica or something. Something manmade.

He made a muttered sound of irritation that, if it had become a word, would have been "Naturally," set that shovelful of dirt aside carefully, without any *shrrp*, then offset his point of attack slightly and tried again.

Clack!

"Aw, fuck!" he groaned.

No, *no,* she wanted to say. *"Fuck!" is the sound of an axe sinking into a tree. That was "Clack!"*

As if insisting on his point of view, he said "Fuck!" again, louder. But this time, the way he said it was so different, and so incongruous, so full of an almost religious awe, that it caused her to focus her attention on him. Because of that—remarkably—she actually recognized what happened to him next. It was a thing she had never expected to see in quite that context, but if you were looking right at it and paying close attention, it was unmistakable.

Standing up, hip-deep in an unfinished grave, fully dressed, shovel still held in both hands, the mook threw back his head, keened like a forlorn kitten, and had an orgasm.

It might even have been the orgasm of his life. As she stared, marveling but never doubting, June was impressed. Thanks to her mother, she had been confident in her own sexuality since the age of fourteen, but she had to admit that in a varied life she had never received applause quite as enthusiastic and sincere as the mook was now awarding to . . . no one at all. It was more than vocal: his body language was so emphatic and so explicit that she decided he might well have found work as a male erotic dancer, even with that body.

I've heard the expression "Fuck the world" countless times, of course, she thought, *but I'd never actually seen it done before.*

He was not even rubbing his groin against the wall of the pit in which he stood, though he could have. Instead he simply thrust, violently, at the air itself, and seemed to find it a more than adequate lover.

For all its intensity, the event seemed to take somewhat less time than usual, at least in her experience, and when it was over, he simply let go of the shovel and sat down in the hole, his head disappearing almost completely from view. As the top of it bobbed up and down with his slowing respiration, its coconut-husk hair made it resemble a hedgehog trying to frighten off an intruder with a display of puffing bristles.

Something in that hole, June thought, *causes men to have instant orgasms, of higher than usual quality. I might just find a use for such a thing. God help me: I am starting to feel consoled. . . .*

She waited, and watched, her vision so narrowed and focused that she seemed to see him in the crosshairs of a periscope, her hearing so acute she became aware of a mosquito hovering near her left wrist (the silenced headphones passed ambient sound so well, she had forgotten she was wearing them), her attention so concentrated she ignored the mosquito.

"Angel Gerhardt," he said aloud, his voice hoarse but happy.

Of course. After you have sex with the universe, it is polite to offer your name. He must be a nonsmoker.

"Heinz," he said, "but everybody calls me Angel."

I see, she thought. *And your address?*

"Nine four seven four Williams Street. Two two two, fourteen hundred. Frosty at eWorld dot com." Despite their prosaic nature, he spoke each of these factoids blissfully, as though they were special joys to be shared in afterglow. "No, there's my old lady and another couple and a dog and three cats. Linda Wu. Tony Solideri and Mary Carry-the-Kettle."

There were short pauses between each sentence. By now she understood that something silent in that hole was interrogating him, somehow, and she memorized every syllable. Whatever it was, was a potential enemy, and she did not want it better informed than her.

"I was looking to bury a couple o's of flake till it cooled off a little," he said, still lazily ecstatic. "Yeah. No. Yeah, they do. No, they don't. Yeah, I'm sure. I don't trust them. Well, Linda, a little." Even those last two sentences sounded happy.

The next pause was long enough to give her time to work that out. Yes, his lover and housemates knew he was out burying cocaine. No, they didn't know, or even suspect, just where. This suited June. She was much less interested in even two ounces of coke than in whatever the *hell* was in that hole . . . but either way it would be nice never to have to meet anyone who would have Angel Gerhardt for a friend.

Then she caught herself, remembering the e-mail handle he had revealed: Frosty. Admittedly, it was more energy-efficient than walking around wearing a sandwich sign that read, "I deal cocaine in felony weight"—but not much smarter. Angel could not be considered a reliable judge of *what* his lover and housemates did or didn't know. Worse, all the neighborhoods that bordered on Pacific Spirit Park were upscale: he had probably attracted attention on his way into the woods. She did not believe anyone could have tailed her the way she had tailed him; nonetheless it came to her that it might be well to complete her business here and be gone quickly.

Angel seemed to agree. He said only one more word—" Okay"— then stood up in the hole, set down the shovel and began taking off his pants. A strange dread clutched at her, though she could not have explained why undressing was weirder than having a spontaneous orgasm dressed—but all he did was remove his threadbare boxer shorts, wipe himself off with them, drop them into the hole and put his pants back on. He was so skinny that he seemed to have no difficulty getting the pants off and on without removing his sneakers. Then he hoisted himself out of the hole and began hastily filling it back in. He did it more intelligently than she would have expected. When he was done, he collected underbrush and sprinkled it over the fresh-turned earth—again, more artistically than she'd have predicted. Then he put his backpack back on, picked up his shovel and walked away.

His course, apparently randomly chosen, brought him rather near to June before he reached the path again, but somehow she knew he was going to walk right by without seeing her, and he did. He wore a vague, fatuous smile, and his eyes were unfocused.

She glanced briefly toward the huge drunken tree. Whatever was down there under its uprooted base would probably stay there awhile. In any case she was not ready to confront it. She followed the backpack.

She was tempted at first to just stroll along beside Angel, since he seemed oblivious, but she resisted, and took up stealthy station fifty meters behind him again. She was glad when, a few hundred meters later, he stopped and shook himself like a man coming out of a deep reverie. She had plenty of time to become invisible before he turned and scanned his surroundings. His expression was inhabited now, but still serene. For an instant he reminded her absurdly of her mother in her hospital bed. He checked his watch then, muttered something she couldn't hear, and resumed walking.

Shortly he found another exposed bank, took out his shovel and began digging again.

As she watched, she noticed something subtle. He was not digging like a man who had already dug one hole this size this afternoon. Something seemed to have returned to him the energy he had expended earlier.

This time his task was accomplished without incident. She was not much surprised when he buried the entire backpack: now anyone who had noticed him enter the woods and saw him leave would know he had left something behind. The trick in finding it would then be to go to the only dry trail in the forest, and proceed as far as the *second* easy place to dig. The world had lost a great rocket scientist when Angel Gerhardt decided to go into the crystal trade. Sure enough, when he was done he left the shovel about five meters away (concealed by a mound of leaves that would stay there for at least an hour, unless a breeze came up), both to mark the spot and to make it easy for anyone who found the stash to dig it up.

Then he went away. He no longer looked serene; now he looked pooped. He dragged his feet. But he moved.

After she was certain he was out of earshot, June took her cell phone from her hip holster and dialed Paul's number, irritably removing her forgotten FM headphones when she hit them with the phone. Self-contained, with no wires to a Walkman or CD player on her person, they fell to the forest floor. She expected to get his machine and did; she suffered through the outgoing message with even more than her usual impatience, wishing for the thousandth time that he'd get a modern machine, which allowed your friends to cut off the message by pushing the proper key. The moment she heard the beep she began talking quickly and quietly.

"Honey, I'm into something heavy here. I'm walking in the Endowment Lands, and I ran across a mook looking to bury something nice just off the Lowrie Trail, Dorothy twice, but that's not the good part. He was digging away at the base of a huge old toppled elm tree, and he hit something with his shovel that made a sound like *clack*, something like plywood or plastic. And then—" She knew how all this was going to sound, but didn't want to edit it. "—I know this is nuts, but then he had an orgasm, all by himself, standing up. And then he started to talk out loud, as if somebody was grilling him— only I was only fifty meters away and I swear there was no one else there. He said his name was Angel Gerhardt and he lived over in the East End on William Street and his e-mail handle, God help us all, was 'Frosty,' and he named his girlfriend Linda Wu and his two housemates and said none of them knew where he planned to bury the . . . the thing . . . and the weird part was, he didn't say any of this like a mope giving information to the heat, he said it like a guy opening his soul to his new lover, happy as a clam. Then he filled the hole back in and buried the package in another spot. He's gone now. I'm going to put the package somewhere else—but I'm not going near that goddam fallen elm without you, and maybe Rosco. I don't know what we've got ahold of here, but whatever it is is very very big. Call me as soon as you get in, okay? I hope everything went okay."

She put the phone away and squatted there in the woods, thinking hard, for a minute—almost but not quite long enough. Then she got to her feet, went to the shovel and picked it up.

If she had thought just a little longer, it might have occurred to her that in fantasy stories, it is generally unwise to tamper with the belongings of one on whom a geas has been placed. The moment her fingers touched the shovel, she came.

⚜CHAPTER 2⚜
Silent light, Holy light

WALLY AND MOIRA had, in a sense, spent most of their adult lives training for the advent of the naked bald man. That didn't help them much.

Happy round people in their mid-forties, they were hard at work at 11 p.m. on Halloween night, side by side at their respective computers in the study of their Vancouver home—popularly known as The Only Dump In Point Grey—when a short sharp silent blast of very bright light burst in the big window behind them and momentarily washed out their screens. As it faded, they saw that they were both hung, their mice impotent; each rebooted at once, then used the brief interval of startup to adjust their blood-sugar levels, Wally with a bird's nest cookie and Moira with coffee.

"More Halloween nonsense?" Wally suggested as he chewed.

Moira frowned. "Thought we paid off the last of the little thugs hours ago."

"Maybe we should have given that Ace Ventura chocolate instead of rice cakes."

"It was instinctive. I see Ace Ventura: I think bowel movements: I reach for the fiber." She gulped coffee and glared at her monitor. "No, a smart-aleck kid going to that much trouble would pick something with bang, not flash. Why waste that much magnesium to not annoy somebody very much?"

"Right. Got to be a fan or fen, then. Dr. Techno, or one of the Latex Goddesses."

She shook her head. "Any other time of the year, I'd say sure. But this close to VanCon, all the fans bright enough are too *busy*. Like us. At least, they'd better be."

Wally finished his cookie hurriedly; his system was back up. "Maybe we should duck and cover," he suggested, typing furiously.

"Eh?"

"Maybe somebody just nuked Coquitlam. Or points east."

"Huh." She gave it half her attention; her own desktop had finally come up and typing with a coffee cup in one hand took some care. "Nah," she decided, reopening her application, "if the sound wave hasn't gotten here by now, we're okay. I gotta get this thing uploaded."

"Damn," he said. "It didn't save." He poked futilely at his own keyboard. "I lost the whole flippin' file."

Moira smirked and kept working. "You should get a Mac."

"I hate obsequious machines," he said automatically, and let it go. Mixed marriages can work, with enough good will. "You're right: if it was a nuke, it was way out in the Okanagan somewhere. Come Spring we'll have peaches the size of pumpkins."

"And use them for lawn lanterns," she agreed. "Seriously, what the hell do you suppose that was?'

Wally typed twelve lines before her question caught up with him, then shrugged. (She saw it; they knew each other's rhythms.) "Bright. Short. Sharp; no perceptible waxing or waning. No sound at all that I heard. Magnesium . . . big laser . . . searchlight, maybe. None likely in our alley, even on Halloween." He typed some more, then cycled back again. "No, I don't come up with *anything* that makes sense. Except fannish humor, and you're right: there's no punchline to this one."

Moira finished a flurry of her own, played back his answer, and frowned. "So . . . what? Elvis has just entered the building?"

"No, he was here four hours ago—and *he* got a Mars Bar. Seriously, hon, my honest best guess is that Captain Kirk just beamed down to ask for directions." He resumed typing at top speed.

Moira frowned fiercely now, and actually stopped typing for several seconds, even though she was paying connect time again by now. This was a perfect example of one of the Great Differences on which her twenty-year marriage to Wally was founded. He found the irrational, the inexplicable, amusing. She found it barely tolerable.

"We ought to take a look out the window, at least," she muttered, and resumed netsurfing.

"Sure thing," he said, and kept typing. "Just as soon as I upload my column for the LMSFSazine, finish that web-page upgrade for the SCA, answer all the e-mail rumors on the new Beatles stuff, and—oh, yes— download about twenty megs of current VanCon traffic and route it to the proper serfs, I'll join you there at the window. Save me a seat."

She didn't bother to recite her own litany of tasks; she had already dismissed the matter and was deeply engaged in a rather tricky attempt to hack her way into NASA and sniff out information regarding the first live guitar jam—the first musical interaction— ever to be performed in space (scheduled, according to rumor, to occur aboard Mir, during the next visit by the shuttle *Atlantis*; a Canadian and a Russian trading off on acoustic and electric). It was her intention to obtain the best possible recording of the event, and play it at VanCon, the annual Vancouver science fiction convention she and Wally helped run.

He was editing his column, and she had just settled on a promising line of attack, when they heard the wail.

It came clearly through the window behind them: the unformed sound of a baby in distress. Odd that they both thought "baby" the instant they heard it—for both the volume and pitch of the sound were unmistakably adult (though the gender was indeterminate). But that cry was not even an attempt at a word.

"There is a baby the size of a football player in our alley," Wally said calmly, fingers poised over his keyboard, "on Halloween night."

Moira caught herself trying to use her own keyboard as a breed of Ouija board. "One of us should really look out the window."

He began to tap his keys without quite typing them, a nervous mannerism she was sure she would learn to accept in no more than another decade at most. "That's the requisite number," he agreed, and poked a key tentatively.

Her face clouded up . . . then smoothed over. "And babies are my department. I see." She disconnected from the net, treating her mouse with elaborate gentleness, and rose from her seat.

Although their workstation was large by most home standards, so were Wally and Moira; she could not move her chair out of her way unless he got up too, so the only way she could get a look out the window was to kneel up on the chair and lean forward until her cheek pressed against the chilly pane. She did so.

Several seconds passed. Wally typed, but his heart clearly wasn't in it.

"What do you see?" he asked finally.

"Bad news," she replied slowly. "I think I'm getting a zit."

"Oh, for—" He got hold of himself, and saved his changes. "Right. Sorry. You're quite right: we *do* have to take up the tacks before we can take up the carpet." He darkened both monitor screens, extinguished both gooseneck lamps, levered himself up out of his own chair and went to dial the overhead light down. He waited there by the rheostat, in near darkness, watching his wife look out the window and down into the alley. "It's Captain Kirk, right?" he said.

More seconds passed.

He was beginning to become irritated by the time she stirred slightly and spoke his name; but then his irritation vanished at once, for there was something wrong with her voice. "Yes, Moira?"

"We've spoken of my ongoing ambiguity with regard to certain of the so-called assigned gender roles, right?"

"Yes, dear. And I am sworn not to break your stones about it."

"Thank you. With all due respect to sisterhood, I think this is one of those times when a Y chromosome is called for. He's naked, and he looks dead, and he's bald—so for all I know he *is* Captain Kirk, but this is definitely not my department, okay?"

"Our side of the fence, or Gorskys?"

"Our side."

His pidgin, then. He sighed. "Wait here in the cave. Now, where did I leave that stone ax . . . ?"

She turned away from the window. "Wally, seriously—"

He halted in the doorway. "Woman, you have invoked the Y chromosome—now run for cover and get the bandages ready. No, better yet, go to the phone, dial nine one, and wait for my scream." He grinned and left the room, feeling like a Heinlein hero. A Secret Master of Fandom and Permanent Secretary of the Lower Mainland Science Fiction Society had, after all, certain standards to maintain. And how tough could a nude bald corpse be?

She turned her Mac into a voicephone and did just as he had suggested, then went back to the window—moving both chairs out of the way this time—telling herself that at the first sign of funny business she would punch that last digit into the phone and then put a chair through that window and . . . and . . . and rain coffee cups and lava lamps on the naked bald man until he surrendered, that's what.

Wally did take the time to change to better footgear, put on a light jacket, and slide a short length of rebar up one sleeve before leaving the house by the back door. It was a typical Vancouver October night, save that it was not raining; the jacket was useful only as camouflage for the weapon. He rounded the corner of the house cautiously, staying far from the building and crouching slightly. Even with his own den lights extinguished, there was still enough light from the streetlights out front, the moon overhead, and spilling over the fence from the detestable frosted windows of the Gorskys (Gorskies? Gorski?) next door, to illuminate the alleyway with reasonable clarity.

There was unquestionably and no shit a naked bald Caucasian male lying there on his back, just below the den window.

Dead, however, he was not. He was in the slow process of trying to lever himself up from complete spread-eagled sprawl to a sort of sitting fetal position. Wally had plenty of time to see clearly that the naked man was not merely bald but completely hairless . . . and uncircumsized. Wally guessed him to be about twenty-five, and in excellent shape, well muscled and trim. He noted absently that the nude intruder was surrounded by a roughly circular patch of scorched grass, and that the circle of scorching was wide enough to mark both Wally's own house and the fence as well. He further noted, and filed, the depth of the impression the stranger had left in the soggy earth; as if he were made of lead . . . or had somehow *fallen* onto his back from . . . ah, doubtless from the top of the fence: that explained it. Considering that the fence was made of chain link topped by savage little twists of jagged steel, and that the stranger was nude right down to his soles, he must have wanted to leave the Gorsky property quite badly. For the first time Wally warmed to him slightly. (Like nearly everyone else in the district except Wally and Moira, the Gorsky clan lived in a million-dollar stucco-and-plaster steroid monstrosity that looked like the box a real home had come in—and did not trouble to hide their disgust at the property-value-lowering presence of Wally and Moira's shabby human dwelling in their midst. In retaliation, Wally had befriended his crabgrass.)

The naked man saw Wally for the first time. His eyes widened comically, and he gasped, a sound so loud and sibilant it was nearly a shriek. He drew up his knees, buried his head between them, and wrapped his arms around them to keep them secure, like a turtle withdrawing into his shell.

Wally moved, cautiously, to try and get a glimpse of Moira in the study window, thought he saw her wave a hand. He let the chunk of rebar slip out of his sleeve and into his palm, and tapped the stranger with it.

As a lifetime science fiction fan, Wally feared little so much as the prospect of appearing stupid in retrospect. He chose his words with care, and was rather proud of them. "Excuse me," he said gently, "but do I correctly understand that you are Blanched Du Boy, and you have always depended on the blahndness of stranguhs?"

The stranger poked his head back out, and stared fixedly—not at Wally, but at the house . . . or more properly, at the portion of its foundation nearest him, about a meter away. His eyes seemed to be bulging out of his head—or was that just the lack of eyelashes? No . . . no, he was genuinely terrified . . . not of the large homeowner poking him with a piece of rebar, but of a cement wall. He scuttled involuntarily away from it, until he fetched up against the fence.

"John!" he muttered. "Unsnuffingbelievable! One more hackin' meter west, and—" He shivered violently.

Wally thought it was about time; it wasn't terribly chilly out here, this was after all Vancouver, but it shouldn't take much to chill a naked man. "I say—" he began again.

The stranger whirled on him—not easy to do from a sitting position. "*What year is it?*" he snapped.

Wally bunked. "The same one it was when you decided to get drunk," he said.

The man was on his feet so suddenly he seemed to have levitated; he sprang at Wally and took him by the lapels of his coat. "*What year?*" he thundered.

Unused to naked men taking him by the lapels in his own yard while he held a piece of rebar, Wally answered automatically, and very quickly, "1995, its 1995, I swear to God!"

The stranger released him as quickly as he'd seized him, and the strangest thing happened. For just a moment Wally saw him begin to panic utterly, just totally lose it . . . then, confoundingly, he felt his own naked arms with his hands, felt his cheeks, and pulled himself back from the edge. Terror gave way at once to towering rage: he smote himself mightily on the thighs. "Grot!" he snarled. "Total snowcrash! Blood for this, my chop . . . grotty wannabes!" The date clearly displeased him greatly.

On Wally, the light had just begun, dimly, to dawn. This was the moment he had been waiting for since the age of six—here—now! He opened his mouth . . . then glanced up at the window and closed it again.

"Look, cousin," he said after some thought, "it's cool out here. Come on inside like I said, okay? Get some hot coffee in you—you drink coffee? We got *real* good coffee—"

The naked man looked up at him and instantly, visibly, became devious. "Sure, yes, hot caffy, very kind of you, caffy would be optimal. I can . . . uh . . . I can explain all this—"

"Yes, I'm sure you can," said Wally. "I'm looking forward to it." He gestured. "If you'll just walk this . . . uh, in this direction." And then he waved and gestured for Moira's benefit, before leading the way.

Wally watched the stranger carefully on the way into the house. He was one of those people who looks good with his head shaved— in fact, now that Wally noticed, he looked a little like a younger version of Captain Picard from *Star Trek: The Next Generation*. He seemed alert, but some of the things that interested him were interesting. He paid close attention, for instance, to the process by which Wally opened, and then closed, the back door—but did not attempt to hide his interest, as would a burglar casing the joint. He shielded his eyes with his hand from the meager 40-watt bulb in Wally and Moira's back hall. He noticed the stack of newspapers and the recycle blue-box full of waste glass and metal waiting for Garbage Night, and for some reason they seemed to amuse him. The stove in the kitchen made him snort. Then they hung the right into the study, and the stranger froze in his tracks, gaping.

Wally was aware that not everyone admired large women as much as he; nonetheless this behavior seemed rude for a guest. Then he realized that the stranger had not yet noticed Moira. He was staring horrorstruck at . . .

. . . a painting on the study wall. The Jack Gaughan *Analog* cover, for a story called "By Any Other Name"—a simple crouched figure seen from behind, brandishing a futuristic weapon at a number of translucent fireballs. Wally owned many scarier paintings.

But the stranger had clearly never seen anything so utterly terrifying in his life—not even the cement wall of Wally's foundation. "Oh *crash*," he moaned. "Its worse than I thought! You're science fiction fans, aren't you?"

Wally took a deep breath, and drew himself up. "Sir, I'm afraid it is worse than that. My wife and I are SMOFs."

The stranger fainted dead away.

Wally gave Moira a meaningful look. "The first thing he wanted to know was what year it was."

She stared down at the inert stranger, then back up at her husband. "Oh, Wally, *really?*"

He nodded, unable to suppress the grin any longer.

Her own eyes became large and round, and for just a moment it looked as though she might pass out herself. Then she got control, and smiled. "And the con's only a few weeks away!" she cried.

The two Secret Masters Of Fandom raced to each other, joined hands, and began to dance.

When the hairless man opened his eyes, it was in a *white* room which had no windows and only one door. The door had no knob or handle or keypad or other obvious means of causing it to open, nor did it appear to slide on tracks. There was a bare lightbulb in the ceiling, but its switch appeared to be elsewhere.

The room contained no furniture or decorations of any kind.

The balance of its contents were all sentient beings. Specifically, the hairless man himself, Wally, Moira and the Buddha . . . represented in this specific instance by a football-sized and -shaped bronze statue of him which was, ironically, the only purely material object present. Everyone but the hairless man looked generally the same: short, round and smiling beatifically.

He sat up slowly, took in his surroundings, and the fact that he was no longer naked. He now wore an old grey sweatshirt shrunken almost to normal-range size, a pair of sweatpants cinched tight at the waist but with adequate room to store a pup tent and an inflatable raft in the legs, and odd foot coverings that Wally was accustomed to refer to as "sockasins." He seemed to find the coverings tolerable.

"This is my meditation room," Moira said.

He nodded.

"If the beginning of this conversation goes well," Wally said, "we can continue it in more congenial surroundings. Over 'caffy.' But you *did* drop in without an appointment."

The stranger said nothing.

"We caught a burglar once," Wally said. "We left him in here for a week. Took the Buddha out, left him an empty wastebasket. He was very very contrite when we let him go. We had to help him to the sidewalk. Nothing much but solids in the basket by that point . . ."

"I understand," the hairless man said. "Come, let us reason together."

"When are you from?" Wally asked. "Originally, I mean."

The hairless man did a creditable imitation of puzzlement. "What do you mean, '*when*' am I from, Daddy-o? I'm from Frisco; I'm part of a team of long-hairs hacking on a matter transporter at the University of Frisco, and while I was there after hours there was this terrible—"

"Its possible to pipe sound in here," Moira said. "Are you by any chance familiar with the work of the Gyuto Monks?"

Beside her, Wally visibly shuddered. The Gyuto Monks, chanting, sound very much like a sustained short in the circuit that powers the world. Like the Grand Canyon: anyone will be impressed by them, but few can endure them at any length.

The hairless man sighed, and his shoulders drooped. He might not have known the Gyuto Monks, but he knew a threat when he heard it. "In your reckoning it would be the year 2287."

Wally and Moira each outsmiled the Buddha.

"I'm Wallace Kemp, and this is my wife Moira Rogers," Wally said.

"I am Jude," the time traveler said.

Wally and Moira exchanged a glance. "Hey," Wally said softly, making his Paul McCartney face, and she glared at him. To Wally's surprise, Jude seemed to catch the reference too, and looked suddenly wary.

"What was your purpose in time-traveling, Jude?" Wally went on, louder.

"The information would be of no value to you."

"Let us decide that. Unless you're in a hurry to get started meditating? We could get you a wastebasket—"

"I came back in order to drive a taxicab, one time," Jude said. "There. That is the complete truth. Satisfied?"

Wally digested that. "You know how to drive a car?" Moira asked.

Jude sneered. "Primitive mobile—myocontrol—how hard can it be?"

"Does it have to be a cab?" Wally asked.

Jude's face fell. "The discussion is pointless," he said. "My mission is a failure."

"Why?" they asked together.

He rubbed his forehead, where his eyebrows ought to have been. "Because there was a major snowcrash—" He glanced suddenly at Moira. "—pardon me, madam, a fuckup, and I undershot. This is the *wrong ficton*."

Wally nodded, pleased to have confirmed that Robert Heinlein's term for a place-and-time, "ficton," would one day pass into the language. "Yes, I got that. So it was necessary that your cab ride take place in a ficton earlier in history than this?"

"Yes, by several years."

"What year?"

Jude looked stubborn.

"Look," Wally said reasonably. "You must see our problem. I told you we are Secret Masters of Fandom. You are obviously a time traveler. There can only be four kinds of time traveler: idiots, fanatics, criminals and very careful historians—which last does not seem to describe you. Anyone else would know it's too risky. Before we can let you go, we need to know which kind you are."

Jude frowned. "In your terms, I suppose I am a fanatic. I would call myself a religious martyr."

Wally nodded. "And you plan to alter history, for theological reasons. By driving a taxicab. Even though that will annihilate reality."

"*My* reality," Jude pointed out. "Not yours. If I had succeeded, *my* ficton would have vanished utterly, yes—but yours would merely have turned out somewhat differently."

"True," Wally agreed. "Still, you're going to have to tell us about it, if you want to leave this room."

Jude looked distinctly uncomfortable. "May I first ask you a question? Matters of religion can be volatile. I know it is a little early in history for this question to be truly meaningful, but . . . may I ask both of you your views regarding . . . Elvis?"

Looking back on all this in years to come, one of the small things Wally and Moira would be proud of was the fact that neither of them cracked a smile at this juncture. They did exchange a momentary glance which was a promissory note for a shared belly-laugh later, but Wally answered seriously, after only a seconds hesitation, "He *has* left the building. If he were alive, he'd have stopped his daughter's wedding."

"And while he was here," Moira said, "he was a relatively talentless nutbar who happened to get struck by lightning, and didn't do anything important with the energy. Why?"

"Praise John!" Jude said fervently. "Are you, then, by any chance . . . Fab?"

Wally and Moira exchanged another glance. It was getting harder and harder not to grin. The idea that there would be a Church of Elvis in the not-too-distant future had become something of a cliché in recent science fiction—but until now only Wally, in on-line forums and in his column in LMSFSazine, had ever suggested that it might and should be countered by an equally fervent cult that worshipped the Beatles.

"I think you could say that," Wally agreed slowly. "Washed in the Juice of the Apple, you mean? I wouldn't call us devout, strictly speaking—we're fen; we must remain skeptical on all matters of religion, by policy—but I own the Black Album, and all the Christmas Fan Club Messages." He saw that register. "And I was at Shea Stadium in '65, if that helps."

"Twenty-three August, yeah yeah yeah!" Jude cried excitedly. "Oh, thank The Four, some gear luck at last! You *must* help me—*it may yet be accomplished!*"

"What may?" Wally asked, but his eyes were already starting to gleam.

"The Reunification!" Jude said. "The Healing . . . the Reforging of the Bond . . . the utter destruction of the forces of Elvis!"

Suddenly Wally *knew* what he was talking about. It all . . . well, came together, over him. "Oh my *God*," he breathed, thunderstruck. For the third time he met his wife's eyes, and was startled to see that she hadn't caught up yet. "Don't you get it, love? In the future, there's a major showdown between the Church of Elvis and the Church of The Beatles—the anti-Asian Christians versus the pro-Asian Pagans—and we're looking at a kamikaze samurai. God, the most awful Beatles anecdote of all—and Jude here came back through time to change it."

Moira was lost, but game. " ' . . . most awful Beatles anecdote . . . ' John's death? Or something to do with Stu Sutcliffe?"

"No, no—you've heard this one, I'm sure; I've told it a hundred times. John and Paul have buried the hatchet; they're sitting around in the Dakota one night in '79, getting stoned and watching telly while the wives chat in the kitchen. Lorne Michaels comes on the tube: it's the Saturday after Bernstein offered the Beatles a million to reunite, and Michaels makes a counteroffer on the air, live: if the Beatles will come down and play on *Saturday Night Live,* now, he's prepared to pay them . . . union scale, a thousand bucks or so apiece. Rim shot. And across town at the Dakota, John looks at Paul and Paul looks at John and they both start to grin—"

"Oh my God, I remember now," Moira said, "And they called a cab—*but it never showed up. . . .*" She turned pale.

"One of the great Lost Moments of history," Wally said, his voice trembling.

Jude broke the silence which followed. "It's plaintext, right? If the cab had arrived, John and Paul would have appeared on *Saturday Night Live* that night. The planet would have convulsed in its orbit, a generation gone mad with joy. George and Ringo both would have been on the phone before the credits rolled—and sooner or later, *The Four would have gotten together again!* John would have gone back home to England, and that Presleyan crot would *never* have gotten a shot at him *there*." His voice was rising "And sooner or later, they'd have learned the truth about Eppy's death, and in their holy wrath crashed the forces of Elvis forever—"

Wally couldn't help interrupting. "Wait a minute—are you saying that *Elvis Presley* was behind Brian Epstein's—"

"Indisputable proof will be uncovered in another eight years,"

Jude said, "but isn't it obvious? Faggot Jew Commie . . . creator of the Anti-Elvis . . . *pills* as the instrument of death . . . did you think it coincidence that Eppy died *just* as The Four were communing publicly with an Eastern, non-Christian religious figure in India?"

"Elvis *did* approach J. Edgar Hoover, and volunteer to spy on the Beatles for the DEA, that's documented," Wally said softly. He was talking to himself. "And his daughter's flaky husband is the guy who stole the Beatles' publishing rights out from under his mentor, Paul McCartney—"

"Elvis Presley made his evil plans in full, the day he read John's Jesus Quote . . . and from beyond the grave, he triumphed," Jude said in a vaguely chanting tone, clearly quoting from scripture.

Moira noticed that her hand hurt, from crushing Wally's hand, but forgot it almost at once, distracted by horror. "You mean . . . you mean He Whose Name We Must Never Mention really shot John as an agent of—of—"

Jude nodded solemnly. "It will be the chance discovery of his secret memoirs by a prison guard in 2003 that blows the story. I meant to undo all of that—and with your help, *I still can.*"

As unconsciously as they had mangled them, Wally and Moira let go of each other's hands, and sat up straighter, hearts hammering.

"You've got the time machine *on* you," Wally suggested. "Or in you. Implanted, or something."

Jude shook his ironically bald head. "All the assets I have, you see."

"So you're going to automatically slingshot back to the future, or something, and try again."

Another headshake. "Return to my ficton is fundamentally impossible, time travel only works backwards. Even if I had another machine, I could not travel to the future—it isn't *there* yet."

"You're stuck in this ficton, then? But then it's too late, right? John's been dead for fifteen years!"

Jude looked sly. "But there is another time machine—in this ficton—and in this city."

"No *shit*," Wally and Moira chorused. "I mean," Wally went on, " 'speak on, sir, omitting no detail however slight.' Where? And why?"

"Let me table the question of its location for a moment," Jude temporized, "and address your last input first. Authorized time travelers—as opposed to myself—are naturally hyperconscious of the danger of corrupting history. Therefore a clandestine machine is maintained throughout all periods of historical interest—so that if a researcher's cover story should collapse, at worst they can make their way there and escape to an earlier ficton, aborting the hang."

"Smart," Wally said. "So all you really need is a ride across town somewhere?"

Jude sighed. "Well, no. I am not an *authorized* time traveler."

Slowly, Wally nodded. "So then, what you need is . . . ?"

Jude hesitated . . . then took the plunge. "A substantial bribe."

"In what form?" Wally asked.

"Cash. Small bills would be best. . . ."

Wally boggled, shamelessly. He had been very good for a long time, but this just didn't seem *logical*. "Cash? You mean, 1995 dollars? What the hell would time travelers want with *cash*?"

"Think it through," Jude suggested.

Wally frowned fiercely. That one stung: a science fiction fan should never need to be told to think it through. "Apparently I lack data," he said stiffly.

"Okay. You're the guardian of the time machine, stuck in this primitive ficton forever, and if The Fabs are good you will have very little actual work to do: the need for your services had better be rare. Sooner or later you go native. Now: what can I bribe you with? Money in 2287 dollars, that you can bury for your descendants? Unnameable futuristic comforts and delights that you may never even risk letting any local observe you enjoying? Or the means to render this Stone Age existence as tolerable as possible?"

"But why can't I generate as much cash as I want?" Wally said, falling into the Socratic spirit of the thing. "If I'm from the future, surely I was smart enough to pack some market tips, memorize some important dates—"

"—which you could only capitalize on at the cost of altering history," Jude pointed out. "Calling that kind of attention to yourself is precisely what you must not do. You must be a kind of invisible man—yet you must earn a living, in a ficton with all the privacy of a large bedroom, for altruism's sake. This is a recipe for bribery."

"Ah," Wally said. "I get it. And you're willing to take the risk they aren't, to get money to bribe them with. If you show up with a barrel of cash, they'll think it over and decide what's done is done, and the smartest thing to do with that money is quietly slip it back into the system—by spending it themselves. I guess if I were tending a time machine in the Court of Herod, I might take a hundred goats to bend a rule. You might pull it off."

"If you will help me," Jude agreed. "I need valid financial entities of this ficton to act as my agents. If you will let me give you market advice, I will make us . . . let me see, '95, '95 . . . say, two hundred thousand Canadian dollars, and give you half. And—Julia willing!— the joy of having undone the anagrammatic Evils of Elvis and saved Saint Jock. Will you help?"

Wally's heart was beating very fast. "Hold the phone. Check me out on this: you go back in time sixteen-odd years. You show up at the Dakota in a Yellow cab. Johnny and Paulie make the curtain, and history changes. And *this* ficton—here, now, sixteen years later— ceases to exist, right? Moira and I and everybody we know all disappear like Boojums?"

Jude did not hesitate. "These avatars of you, yes. But there will still be a Wally and a Moira. Have your lives been so good since John's Murder that you would not have them different? In a world with four strong Beatles to inspire it? Stack all the music recorded since 1972 against *Rubber Soul* . . ."

Husband and wife both started to answer, and fell silent. They *had* met, fallen in love and married well before the date in question. It wasn't as though the proposed alteration in history would cost them their marriage. Merely some dispiriting shared history . . . which would be replaced with—

"You live here; I don't. Is this ficton, in your opinions, gear? Or grotty? When do you believe the Sixties died, and why? Would you not see that undone, the Yellow Submarine relaunched?"

Wally found that tears were trickling, silently and unobtrusively, down his cheeks.

"Please help me," Jude said softly. "It is my destiny. I was born and named to do as Paul commanded: to make the sad song better."

"We'll do it," Wally and Moira both said at once, and took each other's hands again. They shared a grin that began as a promissory note for a kiss, and began inflating in value almost at once. Perhaps they had not been so happy since the day Moira proposed.

Jude, for his part, appeared to go into something like religious ecstasy. He shivered all over, smiled hugely, and began rocking gently from side to side, seeming to glow. "Then you shall live out the year," he said happily.

Through his own warm glow, those words reached Wally. He stopped grinning long enough to say, "Beg pardon?"

Jude waved his hands in the air, as one who would say, *no, no, it's nothing.* "Vancouver will be destroyed later this year. Not a problem."

"*The Big One?*" Moira squealed. "Juan de Fuca Fault? *This year?*"

"Yes, yes—but you will have a hundred thousand dollars with which to flee. And I will tell you when. Save as many friends as you like—as long as they are absolutely discreet."

An extraordinary cascade of thoughts went though Wally's brain in a short time.

Jesus, they do *say it's overdue—the whole Pacific Rim's going up lately—*

—Our home here in Point Grey sits on the only rock around: the only part of the greater Vancouver area that would not immediately liquefy and submerge in the event of a quake. Of course, we'd get some thirsty by and by—

—After we agree to help Jude, he gets around to mentioning cataclysmic earthquakes in the near future?—

Oh no, I see: he wanted us to be able to know and honestly say that our choice was pure, wasn't based on selfish motives—

—except for a piddling hundred grand—

—ohmyGod, to have the Beatles back! How many albums would they have put out between 1979 and now? Oh Jesus . . . imagine hearing Tug of War *without "Here Today"—but with John himself! Hell, those new tracks we're supposed to hear next month could have been out fifteen years ago—*

—get a grip, boy. Now which, if any, of my friends can I trust to keep their mouth shut about this? Oh, shit—

—can I condemn the rest to death for being gabby? Justice, perhaps, but rather harsh—

—is there some way to get them a warning at the last possible moment? Or can I come up with some alternate explanation for how I know for sure a quake is coming? A prediction I got from the Internet, maybe? Or—

—I'll miss this soggy town—

—where the hell will we go? Will Vancouver Island survive? Go-to-the-States or tolerate-Canadian-weather is a choice it's been nice not to have to make—

—no wonder Jude freaked when he learned what year it is—

—that's funny . . . why did he calm down, though, almost at once? He didn't even ask me the exact date: he just thought for a second, and relaxed—

—oh my dear God, he's not from Vancouver! *And there's not much of 1995 left* anymore—

"Jude," he said, enunciating carefully, feeling his lips and tongue starting to go numb, "what is the date of the earthquake?"

Jude was still ecstatic. "Oh, we'll have more than enough time, I should think, assuming you have any reasonable amount of capital. Point two megabucks shouldn't take more than a few weeks. You *do* know . . . um . . . a flexible broker?"

Moira started to answer, would doubtless have expressed amusement at the notion that there could be any difficulty locating a shady broker in the city which held the Vancouver Stock Exchange, but Wally overrode her: "*Tell me the date, Jude.*"

"Really, don't worry," Jude assured him. "It's not until Fall."

Wally groaned.

"Wally, what is it?" Moira said.

He turned to her. "I told him it was 1995, and he freaked," he said. "And then he felt the air with his skin, and relaxed . . . because it couldn't possibly be later in the year than late Summer. Don't you get it, love? Either he isn't from Vancouver—or in his ficton, Vancouver is as cold as the rest of Canada."

Moira's eyes grew round. "Oh my stars and garters. Jude!"

"Yes, Moira?"

"This is Halloween Night."

He nodded. "I have read of it. Anti-Christian ritual holiday, yes? Dress up, like Sergeant Pepper, take Magical Mystery Tour. We have a similar ritual in late October. And your point is—"

"Halloween Night falls on 31 October."

Jude grasped the floor on either side of him to keep from falling through it. "WHAT?" Gravity reversed itself; suddenly he rose like a launched missile, clutching at the floor with his soles to keep from flying away. "This is *October*?" Even internal gravity failed him: his trunk repelled his hands, and they flew out to either side. "The *end* of October?" He forced them to his will, brought them back in and beat them on his thighs. "The LAST FUCKING DAY of October?'

"It almost never gets cold here," Wally said apologetically.

Physics restored itself in Jude's vicinity: he went inert, *fell* back into his seat, with a thud, and kept collapsing, like a dropped dummy.

They gave him a moment with his despair. They wanted to ask, but the question was too obvious. To ask it would have insulted all three of them. Finally, Wally cleared his throat as discreetly as he could.

"Less than forty-eight hours," Jude said hollowly.

They both sat perfectly still. How appropriate a place in which to receive the news, Wally thought. Except the clothes on their backs, a statue of Siddhartha and a forty-watt lightbulb, there was not a single material possession in the room.

All right, then: it was a good place to think. Wally thought, as hard and fast as he ever had in his life. This time, even a summary of the resulting cascade of cogitation would be impossible, but he was through within a matter of perhaps ten seconds.

"All is not lost," he said then.

Jude nodded dispiritedly. "There is time to save ourselves, yes. With your help, perhaps I can establish a cover identity that will hold. I suppose it is possible that later, when things settle down and you rebuild your credit standing, we might try to . . . but then the problem becomes vastly more complex, you see. *This* time machine will be destroyed by the quake—and since its replacement in Halifax will just be entering operation, enforcement of regulations will be at its strictest: it'll be *years* before I'll even dare try to . . . oh *crot*, if only I'd arrived even a *week* earlier—" He was near tears in his frustration.

Wally turned and caught Moira's eyes. "Tomorrow morning we can put eighty-seven thousand dollars in cash into your hands," he said. Moira's eyes widened—and then slowly, she nodded. They turned back to Jude.

Burned once, he was reluctant to let hope back. "That . . . thank you, but I don't think that would quite be enough to—"

"You were always lousy at math, love," Moira said to Wally. "The correct figure is ninety-six thousand, seven hundred and fourteen dollars and fifty-two cents."

Wally nodded, mortified. In his haste, he had neglected to include their own personal net liquidity in the equation. The figure he had named represented only every penny presently in the Lower Mainland Science Fiction Society's VanCon account, entrusted to him and Moira by a couple of thousand Pacific Northwest science fiction fans. In his heart, Wally did not feel there was anything really dishonorable about offering that money. There was not going to *be* a VanCon in two weeks . . . and only a handful of chronic pains in the ass were ever even going to *ask* for a refund. Nonetheless, he knew the moment Moira spoke that, having pledged both his life and his sacred honor, he really should have thought to include his fortune as well. He excused himself on the grounds that the sum was so negligible it might have escaped anyone's attention. "Actually, darling," he said, anxious to redeem himself, "we could hit a few cash machines, and get another two grand before we max out. So the correct figure is ninety-*eight*-seven and change."

"Well," she said, "I thought we might—"

"We can charge our plane tickets out of town," he pointed out. "We can even put movers on plastic, to ship the books and music to a safe place. There's enough walking-around money in the house." He turned back to Jude. "Can you pull it off with ninety-eight-seven?"

Jude frowned in concentration—then all at once, shockingly, he giggled. "I'll tell them I have to charge them G.S.T.," he said puckishly.

Wally and Moira dissolved a lot of tension in that burst of laughter. (Canadians in 1995 regarded the Goods and Services Tax with all the affection Bostonians in 1776 had held for a similar levy on tea.) Each felt rather as though they had gnawed a leg off to escape a trap—but there was a sort of dizzy calm in that . . . and a quiet joy that the sacrifice would be sufficient after all. For think of the prize! New Beatles songs—not a lousy pair of them, but albums and albums—conceivably even some kind of *tours* again, with a living John Lennon, and stage technology the Beatles had never dreamed of in their touring days. *A world healed of disco.* A reconsolidation of the hopes and aspirations of the Sixties, tempered by experience—

—and it would be Wallace Kemp and Moira Rogers, Secret Masters Of Fandom, Secretary and Treasurer of LMSFS, who had helped to accomplish it! (Even if they never got to remember that . . . talk about your selfless sacrifices . . .)

In less than an hour, Jude had been fed, taken on a tour of the house and the hard drives, shown to a guest bedroom, taught to use a primitive contemporary cable-TV remote and a flush toilet, and left alone to sleep. Wally and Moira talked for another half an hour in bed, making plans, but they knew they needed rest and it had been a long night; they put out the light at around midnight, and were both asleep in a matter of minutes. Wally's last fleeting thought, before he slipped over the edge and into Strawberry Fields, was the bemused recollection from a Catholic childhood that, in that myth-structure, Jude was the patron saint of the impossible.

Realizing their total liquidity in small bills the next day required some ingenuity as well as effort; fortunately Wally, a professional hacker, had "social engineering" skills which proved useful. He and Moira left Jude alone with the TV and Moira's Mac (to Wally's disgust, he was told that the basic Mac interface would triumph in the future—as indeed it had already begun to do in his own ficton), and Wally spent the day stalking money while Moira worked the phone. By nightfall, just as movers were arriving to ship their most precious possessions to Toronto at outrageously padded emergency rates, he was able to hand Jude a large Tourister suitcase stuffed with cash.

"How does it feel," he asked as he passed it across, "to be one of the beautiful people?'

Jude grinned. "Baby, you're a rich man, too."

Wally handed over a bulky envelope. "Just in case you fail—in case they won't take the bribe—here's a plane ticket to Halifax, and cab fare to the airport. You can always sit on that cash until it's safe to try again." He smiled. "Keep it in a big brown bag, inside the zoo."

Jude's eyes were misting. "What a thing to do. Thank you, brother."

"Driving a cab is a little harder than it sounds. Try and arrive a week or so early, give yourself time to practice. Watch it done a few times, first. I typed out some tips; you'll find them on a sheet headed 'Baby, You Can Drive Their Car.' There's a tube of pepper spray in the envelope with it: don't use it until he's stopped, on a dark street, then reach past him fast and turn the key counter-clockwise. Our temporary new number in Toronto is in that envelope, too. If we don't hear from you in a few days, we'll assume you were successful." He caught himself. "Excuse me. Dumb: if you succeed, we'll never know it. Never have known it. Boy, that's a hard concept to get my mind around. And I'm going to hate to lose the memory of the last twenty hours or so."

"I know it seems paradoxical," Jude said, taking his hand, "but I feel in my heart that if I succeed in my mission, somehow, in some way, you will remember your part in it for all the days of your life."

Wally did not agree, but it was a pretty thought; he let it pass unchallenged.

Moira looked up from her sorting and packing. "Get a move on, Jude. John and Paul are waiting. Give our love to Yoko and Linda."

Jude nodded and left without another word, threading his way through the movers.

"Have you noticed?" Moira said. "He has a passing resemblance to Jean-Luc Picard. . . ."

His last words came back to them both with great vividness and force . . . on the very next evening, as they sat up late into the night, in the guest bedroom of a friend and fellow SMOF in Toronto, listening in growing horror to a television and a radio and an Internet Reuters feed that all doggedly *refused* to report anything whatsoever about an earthquake in the Pacific Northwest. They tried desperately for hours to persuade each other that Jude had merely made some small error in the date, or that the authorities were censoring the news to prevent panic, or . . .

But they were not stupid people, only silly ones. By dawn, shortly after Wally realized and pointed out that only in the unlikely event it finally provoked Canadians to open Boston-Tea-Party-style insurrection could the G.S.T. reasonably have been remembered in history long enough for someone from the year 2287 to have heard of it, they had both finally conceded that love is not all you need. Wally gave Moira the chore of booking transport back home, while he went down to Bathurst Street and, with some difficulty, bought a handgun.

❈CHAPTER 3❈
What'd I Say

JUDE CEASED to exist about a hundred meters from Wally and Moira's house. Operation of his physical plant was taken over then by Paul Throtmanian, who made a point of existing whenever it was not inconvenient. It was he who conveyed the bag of swag a kilometer or two, from one end of Point Grey to the other (passing within a block of the edge of Pacific Spirit Park), softly and triumphantly singing John Lennon songs every step of the way. When he got within two blocks of his current home—just as he got to the words, "I don't believe ... in Beatles"—Paul too ceased to exist, and became Ralph Metkiewicz, programmer, solid citizen, and tenant-of-record for that address.

Ralph was the only safe person to be in this particular neighborhood—was a considerably safer identity altogether than either of the other two. (Though there were no warrants outstanding for him under any of those names.) Nonetheless he kept the lowest possible profile, walking in shadow whenever possible, and using every trick he knew to make himself unobtrusive when he could not. He knew it would not be safe to openly enter his home tonight, even in darkness. Moira's sweatshirt and Wally's parachute pants and sockasins were just too weird for his persona, too memorable should certain questions ever be asked. Not that they would be, but he was an artist ... and a professional pessimist, besides.

Happily, Ralph's home had been chosen specifically because one could leave it without being seen, even if it were surrounded by many policemen ... and the process worked just as well in reverse. He entered the underground parking garage of an apartment building on West Fourteenth, used a key to open a knobless maintenance door on its far wall, let himself thereby into a long concrete corridor that led past the building's boiler room, and then turned left. Halfway along this corridor, which ran the width of the building, he bent and picked up a small unobtrusive piece of articulated wire from the filthy floor, about the length and strength of a paper clip and bent at six places. At the corridor's end he came to a blank wall, seemingly made of particle board sealed somehow to the raw concrete. There was a heavy-duty electrical outlet set in it at about chest height, inset perhaps a quarter of an inch as if sloppily installed. He inserted the bit of wire into the right-hand slot of the socket in a certain way, rotated it clockwise, twice, and heard a small *clack*! sound. Then he repeated the procedure, counterclockwise, with the left slot. He removed the lockpick and tossed it behind him toward the spot on the floor where he'd found it. He set down his bag, put his fingertips into the shallow space formed by the wall socket's inset, braced himself, and heaved sideways. The wall slid away smoothly and noiselessly to the left. He reclaimed his satchel of swag, stepped through the resulting opening into a tunnel, turned and slid the false wall back into place, and continued on without troubling to turn on the lights. At the end of the tunnel he found the keypad in the dark, tapped the combination, and was admitted into his own basement.

The moment the door locked behind him, Ralph was tempted to become Paul again. But he waited until he had queried the security system and confirmed that his was the only entry, authorized or otherwise, since his departure. *Then* he morphed back to himself, losing Ralph's slouch and outthrust jaw, and emitted a sustained whoop of triumph and glee that made the basement ring.

It was more than the ninety-eight large. His place in the annals of the great was assured. As of this moment, Paul Throtmanian was legend. He had detected, perfected, and just now effected *the first new con in at least a hundred years.*

With any luck, the bulk of the fame—the on-the-record portion— would be posthumous. Ideally his achievement would not reach the ears of anyone who wasn't bent until Paul was comfortably in the ground, or at least past the statutes of limitations. But the players would all know, well before then. In the bucket-shops of Vancouver and Melbourne and Markham, at all the major stock exchanges, in the great seine of Times Square, in the cabs of Florida pickup trucks painted with the names of hurricane-repair contractors, backstage at alien-abductee conferences, after hours in Alternative AIDS clinics and Stop Smoking clinics and Facilitated Communication clinics and Cure Cancer clinics, on cruise ships and in revival tents and in Vegas and Key West and along Bourbon Street, in between dropping wallets or recovering memories of fetal rape or pretending to treat frozen shoulder or dispensing market or other psychic advice, the grifter elite of the English-speaking world would sooner or later speak of Paul Throtmanian with respect, and even admiration. The beauty of the sting, the sheer joy of it, the thing that would sell it, was that the higher the mark's IQ, the *more* likely he was to bite. Pleasure without guilt, like Pepperidge Farm cookies. You could almost use MENSA's mailing list for a hit sheet. It was possible that his fame would become planetary, for the gag would work in any culture which had been exposed to science fiction. It was even conceivable that the gambit might come to be known as a *Throtmanian* . . . the way Murphy's and Vesco's and Rockford's names had entered the language. Today, Paul had become one of the immortals.

For *once*, he would outshine his partner.

That thought came close to derailing his joy, for he loved her and respected her professionally and did not *want* to envy her, and besides there was darkness in her life just now. But he also knew that she would not begrudge him his triumph—she would probably take some of the credit for it, and probably deserved it—and perhaps his glow would brighten her present darkness just a bit. If not, perhaps ninety-eight large in cash would. And he had to share the news or burst.

She must be back from California by now, was probably at her own apartment waiting for his call. (They had learned, early on in the five years they'd been a team so far, that both their personal and professional relationships went better if they maintained separate addresses. Aside from that they were practically married.) So: check in with her at once. Or nearly . . .

He left the cash in a place even the building's architect could not have found without deep radar, and set demons to guard it. He stripped off Wally's and Moira's clothing and fed it to the furnace, along with the air ticket to Halifax, the Toronto phone number, the cab-driving tips and the envelope that had contained them. The pepper spray and the cab fare he took with him as he padded naked up the stairs. He went straight to the phone machine, which greeted him with four blinks. The first call was a hangup—no manners left in the world. The second was an infant or small child, happily pushing buttons at random—no parents left in the world. The third caller warned him that the opportunity to buy into lucrative lottery ticket syndicates in other, tax-free nations was about to slip through his fingers—Paul recognized the voice, and grinned. The fourth, at last, was his lady love, who said:

"*Honey, I'm into something heavy here. I'm walking in the Endowment Lands, and I ran across a mook looking to bury something nice just off the Lowrie Trail, Dorothy twice, but that's not the good part. He was digging away at the base of a huge old toppled elm tree, and he hit something with his shovel that made a sound like* clack, *something like plywood or plastic. And then . . . I know this is nuts, but then he had an orgasm, all by himself, standing up. And then he started to talk out loud, as if somebody was grilling him—only I was only fifty meters away and I swear there was no one else there. He said his name was Angel Gerhardt and he lived over in the East End on William Street and his e-mail handle, God help us all, was 'Frosty,' and he named his girlfriend Linda Wu and his two housemates and said none of them knew where he planned to bury the . . . the thing . . . and the weird part was, he didn't say any of this like a mope giving information to the heat, he said it like a guy opening his soul to his new lover, happy as a clam. Then he filled the hole back in and buried the package in another spot. He's gone now. I'm going to put the package somewhere else—but I'm not going near that goddam fallen elm without you, and maybe Rosco. I don't know what we've got ahold of here, but whatever it is is very very big. Call me as soon as you get in, okay? I hope everything went okay.*" Paul frowned. It was a good thing for her, he reflected, that he loved her. . . .

His phone had no redial button (it was barely a touch-tone), and he had a mental block against remembering her cell phone number. So it was necessary to go consult the tackboard in the kitchen, again. Along the way he stopped in his bedroom and threw casual clothes on, chiefly to give him time to deal with his irritation.

Even for God, this seemed low comedy.

He didn't have the slightest idea what the hell June had stumbled onto—any more than she seemed to. But it never entered his mind to doubt for an instant that *whatever* it was, was of greater and more lasting significance than ninety-eight large in small bills. Or even maybe the first new con of the century. That much was obvious. This was his punishment for being a male chauvinist pig—penance, for the sin of Pride.

Most infuriating of all, the mystery fascinated him.

It seemed clear that her mook had triggered some kind of security system light-years beyond anything Paul had ever heard of—and security was a field he had given diligent study. Whoever had designed the system possessed technology the RCMP or American NSA would unquestionably kill, maim and/or torture for. Paul's most plausible first-hypothesis was aliens, and he emphatically did not believe in flying saucers.

What that system was meant to protect, he could not even begin to guess. He did not waste time trying. It would be more efficient to just go find out. He was already scheming ways to beat the system as he returned to the kitchen.

There he made and drank Ghimbi coffee while he replayed the relevant tape, twice. At the third mention of Rosco's name, he went to the bedroom and got him. Then he sat in the kitchen again and thought hard for several minutes, occupying his hands and eyes by cleaning and oiling Rosco and practicing with the speed-loader.

Maybe he was looking at this the wrong way. Just backwards, even. Maybe he was going to become *twice* as immortal as he had thought. How many players had ever hit two world-class jackpots on the same day?

He read June's number off the wall and dialed it.

She answered at once. "Hi, hon."

She sounded depressed—more accurately, chipper: the way she sounded when she didn't want you to know she was depressed. June said depression was like farting: that all humans are subject to it, but it is not done in polite company. He knew it ran deeper than that, for they had long since reached that point of intimacy at which they could fart unself-consciously in each other's presence. But he respected her need to suffer in silence, and tried not to be insulted by it. "After considerable reflection, I've decided to let you live," he said.

"That's nice."

"I will, of course, do my best to ensure that your every moment is infinite agony—but it just seems to me Hell doesn't deserve you."

"It never will. What'd I do?"

"What did you *do*? Only you could have done this to me, bitch. I pull off the triumph of my career, dead bang perfect the first time—and you top me before I can even tell you the news. It's fucking typical, I tell you. You're a menace."

"Paul, what the hell are you talking about?"

At once he inferred that she was not alone. Something had gone horribly wrong since she'd left her message. It was now imperative to know whether the third party could hear Paul's end of the conversation too, or only June's. "I see. Good as a nod, is it?" he said, hoping to hear an "Uh huh," that would mean they could communicate safely as long as he could phrase his questions to require yes/no or similarly cryptic answers.

Instead she said, "What?"

Confused, he tried, "You're alone?"

"Yeah, I'm out for a walk, over in the Endowment Lands. Why?"

He had to nail it down. "Where did we first meet?"

This should do it. If someone were listening, she would answer with the Official Version: the one they gave to strangers, straight acquaintances, and casual friends.

But she answered accurately. "Fogerty's. I'm really me, okay? So what's going on? Did something go sour with your thing, or what?"

Now he was baffled. "No. No, it went just great . . . right up until I got home heavy and found your message."

"What message?"

"—," Paul said, and then repeated it for emphasis.

"I just got out of Customs three—no, four . . . that's funny—four hours ago. It didn't go real great down in San Francisco, so I dropped my stuff at my place and came out here to think. Did this message actually sound like me? What did I say?"

The one thing he was certain of was that the phone message was from June. Not an impressionist, not a computer-assembled matchup of voice recordings: June. In speech pattern, emotional nuance, it was unmistakably his lover. He knew he might be wrong, but he was positive.

She was an amnesiac or a zombie. There was no third choice.

"Look," he said slowly, "I think it would be best if we discussed this in person. I really really do."

Brief pause. "Okay. My place or yours?"

Paul thought quickly. They had long since agreed and arranged that, for reasons of professional risk hygiene, neither should be able to enter the others home in its owner's absence—the stated theory being that what you do not know, you cannot babble if drugged or otherwise coerced. Paul had never quite been certain that security was the only reason for this arrangement, but had never pushed to find out. June was the senior partner of the team; it was enough that she always let him in when he knocked, and usually came when he called. But now he was seeing things through new eyes. If someone else *were* operating her now, the tactical advantage for him lay on his own turf.

"Come in the front way, okay?"

Longer pause than before. "Paul?"

"Yeah, love."

"What *time* did we meet at Fogerty's?"

He blinked. Okay, fair enough. "Twenty minutes after closing."

Her relief was audible. "I'll be there in about fifteen minutes."

He hung up the phone and glowered at Rosco, so frightened and angry that holding him did not make Paul feel as ridiculous as it usually did. Dammit, he had not expected to have to be this paranoid again for months, yet! A man deserved a break after a big job.

Mess with my *woman's head, will you? I'm coming for you, pal. I don't care* who *you are: I'm bringing it to you.* You *just bought the whole package. Batteries* are *included.*

The living room projected out four feet from the rest of the house, with a big bay window facing north that wrapped at east and west ends. Someone sitting in the rocker by the window could see a pedestrian or motorist approaching the house, from either direction, from at least a block away. So could someone crouching beneath the window with a toy periscope in one hand and Rosco in the other.

She came from the right direction. It was for sure her. She was alone. She did not appear to be under any kind of duress or constraint, did not look drugged or at gunpoint. She looked totally serene, in fact, until she was within a few feet of the door, at which time she allowed an expression of mingled curiosity and weariness to cross her face. It was still there as she let herself in the unlocked door and locked it behind her. Then it was gone, for you cannot look curious and weary and hoot with helpless laughter at the same time.

"I'm sorry," she said when she could. "I know you told me, but I guess I didn't—I hadn't—" She lost it again, and sat in a nearby chair.

Under other circumstances he might have been irritated—but he was too relieved. So far as he understood, zombies did not giggle. Or break their lover's balls. "Issss," he said in a hokey baritone, and rubbed his free hand across his bald scalp, "a pozzlement!" The hand she could not see put the safety back on and put Rosco away in his small-of-the-back holster.

She got the *King and I* reference, and giggled even harder. "Thanks," she said when she was done. "I needed that. You look like that guy from Star Trek, the one without the wrinkles. 'Make it so!'—that one."

"It'll grow back," he said in his own voice. "And it was worth it, believe me." He got up from his crouch, went to the door and rearmed the security system.

"The scam worked? Oh, that's great, honey—you're a genius! A bald genius. How big?"

"Ninety-eight kay," he said smugly, buffing his nails on his chest. "Perfect blowoff. They won't even know they've been stung for hours yet." He admired his manicure. "I'm so smart I make myself sick."

Suddenly she was serious. "You're not wrong. I take my hat off. Do you have any idea how many people spent their whole *lives* trying to think up a new bit?"

He had not meant to be sidetracked by this, but he couldn't help himself. "Aw hell," he said, "it's really just a refinement of the Horse Wire."

By this he referred to the classic con outlined in the film *The Sting*, in which the mark is led to believe the player has secret advance access to telegraphed racing results. It is indeed the historical grandfather of most "insider-information" cons, and a case could be made that Paul's creation was merely another, admittedly highly refined, variant.

But June answered as if he had primed her. "The hell it is. It looks a little like a Horse Wire, but it's fundamentally different. It's about the only con I ever heard of *that doesn't require the mark to be corrupt.* Your sting works on *altruists.* You've broken new ground!"

For some reason her praise made him flinch. Okay, he thought, you've had your minimum daily requirement of stroking. Back to business!

"So have you, love," he said.

She frowned, shifting gears at once. "Oh yeah. What's this about a message?"

"You better listen to it yourself."

"I guess so." She got up.

He pushed away from the door, and just in time remembered to say, and just in time had the wit not to preface it with *By the way,* "How's Laura?"

She winced, and came to him, and they hugged. "Later, okay?" she murmured into his neck.

Sure. Maybe in their golden years. "Yeah."

They held each other for a long moment, each relishing the physical comfort, each wishing it could be prolonged. Then they went to the kitchen, and he started a pot of coffee while the tape played back.

She played the whole message twice, and after she shut the machine off, for several minutes the only sound in the room was the merry bubbling of water. Just as he was about to set out cups and spoons, she shook her head as if coming out of a trance.

"You said there's a priest's hole in this dump," she stated, fiddling with the machine.

"Yeah. Down cellar." His blood began to pound: she was using command voice.

"*Now.* Bring Rosco!"

"I'll get a jacket—"

"Fuck the jacket. *Let's go.*" She was already heading for the door to the basement.

He caught up with her at the foot of the stairs: she did not know which way to go from there. But she was right on his heels as he led them to the emergency exit, one hand in her purse, looking back over her shoulder. He had caught her urgency now, and didn't bother to conceal the code he punched into what looked like a broken calculator. A slab of paneling became a door, which opened to reveal the unlit tunnel. As he reached to turn the tunnel light on, they both heard the horrid sound of an alarm echoing through the house, and probably the neighborhood.

"Son of a *bitch*," he said. "Somebody just came through the front door." A different tocsin. "The fire alarm too! Damn—I *liked* this place." Suddenly his eyes widened. "Oh, shit—cover me! *The ninety-eight large*—" He began to turn back . . . and found that June was pointing her own gun at him.

"Did the brain fairy leave you a quarter last night?" she snarled. "Fuck the money."

She was right. He knew she was right. "But—"

She took the safety off. "Move move move move move—"

He moved.

The best car in the underground garage was a '94 Honda Accord. June was better with cars, they'd settled that long ago, so Paul guarded her back while she got in and got it running, a matter of seconds. She had it on the street and accelerating before he could get his seat belt buckled. "Where are we going?" he asked.

"How the hell do I know? Downtown, for now: try and maximize witnesses, disappear in the crowd. After that, who knows?"

He nodded and watched out the window for cops. A few blocks later, he said, "You don't remember it at *all*?"

She took her eyes off the rearview mirror long enough to throw him an agonized look. "No! Not any part of it. If it wasn't my voice, I wouldn't believe it. Except for one other thing."

He nodded. "Our visitors."

"No, they only confirmed it. I believed it before we ran—that's *why* we ran."

"Okay: what's the one thing that convinced you?'

"The part about Angel Gerhardt having an orgasm."

"I don't get you. That part almost convinced me you were hallucinating."

"When I left Dad's house this morning, I was wearing panties. I'm not, now."

Paul turned pale, and then ruddy. "Jesus."

Suddenly she started to laugh. "You want to hear something stupid?"

"Sure."

"I actually feel better now than I did when you called. And I'm scared shitless."

⚜CHAPTER 4⚜
Strike One

AS THEY CAME through the door they knew they were too late.

They did what they could—hurled orgasms after both their targets, *hard*—but were unsurprised to miss. Too much distance, too much building and wiring in the way . . . and almost at once, the targets were enclosed in something that insulated them from the tasp.

Knowledge of the certainty of failure slowed them no more than the door had—that is, not at all: they burned the living room floor away beneath their pounding feet and hit the basement running. Walls received no more respect. But the door they finally came to was made of sterner stuff, fighting a heroic fifteen-second rear guard action before it too succumbed. So did the one at the far end of the tunnel. By the time they emerged into the underground parking garage its robot door had fully closed again.

They let it live. To go quickly through so public a door would court attention; to trick it into opening normally would take too long. Without hesitation they backed out of the garage and retraced their steps toward the single-family home they had just renovated.

Once they were back in the tunnel, and its door to the world was fused shut again behind them, she put away a weapon widget and took out a scanning widget. "Lead lining," she announced. "Not just this tunnel: half the basement. Positively Murphian."

"This whole set-up has to be a Cold War relic," he said. "Basement bomb shelter with a secret way in and out."

"Thanks," she said. "I didn't quite have enough irony to choke on. Somewhere, Joe Stalin is chuckling. I don't like this."

"We'll reacquire," he said as they reentered the house proper and sealed the tunnel behind them.

"Of course we will. But meanwhile we have *two* active leaks—and the second target we know nothing about."

"We know everything June knows about him," he said soothingly.

"Yes, and she thinks he's an endearingly helpless boob. Do you think a boob outfitted this house?"

The house's security measures *had* been impressive, for this ficton. Impressive enough to keep their preliminary site surveillance shallow, for fear of being spotted. For that reason, the priest's hole had come as a rude surprise. And the speed—no, the quickness—with which it had been used was certainly unsettling. "No," he admitted.

"This is ungood," she said. "Two competent paranoids, in a fairly sophisticated ficton, on the loose with a Time bomb in their heads."

"So let's learn all we can about target number two," he said. He waved his hand like Peter Pan scattering fairy dust, and multicolored sparkles dispersed in all directions.

Upstairs in the den, Paul's hard drive powered up. Elsewhere in the building, photos of him were identified and scanned; samples of his DNA were collected and analyzed; his belongings were inventoried. In the basement, in the room where they stood, a barely visible trail of red sparkles began to form in midair, denoting where a heat-source of human temperature had recently passed. The brighter the sparkles, the more recent the passage. The *redder* the sparkles, the longer the human had tarried there. She traced it down a hallway to a place faint but carmine, and used her scanning widget. "There's something good here," she said, deactivating an excellent booby-trap.

"Be careful," he said, approaching.

"Don't b—" she said, and the second booby-trap blew her through a wall. He was barely able to cancel most of the sound. A lot of upstairs came downstairs onto both of them. He fought through smoking rubble to reach her side.

She lay on her back, blinking up at him. "I am finding it very hard not to dislike Paul Throtmanian," she said, her voice gentle in the sudden silence.

"Are you all right?"

She scanned herself—and winced. "I came through fine—but love . . . I'm afraid that was the Last Straw."

He turned to stone, and it did not help enough. "You're sure."

"My whole defensive system overloaded. For good. I'm an ordinary mortal."

He flinched, but said nothing. He owned no words equal to the occasion. He dropped to his knees beside her and took her in his arms.

This was a body blow, for her and for him and for their marriage and for their mission. They had both known this day might come, for either or both of them—had spent centuries preparing themselves for it, knowing that preparation would be no help. Sure enough, it was not. Suddenly it was a very sad day . . . and nowhere near over, with utter disaster on the horizon.

They shared their heartbreak in silence for several seconds.

"I dislike Paul Throtmanian," she said then, her voice even gentler than before. "Let's go see what he was protecting."

He helped her up. Her clothing was already starting to repair itself—as if to underline the point that she no longer could. Her temper was not improved when she found that Paul's hiding place had concealed money. "Oh for God's sake," she snapped. "I thought it was something *important*."

He was almost as annoyed that the cash had been destroyed—it certainly could have come in handy for *them*, particularly just now— but he could not say so without implying criticism of her judgment. Worse, accurate criticism. Fortunately the stream of incoming data still being assimilated and analyzed throughout the house picked then to yield up a useful distraction. "Ah," he said gratefully, "there's a lead."

She held the flagged datum before her mind's eye, studied it, and nodded just as gratefully. "Good. It's a place to start, at least."

"Do we want to involve the law?" he asked.

She started to answer . . . caught herself. "You decide. My judgment is a little off tonight."

It was one of the bravest things he had ever heard her say. He saluted it by ignoring it. "I'm on the fence," he said at once. "My inclination is obviously to go for a full-court press; I'd call out an air strike on them if I could think of a cover story. But the way they bugged out of here, on a second's notice, without even stopping for the cash . . . maybe our only chance is for them to think they've gotten clear, and relax just a hair. I think the cops might simply keep those two alert."

"Tough call," she agreed. "Make it."

He juggled the universe, backstopped but all alone. As he thought, he heard a clock ticking, louder than one had ever ticked for him before. Sweat sprang out on his forehead for the first time in decades.

"More data," he said. "We *know* one of them; we know *about* the other—the one with the testosterone. We need to integrate everything we just got here with everything June knows about him."

Ignoring the ticking, they closed their eyes, joined hands, joined minds, and did as he had proposed.

❈CHAPTER 5❈
Cute Meat

MEMORY SHARD:
JUNE BELLAMY, 08 JULY 1993:

JUNE TRIED TO WALK as if the right shoe still had a high heel, and scanned both sides of the deserted street, searching the shadowed places for danger and the arc-lit places for a door out of the world.

At age twenty-eight, she had just made what she intended to be her last professional mistake, overestimating not the character but the intelligence of her partner. The Slider was so innately lazy, she had assumed he realized what a valuable asset she was to him. She had trusted him completely to handle the blow-off; it was well within his talents. Instead he had simply skipped, left her standing there to take the gaff when the mark tipped. Caught flatfooted, she had been lucky to get clear with nothing worse than a couple of slaps, one good punch, and a broken high heel. In the Slider's stupid estimation, the extra half of the take was compensation enough for the inconvenience of having to find and train another skirt at his next address; never mind that the new girl would have *half* June's brains, skills or talent at best. As a result June herself was on the street at 4 AM in Toronto with no money, no safe address or identity, no local friends, and a dull nauseating ache on the left side of her face where the fist had caught her.

She understood her error, and looked forward to explaining his to the Slider one day. Some equations, she would tell him, contain certain terms so valuable that they *cannot* safely be subtracted or replaced. Or perhaps she could match his own laziness and say it even more succinctly: a good place to carve an "equals" sign occurred to her . . .

But first she had to make sure she *was* clear, get off the street. The mark might have yelled copper—or he might be in his Porsche now, casting through the night streets for a redhead with a hitch in her walk. Her hair and makeup would probably pass under streetlights—if she kept the unmarked side of her face to the street—but even the option of playing hooker and flagging down one of the rare motorists was closed to her: she looked like after the rape rather than before. It was so late, other pedestrians were rare, and none she saw looked like a serviceable champion. The cabs had all melted or corralled up or whatever it was they did when you really needed one.

That left a rabbit hole. Scarce, at 4 AM in downtown Toronto.

Up ahead on this side of the street. A bar with a faint light on inside . . .

Horse Shoes & Hand Grenades, it was called. The owner had hubris—June was absolutely certain every male who had ever spoken of it had referred to it as "Horseshit and Handjobs." She squinted through the partially frosted window, saw a shadowy figure behind the bar. Thank God—someone as lazy as the Slider, still cleaning up at this hour.

Her knock startled him; he spun and stared from side to side of the vast window that fronted the street, trying to locate her. He looked young and dumb and just cute enough to believe himself irresistible.

Perfect.

She knocked again, more weakly than before, and allowed herself to slump.

This time he located her, and at once began shaking his head and waving his hands in a reasonably impressive catalog of all the myriad ways there are to pantomime *Go away; we are closed,* a statement so self-evident as to be insulting. Marceau himself could not have returned the serve more powerfully: she managed—long distance, in bad light—to convey *need, desperation, apology, tremulous hope* and *earnest entreaty,* without so much as raising her hands or ever drawing undue attention from her sexual desirability.

It might not have worked in America, say, but in this blessed country even the bartenders were candy. Knowing he was defeated, but unwilling to acknowledge it yet, he stayed behind the bar and gave her *harassed* and *frustrated*. She riposted with *abject surrender*, and saw him fold. She was already digging tissues and another item from her purse as he put down whatever he was fooling with and came around the bar, and by the time he got the door open the tears she was wiping away looked genuine.

He was still doing *harassed*, but now that he could see her left cheek and general state of disrepair, felt obliged to add *concerned* and just a touch of *generically gallant*. Nonetheless he began by wasting his breath. "I'm sorry, miss, but we're closed."

"I know," she said, wasting some of her own. "But I just . . . I . . . look, I just had a really bad experience, okay? I'm a little shaken up; I thought he was going to . . . look, can I just duck inside for a second and clean up? Maybe after that I can figure out what to . . ." She let her voice trail off.

"Look, lady, I'd really like to help, okay? but the boss is gonna be back any minute, and honest to God, if he finds out I let anybody in here after closing he's gonna—"

He certainly had a lot of breath to waste. "I'll only be a minute, I swear." She paused a moment to let him begin his response, then overrode him with, "Look, I got female troubles, give me a break, okay?" and took a deep breath of her own to set the hook.

He emptied his lungs in a sigh (breath smelled okay, a good omen) and, in the Slider's memorable phrase, folded like a full wallet: slowly but thoroughly. "Jesus Christ, you're breaking my stones, lady. All right, look, come on in, the ladies' can is, uh, over there, just make it *quick*, all right?"

"You're very kind," she lied, and brushed past him, leaving him to close the door.

Once in the toilet, she relaxed and took her time. The cheek wasn't as bad as she had feared (thank God the son of a bitch wore the diamond on his other hand). She decided it would pass with a little work, and did it carefully. Then she addressed the shoes; by wedging the remaining heel under the sink tap, she was able to snap it off— lowering her apparent height by an inch or two. The tear at the collar she managed to repair with a safety pin, although it required taking off the blouse. Since it was off, she took off her bra too and treated herself to a full field bath, swabbing the sweat and fear-stink from her armpits with paper towels and rolling on fresh deodorant. The bra went into her purse, and several buttons were not rebuttoned when she put the blouse back on. She brushed out her hair and restyled it to present an altered silhouette. She removed and reversed her skirt, changing its color, and rolled its waistband under to shorten it by a couple of inches. She redid her lipstick with care. As an afterthought she slid a finger down her panties, moistened it, and rubbed it off on each earlobe. She assessed the results in the mirror, and felt some of her self-confidence flowing back.

Time to boat this sucker, she thought. She made sure her purse held condoms, and left the toilet.

He was exactly as she had imagined him: pacing behind the bar, muttering to his feet, drumming his fingers on every flat surface he passed, miming *impatience* to an empty house. He spun at the sound of her approach and stumbled slightly. When his eyes locked on her, there was an audible click. He had clearly been preparing to resume their Dueling Mimes with a strong combination of *put upon* and *endangered by your thoughtlessness* and *in no mood*, but the impression collapsed as his targeting computer claimed all available processing power.

She waited, let him speak first, and as soon as he did she overrode him with a husky "Thank you, kind sir. I really . . . owe you a lot."

"You're welcome," he had to say. "But look—"

"I really hope you mean that," she said. "Because right now I'd do just about anything for a stiff bourbon."

He wanted to say no firmly and at once, but was distracted by the half-grasped changes in her appearance; by the time he refocused, too much time had passed and it came out ineffective. "Jesus, lady, my boss—"

"I'm sure he wouldn't begrudge a lady a single drink," she said. "Not if he knew what I've been through tonight."

"Look, a cop glances in and sees you here this time of night and we got license trouble—really, they already gave us a couple of warnings: this time they're gonna—"

"I'll sit over here out of sight, then," she said, and at once took a seat at a table which was both well outside the cone of light from the single lamp above the register, and shielded from the window by a cigarette machine.

He glared down at his shoes and relaxed to the inevitable. "One *short* one," he said, and turned to hunt for a bourbon bottle.

She studied him as he built her drink. He was younger than her; call it three calendar and about a century subjective. He was of pleasing height, shape and aspect, in shape but not obsessive about it. He was clean shaven, wearing a black turtleneck and dark slacks. He moved with easy grace, light on his feet, but appeared very tired, fumbling for things he needed and pouring with only a sketch of professional elegance. As he went by the register, she noticed the key sticking out of its lock, giving it the absurd air of a windup toy. Something indefinable about his upper lip gave her a mild but distinct urge to bite it. When he brought her the drink, she noticed the bulge in his pants, without being caught at it.

She thought about all these things, and then she made him sit down and told him a long and gaudy and quite fictitious tale about how she had come to need succor at this hour, sipping her bourbon slowly as she created. The story might well have produced an erection on a statue of John Diefenbaker, and when she was sure he had one, she slid a hand into her purse. "I've taken up enough of your time," she said. "Let me just pay for my drink and I'll let you finish up and go home." She stirred the trash in her purse. "Do you have change for a twenty?"

He bunked at her, turned to look at the locked register, turned back to her. "You don't have anything smaller?"

"Afraid not," she said, smiling sweetly.

"Forget it, it's on the house."

"No, really, it's the least I can do. You want your accounts to balance."

"I already closed out the register. Thanks for offering, but it isn't necessary."

"Well, let me give you something for your trouble, then. Really, you've been a life-saver: just give me back a ten and a five." She began to take out the imaginary twenty. This was *fun*.

"I wouldn't dream of it," he said quickly. "Look, have you got some place you can go for the night? That creep could still be back at your apartment—"

"I . . . I'll think of something," she said.

"Why don't I go back there with you, right now, make sure the coast is clear?"

"But didn't you say you have to wait for your boss?" she said sadistically.

He blinked twice. "Uh, well, if he's not here by—" He glanced at his watch. "—now, it usually means he's not coming. Really, I'd be glad to lock up here and—"

"I don't think I want to go back to my place, just yet. I don't think I'm ready. You wouldn't know of anyplace else . . ."

He went for it like a starving trout. "Uh . . . look, what's your name?"

"Angela," she said.

"Angela, I know how this might sound, but . . . there's a fold-out couch at my place." He met her eyes squarely. "And I swear you can trust me."

She looked him over carefully. "I almost believe you," she said softly.

"You can," he said. "I've got my share of faults, but I won't ever lie to you."

"I hope you mean that," she said.

"I do," he assured her, quiet sincerity in his voice.

She took her time deciding, for the pleasure of watching him mime *steadfast*, and finally said, "I don't even know your name—no, don't tell me yet—but I'll go home with you, if you'll give me a truthful answer to one question."

"I'm not," he said. "Never even been engaged."

"Good, but that wasn't the question."

"What, then?'

"How much did you clear?"

He shook his head slightly a few times. "Beg pardon?"

"How much did you take off the guy tied up and gagged on the floor behind the bar?"

His eyes went to her right hand, still deep in her purse. They were the only part of him that moved. His own hand must have yearned to go to the bulge in his pants she had seen earlier—the one a few inches from his erection—but it didn't even twitch. She was impressed. "You heat?"

"No," she said. "And *I'll* never lie to *you*, either. Not anymore. Sound like a plan?"

It was his turn to take his time making up his mind. "Yeah," he said finally. "I guess it does. When did you tip?"

"You were too graceful to be such a lousy bartender. And you left the key in the register."

He was impressed. "You're good."

"Yes," she said.

"I figure I'll probably net somewhere around two large."

"Chump," she said fondly. "It's time you went professional. Let's book."

"I'm sick of the place," he agreed. He rose, got a briefcase from behind the bar, said, "Sorry 'bout that, cap," toward the floor, and came back to take her arm.

As they walked out the door they nearly collided with a cop. He glanced at them with idle curiosity, looked away politely, then registered the briefcase and began a double take. Before he could complete it his jaw collided with a male fist, distracting him so much that he failed to notice June's foot rising like a Shuttle launch toward his groin. Its impact folded him like an *empty* wallet, presenting the nape of his neck to her companion's elbow, and he ceased to be a significant part of their lives.

"*Now* you can tell me your name," she said, when she had made sure the cop was out.

"I'm Paul Throtmanian." He was breathing audibly but under control.

"I'm Susan Hughes."

"Want a gun or a badge?" Paul said cheerily.

"What would I need with a gun?"

"Good point." He flexed the fingers of his right hand, winced, and started to walk away.

"Chump," Susan said—but softly, to herself—and got the cop's wallet and pocket change.

She told him her right name after the third orgasm. His third; she had long since lost count.

ABSTRACT, ACQUIRED DATA:
PAUL THROTMANIAN, 31 OCTOBER 1995:

BIRTH NAME:
Paul Donald Throtmanian

BIRTHPLACE:

Riker's Island (holding cell, Women's Corrective Facility)

BIRTHDATE:

1 April 1970

MOTHER:

Lada Loven (apparently legal name; birth name: Ilse Throtmanian; deceased)

FATHER:

not known

CURRENT LEGAL NAME (THIS ADDRESS):

Ralph Metkiewicz

KNOWN ALIASES:

Peter David Talbot; Philip Dwight Tanager; Sebastian Tombs; Richard Stark; Dick Starkey; John Archibald Dortmunder; Samuel Holt; Ernest Gibbons, Sr; James Tiptree, Jr.; Dr. Lafe Hubert, M.D.; Neil O'Heret Brain; B.D. Wyatt; Edward Hunter Waldo; Preston Danforth Tomlinson; Parker Meyer Spenser; Travis T. Magee; Tak Hallus; Penforth Naim; Susan Donim; Dr. Winston O. Bourgee; Paul Nurk; John Nurk; Edison Ripsborn; Marcus Van Heller; Paul Teale

CURRENTLY ACTIVE ID:

Metkiewicz; Gibbons; Hallus; Naim; Donim; Smith; Teale (various)

REGISTERED VEHICLES:

- 1994 Toyota Camry to Metkiewicz (this address; disabled)
- 1995 Porsche to Naim (location of record: 10659 Point Grey Rd.)

KNOWN RESIDENCES, LOCAL:

- this address; expired
- 10659 Point Grey Rd., Vancouver, BC V8U 4R6 (legal residence of June Bellamy as "Carla Bernardo")

KNOWN RESIDENCES, NONLOCAL:

- 9787 Flagler St., Key West, FL [zip unknown] (summer home of "Ernie and Dora Gibbons"; currently sublet)

CITIZENSHIP:

Canadian (2); American (3); Cuban; Japanese; all valid and current

EDUCATIONAL HISTORY:

entered Chaminade HS, Mineola, NY, 5 September 1982; withdrew two months short of graduation; no further formal study indicated

CREDIT HISTORY:
labyrinthine; no credit history as Paul Donald Throtmanian
after 1982
MILITARY HISTORY:
none recorded; inventory suggests advanced weapons training
WORK HISTORY:
various; all apparently virtual except for a summer job as shipping
clerk, K&K Chemicals, Syosset, NY, as Paul D. Throtmanian, 1985
TAX HISTORY:
none, any jurisdiction
ARRESTS:
- 1 April 1986, Old Bethpage, NY: Suspicion of Arson (NYS
  orphanage), as Paul David Throtmanian; dismissed LOE; file
  open
COMPLAINTS FILED:
none, any jurisdiction
CONVICTIONS:
none, any jurisdiction
WARRANTS OUTSTANDING:
none, any jurisdiction

⚹CHAPTER 6⚹
Grok and Roll

"THERE IS NO POINT in mobilizing the authorities," he said. Upstairs, the Throtmanian/Metkiewicz computer reformatted its hard drive three times and then boiled its own ROM; flames began whispering in two nearby floppy disk caddies, two filing cabinets, a lockbox under the bed in the master bedroom, and at three points in the basement.

"There isn't even any point in chasing that pair ourselves," she said. "We need to phone home."

His shoulders tensed, then slumped as he realized he agreed. Centuries of success, ended. Only the third full-scale Red Alert in their entire tenure, and the first time they had *ever* needed to yell for help.

The day had begun so *well.* . . .

Their own vehicle, a generic grey Honda Accord, was parked immediately across from Chez Metkiewicz, and their clothes had finished regrowing themselves by now. Nonetheless they left the building by the discreet route, and circled a total of seven blocks to approach the car. They would have abandoned it, but it was registered to his current identity. Several local residents and pedestrians passed them as they reached it, and they were alert and ready with the tasp . . . but it proved unnecessary, as everyone's attention was focused on the smoke and flames emerging from the shattered door of the house across the street.

They left that block with care, scanning the sidewalks to make sure no disaster fans would need to notice them to cross the street safely. Even after turning the corner he drove just enough above the speed limit to avoid being conspicuous, and maneuvered conservatively, until he found a spot on West 10th where an Accord could remain parked indefinitely without attracting interest. The distant sounds of the fire engines leaving the substation were audible as they got out of the car; for once that fine brigade would be too late. They rounded the corner and walked south at a speed appropriate to their personas, and for another twenty meters into the dark mews between West 10th and West 11th. They stopped abruptly there, and stood in perfect silence and stillness for five seconds, making quite sure they were unobserved.

Then they became invisible and rose into the air and flew southwest at barely subsonic speed.

Like circling seven blocks to get the car, stashing it *felt* like a waste of time and energy. But the roundabout method got them home nearly two full minutes sooner, without compromising security.

There they found no good news.

⊰CHAPTER 7⊱
Woolgathering on the Lam

PAUL SAID, "I think it's time to stop underestimating these people."

June, involved with a "footlong" sub (nineteen centimeters, counting projecting silage), did not respond. They were in the safest place they could think of to dine at 10 p.m.: on a bench by the harbor at Jericho Beach. An overhanging tree shielded them fairly well from the intermittent rain. People approaching on foot could be observed for hundreds of meters in silhouette before they reached small-arms range; there were a hundred and eighty directions in which to flee at need; innumerable cloutable cars were parked nearby; there were even cloutable boats moored at hand, and three different places of concealment to which one might swim underwater if need arose. The twinkling panorama of Vancouver's downtown—the Emerald City indeed—was arrayed on their right, with Stanley Park jutting out into the water to the left of it like Nature's Last Stand. Distant lights twinkled and shimmered at the tops of the ski runs across the water in North Vancouver. A tiny Asian man waded with rolled trousers at the water's edge well to the west, ignoring the drizzle, stalking tomorrow's breakfast. Dark water lapped at the shore, too gently to obscure approaching footsteps.

"I think it's time to change tactics, too," he went on. "I've been on the defensive for over an hour, now, and that raises my lifetime cumulative exposure to damn near a whole waking day. I think it's time we scared the shit out of *them*."

"Paf 'ime," she said, then swallowed and repeated, "Past time."

"So we need a plan," he said, and took a bite of his own sub. He

504

hoped that she would take up the conversational ball while he chewed, but she took another big bite of her own food. When he had cleared his mouth again, he tried, "So what are our assets?" and took another mouthful.

"I come up with bugger-all," she said.

"Zheevuf, Zhu'," he said, and then, "Jesus, June!"

"Am I missing something? As an asset, a hot car has the shelf life of a donut. We have to consider both of our addresses blown. All three cars gone or useless. Every ID we have is hot, including passports. Chump change. No weapons. No good way to get out of town without new ID. Three real friends in the world, each of whom would regard us as radioactive typhoid HIV-positive lepers with Ebola fever if they knew what's after us. And I wouldn't blame them."

"Hell, *I* don't know what's after us. Maybe we're all of those things. All I know is, I'm a dog who just got chased out of his own damn house, and if I don't do something about it I gotta lie down and die."

"I agree," she said. "I simply said we have no assets. Except fear, terror, and a fanatical devotion to the Pope. So how would you like to start?"

He looked down at his sandwich, and gave thought to pitching it into the sea . . . following it, perhaps, with the portion already consumed. Then he sighed, and took a deep breath, and bit off another hunk.

"Okay, no asshetsh," he said, chewing vigorously. "Exshep Key Wesh, maybe, if we cang 'et there . . ."

"I think we have to consider that blown, too," she said.

"Not for awhile, maybe," he said. "There's no paper on it back there at home."

"Its in the computer."

"Jesus, June, the fucking *NSA* couldn't hack into my private partition in less than a week: even *you* might have some—" His voice trailed off. "Oh."

She nodded. "We've already *seen* them do things the NSA couldn't do."

"I said I was going to stop underestimating them. Right." He resumed eating, frowning.

She corrected him. "What you said was, 'It's time to stop underestimating these people. . . .' Maybe that's doing it again."

"Huh?"

"I've stopped assuming they're people."

He spat out a mouthful of sandwich and stared. After a moment, he wiped his mouth and said, "What, then? Martians? Sauron of Mordor? Cthulhu? Christ, Scientist?"

She shook her head impatiently. "I don't *have* any labels for what's after us. And I'm not looking for any. If I think of them as humans, I'll be subconsciously expecting them to have human limitations. If I let myself think of them as Martians, I'm liable to hunt them with a water pistol. If they're Sauron, I'll start looking for the Ring—you see? I can't afford preconceptions: this is more than our lives on the line."

"There *is* nothing more than our lives."

"Yes, there is!"

"Not so loud—"

She lowered her volume to a passionate whisper. "I'd rather the bastards rape me and torture me to death and crap on my corpse than monkey with my mind. They're welcome to anything else they're smart enough and strong enough to take *from* me, including my life—but they *can't have my memories*. Those are all I've *got* out of all this."

He kept silent, from surprise at her passion and confusion at her words and a general instinct to lower their average sound production. He had known that what had happened to June was very bad; awful, sure. He had not realized until now it was skin-crawling. . . .

Well, which *was* more important to him? Staying alive? Or preserving the integrity of his mind? You *can live, Mr. Throtmanian, but you'll never be able to trust your own memories again as long as you live . . . never know for sure what has been or will be taken from you— or, if you prefer, we can put you out of your misery right now. . . .*

What finally brought him out of his thoughts was the classic Sub Eater's Dilemma. (You've finished the sandwich; your hands are greasy; the paper napkin you were using is a sodden, useless mess; you have another napkin, but can't get it without soiling your shirt by reaching into your pocket for it with greasy hands.) He solved it as he did most problems, impatiently, running his fingers through the stubble on his head until his hands were clean. June regarded him with fond distaste. "Can't take you anywhere," she said softly.

"Do we even know it's a 'they'? Do we know for a fact that there's more than one . . . Jesus, we have to call it *something*—more than one monkey demon?" He knew she would get the reference, having lent her the book. In Richard Farina's novel BEEN DOWN SO LONG, IT LOOKS LIKE UP TO ME, the monkey demon was the symbol of all ancient evil; it *had* no limitations.

"Good point. Let's think it through using one, and see if we stumble. Okay: I trip over the demon in the woods, and I—" She hesitated. "—I have an orgasm, and it takes over my mind. It interrogates me until it's happy, disposes of my damp underwear, and lets me go. It doesn't need to follow me any more, any more than it needed to follow Angel Gerhardt. But now it knows I phoned you. It knows everything I said. It wants me to erase the message, but I have no way to do that because your machine is so primitive. So it goes to your place, but you're not there, you're out cleaning the sci-fi people. So the monkey demon stakes you out."

He held up a hand. "Interesting point. Why? Why not just enter the house, find out everything it can about me, and wait *inside* for me to come home? Or just erase the phone machine and tiptoe away?"

"I don't know," she said, "and it's the first thing like a limitation we've spotted on it. Maybe it could smell your alarms, and decided to let *you* turn them off. Mark for later analysis; onward. Then you come home—but it doesn't know you have, right away, because it doesn't know about your back way in, because *I* didn't—you'd hinted you had a bolt-hole, but you never showed it to me. For all we can prove, there was a second demon *behind* the house, with no idea you were strolling by under his feet."

"There was a back door alarm too," Paul said, "and I never heard it go off."

"To notice you were home only after a while suggests the demon or demons were monitoring the house with something like thermal gear, from outside: it took time for you to set it off. They thought I was in there alone, waiting for you."

"Okay, I buy that. I still see only one set of tracks."

"You're right," she said. "There's no reason to assume there's more than one monkey demon. On the other hand, there's no reason to assume there aren't fifty. And my mother is dying." At the non sequitur, she flung the heel of her sandwich from her, so heedlessly that it fell short of the water, providing not even the satisfaction of a splash. "So what I say is, screw the bastard or bastards. You want vengeance; I can relate. Let's deal with it in our next lifetime. Let's abandon our luggage, figuratively and literally. Forget Key West. Forget any plans we ever had that got as far as being spoken aloud. Forget anybody we ever knew. Let's just hit the restart button on our lives, right now. Make it didn't happen. Go someplace we've never been and create new personas and go back to what we were doing: educating the gullible. Yellow alert: I think the distant silhouette approaching from the west is a cop." Her voice did not change in pitch or tone in the slightest, on the last sentence.

Paul scratched his neck and peeked. "Still a ways off."

"Alone. Fat. Moving slow. I think he's just strolling his beat."

"Back to business, then: can we do that, you think? Just walk away?"

"There's only one weakness I've noticed about the monkey demon. I don't understand it, but I'm sure of it: somehow, despite all his power, he's as afraid of The Man as we are. He could have taken either of us out at any time, with anything from an axe to a nuke—but he doesn't want to attract attention to himself for some reason. I won't be terribly surprised if he sends a fucking curse after us . . . but he can't put out an APB. I don't think that cop is looking for us. About forty meters away now."

Converting that laboriously in his head to a hundred and thirty one and a quarter feet, a hair under forty-three and a quarter yards, Paul decided the metric system could stand to be damned one more time. "And maybe if the monkey demon notices we've disappeared, and after awhile nothing he doesn't like has happened, he'll decide we're not a threat and let us live. It plays. So let's see if it's safe." He stood and walked like a numbskull directly toward the cop.

June sat still, and discreetly put a hand into her purse.

"Excuse me, Constable," Paul said, pitching his voice just a little too loud for the time and place, the way a real numbskull would do. "My name is Ralph Metkiewicz, and that's my fiancée June Cleaver, and we've been talking about our relationship for hours, you know how it is, and we were just starting to wonder, sitting here trying to remember, whether we turned the gas off before we left my house, or . . . what I'm getting at, I'm sorry to bother you, I know this must sound stupid, but have you heard anything about a house fire or some kind of commotion up on West Thirteenth tonight?"

June held her breath. *That's my warrior,* she thought. *A hair trigger—everywhere except in the rack, thank God! Hope it doesn't get us killed . . . or even pinched. This is a lousy time to be trapped in a known location and have our faces on the news.*

The cop sized him up. After an endless few seconds, the registers of his eyes displayed: *Numbskull.* "Friend, if it doesn't concern this particular stretch of shoreline, I tend to get most of my local news from the TV, just like you. I was in your shoes, though, I think I'd conclude it was something worth going home to check on."

"You know, you're probably right," Paul told him. "Joan—Miss Cleveland there—excuse me, honey, *Ms.* Clevelyn—was just saying something like that. Risk versus game, or something like that. Weren't you, honey?"

"The term 'honey' is a demeaning sexist put-down, you *know* that, Ralph," she said. "It is not flattering to be compared to something wild bears paw and slaver over. And I think the constable is quite right—aren't you, Constable?"

For her the cop took no time at all: *Numbskull.* "Well, ma'am, all's I'm saying is, it wouldn't hurt to go check. I hope everything turns out alright for you both. Goodnight, Ms. Clevemumble—good night, Mr., uh, Metka . . ."

"Meskavitz," Paul said. "Thank you, Constable. Have a nice night."

"Anybody ever tell you you look like that starship guy on TV?"

"What guy?"

"Never mind. Good night."

Paul and June left their bench and headed west, listening carefully to the tired footsteps behind them. When Paul calculated that the fat cop was once again a shade under forty-three and a quarter yards distant, he murmured, "See? Good news: we were right about something."

"I *said* I didn't *think* he had us on his hot list," June said, a wonderful sentence to hiss through one's teeth.

"And that was good enough for me . . . 'honey.' What would have been better: wait a few hours for the morning paper to come out? Now we know we're not law-type hot, and we can plan our getaway."

"Fine. Go ahead."

"Jesus, do I have to do *everything* around here? You start. We want to go far far away. Tell me where."

"Not there."

"Huh?"

"Far far away is where the monkey demon will expect us to go. We want to get clear, sure—but some place so close to the known Danger Zone that only a numbskull would run that far and then stop. The monkey demon thinks he knows we're not numbskulls: that's our secret weapon."

He snorted. "By that logic, the smartest thing for us to do is pick up some marshmallows and wieners and go back to my place to toast 'em. We can join the crowd and ask in a loud voice if anybody's seen a monkey who can suck your brain and make you forget you saw him."

"Maybe that would be the smartest thing we can do," she said dryly. "I have a feeling the least threatening place we could be right now, in his estimation, is in a nice snug VGH mental ward with heads full of thorazine. It's something we *know* that makes us dangerous to him, and mental patients don't have any information anyone else cares about." She stopped, confused; instead of being squelched, he looked almost cheerful.

"You think he considers us 'dangerous'?" he said.

She suppressed an urge to smack him. "Amend that to 'annoying,' all right, Tarzan? 'Worth hunting and mindraping.' You want to pick up those marshmallows and franks? We'll have to pull a short con on a Seven-Eleven guy. . . ."

He sobered. "As Oberlin Bill used to say, it never pays to be *too* smart. Maybe a shade less audacity wouldn't hurt anything. Okay, nearby, but not too near—someplace we can get to without leaving a record or passing a security camera, with no ID and chump change. Well, I know one last good border crossing I think I can afford to use up—but I'm afraid we're going to arrive in the Land of the Fee smelling just like everything else that comes out of that pipe. Let's try and clout something with two changes of clothes in it—"

"The border's too far and too intelligent," she said. "Everybody tries to disappear to a crowded place where you can blend in easy. Let's go to someplace we'll stand out—to the *locals*, who we don't care about—and where we can hang out a lot of tripwires, where we'll hear early about any *other* odd strangers in town. We're both city kids, so we'll hide in the boonies."

"The Gulf Islands," he said. "A ferry."

"That'd work," she said. "But I've got something better in mind. Cast your mind back about a million years, to when we were free human beings, loose on the earth. What was I working on, when I had to go visit my mother?"

Paul stopped short, and stared in admiration. "Jesus. Of course. Whatsisname! Bonehead Island!"

June's recent trip south to visit her mother had forced a working con onto the back burner: the mark had been ripe but June was too busy to pluck him, so she had been forced to reschedule. He was a yuppy software baron named O'Leary, presently away with his beloved on a long-planned trip around the world which would take him three months even in the absurd event that everything went as planned. Postponed opportunity had proven to be a blessing in disguise: O'Leary's luxury A-frame home stood unoccupied until his return.

"*Bowen* Island," June said. "Henry O'Leary."

"Where is that one?'

"It's one of the Horseshoe Bay jobs."

"Better and better," he said. "A little one. This likes me well. Have you noticed that things always start to look better after you eat a sub?"

"First we have to get there," she said. She was cheering up too, but was not yet ready to admit it. "Let's go find a doss. Tomorrow we scrounge a little, and then catch a ferry."

"Scrounge what?"

She thought. "We need a backpack, maybe an overnight bag, some binoculars, sunglasses . . . an ice chest wouldn't hurt. And cash, of course, at least enough for two pedestrian ferry tickets. And as much L.L. Bean as we can lay our hands on." She looked him over critically, and suddenly started to laugh. "And you'll need to shave." The laugh built as he stared in incomprehension. He had forgotten. "Nothing looks less respectable than five o'clock shadow all over your fucking head," she managed, and then lost it.

So did he, of course, and the shared laugh grew until they had to stop walking and hold each other up, and in no time at all they were kissing, still laughing but really kissing.

"Are we having fun yet?" he asked when they broke for air.

"Who stopped?' she said. But there was something indefinable in the placement of her eyebrows, or possibly her lower lip, that cued him it was time to stop kissing and get back to business.

Besides, the rain was starting to really come down, now.

The Lower Mainland of the province of British Columbia is more than generously supplied with islands; if you're missing one, it's probably there, somewhere. There ought to be a Lower Mainland salad dressing.

In 1995 one could drive thirty minutes south from Vancouver, almost to the U.S. border, and take a large ferry from the immense ways at Tsawwassen (providing one resisted the urge to attempt to pronounce it) southwest to any of the medium-size, generally well-populated Gulf Islands; these gathered like hungry pilotfish around the anus of the leviathan Vancouver Island, whose immense torso enclosed the Strait of Georgia between it and the mainland. Alternatively, one could drive twenty minutes north and then west to the feverishly picturesque Horseshoe Bay, and take a small or medium-size ferry from more modest docks than Tsawwassen's to an assortment of smaller and less populous (thus more interesting) islands in Howe Sound. These varied widely in state of development—from rustic Gambier Island, accessible only to foot traffic, to Bowen Island, relatively built up and well built. People were starting to call it Commuter Cay: it perfectly met the needs of the yuppie commuter, being as far from Vancouver (in every sense of the term) as one could get and still be within reasonable travel time. There was more than one Porsche on Bowen Island, and you could rent Buñuel movies or buy fresh Jamaica Blue Mountain coffee beans at the general store—but you could also get Cheese Whiz, frozen waffles and King Red Man chewing tobacco.

The Horseshoe Bay terminal was ideal for a fugitive, big enough for one to hide in the crowd but not big enough or important enough to be watched. Paul and June, carefully dressed and outfitted to suggest fairly rich people who had dressed down for the trip so as not to appear pretentious, would have been effectively invisible even without the drizzle.

Paul could not *believe* the security.

"There *isn't* any!" he exclaimed almost angrily. "Look at this place! No ID check, no cameras—I swear to God I don't smell a single cop, uniform or plain. There must be some, but they're all cooping." They were strolling along the edge of an immense parking lot which had filled in the last half hour and would empty in fifteen minutes, on the opposite side from the long row of washrooms, "restaurant" and other dollar-traps that were currently milking most of the cars' passengers while they waited for the ferry.

"They're probably helping a trucker with his engine," she said. "Usually they try to stay visible. In case someone needs to ask them a question."

Paul stared at her. "I will never in my life get used to this country. It isn't fucking natural."

"Thank God!"

"Christ, we could clout a car right here in broad daylight, if we had any use for one. I've seen three with keys in them."

"Where the hell are they going to go? Every one is boxed in."

They reached the front of the lineup, found a spot from which they could admire Horseshoe Bay. It was easy work. The stage-prop binoculars proved useful. The ferry was in sight in the distance, looking rather like Roseanne Barr—a white tub and proud of it, with great bumpers—and a cinch to beat the napping Hare in the swimming race, approaching Horseshoe Bay with the speed of the bell at the end of Geometry class.

"June?"

"Mm?"

"About your mother . . ."

She kept staring out across the gunmetal water. "She's still here. I can feel it. Still hanging on."

He nodded uselessly. He began to speak three times, producing nothing at first, and then, "We could," and "If."

She nodded, and put the binoculars on a bird. "Pop has enough on his plate just now," she said, tracking it. "He can't believe they moved to a country without socialized medicine."

"Yeah. I just . . ."

"I know." She put down the glasses. "And what I'm supposed to do is come into your arms and let you comfort me. You deserve that. You really do. I'm sorry."

He said nothing.

"I don't know if this is going to make sense," June said. "I want to try and say it just right." There was a long pause, and then the words came out quickly. "You and me. When we're together I want you inside of me, and me inside of you. You know that. When we're together and it's good I want to be naked for you, naked to you. I want you to come inside of my skull and *know me*, know me better than anybody else, know me better than I've ever been able to make myself known to anybody else, know all my secrets and all my sorrows." She stopped speaking, bent her head. The ferry was 25 percent nearer when she continued. "Well, it happened to me, the real deal, and it sucks. I feel like I've been raped by a column of ants, like a burglar left turds on the carpet of my brain on the way out. I don't know, it—" She broke off again. When she resumed, her voice was thicker, her words clumsier. "So what I mean, us, it's for a while it'll be a little hard, okay? I'm trying to say hard the way it was, like before, feeling that way again for a little while, with *anybody*. I just—I've only *got* the two speeds, flat out and neutral, and I'm scared to touch the pedal. . . . I hope you can deal with that."

He had trouble enough dealing with the simple urge to reach out to her with his hands, then and there: the lunatic certainty that if he only touched her he could draw out some of her pain even if she said otherwise. And he did have the fleeting, guilty thought that running for your life is much more fun if you can get laid during the lulls. But he was a strong man, and loved her enough to give her anything she asked that would not kill him outright or spoil his opinion of himself. He took several deep breaths without being caught at it, and when he had himself under control, he said, as if agreeing on a restaurant, "Space. Sure."

The ferry was near, now. She checked his backpack, then picked up her overnight bag. "Thanks."

"Yowsah."

Then neither of them said anything until he said, "Say when," and she said, "You'll know." By then the ferry was beginning its approach, snorting foam, and he picked up the cooler and they joined the rest of the foot passengers lining up at the gate.

They were much more plausible as rich people, walking a couple of feet apart.

Snug Cove, the ferry terminus at Bowen Island, was a lovely, sleepy little place, quaint but not yet aware of it, its "downtown" small enough that there was nowhere you could stand in it and not see forest, but just large enough to offer a choice of "restaurants." They dined in silence (as was expected of people dressed like that) at the least worst. The deck view of a rustic duck pond guarded by a magnificent old grandfather tree was splendid, but Paul was still moved to swipe tips on the way out. As they stepped back out onto a sidewalk which, between ferries, was empty as a politician's word, he spoke to his lady for the first time since they had left the mainland. "So how far is this place?"

"About a fifteen-minute drive, I think. I've never actually been there."

He groaned. "Naturally. We can't go around clouting cars, either; we have to *live* here. Is there any point in my even asking whether they have cabs on this overgrown speed bump?"

"Nope." She headed off uphill through the drizzle, toward the beckoning wilderness. He followed with as much good cheer as he could muster. Within what he thought of as a city block, the terrain leveled off—but the buildings and sidewalks went away. He was too much of a city kid to be comfortable walking anywhere that didn't have sidewalks, but his guru had once drummed into him that he must never complain (because she was sick and tired of listening to it), and so he soldiered on, scheming ways to humiliate an irresistible force. *Any place that has fifteen-minute drives should have cabs,* he thought from time to time, as the blisters began to form.

Suddenly June stopped, for no reason he could see. Distantly he heard the sound of a motorist, and envied him or her fiercely. "What's up?"

As though it were an answer, she moved a few steps to the edge of the roadbed, held out her hand, and stuck up her thumb.

He blinked, puzzled. "What are you doing?"

She sighed. "Just wait. And pray."

The vehicle, a truck that had emphysema too bad to be singing that loud, was almost upon them now. All at once it dropped its pitch, like Tom Waits nodding off in the middle of a song, and slowed to a complete stop beside them.

The driver, a senior citizen, stared at them. At a loss, Paul stared back. Both the old man's hands were visible on the steering wheel.

"Where you folks headed?" he asked.

Paul was too flustered to remember his cover; June supplied the name of the man whose house they were supposed to be sitting, and described its location. At once, as if some sort of agreement had been negotiated, the old man leaned to his right and opened the passenger door of his pickup, clearly offering them a ride. Up front, with him.

When June began walking around the front of the truck, Paul decided people must just do things like this in the country, in Canada anyway, and followed her.

Sure enough, without so much as displaying a weapon, the old man put the truck very neatly in gear and took them where they wanted to go. He did talk nearly as much as a New York cabbie, in a voice clearly audible above the roar of the truck's renewed Waits imitation, but was willing to listen to June bullshit back—he even gave her something like fifty percent of the airtime. In the course of his own rambling he disclosed at least three pieces of information of use to anyone who wanted to come clean him out some night. He even waited to offer his name until June gave their current names.

"And it's all right to laugh when I tell you," he prefaced it.

"I wouldn't laugh," June assured him.

"Aw, go ahead, I wouldn't want to see you folks hurt yourself. My daddy's name was spelled L-Y-C-O-T-T, and he always pronounced it 'like it'—'like it is,' he'd say, 'and you can Lycott or lump it!' And then my ma decided she just had to name me after her dead little brother Maurice. . . ." He waited until their faces showed they'd got it, thumped the dashboard and cackled. "That's right: I'm Moe Lycott!"

After a polite pause, they used the dispensation they'd been given and began to giggle. "You don't seem mad about it," June said.

"Hell, no," he said. "All my life, whenever I walk by, people point and say, 'Now, *that's*—' "

June obligingly supplied the punchline, and giggled some more.

Paul did not really think the bald husband of a chirpy yuppie woman who kept silent himself would be out of character, but eventually he felt he should produce at least a token attempt at polite discourse, to make clear that he was not the world's only wealthy skinhead. He cast through his mind for movies he'd seen involving country life, and at the next gap in the conversation, he said, "So Moe, do you have any cows?"

The truck was allowed to take a solo for the next forty-three and a quarter yards or so.

"I been a widower twenty year," Moe finally said, and immediately asked June something about her imaginary job back in the city.

Although June's directions had been general, Moe spotted the right mailbox with his cataracted eyes and let them off exactly where they wanted to be. He drove off before Paul could even begin to embarrass himself by offering to pay for the ride, leaving them the single word, "Goodnight," as though he no longer had a right to talk their ear off now that they were no longer locked into being with him. June turned at once and started down the weeded driveway, but Paul stood where he was for a moment, frowning.

"What?" she said, turning back.

"Nothing," he said. "I just feel like a tiger trying to hide in a slaughter-house. This island is *candy*. Hell, Hopeless *Harry* could get healthy, here." He blinked. "I can't believe I just said that sentence." Hopeless Harry was the worst grifter either of them knew, a man with a face so quintessentially dishonest that he had once been stopped and frisked while dressed as a priest in a wheelchair; you had to admire his doggedness, but then you were done admiring him.

"Down, boy."

"I know, I know," he said. "I feel like the Invisible Man in the girls' dormitory, though."

As he had prayed, that got a faint grin. "Up, boy. Come on, let's check out our lovely new home."

The keys, as expected, were where people hide keys.

Much money had been both thoughtfully and tastefully spent on that home. The location itself was a postcard. The A-frame was a sketch drawn on the back of the postcard by a master. It had *two* decks out back, both cantilevered out over a dizzying slope that dropped what Paul thought of as about fifteen stories in about one block to Howe Sound; lush forest on either side framed the view perfectly, making it endurable. Next stop, Japan. Hi, birds.

"I can't believe this clown *didn't* actually get someone to watch a house this nice for him while he was away."

"Why? To make sure nobody moves in and trashes the place, or something? What do you think this is, civilization?"

There was a hot tub built into the lower deck, big enough for seven people or four programmers. The barbie on the upper deck enabled a reasonably bright child to cook half a beeve at a time to perfection, and the deck itself had a built-in cable-and-power hookup in its railing so you could take the portable TV/CD/tapedeck/tuner/VCR out there without stringing unsightly wires from the bedroom. There was an Aptiva in the den, with Pentium 133 chip and 32 megs of RAM, a ten-gig hard drive, a 25-inch monitor and an 800-dpi printer. There was a similarly equipped Power Mac in a corner of the living room; apparently O'Leary had taken all of his Powerbooks with him on his world tour. The brand-new state-of-the-art high-end entertainment console beside the Mac produced sound you could taste and video you could smell in any room of the house including both bathrooms, and could be remotely programmed from most of them. The fridge and freezer could have supported a midsize restaurant; the microwave could have accommodated the other half of the barbecued cow, with the gas stove for the potatoes and vegetables; there was no room in the house without at least one ceiling-high shelf of books (most either old friends or intriguing); the construction and carpentry were ostentatiously breathtaking throughout; the interior decor said *you deserve this* quietly but very persuasively, and it came as something of a relief to Paul when he managed to find (in the garage) a single, inexplicably uncomfortable chair.

"I don't want to con this guy," he said to June, when he found her sorting through excellent drugs in the drawers of the guest bedroom. "I want to *be* this guy." He smelled a bag of marijuana, and sighed. "I love this part of the world."

"You haven't seen what he's sleeping with," she said.

"True. What *is* Mrs. O'Leary like? You never told me."

"What's that got to do with what he's sleeping with?"

"Ah," he said. "You were working a Diabolique."

"A modified Diabolique," she agreed. "What he's sleeping with has a Y chromosome. Likes girls just as much as Henry does, thank goodness, or I'd have had to be big sister fag hag."

Paul nodded. "I wondered how old Henry was dealing with the problem of bringing his mistress along on a world cruise."

"By the time they all get back from being locked in a hotel together for three months, all the way 'round the planet, the boyfriend will be happier than ever to have me help him set up a burglary-gone-wrong on the happy couple, and run away with me. I just hope he stays greedy and half-smart, doesn't decide to ad-lib and lever them both over the rail somewhere along the way. I won't blame him if he does, but I want this place for the whole three months if I can get it."

The turn of this conversation was giving Paul a powerful warm furry urge to tear off all that L.L. Bean, peel his lady like a grape and throw her on the guest bed, so he put down the bag of marijuana and said, "I've got the water and heat back on, and the hot tub is warming. Is it time to go next door—wherever the hell *that* is—and start establishing our cover, so nobody has the cops swing by?"

She shook her head, and dropped a large chunk of hashish on top of the cocaine in the drawer. Coke was just money one shouldn't flash, to both of them. "That's covered."

"What, you mean Mo' Like It? We don't even know how far away he lives; he could be a hermit at the other end of the island."

"Doesn't matter. On an island this size, the jungle telegraph is like the Internet: all users are equidistant. Twenty bucks says at this moment, one of the neighbors is asking what the world is coming to, when even decent people are shaving their heads."

"Twenty Canadian? Or American?"

June shut the drawer. "Whatever. And I have a much better idea than borrowing a cup of credibility."

"Go."

"Why don't you tear this goddam L.L. Bean off me, peel me like a grape, and carry me upstairs to the master bedroom?"

Don't ever let anybody tell you enough money can't heal, sometimes, Paul thought. "That bed there's a lot closer," he pointed out.

"Yeah, but I want to be carried further than that."

He shrugged. "Works for me."

Even for a strong man in love and his prime, yuppie clothing is oddly hard to tear; Paul had to settle for merely rumpling everything but the panties. June didn't seem to mind.

He was very careful, very alert, until she signaled clearly that he did not need to be; then he burst open and died and was annihilated and, timeless time later, painstakingly reassembled from a kind description. Perhaps it should have been disappointing to both of them that she didn't come, too. But she did not always, when they made love, and often didn't care, and could be relied on to cue him if she did. He offered anyway, licking her throat in a way that was one of their signals, but she declined with a warm hug and an uncounterfeitable kiss, and reached for the remote.

"*That's* why you wanted to come up here," he said sleepily. "Better TV."

"You know me so well," she said, and gave him a friendly tweak.

He fell asleep watching a genuinely astonishing commercial, in which an immensely fat hairy jolly man (immensely all those things) wearing only a jockstrap and a skipper's cap did—for a Pacific Rim audience—a *sumo* shtick that must have been to a Japanese what Step'n'Fetchit is to a brother. It turned out he sold junk. *What a country!* was Paul's last coherent thought.

Then he slept, and dreamed that he was Gnossos Pappadapolous, and the monkey demon was chasing him and his buddy Heffalump through New Mexico desert. When it turned into Batista's Cuba and guns started going off, Paul tried what Gnossos had done in the book—run in circles; scream and shout—and it worked: he became Exempt. But not Heffalump, the only human being Gnossos ever genuinely loved: Heffalump was down, and Gnossos was hip too late. He tried to change the dream channel, and found himself in Heinlein's JOB: A COMEDY OF JUSTICE, he and Margrethe on an ocean liner, suffering from *mal de merde*. This was insufficient improvement: Margrethe was stacked but so was the deck, which promptly sank out from under them. So he went deep, and found darkness and quiet for awhile.

June switched to headphones when she saw he was asleep, found the satellite channels and watched a Japanese porn movie dubbed into Chinese for an hour, marveling at the endless variety of ways different cultures have evolved to make idiots out of themselves while doing something necessary, all in the name of a little quiet in the pants. *Hasn't there* ever *been a sexually sane culture?* she wondered for the thousandth time in her life. *Will there ever be one?*

Just before she drifted off, she thought, *I almost came. Next time I will. I won't let the bastard take that away from me, too.*

Her sleep was dreamless when it came, and she woke hungry.

⊀CHAPTER 8⊁
The Fans Hit the Shit *Back*

PACING IN HIS BEDROOM, the evening after the con, Wally said, "Let's total up everything we know for sure about the son of a bitch."

He's uncircumsized was Moira's first thought, but she probably would not have said that even if her husband had not been armed. "He's very smart; he probably has five o'clock shadow all over his body right now; he has our lives, AKA ninety-eight thousand dollars, in a big brown bag; and with his head shaved he looks a little like Captain Picard. And he was raised in America. That's all I'm sure of." She rearranged the pillows behind her.

Wally stopped pacing. "You think he's American?"

"I didn't say that. Maybe he's a Canadian citizen, maybe he's a Landed Immigrant, maybe he's just a visitor come north to shear the fat stupid sheep of Niceland for a few weeks. But he was raised in the Untied Snakes." The pillows were giving her trouble.

"What makes you say that?"

She burrowed her shoulder blades into the pillow mass, and finally achieved comfort. "He used the word 'table' to mean 'temporarily remove from consideration,' rather than the correct, rational, AngloCanadian meaning, 'put forward for immediate consideration.' He was raised in America, all right."

Wally smiled. "By God, I think you're right. He *did* say that, I remember. It didn't take at the time. Very good, love." He frowned. "Wait, now. What about that G.S.T. line?"

"Misdirection," she suggested. "He's subtle."

"Which one?" he argued. " 'Table' or 'G.S.T.'?"

She echoed his frown.

"Let's mark that one 'tentative,' for now," he said. "I'm considerably more confident that he's a fan, possibly even a Truphan. Inactive, maybe—about as gafiated as you can get, now, thanks to us—but at some time in his life he smelled corflu, I'd bet my collection on it."

"Not necessarily," she insisted. "Ten or fifteen years ago, I'd have said anybody who could sting us like that would *have* to be a fan. Who else would try? But fandom's had a lot of media exposure, the last decade or so. A lot of mundanes have noticed us going through hotel lobbies in costume and asked the desk clerk what was going on. Anybody on the Internet could have stumbled over all that PR we tried so hard to make eye-catching, and found out about VanCon. From the membership data he could infer the size of the nut in the bank, and even the bank . . . and the names of the only two chumps with signing authority."

"Sure, maybe," he said. "But constructing the scam itself . . ."

"—doesn't even require that the bastard ever read a book in his life," she said. "The movies are full of time travel these days."

"He used the word 'ficton,' I'm sure of that," Wally said.

"True," she said. "Okay, so he's read Heinlein. That just makes him literate and lucky. It doesn't mean he reads sf for pleasure, let alone make him a fan. Much less a Truphan. No fan could be capable of this. Not even Splatt."

Wally resumed pacing. "Dammit, you may be right. But even so, I think we have to put out the Word."

"To *fandom*? Come clean? *Why*? Didn't we just get through begging Steve and Sybil in Toronto to keep the story to themselves? And apologizing to a dozen friends for terrifying them with hallucinatory warnings about an earthquake? They already all think we've started taking drugs." Suddenly Moira's stomach hurt.

"Moira, our fannish reputations are dead, forever, the moment the first major VanCon bill comes due. *We have no other explanation for where the money went.* We can't even say *we* stole it, unless we can explain why we haven't got it any more. There's only one way we can prevent our names becoming *the* fannish byword for Stupidity for the next century, now. The only hope we have in the world of ever being allowed in a Con Suite again, the rest of our lives, is to catch that hairless ape, ourselves, personally, and get back every cent we handed him—in time for the con to go on. That gives us two weeks, absolute max. And I think fandom is our only lead."

"Beatles," she said. "Internet Beatles forums—chat groups—"

He shook his head. "You don't have to leave traces *anywhere* to know all about the Beatles. The information's in the water supply. I mean, there are probably starving hermits in Pakistan who know what the original title of 'Get Back' was, for—"

Moira's choices were, get up and get the Pepto Bismol, or come up with an idea. "I got it!"

Wally misunderstood. "Okay, I was just trying to—"

"No, no, I mean I got an idea. Another lead, besides fandom!"

Wally stopped in his tracks. If he had been the protagonist of Jack London's "To Build A Fire," suddenly confronted with a Zippo, he could not have become more alert, more hopeful, more frightened. ". . . tell me," he whispered.

Moira began to—and from nowhere came the thought that it would be kinder to let him guess it himself, and that her husband could use some kindness now. "'Fool, fool—back to the beginning is the rule,'" she quoted softly from their favorite bedtime story.

For a moment she could *hear* his neurons firing . . . and then his eyes began to glow, as if in illustration of the memory behind them. "Yes!" he cried. "*Magnesium* . . ."

"How many places could there be in the greater Vancouver area where a man could buy that much?"

The question hung in the air for a moment. And then they chorused together: "I don't know, but I know somebody who'll know somebody who will!" and raced for their computers.

Wally, having been both standing and nearest the door at the starting gun, won the race handily; Moira arrived (looking not unlike the Bowen Island ferry) just in his wake, to find that he had already booted both their machines. She slapped her modem to life and waited for her Finder to load.

"I'm tryin'a think, but nothin' *happens*," it reported truthfully, in the voice of Curly (the real one), and began rebuilding her virtual desktop.

As always, it took too much time. By the time the desktop

appeared on-screen, she had begun to leak helium. "This may not work out as well as we hope," she said slowly.

Wally's system had loaded faster; it just took much longer to *do* anything. "Why do you say that?" He moused like Monk taking a solo, off-rhythm but strong.

"Think about Jude. Or whatever his name is. That's my point: can you see a con-man that good buying a kilo of magnesium *in this town*? Under his own name? And leaving a valid address?"

Monk let the bass player have it. "Oh shit." Wally pushed his chair back from the desk, and rubbed his eyes. "Any two, possibly, but not all three." He looked like he was going to cry.

"We should still try, though," she said hastily, and opened her Net browser. She wished she had gotten the Pepto Bismol on the way there.

"Yeah, we will," Wally agreed, his voice tired and defeated. "And we'll check the Beatles forums, and we'll search the Net for 'con-man' and 'grifter' and strings like that, and maybe we can even get Vicki's brother Jack to hack us into the cops' network and look for Jude's footprint, and none of it is—"

"Genius," she said. "I married an intuitive genius."

Wally blinked. "Certainly. What I say?"

"What does Vicki's brother *do* for the cops?"

Wally was hesitant to let hope return, but this was good. For the second time, he chorused along with her: "He draws pictures of people you didn't think you remembered!"

Jack was a police sketch artist—one of the first to realize that the WYSIWYG revolution had transformed *his* profession as much as any other, for no other image-medium can be as quickly and easily changed, fine-tuned, as a computer paint document. He was by training as good a psychologist as he was an artist: he had once, as a parlor trick, drawn Wally and Moira a sketch on his Powerbook of a waiter who had served them the night before, using only the memories he drew out of them with his questions and his trackball. An hour later, a friend who'd had the same waiter a week earlier had ID'd him from the sketch.

"That's really good, love," Wally went on, excited again. "He can even add hair and stuff, or show ways the guy could disguise himself, beard and glasses and like that. We could show them to the clerks at all the chemical supply houses, and—" He broke off.

"And?" She didn't want to ask, but it was the only question she had.

He took his time answering. "And let's face it: unless and until some clerk says, 'Sure, I know that guy; I got his address and his Visa number, and come to think of it, his fingerprints are on the slip,' we still have *shit*."

For the first time in decades, Moira searched for words.

Wally switched his computer off cold, swiveled his chair to face her, and when he spoke his voice was awful to hear. "Let's admit it. We're screwed. The Yankee son of a bitch is just too smart for us."

CHIRRRKRRUP, said the phone.

Oh Finagle, NOW? Moira thought. *Five seconds earlier and whoever it is would have gotten a busy signal on that line. When the luck goes bad, boy—*But almost instantaneously she flip-flopped. Nuisances have their place. When your husband has just made the most terrible, humiliating admission he has ever made or could make, perhaps a good distraction is not unwelcome. Even a poor one. "I'll get it," she said, and started to rise.

"I've got it," he said bitterly, and picked up the phone. "Yeah, who is it?"

The caller ignored the perfectly reasonable question, but identified himself nonetheless. "Enough I had," came a voice with what Moira had always called a pronounced Martian accent. "No more, you are hearing? Any more shenanigans like the last night, police I call, yes? My wife is upset, I am upset, you should be disgrace. You are hearing me, flying saucer boy?"

"Gorsky!" Wally groaned.

Well, I asked for a nuisance, Moira thought. *I hit the Lotto.*

"Dem right Gorsky. Too much, too long I put up. This is decent neighborhood, Kemp, till you come with science fiction condom people. No more! I tell you: you tell wife who has different last name: police come next time. You tell naked Metkiewicz too: police come *his* house too—and one more thing: my dog puke one more time, I come punch you face. You got no right poison lawn where dogs live around, you—"

Moira had turned to stone. It was Wally who found his voice first: an eerily calm, peaceful voice. "Naked who?"

"Naked Metkiewicz—how many naked men play big joke with you last night? You tell him I know where he lives: they got special prison for naked men, what is call? fleshers. He will—"

"You know where Medgawhatsis lives."

"*Metkiewicz,* Jesus, M-E-T—" Gorsky spelled it, contempt plain in his voice for anyone who needed to be told how to spell Metkiewicz. "You bet I know where he lives. Ha ha. He is not so smart he thinks, yes?"

"How do you know where he lives?" Moira heard herself say, and cursed herself because it was the wrong question.

He answered it anyway. "Ha ha. Big surprise, yes? He buys chemical for big boom from my warehouse in Surrey. His Visa I have . . . address I have, God damn, from sign for chemical . . . his fingerprint on paper. Police find easy. No more naked Peeping Dick nonsense, you tell him, are you hearing?"

Wally asked the right question. "What address did Mr. Metkiewicz give you, Mr. Gorsky?"

"What?"

His voice had been too dreamy; Moira repeated the question.

"How do I know what address? Is in warehouse. Why you don't know where your friend lives?"

For a fraction of a second Moira debated telling Gorsky that "Metkiewicz" was a thief, who had stolen their money. The scent of a burglar in the neighborhood would elevate even her and Wally to the status of provisional human beings in Gorsky's eyes. But he would insist on handing over his evidence to the police at once. "He's not a friend, Mr. Gorsky. He's an acquaintance. Someone we know from science fiction. He's having trouble with his mind, you understand?"

"I understand good, you bet it. Big trouble, sure."

"He was acting so crazy last night, after he left we thought maybe we should make sure he got home all right, but we don't know where he lives."

"He go home naked, I know where he lives now. In hose goo."

He couldn't say "hoosegow" when I had time to laugh, Moira thought. "No, he wasn't that crazy. But I really think we ought to check on him. Is there someone at your warehouse at night?"

"Is watchman. But he can not get paper. Is lock."

Moira briefly explored her decision tree. Branch A: try to persuade Gorsky to give them the key to his Restricted Substances records and phone the watchman to expect them; rotsa ruck. Branch B: try to draw the address out of Gorsky's murky memory; forget it. Branch C: give up and hand the whole thing over to the police, like a civilian; make herself and Wally—and by extension, God help them, VanCon and the entire Lower Mainland Science Fiction Association—international laughingstocks within and without fandom.

Without fandom . . .

"But crazy naked man is bad thing. Hokay. You come over, I give you key, phone watchman to wake up."

Absurdly, Moira found herself thinking of the silly joke Wally had once made after they'd seen a video of Stallone as a mountain-climber, endlessly going up and down ropes to display his biceps. Wally had held up the video box, moved it up and down a few times, pointed to Sly's picture, and said, "Yo. Yo. Yo. Yo—*Up, down; up, down—*" That's very kind of you, Mr. Gorsky. Thank you very much. We'll be right over."

"No crazy nakeds in this neighborhood I want."

Wally ended the conversation the way he religiously ended conversations with that man. "Good luck, Mr. Gorsky." He disconnected.

They swiveled to face each other, and simultaneously reached to take each other's hands, and as their fingers touched they allowed themselves to smile.

"Hose goo," she said. "Oh, that is precious."

"The man next door has just walked on the Moon," Wally said, smiling bigger.

"Every once in a while, maybe a good deed goes unpunished," Moira said.

"We are going to explain to Jude that it's a fool who plays it cool, by making his world a little colder."

"Lets go get under his skin," she agreed. They put their silicon servants to sleep, and left the office. Like any Vancouverite about to leave home unexpectedly at night, Moira zapped the TV on to access the cable weather channel to find out whether rain-gear was required. It came on with a shriek of sound, tuned to the local news channel; the last time the set had been used, they'd been listening for earthquake warnings while running around the house packing. The screen filled with a long shot of a smoking ruin, and an earsplitting voice bellowed, "*OINT GREY COMPUTER PROGRAMMER RALPH METKAVITCH'S HOME WAS DESTROYED BY FIRE FOLLOWING*

*AN UNEXPLAINED EXPLOSION LAST NIGHT, AND THE PRE-
LIMINARY INVESTIGATION REPORT SAYS THAT ARSON
QUOTE CANNOT BE RULED OUT UNQUOTE. SO FAR POLICE
HAVE BEEN UNABLE TO CONTACT MESKOWITZ, WHOM
NEIGHBORS SAID HAD RECENTLY SHAVED HIS HEAD—*"

Moira tried for either the volume down or mute buttons, and
missed both; the set went off. She thought about turning it back on,
and could not think of a point. She turned to her husband, and at the
sight of his face she blanched. "Oh, Wally."

"It's not the despair," he said, his voice placid, conversational. "I
can deal with the despair."

She nodded. "It's the hope."

"Yeah. It's killing me."

Sigh. "Me too, Wally."

CHIRRRKRRUP, said the phone.

"Do we answer it?" she asked.

Wally sighed. "Why not? We haven't got anything better to do.
Maybe it's a Psychic Friend, calling to tell us where to find Jude.
Maybe it's Dr. Kevorkian letting us know he's going to be in the
neighborhood, *that'd* be useful—"

"I'll go."

"No, I'll get it."

She compromised, waiting until he caught up and then putting on
the speakerphone. "Is this someone with good news or money?"

"*Both,*" said the phone.

"Steve?"

"*I got a lead on your guy.*"

Silence.

"*Hello?*"

It was Moira who reinvented breathing first. "Say again, Steve."

"*I got your guy. Got an address and an accomplice, anyway—from
the Net.*"

Moira would not have believed, if informed beforehand, that a
heart could so simultaneously rise and fall. This might just possibly
be good news—but it was probably worthless, and its cost could be
dear. Had Steve started a fannish clock ticking on their amateur
manhunt? Had he told anyone *why* he needed the data? "Steve, just
how did you get this—"

Wally overrode her, slapping the *record* button on the phone machine. "What's the address you have?"

The vibrations of his voice had to be translated by the phone into a pattern of electrical signals; these had to cross half a continent, starting at the speed of light but arriving much slower due to switching delays; converting them back into sound waves took more time, then Steve needed at least three times as long to hear, grasp, and respond to them—whereupon the whole weary process began in reverse. All this time, Moira waited, absolutely certain that if she were just patient enough Steve would give them the late address of the former Ralph Metkiewicz, and they could hang up and get back to contemplating suicide. She and hope were quits for the night; maybe for good.

"*Pencils ready? One, zero, six, fi-yuv, niner, Point Grey that's ee why Road, Vancouver; postal code Varley eight Unicorn, four Rotsler six. Owner of record is a Carlo with a sea Bernardo. He got mail there through an account registered to 'Penforth Naim,' that's en-nuh, eh, eye, em-muh, but obviously that's not gonna do you much good. Still, it's a start. You want me to repeat any of that?*"

Moira's operating system was hung, her cursor and her cursor both frozen; Wally had to take it. "No, that's okay, Steve-o, it's on tape. I'm genuinely impressed. Tell me, though, how *exactly* did you dig all that up?"

"*Relax: I know what you're thinking. It's cool—really. I understand this is . . . uh . . . a sensitive matter. What I did, I logged onto the Net and tapped the fannish grapevine—*"

Moira moaned.

"*No, really, wait a minute and listen. I didn't say anything about . . . about what happened to you guys, okay? Not a word.*"

When it was clear that Steve would wait until someone reassured him or hell froze over, whichever came first, Wally said. "You have our complete confidence, Steve. What *did* you say then?"

"*I said I was putting together a Next Generation parody for VanCon, called 'Data Takes A Dump,' and I wanted to know if anybody had seen anyone around a con lately that looked like Picard and either was bald or wouldn't mind shaving his head.*"

The metaphorical lightbulb that appeared in the air over Moira's and Wally's heads baked their shadows onto the wall.

"Bless my soul!" Wally exclaimed. Moira backed up involuntarily until she hit the fridge, and gave thought to sliding down it to a sitting position. But she couldn't face getting back up again. "Steven," she said weakly, "would you and Sybil like a couple of sex-slaves for a year or so?"

"You'll have to take a number—damn city building-code won't let me expand the dungeon without a permit. Now, naturally I got about two dozen hits—hell, I got people who were willing to have plastic surgery to play Picard at a Worldcon, and have you noticed? there's no shortage of bald guys in fandom. But I'm pretty sure if any of 'em is your guy, it's the one I gave you. Yin the Stomach-Settling talked to him at the Registration Table at Vikingcon, down in Bellingham. You know her thing for Captain Picard: she remembers the dude good, even though he had hair then. She says he came on like a mundane, asked all kinds of general questions about fandom . . . but then at one point she started a Lazarus Long quote and he finished it. He gave her his e-mail address so she could send some stuff about how to go about starting your own con, how to finance it and stuff. And some promo for VanCon."

"As far as I know," Wally said, "that may be the second sign of sloppy workmanship he's shown."

"Well, actually it wasn't all that sloppy. He must have thought it was safe: the address he gave her went through anon.data.ru." This was a Moscow-based free Internet service, created and run by a volunteer and funded entirely by donations, which relayed e-mail after stripping off its identifying header—conferring effective anonymity on its users. *"Yin said on the strength of that she included some of her private porn in the stuff she sent him, but she never heard back."*

"Then how did you get a meat address?" Moira heard herself ask.

Steve made the vocal equivalent of a suicide's hesitation marks.

"Steve?" Wally said.

"Look, this is completely DNQ, all right? I mean, really. *I keep your secret, you keep mine, okay? The guy that runs* anon.data.ru *is a friend of mine."*

The metaphorical flashbulb attempted to flare again, but it was shot.

"You told him the truth," Wally said.

"I had to. *He wouldn't have breached security to help me find an*

amateur actor. He's only EVER opened his files twice, and nobody knows about either one or he'd be out of business. Both times were to stop criminals in progress—and I mean, he's got a comfortingly narrow definition of 'criminal.' But 'thief' fits. He says this guy is too clever to be walking around."

"Roger that," Moira muttered.

"Did he let you browse 'Mr. Pen Naim's' traffic?" Wally asked.

"Negatory. He says catching crooks is one thing, reading their mail's another. I have to agree."

"Yes, I suppose so," Wally agreed, rubbing his forehead. "I'll settle for reading his entrails."

"Well, I'll tell you what my friend in Moscow said."

"Please do."

"He said 'bolshoyeh luck.' "

"Thank him for us. Discreetly but profusely. No one will ever know where we got the information, I promise him that. As for yourself, I would begin to outline a summary of just the highlights of all the many ways we thank you, but this is your dime. We owe you big-time."

"I'll relay your offer to Sybil. She happens to have an opening . . . and, a position available, too. Good hunting, you guys. Remember, if you lose him, you're no worse off than you are now—you can't *be—but if you get* him, *you'll live forever. Later."*

The speaker clicked off. There was silence. Wally reached up and shut off the phone machine, hit rewind.

Moira said quick "OhWallyifthefuckingtapedidn't—"

Wally cut her off. "One, zero, six, fi-yuv, niner, Point Grey that's ee why Road, Vancouver; postal code Varley eight Unicorn, four Rotsler six. Carla with a sea Bernardo: cute. Penforth Naim: too cute. Let's go see Ms. Bernardo."

Moira saw his hand twitch toward his pants pocket, toward the little .22 he had bought from a helplessly giggling Rastafarian on Bathurst Street. She kick-started her brain. "Let's walk around her and kick the tires, first. And let's let our fingers do the walking." She pointed toward the office.

He hesitated, and his hand twitched again. And then he relaxed. "Never make decisions in haste that don't call for haste. If she's there now, she'll be there in an hour. You take municipal and provincial, I'll take federal."

"The other way round," she said, already on her way, physically and mentally.

An hour later, they parked their Toyota across the street from Carla Bernardo's house, which lay on the water side of Point Grey Road. It was, even more than its companions along this stretch, shamelessly opulent. It did not even have the decency to wear hedges, and its floral display was positively obscene even by streetlight.

"What's 'cute' about the name Carla Bernardo?" Moira asked.

"You don't want to know. Dammit, I don't see any lights on in there."

"Well, it's late."

"Not to a thief. Maybe they're out working; we can wait here and ram them in their own driveway."

"We could look through the garage window and see if there's a car in there."

"Screw it; let's just go knock on the door and see what happens." He started to get out of the car, but Moira could be a very effective anchor. "What?"

She looked him in the eye. She kept her voice very low and calm. "Wally? Do you want to out-think this guy, for once?"

"More than I want to win a Hugo."

"Give *me* the gun."

He opened his mouth . . . and in spite of himself, he began to smile. "Oh, that is good. That is smart. I smell like fear and testosterone: if he's there he'll watch my hands and you can put one through his knee."

She was mildly surprised to realize that she was actually prepared to do that. "You remember how good I was with a paint-gun that time in Biloxi." They had once and only once attended a con that was eighty percent War Gamers, drawn by a special GoH; to her own surprise, Moira had ended up *winning* the only paint-gun stalk she'd ever been on, nailing the enemy commander square in the groin. (He had earlier made a remark she found offensive.)

"You hit what you aim at," he agreed. "Here." With some difficulty, he extricated the gun from his pants, checked the safety, and passed it across. As he did so, his smile turned wry. "It's technically a lady's gun anyway, the Rasta said."

She moved her hand from his shoulder to his cheek. "Wally . . . I

promise you I won't shoot him until you hit him at least once, okay?
Unless he runs."

He turned his face and kissed her hand. "Thank you. The safety's
on the right."

"I saw how it works." She placed it carefully in her purse, and hung
the purse from her right shoulder, unzipped.

They left and locked the car and, since it was late at night, crossed
Point Grey Road on foot without the customary side effect of dying.
There was a light drizzle in the air, but both ignored it. "There's one
in the chamber and four more," he said. "I insisted on firing it before
I bought it. He just laughed and turned his boom box all the way up.
It put a hole in a dumpster."

She stopped on the minuscule sidewalk and looked at him. "In a
dumpster?"

"Well, it didn't come out the other side. But I think I heard it hit
the back."

"Did it shoot straight?"

"I don't know. Uh . . . I was aiming at the dumpster."

She nodded. "Good enough. Five rounds, got it. Let's check the
garage before we knock."

They walked through a florid floral quotation from Butchart
Gardens and circled around to where they could squint in the
window set into the center door of the three-car garage. "Jesus,"
Wally said. "A Porsche. And something else generic on the right,
maybe only a lowly Thunderbird or something."

"Looks like a Camry to me." She took her hand from the gun and
rummaged in the purse until she found her Swiss Army knife; went
over to the edge of the door and examined its track. She found a place
to wedge the knife, and opened some of its extensions to tighten it in
place, trapping the Porsche in its bay. "There. Now if they get past us
and make it to the garage, we only have to catch another Camry. *Now*
we ring the bell."

Wally examined her in admiration for a moment—she felt it—
before he followed.

She let him ring the bell. Its melody was like a commercial for a
laxative—lovely on first hearing, cloying at the fifth repetition . . .
binding by the tenth.

She was afraid he might get angry then—his face was dark as he turned away from the door—but his voice was calm. "Okay, we gather information. Let's try neighbors. Wake 'em up if we have to."

"What do we tell them?"

"Whatever they want to hear."

To their surprise, they hit pay dirt on the first try. The neighbor immediately to the west of Casa Bernardo was a find from the point of view of just about any collector.

Her face alone was worth driving a long way to see: it had started out pretty once, many years ago, and then she had dieted until the bones showed clearly, and then she had had it repeatedly lifted until, on first viewing, one felt the cruel impulse to bounce a quarter off her cheek. Even in the doorway light, the line where the nasal region of her skull gave way to cartilage was clear; in better light, Moira was confident she could have traced the way that cartilage had been rebuilt. The woman looked overall like a concentration-camp survivor onto whom absurd balloon breasts had been grafted by Dr. Mengele, dressed in the Bitch of Buchenwald's housecoat and given Szell's cigarette holder. For their purposes she was the ideal menagerie: mean as a snake, nosy as a cat, territorial as a pit bull, shameless as a ferret, loud as a gull, smart as an ox, and drunk as a skunk. They had won the Blotto.

She opened the door talking; it was a full minute before they were able to fold and insert their names. The moment she grasped that they were interested in any gossip she might have about That Pardon My French But Cunt Next Door and/or Her Stud Gigolo, it ceased being necessary for Wally or Moira to do anything but murmur and nod from time to time, with an occasional cluck or tsk as seemed indicated. She even reeled away into the house—waving them sternly to wait where they were—and returned with several photographs of an astonishing zoo-parade of zombies at a recent Do in her backyard: three shots had Carla Bernardo in frame in the background, and one of those included a clear shot of Jude/Metkiewicz/Naim with a full head of hair. They were in their own yard, at a raised poolside, visibly sneering at the party. Mrs. Never Mind What My Name Is, I Live Here was unwilling to give Wally and Moira any of the photographs—but *was* willing to sell them the shot with both targets in it for the approximate cost of an exclusive McKinnon, since it also depicted guests she particularly despised (for reasons they were obliged to hear). She even took one of Wally's cards—Moira's she ignored—and swore to call him the *instant* That What I Said or Her Love Slave came home. She assured them she would know, day or night; they did not doubt this. Then she gave Wally a quick but nonetheless sloppy bourbon kiss he was too shocked to dodge, and closed the door in their faces, but Moira did not shoot her through it.

"You know," she said as they walked back to their car, "I hate to say it, but I'm almost starting to enjoy this. Stephen Cannell couldn't have written her dialogue better."

"Monologue," Wally corrected, wiping his mouth and spitting.

"We were getting *stale*, Wally: we gotta start hanging out with mundanes again. You know, if a pygmy shrunk her, she wouldn't get any smaller."

Wally began to giggle. "If you unscrewed the top of her head, her whole skeleton would come squirting out from the pressure—" He chortled. "—and there'd be this little glove left, shaped like Linda Hunt—" He whooped. "Unzip the *back* of her head, and her face would be in your face—"

"Keep it down. A sincere laugh in this neighborhood is unusual enough somebody might call the cops—and I'm holding a firearm."

He reduced his mirth by increments to a silly grin, and they got in the car. "Okay, now we're getting somewhere. We know there's two of them, we have their pictures, we know a lot about their habits, and we have their house staked out for us by a force of nature. All we have to do now is—

"Honey, I, uh, I have a bad feeling about that part."

His grin flickered.

"Maybe you'll think this is hard to buy, with that Porsche sitting there in that garage and all that money blooming all over the place . . . but I think maybe why I *buy* it is that Porsche, just sitting there. . . . Wally, honey, I don't think they're coming back here. I think something happened, something spooked them, some other con blew up in their faces, probably. Jude's house got torched last night, and according to Robo-neighbor they left here on foot a few hours later. I think they're on the run."

"We have competition," Wally said, in his testosterone voice.

"But maybe we're a jump ahead of them," she said quickly. "That . . . life-form back there would have mentioned anybody else asking about Carla, so we have information nobody else does."

"Sure—about why Motormouth doesn't like her other neighbor Mrs. Wong."

"Think, Wally. She said they left in the middle of the night dressed for a day of hiking. . . . I remember distinctly the way she made five syllables out of 'L.L. *Be-ean-uh*' . . . and she said they were carrying an ice chest and a backpack and an overnight bag. Carla's a Canadian, from Vancouver, she knows you can't get cabs on the street here. They're running for the country somewhere, on foot."

"Terrific," he said. "That narrows it down to three hundred and sixty possible degrees. Maybe they dug themselves a bunker over in the Endowment Lands—excuse me, Pacific Spirit Park."

"It means wherever they run to, it won't be far. And not where anybody else would expect a con-man to run to, not downtown or the 'burbs or another city altogether."

He nodded. "Yeah. That's good."

"Everybody else will be watching the airport and the bus station and the highways and the Tsawwassen Terminal . . . and meanwhile they'll take the bus or Skytrain or the Seabus or . . . I don't know, the Horseshoe Bay Ferry."

"But we still don't know which, or how far."

"No, but look on the bright side. Country grapevine works even better than city grapevine—if you're listening to it."

His fickle grin returned. "Wherever there's a Nowheresville . . . there's a fan with a modem. Those two will stick out *more* there—to us. Oh, I like it, darling. Let's go get their pictures scanned in and cropped, and put them—no, get Steve to put them out on the Net. You're right. Maybe our luck is finally starring to turn."

He should really have known better than to make a U-turn on Point Grey Road at night. On that long straight pipeline they were visible for a kilometer in either direction, and the cops' end-of-shift was approaching, leaving them with tickets to unload.

Fortunately, Canadian cops do not search stopped vehicles—or their passengers' purses—without a good reason. The pair got back home with nothing worse than a ticket that would put points on Wally's license . . . and one set of slightly damp underwear. His, if you must know.

⚜CHAPTER 9⚜
Peeking Ahead

RAIN WAS JUST beginning to fall as they arrived. Ignoring it, and being ignored in return, they landed in front of their home in Pacific Spirit Park, entered the house, and became visible again.

She found that she was both exhilarated and exhausted. (These terms relative to her normal emotional state: any human observer would have thought her serene.) The simple intellectual knowledge that one has become mortal, can die, changes a thing like flying. The sensation was oddly invigorating, as if in pathetic compensation for its cost.

He did not notice, nor did she hold it against him. He was too worried for her to empathize with her fully right now; she would have to do something about that when she had time. And they were both too busy.

"I'll make coffee," she said. Human domestic customs, adopted for cover and practiced for drill, had worked their insidious comfort over the centuries. The ritual would help her ground herself, and him as well, even if the caffeine itself was superfluous.

He nodded, understanding. "I'll build a fire." He used his hands.

Both had long practice in achieving and sustaining calm; it was a large part of what they did. By the time the hearth was crackling and the coffee was steaming, they were ready to see the humor in the situation, and nearly ready to appreciate it.

"E.T.," she said. She blew across the surface of her cup, grateful for the professionalism which had caused her to develop that habit, now that her lips could be burned, "Only it's Extra Temporal, rather than Terrestrial."

He smiled, understanding the reference. "Yes. Time for us to Phone Home. Talk about call forwarding!"

She sighed. "Never expected to do it."

"I know. I haven't tried to peek ahead to the end of a book since . . . well, a long time ago."

"And we made it necessary."

Another would have accepted her tone as flat, neutral—but he did not need ears to hear his mate's pain. He spoke sharply, for him. "We cannot afford to be ashamed of our failure just now. The stakes are too high. The least important thing about this disaster is whose watch it happened on. The most important thing is to report it fully and try to get it dealt with. I love you."

She steadied. "Agreed. I love you."

He gestured, and a small piece of polished quartz left the rock collection on display in a corner of the room and came to them. It hovered directly between them, picking up flickering highlights from the fire, so that to each it appeared a sparkling third eye of the other.

They began to fill it with thought together.

Even as the first datum was entered, the message began containing information. Its very formatting structure said that it was composed of purely human thoughts, thus largely in words, these words being late 20th Century Canadian English. This declared the identity of its senders, strongly hinted at the nature of the problem itself, and implied the mode of thought that would have to be adopted in order to consider it effectively.

Having created a self-explaining "blank sheet of paper," they began to "write" on it.

First, in the largest type, the addressee:

Everyone.

Next, the desired delivery time; i.e., the specific (sidereally expressed) date on which the quartz beacon was to begin announcing itself, and continue until acknowledged:

The instant we left.

Then, priority:

Ultimate.

Next, summary of text. This was the first part they hesitated over long enough for a contemporary timepiece to measure the interval. Finally:

A Class One Paradox threatens. We urgently request Anachrognosis to resolve it; delivery soonest.

They *had* to pause, there. One simply cannot make a truthful statement on the order of *it will now be necessary to rape God* and then go on to explain why and just how, without stopping for a moment and waiting for the unprecedented thrill of awe and horror to fade. They had just asked that one of the most fundamental principles of their society of origin be massively violated, in order to preserve it. Since the whole point of their present existence was to make such a request unnecessary, they felt the antinomy perhaps more strongly than would anyone who heard it.

Thunder sounded outside, somewhere to the north.

Statement of problem:

Here they dumped everything either had experienced since the Tar Baby had shrieked. Literally everything. The context from each of their points of view. Every single vagrant thought or sensation the mook had ever had, up to the instant when his shovel had said *clack* and he had said "Aw, fuck." (He'd had no thoughts after that which were relevant.) Every single random thought or sensation June Bellamy had ever had, up to the instant when she touched the shovel. Everything they had done in response to this catastrophe, and every thought they'd formed while doing it. All the data they had gleaned from Paul Throtmanian's house and ancillary sources.

Summary of conclusions:

The targets Throtmanian and Bellamy are much too intelligent and educated to be permitted to know what they know. Given time, they will draw obvious conclusions. They are top professionals at escaping capture by any reasonable contemporary means, and have proved themselves resourceful in evading the most sophisticated methods available to us. One of us has already been rendered mortal while tracking them.

Prognosis broke down into two sections. First:

(Without Anachrognosis—) Exposure. Paradox. Catastrophe.

(With Anachrognosis—) A very good chance of salvage and safety.

And at last, they came to the part they metaphorically sweated most over: their specific request. The heavens outside wept inconsolably onto their roof as they thought it over. There were several ways to approach it. After agonizing for nearly a full minute together, they selected the one which seemed to them to require the absolute minimum of anachrognostic disturbance, and the smallest possible outrage of human free will.

We request that Paul Throtmanian and June Bellamy advise us on how to catch them.

It was done, now. All that was left was a final trivial detail: specification of the delivery date for the requested information. They had already asked for "soonest"—but now they must tell the addressee specifically when "soonest" would be.

He glanced over at the TV by learned reflex, snorted, glanced upward through the ceiling to a satellite with considerably better raw data, and made his own analysis.

She saw his face change, checked his figures—and reached the same conclusion.

It had long been established—indeed, since the very first attempt—that it was a Very Bad Idea to hurl a parcel back through time to a ficton where it was raining . . . or snowing, though that was rarely a problem in the Pacific Northwest. In that historic instance, in Nova Scotia in 1972, the energy liberated by the simultaneous annihilation of several hundred snowflakes had been sufficient to offset the Egg's terminus by a crucial few meters, into a tree—nearly killing its occupant, the first-ever time traveler.

For as long as there was rain, or even mist, in the air, they could hope for no package from home. They could not even submit their request for one until they could confidently specify dry target ficton coordinates.

"Why am I not surprised?" she asked. And then for the first time in more than a hundred and fifty years, she began to cry.

He swept the coruscating bit of quartz out of the way and took her in his arms. "It will be okay," he said, the way you say something when you hope saying it will make it true.

"After all this," she sobbed against his neck, "are we going to be ruined by the damned *weather*?"

"We've always had that hazard here," he said. "We can shorten it a little. Three days. Maybe two; let me work up a first approximation."

She struggled against his embrace. "If those two get *one* whole day to sit and think about what they already know, it's all over."

"Not instantly," he insisted, the muscles of his upper arms and shoulders bulging like kinked hoses. "Even if they figure it out, we could have *days* to get to them before they *do* anything about it."

She gave up the physical expression of her struggle. "Sure. And right now they could be gaping up at the clouds and drowning, like turkeys."

He did not slacken the physical expression of his caring. "Things are bad. We will do our best. And then we will wait to see what happens. Shall I refine that approximation now, or would you like to do it?"

She squeezed her eyes shut until the mandalas came. "I'll do it. I was always better with weather."

❧CHAPTER 10❧
The Biter Bit

IN PARADISE, Paul was in a funk.

He didn't do it often, for a man. June's inclination was to let him indulge himself. But he seemed to *want* to be busted for it.

He had thrown himself savagely into his period of enforced play, as if determined to have run or die in the attempt. He had hot-tubbed until he pruned; eaten till he creaked; drunk till he puked, and screwed till he couldn't any more for awhile. Then he had filled the house with Wagner at terrifying volume while filling the huge satellite TV screen with German porn—some of the really astonishing stuff; the kind that would in a few months embarrass the Munich police into harassing CompuServe for letting foreigners export disgusting hard-core erotica to their God-fearing nation. Then, of course, he had screwed some more. (She'd been forced to admit, howling along with the Valkyries, that the Master Race had its points. As she'd hoped, the ability to climax had returned to her— Hoyoto! But it hadn't been especially *friendly* sex.) Afterwards he'd switched the music to the Beatles, and dived into O'Leary's books for several taciturn hours. When he emerged it was only to boot up the big Mac in the living room and sample his host's games. He found an alpha version of a WWII submarine simulator with superb graphics called War Patrol, designed by Gordon Walton, and became impervious to human contact for half a day, happily stalking defenseless convoys and torpedoing hospital ships.

June joined him for half an hour, out of loneliness, and the game was diabolically interesting. But it was a prerelease version, even more prone to crashes than Wagner, and she could not see the point of a game that would kill her sooner or later no matter how smart she was. She drifted off and watched the rain fall on the lower sundeck. The next time she wandered by he had stopped playing and was typing some sort of text document, but she knew from the set of his face that it would not be a good idea to read it over his shoulder. A little while later, reading in the bedroom, she heard the keyboard-tapping downstairs cease abruptly, and the door to the lower deck slide open and close again. When he did not return within five minutes, she left the TV and went to make sure he hadn't fallen over the side.

She saw him at an angle through the glass of her own sliding door, wearing a mackinaw, standing down on the lower deck by O'Leary's big Zeiss telescope, a hand resting on it. It was aimed not at the drizzling sky, but at the bay laid out below. His other hand held a pair of binoculars, through which he seemed to be examining the horizon. As she watched, he took a look through the scope, visibly sighed, and went back to the binoculars.

For the first time it began to dawn on her that he was in some kind of trouble. Paul was a city lad to his bones; he enjoyed looking at nature as much as she enjoyed looking at blood.

But what the hell could his problem be? They had been on the run before. They had even been on the run from superior forces before, and taken shelter in much meaner quarters than these. Okay: so Something Bad was out there, and for all they knew might be vectoring closer even now—was that any reason not to enjoy life in the meantime? Why was he acting like a citizen?

She slid her door open and stepped out onto her own smaller deck, and was shocked. He was smoking marijuana! The light rain and the roof overhang that shielded her from it combined to enclose the smell. It was not the first time he'd ever gotten high—but it was definitely the first time she could recall him doing so while danger was known to threaten. They were both firm believers in alertness during working hours: God knew nothing else had saved their bacon only two days earlier. "Jesus, Paul," she said, leaning over the rail and waving at the thick fruity scent.

Red eyes blinked up at her. "Hey, baby. Wanna toke?"

He looked so miserable her heart softened. "One of us better stay on duty," she said gently. "You have fun."

He snorted and looked away. "Yah. Fun."

She let that line sit there for a little bit. When he raised the binoculars again, she asked, "Whatcha looking at?"

"The only straight line God ever made," he said, resting his elbow on the Zeiss to steady himself.

She found herself thinking about that. Were there any straight lines in nature besides the horizon? Come to think, even raindrops didn't fall straight, did they? "Curved," she said thickly. God, was the stuff *that* good, that two breaths of his exhaust were zonking her? Or was it just empathic contact high with her lover?

"Technically, yeah, but you can't see that from here. Looks straight as a citizen, doesn't it? Has to be where humans got the idea for straight lines . . . and without them, what would people like you and me color outside of?"

"Go easy on that stuff, okay? It smells powerful."

"The year I was born," he said, "New York State did a study comparing the effects of alcohol and marijuana on drivers. I ever tell you about that?"

"No."

"They assigned five levels of stonedness for each drug, and learned how to reliably bring experienced volunteers to each level—from barely buzzed to shitfaced. Then they had 'em all drive an obstacle course, sober and at each of the five levels of intoxication for both drugs, and compared results. At levels one and two, grass made you a *better* driver. Faster reflexes, wider peripheral vision, expanded depth of field, more caution. After careful thought and due determination, the state decided the study was too good to publish or release. They prefer the ones where you count how many fatality-accident victims had smoked pot in the previous forty-eight hours: the more people get high, the more 'proof' they have that it 'causes' all those accidents. My mom happened to type most of the raw data while she was in the joint, and she told me about it."

"I wouldn't dream of arguing with your mother," she said, "but remember: that's B.C. boo you're smoking. They didn't have that shit in the '70s."

He put down the binoculars and looked up at her. "True. Maybe I better check the old reflexes, huh?" He slipped off his mackinaw, faced her and crouched.

"Paul—"

Nothing wrong with her own reflexes; she managed to get out of his way, and still had a whole half second to appreciate the beauty of his tumbling flight and the catlike grace of his landing. Dizzily, she reconstructed what she must have seen: he had sprung high, used the floor of the deck on which she stood to continue his ascent, and grabbed the rainslick upper railing just long and hard enough to let his legs come up and over and fling his body forward, finishing up in a half crouch before her. "So," he said, not even breathing hard, "you sure you don't want a hit?"

"Christ," she said, annoyed at her momentary fear and at him for causing it. "I hope you don't develop a taste for coke, next."

"Right. I'm just trying to relax and have a little fun, alright?"

"I noticed," she said. "You getting anywhere?"

His cockiness drained from him. "As the fella said after a *ménage á trois* with a porcupine and a skunk, 'I reckon I've enjoyed about as much of this as I can stand.' I feel like a guy who's had his leg cut off—I itch, but I can't find the place to scratch."

Good. Keep him talking now. Anything at all. "So what's all this about straight lines?"

Paul made that sound which can be either an aborted chuckle or suppressed nausea; context offered no clue which. "Well, it just seemed like there had to be one, right?"

"In nature, you mean? I guess so. Why?"

"Hey, think about it. The greatest joker Who ever lived—" He waved upward at the weeping sky. "—I mean, the truly *funniest* sonofabitch of all time . . . the guy Who filled the universe with punch-lines—" He mimed boxing. "—pow, pow, pow, punchlines . . . shit, there'd just *have* to be a straight-line around *somewhere*, now wouldn't there?" He pointed at the horizon, where grey day was becoming rainy night. "There it is. The set-up for the cosmic joke. The sweet salty place we came from, that tries to kill us every time we try to go back." He began to laugh, the helpless belly laugh of a driver who wakes after the crash to see his toddler wearing the dashboard for a hat.

She took him in her arms and tried her best to stop the ghastly laughter with compression of the thorax. "*Good* straight-line—" he choked out between spasms. "—stare at it—long as you want—*still* won't see that old punchline comin'—oh God, baby—"

She held on, searched her memory for soothing things her mother had said to her when she was a heartbroken child. "Better soon . . . better soon, honey . . . I'm here . . . we're okay so far . . . it'll be all right . . . we'll figure out what's the matter, we're too smart not to . . . and once we do, we'll know how to fix it, you wait and—" She broke off. He had stopped sobbing, was looking at her with astonished eyes from a distance of three inches.

"You don't get it yet," he said. "You really don't get it." He worked a hand between them and wiped at his nose. "Jesus, I'm really surprised."

"Get what?" She wasn't going to like this. She let go of him.

"You haven't worked out the punchline yet." He grimaced, covered it by rubbing at his eyes. "Hey, why should you? I'm the one it was aimed at. 'You just happened to be comin' along at the right time, sucker.' You want me to spoil it for you? Or you just want a hint?"

She took a deep breath. "Spit it out."

"How did I get Wally Kemp and Moira Rogers to give me ninety-eight large?"

There having been no part for her in the Jude sting, Wally and Moira had never become real to her. She fell back on first principles: "By selling them something they wanted that much."

"No, I mean, who was I? Who did they think I was?"

"A time traveler. It really was brilliant, you know."

He waited for her to get it, so she tried. Finally she lifted her eyebrows: I'm stumped, get on with it.

"Who," he said, "are we running from?"

At first she thought he was crazy. The more she thought about it, the more terrified she became that he was not.

"Tell me something else it could be," he said, "that fits the facts we have so far."

She flailed. "Mad scientists," she tried. "I don't know, aliens, maybe." She was horrified to hear herself suggesting something even more X-Files than his notion, but could find no better.

"If you find star travelers who have some reason to be afraid of us monkeys more plausible than time travelers, hey, go for it," he said. "I figure like this: you tell people you came across an alien artifact, either you end up in a shirt with real long sleeves and buckles, or you end up in the same room with Maury Povich: either way there's no reason for anybody to burn your house down. But you tell people you stumbled across a *human* artifact that can't be made yet, an anachronism of some kind . . . and maybe you end up making a paradox, and the universe goes away."

June had endured just enough sci fi in her life to understand the argument. Time travel had to be stealthy if it was to be done at all. Change history, and all hell broke loose. Whoever wanted them dead was trying to move like a virus: with *discreet* deadliness. Oh God, it made sense . . . more than anything else she could think of.

The word "denial" was in her vocabulary—but only as a legal strategy. She had spent her life training herself to face facts. She couldn't stop, just because the facts had turned weird . . . could she?

"My brilliant idea," Paul said sourly. "I'll tell you something I wasn't ever gonna tell anybody: it wasn't even original. I got it from a fifty-year-old story by a writer named Cyril Kornbluth—the guy that wrote 'The Marching Morons.' I figured it was okay to lift the gimmick in this other story because what he did with it just wasn't practical. His grifter pretends to be a time traveler, and pulls off a sting—a lot crummier sting than the beauty I put together, by the way: it never woulda worked in real life—and then the punchline is, the real time travelers hear he's blowing their cover, and they come boil his brain. Naturally I didn't waste any time worrying about *that* little hazard—hell, no! I'm a rational man. Only in a science fiction story would time travel turn out to be real—and unlike Wally and Moira, I don't wish my life were a science fiction story. Guess what, honey: it is anyway. Whether we like it or not."

The true horror of their situation washed over her, and she began to laugh herself.

Unlike Paul, however, she had no trouble at all stopping. She sat down on the deck with her arms wrapped around her knees and thought, *hard*. He sat beside her and let her think, silently watching the dull grey glow go out of the world to the west.

"I don't get it," June said finally, breaking the silence. "I believe you, I guess, but I still don't understand it. How the hell does this time traveler think we threaten him? By knowing he exists? How does that make us any different from Kemp and Rogers? What are we supposed to do with the information? Sell it to Geraldo?"

"We know where he has something buried. We don't know what, but it must constitute proof he's a time traveler."

"So what? Everybody who sees it forgets."

"You didn't—for long enough to phone me."

"So why doesn't he just move whatever it is fifty meters east? We'd never find it again."

Paul shook his head. "I don't know. He must like it right where it is, for some reason. Maybe it's his time gate, and once you set it up you can't move it." He frowned at the rain. "I wish I could call up Wally and Moira and ask them. They've had experience thinking seriously about this shit."

She shook her own head, impatiently. "Horseshit. They don't know any more about time travel than we do. And they probably don't even realize *that*."

"Maybe not, but they can think about this kind of stuff logically without boggling," he said. "They actually know some real science. I haven't got a good enough sense of what's really ridiculous, and what's only weird."

"So we do that: stick to what we know, and apply logic. How about this one—this is the one that keeps sticking in my craw: how come we know as much as we do? How come we know anything at all?"

"Huh?"

June went into lecture mode. "You're a time traveler. You have powers beyond those of mortal men. You bury something you want to stay buried. So you booby-trap it: if a guy hits it with a shovel, he gets hit with a mind-ray or whatever, he forgets what he was doing and wanders off. Now: won't you give the damn mind-ray a large enough radius to *also* get his buddy who wandered off a few meters to take a pee?"

He nodded. "That bothers me some, too. You shouldn't have had time to make that long a phone call before you got bagged."

"Maybe it was just a robot security system that mook triggered—"

"Even so. It obviously read his mind; it should have noticed a better mind nearby. It would have if *I* designed it, and I'm probably not as smart as a time traveler."

June winced at the last clause, and spoke quickly to distract him, lest he hear what he had just said. "So we want to figure out why it didn't notice me at first. Let's just riff and see what happens. How am

I different from Angel Gerhardt? I'm smarter . . . right, and the mind-ray only notices stupid people. It'd be getting a great reading off of me, now. Uh . . . let's see: I'm female, I weigh less, less upper-arm strength, I probably have nicer tits—"

"Try it this way," Paul said. "How were you different from him *that afternoon*?"

"Okay, let's think about that. I probably had less cocaine in my system . . . I wasn't planning to commit a crime, not that day, anyway . . . I was depressed from thinking about my mother . . . I didn't have a backpack or a shovel—"

"The depressed thing might be something," he said. "I admit I can't imagine what—but it's something mental, and this is a mind-reader we're talking about. I think so, anyway. Maybe depression is something he blocks out as long as possible."

"Great. In that case, I could walk straight up to him, right now, and he'd never even notice me." Thoughts of her mother were trying to steal her attention, but June pushed them back under the covers. She knew—somehow—that Laura Bellamy was still alive, down there in California, and she had made up her mind not to start grieving until it was grieving time. But the mental association did give her an idea of what to do next. "Look," she said, getting to her feet, "I'm coming up empty. It's time for me to do my thinking thing."

"Not a bad idea," he agreed, remaining where he was. "It's what you were doing when this whole clem started. And this is a good place for it, as long as you stick to the path. Take an umbrella and a flashlight." June's "thinking thing" was a ritual he was familiar with, and respected, even if it didn't work for him. Faced with an intractable problem, she liked to surround herself with the physical, visual, olfactory and aural stimuli she found most conducive to thought—by walking in woods (for preference; a park or picnic area would do in a pinch) or along the shore while listening to good music on headphones. "I think I saw a Walkman in the bedroom," he added.

"Yeah," she snorted. She took hold of the railing and did some stretches to work the kinks out. "I noticed it, too. What the hell is the point of *owning* a Walkman if you're going to leave it behind when you go on trips? I swear, the ones with the money are always the least—WOW!"

He rolled away from her, came to his feet in a half crouch and spun twice like a ballet dancer, snapping his head around for each turn. "*Where?*"

"No, no, relax—I just had a rush of brains to the head. I was wishing I had my own FM headphones with me, so I wouldn't have to go put on something with a pocket to put that heavy Walkman in, and deal with the cord, and so on . . . and that made me miss my headphones, sitting back home in Vancouver . . . and that reminded me that as I was leaving the house for the last time, right after you called, I looked for those 'phones and couldn't find them. They weren't where I always hang them by the door."

Paul straightened, shivered slightly, and shook adrenalin-energy from his fingertips, but kept his temper. "Okay. And from this you infer . . . ?"

"I know I had those 'phones on my head when I walked into Pacific Spirit Park. The jockey had put on a whole side of Coltrane ballads." Her voice was becoming dreamy as she forced the memories to the surface. "I remember 'Nancy With The Laughing Face,' and 'Little Brown Book,' and something I didn't know, and then another Strayhorn . . . 'Lush Life,' that was it . . . I remember 'Lush Life' starting . . . and then the next sound-memory I have is walking out of the Park . . . and thinking for the thousandth time in my life that Philip Glass must have stolen half his lick from listening to birds! Paul, I was hearing birds—"

Paul's eyes glowed. "You didn't have the radio on anymore. Oh, I *like* this. You're absolutely right: this is a 'WOW.' " He began to pace the deck. "Check me out on this. This Gerhardt mook starts to bury his stash. In doing so he triggers . . . I know it's a feeble pun, but let's call it a mental detector. It reads his mind, erases the parts it doesn't like, and sends him on his way, clueless. It ought to pick *you* up, too, what did you say, fifty meters away, call it fifty yards, right? Only *you have an FM radio right next to your skull,* and that screws up the mental detector for some reason. So you get to watch the whole show. The mook buries his stash somewhere else, and goes home, and you put a message on my machine. Alright: for the Hawaiian vacation and ten thousand dollars cash, what does June Bellamy do next?"

"I dig up his stash," she said at once, and then, more slowly, "and maybe I take my radiophones off to wipe away the sweat—"

"Or maybe a *second* mental detector has been put on the stash, now, to keep tabs on the mook if he should ever shake off the whammy and come back—and the FM radio gag only works at fifty meters."

"I like the first one," she said. "It explains why they take the risk of not giving me my headphones back after they're done."

"Okay," he agreed. "I like it, too. You realize what this means? For the first time, we have a *clue* how we can possibly defend ourselves, if the bastard catches up with us."

"We're doing it again," she said.

"Doing what?"

"Thinking of him as 'him.' I said I wasn't going to do that."

"Hard not to."

She nodded. "Well, now that we're agreed he's not a monkey demon or a spaceman, 'it' doesn't work anymore . . . and who knows better than I how few women warriors there are in North America? But we still ought to keep reminding ourselves that 'he' could just as easily be 'they,' at least."

"Point taken. Tell you the truth, I kind of hope there *are* two of them."

"Really? Why?"

"Well, we seem to have found a counter for the mental detector slash obedience ray slash brain-washer."

"Maybe."

"Without that, the best these guys can possibly be is supernaturally good . . . so if there's two of them, that makes it a fair fight." Even in the growing dark she could see his grin. "I *like* a fair fight."

"God, testosterone is an amazing thing. I'll settle for there's only one of him and we kick his ass without working up a sweat."

He shook his head, still grinning happily. "One way or another, I'm working up a sweat. I disapprove of people who do B&Es on my sweetie's skull."

It came to her that testosterone had its uses. "Not to mention people who spoil your greatest triumph and burn your house down."

He shrugged. "Those things too. For them I'd hurt him. For you, I'm going to kill him."

A primitive thrill made her tingle, and a few more uses for testosterone occurred to her. "You say the sweetest things," she murmured, and moved nearer.

But he was not quite ready to segue from blood lust to the other kind. "I'm glad it pleases you," he said, "but I have to be honest: I think my motives are more selfish than anything else. *Nobody* is going to know you better than I do."

She pressed her attack, ignoring his body language. "Darling, our relationship is based on enlightened mutual selfishness, you know that." Her tongue made a demand of his neck. "Our interests coincide." She could smell him shifting gears. "You kill him, and I'll make you a lovely loincloth from the hide." Her fingers asked a question of his penis. "Now drag me into the cave and exploit me, you brute."

As she was being carried in from the deck, she remembered that he always lasted forever when he was stoned, and she shivered with anticipation. Her lover's funk was definitely over. They had a plan . . . and just possibly the beginnings of an edge.

"The first thing we do tomorrow morning," he said sleepily, "we find out where's the nearest place to score a couple of sets of FM headsets. Shit, one of us may have to go back to Vancouver; I'll be surprised if they stock 'em out here on Gilligan's Island. Maybe I could work up some kind of headband rig to hold a Walkman against our skulls—did you notice whether O'Leary's has FM? Or is it just the tape kind? June? Are you listening to me? Hey—are you *crying*? God, was I that good, or are you—"

"Mom is down."

He stared.

"I just know, okay? She's gone."

"Aw jeeze—"

"Shit, I can't even call Pop and console him."

And *her* funk began.

By the middle of the next day, it had so thoroughly thickened the atmosphere in that lavish little A-frame that Paul volunteered to walk to "town" in a low-probability search for headphones with FM radios built in, despite the ever present rain. Better to soak than choke.

Although he kept his ears open for the sound of Tom Waits along the way, he was not fortunate enough to encounter Moe Lycott, and he could not quite suppress the instincts of a lifetime enough to stick his thumb out for the occasional stranger who did drive past. Consequently it was midafternoon, and he was footsore and sweaty under his mackinaw, by the time he reached the cluster of shops by the ferry terminus. He looked with longing upon the first tavern he came to . . . then remembered his marijuana binge of the night before, reminded himself sharply that he was on combat-alert, and began to walk on by. But the first step hurt so much, after the momentary respite, that he converted the second into a pivot and trod heavily into the welcoming shade where ice-cold beer lived.

He emerged with a much lighter step half an hour later, scoped the street without seeming to, and made his way to the general store the bartender had suggested, humming softly.

Two beers was not enough, however, to make him follow the bartender's suggestion that he ask for "Space Case," despite assurances that this was the name of the clerk most likely to be able to help him. Instead he simply looked over the two clerks available in the little shop, figured out which a yokel would be most likely to call Space Case, and approached that one. "Uh, excuse me—I wonder if you could help me out."

"I can try. Define the problem."

Ah, a technical mind. "My wife and I have decided we prefer radio to tape. It's more unpredictable, eh? And we do a lot of walking, and gosh, to get the same amount of choice from a Walkman that a radio offers, you need an extra pack just for cassettes. Plus I always get the cord caught. You wouldn't by any chance happen to have a couple of sets of dedicated FM headphones around the shop, would you?"

Space Case grinned, brushed stringy hair from his face, and pointed to the wall behind him. "Ask me a hard one. Panasonic okay?"

Paul squinted. "Are they powerful?"

The grin widened. "Well, that's your basic good news/bad news situation. The good news is yes and yes, and the bad news is yes."

Paul reminded himself that he was supposed to be a Canadian, too polite to mind having his chain yanked. "Beg pardon?"

"You ask me if it's powerful, you're asking three things. First, does it play loud? Answer: yes, it'll play just as loud as anything else in the world with earphones—as loud as the law allows, and no louder. Second, does it pull in all the signals, even the weak ones? Answer: maybe better than the tuner you have back home; your whole skull kind of acts as an antenna, fillings and all. Those are the good news. Part three: does it put out a strong field? Answer: well, yeah, kind of, relatively speaking."

Paul's ears grew points. "I don't think I follow you. A radio receiver puts out a signal of its own?"

"Well, a weak one. So does a Walkman, or a CD player, or a computer. It's why they don't want you to use one in a plane during takeoff and landing. Which by the way is a total crock: the field strength falls off so fast with distance, you're as likely to interfere with the pilot's electronics as you are with his menstrual cycle. Airlines are just lawsuit-happy."

"So why is this bad news?"

Space Case took two sets of FM headphones from the wall and set them on the counter, then recaptured his hair and tucked it behind his ear again. "Well, a lot of experts say it isn't, actually. But I notice that your personal skull gets a lot closer to one of these than the cockpit does. Even a Walkman at the end of one of those little cords gives you more distance. And there's this cube-square thing happening."

"So if the experts are wrong, and there *is* any danger in low-level electromagnetic fields . . ."

"This is about as good a test as you can get," Space Case agreed. "Short of building a cabin under a power line."

Paul frowned. He wanted the things more than ever, now . . . but staying in character required him to appear dubious. "Are you saying they're dangerous, then?"

Space Case shrugged. "I'm saying, anybody who claims to know that *for sure* either way at this point in history is lying or kidding himself. Put it like this: Panasonic is willing to undertake the risk of selling them to you . . . and I'm willing to accept the karma of taking your money. I'm just into full disclosure. Like I say, a lot of experts say they're perfectly harmless. But the way I see it, an expert is an ordinary person, a long way from home."

Paul considered, wrestling with a tiny, absurd dilemma. In New York, he would simply have bought the headphones now—long since, in fact. But as a putative Canadian, he needed a polite reason to ignore the salesman's clear reluctance to sell them, to override the other's judgment. He took refuge in quotation. "Well, as a great man once said, 'You can go as far wrong by being too skeptical as by being too trusting.' I guess I'll give Panasonic the benefit of the doubt: let me have two sets, please."

Space Case grinned even wider. "A fan!"

Paul blinked. "Beg pardon?"

"That was a Lazarus Long quote. You're a fan, right?"

Very faintly—in fact, almost below the conscious level entirely—an alarm went off in the back of Paul's mind. Those who lie for a living must pay close attention to any mental notes they leave themselves . . . and one part of the prophylactic debriefing procedure he'd automatically put himself through as he had walked out Wally and Moira's door with ninety-eight thousand of their dollars in his hand had been to instruct himself: *For the next little while, if anyone asks you if you know anything about science fiction, say no.* "Sorry," he lied fluently. "I don't know this Nazareth fellow. I was quoting an English teacher I had once, Mr. Leamer."

"Ah. Well, never mind; it's a long story. Pun intended. Several books long, actually. Will that be cash or charge?"

"Cash, please."

"How are you fixed for goo?"

Paul stopped sorting bills by color, and stared. "Could you run that by me again?"

"You said you and the wife walk a lot. I got some great blister goo."

Paul had made up his mind over an hour ago: he was going to walk back to Casa O'Leary with his new radio headphones, and then he was never ever going to walk anywhere again as long as he lived. Painkiller he already had. So the only operative consideration was, what would a *real* walker say to an offer like this? "No, thanks," he said. "We've got some prescription stuff her sports medicine doctor gives her."

"Oh yeah? What's it called?"

He took refuge in incompetence. "I know it as 'foot gunk.' It's white, if that helps any."

Space Case kept his face straight. "Yeah, that narrows it down some."

Out of professional admiration, Paul kept his own face straight, and kept playing dumb. "Really?"

"Yeah, all them white ones are only manufactured on days that end in y."

He did his double-take so beautifully he drew a shout of laughter from Space Case. "I suppose they *are* just about all white, eh?" he said with a great show of rue. "I wonder why that is."

"I'd imagine," Space Case said, still chuckling, "for the same reason every brand of creme rinse you can buy for your hair looks exactly like ejaculate. You want powerful magic, invoke semen."

Paul obliged by looking mildly scandalized but too ashamed to admit it, and left, well pleased. Even the nosiest clerk tended to forget the dull ones quickly.

All the way back to O'Leary's A-frame he strained his ears for Moe Lycott's truck, without success. Halfway there the rain suddenly went from drizzle to downpour. He went through a kind of epiphany, and by an act of the will forced himself to stick his thumb out, the way he'd seen people do in old movies. This turned out to be sound strategy: the savage satisfaction he achieved when fourteen successive cars blew by him without slowing was more comfort than a ride would have been. Even here, there were traces of civilization. . . .

He arrived home lamed but in a fine sour spirit that tasted like unsweetened chocolate, and hung up his mackinaw prepared to resume the burden of not being permitted to comfort his lover—

—only to find something out of a nightmare.

Sitting, safe and sound, in the chaise lounge on the lower deck, under the overhang of the deck above. Serene and tranquil, internal thunderclouds past, funk miraculously over, days ahead of schedule. Heartbreakingly lovely in the grey light of rainy afternoon: his lover, his partner, his best friend June. Who at his approach looked him square in the eye, and said, quietly and without a trace of humor, words which frightened and shocked him more than being stalked by a brain-raping house-burning time traveler had:

"Paul, I'm getting out of the business."

Paralysis. There were so many possible responses—so many sheafs of different *kinds* of possible responses—that his quick wit and quick body alike were mazed, and he made no response at all. He stood there expressionless and motionless and almost thoughtless, for the first time in years simply waiting to find out what would happen next.

"However this thing with the time traveler works out, I'm

through," she said. "I'd like to keep half title to the Key West place, if we're alive when this is over, and the stash in Chicago. The rest is yours. The store, all the other cushions, the software, everything. I'm cashing out."

His eyelids closed of their own accord. He could think of no reason to raise them, but then he heard a voice rather like his own, miles away, croak, "You're leaving me?" and opened his eyes to see who had said that and what she would answer.

It must have been one of those two tiny copies of him swimming in her eyes who'd spoken. "Not unless you ask me to," she said carefully. "We can keep separate finances, and you won't talk about work at home. I'll go where you go, and lie for you, and cover you when you have to run, and catch up when I can. I'll bind your wounds and tolerate your bullshit and I'll bury you if it comes to that. But I won't so much as rope for you: I won't even consult. I'm through."

Idly he wondered what new—legit!—profession she would dream up for herself, flexible and portable enough to be compatible with a mate in The Life: he knew it was certain to be interesting. But that was a consideration for the distant future—whole minutes from now. At the moment the important thing was to get his heart restarted.

Unh. There . . .

"You want to hear something amazing?" his voice said. Yeah, it was coming from one of those little reflections in her eyes: the distance and volume sounded about right. "My feet don't hurt a bit. Not at all. You feel like going for a hike in the rain, I'll be glad to come along."

"Paul—"

"It's like the old joke," the reflection interrupted; he lip-synched along. "You're supposed to lead up to a thing like that. First you say, 'I've found Krishna; please call me Moonbeam now.' Then you say, 'Your test came back: it's cancer of the penis.' *Then* you say you're retiring."

She returned his gaze steadily, and said something so absurd he and the reflections all had to smile: "I'm sorry."

For the first time Paul understood why the commander of the Light Brigade had followed those blundering orders and mounted an impossible charge. Because there is no despair so vast or cold or stony that some drifting idiot seed of hope cannot take root, wither, and decay there, all in an instant. "June," he said, in the freedom of futility, "your mom—"

"She didn't like what I do, Paul. She never said so. Not once, or we could have argued it, and maybe I could have persuaded her. But we both knew."

"Of *course* she didn't like it: she's your mother, she was scared for you—"

"She was ashamed of me. I think she was wrong, most of the time, but she was ashamed of me. Not because she had to lie whenever her friends asked what I was up to; she didn't mind lying at all. Because the truth hurt her. She wanted to be proud of me. And she was—but not all the way."

"If she'd understood—"

"I'll tell you the worst. I've been sitting here reviewing the last year or so, and I'm ashamed of me, too."

He had been stunned for some time, now he was shocked: different things. He raised his arms as if to summon divine witness. "*Why?*"

His reflections, thrashing around in their tubs like that, made them spill over and run down her cheeks. "Our standards have been slipping."

"Bullshit."

She shook her head hard enough to displace the tears, but they were replaced almost at once. "What did we say, back at the beginning? *Only jerks*, right? Only people that deserved it."

"That's right," he agreed. "You're the one who taught me that. I was feeding on anything with blood when you found me. And feeling shitty about it."

"Think about my last two games. How about Frazier?"

"He hired us to kill his wife!"

"And you said yourself it was a shame not to go through with it."

"But—but then it wouldn't have been a sting. It would have been . . . *work*."

"The point remains. Being driven beyond his endurance doesn't make a guy a jerk. Remember, he even asked us to make it quick and painless."

"Sure—till I told him that'd be extra."

"Being on a budget doesn't make you a jerk either. She had no money, there was no real insurance on her to speak of: all he wanted was his sanity back. We didn't even leave him enough to try again."

Change tack. "Well, what was wrong with Wo Fat? *He* had it coming."

"Sure, he deserved to get stung. I *ruined* him. Not because he ripped off immigrants. Because he offended me. Because he treated me exactly the way his culture had raised and trained him to treat women. The way I encouraged him to treat me, to set up the gaff. What I was trying to do was sting his whole sexist society."

"So?"

"So I forgot it's half women."

Paul was lost. "Okay, so maybe you've slipped into a couple of grey areas, lately—"

Water had continued to leak, silently and slowly, from her clear eyes. Now she began to cry: different thing. "I've even got you doing it lately."

"*Huh?*"

"It really was brilliant, honey. I never wrote a better scam in my life. But tell me: just what did your Wally and Moira do to deserve to lose ninety-eight large that wasn't even theirs?"

For the second time he waved his arms. "Are you nuts? They're true believers. Sci fi fans, for God's sake."

"Those are lapses of taste, not lapses of morality. And you didn't just take their money. You also took their friends' money, entrusted to them. Right now their universe is forever fucked because they wanted John Lennon alive and the Beatles back. Accept that criterion and we can sting anybody over thirty, and anybody younger than that with taste."

He got a grip, and patiently began to explain to her why she was wrong. Assembling his arguments, he discovered she was right.

The only trouble with owning an unusually acute and flexible mind (aside from the loneliness) is that you can't make it blind or stupid when you need to. Paul Throtmanian shifted gears instantly for a living. Against his will, his universe now processed about two degrees, and clicked into a new alignment, for the second time in as many minutes. He tried desperately to put it back the way it had been, but it wouldn't go. He had been stunned and shocked, now he was horrified: different thing.

"My God," he breathed. "We *have* been slipping. You're right. We've been acting like . . . like executives, or muggers or something. Robbing anybody who comes along." He shook his head, in awe as much as horror. "Haven't we?"

Her crying escalated to sobbing. "I never got to work it out with her. She died ashamed of me. It has to stop."

He had *never* seen her sob, not even when that mark in Calgary had broken her finger. After stunned, shocked and horrified comes terrified. "Okay," he cried, and threw himself on his knees to embrace her. "Okay," he kept saying, over and over. "Okay, it stops now."

He didn't mean it yet. But he already knew he would, eventually.

After they had been silent and still for awhile, he suddenly began to giggle. She pulled away and searched his face, more than glad for something to laugh about. "What?"

"J-just one thing b-bothers me—"

All of a sudden she got it, and began to giggle herself. "The time traveler—"

He nodded. "If he gets us—"

"—we'll forget we ever made this decision!"

They howled.

Later, as he helped her to her feet, she gripped his shoulder. "So we won't let him get us. Right?"

"Well, now that we've finally got a good reason . . ." He stopped smiling, then, and put his hand over hers. "We won't let him get us."

"I love you," she said.

He squeezed her hand tightly. "And so well."

As they cleared the doorway, his feet began to hurt again.

❊CHAPTER 11❊
The Immortal Storm

"EXCUSE ME, MA'AM," Wally said. "I'm sorry to bother you a second time, but I intend to break and enter Ms. Bernardo's home shortly, and I was wondering if you could help me."

He held his breath, poised like a cat to spring to safety, while she blinked blearily at him.

In America it might not have worked. But Canadians could still afford a romantic view of crime. "Why, yesh," she said finally. "I believe I could be of shome asshistance."

He had to wonder why she had failed to slur the last two sibilants. For that matter, why hadn't she shooshed last night, when she'd been just as drunk? "Thank you, Mrs. Live Here. That's very kind of you."

He still did not relax. He was not poised to escape an adverse reaction, but to dodge any more attempted bourbon kisses. Moira had agreed with him that this audacious approach, long shot though it might be, was the only possible way to burgle a home on Point Grey Road, but she had been extremely emphatic on precisely how far he was and was not authorized to go in securing assistance. If her sensitive nose detected a single molecule of bourbon—or worse, soap—anywhere above his collar or below his belt when he got home tonight . . . well, he wouldn't be able to go home, no matter what he found out at the Bernardo house.

"Why do you call me that?"

He slapped his forehead. Clumsy start. "I'm sorry. I have this . . . well, odd sense of humor. When I asked your name last night, you

561

said, 'Never mind, I live here,' so I'm afraid ever since, I've been thinking of you as 'Mrs. Live Here' in my head."

She pursed her lips and blinked some more. "All thingsh considered, that'll do. But it's Ms. Live Here. Call me Liv for short."

"Ah." Oh God, don't let that mean she's single. "Well, Liv, is there any particular method of entry you would recommend? I'd prefer to keep this as discreet as possible. Actually, I'd like it if no one ever finds out I was in there; frankly, we're sort of hoping to come up on Ms. Bernardo's blind side. If you should know anything about the nature of her alarm system, for instance—"

"I only know one thing about it," she said, blinking, "but it's a pip. There ishn't one."

Wally blinked back at her. "Bless my soul. Really?"

"She told me once it was ludicroush to spend a penny on shecurity on Point Grey Road. She said she had no alarm, never locked her windowsh, and, for icing on the cake, as she put it, she always left the back door shlightly ajar."

"You know," Wally said slowly, "that makes a kind of sense. You see an open door, unlocked windows, you assume someone's inside."

She nodded so savagely she nearly unbalanced. "Damn right it make shense! Spesh'ly here. There hashn't been an *attempted* break-in on thish shtreet in . . . well, shince I've been here. Early this century. And do you think my fucking inshurance comp'ny'll let *me* do the same goddam thing? Bugger, they will! That'sh why I'm gon' help you: I wanna see *her* 'shurance comp'ny get what they desherve for being so shenshible and decent."

His brain kept trying to find the pattern in her intermittent slur; it was giving him a headache. She seemed most successful with sibilants spelled with a c. Could her tongue *spell*? "Of course. So you think it would be safe for me to just . . . pop next door, go round back, and try the door?"

"Long ash you don't look furtive," she said. "That'll get you shot anywheres around here."

"Oh, I won't," he assured her.

"You're poor," she said suddenly, as if challenging him to disagree.

"That's right," he said.

She snorted, fruitily, like a small horse. "You poor guys alwaysh got more intreshsting minds than the kind o' jerksh I gotta hang out with. Why'sh that, you think?"

"We need to," Wally explained.

She nodded as thoughtfully as if provisionally accepting his solution to Fermat's Last Theorem. "That soundsh right. Anybody on thish block wanted a break an' enner done, they'd hire it done. Too damn rich to be intereshsting."

He wanted, badly, to ask her how she had conceived the notion of both slurring and not slurring the sibilant in "interesting," and whether it required practice or had come easily to her—but he knew it would constitute a digression, and in any case, artists are seldom able to explain their methods satisfactorily to the layman. "It hardly seems like break and enter if I don't have to break anything, does it?"

She smiled her feral smile, tightening her face so much that for a moment he feared her eyeballs would pop out. "Far'sh I'm consherned, you can exshplore that ashpect of your artishtic vision once you're inshide. I promish not to hear a thing. And the old Chink on the other shide's deaf as a boot. Wing Wang Wong, or whatever her name ish."

Now she was slurring c's—and even an x! "I really appreciate your help," he said. He was already backing away as he began the second syllable, out of the sheltered doorway and into the rain. This proved to be nice timing: her aborted lunge was unmistakable. "Goodbye, Liv, and thank you."

"Good luck, Handsome."

Wally had last been called handsome by a woman not Moira while auditioning for a part in a fannish play that was to have been performed at a small regional relaxacon, some eighteen years before—and he had not gotten the part. "Cuddly" he could aspire to; "handsome" exceeded even his fantasies. Nevertheless he was within ten steps of Carla Bernardo's back door before he next remembered to be terrified again. There was something to be said for drunken myopia—and nymphomania, too, if it came to that.

His pulse quickened when he saw that the door was not, as advertised, actually ajar. Liv Here might—in fact, almost certainly did—suffer from that condition Moira called rectofossal ambiguity. ("Fossa" being Latin for "a hole in the ground.") If he tried that door ... was he going to trigger the alarm system Liv had assured him didn't exist, and end up with his own rectum in a torsa ("sling")?

Did he have any choice?

The door opened at his touch like a nymphomaniac's legs, easily, thoroughly, and silently.

Wally stood there before the open door, absolutely motionless, in drizzling rain, for a full five minutes. He told himself he was listening, but the rain and his pulse would have drowned out anything short of a pistol being cocked next to his head. It took him nearly the whole first minute to realize that there was a radio playing in the house, a talkjock whose topic tonight seemed to be the old Canadian standby, "America: Threat or Menace?" If Wally had merely been a junkie with his whole body screaming for a fix, he'd have left. Only one thing finally had the power to drive him inside: the vision of Moira's face when he reported back. He found that he wanted, very badly, to hear her say, "My hero!" so that he could say, "Aw, shucks."

Once in the house, however, he simply doffed his rain gear and got to work. He lost some time and some shin skin to his reluctance to turn on any lights—successfully establishing by way of consolation, however, that anyone else in the building was dead or deaf, and that a human heart can't actually explode. He also managed to silence the talkjock, at least locally. But once he penetrated to rooms with no exterior windows, where he felt safe turning lights on, things picked up quickly. Not only did he locate the computer in the second room he tried, and not only was it a make and model and operating system he was reasonably comfortable with, its security encryption program yielded to him even more skittishly than the door had.

As he had guessed, "Carla Bernardo" had characteristically been a hair too cute for her own good: the password that cracked her shields was "Tammy Lynn." It was an obvious choice, if you had some experience at what hackers and crackers called "social engineering"—and if you realized "Carla" had made up her name by reverse-combining those of the notorious, recently sentenced Canadian monsters Paul Bernardo and Karla Homolka. The first of the young girls they had raped and murdered together—a few weeks before their wedding— was Karla's fifteen-year-old sister Tammy.

Wally didn't even bother to read a thing: just fired up the modem and uploaded everything he could decrypt to one of his own hard drives back home. It came to something over fifty megabytes. Then he scanned the stuff which had not been encrypted, and uploaded some of those files to a separate folder at home. He could see Moira smiling, in his mind's eye, and grinned back at the screen.

When he was satisfied he had every byte he could locate and wanted, he reformatted Carla's whole hard drive three times—wiping it irrecoverably—and entertained himself as it churned by thumbing through the Japanese pornographic comic book collection he found in a drawer. She had some better ones than he and Moira did.

Finally the computer chirped for the third time and drew him back from a particularly absorbing *manga*. He nearly left, then, but things had gone so well thus far, he was in the mood for a little adventure. So he searched Carla's office, finding nothing of lasting interest, and then her bathroom, learning only that she was not a natural blonde, and then her bedroom, where he found behind the false back of a bottom dresser drawer a lockbox whose combination was the same as her computer password. Its contents caused Wally to leap to his feet and dance the Monkey, for the first time in twenty years. A little work before a full-length mirror distributed these things about his person so well that even a sharper observer than Liv might not have noticed Wally was a bit more cuddly than usual.

On his way out, he stopped by Carla's office again, stole three of the *manga*, and added them to the swag, tucking them inside his belt in the back, under his shirt.

He recovered his rain poncho and left by the back door again—leaving it ajar—and returned to the street around the opposite side of the building from the one by which he'd entered. By the time Liv saw him and began cawing, he was within twenty steps of his car. Even walking carefully so as not to spill his pornography, he was able to make a clean getaway.

Halfway home, stopped at a traffic light on Broadway, he found himself unable to suppress an impulse to beat his fists on the steering wheel and howl with animal glee. He glanced to his left and saw a pedestrian staring at him from the sidewalk. "Vancouver," he cried happily through his rain-streaked window.

The pedestrian smiled, nodded, and waved.

The light changed and the mighty hunter went home to his mate.

Who literally greeted him with open arms. And open nostrils.

"My hero!" she cried.

"Aw, shucks, ma'am." Wally knew he was grinning the uncontrolled grin, the one that made him look goofy, but he couldn't help it. He had successfully carried out his first burglary, and he had passed his sniff test, and he had just heard and spoken two of his very favorite clichés—and the best was yet to come.

Moira hugged him tightly, putting english on it. "Really, Wally, you did great. I've been going through some of what you sent, making a start, anyway, and there's—what?"

He had disengaged from the hug just far enough to silence her with an upraised finger. "Go to the meditation room," he said, "and wait for me there."

She frowned, studied him carefully, and one eyebrow lifted slightly in alarm. "Wally, that's the goofy grin. Am I gonna like this?'

"Want to see another grin just like it? Bring a hand mirror to the meditation room and wait for me there."

"Hey, where's your coat?"

"Read on," he suggested.

She sighed. "Should I put on music?"

He shook his head. "There'll be plenty. Trust me."

She looked exasperated. "That's the trouble. I do."

He went back to the car, recovered his coat, and carried it inside in his arms. He locked the door behind him and made sure the phone machine was armed before joining Moira in the meditation room. He found her there, sitting on her *zafu*, measuring her breath. She had not fetched a mirror. Again he made sure the door was sealed behind him, then dropped into tailor's seat opposite her, setting his bundle down between them. Declining to feed him any more straight-lines, she waited serenely.

He adopted his Panel Moderator voice. "Having stolen all the really *important* items—that is, the data—of which you were just about to deliver a preliminary summary that I am, I promise you, most eager to hear—I turned my attention briefly, before I took my leave, to mere material things."

She kept waiting, but her lips seemed to tighten ever so slightly.

He nodded as if she had said something. "I hear you. You're thinking: no matter how lavish or fine they may be, I don't want any of the possessions of those people in my house. I felt much the same way when I began my search. Doubtless you're wondering why I'm going around Robin Hood's barn like this, why I've got what I found bundled up in my coat. If I'd left it all where I had it stashed when I left the place, you'd have felt most of it as soon as you hugged me a minute ago, and then there might have been trouble. I thought it would be better all around if we did this here. Are you ready?"

She took one more deep breath and nodded.

He unwrapped his booty.

He let her have five seconds to absorb the basic gist of the contents, and then placed his fingers in his ears, and in a loud clear voice, provided inventory details. "The Canadian is forty-seven thousand five hundred in used nonserial fifties. The American is thirty-five thousand in new nonserial twenties. The handgun is a Glock nine millimeter, fully loaded; there was no extra ammo. The comics are great. The passports are all—" That was as far as he got.

One of several reasons Moira had been in more or less constant demand for fan theatricals over the past few decades was her scream. It might have made a Hammer Films alumnus weep with nostalgia, or won a nod from Coltrane—evoking all the stark despairing terror of a virgin accosted by the Ripper on her wedding night, yet delivered by a vocal instrument with the raw pneumatic power of a Sophie Tucker or a Mama Cass. At the previous year's Worldcon Hugo ceremonies, where she had performed for two thousand pros and fans in an immense hall, the tech crew had not found it necessary or even advisable to mike her. The effect in a small soundproof room was impressive. Even with his fingers deep in his ears and his palms cupped over them, Wally paid for his fun. He had expected to, and paid up like a man. But then he made a very bad mistake: he took his fingers out of his ears—just as she did it again.

Shortly he managed to pry his eyelids open again, but he kept on seeing paisley swirls and neon mandalas. Gradually, as in one of those tests for color-blindness, some of them resolved into Moira's face. The lips were moving. He waved and gestured to indicate the transmission was unsuccessful, but they kept moving. He closed his eyes to conserve processing power and concentrated. White noise slowly arrived from the far end of the universe, rose to the level of static—then, as with the visual data, some of it coalesced into a parody of Moira's voice.

"—alize what this means? *This is wonderful. This is horrible. It couldn't be better, and it couldn't be worse. Who's writing this mess, Wally? What did we ever do to deserve this? Stop grinning, dammit!"*

He hadn't realized he still was. He made it go away with a massive effort, and his hearing improved slightly. "You understand why I did this *here*?" he asked. His voice sounded to him flanged, distorted, like John Lennon in "I Am the Walrus," a comparison that irritated him.

She nodded impatiently. "Of course. Everyone on the block would be dialing 911 right now if we weren't in a soundproof room. But Jesus, Wally, the way you set it up I thought it was gonna be something *good*."

What in Finagle's name did he have to do to *please* this woman? "This isn't good? One: sitting right there on the floor is on the close order of ninety-five percent of what we got taken for; I did the math. As far as I can tell it's all real and it all spends. Two: it's enough—as of now, VanCon can happen after all, and we even got some of our own money back! Three: that means hereinafter, I can be assured that my motives in continuing to stalk these bastards are at least eighty percent pure personal vengeance; I don't know about you, but that gives me a lot of spiritual satisfaction." His hearing was improving; by now he sounded like Lennon in "Strawberry Fields." (The first half.) "And four: now we *each* have a gun, and neither can be traced to us. Tell me the downside, because I don't—oh wait, I get you. Here we are in the middle of a manhunt, and we have a convention to run again. Okay, so we give up sleeping on alternate days, instead of every third—"

She cut him off. "What would have happened if we'd gone on the Net this morning and announced exactly what had happened to us? That we got taken, and VanCon was vaporware?"

He frowned. If this was a sequitur, the connection escaped him. "Well . . . put it this way: the only upside would have been that we'd never have heard another live filksong in our lives."

She nodded. "Total humiliation, and lifelong expulsion from the councils of fandom. Possibly even total excommunication from fandom itself. We'd have had to have plastic surgery and change all our ID to ever see another huckster room."

"And your point is . . . ?"

"Obviously that's unthinkable. But what would happen if we went on the Net right *now*, and truthfully reported events as of this minute? VanCon's still on, but here's why it almost didn't happen?"

He flinched slightly, and then made himself think about it dispassionately. If she wanted to be Socrates, he could bat around a theoretical proposition as well as Phaedrus. "Uh . . . let's see . . . still total humiliation, for sure . . . but probably no banishment. It'd be just too much fun to have us around to laugh at. Best guess, I'd say we'd be making significant progress toward living it down in—I don't know, ten years? Twelve? A couple of fannish generations, call it, before we'd ever be given anything but scutwork to do again. Long after we died, they'd still be telling neos about us. And the neos would be laughing. Except for the occasional sweet one who would pity us."

She reached out and took his hand. "Wally?" she said. His hearing was now nominal; nonetheless her voice sounded strained. "Those two jerks are still out there someplace, with new names and maybe new faces. We're looking for them, granted, but we don't even really know for certain they're still in *Canada*, much less in the Lower Mainland. They're experienced, professional vampires, and they've just learned how nice fans taste, and perhaps you'll join me in flattering ourselves that they are very fucking good." She had his complete attention; Moira rarely used that word. "Answer me this, honey: *how important is it that fandom be warned?*"

Wally screamed. Not in the same league with one of hers . . . but it was closer to his ears.

That postponed the first real quarrel they'd had in months for another several minutes.

It escalated, when it finally came, to yet another iteration of The Quarrel. Their version, that is, of the one all couples lucky enough to have the privilege will write together and perfect over the years granted them: the basic chord structure over which they would improvise The Dozens together, every time fate lashed them into song. It was no more interesting than any other couple's quarrel, full of You're Always and You Never and If You'd Just Once; its chief function was to allow them each to say things of which they would later be intellectually and/or emotionally ashamed—an instinctive human response to crisis so primitive it makes fight-or-flight look like an intelligent advance. By now they knew where each other's vulnerable places were, and were reasonably confident they could take each other's best shot. (Pity the singles and loners, who must make do with bar fights or politics.)

As in postmodern music—indeed, postmodern art of most kinds—communication was subordinated to personal expression; the results were thus unlistenable for anyone but the artists, and will not be recorded here. When this set had had time to seep into long-term memory storage, each would forget most of what they had said, and remember most of what the other had said, but they would process it differently. Wally would be deeply scarred by the very worst of her barbs—but would almost never consciously think of them again until the next jam session, and thus would take decades to deal with them. Moira, on the other hand, would replay his cruelest words over and over in her head daily for several weeks, until she had worn them smooth, then string them with the others on a secret necklace she could finger whenever it suited her to be depressed.

Fortunately for them, they both suffered from a chronic condition that might be called stupidity fatigue. Even driven by fear, frustration and shame, half an hour away from rationality was about the maximum either Wally or Moira were built to tolerate. This session followed their basic pattern: two extended solos, a spirited duet, a reprise of the theme, and then a smooth segue into their trademark ending. Wally always won the putative argument, whatever it happened to be, and then discovered his prize was a barren, blasted desert, and scrambled to apologize and surrender. This allowed her to apologize and accept his surrender, and at last they were free to return, tired but oddly refreshed, to whatever their actual problem was.

Which usually had neither changed in the slightest, nor suffered visibly from being used as an emotional dodgeball.

"Alright," he conceded finally, and swallowed a mouthful of the coffee cake she had fetched to seal the truce. "We have to warn fandom. It is our fannish duty. But do we have to do it *immediately*?"

"Let's use worst-case analysis," she suggested. "Say Jude and Carla walked from Point Grey Road down to the water, climbed into a float-plane and flew straight to—lets say, Edmonton. Okay, how long does Jude need to set up his next victims? How long did he need to set *us* up?"

He stopped a forkful short of his mouth. "Well," he said, "it must have taken him awhile to select us as targets, and research us both—"

"Worst-case scenario, I said. Assume he selected and researched multiple targets, and now he's going across the checker board: jump . . . jump . . . jump. Or maybe she does the research in advance for him. Like a celebrity surgeon: he holds out his palm, she slaps the next scalpel onto it. Whatever: once he knew he was coming after *us*, once he knew which window we'd be sitting beside, how much time did he need to take us?"

He took the bite, and chewed and swallowed it, before he was ready to say, "Half an hour to shave all over. Maybe an hour or two to buy and set up the magnesium. Then he could go as soon as it got dark enough. Oh, damn."

"We have no way to be sure we're the first fans he's hit, Wally."

"Butter me!" He spilled tea on his lap. "Ow. Oh, Moira, that's a horrid thought."

"And even if we are, he could have destroyed two more clubs already, by now. Every convention in North America with a Beatles fan on the concom is at risk, this minute."

He prodded futilely at his soggy slacks with a handful of kleenex she'd given him, and gazed morosely at the results. "Heaven help me, I think I'd actually rather be a monumental sucker, than *just another* monumental sucker." He shook his head. "Isn't that appalling?"

"Well," she said grimly, "if we are, we can at least be the first ones who didn't fail the test of honor." She turned and looked pointedly toward the office, where the computers waited. "We can sound the alarm. Even if we have to pull our pants down to the world to do it."

For the first time he could recall, Wally didn't feel like finishing his coffee cake. He sighed, assessed the results, and sighed again. "I guess it's time to put my Asshole Principle to the test."

Some years before, he had suddenly stopped their car on a country road, gotten out and walked around it several times, shaking his head and mumbling, then slowly climbed back in and propounded to his wife the stunning new insight he had been vouchsafed: that every living human, and every one who had ever lived, was an asshole. He had challenged her to name a single exception. Jesus? Trashed a harmless currency exchange, which merely let foreigners give sacrifice to God in legal tender. Handpicked a round dozen custodians for the most important words ever spoken: every man jack of them both illiterate and too stupid to find a ghostwriter—staged the most important event in history and forgot to invite the media. What an asshole. Albert Einstein? Instigates Manhattan Project; says Oops: major asshole. John Lennon? Saw his future with utter clarity—began the last Beatles album with the whispered words, "Shoot me," wrote and recorded a prescient solo song called "I'm Scared"—then a few years later, forgot and stuck his head up again: poor asshole. Robert Heinlein had given Wally's theory the most trouble—but even the First Grandmaster of Science Fiction had disparaged marijuana, and once permitted one of his more authoritative characters to refer to homosexuals as "the poor in-betweeners." To be sure, Heinlein had more class than any other three assholes put together, but . . .

Once Moira had accepted her husband's basic premise, that *everyone* is an asshole—and she could not dispute it; she had a fair amount of self-honesty—she'd seen the obvious corollary. The trademark of the true, dyed-in-the-wool, hopeless and irredeemable capital-A Asshole (Wally had explained) is the fixed belief that there exist some people, somewhere, who are Not Assholes. This immediately gives rise to the passionate desire to be mistaken for one of them. Wally himself—he now saw—had been wasting enormous amounts of energy, time and invention on *trying to keep anyone from suspecting that he was one of the Assholes.* "Dignity doesn't have to be a suit of armor," he had told her. "It can be as weightless and transparent as a force field." And from that day forth, both had tried to refocus their efforts—to settle for being perceived (by anyone whose opinion mattered to them) as a pair of competent and pleasant and capable assholes. Assholes with class.

And, damn it, with senses of personal honor.

Building on his anal metaphor, and punning on a joke they both knew, so ancient it was almost due to come around again, she gestured with her head toward their office and said, "Time to answer the question, 'How far is the old log-in?' "

He took one last look at his coffee cake and heaved up from his chair. "About thirteen steps away, I'd say." He helped her out of her own chair, and they each put an arm around the other as they walked those steps to the gallows.

"Let's compose it on your Mac," he said as they waited for their machines to boot. "Then we'll save it as text-only, and both upload it.

Gee, there are still a few clubs that aren't online yet, too—we better fax them. Don't you have a database for them somewhere?"

"First let's just sniff the Web and make sure we aren't too late," she said. "Maybe we'll get lucky: somebody else will sing first, and we can go down as a subtitle instead of a headline." Her browser stabilized on-screen and she began a staccato composition for keyboard and mouse.

He knew she could netsurf better and faster; he left her to it, and began to triage their e-mail. First he identified the VanCon traffic, which had to be sorted into business (hotel and other subcontractors), pro (the Guests of Honor and honored guests), and fan (everybody else with a right to yank on their chain). All three folders bulged with unread posts which he was just beginning to realize he was going to have to deal with after all, now that the con was tentatively back on. But he left them all unread and pressed on. Next he culled out and filed several professional messages—related, that is, to the cottage industry by which he and Moira earned their bread: writing and distributing stable software patches for existing computer operating systems, which made them more useful for the handicapped. He was briefly tempted to stop and read one of these messages, a beta-tester's critique of a new program intended to assist one-handed typing and eliminate mouse-work altogether in Mac System, but restrained himself. Finally he was down to personal mail, and began to read it—for once leaving his Joke of the Day subscription for last. If there were going to be a report of a major fiscal fiasco anywhere in fandom, this was (after the Web) where it was most likely to be.

Two sentences into the third message, he turned to stone in his chair.

Even a statue can read good news, though, given enough time, and happily the text of this message was short enough to fit on Wally's oversized screen without scrolling.

When his screen began to shimmer at the edges, he remembered to bunk. He stopped when he realized he was making it strobe. "Darling?" he said faintly. "Anything?"

"Bugger all so far."

He reached out, groped, found her wrist and clamped down hard. "Have you committed us to anything yet?"

She stopped work, looked down at his hand on her wrist, then up at him. "Of course not—we said we're going to write it together, didn't we? Aren't we?"

"Maybe not."

Her eyes widened, and she gripped his hand with her other one. "Tell me."

"Take a look at this e-mail from Steve."

Subject: Forwarded message from Space
Case
To: moira@eworld.com (Wallace Kemp)
Date: Tue, 14 May 1996 06:58:30 -0700
(PDT)

Found this in my mailbox this morning. Will be happy to forward any reply you want to send.

—Forwarded message from Space Case
(John Edw. MacDougal, III)—

From spacecase@teleport.com Mon May 13
22:33:15 1995
Message-Id:
<999605140533.WAA05535@desiree.teleport.com>
From: spacecase@teleport.com (John Edw.
MacDougal, III)
To: stevethesleeve@eworld.com (Steve Tomas)
Subject: smooth fen
Date: Tue, 14 May 1995 05:29:51 GMT
X-Newsreader: Forte Free Agent 1.0.82

Dear Sleever:

On 31 October 1995 00:19:57, you wrote:
>If you happen to run across any new fans, or even just
>fellow travelers, who look like they'd cast well as
>Captain Picard, let me know ASAP. (Please route thru
>me as Wally and Moira are busy with VanCon coming up.)
>As you might imagine, close facial resemblance is not
>as important here as willingness to go bald for awhile
>—and if he's articulate, so much the better. Please

>pass the word.<

Don't know if helps, but am out here on Bowen Island,
hard by your friends' meat address, and gent just walked
into my store today with 3-4 days' beard - all over head.
Backs of hands, too. Not stilyagi: if had to guess, would
say he bet Reform in last election. Late 20s, tall, in great
shape, narrow face. IMHO, with right makeup could
make wizard Picard—and if wife he mentioned let him
shave head once, might again if asked quickly enough.

Funny thing: specifically stated was NOT fan —but quoted
Lazarus Long . . . accurately. Perhaps one of those
legendary poor bastards who got self de-fan-estrated
for life, for some ripoff or cosmic concom blunder. Or
perhaps, as he claimed, favorite English teacher once
passed off Heinlein quote as own. Pleasant cobber,
seemed a little dull to be fan. But note for whatever may
be worth he also claimed to be hiker, and was full of shit
about that. Still, get that lie all time out here . . .

Want me to ask grapevine for his 20?
Probably take <5 minutes and .5 droplet of sweat. Please
advise.

CU at VanCon; will have latest NSS updates for our
panel as promised.

—Space Case
Regional Rep, National Space Society

—End of forwarded message from Space Case (John
Edw. MacDougal, III—

"He's on Bowen Island," Moira said, pounding on a thigh
(Wally's) with a fist (hers). "With his girlfriend, enjoying the spoils
of war. There's only one or two ways on and off that island. And we
have a large war chest to hunt him down with."

"And two warm guns," Wally murmured dreamily, temporarily immune to physical pain. "Double happiness." He began to sing. "Bang bang, shoot shoot . . ."

She had to lean past him and use his keyboard to reply to Space Case.

⚹CHAPTER 12⚹
The Lifehouse

JOHNSON WOULD have found the successive days of almost relentless rain frustrating—even though waiting was his life, and his life was long—had it not freed him up to devote most of his time and attention to cheering up his dying wife Myrna. This had the side effect of cheering him considerably as well.

Their emotional state during this period is difficult to convey to a normal human; different postulates controlled. Most adults who mate know, and sometimes reflect, that they will one day see their loved one die, *if they are the lucky one of the pair;* it has been thus since before we invented language. Johnson, however, had lived several long centuries without ever truly believing in his heart that this fate could come to *him* some day. (And in that respect, at least, was like all other men— save that in his case it had not been denial, but only optimism.) The fact was emotionally wrenching—could have been devastating, if he had not regarded death as a correctable nuisance.

Myrna did, too . . . but understandably, she needed more cheering up than he did. She was the one who was probably going to have to do the dying.

And even that (maddeningly) was not certain. Her body was newly mortal, but not particularly fragile—especially for its age—and the Great Change was not impossibly far away. With luck and good management, she might very well survive, enfeebled, until the day when the long Masquerade could end, and she could have not just immortality and invulnerability and youth again, but literally anything she could conceive.

Unfortunately, luck and good management did not appear to be in inventory just at present, which was where/when they were needed. "Might not die" is admittedly better than "will certainly die"—but not a hell of a lot better, for one who has long been immortal.

So Myrna's husband did his best to cheer her.

Music was one of his favorite methods of sharing, a nonprescription mood-elevator almost as potent as sex and laughter themselves. The artistic challenge he faced was that he had been writing her love songs for some seven hundred years, during which he had been perpetually on duty but almost never busy. The subject had been picked pretty clean: believe it or not, there are a finite number of ways to say "I love you."

Happily, the dilemma itself suggested a line of attack, and by the evening of the third rainy night, he was able to take up his current guitar, borrow a sprightly tune no one was using at the moment, and sing to her:

> *I want to tell you how I feel, love*
> *But it ain't exactly news*
> *Got no secrets to reveal love*
> *But I'm gonna say it anyway,*
> *'cause I'm alone and you're away*
> *I haven't got a blessed thing to lose . . .*
>
> *(so here goes:)*
>
> *Water ain't dry, the sky goes up high,*
> *And a booger makes pretty poor glue*
> *You can't herd cats, bacteria don't wear hats*
> *—and I love you*
>
> *Sugar ain't sour, it's damp in the shower*
> *And murder's a mean thing to do*
> *Trees got wood, and fucking is pretty good*
> *—and I love you*
>
> *I'm belaboring the obvious:*
> *You will have noticed all the good times*
> *This is as practical an exercise*

As taping twenty cents to my transmission
so that any time I want to
I can shift my pair o' dimes . . .

(but God knows:)

Goats don't vote, and iron don't float
And a hippie don't turn down boo
Dog bites man, the teacher don't understand
—and I love you

Sickness sucks, it's nice to have bucks
And the player on first base is named Who
Kids grow up, and fellows pee standing up
—and I love you

Guess I didn't need to say it
Just a message that my heart sent
And I kinda like the way it's
More redundant than is absolutely
necessary according to the Department
of Redundancy Department . . .

(I must close:)

Fun is nice, you can't fry ice,
And the money will always be due
Bullshit stinks, and no one outsits the Sphinx
—and I love you

Living ain't bad, and dying is sad
And little we know is true
But that's just karma—baby,
you can bet the farm on this:
I do love you.

"I call it 'Belaboring The Obvious'—or is that redundant?" he said, after the last notes echoed away.

He had already gotten the smile he had hoped for. Once he had set down the guitar, he got the kiss, too.

Smile and kiss were both like oil of cloves on a toothache, like the warm bath of pharmaceutical morphine, melting pain for each spouse. Their telempathic connection caused this analgesic energy to oscillate back and forth between them like alternating current, reinforcing itself, and generating a third, resultant field that acted to stabilize both. Their vibrant love had been the sole constant in a millennium of slow tedious change; they knew well that it was stronger than death, and that they differed from all the other lovers alive only in that they could explain why. Johnson, a scholar of his wife's body language, decoded runes in their hug which indicated that while this was not yet the right time to proffer an erection, a fellow who was patient and played his cards right might not die of waiting. Every songwriter loves applause, however promissory.

As they disengaged, he caught himself reaching for a cigarette. He was not addicted to nicotine, of course—he and Myrna could self-generate any desired drug effect they wished—but his cover persona appeared to be, drawing smoke deep into his lungs in public without ever actually metabolizing a molecule of it. And he was meticulous enough about tradecraft that he had formed the policy of smoking even when in private, sometimes, so his home would smell right to the rare visitor. It was that (true) habit which had caused his hand to start toward his breast pocket.

What stopped it was the realization that his mate no longer had the power to decide which of the molecules she inhaled might have her leave to remain, and which must depart.

Well, irrational anti-tobacco hysteria was currently epidemic in this ficton anyway, part of the general paranoia inevitable in a large complex society of innumerates and scientific illiterates. It would actually be good for his cover to quit smoking, at this juncture in history, make his persona even less interesting. And their home less musty—not that either ever smelled anything they didn't choose to. He mentally accessed the housekeeping nanobots' controller, and added cigarettes and related materials to the list of objects defined as "trash," to be disassembled for parts the next time it was convenient.

—and was surprised to feel a pang, almost as sharp as an addict might have felt. The small change in habit was his first overt acceptance of the great change that had come into their lives, his first tacit admission that he was helpless to cure, and must endure, this thing.

Myrna caught all this, of course, and instantly took over as morale officer. "Honey," she said, referencing a book they had both enjoyed, "let's go and look at the kids."

He hesitated a fraction of a second. Was it appropriate to comfort a dying woman by taking her to visit one of the world's great mausolea? But he knew her intuition was superior to his own. "Sure."

The Lifehouse lay less than half a kilometer from their home. They walked the distance, as humans would (under an umbrella Myrna would actually have needed if she'd been alone), not just for the sake of their cover, but simply because they wanted to walk in the forest in the rain together. It was always best, they had found, to approach the Lifehouse slowly, and with humility.

The rain had dwindled for a time to a barely visible mist, that did not so much fall as roil. This should have been frustrating—for if it would only clear up that last little bit, even for a few minutes, they could inscribe their quartz beacon with a requested delivery date of *now*, stomp it into the mud, and receive an instant response from the future. But one of the first principles of Waiting is that there is no such thing as *almost done*. The rain would stop when it stopped; very sensitive detectors would alert them the instant that occurred; meanwhile downpour or mist were the same.

The damp forest was full of trapped ozone; they allowed it to mildly exhilarate them. Everything had that strange muted vividness that comes of poor light passed through a billion tiny prisms. The rain-sound that had been blanketing the high frequencies like a treble filter was suspended now; viridescent trees still dripped their accumulated moisture, but those sounds arrived with crystal clarity. So did a rich stew of smells. The rain forest ecology could be *felt* going about its business all around them, industriously making hay while the sun didn't shine.

And so, hand in hand beneath their umbrella, mud sucking shamelessly at their boots, the scent of sweet rot in their nostrils, they came to the place where the mook Angel Gerhardt had recently tried to bury two ounces of something laced with cocaine.

They perceived that the repairs they had made to the site were holding up. The great elm was vertical once more, the bank on which it stood rebuilt to a convincing naturalness. They stepped up detector range and sensitivity to the maximum, satisfied themselves that the most intelligent life-form besides themselves within a kilometer was a bull raccoon—and, this time, that there were no electronic devices save their own functioning anywhere within the same range. Then Johnson gestured, and a yonic tunnel gaped in the side of the bank with a lewd wet sound, opening like a man-sized mud sphincter to reveal the stainless surface of—

—the Lifehouse.

Their Lifehouse.

Their child, in a sense. Many children and children's children, in another. In yet another—just as valid—merely a highly evolved descendant of a hard disk, packed with a great many zeros and ones.

It was a crystalline sphere two meters in diameter, externally identical to the Eggs used to travel back through time, but it had never carried a living passenger—in that direction. Now, after a millennium of creeping *forward* through time again in the only way possible—like everything else, at the rate of one second per second— it held millions of passengers . . . albeit only potentially living, at present.

This particular Egg, like all the other Lifehouses on earth, was packed absolutely full of the most dense and stable information storage medium permitted by the laws of physics. Its capacity was most meaningfully expressed not in giga-, tera-, peta-, exa-, or even zettabytes, but in yottabytes, or sextillions of bytes. It could hold a *lot* of yottabytes—so securely that the society which designed it had actually abandoned, presumably forever, the concept of data backup.

Paradoxically, this sphere of ultrastable memory visually resembled nothing so much as a translucent model of Jupiter: a slow, majestically churning globe of chaotic milky fluids, that appeared dimly lit from within, as if for the convenience of the student.

Suspended in those roiling fluids, as incorruptible patterns of data, were virtually all the human beings who had died in the Pacific Northwest since the dawn of time.

There in the Lifehouse, if all went well, they would wait safely, in something very like the Christian concept of Limbo . . . until the day came when their descendants were ready to grow them new bodies and resurrect them to life eternal.

And if, through Myrna's and Johnson's failures as guardians, that day should never come . . .

Well, the dead would never know they had died a second time, at least.

Was there any consolation in that? Or not?

Myrna had always loved to visit the Lifehouse, always wished they dared do so more often. It did *not* put out any trace of any field that any instrument could detect . . . but it always seemed to. Whenever she felt overwhelmed by that profound melancholy which sooner or later must come to any immortal, who watches everything around her dying in pain and needless terror, she would come to the Lifehouse and put her hand on its cool surface and feel better. This was part of the antidote to Death. A monument to monkey defiance of entropy, to the stubborn, eternal refusal of the human spirit to surrender to fate.

She had wondered if it would feel any different, any less comforting to be here, now that she knew in her guts she might well end up in that glowing milky swirl herself one day. She found that it did not. Mentally she compared the Lifehouse to every popular human conception of afterlife, including utter nothingness, and found it a reasonably congenial place to be dead for a few decades. No hymns to memorize, no harp lessons. No hellfire. No petulant paranoid demanding hosannas. No houris forcing figs and camel milk on you. No grinning Krishna with a rampant erection. No Great Wheel, no Eightfold Path. Absolutely no sensation of the passage of time at all, by all reports. Simple suspended awareness, like a paused CD.

She found herself picturing the way it would probably be.

One silly thing or another would kill her. Whatever the proximate cause, her heart would cease to beat, and decline to restart. Blood pressure would fall to zero, along with cranial oxygen supply. Brain temperature would begin to drop. At some point, an indetectably tiny but quite sophisticated nanocomputer in her medial forebrain bundle—precisely like the one to be found in the brain of every living human being older than minus eight months—would conclude that she was a goner.

And, as with everyone else who had ever died, her whole life would pass before her eyes . . . as a high-speed data dump.

Forewarned, and used to thinking at computer rates when necessary, she would probably be one of a bare handful who had ever been in a position to fully appreciate that particular show—and hers would last considerably longer than was customary. Even at the ferocious speeds that would be employed, and even though she had been in the habit of making regular deposits in the Lifehouse's memory bank every century or so, it would take nearly five whole seconds of realtime to squirt a perfect copy of her *self* from her played-out body—wherever it happened to die—to the indetectable satellite that was always in the sky, and another ten seconds for the satellite to perform integrity tests and relay-bounce her back down to . . . *here*, to this very Lifehouse.

Where she would remain in stasis, in the form of Read-Only Memory, along with all the other dead. Until the time—subjectively, only an instant after her death—when she would come to awareness again, to find herself floating down a long tunnel diode, toward a bright light . . . being greeted by departed relatives and loved ones . . . being welcomed (in her case, back) into The Mind, the telepathic family of nearly all the humans who had ever lived . . .

It didn't sound that bad, actually.

Oh, the dying part itself would doubtless be unpleasant. But she had known unpleasantness before, in her near-millennium of stewardship. And it would probably be the *last* unpleasantness she would ever know. In effect, she would be trading some moments or days or weeks of pain for the privilege of fast-forwarding through some history that was becoming increasingly oppressive: the final darkness before the dawn of the Great Change. It might almost be worth dying, to miss the rest of the Nineties—let alone the decades that would follow.

But poor Johnson would be so lonely in the meantime!

"I keep wishing we could just talk to them," she said aloud.

"To Paul and June, you mean?"

"Yes. If we could just *explain* to them . . . bring them here, show them this, explain the stakes . . . perhaps they'd submit voluntarily to editing. You never know."

In her mind she constructed the argument.

Elsewhere in this country, right now, a man is learning to decipher the information storage code of the human brain. Before long he will know how to erase memories . . . and shortly after that, how to read and write them. In time he will have technologically assisted telepathy. By great good fortune he will be an ethical man: he will exercise the resulting power to conquer the world undetected—but only long enough to successfully give away his secret to everyone, everywhere, at once. Soon thereafter, inevitably, nearly all men will be telepathic, and nontelepathic man will join Neanderthal. The Mind will form: several billion brains, all equal, all forever free, all able to transcend solitude and death and pain and the need to sleep, working together without friction or language barrier. Soon, inevitably, they will understand the universe well enough to travel backward through time. Soon, inevitably, they will realize that almost as many brains' worth of memories as the Mind began with were trashed unnecessarily before it formed—and they will decide to conquer death retroactively. *They will come back and make pickup on all their fallen comrades who will consent to live again in a different way. They will tailor a nanovirus that makes backup copies of human beings, and stores them in Lifehouses until there is a Mind to restart them, and they will release it ten thousand years ago. And the very hardest and most necessary part of the whole project will be concealing that knowledge from terrified ancestors, who needlessly believe themselves doomed to extinction.*

Johnson knew her thought. He did not even bother to disagree. They both knew it was wishful thinking. Though they had never physically met either Paul or June, they knew both of them very well: they knew June at least as well as she knew herself, and knew Paul a little better than she knew him. Each human had the kind of fiercely independent, paranoid temperament that would find The Mind— the author and point of all this—a thing of horror. Both believed deep down that identity was a thing made of borders and limits; both would flatly refuse to believe that an ego could blend with any other without losing its integrity. To them, a self-cherishing telepathic species-wide family would seem an ant-like hive mentality: inhuman rather than superhuman. If they were apprised of all the facts, and given a simple choice—forget this ever happened, and wake one day to life eternal in the company of everyone you ever loved, liked or respected . . . or sound the alarm, and vanish forever along with the whole universe—well, humans could never be perfectly predicted, but the strong probability was they would proudly choose the latter.

When and if they were tracked down, they would have to be mind-raped: both were incapable of surrender. The irony was biting.

As Myrna and Johnson stood there in silence, contemplating the Lifehouse together, souls of the recently deceased rained down invisibly from the sky at random intervals, striking the receiver at the peak of the elm and racing down the heart of its trunk to the Egg beneath. Each time this occurred, a short report was generated and squirted to a database in the attic of their caretaker's cottage, a process designed to come to their conscious attention only in the astronomically rare event that the report read "file could not be written and was skipped." Idly, now, perhaps feeling that it would bring her into a slightly more intimate contact with the whole ongoing process to which she'd dedicated her life, Myrna tuned a fragment of her mind to that "channel," and monitored the names and vital statistics of the incoming new dead.

Just as one byte in particular tried to claim her attention, an alarm went off. Think of the alarm clock you've hated worst in your life, surgically implanted in your skull. Even as she and Johnson flinched, their hearts leapt with joy and relief.

The humidity had finally fallen below the critical value.

Johnson whirled and gestured toward home. The chunk of coruscating quartz crystal arrived in less than a second, decelerating smoothly to a dead stop in midair at a point precisely equidistant from them both. Their eyes met around it. Together they mentally inscribed it with the tick that described this particular instant of side-real time. Johnson gestured again, and the crystal slammed down into the earth and buried itself deep.

At once, both began to back away from the spot.

The air became electric. A prickly scent, like toasting basil and cinnamon, came from everywhere. A faint, high, vaguely metallic sound converged slowly from all directions at once. Local temperature rose. Tendrils of steam rose from the damp grass. The sound swelled and contracted, like an explosion played backwards—

At the last moment, Myrna remembered to avert her eyes.

CRACK!

"Oh, shit," Johnson said.

She opened her eyes again. An Egg sat on the earth, directly above the spot where the quartz beacon had buried itself.

"Oh, shit," she agreed.

They had *not*, in their wildest dreams, expected to see two actual, corporate passengers in that Egg. A person could exist only once in any given ficton. But they had hoped—hoped *hard*—to see a chunk of quartz very like the one they had used to summon the Egg here/now: a memory-crystal containing the best advice of the future June Bellamy and Paul Throtmanian on how to track and capture their past selves.

What had arrived instead both looked and was considerably less impressive.

"Well," Johnson said philosophically, "like they told us back in training, the operative syllable in 'Anachrognosis' is the next-to-last one. Can't fight a big paradox with a little one. We should have known The Mind would turn us down."

Myrna said nothing.

"Look on the bright side," he said. "The situation just improved: from 'hopeless' to 'outcome uncertain.' "

"Yes," she said softly. "That is good news."

"We're going to get to repair our own mistake after all."

She noticed, just at that moment, that her neck hurt, and automatically tried to fix it herself so she wouldn't have to ask Johnson for a rub. And failed. For the first time in her long life . . . and not the last. "It's purely a coincidence those things usually home on shit," she said, suppressing a wince.

"Well," he said, apparently deciding that sardonic humor was better than none at all, "at least nobody can say we don't give a fucking fly."

The humor was metaphorical, of course. The thing that hovered in the center of the new Egg—its sole contents, save for air—was not in fact a housefly. It just looked and acted precisely like one.

Externally, at least. But not superficially. If, somehow, it had fallen into the hands of a drosophilist, he might have needed several days of study to notice there was something distinctly odd about that particular specimen. He would probably never have identified the weaponry, would certainly never have located either the detection gear or the onboard computer, and could not have comprehended the power source if it had been explained to him. His best guess at its top speed would have been short by at least an order of magnitude or two.

For a climate so kind that even in November a single passing fly would elicit only mildest surprise, it was the perfect tracking device. The ultimate snitch: in cop slang, a shoo-fly. Or perhaps "gumshoe-fly" was more accurate.

If time travelers had the luxury of being allowed to alter the historical date of anyone's death, it might also have made a perfect Terminator. It was quite capable of saying "No problemo" in a German accent if the need should arise . . . and could not be stopped or destroyed by anything currently living or manmade. But while it would fight like a wolverine to avoid capture, it could not kill any life-form as advanced as another fly, even to save itself.

Given enough time, however, it could *locate* any life-form whose DNA parameters it knew, anywhere on earth or in its atmosphere, clear out to Low Earth Orbit.

It already had DNA and gross physical descriptions of June and Paul in memory. It could identify their skeletal profiles under any conceivable disguise, their retinal patterns through even opaque contacts, their fingerprints on a car door handle from treetop height. It knew every pheromone or sebaceous volatile their bodies were capable of emitting, far more intimately than the lovers themselves did, and could positively identify them in concentrations of less than one part per octillion. Like a Bussard ramjet, its high speed made it an excellent molecule collector. If either grifter were presently in Vancouver, it would have them pinpointed in less than a day. If they were within the Lower Mainland area, two days, or three at the outside. Perhaps a week, if they were somewhere in China. Worst case— say, a nominally airtight enclosure buried deep on the other side of the planet, with sophisticated countermeasures—call it ten days.

The question was: did Myrna and Johnson have as much as a whole day left, before some form of all Hell broke loose?

" 'Said the flea, "let us fly!" Said the fly, "let us flee!" . . .'" Myrna recited.

". . . 'So they flew through a flaw in the flue.'" Johnson said, giving the tagline of the ancient limerick. It so happened that he had written it. "This fly won't leave a flaw in the flue, Flo. Slim Gaillard would have called it a 'flatfoot floozie with the floy-floy.'"

She wasn't really in the mood for word games—her neck was quite stiff, now—but he was trying his best. "Reet," she agreed. "Let's turn it loose-a-rootie."

He heard the subtext in her voice, dropped the banter, gestured sharply at the Egg. It promptly ceased to exist, utterly and forever. The Superfly, without so much as pausing to dip its wings in salute, took off like a silent bullet, reappeared briefly above the nearby spot where Angel Gerhardt's coke-laced baby laxative lay buried for all time, and departed in a northerly direction at just under Mach One.

They stood there in silence together for a minute or two, looking deep into each other's eyes. She found the strength for one last effort. "Well," she said, "the fly is cast."

He winced obligingly. "Very dry."

And of course, just then it began to rain again, wringing genuine giggles from both of them.

"Come on," he said, taking up the umbrella and putting an arm around her. "Let's go home. You look like you could use a neck rub."

She put her head on his shoulder, her own arm around him, and squeezed *hard*.

In the distance a faint false thunder was heard, as the trackfly exceeded the speed of sound. . . .

⚜CHAPTER 13⚜
The Shithouse

IT WAS SUCH A BRIEF and such a kindly note, to have generated so much adrenalin:

Dear Mr and Mrs Dortmunder
somebodys askin around the island tryin to find you two without you knowin. I didnt say nothin but they will find you sure by tomorrow or the next day. You seem like a nice young couple. I thought youd want to know.

Regards,
Maurice Lycott

June always took a secret special pleasure in blowing her lover's mind. So few people could manage it. Even she, who could blow just about anybody's mind, usually had to work at it with Paul. The look on his face now, the color in his forehead, the little squeak in his voice as he said, "You want to *what*?" were enough to calm her down, and almost enough to cheer her up.

"Call Wally and Moira," she repeated.

He made three successive sounds, two moist and one dry, none of which graduated to the status of a proper syllable.

"You said it yourself: they've got the kind of minds that can think about time travel without boggling. For sure they've been thinking about it longer than we have—and reading the ideas of better minds than their own, too. The more I think about this, the more my head hurts. You need a getaway: you call in a wheelman. You need

590

something moved: you hire muscle. Right now, we need a time travel specialist in the string, *fast*. Two would be even better."

He closed his eyes, sighed, and opened them again. He began quietly, but built to a crescendo by the end of his question. "And you don't suppose the fact that both those airheads are presently consumed by a *passionate* desire to examine my giblets with rusty fucking *tongs* might present a few *trivial fucking obstacles?*"

She ignored his anger: it was not really directed at her. "You tell me—you know them better. Which would a true-blue science fiction fan rather do, in his or her heart of hearts? Avenge a sting—or meet a no-shit time traveler?"

"No *way* they're going to believe me a second time—"

"*Way*," she said, knowing he hated that particular neologism. "They're not stupid, you said. You *steam-cleaned* them, Paul, down to the last peso. They're wigless, gigless and cigless now. You know it, and they know you know it. The only possible motive you could have for coming back on them again with the same tale is if it's the truth this time."

"That's not—"

"That Kornbluth guy—was he a big name in sci fi?"

"One of the very very best. So what?"

"How much do you want to bet Wally or Moira once read the same story you did?'

He frowned and squinted ferociously, as at a sudden blinding light.

"Think about it, Paul. Everything I know about time travel, and half of what you know, we got from the movies and TV. They're lousy sources of information about *real* science, for God's sake. You want to blow this, through some equivalent of expecting to hear sounds in vacuum, or thinking cars blow up in real life?"

He gestured, like a beggar seeking alms. Shylock, crying, "My daughter! My ducats!" could not have sounded more conflicted. "But June—*ask a mark for help?* It's . . . it's not *decent*."

She shared his pain, but pressed on. "You don't like that argument? Here's one you're gonna love: it goes right to the root of your favorite root. So far we *think* we've worked up a few field tactics useful for defending ourselves against this guy's mind-ray— maybe—for as long as a pair of AA batteries hold out—maybe long enough to slip in under his radar. All to the good. But wouldn't you like to have a way to *threaten* the bastard?"

His frown eased slightly. "With what?"

"Look, we know he's afraid of exposure. Maybe even more than we are: we could go to jail, he could go to Never-Never Land. That in itself doesn't give us a whole lot of leverage, though . . . because ninety-nine people out of a hundred, we could tell them everything we know, in detail, with a straight face and corroborating exhibits, and all they'd do is call the men with the thorazine. *But suppose we convinced a science fiction fan, who's wired into the Internet?*"

Paul's frown released altogether; so did all his facial muscles. "Oh, my," he said softly. "Oh la." He pulled his jaw back up, and shaped it into a grin. "Oh angel, I *like* it. That might be just about the only thing we could possibly do that would scare the living shit out of the son of a bitch. Will you marry me?"

"No."

His grin faltered. "Huh? Why not?"

"Paul, don't ask me that now, okay?"

Back to a frown. "I think it constitutes what I'd call a valid point of order," he said. "I may have been smiling, but it wasn't a joke question."

"I know."

Hurt twisted his features. "So?"

"I gave up on marriage a long time before I met you: it just isn't in the cards for me, alright? Please, baby, can't we just go on living in sin and get this fucking zombie off our backs and then see what happens?"

He turned on his heel and walked away.

"Paul?"

He reached the telephone's base unit and thumbed the intercom; a loud repetitive whoop in the next room announced the location of the wandering handset.

"Aw, come on—Paul?"

He retrieved the phone, punched keys. "Yes, in Vancouver, operator, I'd like a residential listing for a Wallace Kemp, that's kay ee em pee, on West 12th, please?"

"Paul—"

He held up a hand. As the digits were read to him, he punched them into the phone. When he had them all, he hung up, poked redial and returned the thing to his ear. "Ringing," he said.

"Paul, damn it to hell—"

He held his hand higher and turned his face away slightly.

They waited, alone, together.

After what seemed like an eternity, he disconnected. "Answering machine. They stayed in Toronto. Oh *damn*."

"Paul—"

"They *gave* me their fucking number there—and of course I burned it the minute I got home. Oh—" He began his swearing litany. It was different every time, and she had once heard him continue it for three solid sulphurous minutes before he slipped, and repeated an obscenity. Another time, the victim—a grown man— had fainted dead away, midway into the second minute. It was going to be impossible to interrupt him now until he had finished wringing the English language dry of its power to express his frustration.

She gave up and left the room, to attack the same task from a feminine perspective. Somewhere she couldn't be interrupted either, with a door that locked, and lots and lots of kleenex.

But of course she was wrong. One simple knock at the front door, and she and Paul were both as interrupted as they could be.

"Look," Paul said wearily, when they had all seated themselves, "the sooner you put those silly things away, the less chance you'll end up using them as suppositories."

"You're probably right," Wally agreed. "But I'm feeling reckless." His gun-hand looked dismayingly steady.

"It's not necessary, you know," June said. "We were just trying to call you when you showed up, only we lost your Toronto number."

Wally looked at her for a long moment. "That is such a preposterous assertion, I think I almost believe it." He glanced to Moira.

She shrugged. "My experience is that the really ridiculous is usually true. But I'm not losing the gun."

Her husband nodded, and turned back to June. "Why were you going to call us? You don't look like gloaters. You *know* you tapped us out. Oh, wait, I get it—you must have found out somehow that we hit your other place on Point Grey Road. What, you were going to ask us to give you *your* money back?"

June groaned. Another perfectly good address and identity, blown for good. Not to mention another large cash-stash gone. "You know," she said to her own partner, "I've had better weeks. Lots of 'em."

"Tell me about it."

"Our own has been excessively eventful," Moira pointed out.

"Let me take this," June said.

"Of course," Paul agreed.

There was no more than that to the exchange: half a dozen banal words, absolutely no ironic vocal undertones or pained expressions. But June clearly saw Moira grasp that she and Paul were presently in the middle of a quarrel. From this she inferred that Moira was no fool, and reconsidered her opening.

"Wallace, Moira, my name is June Bellamy, and this is Paul Throtmanian. I can't think of any reason why you should believe those are our real names, because I'm as good a professional liar as he is. But you have to call us something. It's a place to start."

"Call me Wally, June," Wally said.

She felt relief. She did *not* want to address herself principally to Moira, to seem to be trying the lame *let's us girls work this out while the boys hold weapons on each other* ploy. "Thank you, Wally. As I said, Paul and I were discussing phoning you and Moira. Not because you have brains—we have brains—but because you both have a particular *kind* of brains. And I think you've proven that, by tracking us. Frankly, I don't know how you pulled it off—and please don't think I'm asking how you found us: I haven't earned the right. But we have a problem we need your kind of brains to solve, and I'd like to explain it to you."

"Pardon me," Wally said, "but I want to get this straight. We're holding guns on you, and you're trying to *hire* us?"

"Basically," she agreed.

He nodded. "I'm beginning to like you, June. Proceed."

She carefully did not smile. "Thank you, Wally. Since you say you got as far as the Bernardo house, I assume you must know what happened to Paul's Metkiewicz place." She glanced to Moira for confirmation, got back nothing, glanced away. "From that and our hasty departure for here, you must have deduced that someone else is after us. Someone we are very respectful of."

"And you want to hire us as consultant hackers," Wally said. "Oh, this is lovely."

"Would you like to hear our minimum fee?" Moira inquired.

June turned back to her. "Please, let me define the job correctly first. It may not involve any hacking as such, for instance. What we really need is your expertise as science fiction fans." She saw Moira begin to frown. "Please," she said quickly, holding up a hand, "I *know* that sounds like exactly the same sort of grifter technique my partner used on you: tell the mark what she wants to hear. Unfortunately, it happens to be the truth. Paul and I need a fan, badly. All I have to overcome your reasonable suspicion is logic. If you're really who we need, you'll see that logic. Will you listen?"

She was quietly elated when Moira shared a glance with her husband before saying, "Yes."

"Again, thank you. I'm going to make another assumption. I'm guessing you've both figured out where Paul got the idea for the game he ran on you. A story by . . . what's his name, honey?"

"Cyril Kornbluth," Paul supplied.

"*Told* you," Wally blurted, and flinched at the glance it got him from Moira.

"Thanks," June pressed on. "Kornbluth." She began slowing the pace of her speech. ("June," her mother had once told her, "it is almost impossible to speak foolishness slowly.") "I haven't read it, but Paul's told me about it. You've read it. A grifter pretends to be a time traveler. He works a long con." Beat. "*What happens to him?*"

Moira's eyes began to glitter a whole second before Wally's did. She covered superbly, kept her face serene and body relaxed. Wally managed to keep silent, but allowed his eyes to widen and his knuckles to whiten on his Glock, which happened to be pointed at his own ankle. Neither said anything for several seconds. Then simultaneously they turned to each other, exchanged a silent highspeed transmission, and turned back to June together. Wally's gun was no longer pointing at his ankle.

"You allege that the Time Police are after you," Moira stated. Her own gun was smaller, but nearer; June felt she could almost see the .22 bullet in there in the chamber. Dammit, this *did* sound exactly like another con, improvised to fit their known weakness. They were right to be angry. It was time to go for broke.

"I have a . . . call it a skill," she said. "I call it the eye of power, or just the eye. I have not tried to use it on you so far—" She did so now, on Moira, gave her both barrels. "—but you can see that it is very powerful. I can sell a turd to a perfumier with the eye of power." Moira nodded involuntarily. "I am now going to look away from you both and talk to the bay out there for a few minutes. You can shoot me any time you become convinced I'm lying to you. If you can think of any other explanation for what's happened to us, I promise to believe it." She switched off the eye, continued to meet Moira's eyes long enough for her to grasp that, then slowly swiveled her chair until she could just see Moira's gun in her peripheral vision.

And then she told them, as concisely and accurately and dryly as she could, everything that had happened to her since she had first seen the mook in Pacific Spirit Park.

She was quite surprised not to be interrupted even once. Her opinion of science fiction fans rose somewhat, in consequence. She did not try to hide her own complicity in Paul's sting. When she came to the only part she had intended to gloss over, how she and Paul came to be in tenancy of this particular dwelling, she changed her mind and told that straight too, giving O'Leary's name and a rough sketch of the game she had been planning for him, blowing it thereby.

For her finale, she got up, went to the phones base unit, and activated the speakerphone feature. "I just thought of one small piece of evidence that can corroborate at least one tiny thing we've told you," she said, over the sound of dial tone. "I wish I had more." Signifying for them like a mime, she pushed the redial button. After four rings, they all heard a click, and then Moira's recorded voice saying, "This is what it sounds like. Do the obvious at the standard cue." June disconnected before it could beep at them.

Wally and Moira exchanged a glance.

"You both must know the Sherlock Holmes quote about eliminating the impossible," June concluded. "Paul and I are down to the X-Files, ancient hairy gods, a mad scientist, or a time traveler. I don't know about you two, but time traveler is the only one of those I can live with. I would reject *that* as impossible . . . if I had anything at all to replace it with. Do either of you see any possibility I missed?"

There was a long silence.

"And you see why we need *you*?"

Outside, the rain stopped.

She was mildly surprised when it was Wally who broke the silence.

"You've defined the job. I will stipulate the problem is interesting to us. Will you hear our consulting fee now?"

She swiveled back to face them, and took Paul's hand. "Please."

"Ninety-nine thousand Canadian dollars."

Paul's hand tightened on hers. She squeezed back. "You've already—" she tried.

"—recovered a large fraction of what you took us for, yes. That's a separate transaction. That's why we're probably not going to shoot you. This is different. Ninety-nine thousand dollars is the fee your partner set for giving us an education, in *his* area of expertise. We won't work for less."

June looked at Moira's eyes. They meant it.

Paul groaned, and made one last try at preserving a shred of self-respect. "The correct figure—"

"Excuse me," Wally said mildly, but it was the gesture with the Glock that cut Paul off. "I am not going to shoot you unless you absolutely insist. And I may work for you if we can agree on terms. But if you want to dick me around over *change*, I may be moved to pistol-whip you a little. Can we keep this friendly?"

"Sorry," Paul said. He turned to look at June. She felt his pain, like a blow to an already weary heart. His hand was limp in hers, now. "That's about everything we've got left," he said.

Technically he was lying; there were a few stashes here and there, though none easily accessible. But in another sense he was correct. There could be no more humiliating fate for a grifter than to have to pay the mark double. If they agreed to this—even if they swore Wally and Moira to secrecy—it would be the irrevocable end of both their careers. No one but the people in this room would ever know what a genius Paul Throtmanian was. She groped for words. As she did so, her eyes met his squarely for the first time since Wally and Moira had arrived . . . and she fell in.

"Yes, I will," she heard herself say.

He understood her perfectly and at once. His smile was a beautiful thing to see. "Then everything's okay, then."

"Yes, Paul," she said. Her pulse thundered in her ears.

"I was broke when I met you."

"So was I," she agreed. "Ow."

He eased his grip on her hand, snapped their gaze-lock with a visible effort, and turned his smile-beam on their guests. "It's a deal. You'll want it up front." Both nodded firmly. "It'll probably involve a little pick and shovel work: the bastard burned my house down around it. But it should still be there, perfectly safe, untoasted and undiscovered, not far from a basement entrance I *know* survived. Best done in darkness; if we catch the next ferry the timing should work out." June had tuned out, distracted by the stunning awareness that she had somehow, despite a lifetime of wariness, become a fiancée. But her attention was caught again when Paul went on, "I guess the only thing left to be settled is whether you need to pistol-whip me before we can put the heat away and get this show on the road."

Moira visibly deferred to her husband. He considered the matter, frowning speculatively. "You're a prick," he said finally, "but I've worked for pricks without violence all my life. And for about twenty-four hours, there, I thought I'd saved John Lennon's life. Maybe that is worth what it cost me." He engaged the safety catch on his gun and put it in his lap. (Moira, startled, started to take her own safety *off* . . . then left it the way it was, and put the gun in her purse.)

June was so relieved she shamelessly allowed it to show.

Paul nodded. "In that case, I believe the moment has come when honor will permit me to apologize, to you and your wife, for what I did to you. I don't have any excuse, and I don't expect you to accept the apology, but I give it gladly."

No response.

"So do I," June said, largely to see if her numb lips could produce speech. "We're quitting the business."

"One last thing and then we can head for the ferry," Paul went on. "You're the first to know: we just got engaged."

Wally and Moira both raised their eyebrows and exchanged a glance. And began to smile.

"June," Moira said, "all your sins will be satisfactorily atoned for."

"You lucky duck," Wally added.

She found her cheeks were being squeezed up so tight by the corners of her mouth that water was threatening to leak from her eyes. "I hope we're as lucky as you two."

"Not a chance," Wally said. "But it's something to shoot for."

"Then I take it we're adjourned?" Paul asked.

"Just one thing," Wally said. "That PC I saw in the den—is that the one with the Pentium 133 chip?"

Moira smacked him on the shoulder. In spite of herself, June giggled. After a moment and a few blinks, so did Wally.

This might, June decided, just work out.

The ride to the ferry terminus in Wally and Moira's Toyota was undertaken in a slightly strained silence. All four knew that further discussion of the time traveler would be improper until the consultants had received their advance, and the only other interest they all seemed to have in common was the Beatles, which seemed inappropriate under the circumstances.

But by the time they shut off the engine at the tail end of the line-up waiting for the next sailing (at this end of the trip, perhaps thirty whole vehicles—for which no accommodation whatsoever had been provided, stacked up in most of the downhill lane of "downtown" Snug Cove's "main street"), the women could stand it no longer. "How long have you and Wally—" June began, at the same instant Moira asked, "How long have you and Paul—" and everyone laughed, and that broke the ice. Then they swapped How We Met stories. June went first, and gave both the version they told people, and the truth. So Moira felt compelled to do the same when it was her turn. Sharing embarrassment forged another small bond. Yet another formed between Paul and Wally as each attempted and failed to edit his mate's account: that peculiar, wry late-twentieth-century brotherhood of shared public submission.

Whatever their business differences, it is difficult for really intelligent people not to enjoy each other's company. Each couple had good and recent reason to respect the other's intelligence. None of the four ever quite completely forgot that there were loaded firearms in the vehicle, or just where they were located; nonetheless they were all about as relaxed with each other as crime partners, for instance, ever get by the time the Queen of Something-or-Other snugged itself into its tire-studded berth, stuck out its steel tongue and began vomiting Jaguars, Ladas and 4X4s onto the land.

As Wally parked in the vehicle bay, they agreed they were all hungry, but not enough to eat ferry food. The two grifters went first up the steep narrow stairwell, out of an intuitive sense that they were still not fully trusted yet. The first time you climbed those stairs, you wondered why the handrails had studs along most of their length; halfway up you came to appreciate the pitons. June became slightly aware of Wally's nose only a few inches from her buttocks, and tried to climb as unprovocatively as possible. Apparently she succeeded; when they all sat together on a life-jacket locker outside on the upper passenger deck, Moira did not interpose herself between them.

It was quite pleasant on deck, no cooler or windier than they were dressed for. The rain had been over for so long it was not necessary to dry the surface of the locker before sitting on it. The sun was just settling toward the treetops, behind the ferry, crowning Bowen Island with glory. They were on the south or starboard side of the ship as it left Snug Cove and headed out into the bay; thunderheads comfortably far away on the horizon produced a Disney sunset. June mentioned that it reminded her a little of Key West; Moira said it reminded her of her and Wally's summer place in Nova Scotia. Paul observed that both couples seemed to look for similar sorts of things in a vacation home: remoteness, simple circumstances, few and tolerant neighbors. Wally suggested the needs of con organizers and con artists were not all that different—using the latter term somewhat shyly until he saw neither Paul or June took offense at it. Conversation became general; each of the four performed a few of their standard anecdotes, and was pleased with their reception. Wally beta-tested a new pun he was working up, to the effect that if the promised paperless digital world ever materialized, writers would all be The Artists Formerly Known In Prints. He lived; the only one armed besides himself within earshot had married him knowing of his affliction.

Shortly, the captain made a general announcement over the loudspeakers, and the four got up and joined ninety percent of the vessel's passengers on the north side to gawk in awe and inexplicable pleasure at a whale. A bitter argument broke out among several of their fellow passengers as to just which sort of whale it was. An elderly man loudly demanded to know why, for this kind of money, the captain couldn't for chrissake drive the damn boat closer so he (the jerk) could get some better shots of the fish. The air was cooler out of the cove, and the wind was from the south, so it was somewhat less nippy there on the port side; they remained by tacit mutual consent even after the whale had gone about its business, and most of the other passengers had gone back indoors to enjoy "food" or videogames or virtuously display their nonsmoking status.

It would not have made the slightest difference if they had remained where they'd started. The trackfly passed the ferry on the south side, no more than half a kilometer away at closest approach, but as stated, the wind was from that direction. The fly was not quite bright enough to change course to pass the ferry to leeward; in order to bring the search down to something manageable, it had been programmed to regard bodies of water as null areas, to be traversed as quickly as possible. Ignoring the can of pheromones downwind, it continued on a straight line toward Bowen Island.

If it had so much as glanced their way, even its rather poor vision might have picked out Paul's fuzzy skull, decided that it fit the parameters of a male head which had been bald three days ago, and vectored in for a quick sniff. If any of the four had been scanning the right quarter of the sky with good binoculars at precisely the right instant, and known what to look for, they might just have glimpsed the fly. They did, in fact, like all the other passengers out on deck, hear a muffled sound that might be termed a sonic poof, and like everyone else dismissed it as some sort of ferry noise, or perhaps a far-distant Canadian Forces jet.

It was—as it had been at the very start—just that tantalizingly close. But they were sailing to Horseshoe Bay, not playing horseshoes, and so again "close" was simply not good enough.

They ate in a *wonderful* place Wally and Moira knew just outside Horseshoe Bay. (A law of nature states that all sf fans know all superb and most good restaurants within a fifty-kilometer radius of their home. SMOFs generally at least double the radius.) The food was so good that it was not until the check was actually on the table that Paul remembered to blush.

"Wally?" he said. "Are you familiar with a condition called shell-out falter?"

Watty's eyebrows rose sympathetically. "You suffer from a reach impediment?"

"Well, it's been a hard week."

Wally waved a hand, and grinned. "Take it from your mind. I cannot tell you how much you will have improved this whole anecdote if you will allow me to buy you dinner."

Paul and June considered that . . . and burst out laughing.

Moira joined in too, but when the laughter had subsided she said to June, "So you two took off so fast you didn't have time to grab any cash?"

June nodded. "There are still a couple of small accounts around town we could tap in theory—but none I'd dare access until we settle this."

"So what were you going to do when O'Leary's fridge emptied out?"

"Pocket cash has never—" Paul began automatically, and then trailed off.

"What?" Moira said.

"Pardon me," he said slowly. "A phantom ache in an amputated limb. I said goodbye to my life out there on Bowen Island, but I'll be awhile unlearning old habits, I guess." He looked away.

June took his hand. "What Paul means," she said quietly, "is that he started to say cash has never been a problem for us, we'd just have worked some short con or other on some mark for operating capital. And then he remembered that we've retired, and there's no answer to your question anymore."

After an awkward silence, Moira spoke up. "You meant that about quitting your line of work?"

June nodded.

"*Why?*" In spite of herself she giggled. "I mean, you're *good* at it," she tried to explain. "That eye of power thing is awesome. And you had no way of knowing Wally and I were going to catch up with you. Why were you thinking about retiring?"

"To change your pattern, make it harder for the time traveler to track you?" Wally suggested.

Still looking at her fiancé's expressionless profile, June shook her head. "Basically," she said, "we woke up one day and found ourselves stinging nice people. People who we could have liked. We always swore we weren't going to. Maybe every grifter swears that, starting out—the good ones, anyway. Maybe not. But over the years, your standards slip, a centimeter at a time, while you aren't paying attention. Your partner's standards slip, too. Soon you're like two drunks trying to hold each other up, each certain you're sober. The next thing you know, you find you've written a truly brilliant new con . . . that only works on smart, kind people." She reached out and stroked

Paul's cheek. "So you look back to see just where you lost control, and you can't pin it down. So maybe you've had it all wrong from the start, and *nobody* deserves to get stung."

"I'm not certain I agree with *that* part," Moira said. "There are bastards on this planet. Maybe you've just lost faith in your own wisdom to judge."

It was not said unkindly; June considered it, and shook her head. "My right to."

"It isn't right to be Simon Templar, and smite the Ungodly," Wally suggested, "unless you're in a book, where you don't make mistakes, and you can guarantee there won't be any innocent bystanders."

"Exactly," Paul said, and turned back to face the table. "There's a song James Taylor's brother Liv wrote, that goes, 'Life is good—when you're proud of what you do . . .' " he said to Wally. "Well, for a long time now, I've been trying to skate by on being proud of how I *do* it, instead. It just stopped being good enough."

"I see," Wally said.

"I mean, look at my masterpiece. My most brilliant artistic creation. Like June says, it only works on bright sensitive misfits with unusually flexible minds. I mean, it's pretty obvious who I'm really trying to sting, isn't it?'

"Your mother," June said.

He spun on her, thunderstruck, and started to cloud up—then his face went blank. "Good one," he said after a few seconds of thought. "I was going to say me, but that was infuriating enough to have some truth in it."

"Maybe some of both," she suggested.

"You two are going to be good at this marriage business," Moira said.

"And the rest will fall into place," Wally agreed. "It always does, if you've got the *basic* stuff covered."

June found herself smiling. "Well, if we don't get caught and killed, or shipped off to the Stone Age or something, I think we've got a shot. That's why I accepted his proposal."

"Oh, don't worry about that," Wally assured her. "I think we can deal with that."

Paul and June stared at him.

"Oh yeah," he said, somewhat abashed. "I worked it out on the way to the ferry. A plan, I mean. It needs a little polish, but it ought to work."

Moira's eyes were gleaming. "My heroin," she said in a swooning, theatrical voice.

Her husband smiled at her. "Aw, shocks."

The good fellowship that had grown up between the four of them made it sort of necessary for Wally to outline his idea then, even though he and Moira had not yet been paid their consulting fee. His scheme was not, at first, received with great enthusiasm, since it required large amounts of trust and faith and hope—ingredients Paul and June were mostly accustomed to selling to other people. But eventually they were forced to concede that their only other option was to cut their own throats, right now. June then spotted a potential hole in the scenario, but Moira was able to patch it brilliantly. They all left the restaurant feeling confident, and with that special warmth that comes from having made good new friends. Wally and Paul talked together in the front of the Camry, and Moira and June talked in the back, all the way back to Vancouver. When they reached the building behind Paul's former address, the ladies split the chore of keeping lookout—June in the parking garage, Moira on the other side of the burned-out property—while Paul and Wally excavated together, armed with a shovel and a good tire iron Wally kept in his trunk. Wally was poor at gruntwork, but turned out to be world-class at thinking of easier ways to do things.

The camaraderie thus engendered helped considerably to smooth over the awkward moment that arose when they reached the site of Paul's secret stash, and found only shrapnel.

After several minutes of silence, during which Paul considered using his swearing litany—after all, the house had already burned down—but couldn't work up the heart to begin, he felt Wally's pudgy hand on his bowed shoulder. In all the countless permutations of the English language, there was only one right thing Wally could possibly have said just then, and Paul was immensely gratified to hear him say it.

"You can owe us."

Too moved to speak, he nodded.

"Let's get our women and go to war," Wally said.

Paul nodded again, and they left.

⚡CHAPTER 14⚡
"... Danny Boy, this is a showdown ..."

MYRNA AND JOHNSON were alertly waiting—desperately hoping—for word of June Bellamy and Paul Throtmanian; indeed, they had done very little else in the thirty-six hours since they'd loosed the trackfly. It didn't help them much.

The one thing they'd thought they knew for sure about June and Paul's location was that it was *distant*. The fly had long since swept the entire Greater Vancouver area in a Drunkard's Walk pattern, conclusively reported null results, and expanded its search area to encompass all the inhabited islands nearby. It had scanned most of the small ones, was already halfway through the immense Vancouver Island. If it came up empty there as well, it would begin quartering the Lower Mainland and upper United States. The more infuriating minutes dragged by without news of success, the more distant became June and Paul's proved location. By now, it was certain they could not be within eighty kilometers of Pacific Spirit Park—or so the Lifehouse Keepers believed.

The truth came as a rude shock. A similar emotion might be experienced by a submarine skipper who—having lobbed a deck-gun round through the night at a distant gunboat, and while waiting out the endless long seconds before he will know for sure whether or not he has scored a hit and is committed to battle, or has wasted a round but is still safe—feels the cold muzzle of a pistol against the back of his own personal neck, and hears the click of the hammer being cocked. By the time Myrna and Johnson's own personal alarms—which had seemed perfectly adequate for nearly a thousand years, and which had been tuned most carefully—sounded in their skulls, June was standing about half a kilometer from their home.

And about a hundred meters from the Lifehouse . . .

She got that far without being identified as more than just another passing hiker, biker or stroller because Myrna and Johnson's own sentries were nowhere near as sophisticated as the trackfly. A change of hair and eye color, cheek inserts and lifts sufficed to fool them on the physical level, as they would probably have fooled another human. They neither knew nor cared what she smelled like.

And she had obviously remembered her lost FM radio headphones, and somehow deduced what they could accomplish on the mental level.

The set she wore now had been altered to generate a much more powerful signal than usual. It did not merely mask, but completely shielded her thoughts. Indeed, what had finally triggered the alarm was the sentries' belated perception that a human-sized animal with a sentience level around that of a bluejay was probably a significant anomaly.

But Myrna and Johnson absorbed all this information *after* they perceived the message June meant them to get, so efficiently did she deliver it.

First, they saw the white flag she was waving in her right hand.

Next, they took in the modified cellular phone that hung from the belt of her jeans, to which she was speaking continuously.

And finally they noted the extra-extra-large black tee-shirt she was wearing, big enough to be a Rubenesque sf fan's convention souvenir. It was gathered and tucked in in back, so the white lettering just below her left breast could be clearly seen. It spelled out the simple words:

The Place
because it's time

She and Paul wanted to parley.

Knowing her as they did, they were at once dismally certain that she and her partner had rigged some sort of ingenious stalemate to protect themselves. The Lifehouse Keepers sent their awareness hurtling pessimistically out to trace it as far as they could.

Somewhat to their surprise, the cell phone's signal went less than a hundred meters, at first—to a phone Paul wore as a headset with a throat mike, very sophisticated gear indeed for a grifter. So was the high-powered rifle on a tripod, through whose sniperscope he was taking dead aim at the back of June's skull. (All the gear seemed brand-new; there was still a price tag on the tripod.)

But from there the phone signal went off on Hell's own journey. They followed it awhile, but gave up when it crossed its own trail for the third time in Singapore. The point was made: June and Paul had a third confederate Myrna and Johnson could not quickly affect, locate or identify save by overt telepathic conquest.

Worse: the existence of a third, combined with the fact that neither grifter had ever once been so much as indicted for any felony in any jurisdiction, strongly implied at least a fourth party as well. Both Paul and June were suspenders-and-belt types. Myrna herself was going to die because Paul's money stash had been doubly booby-trapped; he was clearly a man happiest with an ace up *both* sleeves at a minimum. He might, for all Myrna or Johnson knew, have enlisted an entire army of grifters, grafters, hucksters and dips, who could communicate in ways even a thousand-year-old layman could not hope to grasp.

This was very bad.

A Quaker watching her family tortured could not have felt more profoundly or primitively conflicted. Myrna had seen so much sorry death in her millennium of service that it had been centuries since she had even recreationally fantasized dealing it out to anyone as punishment for their silly human sins. Nonetheless she was a true descendant of a redhanded ape and his bloodthirsty mate, mortal as them now into the bargain, and to *hell* with the fate of all the sleeping dead and all reality: *these clowns were messing with her personal lifeboat!* If killing had been of the slightest use to her, she'd have used her teeth and fingernails.

Johnson, similarly, was descended from two million years of primates who had unanimously felt that anyone who killed their mate should be treated with great rudeness. Since his and Myrna's personalities had been tailored to pass without comment through the past thousand years, and not merely the last thirty-odd, he had been crafted with a normal amount of male dominance: he was not merely the titular but the effective leader of their team, and knew the ancient commander's desire to avenge his wounded as strongly as he knew the even more ancient protector's desire to avenge his mate.

Dealing with such emotional disturbances would never be impossible for either of them. At times it could be extremely difficult. Myrna, in particular, had lately had to do much more of that sort of thing than usual, as small bodily damages she was no longer able to heal sent chemical messages of unease to her alarm system. Emotional control was somewhat like a muscle that can be worn out to the point of spasm. She managed to master herself, now, but it cost her great effort.

And the shared knowledge made it that much harder for Johnson to do the same.

So it was that several seconds passed before they acted.

Then Johnson enveloped her in his field and flew them together like bullets, and at a similar velocity, through the forest toward June Bellamy.

There was no deceleration. Their velocity was simply canceled, at a point just out of sight and just out of earshot of June. As smoothly as children stepping off an escalator, they were walking hand in hand toward her at a slow pace, making no effort to muffle their footsteps in the (finally) drying underbrush. Their acute hearing picked up her muttered telephone monologue about the time she became aware they were approaching. They heard her alert Paul, and tell him to stand by.

"If I come, I die," she yelled then.

They had to admire the absolute absence of self-consciousness in her voice. She was stating a fact, and could not care less if some distant hiker thought she was kinky.

Johnson, who knew there was no other human within earshot, called back, "Understood," and he and Myrna kept walking.

They expected June to start visibly when she finally saw them. It was clear that she and Paul had *not* deduced their antagonists' cover identities, or they would have come directly to the park caretaker's cottage. Therefore, however she had been visualizing their pursuers, it could scarcely have been as a pair of snowcapped senior citizens.

But she betrayed no surprise. Professionally immune to surface appearances, she would not have lost her poker face if they had manifested hand in hand as Janis Joplin and Jimi Hendrix, on fire. Her only reaction was to give target coordinates to Paul, who shifted aim from the back of her head to Johnson's forehead the moment it entered his field of view.

Paul was largely visually concealed from them by undergrowth, though not of course from their sentries. He was a memorable sight. His headset phone sat atop a bright skull-hugging helmet of some sort of crinkly golden metal foil, almost a metal-maché, with small holes for eyes and mouth and absurd sculpted ears that came to Vulcan points (the phone's earbead cord disappeared into the one on his right), and to whose preposterous appearance he was plainly as indifferent as any holdup man in a Nixon mask. It shielded his thoughts even better than June's radio headphones did hers: the sentries rated him a rather bright shrub on the sentience scale. He seemed to sense that he was under remote surveillance of some kind—and didn't give a damn.

Johnson kept his own face blank, maintained his leisurely pace, and shifted their course slightly so that Paul could continue to track him without needing to move the tripod.

Myrna's grip was tight in his. They both knew a bad shot or a bad ricochet could kill her. They also knew if one did, it would be his immediate task—*before* he could so much as say goodbye—to try to reason with her killers.

They stepped out of the woods and onto the path together, stopped six meters from June, and perhaps ten meters from the great tree under which the Lifehouse lay hidden.

"I'll bet you can force your way through this," June said, pointing at her headset. "But I bet you can't take me over *instantly*." She pointed to the cell phone at her hip. "If anything makes Paul suspect a struggle for control of my mind is taking place, he will try to kill one of you, and failing that will take me out with the second slug."

Johnson nodded.

"If that happens," June went on quietly, "someone else far from here—someone who *doesn't even know where he is himself*—will make a single mouse-click, and spam the planet with everything we know about you time travelers. Every science fiction or fantasy writer or fan, every scientist, science writer, news medium and national security agency with an Internet address will know everything we knew up to the moment of the mouse-click."

Determined to keep his features expressionless, Johnson found that his eyes had closed of their own volition. It took immense effort to force them open again. He did have the power to take over the minds of both June and Paul by brute force, despite radio headphones or metallic masquerade masks, whenever he wanted to badly enough to permanently lower their IQs by fifty or sixty points—but no longer dared use it, whatever the need. This was Armageddon. Here. Now.

"You understand that would make a hole in history too big to mend," he said softly. "Even if not one person believed you."

It wasn't quite a question, but she nodded superfluous agreement, "That's how little I'm prepared to tolerate another hole in my mind."

"Do you have a proposal?" Myrna asked.

"Do we have a truce?"

Again, Johnson nearly showed surprise. "You will accept our word?"

June nodded. "What choice do we have? If your word is no good, there's no point in bargaining. Besides, if you are time travelers without honor, *everything* is already fucked . . . and the problems of two little people don't amount to a hill of beans."

He exchanged a glance with Myrna. June was emphatically not a science fiction reader, and Paul only a recreational one, like a social drinker: that last sentence was reasoning more sophisticated than expected for either of them. At once the Lifehouse Keepers began to suspect who the pair's new allies might be. A pity that when they'd last read June's mind, she had not then known the specific names or addresses of the sf fans Paul was about to sting—or that Paul had not left any useful clues even in the encrypted partition of his hard drive. If only the couple had trusted each other a little more, been a little less paranoid by nature, the Keepers might now have a lead on their new antagonists.

The absurdity of that last thought caused them to spend a precious half-second smiling ruefully at each other. (Inside only.)

"We have a truce," Johnson said then.

June insisted on spelling it out. "You won't try to monkey with our memories any more?"

She was too good a liar to lie to. Johnson shrugged and spread his hands. "We *must* try, or die in the attempt. But we won't do it *now*. If this parley is unsuccessful, we'll give you an hour for a head start."

"A lot more than you needed the last time," Myrna pointed out. There was just a hint of an edge to her voice.

June nodded, and gave her just a touch of the eye of power in return. "If it goes that way, we'll suspend our upload for the same period." *Wanna play hardball, Granny?* said her gaze.

"Agreed," Johnson said. With eyes locked, both women said it together, and Paul's echo came in stereo, from June's hip and from a hundred meters away.

When he emerged from his place of concealment, his hands were empty, and he no longer wore the comedy space-monster mask. But his phone now rode directly on his own bristly scalp, and its circuit was still open. Johnson counted two hidden weapons (lethal to a human—such as his wife), and wondered how many he was over-looking.

Being impressed by an opponent was, for him, a novel and not utterly unpleasant sensation.

As Paul joined them there was a brief subtle dance that ended with the men confronting each other directly, each with his mate slightly behind him and to his left. Neither male consciously noticed it hap-pen; neither female missed it.

"Had you actually already stung them?" Johnson asked.

Paul took his meaning at once, and if he found it an odd opening, he showed no surprise. "Yes," he said. "Ninety-eight thousand Canadian."

Johnson allowed his own surprise to show, in the form of a lifted eyebrow, and tried another gambit. "So that's, what, seventy-five in real money?"

Again Paul was impervious. "Call it seventy-three five American."

"Mr. Throtmanian, I am impressed. Even for you, conceiving of enlisting your victims as allies was uncharacteristically brilliant. Pulling it off was . . . As I say, I'm impressed."

"And I'm impressed by how well you know me, okay? As the say-ing goes, you must be reading my mail. Can we move on?"

"Certainly. My name is Johnson Stevens, and this is my wife Myrna. I'm afraid we don't *have* 'real names'—but we've been using those for nearly two centuries now."

June spoke up. "You're old: we get it." Her eyes were still locked on Myrna's. "We knew that anyway. We would not have gone to all this trouble if *we* were not impressed with *you*, alright?" She switched off her eye of power. "You're Myrna and Johnson; we're June and Paul. Like he said, can we move on now?"

Myrna blinked her own tired old eyes for the first time in a long while, and shivered slightly as if throwing off a chill. "Please go ahead, Paul," she said. The edge was gone from her voice now.

"In Minneapolis," Paul said, "in a joint called Palmer's Bar, I heard a guy sing a verse once that stuck in my head. It went:

> *Very old man with money in his hand*
> *Lookin for a place to hide*
> *Along come a young man,*
> *a gun in his hand*
> *They both sat down and cried*
> *Cryin all they had in this world*
> *done gone.*"

Johnson nodded. "Neither side in this matter much likes the role fate has cast them in. We don't want to edit your memories by force. You don't want to risk paradox to prevent us. Neither side can see a choice. But you did not come here to suggest we sit down and weep together, Paul."

"We came to see if there is any give in your position," Paul said.

"Is there any in yours?"

For the first time, Paul betrayed surprise.

"Can you conceive of circumstances under which you would consent to specifically limited memory-edit?"

"Cover me," Paul said softly, and closed his eyes to help him visualize. At the cue, June increased her own alertness, expanded her peripheral vision to encompass Johnson, and moved her right hand fractionally *away* from her own hidden weapon . . . presumably toward one the sentries could not detect.

"I can think of only one case," Paul said, reopening his eyes, "and it doesn't seem to pertain here. Can you conceive of circumstances under which you would consent to let us keep our present memories?"

"I'm afraid my answer is the same," Johnson said, allowing as much of his own sadness as they would find credible to come through in his voice.

"Then we have two choices," Paul said. "Say goodbye now, and start fighting to the death in an hour . . . or try and persuade each other that the unique solution we each find imaginable might somehow be made to exist. I would prefer the latter. I assume you feel the same."

"Very well," Johnson said. "I will go first."

He held a hasty telepathic conference with Myrna. They had no contingency plan for negotiation; had not until this minute considered it a possibility. But their minimum requirements seemed clear—and highly unlikely to be acceptable. No point in pulling punches.

"I would let you and June and your allies walk the earth unedited under the following circumstances: you permit me to enter each of your minds, satisfy me that you will never voluntarily divulge any datum I label critical, to anyone under any circumstances, and permit me to insure you against drug or hypno interrogation. Not lethally— but any such attempt would leave you a very happy fellow with no memory of anything at all, for life. I realize that could be a significant hazard for you and June, given the nature of your profession, but after all you both *have* gone undetected by the authorities up to this—"

"That part's not a factor," Paul said. "My fiancée and I are retired. For good."

Johnson's face did not pale; it never did unless he told it to. But he was shocked. His superb and trusty Bullshit Detector told him Paul was not lying . . . but if this was a true statement, then he and Myrna did not know June or Paul nearly as well as they'd thought they did, could not hope to reliably predict what they might do. This might actually work! "Congratulations, twice," he said automatically, while his mind raced. "Then I see no problem. Our minimum requirements are, one, absolute assurance of your sincere will to be permanently discreet; two, assurance that you cannot be compelled to spill what you know of us against your own will; and three, your promise that when our business is concluded, you will never have anything to do with this park again as long as you live, or cause others to do so. We will trust you to keep the most important secret we know, our existence—*if* you will prove you can be trusted by opening your minds. In all candor, we might not require this of ordinary civilians . . . but I hope you'll take it as the compliment it's intended to be if I say that, for you two and your allies, nothing less will serve: you are two of the greatest liars we've ever encountered. Your turn."

Paul inclined his head. "Thank you. Coming from thieves of your caliber it is indeed flattering. I would permit you to enter my mind under the following conditions. One, you must first restore every second of the memories you stole from my fiancée."

Johnson nodded. "Acceptable." June had never learned anything more damaging than the simple fact that something was buried here.

"Two, you must give me your word that neither of you will ever use anything you learn from my mind in any way that, *in my opinion,* would harm me or anyone I care about. I don't have to define that any closer, because you'll *know.* And the same for the others."

Johnson nodded again.

"Three, it must be two-way."

"In what sense?"

"*I* get to walk around inside *your* head too."

Johnson shook his head sadly. "I'm sorry. That's impossible."

Paul's voice went flat. "Gosh, that's a real pity."

"*Please!*" Johnson said quickly. "I do not mean that word as a euphemism for 'unacceptable'—it literally is not possible."

Paul nodded. "I believe you. Like I said, a real pity. But a deal-breaker."

Johnson wondered why; was startled to hear himself ask, "Why?"

"Two reasons, either one sufficient. First, thanks to June here, and everything she has taught me in our time together about subordinating my precious ego, I am just barely willing to consider telepathy—*with an equal.* Wide-open two-way . . . or strictly limited on *both* sides. You want me to get naked in front of your brain, I'll consider it. But you don't get to keep *your* shorts on."

Johnson sighed. "I understand your position. And your second reason?"

"You want me to keep your dark secret for life. Only *I don't know shit.* All I know is, there's something from the future buried over there that's worth brain-rape to protect. Before I agree to keep my mouth shut about it, I have to know what it is, and why it's so important. For all I know, you came back here in your time machine to start the plague that'll solve your real estate problem. I have to be as sure of your sincerity as you are of mine."

Johnson knew more about serenity than most Zen masters. Nonetheless he was conscious of a powerful urge to bite himself on the small of the back. If any particle of him had believed in an external deity who was supposed to punish vice and reward virtue, he could have taken refuge in rage at that Being. Lacking this (expensive) luxury, he was instead so overwhelmingly sad it seemed his ancient heart might stop of it. There were very few bodily functions he could not control absolutely, but tears leaked against his will from his eyes as he said, "Paul, you break my heart. Everything you ask is perfectly reasonable, nothing more than you deserve, and the least I'd probably settle for in your shoes. And I wasn't lying—it just isn't possible. I'll be honest: I wouldn't do it if I could. But I can't."

"You want to amplify that a little?" Paul asked. "Or are we done here?"

As far as Johnson could tell, they were. But he did not want to admit it, even to himself, so he allowed himself a few more sentences, to buy time. "I can't drop my shields and let you in, because I can't do it partway. It's like being a little bit pregnant, or somewhat dead. You would get everything at once."

"Your point being?"

Johnson pointed at his own head. "This is not a brain like yours. It has been gathering memories more detailed and vivid than yours for a thousand years—and it was never really human by your definition to begin with. Furthermore, I am inextricably interwoven with Myrna: you'd get most of *her* thousand years, too. If I opened my mind to you, it might take you several seconds to actually hit the ground . . . but only because your knees would probably lock when the first seizure hit. Beyond doubt, what would finally fall to earth would be a vegetable with your face. A dying vegetable, too stupid to breathe."

Paul seemed to be listening to his earbead. "There *have* to be people trained to initiate new telepaths without burning out their brains," he said.

Damn. It would be one of the kibitzing fans who had realized that. "Yes," he agreed. "But none in this time. Nor would I be permitted to so initiate you, if I were able. Think it through. There would be no way but mindwipe to make you *unlearn* it again, afterward, and it would no longer be possible to mindwipe you."

As he had expected, the words "Think it through" shamed the unseen fans into silence again. It was June who spoke next. "Is that what you meant by, 'you wouldn't if you could'?"

He was tempted to agree just for the sake of simplicity, but something made him answer more honestly. "No. Forget telepathy for a moment. I would not even verbally *tell* you any more than you already know about our mission here."

"Then you better give me a better reason why not than, 'I might want to stop you if I knew,'" Paul said inexorably.

Fair enough. But *how*? "Paul, listen to me. I'll try to explain as much as I possibly can. The knowledge you want is knowledge that . . . that would change the coloration of every second of the rest of your life. It is a secret so . . . so precious, so *wonderful*, that a hundred times a day for the rest of your days you would be tempted to share it." He saw Paul's face twist into a grimace of insult, and went on hastily. "I am not disparaging your self-control! Please believe me—"

Myrna spoke. "Paul, we stipulate that you can hold out against needles under the fingernails. That's not what this is about. Knowing what you want to know would *change* you. In ways you would come to regret."

"Grandma knows best," Paul said flatly. Distant thunder was heard from the west, threatening rain.

"I will make one more try," Johnson said, "and then we'll give up and move on. Paul, by your standards I am not a human being. I was not born of woman. My personality was assembled from parts, and poured into a body whose DNA configuration had never existed before, designed for the occasion. The same is true of Myrna. A normal human given longevity and required to do our job would have gone insane about nine hundred years ago. Now that you are engaged, it may mean something if I tell you that I have been happily faithful to my wife for all that time. I was, if you will, *built* to accomplish one specific purpose: to preserve the secret you want to learn, for a thousand long, slow years." He met Paul's eyes squarely.

"But *this* human I am: keeping that secret has been the hardest thing I've ever had to do. Even harder than the loneliness of being penned up inside a single skull."

"I promise you," Myrna said. "It would tear you apart. June too. The nicer a person you are, the worse it would tear you up."

"Cover me," Paul murmured again, and again went away inside to his thinking place. His features smoothed over. June's hand went this time toward the hidden weapon Johnson could identify, rather than away from it. Did that mean she was closer to attacking? Again, thunder rumbled faintly, to the north this time.

"The hell of it," Paul said finally, "is that I think I believe every word you say. But I cannot bet my species on it . . . and that's what you're asking me to do."

Johnson was in constant rapport with Myrna. Nonetheless he turned his head toward her now, and used his mouth to say, "He's right," in mournful tones. Meanwhile his awareness was reaching out—

The trackfly had nearly succeeded in executing its new programming, by now—as he had known when he'd heard its thunder a few moments ago. It had returned from Vancouver Island, and located and identified both Wally and Moira; their brilliant antitelepath strategy of Moira driving Wally blindfolded to a location he himself did not know had not been of any help against a nano-dreadnought trackfly's hypersensitive nose. It was prepared to interdict and erase their Internet upload on command, and 100% confident of success. It was ready to help hold all four people immobile and helpless until the one-hour truce ran out, and Johnson could honorably begin mindwipe. There was only one . . . well, fly in the ointment: it reported that Moira seemed to be holding a *second* phone a bare half inch above its own cradle.

If forced to it, Johnson was barely able and barely willing to take over the minds of Paul, June, Wally and Moira at once—rendering them permanently autistic in the process. But even if he focused his full attention on Moira alone—allowed Paul to shoot Myrna dead, took the chance that a ricochet from his own body might kill one of them prematurely and ruin everything—he still could not seize control quickly and smoothly enough to prevent Moira from dropping that second phone, and thus hanging it up. If there were a *fifth* confederate somewhere, with a high-speed modem programmed to dial Moira's number continuously—and there was no way for even the trackfly to know where such a person might be—the instant it reported success, the fifth man could, and probably would, upload The End of Everything to the Worldwide Web. There was no way to stop him.

Yet Johnson knew if he did nothing, sometime in the next thirty seconds Paul Throtmanian was going to break the truce and try his best to kill him, fully expecting to die in the attempt but determined. Paul lied brilliantly in body language, but Johnson had been decoding that language for twenty lifetimes longer than Paul had been lying in it. He was going to have to risk everything whether he liked it or not, and there was nothing to be gained by letting Paul force his hand. He told the trackfly to hover, await his command, and then do its best to destroy Moira's second phone as she thrashed. He bade Myrna good-bye, and started the process of turning part of his consciousness into a long-distance sledgehammer—

"Wait," Myrna said, in his mind to him and aloud to all of them. "Don't just *do* something: stand there. All of you. I know one last thing I can try." She pulled her gaze from her husbands. "June—will you trust me, for about thirty seconds?"

June studied her for a long moment. "Give her thirty seconds," she said to Paul, not taking her eyes from Myrna's.

"Johnson, will you trust me?"

The question was so simple it confused him briefly. "With the universe," he said simply.

"Thank you, beloved." She turned back to the grifters, spoke slowly and calmly. "June, Paul, I'm going to cause a utensil to come to me. It will stop in midair, right in front of Johnson and me. After a few seconds, it will drop and bury itself in the soil. When that happens, we will all back away from the spot, and a time machine will appear on it. There'll be some special effects—but nothing that will hurt you, if you close your eyes when I tell you to. All right?"

"Go ahead, Myrna," Paul said. "I really hope you've got something."

"That's why I'm doing it," she said.

A chunk of quartz arrived from the house, took up station in front of her and Johnson. June and Paul regarded it with close interest, and Paul muttered a terse description of it to Wally.

Concealing her thought from Johnson for the first time in centuries, Myrna composed a message, impressed it into the quartz beacon, and planted it in the earth. They all backed away, Paul and June taking their cue from Myrna and Johnson as to how far away was far enough. "Here we go," Myrna said.

The air crackled. The scent of toasting basil and cinnamon stung their noses. A faint, high whine converged slowly from all directions at once. The temperature rose just perceptibly. The sound swelled and contracted, like an explosion played backwards—

"Close your eyes," Myrna called, and everyone but Johnson obeyed.

CRACK!

"Oh, shit," Johnson said, quite unable to help himself.

This time the Egg held a passenger.

It appeared to be the fetally curled corpse of a woman about twenty years older than June, with similar features and short thick chestnut hair, dressed in a white garment that somehow was able to suggest a hospital gown and still preserve dignity. At first blink the body was floating in a translucent fluid—then that was gone, and it slumped bonelessly to the bottom of the Egg. Inside his head, Johnson heard a sound very like the squeal of a modem connecting. For the first time ever, one of the buried Lifehouse's files was downloaded from it. Nearly at once the corpse stirred, lifted her head . . . glanced round and spotted her four observers. Her eyes locked on June.

June made a small sound in her throat, somewhere between a sob and a snarl.

The Egg sighed and vanished. The woman in white stood up. She turned slowly in a full circle, took in her surroundings, turned her attention to June again. Slowly she smiled, and started walking closer to June, who visibly turned to stone.

The wrinkles framing that smile were fake. That body had never been used before. Nevertheless it was somehow inexplicably and inescapably an *old* smile . . . and the brand-new body that bore it walked and carried itself as if it belonged to a woman in her fifties who had been ill recently and was still in recovery. She stopped before June, and put her hands on her own hips.

"You see, darling?" she said serenely. "I *told* you we were going to get it all said, someday."

⚜CHAPTER 15⚜
Call or Fold

JUNE DID NOT quite lose consciousness, merely misplaced it for a few moments. And she didn't quite go down, for Paul caught and steadied her. But for the longest interval in her life, perhaps ten whole seconds, she did not think anything whatsoever. Johnson could not have more effectively stunned her consciousness with his mental sledgehammer. Paul was somewhat less affected; his mind produced not only gestalts but words . . . but just the two, over and over: *Holy shit holy shit holy shit—*

By the time June was sentient again, she was in her mother's embrace, squeezing back fiercely. (She heard, but did not register, Paul behind her muttering, "Her fucking dead mother just showed up, okay, Wally? Shut up and stand by.")

This is a lie, was her first verbal construct. And then:

This is the most precious lie I have ever been told, and I must not waste a second of it!

She stepped back and looked.

It *had* to be a lie. It was just too perfect. Laura Bellamy in a brand-new replacement body, she might have been able to rationalize with Star Trek logic. The wasted, half-animate doll she had said goodbye to only days ago, she might also have accepted. But this Laura looked *precisely* the way she had in the childish wish-fulfillment fantasy June had been having repeatedly ever since her death: neither rejuvenated nor ruined, but partly recovered, as though her illness had miraculously remitted a week or two ago and she was nearly ready to be released. This was, at best, a very good model of Laura Bellamy, who was herself in fact dead.

620

Okay. Just now June was prepared to settle for even a fair model of her mother—gratefully. Any booby-prize is much better than total defeat. Too good to be true is the best kind of false.

"Are you all right?' she asked.

"Of course." A very good model. Even Disney's audioanimatronic boys couldn't have gotten that twinkle at such close range—much less the *scent*, the oldest and largest file in June's olfactory memory— or the skin temperature. "But you aren't. What's wrong, Junebug?"

"Don't *call* me th—" June automatically responded, and then caught herself and began to giggle.

Paul came up from behind her and put an arm around her, and that helped her stop and get her breath back. *Okay, I'm in the Twilight Zone. Time to stop acting like a protagonist, and go with it, then.* She came to a decision.

"Mom," she said, "this is Paul. We're retired, and engaged."

Her mother's smile nearly took her breath away again. "Oh, I'm *so* glad! Hello, Paul," Laura said, and embraced him. After a frozen second, he returned it. "Welcome to the family," she said. "Call me Laura."

"I'm . . . glad I got to meet you after all, Laura," he said gravely, and released her.

"Oh, so am I." She took both their hands in hers. "Now, what is wrong?"

"Well . . ." June gestured vaguely toward Myrna and Johnson, and Laura appeared to become aware of them for the first time. ". . . these are Myrna and Johnson Stevens. They're from the future. They say they *must* invade our minds—and will—but it won't hurt a bit, and they'd rather we let them. We say fine, let us into yours so we know we can trust you, and they say that's not possible, we'd go insane. We say, then at least tell us, in words, what you're doing here in our time, so we can be sure it's okay with us, and they say we'd be sorry if they told us and they can't anyway. They're at least as slick as I am, Mom, and I just can't tell if I can trust them."

Laura had nodded after the statement, "They're from the future," and continued to nod after each sentence to indicate that she was following the tale. After June stopped speaking, she nodded one more time, and then turned to face Myrna and Johnson.

"Mr. and Mrs. Stevens," she said, raising her voice but speaking in a polite, conversational tone, "from what I've read and been told by a dear friend of mine, I understand I am late for an appointment with a bright light at the end of a long tunnel, so I'll be brief. Are you conning my daughter?"

Myrna did not hesitate. "Yes, Mrs. Bellamy. We must."

"Is there no way you could tell them what they wish to know, and then, if they are indeed sorry to know it, cause them to forget it again, with their consent?"

"I'm sorry, ma'am," Johnson said. "At that point, the only thing that would serve would be to completely remove every memory they've formed in the last week—no, excuse me, the last several weeks. They would become different people than they are now. They've grown and changed a lot, in the last few days. Several weeks ago, for example, they were not retired. They would notice a memory gap that large, identify it as a wound, put their talented brains to vengeance, and sooner or later we'd be right back where we are now—at best. The only thing that will serve is for *that* Paul and June standing there beside you now—and all their friends listening in—to all agree to walk away and spend the rest of their lives knowing nothing more than they do right now. And we must be certain they mean it."

"But you state that if you could and did satisfy their curiosity, they would *ask* you to perform surgery to remove the knowledge again?"

"Yes," Myrna and Johnson said together.

"Thank you."

She turned back to her daughter and prospective son-in-law. She chose her words, and when she spoke her voice was firm and strong.

"Junebug, if you won't listen to your mother, listen to your great-great-grandchildren. Do what these people tell you. Walk away. You and Paul and whoever else is involved. They mean no harm, to you or anyone."

It never occurred to June to ask her how she knew. Her mother's people-radar had always been infallible. Instead she heard herself cry, "But how do I know you're not a hallucination?"

Laura Bellamy considered the question . . . and smiled. "How do I know *you're* not?" She thought about it some more, and her smile wavered. "This does seem an awful lot like the kind of dying fantasy I'd concoct. You're retired. And engaged. And only my wisdom from beyond the grave can save you." Her smile firmed again. "Only we both know it isn't a hallucination, don't we? We both know this is real, however it's happened. Just like we both somehow know I'm going to have to go again, soon. Tonto, our work here is done."

"No!" June cried.

Oh my God, she thought frantically, *I finally got one last chance to have that Last Conversation after all, without Daddy around . . . and just like last time, it's going to be over before I've even had a chance to remember all the things I needed to say, all the things I needed to ask—*

"Wait!"

"As long as I can, dear," her mother agreed, glancing at Myrna.

"Mom, you were wrong a minute ago. I *did* listen to you. Always. I know I gave you hell. I'm sorry. But I always listened. Hardest when I pretended to be deaf, maybe. You won The Fight, you know. Stubborn bitch that I am, I held out until the day after you died—but you won. I always knew you would. I just didn't want you to have the satisfaction."

"But I did know."

June blinked. Something knotted began to ease, deep within her. "Well, I'm sorry."

"I absolve you. Now ask the question you want to ask."

There's only one? she thought dizzily, and opened her mouth to let it emerge of its own accord. "How could you stay with Daddy, all those years?"

"It was my privilege," she said.

"Mom, forget the fact that on his best day, his brain was half as good as yours. The man is an emotional basket case. He needed round-the-clock care just to keep him functional, my whole life— hell, he managed to screw up your death scene! How could you waste a mind like yours on propping him up all those years?"

Laura took her time answering, seeking the right words. "June," she said finally, "you greatly underestimate my own selfishness. I got more from your father than I gave."

"But *what?*"

"The thing I married him for. The thing I never had much of myself, until he taught it to me. The thing I hope Frank and I together managed to pass on to you. His kindness. His clumsy warm never-failing kindness."

June stared "But there's kindness everywhere," she protested. "The world is full of kindness."

"Oh, it certainly is," Laura agreed. "And most marriages still end in divorce. Most people can *be* kind, honey. Your father *is* kind. That's a different thing—and it's worth more than rubies." Seeing that her daughter still didn't get it, she went on. "Okay, yes: you have to hang a sign on a joke for Frank to recognize it. But dear, once you do, *he always laughs,* even if it's a poor joke. One time I'd gone with him to one of those awful sales conventions, and we were sitting in the most expensive restaurant in the convention complex, and by some accident they had a genuinely wonderful jazz combo playing. I looked up and saw a young couple we knew, a new salesman and his fiancée, standing in the entranceway, listening to the music and nodding. I started to wave and invite them to join us, quite automatically . . . and just as automatically, your father caught my hand and stopped me. 'But that's Jim and Shirley,' I said, 'You like them.' And Frank stopped and thought about it and said to me, 'Laura, look at the way they're dressed. Look at the way we're dressed. Why are they standing there in the doorway? If you wave to them, they're going to have to come in and sit down and blow half their weekend's budget on two drinks they don't want, just to hear the music for a few minutes. Kindest thing you can do just now is ignore them.' Once he explained it, I saw he was right, of course—but June, *he had to stop and think to explain it.* It's instinctive with him. If anyone in a room with him gets their feelings hurt, it's because his best wasn't enough to prevent it.

"Take the example you mentioned. Dear Frank tried to protect me from the terror of death. Clumsily, transparently, yes—and to the very best of his sweet ability. Even though it cost him his right to share his own crushing grief and loss with me. I had no choice but to let him think he was succeeding." She took June's hand again. "And in consequence, I could not allow myself to indulge in that terror. Do you see? For his sake, I kept whistling as I approached the grave-yard—and so in the end he succeeded, and I died with as little fear as I could. Honestly, it wasn't nearly as hard as I'd thought it would be. All our married lives, he did things like that for me. Without him, I might have been you without Paul." She took his hand again as well, but kept speaking directly to June. "I approve of him as a son-in-law—but not because the boy is *clever*. Because I can tell he is kind."

"There are people who would disagree with you," Paul said softly. "Some of them are listening right now."

She met Paul's eyes. "Ah. I see. You were trying to unlearn the kindness . . . to impress June. She has always had enough mischief in her to get her boyfriends in trouble. Well, it didn't work this time . . . did it?" She watched his eyes, and nodded. "Kindness does you less credit than it does Frank, because you're smarter and more confident and less afraid: you can *afford* to be kind. But it's still a rare and sweet thing to be by nature. Teach her everything you know about it, teach her to respect her father and you . . . and forgive her what she finds hard to learn."

"I do," Paul said.

"I will," June said.

Laura smiled again—beamed, this time. "I now pronounce you man and wife," she said.

June felt herself beaming back, and burst into tears. "I love you, Mom."

"I love you, dear. And you too, son." She reached up, captured one of June's tears on her fingertip, and licked it. "We're done, aren't we?"

"Yes," June said in wonder, "I think we are."

At once her mother was gone. The pilot light went out behind her eyes, and as her vacated second body began to fall, it dissolved. There was no sound or heat. It was as though she simply turned to ash-laden smoke and blew away, like a digital special effect. In seconds, the last wisp was gone.

June kissed her fiancé firmly, and was kissed back. Then she pulled away and faced Myrna and Johnson.

"I'll never know for sure if that was real," she stated.

"That's right," Myrna said.

"I am in exactly the frame of mind a mark is just before I take 'em for everything they've got. Cold logic says I'm being set up, but I want to believe."

"I imagine so," Johnson agreed.

She squared her shoulders. "I'm wide open. Come on in."

Paul said nothing, very loudly.

"Sit down," Myrna said. "Since you are volunteering, it will not be necessary to invest you, the way we did Angel Gerhardt. There will be no orgasm involved. Or any other physical sensation."

June sat by the great ash tree, leaned back against it and relaxed utterly. "Go ahead."

"First, your stolen memories back," Johnson said.

There was a soundless explosion, an inertialess impact, and a vague inexpressible sense of relief, of healing from an unsuspected wound. She probed, and found that she had her missing minutes back. Quite dull and uninteresting minutes, really—but she cherished each one.

"That felt . . ." she murmured, "that felt like . . . like scratching an itch on a phantom limb I didn't know I had. Okay, I remember everything now. Scan away."

"It is done," Johnson said. "You are free to go."

She shook her head in awe, and got slowly to her feet. "So little," she said, "for all that trouble. Maybe I felt a tickle. Maybe I imagined it. I'm sure you didn't hurt anything. Paul?"

His voice was so well controlled that only his fiancée or a telepath could have detected the suggestion of a quiver in it. Wally probably never noticed. "I'm ready." He sat.

"It is done," Johnson said again. "Thank you. Mr. Kemp? I can hear you directly. . . ."

Suddenly, so could June—with crystal clarity, as though he were present. "Well, it's going to drive me nuts, that's for sure—but I'd like to put this whole thing behind me as quickly as possible. Moira and I have a convention to run in two weeks, and we've already lost about all the time we can afford. Go ahead: I'm dropping my shields."

"It is done. Thank you, Wally. Ms. Rogers?"

"The greatest puzzle of my life? And I can never ever know the answer? And never ever share it with anyone I haven't already? Johnson, you know more about what makes a SMOF tick than even Paul, there. Besides, I go anywhere Wallace goes. Make it so."

"Thank you, Moira. Mr. MacDougal?"

"You guys got a space program in the future?" Space Case asked.

Johnson seemed to grin in spite of himself. "At the time we left, pretty much anyone who wanted to had spent at least a decade or two off Saturn, in the Ring, just gawking."

"That's all I want to know. My lips are sealed, and I'm gonna die happy."

After a second, Johnson said, "I believe you will. Done."

June knew the meeting was over. She found herself reluctant to leave this place, this tranquil spot, these people she had wished dead for so many hunted days. Something wonderful was near here, and she would never know what it had been. "Will we ever see you again?" she asked Myrna and Johnson.

Myrna shook her snow-white head. "Not for a very long time," she said. "And not here."

"Is there anything you two need, that we can get you?" Paul asked.

June turned and looked at him with new and growing respect.

"One thing, perhaps," Johnson said. "And I'm afraid it's a dreadful cliché."

"Name it," Paul said.

"When you remember this—" he said.

"—and you will—" Myrna said.

"—think of us with kindness."

"We will," June said, and took Paul's hand, and they left Pacific Spirit Park without looking back, and with the firm resolve never to return.

They did, of course—but did not bring their bodies with them when they did, and never experienced a subjective instant of all the long years they spent there together in the Lifehouse. The answers they had wanted so badly would be granted them only in the next life—the longer and happier one. But their reward had already begun. For the remainder of their short first life together, they would display such uncanny talent at remaining married that their many close friends would often say it was as if they had been granted some secret knowledge no one else had.

❧CHAPTER 16❧
Dead Dog

EVERY *OTHER* HOUSE on the south side of the block had a front balcony or deck on its upper story, facing north toward the harbor and North Vancouver on its far side and the magnificent mountains beyond. Paul or June could turn their heads and see all those decks and balconies, up and down this side of the street—all quite empty, at sunset after a sunny day.

To get the same view from Wally and Moira's house, one climbed out an upstairs bedroom window and stretched out on the sloping roof. The roof showed signs of hard use, and was extremely comfortable. There was, for instance, a nook sheltered from the rain, up against the house, in which stood a minifridge, thermal mugs, and a coffeemaker Wally had connected to the house wiring and water systems: one need only bring a basket of grounds, and remember to leave the carafe out for the rain to rinse afterward. The nook also held a large bottle of John Jameson's Irish whiskey, whose continued existence was in doubt, and the controls for a set of external speakers. At the moment they were rendering Don Ross's percussive acoustic guitar, an excellent choice for a sunset.

Early November is right at the end of Vancouver's six-month spring, and the beginning of its six-month fall; it was chilly enough for the Irish coffees to be welcome. Paul took a gulp of his, and felt warmth spread through him—especially to his scalp: though furthest to leeward of the four, he was still unused to being bald. "Wally," he said, "my hair's off to you. It worked like a Swiss watch. I'm not sure how far they got on their own—but I'm certain they never got

628

a definite count of how many of us there were, let alone where we all were, until we let them in."

"I don't think they even got as far as me," Moira said, "and even if they had, they'd never have found Space Case."

"Not even if they'd taken over your mind," Paul agreed. "It was a sweet bit, and I could never have thought of it in a hundred years."

"Aw shucks," Wally said, and something in the tone of his voice made June recall her mother's words about her fiancé's kindness. She tightened the arm she had around Paul, and grinned fiercely at the sunset. "I think the alien mask worked good, too," she said. "Did you see them *frown* at that, Paul?"

"Well, I just had it lying around in my masquerade trunk, and I happened to think of it," Moira said, clearly as pleased as Wally. "So what will you and Paul do now, June?"

"Haven't the foggiest," she said happily, and took a swallow of Irish coffee. "Something good."

"Shouldn't be a problem," Paul said confidently. "Our requirements are modest. All we really need is identities, a house, a car, and a modest income, ideally in the next twenty-four hours. Oh, and one other detail: I owe a guy ninety-nine large."

"Aw Jeeze, look—" Wally began.

"Even worse," Paul went on, "the guy is a friend of mine, so I can't just weasel."

Wally subsided, but bit his lip.

"You can't go back to the Point Grey Road place?" Moira asked.

June shook her head. "We were going to have to leave there soon anyway. Any time now, the bank and the realtor are due to figure out the money we bought it with was imaginary. I don't even think it's safe to go back and get my dirty comic books."

Wally coughed, and bit his lip some more.

"But like I say, I'm in the mood to scale back a little," Paul said. "A Honda gets you the same place a Porsche does—cheaper—and you don't have to keep it locked up as tight. I don't need a really good house, like this one—I'd settle for one of those modern pieces of crap." He gestured casually to his right. "As for work, the first thing that occurs to me is that this is a big movie and TV town, and June and I both have relevant skills."

"WOW!" Wally cried, loud enough to startle Paul and June.

Moira merely turned to him and raised an eyebrow.

"I almost got it," he said excitedly. "Help me, spice!"

Moira nodded, and he turned to present the back of his head to her. She quickly surveyed the tools available to her, finished her coffee in a long draught, and used the soft thermal plastic mug to whack her husband solidly on the occiput.

He caught his glasses as they flew off, and put them back on. "Got it—thanks," he said, and turned to Paul, who was regarding him with a strange expression. "You *are* both excellent actors," he stated.

"Well, actually, when I said 'relevant skills' I meant bullshitting—and I was thinking of bullshitting on a more serious scale than mere acting," Paul began. "I was thinking producer, or—"

"I have two jobs for you," Wally said. "I would also take both of them as personal favors. The first one requires acting—*and* bullshitting: specifically, writing."

Paul pursed his lips. "Well . . . I believe Heinlein said the difference between a writer and a con man was, the writer could work in bed and use his right name if he happened to feel like it. What did you have in mind?"

"Remember the story we gave the Net to track you down?" Wally said. "If Moira and I don't want to have to waste a whole lot of the precious two weeks left before the con doing a lot of fast talking, *somebody* is going to have to write and produce a play called 'Data Takes A Dump,' that stars a guy who looks like Jean-Luc Picard."

In spite of himself, Paul smiled. "Well, it's a little out of our line."

June was smiling too. "What the hell. Dad'll let us use the barn; I can sew costumes—"

"Wait," Wally said. "You haven't heard the second job. It goes along with the first. Both or no deal."

"Go ahead," Paul said.

"That house you just pointed to next door belongs to a life-form named Gorsky. He's the one you bought your magnesium from, and he's the one who gave you up as Metkiewicz."

"Oh, really?" Paul said, turning to look more closely at the Gorsky home. His smile had become faintly feral.

"He's also sued Moira and me half a dozen times in eight years. Now I realize that you are both retired. But if you're willing to skirt grey areas like movie producers . . . would you be willing to lecture other citizens on the tricks of your former trade? Could you, for instance, explain to me how an unscrupulous enough individual could con, say, someone who lived on a block like this out of their house and land?"

Paul looked at June; she looked back. "You want him in jail?"

"No. Just somewhere else. And I want that property."

Paul's smile became positively vulpine.

"If you and June will do those two jobs for me," Wally said, "I will pay you ninety-nine thousand dollars Canadian, and lifetime free rent in that house—on the condition that you plant crabgrass."

"And we'll throw in free room and board here, until both jobs are done," Moira said. "Paul, you know what our guest room is like."

Paul and June exchanged another glance, finished their coffees, put their cups down, and stuck out their hands.

More coffee was poured, considerably more whiskey was poured, and the sunset was roundly toasted. As the sky darkened, conversation became general, veered around for awhile, and inevitably wandered back to the events of the day just finished.

"You know," Paul said, "I almost wish there was some effective way they *could* have edited my memories, without leaving gaps too big to shrug off as a bender. I mean, in a way I'm almost glad I'm never going to know any more than I do right now . . . but at the same time, the little I *do* know is going to stick in my mind like a burr under my saddle for the rest of my life, and drive me crazy."

"Tell me about it," June said. "I *know* my mother was dead. But that was *her*, today. How do you make sense of something like that?"

Wally sent Moira a glance she could read even in the dark, that meant, *They haven't figured it out.*

She sent one back that meant, *That's good.*

He sent, *But knowing is going to drive us crazy!*

She sent back, *So who said life was fair?*

And both grinned.

Just then there came a faint crackling sound, and an odor of toasting basil and cinnamon.

Paul and June stirred in sudden alarm. Wally and Moira caught their alarm at once, and guessed its cause. Each of the four freed their right arm and reached for a weapon. "Double cross?" Paul wondered.

A sound at the upper range of perception converged slowly from all directions at once. The temperature rose just perceptibly. Paul started to rise, and June restrained him. The sound swelled and congealed, like a Bronx cheer played backwards—

A small Egg sat on the roof, directly in front of Wally and Moira.

It was about the size of a volleyball, but otherwise identical to the one Paul and June had seen appear that afternoon: a perfect sphere of something more transparent than glass. Paul and Wally both had the same wild thought: that the little sphere would contain a miniature Laura Bellamy, something like Tinkerbell.

But its contents seemed far more mundane.

The Egg vanished like the soap bubble it resembled, and the item within dropped to the roof and began to slide. Wally reached out and stopped it with a foot, leaned forward and recovered it.

It was a compact disk. The caddy that held it had no front or back cover or liner notes, was simply a plastic box. The CD itself was almost equally featureless. No corporate or manufacturer's logo, no catalog data, no copyright warning, none of the standard commercial icons, no printing at all—not even the basic stuff found on a blank CD-ROM. Just a rectangular white block printed on its upper surface, within which someone with careful, Spenserian penmanship had written the words:

Free As A Bird
Real Love
(final versions and original
demos)

"What the hell do you suppose *that* means?" Wally asked.